KU-350-581

Tana French grew up in Ireland [illegible] Malawi. She is the author of *In the Woods*, *The L*[illegible]*ace*, *Broken Harbour* and *The Secret Place*. Her books hav[illegible] the Edgar, Anthony, Macavity and Barry Awards, the *Los Angeles Times* Award for Best Mystery/Thriller, and the BGE Irish Book Award for Crime Fiction. She lives in Dublin with her family.

Praise for THE TRESPASSER and Tana French

'A beautifully wrought murder mystery and investigation into what it means to be a murder detective' *Mail on Sunday*

'A police procedural series from this side of the Atlantic that can rival the best of the Americans' *Sunday Express*

'A clever and well-crafted read' *Sun*

'Another gripping tale, beautifully told, by a woman at the top of her game' *Sunday Independent*

'Its single voice is brilliantly sustained . . . and the book is a clever and intriguing experiment – the default technique of the psychological thriller, first-person female narration, deployed instead in a procedural whodunit' *Sunday Times*

'This is crime writing at its most sublime: spell-binding story-telling with a heroine to treasure in Detective Antoinette Conway . . . Tana French's reputation has been growing steadily in recent years and she is now at her peak, as this superb novel underlines' *Daily Mail*

'Taut, twisty, packed with all-too believable characters and rattles along at breakneck speed' *Woman & Home*

'A gnarly, absorbing read, and a finely tuned slice of wintry gloom from one the best thriller writers we have' *Observer*

'The life and internal politics of a murder squad room are brilliantly portrayed . . . outstandingly good' *Literary Review*

'With so many indifferent crime novels being published at present, we can be grateful for those authors who remind us what the genre is capable of . . . *The Trespasser* is . . . a tense study in paranoia, delivered with French's customary adroitness. It's not hard to see why such writers as Stephen King and Gillian Flynn are admirers' *Crime Time*

'She's fast becoming our fave crime/thriller writer, as this latest offering is flipping brilliant!' *Fabulous Magazine*

'Tough, twisting procedural . . . charged, complex characterisation . . . French is terrific at creating and lacerating vivid characters . . . French's psych-profile shtick is so sharp, she ensures we're wrapped up, too . . . the big reveal can hit you like a loaded punch' *Crime Scene Magazine*

'Get ready to get comfy on the sofa with this clever, compelling and creepy thriller – it's quite possibly French's best to date' *Closer Magazine*

'French and *The Trespasser* merit all the praise we can heap on them. If 2016 has a better crime thriller to offer, I've not yet read it' *New Books Magazine*

'One of this year's most anticipated books' *Stylist*

'This is story-telling at the highest level, packed with sparky dialogue and a feisty heroine who rises above her difficult background and challenging work environment in order to seek the truth' *Irish Independent*

'Uncommonly well written' *Irish Times*

'A tour de force . . . When you read Ms. French – and she has become required reading for anyone who appreciates tough, unflinching intelligence and ingenious plotting – make only one assumption: all of your initial assumptions are wrong' *The New York Times*

'Tana French is the most interesting, most important crime novelist to emerge in the past ten years' *Washington Post*

'[Tana French] inspires cultic devotion in readers . . . most crime fiction is diverting; French's is consuming' *New Yorker*

'Atmospheric and unputdownable' *People*

'To say Tana French is one of the great thriller writers is really too limiting. Rather she's simply this: a truly great writer' Gillian Flynn

'Terrific – terrifying, amazing, and the prose is incandescent' Stephen King

The Trespasser

TANA FRENCH

HACHETTE
BOOKS
IRELAND

First published in Ireland in 2016 by Hachette Books Ireland

First published in paperback in 2017

1

Copyright © Tana French 2016

The right of Tana French to be identified as the Author
of the Work has been asserted by her in accordance with
the Copyright, Designs and Patents Act 1988.

All rights reserved. No part of this publication may be reproduced, stored
in a retrieval system, or transmitted, in any form or by any means without
the prior written permission of the publisher, nor be otherwise circulated
in any form of binding or cover other than that in which it is published and
without a similar condition being imposed on the subsequent purchaser.

All characters in this publication are fictitious and any resemblance
to real persons, living or dead is purely coincidental.

A CIP catalogue record for this title is available from the British Library

ISBN (B format) 978 1 444 79653 7

Typeset in Plantin Light by Hewer Text UK Ltd, Edinburgh
Printed and bound by Clays Ltd, St Ives plc

Hachette Books Ireland policy is to use papers that are natural, renewable
and recyclable products and made from wood grown in sustainable
forests. The logging and manufacturing processes are expected to
conform to the environmental regulations of the country of origin.

Hachette Books Ireland
8 Castlecourt Centre,
Castleknock, Dublin 15

An Hachette UK company
Carmelite House
50 Victoria Embankment
London EC4Y 0DZ

www.hachettebooksireland.ie

For Oonagh

PROLOGUE

My ma used to tell me stories about my da. The first one I remember, he was an Egyptian prince who wanted to marry her and stay in Ireland forever, only his family made him go home to marry an Arabian princess. She told a good story, my ma. Amethyst rings on his long fingers, the two of them dancing under turning lights, his smell like spices and pine. Me, spreadeagled under my bedsheet, coated in sweat like I'd been dipped – it was winter, but the Corpo set the heating for the whole block of flats, and the windows on the high floors didn't open – I crammed that story into me as deep as I could, and kept it there. I was only little. That story held my chin high for years, till I was eight and told it to my best friend Lisa, who broke her shite laughing.

A couple of months later, once the sting had faded, I marched into the kitchen one afternoon, stuck my fists on my hips and demanded the truth. My ma didn't miss a beat: squirted Fairy liquid and told me he was a medical student, over from Saudi Arabia. She met him because she was studying nursing – lots of nice details there, the long shifts and the tired laughs and the two of them saving some kid who'd been hit by a car. By the time she found out I was on the way, he was gone, back to Saudi, without leaving an address. She dropped out of nursing college and had me.

That one kept me going for another while. I liked it; I even started making secret plans to be the first person from my school ever to become a doctor, seeing as it was in my blood and all. That lasted till I was twelve and got detention for something, and got an earful from my ma about how she wasn't having me end up like her, with no Leaving Cert and no hope of anything but minimum-wage cleaning jobs for the rest of her life. I'd heard it all a thousand times before, but that day it occurred to me that you need a Leaving Cert to study nursing.

On my thirteenth birthday I sat across the cake from her and told her this time I wasn't messing, I wanted to know. She sighed, said I was old enough to know the truth and told me he was a Brazilian guitarist she'd gone out with for a couple of months, till one night at his flat he beat the shite out of her. When he fell asleep, she robbed his car keys and drove home like a bat out of hell, the dark roads rained empty and her eye throbbing in time with the wipers. When he rang sobbing and apologising, she might even have taken him back – she was twenty – only by then she knew about me. She hung up on him.

That was the day I decided I was going to be a cop when I left school. Not because I wanted to go Catwoman on all the abusers out there, but because my ma can't drive. I knew the cop training college was somewhere down the country. It was the fastest way I could think of to get out of my ma's flat without taking that dead-end cleaning job.

My birth cert says *Unknown*, but there are ways. Old friends, DNA databases. And there are ways I could have kept pushing my ma, turning up the pressure every time, till I got something near enough to true that I could work from it.

I never asked her again. When I was thirteen it was because I hated her guts, for all the time I'd spent moulding my life around her bullshit stories. By the time I was older, by the time I made it into training college, it was because I thought maybe I knew what she had been doing, and I knew she had been right.

I

The case comes in, or anyway it comes in to us, on a frozen dawn in the kind of closed-down January that makes you think the sun's never going to drag itself back above the horizon. Me and my partner are finishing up another night shift, the kind I used to think wouldn't exist on the Murder squad: a massive scoop of boring and a bigger one of stupid, topped off with an avalanche of paperwork. Two scumbags decided to round off their Saturday night out by using another scumbag's head as a dance mat, for reasons that are clear to no one including them; we turned up six witnesses, every one of whom was banjoed drunk, every one of whom told a different story from the other five, and every one of whom wanted us to forget the murder case and investigate why he had been thrown out of the pub/sold bad skunk/ditched by his girlfriend. By the time Witness Number 6 ordered me to find out why the dole had cut him off, I was ready to tell him it was because he was too stupid to legally qualify as a human being and kick all their arses out onto the street, but my partner does patience better than I do, which is one of the main reasons I keep him around. We eventually managed to get four of the witness statements matching not only each other but the evidence, meaning now we can charge one of the scumbags with murder and the other one with assault, which presumably means we've saved the world from evil in some way that I can't be arsed figuring out.

We've signed over the scumbags for processing and we're typing up our reports, making sure they'll be on the gaffer's desk all nice and tidy when he comes in. Across from me Steve is whistling, which out of most people would make me want to do damage, but he's doing it right: some old trad tune that I quarter-remember from sing-songs when I was a kid, low and absent and contented, breaking off when he needs to concentrate and coming back with easy trills and flourishes when the report starts going right again.

Him, and the whispery hum of the computers, and the winter wind idling around the windows: just those, and silence. Murder works out of the grounds of Dublin Castle, smack in the heart of town, but our building is tucked away a few corners from the fancy stuff the tourists come to see, and our walls are thick; even the early-morning traffic out on Dame Street only makes it through to us as a soft undemanding hum. The jumbles of paperwork and photos and scribbled notes left on people's desks look like they're charging up, thrumming with action waiting to happen. Outside the tall sash windows the night is thinning towards a chilled grey; the room smells of coffee and hot radiators. At that hour, if I could overlook all the ways the night shift blows, I could love the squad room.

Me and Steve know all the official reasons we get loaded down with night shifts. We're both single, no wives or husbands or kids waiting at home; we're the youngest on the squad, we can take the fatigue better than the guys looking at retirement; we're the newbies – even me, two years in – so suck it up, bitches. Which we do. This isn't uniform, where if your boss is a big bad meanie you can put in a request for reassignment. There's no other Murder squad to transfer to; this is the one and only. If you want it, and both of us do, you take whatever it throws at you.

Some people actually work in the Murder squad I set my sights on, way back when: the one where you spend your day playing knife-edge mind-games with psychopathic geniuses, knowing that one wrong blink could mean the difference between victory and another dead body down the line. Me and Steve, we get to rubberneck at the cunning psychopaths when the other lads walk them past the interview room where we're bashing our heads against yet another Spouse of the Year from our neverending run of domestics, which the gaffer throws our way because he knows they piss me right off. The head-dancing morons at least made a change.

Steve hits Print, and the printer in the corner starts its rickety wheeze. 'You done?' he asks.

'Just about.' I'm scanning my report for typos, making sure the gaffer's got no excuse to give me hassle.

He links his fingers over his head and stretches backwards, setting his chair creaking. 'Pint? The early houses'll be opening.'

'You must be joking.'

'To celebrate.'

Steve, God help me, also does positivity better than I do. I give him a stare that should nip that in the bud. 'Celebrate what?'

He grins. Steve is thirty-three, a year older than me, but he looks younger: maybe the schoolboy build, all gangly legs and skinny shoulders; maybe the orange hair that sticks up in the wrong places; or maybe the relentless godawful cheerfulness. 'We got them, did you not notice?'

'Your granny could've got those two.'

'Probably. And she'd've gone for a pint after.'

'She was an alco, yeah?'

'Total lush. I'm just trying to live up to her standards.' He heads for the printer and starts sorting pages. 'Come on.'

'Nah. Another time.' I don't have it in me. I want to go home, go for a run, stick something in the microwave and fry my brain with shite telly, and then get some sleep before I have to do it all over again.

The door bangs open and O'Kelly, our superintendent, sticks his head in, early as usual to see if he can catch anyone asleep. Mostly he arrives all rosy and shiny, smelling of shower and fry-up, every line of his combover in place – I can't prove it's to rub it in to the tired bastards stinking of night shift and stale Spar danishes, but it would be in character. This morning, at least he looks ragged around the edges – eyebags, tea-stain on his shirt – which I figure is probably my bit of satisfaction for the day used up right there.

'Moran. Conway,' he says, eyeing us suspiciously. 'Anything good come in?'

'Street fight,' I say. 'One victim.' Forget the hit to your social life: the real reason everyone hates night shift is that nothing good ever comes in. The high-profile murders with complex back-stories and fascinating motives might happen at night, sometimes, but they don't get discovered till morning. The only murders that get noticed at night are by drunk arseholes whose motive is that they're drunk arseholes. 'We'll have the reports for you now.'

'Kept you busy, anyway. You sort it?'

'Give or take. We'll tie up the loose ends tonight.'

'Good,' O'Kelly says. 'Then you're free to work this.' And he holds up a call sheet.

Just for a second, like a fool, I get my hopes up. If a case comes in through the gaffer, instead of through our admin straight to the squad room, it's because it's something special. Something that's going to be so high-profile, or so tough, or so delicate, it can't just go to whoever's next on the rota; it needs the right people. One straight from the gaffer hums through the squad room, makes the lads sit up and take notice. One straight from the gaffer would mean me and Steve have finally, finally, worked our way clear of the losers' corner of the playground: we're in.

I have to close my fist to stop my hand reaching out for that sheet. 'What is it?'

O'Kelly snorts. 'You can take that feeding-time look off your face, Conway. I picked it up on my way in, said I'd bring it upstairs to save Bernadette the hassle. Uniforms on the scene say it looks like a slam-dunk domestic.' He throws the call sheet on my desk. 'I said you'll tell them what it looks like, thanks very much. You never know, you could be in luck: it might be a serial killer.'

To save the admin the hassle, my arse. O'Kelly brought up that call sheet so he could enjoy the look on my face. I leave it where it is. 'The day shift'll be in any minute.'

'And you're in now. If you've got a hot date to get to, then you'd better hurry up and get this solved.'

'We're working on our reports.'

'Jesus, Conway, they don't need to be James bloody Joyce. Just give me what you've got. You'd want to get a move on: this yoke's in Stoneybatter, and they're digging up the quays again.'

After a second I hit Print. Steve, the little lickarse, is already wrapping his scarf around his neck.

The gaffer has wandered over to the roster whiteboard and is squinting at it. He says, 'You'll need backup on this one.'

I can feel Steve willing me to keep the head. 'We can handle a slam-dunk domestic on our own,' I say. 'We've worked enough of them.'

'And someone with a bit of experience might teach you how to work them right. How long did ye take to clear that Romanian young one? Five weeks? With two witnesses who saw her fella stab her, and the press and the equality shower yelling about racism and if it was an Irish girl we'd have made an arrest by now—'

'The witnesses wouldn't talk to us.' Steve's eye says *Shut up, Antoinette*, too late. I've bitten, just like O'Kelly knew I would.

'Exactly. And if the witnesses won't talk to you today, I want an old hand around to make them.' O'Kelly taps the whiteboard. 'Breslin's due in. Have him. He's good with witnesses.'

I say, 'Breslin's a busy man. I'd say he's got better things to do with his valuable time than hand-holding the likes of us.'

'He has, yeah, but he's stuck with ye. So you'd better not waste his valuable time.'

Steve is nodding away, thinking at me at the top of his lungs, *Shut your gob, could be a lot worse*. Which it could. I bite down the next argument. 'I'll ring him on the way,' I say, picking up the call sheet and stuffing it in my jacket pocket. 'He can meet us there.'

'Make sure you do. Bernadette's getting onto the techs and the pathologist, and I'll have her find you a few floaters; you won't need the world and his wife for this.' O'Kelly heads for the door, scooping up the printer pages on his way. 'And if you don't want Breslin making a show of the pair of ye, get some coffee into you. You both look like shite.'

In the Castle grounds the streetlamps are still on, but the city is lightening, barely, into something sort of like morning. It's not raining – which is good: somewhere across the river there could be shoeprints waiting for us, or cigarette butts with DNA on them – but it's freezing and damp, a fine haze haloing the lamps, the kind of damp that soaks in and settles till you feel like your bones are colder than the air around you. The early cafés are opening; the air smells of frying sausages and bus fumes. 'You need to stop for coffee?' I ask Steve.

He's wrapping his scarf tighter. 'Jaysus, no. The faster we get down there . . .'

He doesn't finish, doesn't have to. The faster we get to the scene, the more time we have before teacher's best boy pops up to show us poor thick eejits how it's done. I'm not even sure why I care, at this point, but it's some kind of comfort to know Steve does too. We both have long legs, we both walk fast, and we concentrate on walking.

We're headed for the car pool. It would be quicker to take my car or Steve's, but you don't do that, ever. Some neighbourhoods don't like cops, and anyone who bottles my Audi TT is gonna lose a limb. And there are cases – you can never tell what ones in advance, not for definite – where driving up in your own car would mean giving a gang of lunatic thugs your home address. Next thing you know, your cat's been tied to a brick, set on fire and thrown through your window.

I mostly drive. I'm a better driver than Steve, and a way worse passenger; me driving gets us both where we're going in a much happier mood. In the car pool, I pick out the keys to a scraped-up white Opel Kadett. Stoneybatter is old Dublin, working class and never-worked class, mixed with handfuls of yuppies and artists who bought there during the boom because it was so wonderfully authentic, meaning because they couldn't afford anywhere fancier. Sometimes you want a car that's going to turn heads. Not this time.

'Ah, shite,' I say, swinging out of the garage and turning up the heat in the car. 'I can't ring Breslin now. Gotta drive.'

That gets Steve grinning. 'Hate that. And I've got to read the call sheet. No point us arriving on the scene without a clue.'

I floor it through a yellow light, pull the call sheet out of my pocket and toss it to him. 'Go on. Let's hear the good news.'

He scans. 'Call came in to Stoneybatter station at six minutes past five. Caller was a male, wouldn't give his name. Private number.' Meaning an amateur, if he thinks that'll do him any good. The network will have that number for us within hours. 'He said there was a woman injured at Number 26 Viking Gardens. The station officer asked what kind of injury, he said she'd fallen and hit her head. The station officer asked was she breathing; he said he didn't know, but she looked bad. The uniform started telling him how to check her vitals, but he said, "Get an ambulance down there, fast," and hung up.'

'Can't wait to meet him,' I say. 'Bet he was gone before anyone showed up, yeah?'

'Oh yeah. When the ambulance got there, the door was locked, no one answering. Uniforms arrived and broke it in, found a woman in the sitting room. Head injuries. Paramedics confirmed she was dead. No one else home, no sign of forced entry, no sign of burglary.'

'If the guy wanted an ambulance, why'd he ring Stoneybatter station? Why not 999?'

'Maybe he thought 999 would be able to track down his phone number, but a cop shop wouldn't have the technology.'

'So he's a bloody idiot,' I say. 'Great.' O'Kelly was right about the quays: the Department for Digging Up Random Shit is going at one lane with a jackhammer, the other one's turned into a snarl that makes me wish for a vaporiser gun. 'Let's have the lights.'

Steve scoops the blue flasher out from under his seat, leans out the window and slaps it on the roof. I hit the siren. Not a lot happens. People helpfully edge over an inch or two, which is as far as they can go.

'Jesus *Christ*,' I say. I'm in no humour for this. 'So how come the uniforms think it's a domestic? Anyone else live there? Husband, partner?'

Steve scans again. 'Doesn't say.' Hopeful sideways glance at me: 'Maybe they got it wrong, yeah? Could be something good after all.'

'No, it's fucking not. It's another fucking domestic, or else it's not even murder, she died from a fucking fall just like the caller said, because if there was a snowball's chance in *hell* that it was anything halfway decent, O'Kelly would've waited till the morning shift got in and given it to Breslin and McCann or some other pair of smarmy little— *Jesus!* I slam my fist down on my horn. 'Do I have to go out there and arrest someone?' Some idiot up at the front of the traffic jam suddenly notices he's in a car and starts moving; the rest get out of my way and I floor it, round onto the bridge and across the Liffey to the north side.

The sudden semi-quiet, away from the quays and the workmen, feels huge. The long runs of tall red-brick buildings and shop signs shrink and split into clusters of houses, give the light room to widen across the sky, turning the low layer of clouds grey and pale yellow. I kill the siren; Steve reaches out the window and gets the flasher back in. He keeps it in his hands: scrapes a smear of muck off the glass, tilts it to make sure it's clean. Doesn't go back to reading.

Me and Steve have known each other eight months, been partnered up for four. We met working another case, back when he was on Cold Cases. At first I didn't like him – everyone else did, and I don't trust people who everyone likes, plus he smiled too much – but that changed fast. By the time we got the solve, I liked him enough to use my five minutes in O'Kelly's good books putting in a word for Steve. It was good timing – I wouldn't have been in the market for a partner off my own bat, I liked going it alone, but O'Kelly had been getting louder about how clueless newbies didn't fly solo on his squad – and I don't regret it, even if Steve is a chirpy little bollix. He feels right, across from me when I glance up in the squad room, shoulder to shoulder with me at crime scenes, next to me at the interview table. Our solve rate is up there, whatever O'Kelly says, and more often than not we go for that pint to celebrate. Steve feels like a friend, or something on the edge of it. But we're still getting the hang of each other; we still have no guarantees.

I have the hang of him enough to know when he wants to say something, anyway. I say, 'What.'

'Don't let the gaffer get to you.'

I glance across: Steve is watching me, steady-eyed. 'You telling me I'm being oversensitive? Seriously?'

'It's not the end of the world if he thinks we need to get better with witnesses.'

I whip down a side street at double the speed limit, but Steve knows my driving well enough that he doesn't tense up. I'm the one gritting my teeth. 'Yeah, it bloody well is. Oversensitive would be if I cared what Breslin or whoever thinks of our witness technique, which I don't give a damn about. But if O'Kelly thinks we can't handle ourselves, then we're going to keep getting these bullshit nothing cases, and we're going to keep having some tosser looking over our shoulders. You don't have a problem with that?'

Steve shrugs. 'Breslin's just backup. It's still our case.'

'We don't *need* backup. We need to be left the fuck alone to do our job.'

'We will be. Sooner or later.'

'Yeah? When?'

Steve doesn't answer that, obviously. I slow down – the Kadett handles like a shopping trolley. Stoneybatter is getting its Sunday morning underway: runners pounding along the footpaths, pissed-off teenagers dragging dogs and brooding over the unfairness of it all, a girl in clubbing gear wandering home with goosebumps on her legs and her shoes in her hand.

I say, 'I'm not gonna take this much longer.'

Burnout happens. It happens more in the squads like Vice and Drugs, where the same vile shite keeps coming at you every day and nothing you do makes any difference: you burst your bollix making your case and the same girls keep on getting pimped out, just by a new scumbag; the same junkies keep on buying the same gear, just from a new drug lord. You plug one hole, the shite bursts through in a new place and just keeps on pouring. That gets to people. In Murder, if you put someone away, anyone else he would've killed stays alive. You're fighting one killer at a time, instead of the whole worst side of human nature, and you can beat one killer. People last, in Murder. Last their whole careers.

In any squad, people last a lot longer than two years.

My two years have been special. The cases aren't a problem – I could take back-to-back cannibals and kid-killers, never miss a wink of sleep. Like I said, you can beat one killer. Beating your own squad is a whole other thing.

Steve has the hang of me enough to know when I'm not just blowing off steam. After a second he asks, 'What would you do instead? Transfer back to Missing Persons?'

'Nah. Fuck that.' I don't go backwards. 'One of my mates from school, he's a partner in a security agency. The big stuff, bodyguards for high flyers, international; not nabbing shoplifters at Penney's. He says, any time I want a job . . .'

I'm not looking at Steve, but I can feel him motionless and watching me. I can't tell what's in his head. Steve's a good guy, but he's a people-pleaser. With me gone, he could fit right into the squad, if he felt like it. One of the lads, working the decent cases and having a laugh, easy as that.

'The money's great,' I say. 'And in there, being a woman would actually be a plus. That's what a lot of these guys want for their wives, daughters: women bodyguards. For themselves, too. Less obvious.'

Steve says, 'Are you gonna ring him?'

I pull up at the top of Viking Gardens. The cloud's broken up enough that light leaks through, a thin skin of it coating the slate roofs, the leaning lamppost. It's the most sunlight we've seen all week.

I say, 'I don't know.'

I already know Viking Gardens. I live a ten-minute walk away – because I like Stoneybatter, not because I can't afford anything fancier – and one of the routes I use for my run goes past the top of the road. It's less exciting than it sounds: a scruffy cul-de-sac, lined with Victorian terraced cottages fronting straight onto patched-up pavements. Low slate roofs, net curtains, bright-painted doors. The street is narrow enough that the parked cars all have two tyres on the kerb.

This is about as long as we can get away with not ringing Breslin, before he shows up at work and the gaffer wants to know what he's doing there. Before we get out of the car, I ring his voicemail – which may or may not buy us a few extra minutes, but at least it saves me making chitchat – and leave a message. I make the case sound boring as shite, which doesn't take much, but I know that won't slow him down. Breslin likes thinking he's Mr Indispensable; he'll show up just as fast for a shitty domestic as he would for a skin-stripping serial killer, because he knows the poor victim is bollixed until he gets there to save the day. 'Let's move,' I say, swinging my satchel over my shoulder.

Number 26 is the one down the far end of the road, with the crime-scene tape and the marked car and the white Technical Bureau van. A cluster of kids hanging about by the tape scatter when they see us coming ('Ahhh! Run!' 'Here, missus, get him, he robs Toffypops out of the shop—' 'Shut the fuck up, you!') but we still get watched all the way down the road. Behind the net curtains, the windows are popping questions like popcorn.

'I want to wave,' Steve says, under his breath. 'Can I wave, yeah?'

'Act your age, you.' But the shot of adrenaline is hitting me, too, no matter how I fight it. Even when you know trained chimps could do your job that day, the walk to the scene gets you: turns you into a gladiator walking towards the arena, a few heartbeats away from a fight that'll make emperors chant your name. Then you take a look at the scene, your arena and your emperor go up in smoke, and you feel shittier than ever.

The uniform at the door is just a kid, long wobbly-looking neck and big ears holding up a too-big hat. 'Detectives,' he says, snapping upright and trying to work out whether to salute. 'Garda JP Dooley.' Or something. His accent needs subtitles.

'Detective Conway,' I say, finding gloves and shoe covers in my bag. 'And that's Detective Moran. Seen anyone hanging around who shouldn't be?'

'Just them kids, like.' The kids will need talking to, and so will their parents. The thing about old neighbourhoods: people still mind each other's business. It doesn't suit everyone, but it suits us. 'We didn't do any door-to-door yet; we thought ye might want it done your own way, like.'

'Good call,' Steve says, pulling on his gloves. 'We'll get someone onto it. What was that like when you got here?'

He nods at the cottage door, which is a harmless shade of blue, splintered where the uniforms bashed it in. 'Closed,' the uniform says promptly.

'Well, yeah, I got that,' Steve says, but with a grin that makes it a shared joke, not the smackdown I would have pulled out. 'Closed how? Bolted, double-locked, on the latch?'

'Oh, right, sorry, I—' The uniform's gone red. 'There's a Chubb lock and a Yale. 'Twasn't double-locked, but. On the latch, only.'

Meaning if the killer left this way, he just pulled the door closed behind him; he didn't need a key. 'Alarm going off?'

'No. Like, there is an alarm system, like' – the uniform points at the box on the wall above us – 'but it wasn't set. It didn't go off when we went in, even.'

'Thanks,' Steve says, giving him another grin. 'That's great.' The uniform goes scarlet. Stevie has a fan.

The door swings open, and Sophie Miller sticks her head out. Sophie has big brown eyes and a ballerina build and makes a hooded white boiler suit look some kind of elegant, so a lot of people try to give her shit, but they only try once. She's one of the best crime-scene techs we've got, plus the two of us like each other. Seeing her is more of a relief than it should be.

'Hey,' she says. 'About time.'

'Roadworks,' I say. 'Howya. What've we got?'

'Looks like another lovers' tiff to me. Have you called dibs on them, or what?'

'Better than gangsters,' I say. I feel Steve's quick startled glance, throw him a cold one back: he knows me and Sophie are mates, but he should also know I'm not gonna go crying on my mate's shoulder about squad business. 'At least on domestics, you get the odd witness who'll talk. Let's have a look.'

The cottage is small: we walk straight into the sitting-slash-dining room. Three doors off it, and I already know which is what: bedroom off to the left, kitchen straight ahead, shower room to the right of that – the layout is the same as my place. The decor is nothing like, though. Purple rug on the laminate flooring, heavy purple curtains trying to look expensive, purple throw artistically arranged on the white leather sofa, forgettable canvas prints of purple flowers: the room looks like it was bought through some Decorate Your Home app where you plug in your budget and your favourite colours and the whole thing arrives in a van the next day.

In there it's still last night. The curtains are closed; the overhead lights are off, but standing lamps are on in odd corners. Sophie's techs – one kneeling by the sofa picking up fibres with Sellotape, one dusting a side table for prints, one doing a slow sweep with a video camera – have their head-lamps on. The room is stifling hot and stinks of cooked meat and scented candle. The tech by the sofa is fanning the front of his boiler suit, trying to get some air in there.

The gas fire is on, fake coals glowing, flames flickering away manically at the overheated room. The fireplace is cut stone, fake-rustic to go with the adorable little artisan cottage. The woman's head is resting on the corner of the hearth.

She's on her back, knock-kneed, like someone threw her there. One arm is by her side; the other is up over her head, bent at an awkward angle. She's maybe five seven, skinny, wearing spike heels, plenty of fake tan, a tight-fitting cobalt-blue dress and a chunky fake-gold necklace. Her face is covered by blond hair, straightened and sprayed so ferociously that even murder hasn't managed to mess it up. She looks like Dead Barbie.

'We got an ID?' I ask.

Sophie lifts her chin at a table by the door: a few letters, a small neat stack of bills. 'Odds are she's Aislinn Gwendolyn Murray. She owns the place – there's a property-tax statement in there.'

Steve flips bills. 'No other names,' he says to me. 'Looks like it was just her.'

One look at the room, though, and I can see why everyone figures this for boy-beats-girl. The small round table in the dining area is covered in a purple tablecloth; two places laid out, white cloth napkins in fancy folds, the gas flames twinkling in china and polished silver. Open bottle of red, two glasses – clean – a tall candlestick. The candle is burned down to nothing, drips of wax stalactited on the candlestick and spotting the tablecloth.

There's a wide splotch of blood on the fireplace surround, spreading from under her head, dark and sticky. None anywhere else, as far as I can see. No one bothered to lift her after she went down, hold her, try and shake her awake. Just got the hell out of Dodge.

Fell and hit her head, the caller said. Either it's true, and Lover Boy panicked and did a legger – it happens, good little citizens so petrified of getting in trouble that they act squirrelly as serial killers – or he helped her fall.

'Cooper been yet?' I ask. Cooper is the pathologist. He likes me better than he likes most people, but he still wouldn't have stuck around: if you're not at the scene when Cooper shows up to do the preliminary, that counts as your problem, not his.

'Just left,' Sophie says. She has one watchful eye on her techs. 'He says she's dead, just in case we missed that. Her being right next to the fire messed with the rate of cooling and the onset of rigor, so time of death is dodgy: anywhere between six and eleven yesterday evening.'

Steve nods at the table. 'Probably before half-eight, nine. Any later, they'd've started eating.'

'Unless one of them works an odd shift,' I say. Steve puts that in his notebook: something for the floaters to check out, once we have an ID on the dinner guest. 'The call came in as injuries from a fall. Did Cooper say whether that'd fit?'

Sophie snorts. 'Yeah, right. The special kind of fall. The back of her head's smashed in, and the injury looks to match the corner of the fireplace; Cooper's basically sure that's what killed her, but he won't say so till the post-mortem, just in case Peruvian arrow poison or whatever. But she's also got abrasions and a major haematoma on the left side of her jaw, a couple of cracked teeth – probably a cracked jawbone too, but Cooper won't swear till he gets her on the table. She didn't fall on the fireplace from two angles at once.'

I say, 'Someone hit her in the face. She went over backwards, smacked her head on the fireplace.'

'You're the detectives, but that's what it sounds like to me.'

The woman's nails are long and cobalt blue, to match her dress, and perfect: not one broken, not one even chipped. The pretty photography books on the coffee table are still nicely lined up; so are the pretty glass whatsits and the vase of purple flowers on the mantelpiece. There's been no struggle in here. She never got a chance to fight back.

'Cooper have any clue what he hit her with?' I ask.

'Going by the bruise pattern,' Sophie says, 'his fist. Meaning he's right-handed.'

Meaning no weapon, meaning nothing that can be fingerprinted or linked to a suspect. Steve says, 'A punch hard enough to crack her teeth, it's got to have banged up his knuckles. He won't be able to hide that. And if we're really in luck, he's split a knuckle, left DNA on her face.'

'That's if his hands were bare,' I say. 'A night like last night, chances are he was wearing gloves.'

'Inside?'

I nod at the table. 'She never got as far as pouring the wine. He hadn't been here long.'

'Hey,' Steve says, mock-cheery. 'At least it's murder. Here you were worried we'd been hauled out for someone's granny who tripped over the cat.'

'Great,' I say. 'I'll save the happy dance for later. Cooper say anything else?'

'No defensive injuries,' Sophie says. 'Her clothing's all in place, there's no sign of recent intercourse and no semen showed up on any of her swabs, so you can forget sexual assault.'

Steve says, 'Unless our fella tried it on, she said no, and he gave her a punch to subdue her. Then when he realised what was after happening, he got spooked and did a legger.'

'Whatever. You can forget completed sexual assault, anyway; is that better?' Sophie's only met Steve the once. She hasn't decided whether she likes him yet.

I say, 'Attempted doesn't play either. What, he walks in the door and shoves his hand straight up her skirt? Doesn't even wait till they've had a glass of wine and his chances are better?'

Steve shrugs. 'Fair enough. Maybe not.' This isn't him diving into a sulk, the way a lot of Ds would if their partner contradicted them, specially in front of someone who looks like Sophie; he means it. It's not that Steve has no ego – all Ds do – just that his isn't tied to being Mr Big Balls all the time. It's tied to getting stuff done, which is good, and to people liking him, which comes in useful and which I watch like hell.

'Her phone show up?' I ask.

'Yeah. Over on that side table.' Sophie points with her pen. 'It's been fingerprinted. If you want to play with it, go ahead.'

Before we check out the rest of the cottage, I squat down by the body and carefully, one-fingered, hook her hair back from her face. Steve moves in beside me.

Every Murder D I've ever known does it: takes one long look at the victim's face. It doesn't make sense, not to civilians. If we just wanted a mental image of the vic, to keep us reminded who we're working for, any phone selfie would do a better job. If we needed a shot of outrage to get our hearts pumping, the wounds do that better than the face. But we do it, even with the bad ones who barely have a face left to see; a week outdoors in summer, a drowning, we go face-to-face with them just the same. The biggest douchebags on the squad, the guys who would rate this woman's tits out of ten while she lay there getting colder, they would still give her that respect.

She's somewhere under thirty. She was pretty, before someone decided to turn the left side of her jaw into a bloody purple lump; no stunner, but pretty enough, and she worked hard at it. She has on a truckload of makeup, the full works and done right; her nose and her chin would be little-girl cute, only they have that jutting look that comes with long-term low-level starvation. Her mouth – hanging open, showing small bleached teeth and clotted blood – is good: soft and full, with a droop to the bottom lip that looks witless now but was probably appealing yesterday. Under the three blended shades of eyeshadow her eyes are a slit open, staring up into a corner of the ceiling.

I say, 'I've seen her before.'

Steve's head comes up fast. 'Yeah? Where?'

'Not sure.' I've got a good memory. Steve calls it photographic; I don't, because I'd sound like a tosser, but I know when I've seen someone before, and I've seen this woman.

She looked different then. Younger, but that could have been because she had more weight on her – not fat, exactly, but soft – and a lot less makeup: careful foundation a shade darker than her skin, thin mascara, the end. Her hair was brown and wavy, done up in a clumsy twist. Navy skirt-suit, a touch too tight, high heels that made her ankles wobble: grown-up clothes, for some big occasion. But the face, the gentle snub nose and the soft droop of the bottom lip, those were the same.

She was standing in sunlight, swaying forward towards me, palms coming up. High voice with a tremble in it, *But but please I really need—* Me blank-faced, leg twitching with impatience, thinking *Pathetic.*

She wanted something from me. Help, money, a lift, advice? I wanted her gone.

Steve says, 'Work?'

'Could've been.' The blank face took willpower; on my own time, I would've just told her to get lost.

'We'll run her through the system, soon as we get back to HQ. If she came in with a domestic violence complaint . . .'

'I never worked DV. Would've had to be back when I was in uniform. And I don't . . .' I shake my head. The searchlight sweeps of the techs' headlamps turn the room sizeless and menacing, make us into crouching targets. 'I don't remember anything like that.'

I wouldn't have been itching to get rid of her, not if she'd been getting the slaps. The slit-open eyes give her face a sly look, like a kid cheating at hide-and-seek.

Steve straightens up, leaving me to take whatever time I need. He raises his eyebrows at Sophie and points to the rectangle of light coming through the kitchen door. 'Can I . . . ?'

'Knock yourself out. We've videoed in there, but we haven't finger-printed yet, so don't go polishing anything.'

Steve picks his way past the techs, into the kitchen. The ceilings are low enough that he practically has to duck, going through the doorway. 'How's that going?' Sophie asks, nodding after him.

'All right. He's the least of my problems.' I let the vic's hair fall back over her face and stand up. I want to move; if I walked fast and far enough, I could catch up to the memory. If I start pacing around her crime scene, Sophie will kick my arse out the door, lead D or no.

'Sounds like a blast,' Sophie says. 'Now that you've seen the place the way we found it, can we turn on the bloody lights and stop fuck-ing about in the dark?'

'Go for it,' I say. One of the techs turns on the overhead light, which makes the place even more depressing; at least the headlamps gave it some kind of personality, even if it was a creepy one. I pick my way between yellow evidence markers to the bedroom.

It's small and it's spotless. The dressing table – curly white-and-gold yoke with a foofy skirt, like something an eight-year-old would pick out for her princess room – has none of that makeup left scat-tered on it, just another scented candle and two perfume bottles that are for looks, not use. No tried-and-ditched outfits strewn across the bed; the daisy-pattern duvet is pulled straight and symmetrical, neatly dotted with four of those scatter cushions I'll never figure out. Aislinn tidied up, when she finished getting ready: hid away every bit of evidence, in case God forbid Lover Boy should figure out she didn't naturally look like something he'd picked out of a catalogue. He didn't get this far, but she was expecting him to.

I have a look in the fitted wardrobe. Plenty of clothes, mostly skirt suits and going-out dresses, all of it mid-range block-colour stuff with one sparkly detail, the type of stuff that gets showcased on morning talk shows alongside blood-type diets and skin-resurfacing treatments. Have a look in the curly white-and-gold bookcase: load of romances, load of old kids' books, load of that godawful shite where the author enlightens you on the meaning of life through the story of a slum kid who learns to fly, few books about crime in Ireland – missing persons, gangland crime, murder; the irony – some urban fantasy stuff that actually looks OK. I flip through the books: the enlightenment shite and the true crime are covered with underlining, but no he-dun-it note falls out. I have a look in the bedside table: daisy-patterned box of tissues, laptop, chargers; six-pack of condoms, unopened. A look in the bin: nothing. A look under the bed: not even a dustball.

The vic's home is your shot at getting a handle on this person you're never going to meet. Even for their friends, people filter and spin, and then the friends filter all over again: they don't want to speak ill of the dead, or they're feeling maudlin about their poor lost pal, or they don't want you to misunderstand that little quirk of his. But behind the door of home, those filters fall away. You go through that door and you go looking for what's not deliberate: what would have been tidied up before anyone called round, what smells weird and what's down the back of the sofa cushions. The slip-ups that the victim never wanted anyone to see.

This place is giving me nothing. Aislinn Murray is a picture in a glossy magazine. Everything in here is managed as carefully as if she was expecting some candid-camera show to burst in and splash her private life across the internet.

Paranoid? Control freak? Genuinely superhumanly boring?

But please couldn't you just, don't you understand how I—

She let more slip and was more vivid in that one moment than in every detail of her home. There was no way I could've known, not like she was wearing a sign that said *Future Vic*, but still: for once I looked a live murder victim in the eye, and I blew her off.

Once the techs finish up we'll do a serious search, which might give us more, but from the looks of things, Aislinn's personality – assuming she had one somewhere – doesn't actually matter. If we can ID Lover Boy and make a solid case against him, we don't need to give a damn who Aislinn was. It leaves me edgy all the same, hearing that high little-girl voice where there should be nothing.

'Anything?' Steve asks, in the doorway.

'Bugger-all. If she wasn't lying out there, I'd think she never actually existed. How about the kitchen?'

'Couple of interesting things. Come look.'

'Thank Jaysus,' I say, following him. I'm expecting the kitchen to be chrome and fake granite, Celtic Tiger trendy done on the cheap; instead it's over-carved pine, pink gingham oilcloth, framed prints of chickens wearing pink gingham aprons. Everything I find out about this woman leaves me with less of a handle on her. Out the back window is the same walled miniature patio I have, except Aislinn put a curly wooden bench on hers, so she could sit out there and enjoy the view of her wall. I check the back door: locked.

'First thing,' Steve says. He tugs the oven open, carefully, hooking a gloved finger into the door crack instead of touching the handle.

Two roasting tins, full of food shrivelled into crispy brown wads: what looks like potatoes, and something in pastry. He pulls down the half-open door of the grill: two blackish lumps that started out as either stuffed mushrooms or cowpats.

I say, 'So?'

'So it's all cooked to leather, but it hasn't actually burned. Because the knobs are still turned on, but the actual cooker's been switched off at the wall. And look.'

Plate full of vegetables – green beans, peas – on the counter. Pan half-full of water on one of the cooker rings. The knob for the ring is turned on high.

'Soph,' I call. 'Anyone turn off the cooker? You guys, or the uniforms?'

'We didn't,' Sophie yells back. 'And I said to the uniforms: anything you touched, you tell me now. I'm pretty sure I put the fear of God into them. If they'd been fucking about with the cooker, they'd have 'fessed up.'

'So?' I say, to Steve. 'Maybe Lover Boy was late, Aislinn turned off the cooker.'

Steve shakes his head. 'The grill, maybe. But would you turn the oven off, or leave it on low and stick all the food in there to keep warm? And would you let the water for the veg get cold, or would you keep it boiling?'

'I don't cook. I microwave.'

'I cook. You wouldn't switch off the whole thing, specially not if your boyfriend was running late. You'd keep the water simmering, so you could throw in the veg the second he arrived.'

I say, 'Our guy turned it off.'

'Looks like. He didn't want the smoke alarm going off.'

'Soph. Can you print the wall switch of the cooker for me?'

'No problem.'

'You check for footprints in here?'

'No, I let you two walk all over it first, to make my life more inter-esting,' Sophie calls. 'Footprints were the first thing we did. It rained off and on last night, so anyone who came in would've had wet shoes, but any prints dried up a long time ago – the heat in here – and they didn't leave any decent residue. We got a few bits of dried mud, in here and in there; but those could've come from the uniforms clear-ing the scene, and there wasn't enough for identifiable prints anyway.'

Lover Boy is changing, in my mind. I had him down as some sniv-elling little gobshite who threw a punch that went wrong and who was probably back in his flat shitting himself and waiting for us to show up so he could spill his guts and explain how it was all her fault. But that guy would have been halfway home before Aislinn's body hit the floor. He would never have been able to make himself stand still and think strategy.

I say, 'He's got a cool head.'

'Oh yeah,' Steve says. There's a leap in his voice, like when you smell good food and you're suddenly hungry. 'He's just punched out his girlfriend. He probably doesn't even know whether she's alive or dead, but he's steady enough to think about smoke alarms and what's in the cooker. If he's a first-timer, he's a natural.'

The smoke alarm is above our heads. I say, 'Why not go ahead and let the food set off the alarm, but? If the place burns down, it's gonna take a lot of evidence with it. If you get lucky, the body might even be too destroyed for us to tell it was murder.'

'Something to do with his alibi, maybe. If the smoke alarm had gone off, someone would've been out here a lot sooner. Maybe he figured the longer it took us to find her, the less we could narrow down the time of death – and for whatever reason, he doesn't want it narrowed down.'

'Then why call it in, this morning? She could've stayed here another day, maybe more, before anyone came looking. By then, time of death would've been bollixed; we'd've been lucky to pin it down within twelve hours.'

Steve is rubbing rhythmically at the back of his head, rucking up the red hair in clumps. 'Maybe he panicked.'

I make an unconvinced noise. Lover Boy is flicking back and forth like a hologram: pathetic wimp, cold thinker, wimp again. 'He's cool as ice at the actual scene, but a few hours later he's freaking out? Badly enough to call us in?'

'People are mad.' Steve reaches up and pokes the tester button on the smoke alarm with the tip of his Biro. It beeps: working. 'Or else the call wasn't him.'

I try that on for size. 'He runs to someone else: a mate, a brother, maybe his da. Tells him what's after happening. The mate's got a conscience: he doesn't want to leave Aislinn lying here, when she might be still alive and doctors might be able to save her. Soon as he gets a moment on his own, he rings it in.'

'If it's that,' Steve says, 'we need the mate.'

'Yeah.' I'm already pulling my notebook out of my jacket pocket: *Suspect KAs ASAP*. As soon as we get an ID on Lover Boy, we're gonna need a list of his known associates. A mate with a conscience is one of every detective's favourite things.

'Here's the other thing,' Steve says. 'She hadn't put the veg in to cook, hadn't poured out the wine. Like we said before, he'd only just walked in the door.'

I shove my notebook back in my pocket and move around the kitchen. Cupboard full of delft with pretty pink flowers on, fridge empty except for low-fat yoghurt and pre-chopped carrot sticks and a twin-pack of M&S fruit tarts for dessert. Some people keep most of their personality in their kitchens, but not Aislinn. 'Right. So?'

'So how'd they have time to get in an argument? This isn't a married couple who've been bickering for years, he forgets the milk and it blows up into a massive row. These two, they're still at the fancy-dinner-date stage, everyone's on their best behaviour. What are they going to fight about, the second he walks in?'

'You think it wasn't an argument? This was his plan all along?' I flip open the bin: M&S packaging and an empty yoghurt carton. 'Nah. The only way that plays is if he's a stone-cold sadist, picks out a victim and kills her just for kicks. And that guy isn't gonna be done after one punch.'

'I'm not saying he came over here to kill her. Not necessarily. I'm just saying . . .' Steve shrugs, narrowing his eyes at a china cat with a pink gingham bow that's giving us a schizoid stare from the windowsill. 'I'm just saying it's weird.'

'We should be so lucky.' Little pink notepad stuck to a cupboard: *Dry cleaning, toilet roll, lettuce.* 'The argument might've started before he arrived. Where's that phone?'

I bring Aislinn's mobile back into the kitchen, out of the techs' way. Steve moves in to read over my shoulder, which is another thing that most people can't do without pissing me off. Steve manages not to breathe in my ear.

It's a smartphone, but Aislinn has the screen lock set on swipe, no code. She's got two unread texts, but I go through her contacts first. Nothing under Mum or Dad or any variation, but she does have an ICE contact: Lucy Riordan, and a mobile number. I write it down in my notebook, for later – lucky Lucy is gonna make the formal ID. Then I go into Aislinn's text messages and start piecing together the dinner-guest story.

Lover Boy's name is Rory Fallon and he was due over at eight o'clock yesterday evening. He first shows up on Aislinn's phone seven weeks ago, in the second week of December. *Great to meet you – hope you had a wonderful evening. Would you be free for a drink on Friday?*

Aislinn made him work for it. *I'm busy that night, might be able to do Thursday,* and then when he took a few hours to get back to her, *Oops just made plans for Thursday!* She had him jump through hoops coming up with days, times, places, till finally she decided he'd done enough and they went for a drink in town. He rang her the next day, she didn't answer the phone till the third call. He begged her into graciously letting him buy her dinner in a pricey restaurant – she messed him around on that too, cancelled on the morning of the date (*Really sorry, something's come up tonight!*) and made him reschedule. Somewhere in this house we're gonna find a copy of *The Rules.*

I've got no time for women who play games, or for men who play along. That shite is for teenagers, not for grown adults. And when it goes wrong, it goes way wrong. The first few games, you have a blast, get your guy panting along after you like a puppy chasing his chew toy. Then you play one game too many, and you've got a houseful of Murder Ds.

In between Aislinn's little games is the rest of her thrilling life: reminder for a dentist appointment; a few texts back and forth with Lucy Riordan about *Game of Thrones*; a week-old voice message from what sounds like someone from work, freaking out because his e-mail account's been hacked and can Aislinn tell him how to reset his password? No wonder she needed to make a restaurant meal into a major drama.

The invite for home-cooked dinner must have gone out in person or in a phone call – the call log shows a bunch of those from Rory, some answered, some not, none from Aislinn to him – but he confirmed by text. Wednesday evening: *Hi Aislinn, just checking if we're still on for 8 on Saturday? What wine will I bring?*

She let him wait till the next day before she got back to him. *Yes 8 on Saturday! No need to bring anything, just yourself :-)*

'If he showed up without a dozen red roses,' I say, 'he'd've been in deep shite.'

'Maybe he didn't know that,' Steve says. 'No flowers anywhere.'

We've both seen murders that boiled up out of dumber reasons. 'That could explain how it happened so fast. He arrives, she sees he's brought nothing . . .'

Steve is shaking his head. 'And what? Going by the stuff on here, she's not the type who'd tell him to fuck off and come back with a bouquet. She'd play it passive-aggressive: freeze up, let him go mental trying to figure out what he'd done wrong.'

The problem with Steve taking contradiction so nicely is that I feel like I have to live up to him. 'True enough. No wonder she got herself killed.' Sometimes I worry that if I work with Steve for too long, I'm gonna turn into a sweetheart.

With her pal Lucy, though, Aislinn dropped the hard-to-get act. Yesterday evening, 6.49:

Omigod I'm so excited it's ridiculous!!! Getting ready singing into corkscrew like teenager w hairbrush. Am I pathetic or wha??

Lucy came back to her straightaway. *Depends what you're singing Beyoncé :-D*

Could be worse . . . tell me it's not Put a ring on it

Nooo!!! Run the world!

Ah well then you're golden. Just don't feed him on celery and ryvita, you don't want him fainting from hunger before you can have your wicked way with him :-D

Ha ha so funny. Making beef wellington

Ooo get you!! Gordon ramsay

Hello it's just from Marks & Sparks!

Ah gotcha. Have loads of fun. And be careful ok?

Stop worrying!! Tell you everything tomorrow xxx

That one went out at 7.13. Just time for Aislinn to put on the last layer of makeup, the last layer of hairspray, stick her M&S dinner into the cooker, swap Beyoncé for mood music and light the scented candle, before the doorbell rang.

'"Be careful,"' Steve says.

When we talk to Lucy, she'll explain why she was worried: how Rory got aggressive that time in the pub when he thought Aislinn was looking at another guy, or how he made her keep her coat on in the restaurant because her dress showed her cleavage, or how he used to go out with a friend of a friend and the word was he had slapped her around but Aislinn figured it was exaggerated and he was a lovely guy and all he needed was someone who treated him properly. 'Same old story,' I say. 'Next time my ma asks me why I'm still single, I'm gonna tell her about this case. Or the last one. Or the one before that.'

Slam-dunk lovers' tiff, just like the uniforms figured. Our boy Rory practically lay down on a platter and stuck an apple in his mouth for us. I've known this was coming since back in the squad room, but some thicko part of me still feels it like a kick in the teeth.

Domestics are mostly slam-dunks; the question isn't whether you can arrest your guy, or girl, it's whether you can build a case that'll hold up in court. A lot of people love that – it pretties up your solve rate, looks good to the brass – but not me: it means domestics get you fuck-all respect from the squad, where I could do with it, because everyone knows the solve came easy. Which is also the other reason they piss me off: they've got a whole special level of idiotic all to themselves. You take out your wife or your husband or your Shag of the Day, what the fuck do you think is gonna happen? We're gonna be standing there with our mouths open, scratching our heads at the mind-blowing mystery of it all, *Duh, I dunno, musta been the Mafia?* Surprise: we're gonna go straight for you, the evidence is gonna pile up way over your head, and you're gonna wind up with a life sentence. If you want to kill someone, have enough respect for my time to make it someone, anyone, other than the most gobsmackingly obvious person in the world.

One thing on that phone, though, doesn't fit on that rock-bottom level of stupid. After the happy-clappy texts with Lucy, nothing in or out for almost an hour. Then, at 8.09 p.m., a text from Rory: *Hi Aislinn, just checking that I've got the right address? I'm outside 26 Viking Gardens but no one's answering the door. Am I in the right place?*

The text's flagged as unread.

Steve taps the time stamp. 'He wasn't running late, anyway. No reason for her to turn off the cooker.'

'Mm.'

8.15 p.m., Rory rang Aislinn. She didn't pick up.

He rang her again at 8.25. At 8.32 he texted her: *Hi Aislinn, wondering if I've got the weeks mixed up? I thought I was due over for dinner tonight but it seems like you're not around. Let me know the story whenever you get the chance?* Unread again.

'Yeah, right,' I say. 'He knows damn well he hasn't got the weeks mixed up. If he needed to double-check, the appointment's right there in his messages.'

Steve says, 'He's trying to make it sound like, whatever's gone wrong, it has to be his fault. He doesn't want to piss Aislinn off.'

'Or else he knows we'll be reading these, and he wants to get it through to us loud and clear that he's a meek little nice guy who could never do anything like punch his date in the face even if he was in the house which obviously he never was, swear to God, Officer, just look at his phone, see all these messages?'

A lot of domestics try to get smart like that: take one look at what they've done, and start setting up a story. Sometimes it even works – not on us, but on a jury. Rory Fallon pitched it nicely: enough messages to show he was really trying to get hold of Aislinn, honest, but nothing after the 8.32 text, so he doesn't come across like a stalker. Again, not rock-bottom stupid.

'Narrows down time of death, either way,' Steve says. 'She was texting Lucy at thirteen minutes past seven. By ten past eight, she was down.'

'Either way?' That makes me look up from the phone. 'What, you think these could be legit?'

Steve does something noncommittal with his chin. 'Probably not.'

'Come *on*. Someone just happened to walk in looking to kill her, at the exact moment when Rory was due to arrive for his beef Wellington? Seriously?'

'I said probably not. Just . . . we've got a couple of weird things, now. I'm keeping an open mind.'

Oh, Jesus. Little Stevie, bless his heart, is trying to convince us both that we've landed ourselves something special, so that our day will brighten up and I'll turn that frown upside down and quit talking about my mate's security firm and we'll all live happily ever after. I can't wait for this case to be over.

'Let's go pick up Rory Fallon and find out,' I say. If we're in luck and the pathetic-wimp version of Rory is the right one, he might even spill his guts in time for me to get in a run and some food before I crash out.

That gets Steve's attention. 'You want to go straight for him?'

'Yeah. Why not?'

'I was thinking the vic's best friend – Lucy. If she knows anything, it'd be good to have it before we start on Rory. Go in there with all the ammo we can get.'

Which would be the perfect way to work this if it was a proper murder case, with one of those cunning psychopaths lurking in the shadows daring us to take our best shot, instead of some gobshite who got his knickers in a twist and threw a tantrum at his girlfriend and who deserves every short cut we can find. But Steve is giving me the hopeful puppy-dog eyes, and I figure what the hell: he'll have his own burnout soon enough, no point dragging him down into mine. 'Why not,' I say. I lock Aislinn's phone and drop it back into its evidence bag. 'Let's go talk to Lucy Riordan.'

Steve slams the oven door. The waft of air shoots through the kitchen, charred and rich with meat about to rot.

Sophie is squatting beside the fireplace, swabbing the bloodstain. 'We're getting out of your hair,' I tell her. 'You find anything we should know about, give us a bell.'

'Will do. No surprises so far. Your vic did a pretty serious clean-up for her little dinner date – practically every surface in here's been wiped – which is nice: if your guy left prints, we can show they hadn't been there long. So far we're getting bugger-all, though; looks like you could be right about him having his gloves on. Keep your fingers crossed.'

'Yeah,' I say. 'Just so you know: Don Breslin's gonna show up any minute.'

'Oh, great. Be still, my beating heart.' Sophie drops a swab into a test tube. 'What do you want him for?'

'The gaffer thinks we could use someone who's good with witnesses.' That brings Sophie's head up to look at me. I shrug. 'Or

some shit like that, I don't know. So Breslin's coming in with us on
this one.'

'Well, isn't that special,' Sophie says. She caps the test tube and
starts labelling it.

I say, 'He's just backup. Anything you find comes straight to me or
Moran. If you can't get hold of us, keep trying till you do. Yeah?'

One of the reasons it took me and Steve so long to close the
Romanian domestic, the reason we're not about to tell O'Kelly, is
that when a witness finally got up the guts to ring in, we never
heard about the call. It was another two weeks before the witness
tried again – fair play to him; a lot of people would have figured
forget it – and got me. He said his first call had been put through
to a guy, Irish accent – which narrows it down to anyone on the
squad except me – who had promised to pass on the message. I
don't think it was Breslin, but I'm nowhere near sure enough to bet
my case on it.

'Not a problem.' Sophie glances back and forth between her techs.
'Conway, Moran or no one. Everyone clear on that?'

The techs nod. Techs don't give a damn about Ds and our relationship problems – most of them think we're a bunch of prima
donnas who should try doing some real solid work for a change – but
they're loyal as hell to Sophie. Breslin will get nothing out of them.

'The same for her phone and her laptop,' I say. 'When they get into
her e-mail, Facebook, whatever, I want it coming straight to us.'

'Sure. There's this one computer guy who actually listens when
people talk; I'll make sure it goes to him.' She drops the test tube into
an evidence bag. 'We'll keep you updated.'

I take one last look at Aislinn, on my way out. Sophie's hooked
back her hair to take swabs, hoping for DNA from that punch. Death
is starting to take over her face, starting to pull her lips back from her
teeth, sink hollows under her eyes. Even through that, she hits me
with that pulse of memory. *Please I just need please—* And me, barely
bothering to hide the satisfaction: *Sorry. Can't help you there.*

'She pissed me off,' I say. 'When I met her before.'

'Something she did?' Steve asks. 'Something she said?'

'Don't remember. Something.'

'Or nothing. Doesn't take a lot to piss you off, when you're in the humour.'

'Fuck off, you.'

'I like him,' Sophie tells me. 'You can keep him.'

Half my head is on where I've seen the vic before. My guard is down.

I duck under the tape, a voice recorder practically takes my eye out and a noise like an attack dog goes off in my face. I leap before I can stop myself, fists coming up, and hear the burst of fake shutter-clicks from a phone camera.

'Detective Conway do you have a suspect was this a serial killer was the victim sexually assaulted—'

Mostly journalists are a good thing. We all have our special relationships – you throw your guy early tipoffs, he leaks whatever you want leaked and passes you anything you should know – but even with the rest, we usually get on grand: we all know the boundaries, no one oversteps, everyone's happy. Louis Crowley is the exception. Crowley is a little snot-drip who works for a red-top rag called the *Courier*, which specialises in printing just a few too many details about rape cases, for readers who want more buzz of outrage or whatever else than they can get off the normal papers. His look is Poet Meets Pervert – floppy shirts and a dandruffy mac, wavy dark ponytail groomed over a big oily bald spot – and his face is permanently set on Righteous Offence. I'd rather brush my teeth with a chainsaw than tip off Crowley.

'Did the killer stalk his victim should women in the area be taking precautions our readers deserve to know—'

Voice recorder in my face, phone clicking away in his other hand, waft of foul patchouli pomade off his hair – Crowley just about comes up to my nose. I manage not to shoulder the little bollix in the gob on my way past him; can't be arsed with the paperwork. Behind me I hear Steve say cheerily, 'No comment. No comment on the no comment. No comment on the no comment on the no comment.'

The cluster of kids scattering again, open-mouthed. The lace curtains vibrating. The hard chill of the air, after that overheated house. Crowley jerks his voice recorder back just in time, before I slam the car door on it. I reverse out into the road without looking behind me.

'That little git,' Steve says, shaking his jacket sleeves like Crowley dandruffed him. 'That was quick. In time for the afternoon edition, and all.'

'"Detectives Refuse to Deny Stalker Rumours. Detectives Baffled by Possible Serial Killer. Detectives: No Comment on Local Women's Terror."' I don't even know where we're going, we don't have Lucy Riordan's address, but I'm driving like we're in a chase. '"Detectives Punch Shitty Excuse for Journalist in the Fucking Teeth."'

Over the last few months Crowley has been turning up at too many of my scenes, too fast. We have history – last year, he was trying to browbeat a quote out of a teenager who'd seen her drug-dealer da take two in the back of the head, I told him if he didn't fuck off I'd arrest him for hindering my investigation, he flounced off making offended noises about police brutality and freedom of the press and Nelson Mandela – but it's not like that puts me in a minority: half the force has told Crowley to fuck off, one way or another. There's no reason he should pick me out for revenge, specially not all this time later. And even if his tiny mind has decided to fixate on me, that doesn't explain how he's finding out about my cases as soon as I do.

Journalists have ways they don't tell us about, obviously. Crowley probably has a scanner that he tunes to police frequencies when he's on duty, and uses to look for couples having phone sex the rest of the time. But still: I have to wonder.

You don't make the Murder squad without having a world-class gift for finding creative ways to get under someone's skin and wriggle around in there till they'd rip themselves open to get rid of you; without being ready and happy to do it, even if the witness you're working on is a devastated kid sobbing her heart out for her da. I'm not the exception – and neither is Steve, much as he'd love to think he is. It's not like I was shocked, the first time I realised that not all the lads save that talent for interviews. It gets to feel right on you, like the gun at your hip that leaves you lopsided when it's not there. Some of the lads can't put it down. They use it to get anything they happen to want, or to get past anyone who happens to be in their way. Or to break anyone they want broken.

Steve is keeping his trap shut, which is a good call. Without noticing, I've got us deep into Phoenix Park, probably because it's the only place around where I can drive without getting snarled up in traffic and idiots. The roads are straight, between wide gentle meadows and rows of huge old trees, and I'm going like the clappers. The Kadett is about ready to have a fit of the vapours.

I slow down. Pull over, nice and neat, signalling well in advance and keeping one eye on my rear-view mirror.

'We need Lucy Riordan's address,' I say. 'I've got her mobile number.'

We pull out our phones. Steve dials his contact at one of the mobile networks and hits speaker; we listen to the even buzz of the ring. Deer watch us from under bare spreading branches. I realise I'm still wearing my shoe-covers – I'm lucky they didn't slide on the pedals and crash the car. I take them off and toss them in the back seat. The sunlight is still thin and warmthless; it still feels like dawn.

2

Steve's contact gives us a home address for Lucy Riordan in Rathmines, a work address at the Torch Theatre in town, and a birth date that makes her twenty-six. 'Just gone half-nine,' Steve says, checking his watch. 'She should be home.'

I'm dialling my voicemail; I've got a new message, and I just can't wait to hear it. 'She'll be sleeping off last night. Like anyone with sense, this time on a Sunday morning.' The park is making me edgy. Outside the car windows the sky is dead, not one bird, and the massive trees feel like they're slowly tilting inwards over us. 'You head up the interview.' Seeing as I don't have a legit reason to arrest Crowley or punch him in the mouth, or to tell the gaffer where to shove his domestics, I'm gonna take the head off the first person who gives me half an excuse, and I don't want it to be our key witness.

I didn't use to be like this. I've always had a temper on me, but I've always kept it under control, no matter how hard I had to bite down. Even when I was a kid, I knew how to hold it loaded and cocked while I got my target in range, lined up my sights and picked my moment to blow the bastard away. Since I made Murder, that's been changing – slowly, I never lose a lot of ground at once, but I never gain any back, and it's starting to show. The last few months, I've lost count of how many times I've caught myself in the half-second before I splattered temper everywhere and stuck myself cleaning up the mess for the rest of my life. I wasn't kidding about telling that witness he was too stupid to live: my mouth was opening to do it, when Steve came in with some soothing question. I know, dead certain, that someday soon neither of us is gonna catch me in time.

And I know, dead certain, that the rest of the squad is gonna be on that moment like sharks on chum. It'll be blown up to ten times life-size and spread all round the force like it's a full-frontal shot of me naked, and every day for the rest of my career someone will slap me in the face with it.

Murder isn't like other squads. When it's working right, it would take your breath away: it's precision-cut and savage, lithe and momentous, it's a big cat leaping full-stretch or a beauty of a rifle so smooth it practically fires itself. When I was a floater in the General Unit, fresh out of uniform, a bunch of us got brought in to do the scut work on a murder case, typing and door-to-door. I took one look at the squad in action and I couldn't stop looking. That's the nearest I've ever been to falling in love.

By the time I made it onto the squad, something had changed. The pressure level means Murder is balanced so finely that it only takes a few new heads to shift the whole feel of the squad: turn that big cat rogue and edgy, set that rifle warping towards its moment to blow up in your face. I came in at the wrong time, and I got off on the wrong foot.

Part of it was not having a dick, which apparently is the main thing you need to investigate murders. There's been women on the squad before, maybe half a dozen of them over the years; whether they jumped or got pushed, I don't know, but by the time I got there none of them were still around. Some of the guys figure that's the natural order; they thought I had some cheek, swanning in like I had a right to be there, and I needed to be taught a lesson. Not all of them – most were fine, at least to start with – but enough.

They tested me, my first weeks on the squad, the same way a predator tests a potential victim in a bar: tossing out small stuff – worn-out jokes starting *Why is a woman like a*, comments about me being on the rag, hints about how I had to be pretty good at whatever I'd done to get this gig – to see if I'd force myself to laugh along. Checking, just like the predator checks, for the well-behaved one who'll take the putdowns and the humiliation sooner than God forbid make a fuss; who can be forced, shove by shove, into doing whatever he wants.

Deep down, though, it wasn't about me being a woman. That was just their in; that was just the thing that they thought would, or should, make it easy for them to push me around. Deep down, this was simpler. This was about the exact same thing as primary school, when Ireland was still lily-white and I was the only brownish kid around, and my first ever nickname was Shiteface. It was about the same thing as everything else humans have done to each other since before history began: power. It was about deciding who would be the alpha dogs and who would be at the bottom of the pile.

I went in expecting that. Every squad hazes the newbie – my first day on Missing Persons, they tried to send me door-to-door asking if anyone had seen Mike Hunt – and Murder was already growing a rep for doing it that bit harder, fewer laughs, more edge. But just because I expected it, that didn't mean I was gonna take it. If I learned one thing in school, it's this: you never let them get you on the bottom of the pile. If you do, you might never get up again.

I could have followed official policy and reported to my superintendent that I felt other officers were discriminating against me and creating a hostile workplace environment. Apart from the obvious – that would have been the perfect way to make things worse – I'd rather shoot my own fingers off than go running to the gaffer whining for help. So when this little shiteball called Roche slapped my arse, I nearly broke his wrist. He couldn't pick up a coffee cup without wincing for days, and the message went out loud and clear: I wasn't going to roll over, belly-up and wiggling and panting for whatever the big dogs wanted to do to me.

So they went shoulder to shoulder and started pushing me out of the pack. Subtle stuff, at first. Somehow everyone knew about my cousin who's in for dealing smack. Fingerprint results never made it to me, so I never found out about the link between my case and a whole string of burglaries. One time I raised my voice at a lying alibi witness; nothing major, no worse than everyone else does all the time, but someone must have been watching behind the one-way glass, because it was months before I could interview a witness without the squad room wanting to know – just slagging, all a great big laugh – *Did you shout it out of him, Conway, bet you had him shiteing his kax, is he gonna get compensation for the hearing loss, the poor bastard'll think twice before he agrees to talk to the cops again won't he?* By this time even the guys who'd been grand were smelling the blood in the air around me, pulling back from trouble. Every time I walked into the squad room, I walked into a thud of instant, total silence.

Back then, at least I had Costello. Costello was the oldest inhabitant, it was his job to show newbies the ropes, and he was sound; no one was going to turn it up too high while Costello had his eye on me. A few months later, Costello retired.

In school I had my mates. Anyone who messed with me was messing with them too, and none of us was the type you wanted to mess with. When a rumour went round that my da was in prison for hijacking a plane, and half the class wouldn't sit next to me in case I had a bomb, we tracked down the three bitches who had started it and beat the shite out of them, and that was the end of that. In Murder, once Costello went and until Steve came on board, I was all on my own.

Before the door closed behind Costello, the lads stepped it up. I left my e-mail open on my computer, came back to everything wiped: inbox, sent box, contacts, gone. Some of them refused to switch into interviews with me when it was time to shake things up, *You're not sticking me with her, I'm not taking the blame when she fucks up*; or they needed every warm body for a big search, except mine, and sniggered *Couldn't track an elephant through snow* just too loud on their way out the door. At the Christmas party, where I knew better than to have more than one pint, someone got a phone snap of me with my eyes half shut; it was on the noticeboard next morning, labelled 'ALCOCOP', and by the end of the day everyone knew I had a drink problem. By the end of the week, everyone knew I had got rat-arsed drunk, puked on my shoes and given someone – the name varied – a blowjob in the jacks. No way for me to know which one of the lads was behind it, or which two or five or ten. Even if I stick it out in the force till retirement, there'll still be people who believe all that shite. As a rule I don't give a fuck who thinks what about me, but when I can't do my job because nobody trusts me enough to go near me, then I start caring.

All of which is why Steve was the one ringing his contact for Lucy Riordan's info. You pick up useful pals along the way, for moments when an official request would take too long, and a few months back I was making nice with this kid who worked for Vodafone; until one day I rang him to find out who owned a mobile number, and he stammered and dodged and tied himself in knots and couldn't get off the phone fast enough. I didn't bother asking for explanations. I already knew; not the details, like who had got onto him or what they had threatened him with, but enough. So Steve rings the mobile companies when we need info, and Steve runs interviews when I'm too wired to trust myself. And I keep telling myself those fuckers will never get to me.

My voicemail message is from Breslin, of course; lucky me. 'Conway. Hi.' Breslin has a good voice – deep, smooth, the news-reader accent that tells you Mummy and Daddy forked out for school fees to make sure he wouldn't have to meet people like me and Steve – and does he know it. I think he fantasises about doing movie-trailer voiceovers that start 'In a world . . .' 'Good to be working with you guys. We need to touch base as soon as possible; give me a bell when you get this. I'll head down to the crime scene, take a quick look-see at what we've got. If we don't cross paths there, I assume we'll have talked by the time I'm done. We'll take it from there.' Click.

Steve shoots me finger-guns and a wink. 'Yeahhh, baby. Touch my base.'

I snort before I can stop myself. 'You know what it feels like? It feels like he's sticking his tongue right out of the phone down your ear.'

'And he's positive it just made your day.'

We're snickering like a pair of kids. Breslin brings it out in us; he takes himself so seriously you're never gonna live up to it, so we don't try. 'Because before he rang you, he spritzed the good eau de cologne on his magic tongue. Just for you.'

'I feel all special now,' Steve says, hand on heart. 'Don't you feel special?'

'I feel like I should've brought my ear lube,' I say. 'What'll keep him out of our hair for another while?'

'Incident room?' Which isn't a bad idea all round: someone needs to nab us an incident room, and Breslin will get one of the good ones with an actual whiteboard and enough phone lines, while me and Steve would get dumped with the two-desk shithole that used to be the locker room and still smells like it. 'But nothing's going to keep him away for long. In fairness, the interviews are why the gaffer has him on board; he's going to want to be there for them.'

'Don't be giving me "in fairness". I'm not in the humour to be fair to bloody Breslin.' Actually, I'm in a better mood; I needed that laugh. 'Incident room is good. We'll go with that.'

'Don't be biting his head off,' Steve warns me.

'I'm not gonna bite his head off. Why shouldn't I bite his head off, if I feel like it?' Breslin isn't one of the worst by a long shot – mostly he ignores the pair of us – but that doesn't mean I have to like him.

'Because we're stuck with him? Because that'll be a lot harder if he's in a fouler with us from the start?'

'You can smooth him down. Stick your tongue in his ear.'

I ring Breslin's voicemail again – if I have to deal with Breslin, phone tag is the ideal way to do it – and leave him a message back. 'Breslin, Conway here. Looking forward to working with you.' I shoot Steve an eyebrow: *See, I can do nice.* 'We're going to pick up the guy who was due at the vic's house for dinner and bring him back to base for the interview. Could you meet us there? We'd really value your angle on this one.' Steve mimes a blowjob; I give him the finger. 'On the way to his place we're going to have a quick chat with the vic's best friend, in case there's anything we should know. Can you use that time to set us up with an incident room, since you'll be heading back to the squad anyway? Thanks. See you there.'

I hang up. 'See?' I say to Steve.

'That was gorgeous. If you'd put in a kiss at the end, it would've been perfect.'

'Funny guy.' I want to get going. The bare trees feel lower, closer, like while I was focusing on Breslin they grabbed their chance to move in around us. 'Let's find out what kind of crap floaters they've dumped on us.'

Steve is already dialling. Bernadette the admin gives him numbers for our floaters – six of them: O'Kelly pulled out all the stops there. A couple of them are good guys, useful; at least one isn't. If we want more, we're gonna have to fill out requests in triplicate, explain why we can't do our own dirty work, and generally sit up and beg like a pair of poodles.

Later on we'll have the first case meeting: me and Steve and Breslin and all the floaters in the incident room, everyone taking notes while I give a rundown of the case and we assign jobs. There's stuff that needs doing fast, though, no time to wait. Steve sends two of our lucky floaters to do a preliminary door-to-door on Viking Gardens, find out what everyone knows about Aislinn Murray and what they saw and heard last night, and another two to pull all the local CCTV footage they can get, before anyone records over it. Meanwhile I send the last two off to get Rory Fallon's address, find out if he's home, sit on the house if he is, track him if he goes anywhere, and try to be discreet about the whole thing. They could just bring him in straight-away, but my plans don't include Breslin spotting him in the corridors and deciding to do me and Steve a favour by getting a confession before we even make it back to the squad. Breslin rings me back; I let it go to voicemail.

The chewed-up night-shift look on Steve gives me some idea what I look like, so before we head for Lucy Riordan's place we do a fast reboot: brush wrinkles out of our jackets and night-food crumbs off our shirts, Steve combs his hair, I take down what's left of my bun and pull it back smooth and tight again. I don't do makeup on the job, but the slice of me in the rear-view mirror seems decent enough. On a good day I look good, and on a bad day you'd still notice me. I take after my da, or I assume I do: I got the height from my ma, but not the thick shiny black hair, or the cheekbones, or the skin that's never gonna need fake tan. I wear good suits, stuff that's cut right and works with my shape – long and strong – and anyone who thinks I should be schlepping around in a sack to protect him from his own bad thoughts can fuck himself. The stuff people think I should try to hide – being tall, being a woman, being half whatever – is the stuff I keep up front and in their faces. If they can't handle it, I can use that.

'Yeah?' Steve says, pointing at himself.

He looks like his mammy spit-shined him for Mass, but he plays that up on purpose. You use what you've got, and what Steve's got is that your parents would be delighted if you brought him home. 'Have to do,' I say, readjusting the mirror. 'Let's go.'

I hit the pedal hard and let the Kadett pretend it's a real car while it gets us out of there. I get a sudden nasty feeling like the trees behind us have snapped together and come down, with a silent roar and a smash of branches, onto the spot where we were parked.

Lucy Riordan lives in one of those tall old terraced houses split into flats. A lot of those are shitholes, but hers looks OK: the front garden's been weeded, the window-frames have been painted in the last decade, and there are six bells by the door instead of a dozen, meaning the landlord isn't jamming people into nine-foot-square bedsits and making them all share a jacks.

It takes two rings before Lucy answers the intercom, in a voice coated with sleep. ''Lo?'

Steve says, 'Lucy Riordan?'

'Who's this?'

'Detective Garda Stephen Moran. Could we have a word?'

A long second. Then Lucy says, and the sleep's fallen off her voice, 'I'll be down in a minute.'

She opens the door fast and wide awake. She's short and fit, the kind of fit you get from life, not from the gym – she wears it like it's owned, not rented. Cropped platinum hair with a long sweep of fringe falling in her face – pale face with clean quick features, smudges of last night's mascara. She's wearing a black hoodie, paint-splashed black combats, nothing on her feet, a lot of silver ear jewellery and what looks to me like a fair-sized hangover. She has bugger-all in common with Aislinn Murray, or with what I was expecting.

We have our IDs out and ready. 'I'm Detective Garda Stephen Moran,' Steve says, 'and this is my partner, Detective Garda Antoinette Conway.' And he pauses. You always leave a gap there.

Lucy doesn't even look at the IDs. She says, sharp, 'Is it Aislinn?' Which is why you leave the gap: it's unbelievable what people will spill into it.

Steve says, 'Could we come in for a few minutes?'

She looks at the IDs then; takes her time checking them out, or making some decision. Then: 'Yeah,' she says. 'OK. Come in.' And she turns and heads up the stairs.

Her flat is on the first floor and I was right, it's decent: a small sitting room with a kitchenette to one side and two doors leading off the others, for the bedroom and the jacks. She had people over last night – empty cans on the coffee table and under it, thick layer of smoke in the air – but even before that, this place was nothing like Aislinn's. The curtains are made out of old postcards sewn together with twine, the furniture is a banged-up wooden coffee table and a couple of lopsided sofas covered in Mexican-looking woven throws, and there are four 1970s phones and a stuffed fox on top of a coil of cable beside the telly. Nobody ordered this place through an app.

Me and Steve go for the sofa with its back to the high sash window, leaving Lucy with the limp excuse for daylight hitting her face. I get out my notebook, but I sit forward, letting Steve know that I'm not gonna be sitting this one out altogether. O'Kelly was full of shite, Steve is great with witnesses – not as flashy with it as Breslin, but he can make just about anyone believe he's on their side – but I used to be pretty good too, not all that long ago, and Lucy doesn't seem like she's gonna piss me off. This girl is no idiot.

'Anyone else home?' Steve asks. After this conversation, Lucy is going to want backup.

Lucy sits down on the other sofa and tries to look at both of us at once. 'No. It's just me. Why . . . ?'

Your basic witness-face is a mix of eager to help, dying to know the story and oh-God-I-hope-I'm-not-in-trouble. Your standard variation, in neighbourhoods where we're not popular, is a sullen teen-style slouch-stare, including from people who are decades too old to pull off that shite. Lucy isn't wearing either of those. She's sitting up straight, feet planted like she's ready to leap into action, and her eyes are too wide open. Lucy is scared, and she's wary, and whatever she's wary about is taking all her focus. There's a green glass ashtray on the coffee table that she should have emptied before she let cops in. Me and Steve pretend we don't see it.

'I'll just confirm a couple of things,' Steve says, easily, giving her his best nonthreatening smile. 'You're Lucy Riordan, born the twelfth of April '88, and you work at the Torch Theatre. That's all correct, yeah?'

Lucy's back is stiffening up. Nobody likes us knowing stuff they haven't told us, but she's liking it even less than most. 'Yeah. I'm the technical manager.'

'And you're friends with Aislinn Murray. Close friends.'

'We've known each other since we were kids. What's happened?'

I say, 'Aislinn's dead.'

Which isn't me being tactless. After the way she opened the door, I want her reaction neat.

Lucy stares at me. So many expressions collide on her face that I can't read any of them. She's not breathing.

I say, not bitchily, 'Sorry to start your day off like this.'

Lucy grabs for a pack of Marlboro Lights on the coffee table and reefs one out without asking permission. Even her hands look active: strong wrists, short nails, scrapes and calluses. For a second the lighter flame jumps and wavers; then she gets it under control and draws hard on the smoke.

She asks, 'How?'

Her head is down, that white-blond streak hiding her face. I say, 'We don't have any definitive answers yet, but we're treating the death as suspicious.'

'That means someone killed her. Right?'

'Looks like it. Yeah.'

'Shit,' Lucy says, low – I'm pretty sure she doesn't know she's saying it. 'Ah, shit. Ah, shit.'

Steve says, 'Why did you assume we were here about Aislinn?'

Lucy's head comes up. She's not crying, which is a relief, but her face is a nasty white; her eyes look like she's having trouble seeing, or trouble not getting sick. She says, 'What?'

'When you came to the door, you said, "Is it Aislinn?" Why would you think that?'

The cigarette's shaking. Lucy stares at it, curls her fingers tighter to keep it still. 'I don't know. I just did.'

'Think back. There has to have been a reason.'

'I don't remember. That's just what came into my head.'

We wait. In the walls, pipes hoot and groan; upstairs a guy yells something about hot water and someone gallops across the floor, making the postcard curtains tremble. Next to Lucy on the sofa is a Homer Simpson stuffed toy with a Rizla that says PRINCESS BUTTER-CUP stuck to its forehead. Last night was a good one. Next time Lucy sees that toy, she's gonna shove it to the bottom of her bin.

After a long minute, the line of Lucy's spine resets. She's not gonna cry or puke, not now anyway; she's got other things to do. I'm pretty sure she's just decided to lie to us.

She taps ash without even clocking the spliff butts in the ashtray. She says – carefully, feeling her way – 'Aislinn just started seeing this guy Rory. Last night she was cooking him dinner. It was his first time in her house; they'd only met in public places before. So when you said you were Guards, that's the only thing I could think of: some-thing went wrong there. I mean, I couldn't think of any other reason you'd want to talk to me.'

Bullshit. Just off the top of my head I can think of half a dozen reasons – the hash, noise complaint from the neighbours, street fight outside and we need witnesses, domestic in another flat ditto, I could keep going – and Lucy's well able to do the same. Here it is: the lie.

'Yeah,' I say. 'About that. Yesterday evening, you and Aislinn were texting about her dinner date.' The wariness goes up a notch, as Lucy tries to remember what she said. 'You told Aislinn to' – I pretend to check my notebook – '"be careful, OK?" Why was that?'

'Like I said. She hadn't known him that long, and she was going to be on her own in the house with him.'

Steve is doing puzzled. 'Is that not a bit paranoid, no?'

Lucy's eyebrows shoot up and she stares at Steve like he's the enemy. 'You think? I wasn't telling her to have a loaded gun in her bra. Just to mind herself with a strange guy in her house. That's paranoid?'

'Sounds like basic good sense to me,' I say. Lucy turns to me grate-fully, relaxing back off the attack. 'I'd tell my mate the same thing. Had you met Rory?'

'Yeah. I was actually there when the two of them met. This guy I know from work, Lar, he published a book about the history of Dublin theatres, and the launch was at the bookshop Rory runs – the Wayward Bookshop, in Ranelagh? A bunch of us went from the Torch, and I talked Aislinn into coming along. I thought she needed a night out.'

Which is more info than I asked for. It's the oldest technique in the book – get the witness pissed off with one of you, she'll give the other one extra – and me and Steve do it a lot, but mostly we do it the other way round. I let Steve take the notes while I enjoy the feeling of being the good cop for the first time in a long time. 'And Aislinn and Rory clicked,' I say.

'Big-time. Lar had read a bit out of the book and he was signing copies, and the rest of us were hanging around drinking the free wine, and Aislinn and Rory got talking. They basically vanished into a corner together – not snogging or anything, just talking and having a laugh. I think Rory would've stayed there all night, but Ash has this rule about not talking to a guy for too long—'

Lucy cuts off, blinking. It's that filter – God forbid we should think bad things about poor sweet Ash – but I know what she's on about: The Rules. 'In case the guy guesses she's into him,' I say, nodding like this makes total sense.

'Yeah. Exactly. I don't know, that's a bad thing for some reason.' A twist of Lucy's shoulder and her mouth, but it's affectionate, not bitchy. 'So after maybe an hour Ash came dashing over to me, and she was all, "OhmyGod, he's so sweet and so funny and so interesting and so *lovely*, that was sooo much fun . . ." She said she'd given him her number and now she had to find someone else to talk to, so she stuck with me and the gang from work, but she spent the whole rest of the night going, "Is he looking over? What's he doing now, is he looking at me?" Which he always was. They were both totally smitten.'

'Lar who?' I say. 'And when was the book launch?'

'Lar Flannery – Laurence. It was at the beginning of December, I don't remember the exact date. A Sunday night, so theatre people could come.'

'Did you meet Rory again after that?'

'No, that was it. Aislinn's only seen him a few times. She was taking it slow.' Lucy's head ducks to her cigarette, a long pull. We've just brushed past whatever she's hiding. We leave a silence, but this time she drops nothing into it. Instead she asks, 'Are you . . . ? I mean, do you think Rory was the one who . . . ?'

The question's natural enough, but all of a sudden her voice is full up and leaping with things I can't catch, and the flash of her eyes under her fringe is too fast and too intent. This means more to her, or means something more urgent, than it should.

Steve says, 'What do you think? Would he be your guess?'

'I don't have a guess. You're the detectives. Is he your prime suspect, or whatever you call it?'

'Was there anything specific about Rory that set off your radar?' I ask. 'Made him seem like someone to be careful of?'

Lucy's twitching to ask again, but she knows better. Smart, capable and used to thinking on her feet: whatever she's keeping back, we'll be lucky to get to it. She takes another drag of her smoke. 'No. Nothing. He seemed like a nice guy. Kind of boring – I thought, anyway – but Ash was obviously seeing something I missed, so . . .'

'She ever say anything indicating that he frightened her? Pressured her? Tried to control her?'

Lucy's shaking her head. 'No. Seriously. Nothing like that, ever. It was always how lovely he was and how relaxed she was around him, and how she couldn't wait to see him again. Are you thinking—'

I say, 'Then I've gotta be straight with you, Lucy. It doesn't make sense that you were this worried about Aislinn. Texting her to be careful, yeah, sure, I can see that. But taking one look at us and figuring we had to be here about her? When you just told me Rory seemed like a good guy, no threat? Nah. When we showed up, you should've been wondering if the guy downstairs was dealing, or if someone got stabbed outside last night, or if one of your family was mugged or hit by a car. There's no way your mind should've gone straight to Aislinn. Unless there's something about her that you're not telling us.'

Lucy's smoke is right down to the butt. She grinds it out in the ashtray, taking her time, but she's not stonewalling; she's deciding.

The light through the window is filling out; it's ruthless on her, scraping away what should be offbeat-pretty, turning her to nothing but eyebags and mascara smudges on white.

She says, 'Is it OK if I get a glass of water? My head's killing me.'

'No problem,' I say. 'We're in no hurry.'

She takes her time running the tap in the kitchenette, her back to us; cups water in her hands and ducks her face into them, stays there while her shoulders lift and fall once. She comes back holding a pint glass in one hand, wiping water off her face with the other wrist and looking a couple of notches more alive. When she sits down she says, 'OK. I think Ash might've been seeing someone else. As well as Rory.'

That flash of her eyes again, checking our reactions, too ferociously intent. Me and Steve don't look at each other, but you can feel your thoughts click together like glances. Steve thinking *I knew it, I knew something was weird here*; me thinking *Not a fucking chance I'm gonna get my run today.*

Steve says, 'What was his name?'

'I don't know. She never said.'

'Not even a first name?'

Lucy's shaking her head hard enough that her fringe falls forward. She shoves it back again. 'No. She never even actually said she was seeing anyone else. It's just a feeling I got; I don't know anything specific. OK?'

'OK,' I say. 'Fair enough. What gave you that feeling?'

'Just stuff. Like the last few months – way before Ash met Rory – I'd ask if she wanted to meet up for a drink, and she'd say no, she couldn't, but without any reason why not – and normally she'd have been like, "Can't, I've got Pilates" or whatever. Or she'd say yes, and then at the last minute she'd text me like, "Change of plans, can we do it tomorrow instead?" She was around a lot less, mainly. And she got her hair done a lot more, and her nails – they were always perfect. And when someone's around less, and gets more high-maintenance . . .' Lucy shrugs. 'Mostly it's a new relationship.'

Aislinn cancelling her restaurant date with Rory, with just a few hours to go. I thought she was showing him who was boss.

I feel it again, that faint pulse that caught at me in Aislinn's kitchen when Steve showed me the cooker. A pulse like hunger, like dance music: something good, away on the horizon, tugging. I can feel the beat of it hitting Steve's blood too.

He says, 'How long ago did this start?'

Lucy draws tight lines in the condensation on her glass and has a think, either about the actual answer or about the one she wants to give us. 'Maybe five or six months ago. Towards the end of summer.'

'Any idea where they might have met? Work? Pub? Hobby?'

'Haven't a clue.'

'Who else did Aislinn hang out with, besides you?'

Lucy shrugs. 'She went for a drink with people from work, sometimes. She doesn't have a lot of friends.'

'What about hobbies? She have any?'

'Not serious ones. She's been doing a bunch of evening classes, the last couple of years: she did salsa for a while, and then some image and styling thing, and she learned a bit of Spanish . . . Last summer I think she was doing cooking. She liked the people, but she never talked about any guy in particular. There was never anyone she mentioned that bit too often, nothing like that.'

Aislinn Murray is sounding like more and more of a laugh riot. I say, 'I've gotta tell you, Lucy, this is coming across pretty weird to me. You and Ash, you were best friends since you were kids, but she tells you nothing about her fella?'

Her eyes come up, wary. 'I said we've been friends since we were kids. I didn't say we were *best* friends.'

'No? Then what were you?'

'Friends. We hung out in school, we stayed in touch when we grew up. We didn't have a Vulcan *mind* meld.'

Steve has this lovely mix of worried and reproachful growing on his face. He says, 'You know how we got your name? Aislinn had you down as her emergency contact. When you're picking that, you pick someone who you think cares about you.'

Lucy's head jerks away from the reproachful frown. 'Her mum died a few years back, her dad's not around, she's an only kid. Who else was she going to put?'

Lying again. For some reason she's trying to make the friendship sound like a leftover stuck to her shoe, but the layer of warmth when she talked about Aislinn's idiot rules said different. I say, 'You're also the person Aislinn texted and rang most often. Like you said, she didn't have a lot of mates. She thought of you as her closest friend, all right. Did she know you didn't feel the same way?'

'We *are* friends. I *said* that. I'm just saying, we don't live in each other's pocket. We don't know everything about each other's life. OK?'

'So who would know all about Aislinn's life? Who was her best friend, if it wasn't you?'

'She didn't have one, not like you mean. Some people don't.'

Her voice is pulling tighter. I leave it: she's holding herself together by her fingernails, and I don't want her going to pieces on us right now. 'Regardless,' I say. 'Me, when I'm going out with someone, I tell my friends, even if they're not my best bosom buddies. Don't you?'

Lucy takes a gulp of her water and gets herself back. 'Yeah. Sure. But Aislinn didn't.'

'You said she was dying to talk to you about Rory, how great he was. Did she tell you about other boyfriends, before him? Introduce them to you?'

'Yeah. I mean, it's been a few years since she went out with anyone, but yeah, I met him.'

'She wanted to talk about him, see what you thought of him, all that. Right?'

'Yeah.'

'But not this time.'

'No. Not this time.'

Steve asks, 'Why did you figure that was?'

Lucy rubs her water glass over a smear of purple paint on the knee of her combats, scrapes at it with a fingernail. She says, 'I figured the guy was married. Wouldn't you?'

She's looking at me. I say, 'That'd be my first thought, all right. Did you ask her?'

'I didn't want to know. As far as I'm concerned, anyone who's taken is well off limits, and Ash knows that. Neither one of us wanted to have the conversation. It would only have turned into a fight.'

'You're saying she might've been OK with seeing a married guy, though. They weren't off limits to her.'

Purple paint flakes away. Lucy rubs it to a smudge between her fingertips. 'That makes her sound like some homewrecker vamp manhunter. She's not like that. At all. She just . . . she's really unsure. Of a lot of stuff. Does that make sense?' A quick glance up at me. I nod. Her face looks older than it did when we got here, dragged down around the edges. This conversation is taking a lot out of her. 'And if the other person's totally sure, a lot of the time she ends up thinking they're probably right. So yeah, I could see her hooking up with a married guy. Not because she thought it was OK, or because she didn't care, but because he convinced her that it might not be *not* OK.'

'Gotcha,' I say. I'm glad Aislinn is the vic and Lucy is the witness here, not the other way round. By this point I would've brained Aislinn with something gingham.

'So you must've been well pleased when she hit it off with Rory,' Steve says. 'Nice single guy, nothing to cause tension between the two of you, nothing to cause Aislinn hassle. Yeah?'

'Yeah.' But there's a fraction of a second before it. Another brush past something Lucy isn't telling us.

I say, 'Did you get the sense she'd finished it with the other fella before she started seeing Rory? Or would you guess she had them both on the go?'

'How would I know? Like I said—'

'Was she still being vague about her social plans? Still cancelling on you at the last minute?'

'I guess. Yeah, she was.'

I say, 'So that's why you were worried about Aislinn?'

Lucy's still messing around with paint smears, elbows on her thighs and her head right down. 'Anyone would be. I mean, juggling two guys, one of them's married . . . that's not going to end well. And Ash . . . she's really naïve, in a lot of ways. It wouldn't occur to her that this was a pretty volatile situation. I just wanted her to be aware of that.'

This is making more sense, but not enough. 'You said Rory didn't set off your alarm bells,' I say. 'What about this other guy?'

'I don't know anything about him *to* set off alarm bells. Like I said. I just didn't like the whole setup.'

She's tensing, digging her elbows into her thighs. Whatever we're circling, she's not happy being this close to it. I'm not happy myself. Lucy is no idiot; she should know this isn't the time to fuck about. I say, 'That still doesn't explain why your mind went straight to Aislinn when we showed up at your door. You want to try again?'

The edge on my voice makes her elbows dig in harder. 'That's why. Because what else was it going to be? Maybe I lead a really boring life, but most people I know don't do anything that could land actual *detectives* on my doorstep.'

I'm less and less in the mood for bullshit. 'Right,' I say. I lean over and give the ashtray a shove so it slides towards Lucy, a little puff of rancid ash rising into the light. 'Like I said: try again.'

Lucy's head comes up and she gives me a whole new kind of wary look.

Steve shifts his weight beside me. I know that shift: *Leave it.*

I consider punching my elbow through his ribs, but the fact is, he's right. I've been getting on well with Lucy, and I'm about to throw that away for good. I say, more gently, 'We're not planning on doing anything about that. We're only interested in Aislinn.'

The wary look fades, but not all the way. Steve – right back in the Good Cop seat, where he's happiest – says, 'Tell us a bit about her. How did yous meet?'

Lucy lights another smoke. I love nicotine. It puts witnesses back in their comfort zone when things get tricky, it keeps the vic's friends and family from going to pieces, it means we can make suspects as antsy as we want and then throw them an instant chill pill when we want them calm again. Non-smokers are double the hassle; you have to find other ways to adjust their dials. If it was my call, everyone involved in murders would be on a pack a day. She says, 'When we started secondary school. So when we were twelve.'

'You're from the same place, yeah? Where's that?'

'Greystones.'

Just outside Dublin; smallish town, but big enough that Lucy and Aislinn were hanging out together by choice, not because there was no one else. Steve asks, 'And what was Aislinn like, back then? If you had to describe her in one word, what would you pick?'

Lucy thinks back. That affection warms her face again. 'Shy. Really shy. I mean, that wasn't the most important thing about her, not by miles, but back then it covered up practically everything else.'

'Any particular reason? Or just the way she was?'

'Partly just the way she was, and being that age. But I think mostly it was because of her mother.'

'Yeah? What was she like?' This is what I mean about Steve being good with witnesses. The way he's leaning forward on the sofa, the tilt of his head, the note in his voice: even I could believe he's genuinely, personally interested.

'She was messed up,' Lucy says. 'Mrs Murray, not Ash. Like, properly messed up; she should've been in therapy, or on medication. Or both.'

Steve nods away. 'What kind of messed up?'

'Ash said she used to be fine, back before we knew each other. But when Ash was almost ten, her dad walked out on them.' Lucy should be relaxing, now that we've moved away from the murder and the hash and whatever she's hiding, but her fingers are still rigid on her smoke and her feet are still braced on the paint-splattered floorboards like she might need to run any minute. 'They never knew why, exactly. He didn't say. Just . . . gone.'

'And that wrecked Mrs Murray's head.'

'She never got over it. She just started going downhill and couldn't stop. Ash said she was ashamed; she felt like it had to have been her fault.' That twist to Lucy's mouth again, through her cigarette, but this time the warmth isn't there. 'That generation, you know? Everything was the woman's fault somehow, and if you didn't get how, then you probably needed to pray harder. So Ash's mum basically cut herself off. From everyone. She still went to the shops and to Mass, but that was it. So by the time we met, Ash had had two years where she spent most of her life stuck in the house, just her and her mum and the telly – she's an only child. I never even wanted to go over there because her mum creeped me out so much – you'd hear her crying in her bedroom, or else you'd go into the kitchen and she'd just be standing there staring at a spoon while something went up in smoke on the cooker, and the curtains were always closed in case someone saw her through a window and, I don't know, thought bad things about her . . . And Aislinn had to *live* there.'

Steve's hit the Go button. Lucy's talking faster; she's not going to stop till we stop her, or till she crashes. 'There was small stuff, too. Like, since her mum didn't go out, and they didn't have a lot of money, Ash's clothes were always wrong – she never had whatever everyone else in school was wearing; it was always charity-shop crap that was two years out of date and didn't suit her. I used to lend her stuff, but we were different sizes – that was another reason Aislinn was insecure: she was always, not fat, but a bit overweight – and my mum bought her stuff sometimes, but there's four of us so there was a limit to what she could do, you know? It doesn't sound like a big deal, but when you're twelve and everyone already knows that your dad's left and your mum's gone off the rails, the last thing you need is to look like some weirdo.'

This is the stuff Steve likes, and the stuff I'm wary of. He thinks it gives us an insight into the victim. Me, I think about those filters. I already know Lucy's got at least one agenda that we haven't pinned down. The Aislinn we're getting here is totally in Lucy's hands; she can do whatever she wants with her.

I say, 'This is gonna sound blunt, Lucy, and I'm sorry about that. But I'm not getting why you two were friends. I'm trying to see it, but I can't put my finger on a single thing yous had in common. What made it work?'

'I guess you had to be there.' Lucy half-smiles; not at me, at whatever she's seeing. 'We did have stuff in common. I wasn't having that great a time in school either. I wasn't an outcast or anything, but I was always into carpentry and electrics, so the boss mares gave me shite about that and called me a dyke, and the people who wanted to get in with them did it too, and it wasn't some major torture thing but overall school mostly sucked. But Ash, right? She thought I was great – for the exact same things that everyone else was slagging me about. She thought I was totally amazing, like some kind of heroine, just because I told the other girls to fuck off and did what I wanted even though they didn't like it. Ash thought that was the coolest thing ever.'

The smile spasms into something wretched. She takes a drag off her smoke to force it back under control. 'And yeah, at first partly I was hanging out with her because I liked her thinking I was amazing, but after the first while it was because I liked *her*. People thought she was thick, but that was just because of what I told you, how she was unsure – it made her seem like she wasn't keeping up. She wasn't thick, at all. She was actually really perceptive.'

Steve is nodding along, all enthralled. I'm interested too, but not like that. Lucy wants us to know Aislinn, or at least her version of Aislinn; wants it badly. Sometimes we get that: the friends and family want to shove a holy innocent in our faces, so we won't think this was all the vic's fault. Usually they do it when they think it was at least partly the vic's fault. Aislinn shagging a married man might be enough to do that for Lucy, or there might be more.

'And she could make even shit things funny. Like I'd have some bitch-off with some cow in our class, and afterwards I'd be all pissed off and adrenaline-y, like "Who does that geebag think she is, I should've punched her face in . . ." And Ash would start giggling, and I'd be like, "*What?* It's not *funny*!" all ready to go off on her; but she'd go, "You were brilliant, like this little furious cat chasing away a horrible dirty hyena" – and she'd do an imitation of me jumping up and down, trying to punch something way above my head. She'd be like, "I thought she was going to run for it, she'd be hiding in a corner screaming for help while you bit the ankles off her, everyone'd be crowding around chanting your name . . ." And all of a sudden I'd be laughing too, and the whole thing wouldn't feel like a big deal any more. *I* wouldn't feel like such a big deal.'

Lucy laughs, but there's a stretched sound to it, like it's straining against the solid weight of pain dragging downwards. 'That was Ash. She made things better. Maybe because she'd had so much practice with her mum, trying to make their life even bearable for both of them; I don't know. But even when she couldn't make things better for herself, she made them better for other people.'

Please I don't know where else to— That woman was still the twelve-year-old that Lucy's describing: chubby, insecure, clothes that wouldn't suit anyone and definitely didn't suit her. The dead woman was a whole different story. I say, 'Things got better for her, too, though. She grew into her looks, got a bit of style, bit of confidence. Yeah?'

Lucy grinds out her smoke, picks up her glass but doesn't drink. Now that we've moved back to the present, the carefulness is creeping back in.

She says, 'Not as soon as she should've. Even after we left school, she stayed living at home – she felt like she couldn't leave her mother, and even though I thought her staying was a terrible idea, I could see her point: without Aislinn there, probably her mum would've killed herself inside a few weeks. So right up until a few years ago, Ash was going home to that house every night, just like when we were kids. It kept her . . .' She turns the glass between her hands, watching the light move on the surface of the water. 'Like it kept her from growing up. She had a job, but it was the same one she'd had since we left school – she was the receptionist at this place that sells toilet roll and hand soap to businesses, which would have been fine except it wasn't what she wanted to do. She didn't have a clue *what* she wanted; she'd never had a chance to think about it. I was scared for her, you know? I could see us being thirty, forty, and Ash still doing this job she'd wandered into and going straight home to look after her mum, and her whole life just . . .' Lucy snaps her fingers, hand lifting through a patch of pale sun. 'Gone. And she could see it too. She just didn't know how to do anything about it.'

'So what changed?' Steve asks.

'Mrs Murray died. Three years ago. This is going to sound bad, but it was the best thing that ever happened to Ash.'

'What did she die of?'

'You mean, did she actually kill herself?' Lucy shakes her head. 'No. She had a brain aneurysm. Ash came home from work and found her. She was devastated, obviously she was, but after a while she started coming out of that, and . . . it was like that was when her actual life started. She sold the house and bought herself the cottage in Stoneybatter. She lost a load of weight, she got her hair dyed, she bought new clothes, she started going out . . .' A sudden grin. 'To really trendy places, even. I mean, this was the girl I had to *drag* out for one pint in some manky theatre pub, and suddenly she wants to go to some super-fancy club she's read about in some social column – and when I said there was no chance the bouncer would let me in, she was like, "I'll do you up, you can wear my stuff, we'll get in no problem!"'

The grin widens. 'And we actually did. It wasn't my scene – tossers in labels seeing who could yell loudest – but it was totally worth it just to watch Ash. She had a *ball*. Dancing, and flirting with one of the tossers, and turning him down . . . She was like a kid at a funfair.'

The grin is gone. Lucy grabs a big breath and lets it out in a hiss, trying to keep herself together.

'She was just getting her chance to figure out what she wanted to do. Just starting to get enough confidence to even think maybe she was *allowed* to figure that out. Just starting—'

She was getting, she wanted, she was. Lucy has switched Aislinn to past tense. It's sinking in. Any minute now she's going to melt down.

'She was going to quit her job – she'd never had much to spend her salary on, so she had a load of money saved up, and she was going to take a year or two out and decide what she wanted to do next. She was—' Another grab for breath. 'She was talking about travelling – she'd never been out of Ireland – about going to college . . . She was *giddy* about it. Like she was waking up after being in a coma for fifteen years, and she couldn't believe how bright the sun was. She . . .'

Lucy's voice fractures. She dives her head down and digs at another smear of paint, so viciously that she's got to be gouging into her leg through the combats. Whatever game she's playing with us, it's used her up.

She says, down to her knees, 'How did . . . ? Whoever did this. What did he do to her?'

I say, 'We can't give out details, for operational reasons. As far as we can tell, she didn't suffer.'

Lucy opens her mouth to say something else, but she can't make it work. Tears fall onto her combats and spread into dark stains.

The decent thing to do is leave, give her privacy while the first wave of grief smashes her down and pounds her black and blue. Neither of us moves. She holds out for almost a minute before she starts sobbing.

We give her tissues and refill her water glass, ask if she's got some-one who could come stay with her, nod sympathetically and stay put when she manages to say she just wants to be by herself. When she can talk again, we get her to make us a list of Aislinn's exes – all three of them, including a two-week summer fling called Jorge when she was seventeen; the girl was a real player – and of everyone she remem-bers being at the book launch. We ask – just a formality, ticking the boxes, have to ask everyone – where Lucy was yesterday evening. She was at the Torch: arrived at the theatre at half-six, did various stuff within sight of other people till the show came down just after ten, went for a few in the pub, then came home around one in the morning with the lighting operator and two of the cast, who hung out doing the obvious until around four. We – meaning the floaters – will check her story, but we won't find holes in it.

I'm about to bring up the formal ID when Steve says, 'Here are our cards,' and shoots a glance at me. I find a card and shut up. 'Whenever you feel like you're ready to make your official statement, you give one of us a ring.'

Lucy takes the cards without knowing they're there. I say, 'Meanwhile, please don't talk to any journalists. Seriously. Even if you don't think you're saying anything important, it could do real damage to the investigation. OK?' Creepy Crowley is still nagging at the back of my mind. If someone's siccing him on me, it's someone who's gonna have access to Lucy's details.

Lucy nods, wiping her eyes with the back of her hand – she used up the tissues a while back. It makes no difference; the tears are still coming.

She says – her voice has gone thick from crying – 'Whoever did this . . . it's like he killed a little kid: someone who never even had a chance to get her life started. He took away her whole entire life. Could you remember that? When you're investigating?'

I say, 'Don't worry. We're going to do everything we can to put this guy away.'

Lucy gives up and leaves the tears to drip off her chin. She looks like shite, eyes puffed half-shut, a smear of purple paint down one cheek. 'Yeah, I know. Just . . . Could you just keep that in mind?'

'OK,' I say. 'We'll do that. In exchange, though, I want you to keep thinking about whether there's anything else you can tell us. Anything at all. Yeah?'

Lucy nods, for whatever that's worth. She's not looking at either of us. We leave her staring at nothing, surrounded by the ashy leftovers of last night.

Daytime's kicked in properly while we were up there. Rathmines is buzzing: students hunting hangover cures, couples making sure the world can see how in love they are, families who are going to enjoy their family time if it kills them all. One look at it drops us both into the morning-after vortex, when your body suddenly realises you've been up all night and shuts down the engine, turning you floppy with fatigue.

'Coffee,' Steve says. 'Jesus, I need coffee.'

'Wimp.'

'Me? If you shut your eyes, you'll fall over asleep. Do it. I dare you.'

'Fuck off.'

'Coffee. And food.'

I hate wasting my time eating on the job, I can't wait for them to come up with some nutrition pill I can pop twice a day, but till then me and Steve both need food and plenty of it. 'Your turn to buy,' I say. 'Find somewhere they serve coffee by the litre.'

Steve does it right: skips the shiny hip chai-and-cronut cafés, picks the smallest, scuzziest corner shop, and comes out with massive medical-grade coffees and breakfast rolls stuffed with enough sausages and egg and rashers to see us through most of the day. We take them to a little park off a side street; it's too cold for that, with a nasty edge to the air like it's just waiting for the right moment to dump sleet down the backs of our necks, but getting out of the car means at least no one can give us hassle over the radio, and we need to have a conversation that doesn't belong in a coffee shop.

The park looks just adorable, all curly wrought-iron benches and neatly clipped hedges and flowerbeds waiting for spring, till you look again: used condom twisted in the hedge, blue plastic bag hanging off a railing with something sticking out that I don't like the look of. The place has a nightlife. In sunshine it would be jammed, but the weather is keeping people wary. On one bench a guy in a Tesco uniform is having a smoke, whipping his head around after each puff like he's checking no one's seen him, and a kid is circling grimly on a scooter while his mother bobs a whining buggy and swipes at her phone. The kid is wearing a hat that looks like some kind of dinosaur eating his head.

We find a bench that doesn't smell like anyone's pissed on it recently. I turn up my coat collar and get half my coffee down me in one swig. 'You were right. Talking to Lucy, that was worth doing.'

'I think so, yeah. It could still be Rory Fallon—'

I give Steve the eyeball. 'It is. Almost definitely, it is.'

Steve wavers his head noncommittally. He's unfolding paper napkins to spread over the front of his overcoat – these are attack sandwiches, and Steve takes his work clothes very seriously. 'Maybe. But the rest of that stuff's worth knowing, either way.'

I'm feeling better already; the coffee zapped my eyelids open like something out of a cartoon. 'At least we know why Aislinn's gaff looked like Working Girl Barbie Playhouse. And why Aislinn looked like Dream Date Barbie. The woman hadn't got a clue; she was putting together who she was meant to be out of magazines.'

Steve says, 'Someone like that, she's vulnerable. Really vulnerable.'

'No shit. Rory could be a full-on psychopath with more red flags than the Chinese embassy, and as long as he wore the right labels and helped her put her coat on, she'd still have invited him over for dinner on Date Three. Because that's what you're supposed to do.'

'Lucy's not clueless,' Steve points out. 'If he was covered in red flags, she'd've spotted them.'

'Speaking of,' I say. The breakfast roll is good stuff, proper thick rashers, grease and egg yolk going everywhere; I can feel my energy creeping back up. 'What'd you think of Lucy?'

'Smart. Scared.' Steve has finished arranging his bib. He props his coffee cup on the bench and starts peeling back his sandwich wrapper. 'She's keeping something back.'

'She's keeping back plenty. And that doesn't make sense. Forget all that hair-splitting crap about old-mates-not-best-mates-no-not-that-kind-of-mates; she cared about Aislinn, a lot. So what the hell? Does she not want the guy caught?'

'You think she knows more about Aislinn's married fella than she's letting on?'

'I think we've only got Lucy's word for it that this married fella even exists.' We're keeping our voices down; Tesco guy and buggy mammy look like they've barely noticed we're here, but you never know. 'She was dead careful not to give us anything we could disprove, you notice that? No name, no description, no dates, no place where they might've met, nothing.'

Steve has his roll opened up across his lap and is carefully decorating it with brown sauce. 'You figure she made him up on the spot? Why, but?'

I say, 'She cares way too much whether Rory's our prime suspect. It's not just that she wants to know who did this to her mate; she wants to know whether we're looking at Rory, specifically.'

'Yeah.' Steve squirts the last of the brown sauce into his mouth and tosses the packet into a bin by the bench. 'I couldn't figure out whether she was hoping it was yes or no, though. She was straight in there giving us Rory's name, telling us he was due at Aislinn's last night; but after that . . .'

'Right. Giving us his name and the appointment was no big deal: she had to know we had that already, or would any minute. And after that, it was all about what a good guy he was, how she never got any kind of threat vibe off him, how happy Aislinn was with him. Could be all true; she could be trying to steer us away from him because she genuinely doesn't think it's him, doesn't want us wasting our time while the real guy gets away. But I'm wondering if her feelings for Rory were as nonexistent as she's claiming.'

Steve's eyebrows go up. '"I thought he was kind of boring, but Ash was obviously seeing something I missed . . ."'

'Yeah, we've only got Lucy's word for that, too. For all we know, she was just as into Rory as Aislinn was. For all we know, she was actually seeing him behind Aislinn's back.'

'We just said: she cared about Aislinn. A lot.'

'And for some reason, she's not happy admitting that. Could be guilt.' I get more coffee into me. 'Like she said herself, that love-triangle shite can go way wrong.'

'She's got an alibi,' Steve points out.

'Yeah, plus the shock was genuine. Lucy's not our woman. But her alibi means she can't give Rory an alibi. So if she wants him off the hook, for whatever reason, the only thing she can do is come up with some mysterious other guy for us to chase.'

Steve chews and thinks. 'We'll cross-check Lucy's and Rory's numbers, Facebook accounts, e-mails, see if they've been in touch. Not that it proves anything if they haven't; Lucy could still be into him.'

'Yeah.' The dinosaur kid is hovering, balancing on his scooter and eyeing our rolls. I give him a hairy look till he backs off. 'And we need to go through Aislinn's stuff ASAP, see if we find any evidence that this other fella existed. If he did, there's gonna be something. Texts, calls, e-mails.'

Steve examines his breakfast roll, picking an angle. 'Well,' he says. 'Maybe.'

'What're you on about, "maybe"? There's no such thing as invisible, not any more. If he didn't leave tracks, it's because he wasn't there.'

'Tell you what I was thinking,' Steve says. 'Just an idea, now. But I was wondering: what if Aislinn's other fella was a crim? A gangster, like?'

Fried egg nearly goes down my nose. 'Jesus, Moran. How desperate are you to make this one interesting? Shame they got Whitey Bulger, or you could've told yourself it was him.'

'Yeah yeah yeah. Think about it. It explains why Lucy doesn't want us going after Rory: she's positive it's the other guy, doesn't want us heading the wrong way. It explains why she figured straight-away we were there about Aislinn. It explains why she texted her to be careful, last night: if Aislinn was two-timing a crim, she'd want to be bloody careful about inviting some new fella around for dinner—'

I still have my mouth open to slag strips off him when it sinks in: Little Mr Optimist is right. It would fit.

'Jesus,' I say. That pulse is hammering right through me, practically lifting me off the bench. Forget coffee; this job, when it's right, this job is the hit that speed freaks throw their lives away hunting. 'And it'd explain why Lucy's keeping stuff back. She wants us to get him, but the last thing she wants is to be up on the stand with some gangster watching her explain how she's the one who dobbed him in. So she throws the idea out there for us to chase down, but she makes a big deal about how she doesn't know the other guy's name, doesn't know anything about him, can't even swear he exists, her and Aislinn weren't actually that close. Fair play to you, Steo. It works.'

'Not just a pretty face,' Steve says, through roll, giving me a thumbs-up. When he's swallowed: 'And if it was a gangster, he might've been careful not to leave a trail. No texts, calls, none of that.'

'Specially if he was a married gangster. Half of them are married to each other's sisters, cousins, whatever. Playing offside could get you kneecapped.' I've got my second wind now, all right. If this pans out, the gaffer is gonna shit a hedgehog; this is about as far from routine as a lovers' tiff can get. 'Jesus. It actually plays.'

'It'd explain why the call came in to Stoneybatter station, too. Most civilians, if they want an ambulance, they'll just ring 999—'

'But a crim, or a crim's mate, he's gonna know that 999 calls are recorded. And he's not gonna want his voice on tape, where we can identify it – specially if he's already known to us. So he rings the local station instead.'

'Exactly,' Steve says. 'The only thing, though. Does Aislinn seem to you like the type who'd go out with a gangster? Nice girl like that?'

'Hell, yeah. She's *exactly* the type. Her life was so boring, just thinking about it makes me want to hit myself in the face with a hammer for a bit of excitement. You know what she had in her bookcase? Bunch of books about crime in Ireland, including a big thick one on gangs.'

Steve lets out a huff of laughter. 'Look at that. Maybe she was the type after all.'

'I thought she was just looking for second-hand thrills, but she could've been reading up on her new fella's job – or maybe the book was just for kicks, but then she got a chance at the real thing. And you

3

The squad room has come alive. The printer is going, someone's phone is ringing, the blinds are open to try and drag in the half-arsed sunlight; the place smells of half a dozen different lunches, tea, shower gel, sweat, heat and action. O'Gorman is leaning back in his chair with his feet up on his desk, throwing crisps into his mouth and shouting to King about some match; King is reading a statement sheet and saying 'Yeah' whenever O'Gorman pauses for breath. Winters and Healy are arguing about some witness who Healy wants to shake up a little and Winters thinks is a waste of time. Quigley is working his way through one of the filing cabinets, wearing a put-out look on his flabby puss and slamming the drawers harder than he needs to; next to the filing cabinet, McCann is hunched over his desk, shuffling paper and flinching at every slam – he looks like he's got a bastard of a hangover, but the permanent eyebags and five o'clock shadow mean he mostly looks like that anyway. O'Neill has his phone pressed to one ear and a finger stuck in the other. Beside Steve's and my desks, two guys who have to be our floaters are leaning awkwardly on whatever they can find, trying to look at home and stay out of the way and laugh at one of Roche's pointless stories, hoping he'll remember next time he needs someone to do his scut work.

No Breslin, but his overcoat is hanging over the back of his chair. He's probably still sorting out the incident room and bitching to himself about being ordered around by the likes of me. I'm not worried: Breslin's been at this game too long to get snotty when it's not useful to him.

A few people glance up when me and Steve come in, then go back to whatever they're doing. No one says howya. Neither do we. We head for our desks and the floaters. When I'm in the squad room I stride, fast and hard, to smack down the instinct to tiptoe along in case someone sticks a foot in front of me. No one has yet, but it feels like a matter of time.

'Hey,' I say to the floaters, who've straightened up and put on their alert faces. They're both around our age: a gym rat already starting to go bald in front, and a fat blond guy trying for a tache that isn't working out. 'Conway, and this is Moran. Got something for us?'

'Stanton,' says the gym rat, doing a fake salute.

'Deasy,' says the fat one. 'Yeah: we brought in your man Rory Fallon a few minutes ago.'

'Poor bastard,' says Roche from his corner, which reeks of aftershave and sticky keyboard. Roche is a big no-necker who went into this gig because the only way he can get a stiffy is by bullying people into tears, but he's no fool: he knows exactly when to keep that instinct chained up and when to let it out for a run, and he gets results. 'Will I tell him to go ahead and cut off his own balls, save himself some time and hassle?'

'It's not my fault my solve rate's higher than yours, Roche,' I tell him. 'It's because you're a retard. Learn to live with it.'

The floaters look startled and try to hide it. Roche shoots me a bull-stare that I don't bother noticing. 'What's the story on Fallon?' I ask, dumping my satchel on my chair.

'Twenty-nine, owns a bookshop in Ranelagh,' says the fat guy. 'Lives above the shop.'

'With anyone?'

'Nah. On his ownio.'

Which is a pisser: a flatmate would have been not only a nice witness to have, but also an obvious candidate for the guy who called it in. Steve asks, 'Anything happen that we should know about, while you were sitting on his house?'

They look at each other, shake their heads. 'Not a lot,' says the gym rat. 'He opened the front curtains around ten, in his pyjamas. No other visible movement. By the time we picked him up, he'd got dressed, but no shoes, so it didn't look like he was planning on heading out.'

'He'd had breakfast,' says the fat guy. 'Coffee and a fry-up, by the smell.'

Steve catches my eye. A guy punches his girlfriend to death, goes home and snuggles into his pyjamas for a nice bit of kip, gets up in the morning and stuffs his face with egg and sausage. It could happen; Fallon could have been dazed into autopilot, or a psychopath, or setting up his defence. Or.

The room is hot, a dry edgy heat that pricks at the skin on my neck. I pull my coat off. 'What'd you say to him?'

'Like you told us,' the fat one says. 'Nothing. Just said we thought he might have some information that would help us out with an investigation, and asked him if he'd mind coming in for a chat.'

'And he just said yeah? No hassle, no questions?'

The two of them shake their heads. 'Accommodating guy,' says the gym rat.

'No shit,' I say. Most people, if you ask them to come in to a cop shop and answer some questions, they want at least a little info before they ditch the day's plans and toddle along after you. Either Rory Fallon is a natural pushover, or he really, really wants to look like a helpful guy with nothing to hide.

'Did he say anything along the way?' Steve asks.

'Wanted to know what this was about, once we got in the car,' says the fat guy. Which is also interesting. Obviously Rory might know exactly what this is about, but he doesn't think we can prove he knows, which means Lucy wasn't straight on the phone to him the minute we left. One point against the Lucy-and-Rory theory. 'We said we didn't know all the details; the investigating detectives would fill him in. After that he kept his mouth shut.'

'We were nice,' says the gym rat. 'Made him a cup of tea, told him how great he was for helping us out, we'd be nowhere without responsible citizens like him and all that jazz. We figured you'd like him relaxed.'

'Lovely,' Steve says. 'Where'd you put him?'

'The interview room down the end.'

'Is he the type who'll start thinking about leaving if we keep him on ice for a few minutes?'

Both of them laugh. 'Nah,' says the gym rat. 'Like I said: accommodating.'

'He's a *good* boy,' says the fat guy. 'Gone bad.'

'Thanks,' I say. 'We're going to need a list of his associates. Can you get cracking on that? I'm specially interested in close male friends, brothers, father, close male cousins. Some guy called this in, and if it wasn't Fallon, we need to know who it was.' The gym rat is taking notes and making sure I notice. I say, 'The incident room should be ready to work in by now. Case meeting at four. If that changes, I'll let you know.'

The floaters head off at a snappy pace, carefully judged to make them look on the ball but not rushed. I remember that walk; I remember practising it, on my way in to make lists and photocopy statements for some Murder D, hoping I could walk myself into this squad room and never have to walk out again. For a weird second I feel something almost like sorry for Stanton and Deasy, until I realise that if they ever make it in here, they're gonna get on just dandy.

Steve has turned on his computer and is clicking away. I say, 'How come you want to keep Fallon on ice?'

'Only for a minute.' Steve is typing. 'He heads home and goes to bed, gets up and makes himself a fry? Whatever way you look at it, that's pretty cold for a good law-abiding citizen. Even if he's just trying to look innocent. I want to run him through the system, see what pops up.'

'Run her, too. I want to know where I remember her from.' I dial my voicemail, tuck the phone under my jaw and start sorting through the statements from last night's scumbagfest – we need to get the file to the prosecutors before our hold on the scumbags runs out. McCann is mumbling into his mobile, clearly taking job-related shite from his missus ('I *know* that. Tonight I swear I'll be home by—Yeah, I *know* about the reservations. Of course I'll be—'), and Roche is miming whipcracks.

I have another voicemail from Breslin – I'm starting to get my hopes up that we can work this entire case without ever actually seeing each other. 'Yeah, Conway. Hi.' Still smooth, in case Hollywood is listening, but just a faint edge of displeasure: me and Steve have been bad little Ds. 'Looks like we're having some trouble liaising here. I'm back at base. I'll go ahead and get that incident room sorted out for us; you ring me back ASAP. Talk soon.' I delete it.

'Rory Fallon isn't in the system,' Steve says.

'At all?'

'At all.'

'Little Holy Mary,' I say. Staying out of the system is rarer than you'd think; even a speeding ticket puts you on file. Rory has officially never done anything naughty in his life. 'That doesn't mean he was actually a virgin till last night. Just that he never got caught.'

'I know. I'm only telling you.'

'Did you run Aislinn yet?'

'Doing it now, hang on . . .'

I ring Breslin's voicemail and leave him a message to meet us in the observation room in ten minutes. Steve says, 'Nah. Nothing there either. Between the two of them, they'd make you heave.'

'Looks like they were perfect for each other,' I say. 'Shame it didn't work out.' I finish flipping through the last witness statement, and stop.

The last page is missing. Without that – the page with the signature – the whole thing is worthless.

I'll never prove I didn't drop it on my way back from the interview room. There's even an outside chance that actually happened – it was late, I was tired and pissed off and hurrying to finish up by the end of my shift. I can check: wander back and forth like an idiot, peering hopefully under desks and into bins, while this roomful of toss-bubbles hide behind their monitors holding back baboon-howls of laughter and waiting to see who explodes first. Or I can go on the rampage looking to string up the fucker who pinched my statement sheet, which is probably what someone is hoping I'll do. Or I can glue my mouth shut, track down my scumbag witness and spend another couple of hours re-convincing him that talking to cops is cool and digging his statement out of him, one-syllable word by one-syllable word, all over again.

'Hey,' Steve says. 'Here's something.'

It takes me a second to remember what he's on about – I'm so angry I want to bite chunks off my desk. Steve glances up. 'You OK?'

'Yeah. What've you got? Aislinn's in the system?'

'Not her, no. It's probably nothing, but her address comes up. Twentieth of October last, one o'clock in the morning, her neighbour in Number 24 rang Stoneybatter station. He was out on his patio having a last smoke before bed, and he saw someone go over Aislinn's back wall, from her patio out into the laneway. The description's not great – there's a streetlamp at the end of the laneway, but the neighbour only saw the intruder for a second, from the back. Male, medium build, dark coat, the neighbour thought he might be middle-aged from the way he climbed; he thought fair hair, but that could've been the way the light reflected. Stoneybatter sent a couple of lads round to have a look, but by then he was well gone. No signs of an attempted break-in, so they figured the neighbour had disturbed him before he got started. They counselled Aislinn on security measures and dropped the whole thing.'

'Huh,' I say. It doesn't tell me where I've seen Aislinn before, but it's interesting enough to push the missing page to one side of my mind. 'Anything in there about how she took it? Scared, panicky? Went round to Lucy's for the night?'

'Nah. Just, "Resident has a house alarm and locks in place but was advised to consider a monitored alarm system and a dog."'

'Which she didn't get.' Roche is trying to earwig; I give him the finger and lower my voice. 'For a woman on her own, Aislinn was pretty chilled out about the whole intruder thing. She sound to you like someone who had balls that big?'

Steve says, 'She sounds like someone who knew there was nothing to be scared of.'

I say, 'Because that wasn't a burglar; it was the secret boyfriend. Will you look at that. Maybe he actually did exist.' That excitement lunges up inside me again. I smack it down. 'Even if he did, though, that doesn't let Rory Fallon off the hook. Maybe he found out Aislinn was two-timing him, and he didn't like it. Let's go ask him.'

'One sec, I just want to check one more thing—' Steve dives back into his computer.

I shove what's left of my statements into my desk drawer, which locks and which is where they would have been to begin with, if

O'Kelly hadn't caught us on the hop this morning. I stick the key in my trouser pocket. Then I flip through my notebook and try to suss out the squad room from behind it.

No one is obviously watching for me to lose the head, but then they wouldn't be obvious. Quigley has found his file and is picking his ear while he reads it, which probably means he doesn't expect anyone to be looking at him, although you never know. Quigley is a turd, O'Gorman is an ape, Roche is the best of both worlds: any of them, or all of them, would think it was hilarious to fuck up my day. McCann looks like he's in too much pain to think about anything else, and O'Neill has always seemed sound enough, but I can't rule anyone out.

Not that it matters. The point, and they know this as well as I do, isn't who exactly is pulling this shit – it'll be a different guy every time. The point is that, whoever it is, there's fuck-all I can do about it.

'Hang on,' Steve says, low. 'Here's something else.'

This time I remember to answer. 'Yeah? What?'

'I figured we should find out if Aislinn's shown up on Organised Crime's radar, right? So I checked if anyone else has run her through the system.' I start to stand up, heading over to have a look at Steve's monitor, but he shoots me a fast head-shake and a warning stare. 'Stay put. And yeah, sure enough: seventeenth of September last year, someone ran a check on her.'

We look at each other.

I say, 'There's got to be a couple of dozen Aislinn Murrays out there. Minimum.'

'Aislinn Gwendolyn Murrays? Born the sixth of March '88?'

My mind is speeding. 'I don't want to bring Organised Crime in on this. Not yet. I've got a pal—'

Steve says, so quietly that even I barely hear it, 'The login was "Murder".'

We look at each other some more. I can feel the same expression on my face that's on Steve's: wary; trying to work out just how wary to be.

'If it was Murder business,' I say, 'then whoever it was shouldn't have a problem sharing.'

Steve's face shuts down into a warning. He's opening his mouth to tell me why this is a bad idea, and he's right – the smart thing is to keep this to ourselves, go at it through back channels – but that missing statement page is still digging at me, and I've had it up to here with keeping my mouth shut and tiptoeing around my own squad. I swivel my chair around to face the room and snap my fingers over my head. 'Hey! Over here.' I make it good and loud: faces turn, conversations fall away. 'Aislinn Gwendolyn Murray, DOB sixth of March '88. Anyone remember running her through the computer last September?'

Blank looks. A couple of the guys shake their heads. The rest don't even bother, just go back to whatever they were doing.

I swivel my chair back around to face Steve.

He says, 'Maybe whoever ran the search isn't on shift. Or . . .' He does some noncommittal thing with his head.

'Or maybe he wouldn't give me the steam off his piss if I was dying of thirst. I know.' I hate when Steve gets tactful. 'Or else it was a personal one, on the QT.'

It happens, a lot. You don't like the cut of the young fella your daughter brought home, or the couple who viewed your rental flat: you run them through the computer, see if anything pops up. We've all done it – my ma wasn't happy about her new neighbour, who did turn out to be a smackhead but at least not a dealer, and he moved out a few weeks later anyway, believe me – and anyone who gets outraged over it needs to get out more, but the fact is it's illegal. If someone's cousin was thinking of hiring Aislinn, or if someone's parents were thinking of asking the nice young lady next door to mind their spare key, all it would take is thirty seconds on the computer; just doing a harmless favour, no reason anyone should ever know. Now that she's a murder victim, though, anyone who's been running illegal checks on her is gonna get a bollocking from the gaffer and lose a couple of days' holiday, minimum. No wonder no one's jumping to put his hand up.

Steve says, lower, 'Or else it was on the QT, but it wasn't personal. That would fit with the gang thing. Say someone from Organised Crime wants to check her out without his squad knowing about it, for whatever reason, so he gets a mate in Murder to do it for him . . .'

I have trouble seeing a way that one could be harmless. The room feels tricky, twisted: corners warping out of shape, shadows flexing. I say, 'And the mate's never gonna tell us about it.'

Steve says, even lower, 'I know a fella in Computer Crime. He should be able to find out what computer the request came from.'

'What computer. Not who was using it. If we had individual logins, instead of this one-squad-one-password shite—'

'You want me to get onto him anyway?'

'No,' I say. 'Not yet.' Everyone's gone back to their conversations or their paperwork; no one is even looking at us. All the same, I wish I'd kept my big mouth shut.

The observation room is small and shitty. It has a sticky table, one lopsided chair and a water cooler that's usually empty. There's no window and the air vent hasn't worked in years; if that was an interview room, the solicitors would start bitching about their clients' right to breathe and it would get fixed pronto, but since no one cares about our breathing, the vent stays banjaxed. The place smells of sweat, years of spilled coffee, aftershave from guys who retired when me and Steve were in training, cigarette smoke from back before the ban. It's worse in winter, when the heating brings out the full bouquet.

Breslin isn't there yet. I throw my coat on the back of the chair – I don't feel like leaving it in the squad room and having to wonder if someone's wiped his dick on it – and head over to have a look at Rory Fallon. Steve moves in beside me, close enough to the one-way glass that our breath leaves mist.

Fallon looks younger than twenty-nine. He's on the short side, maybe five eight, and slight with it. I could take him down one-handed, but all this took was one good punch, and even a wimp can get worked up enough for that. He's got floppy brown hair that just got cut special for his big date, glasses with fake-tortoiseshell frames so old the plastic's gone cloudy, a cream grandfather shirt tucked neatly into faded jeans, and fine, pointy features that make him look like either a lovely sensitive artiste or a wimp, depending on your perspective. He's OK-looking, but he's not what I was expecting Aislinn to go for, any more than Lucy is. I was all ready for a great big chunk of designer-label thicko who worked for an estate agent and couldn't shut up about rugby. Rory looks like the kind of guy who thinks the good bit of a video game is when you're exploring the terrain and admiring the state-of-the-art graphics, before you get to the crude part where you have to blow the baddies away.

'A tenner says he cries,' I say. Me and Steve have started doing this on domestics – gambling on the job is obviously a big no-no, but I manage to live with myself. Half of the suspects take one look at us and turn on the waterworks, and it makes me want to give them an almighty kick up the hole. I have to bite my tongue to stop myself telling them to man – or woman – the fuck up: you were big and tough when you beat your other half to pulp and splinters, where's all the attitude now? If I have to put up with that shite, I figure I might as well make a few quid out of it.

'Ah, arse,' Steve says. 'I hope I've got a tenner. Look at the state of him.'

'Sucks to be you. Get in quicker next time.'

We watch Rory Fallon flick his head back and forth and fidget his feet under his chair while he tries to get a handle on the interview room. Interview rooms are designed so you can't get a handle on them. The linoleum and the table and the chairs are all the plainest, most nondescript ones out there, and it's not just because of budget cuts; it's so your mind can't read anything off them, and it starts reading stuff in. Long enough alone in an interview room and the place goes from nothing to sinister to pure horror film.

There's a black overcoat neatly folded over the back of his chair, and a pair of grey nylon padded gloves lined up on the table. Rory's hands are arranged the same way as the gloves, palms pressed down, thumbs just touching. His knuckles, as far as I can tell from this distance, are perfect: not a scratch.

Steve says, 'See his hands?'

'That doesn't rule him out. Sophie said he probably wore gloves, remember?'

'Ring her. See if they found prints in the end.'

I ring Sophie, hit speaker, keep one eye on the door for Breslin. 'Sophie. Hey. It's me and Moran.'

'Hey. Update: we've basically finished processing the body and the sitting room—' Her voice cuts out, comes back. 'Fucking reception in here. Hang on a sec.' A door slams. 'Hi.'

'How're you doing on prints?'

'It looks like we're out of luck, basically.' Wind whirls around Sophie's voice; she's out on the street. She does something, cups her hand around the phone, and the roar goes away. 'We've got plenty on the dinner settings, the door handle, the wine bottle, wineglasses, but just offhand my guy says they're all too small for a man and they all look like a match to the vic.'

'We were right about the guy wearing gloves,' I say. Steve makes a face.

'We'll keep looking, but I'm guessing yeah. Probably leather or Gore-Tex, something smooth like that. We didn't find any fibres on the vic's face where he punched her, and we should've, if the gloves were wool or anything knitted. Fibres would've stuck to the blood.'

I say, to Steve, 'So thick gloves, probably. Meaning he might not have wrecked his hand, at least not enough to be visible.'

'Meaning you've picked up your suspect,' Sophie says. 'And his hands are fine.'

'Yeah. The dinner-date guy.'

'Did you get whatever gloves he was wearing last night? Because if your killer wore gloves, he's got the vic's blood all over the right-hand one. Even if he cleaned it. That shit sticks around.'

'Today he's wearing grey nylon ones. They look clean, but we'll get them down to you for testing, and if we get a search warrant we'll send you any others out of his place, but I bet we're out of luck there too. He probably dumped last night's ones on his way home.' I've got one eye on Fallon. He's given up trying to get a handle on his surroundings and is sitting still, gazing down at his hands and taking deep breaths. He looks like he might be doing some kind of meditation thing. I give the glass a quick smack, put a stop to that shite. 'Anything else we should know, before we start in on him?'

Sophie blows out an exasperated breath. 'Not a lot. Most of this morning was a waste of our fucking time. The only solid thing we've got is three black wool fibres off the vic's dress: two on the left side of the chest, one on the left side of the skirt. They don't match anything she was wearing, obviously, and she doesn't have a black coat, so it's not like she popped out to the shops for something and got transfer from that. She could've thrown on a jumper to protect the dress while she was cooking, but we checked the bedroom and no black jumpers or cardigans.' She's keeping her voice down; someone is outside Aislinn's place, maybe just the kids, maybe reporters. 'So I'm thinking the fibres are transfer off your guy, from when he hugged her hello or grabbed her or whatever. Check if he owns a black wool coat.'

'He came in wearing one.' I glance at Steve, who shrugs: every other guy in Dublin owns a black wool overcoat. 'We'll send it over to you. Nice one, Sophie. Thanks.'

'No problem. I'm going to head; there's some baby reporter hanging over the tape trying to listen in. You want me to tell him we suspect ninja assassins?'

'Go on, make his day. Talk soon.'

'Hang on,' Steve says, leaning in over the phone. 'Hiya; it's Moran. Can you process the bedroom? And the bathroom?'

'Wow, brilliant idea. What did you think we were going to do with them? Spray-paint them?'

'I mean places that probably wouldn't have been touched last night, but might have been last time the vic had a fella staying over. The headboard, inside the bedside table, the underside of the toilet seat. And can you do the mattress for body fluids?'

'Huh,' Sophie says. 'You looking at exes?'

'Something like that. Thanks. Give the baby reporter our best.'

'I'm going to tell him you'll arrest him for not being in school. I swear to God, he's about twelve, I'm getting old—' and Sophie's gone.

Fallon is giving his meditation thing a second try. Breslin is either building the incident room from the ground up or else punishing us for keeping him waiting. While I've got my phone out: 'One sec,' I say, swiping the screen and moving away from Steve.

The afternoon edition of the *Courier* is out. Creepy Crowley has gone to town.

The front page yells, 'POLICE BAFFLED BY BRUTAL MURDER'. Underneath are two photos. Aislinn, the recent version, wearing a tight orange dress and sparkly eyeshadow and laughing – looks like a Christmas-party shot that Crowley pulled off someone's Facebook. The other one is me, ducking out from under the crime-scene tape, looking my finest: eyebags, hair coming down, fists coming up, and my mouth opening in a snarl that would scare a Rottweiler.

My jaw is clamped so tight it hurts. I scroll down, but the text is just titillation, glurge and outrage – stunning young woman, prime of life, details of her injuries not yet released; quote from a local about how Aislinn went to the shops for him when the footpaths were icy, quote from a local who isn't going to feel safe in her own home until we do our jobs and get this b****** off the streets; a snide little dig about 'Detective Antoinette Conway, who led the investigation into the still-unsolved murder of Michael Murnane in Ballymun last September', to make it clear that I'm incompetent and/or don't give a shite about working-class victims. Down the sidebar: *Parents Panic over Playground Pervert*, plus a splatter of snottiness at the County Council, who should apparently do something about the shite weather, and some celebrity gushing about quinoa and what a normal life her kids lead.

'What?' Steve asks.

I manage to unclamp my jaw. 'Nothing.'

'No. What?'

It's not like I can keep him away from newspapers forever, and hiding it would look like I'm upset that I'm a hound in the photo, about which I don't give one fun-size fuck. 'Here,' I say, and pass him the phone.

His eyebrows go up. 'Ah, Jaysus.' A second later: 'Whoa. *Jaysus.*'

'No shit,' I say.

The media don't ID murder victims till they get the all-clear from us – for the sake of the families, who don't need to find out from a supermarket newsstand, and because sometimes we have reasons for wanting to keep the ID quiet for a day or two. A lot of the time they drop enough info that locals can tell who it is – 'the thirty-year-old father of two, who worked in finance', or whatever – but then the locals knew already. And the media don't use shots of the detectives on the case without permission, either, just in case we might not want to be instantly identifiable from ten metres away. I don't let photos of me get out there, for a very good reason, but when a photo of Ds does go out, it's one where they look professional and approachable and all that good shit; one that would make witnesses actually want to come talk to us, not one that's going to terrify them into hiding because we look like hungover wolverines. If a journalist steps over the line, he pays: no more sources close to the investigation for you, and we make sure your editor knows it. That fuck Crowley has stepped over the line half a dozen ways.

He's wiggled a toe over it plenty of times before, but that was all wimpy little stuff meant to make him feel like Bob Woodward without getting him in real hassle; never like this. Crowley doesn't like cops, because he's a rebel spirit who doesn't bow down to The Man, but he's a rebel spirit with rent to pay, so he keeps himself in check. Either he's suddenly, late in life, grown himself a pair of nads, or he's trying to commit career suicide; or someone is running him. Someone – the same someone who told Crowley where to find me this morning – told him to print those photos. Someone reassured him he won't end up on any blacklist. Someone promised to make it worth his while.

Steve is still scrolling through the article. 'There's no inside info in there.'

Meaning nothing we can trace back to a source. 'I know that. But he's talking to someone on the inside. No question. If I find out who—'

Steve glances up. 'We could swap Crowley for a scoop. Offer him first bite at every break on this case, if he tells us who his contact is.'

'Won't work. Whoever's been onto Crowley, they've promised him plenty already. He's not going to jeopardise that.' I take my phone back and shove it in my pocket. 'You know who had the best opportunity to talk to Crowley about this case.'

Steve says quietly, 'Breslin.'

'Yeah.'

'Breslin likes looking good. That'd be one way to do it: turn this into a story where we're making a balls of the case, till he steps in to save the day.'

I say, and I'm keeping my voice down too, 'Or he just felt like fucking me around, getting a laugh from the lads. Or he's got a deal in place with Crowley and he was due to throw him a bone, and lucky us just happened to be today's bone.'

'Maybe. Could be.' Steve is watching the door. So am I. 'Listen: we need to get on with Breslin. Either way.'

'I get on with everyone. It's who I am.'

'Seriously.'

'I'll get on with him.' I want to pace. I lean my arse on the edge of the table to keep myself still. 'We'll have to use him in the interviews. And we'll have to keep him up to speed on your man in there' – I jerk my chin at the one-way glass. 'Apart from that, he doesn't need to know anything about what we're thinking.'

Steve says, suddenly and grimly, 'Back when I was bursting my bollix trying to get on the squad? This isn't what I was picturing.'

'Me neither,' I say. 'Believe me.' Trying to remember when today started makes my head swim. I get a vicious cramp of craving for cold air, music loud enough to blow my eardrums and a run that doesn't stop till my whole body burns.

Breslin picks that moment to bang the observation-room door open. Both of us jump. He stays in the doorway, hands in his trouser pockets, looking us up and down. The curl to his mouth is a nicely judged balance between amused and cold.

'Detective Conway. Detective Moran,' he says. 'At last.'

I should like Breslin just fine, given that he's one of the few lads on the squad who haven't given me more than the standard ration of shite, but I don't. The first time you meet Breslin, you're well impressed. He's somewhere in his mid-forties, but he's still in shape, all shoulders and straight back and none of the beer belly that gets hold of most Irish guys. He's on the tall side, with pale eyes and slicked-back fair hair, and he's good-looking – if you squint he looks sort of like some actor, I can't remember the guy's name but he plays maverick suits, which is a laugh given that Breslin is the least maverick guy around. But throw in the voice and somehow it all adds up to winner's dazzle, the gold glow that shouts to everyone within range that this dude is something special: smarter, faster, savvier, smoother.

Breslin is so deep into this version of his bad self that he brings it sweeping into the room with him, and it carries you right along. Steve's first few weeks in Murder, he watched Breslin the way a twelve-year-old with a crush watches the captain of the rugby team, drooling for a smile and a pat on the shoulder. I nearly bit my tongue in half not slagging the pathetic little bollix, but I managed because I knew it would wear off. I could practically have marked the day on the calendar. When I started on the squad, I spent a while praying Breslin and McCann would have a row so I could end up partnered with Breslin, on the fast track to glory. It wore off.

Sure enough, three weeks into Steve's boy-crush, a guy in Vice ate his gun, and Breslin – in the middle of the squad room, surrounded by people who'd known the dead guy, worked with him, gone drinking with him – pushed back his chair, balanced a pen between his fingers and enlightened us with a deep and meaningful lecture about how the guy would still have been with us if he'd quit the smokes, got more exercise and put in the time to build up real friendships at work. The smarter guys on the squad kept working; the dumb ones nodded along, mouths hanging open at the genius unfolding in front of them. Poor Stevie looked like he'd just found out about Santy.

Once you realise Breslin is an idiot, you start counting the clichés on their way out of his mouth and noticing that the slick hair is organised over a balding spot, and somewhere in there you realise that he's actually only around five foot ten and his solve rate is nothing special and you start wondering if he wears a girdle. None of that matters – the dazzle does its job on witnesses and suspects, and Breslin's moved on long before it can wear off – but it left me pissed off with myself for being suckered, which left me pissed off with Breslin and everything about him.

'Howya,' I say. 'Shame we didn't manage to talk along the way. Reception's a bastard.'

Breslin hasn't moved from the doorway. 'Sounds like you need a new phone, Detective Conway. But let's move past that. We're all here now.'

'We are, yeah,' I say. 'You got a look around the scene?'

'Yeah. Ten-a-penny lovers' tiff. Let's see how fast we can clear it and get back to the good stuff, shall we?'

'That's the plan,' Steve says easily, before I can open my mouth. 'Thanks for joining us. We appreciate it.'

'No problem.' Breslin gives Steve a gracious nod. 'We're in Incident Room C.'

Incident Room C has a whiteboard bigger than my kitchen, enough computers and phone lines for a major incident investigation, a lovely view over the gardens of Dublin Castle, and PowerPoint facilities just in case you get the urge to show slides. Steve and I have only ever been inside it as someone else's floaters. 'Nice one,' I say.

'Only the best.' Breslin heads over to the glass for a look at Rory. 'After all this, I'm just hoping the best friend – what's her name? – gave you something good.'

'Lucy Riordan,' Steve says. 'Background info, basically. Aislinn's childhood wasn't great: the da walked out, the ma had some kind of breakdown, Aislinn took on the carer role. It left her pretty sheltered – not a lot of life experience, not a lot of confidence. The ma died a few years back and Aislinn started coming out of herself, but she was still catching up, still pretty naïve. Just the type who'd miss a few red flags.'

'And were there red flags?'

'Not that Lucy knows of. Aislinn and Rory met at a book launch six or seven weeks back; they were both smitten, but Aislinn was playing it cool. Rory seemed like a nice guy, seemed to be treating Aislinn well. Lucy never got the sense he was a threat.'

'No shit,' Breslin says, examining Rory, who's started jiggling one knee under the table. 'Little wimp, isn't he? He doesn't look like he could punch out his granny. No reason why Lucy Whatsername should know that those can be the most dangerous ones, if they feel like they've been disrespected. It's not her job to know that; it's ours. What else?'

Steve shakes his head. 'That's about it.'

Breslin's eyebrows go up. 'That's all the best mate had? What about other boyfriends? Disgruntled exes? Jealous women? Work enemies?'

We're both shaking our heads now. 'Nope,' I say.

'Come on, guys. Girls talk – am I right, Conway? I don't even want to imagine what my missus tells her gal pals over the Chardonnay. The vic must've given your Lucy something juicier than that.'

'According to Lucy, they weren't that kind of close. They were mates because they had been since they were kids, and because Aislinn had no other friends, but they didn't have a lot in common and they didn't spill their guts to each other.'

Breslin thinks about that, leaning back against the glass and pinching his bottom lip. 'You don't think she's keeping anything back?'

Me and Steve look at each other blankly. Steve shakes his head. 'Nah.'

'Lucy's no idiot,' I say. 'She knows she needs to give us whatever she's got. The only thing I wondered . . .' I let it trail off. 'Probably nothing.'

'Hey, share with the class, Conway. Don't worry about sounding stupid; we're blue-skying here.'

What a tosspot. 'Fair enough,' I say. 'I wondered if Lucy might've had a thing for Rory herself. She was all about what a great guy he was. I mean, maybe he is, but if my mate had just been killed, I'd be feeling at least a little bit dodgy about the new boyfriend.'

'Huh,' Breslin says. 'Has this Lucy got an alibi for last night?'

'Yeah. She works at the Torch Theatre; she was there at half-six in the evening, in company constantly from then till four this morning. We'll verify it, but like I said, she's no idiot; she wouldn't have given us something we could break that easily.'

'Well then. We'll check for contact between her and our boy there, in case she's mixed up in the motive somehow; but unless some contact shows up, I'm not seeing any way her hypothetical crush could be relevant to us. Are you?' Me and Steve shake our heads, nice and humble. 'Good brainstorming, though. Anything else come up?'

'That's the lot,' I say.

'Well,' Breslin says, on the edge of a sigh but managing to restrain himself. 'I guess your little side trip was worth a shot. Background info's never really a waste. Now, though, I suggest we get our arses in gear and get stuck into the serious stuff. That sound good to you two?'

'Sounds great,' I say. Which it does: another sixty seconds of this and I'm gonna knee the fucker in the guts. 'I'll lead the interview, with you backing me up, Detective Breslin. Detective Moran, you observe from here, and be ready to switch in if I decide we need to mix it up a little.'

Steve nods. Breslin shoots his cuffs. 'Come to Papa,' he says to the one-way glass.

I say, 'This is only a preliminary interview. I'm not looking for a confession; we can push for that once we've got forensics, post-mortem results, all the good stuff to throw at him.' And once me and Steve have done enough private digging to know what we're dealing with here. 'Right now I'm just looking to put the outlines in place. What Rory's like, what the relationship was like, his take on Aislinn, his story on last night. I want to know if he'll admit to talking to anyone between eight last night and five this morning; if our guy didn't call this in himself, he told someone who did, and we need that someone. I want his coat and his gloves – the techs got black wool fibres off the body, and they say our guy probably wore non-shedding gloves, which matches what Rory's got in there; so if we can convince him to hand them over for testing and save us fucking around with a warrant, I'll be a very happy camper. In a perfect world he'd let us go through his gaff and take any other coats and gloves we find, but I don't want to get him uptight today, so if that doesn't come easy, we'll leave it and go the warrant route. OK?'

Breslin considers that. 'Mm,' he says. 'OK; that's one way to work it. The other way would be to try and knock this sucker on the head as fast as we can. I'm not saying I have any problem with being assigned to this case – that's fine, happy to help out. I'm just saying I've put my other cases on hold to be here, and there's a limit to how much time I want to put into a bog-standard domestic. I'm sure you guys feel the same. Am I right?'

I mainly feel he should shut his trap and do what the lead D tells him, but I catch the pop-eyed panic on Steve's face. It makes me want to laugh, which takes me off the boil. 'That's a point,' I say, pleasantly. 'Let's do this: for now, we'll take it slow, like I was saying. As soon as I think we can afford to ramp it up, I promise I'll give the word. Fair enough?'

Breslin doesn't look pleased, but after a moment he shrugs. 'Suit yourselves. In that case, can we get started while there's still some of the shift left?' And, when I straighten up off the table: 'You might want to do something about that first, Detective. Unless it's part of your cunning plan.'

'That' is a dab at the corner of his mouth. I rub at my face: a flake of egg yolk, which I've obviously been wearing since that breakfast roll. 'Thanks,' I say, partly to Breslin and partly to my partner Captain Eagle-Eye. He makes an apology face back.

'First impressions and all that jazz. If we're ready now, let's rock and roll.'

Breslin holds the door open for me to leave the observation room first, so I can't get a last word with Steve behind his back – not that we need to swap meaningful whispers, but still. The corridor should fold around me like home, scuffed sludge-green paint and worn carpet and all; should feel like my marked track through my own territory, leading me straight and safe to the enemy neatly arranged in my interview-room crosshairs. Instead it feels like an unflagged trail through No Man's Land, pocked with ankle-breaking mud holes and booby-trapped all the way.

4

Everyone has an interview shtick. One guy on the squad does a beautiful line in Father Confessor, piling on the guilt and waving absolution like a doggy treat; another one does Narky Headmaster, staring over his glasses and snapping out questions. I do Warrior Woman, ready to rush out with her guns blazing and avenge all your wrongs, if you'll just tell her what they are, and her flipside Stroppy Man-Hating Bitch when we want to piss off a rapist or a Neanderthal; I also do Cool Girl, who's one of the lads and stands her round and has a laugh, who guys can talk to when they wouldn't feel comfortable talking to another fella. Steve does Nice Boy Next Door and variations. With women, Breslin does Gallant Gentleman, taking their coats and bending his head to listen to every word; with guys he does Chief Jock, your best pal but you better stay on his good side or he'll flush your head down the jacks. We size up the target and wheel out the one that we think has the best chance.

Rory doesn't need Warrior Woman, at least as far as we know, and Stroppy Man-Hating Bitch would probably scare him under the table, but Cool Girl should relax him a notch or two. It sounds like he'd get on great with Nice Boy Next Door, but that's out for now. I just hope Chief Jock doesn't intimidate him enough, or piss me off enough, to send this whole thing off the rails.

Rory starts off our relationship by costing me a tenner: he doesn't cry. He jumps a mile when Breslin throws the door open, but when I give him my Cool Girl nod and grin, he comes up with some kind of smile back. 'Howya,' I say, throwing myself into a chair opposite him and pulling out my notebook. 'I'm Detective Conway, and that's Detective Breslin. Thanks for coming in.'

'No problem.' Rory tries to work out whether we're going to shake hands. We're not. 'I'm Rory Fallon. Is—'

'Morning,' Breslin says, heading over to the video recorder. 'You OK to talk? Not too hungover? I know how it goes: young guy like you, Sunday morning . . .'

'I'm fine.' Rory's voice cracks on the word. He clears his throat.

Breslin grins, hitting buttons. 'Disgraceful. You'll have to do better next weekend.'

I nod at his half-drunk cup of tea. 'Can I get you a reheat on that? Or a coffee, maybe?'

'No, thanks. I'm fine.' Rory barely has the edge of his arse on the seat; he looks ready to leg it at the first loud noise, if there was anywhere to leg it to. 'What's this about?'

'Ah-ah,' Breslin says, turning from the video to point a finger at him. 'Hang on there, man. We can't get down to business yet. These days we have to get any conversation on tape and video. For every-one's protection, you know what I mean?'

After a second Rory nods uncertainly. 'Yeah. I guess.'

'Course you do,' Breslin says cheerfully. 'Just give me a minute and we can chat away to our hearts' content.' He goes back to messing with the recorder, whistling softly between his teeth.

Rory's shoulders are up around his ears. He says, 'Do I need a lawyer? Or something?'

'I don't know,' I say, lowering my notebook to give him my full attention. 'Do you?'

'I just mean – I mean, shouldn't I have one?'

I raise my eyebrows. 'Any reason why?'

'No. I don't have anything to— Am I not supposed to have one?'

'You can have one if you want, man,' Breslin tells him. 'Absolutely. Pick a solicitor, give him a ring, we'll all wait around till he can join us; not a problem. I can tell you exactly what he'll do, though. He'll sit next to you, every now and then he'll say, "You don't have to answer that question," and he'll charge you by the minute for it. I can tell you the same thing for free: you don't have to answer *any* of our questions. We tell everyone, first thing: you are not obliged to say anything unless you wish to do so, but anything you do say will be taken down in writing and may be given in evidence. Clear enough? Or would you be happier paying for it?'

'No. I mean—Yeah. I guess I'm OK without a solicitor.'

And that's the caution out of the way. 'You are, of course,' Breslin says, giving the video recorder a pat. 'Okely-dokely: that's working. Detectives Conway and Breslin interviewing Mr Rory Fallon. Let's talk.'

Rory says – just like Lucy did – 'Is this about Aislinn?'

'Hey, whoa there, Rory,' Breslin says, lifting his hands and laughing. I grin along. 'Slow down, will you? We'll get there, I promise. But me and Detective Conway, we're going to be doing hundreds of these interviews, so we need to stick to asking the same questions in the same order, or we'll get mixed up and forget what we've already asked who. So do us a favour: let us do this our way. OK?'

'OK. Sorry.' But Rory's shoulders have dropped – what with him being just one of hundreds, and what with us being just a couple of dumb goons on the verge of losing our place in our script. Breslin is good. I've watched him work before, but I've never shared an interview room with him, and in spite of myself I'm not hating it.

'No problem,' I say easily. Breslin drops into the chair next to mine and we get comfortable, flipping notebook pages, settling our arses into the quirks of our chairs, checking that our Biros work. 'So,' I say, 'let's start at the beginning. What'd you do yesterday? From, like, noon onwards?'

Rory takes a deep breath and pushes his glasses up his nose. 'Right. At noon I was in the shop – I own the Wayward Bookshop, in Ranelagh? Right below my flat, where you – well, your colleagues – came and got me?'

'Been past it a hundred times, kept meaning to go in,' I say. 'I'll have to do it now, or you'll be filing complaints about me.' Me and Breslin have a little chuckle about that. Rory smiles automatically: a good boy, giving us what we expect from him. 'So how was business yesterday?'

'Pretty good. Saturdays I get a lot of regulars – mums and dads bringing the kids in to pick out a book, mostly. We've got a good children's section, if you – I mean, I just mean *if* you were, I'm not—'

He's blinking away anxiously. 'I'll bring the nephews in to you,' I say. I don't have nephews. 'You can recommend them something with dinosaurs. How's business overall?'

'It's all right. I mean . . .' Rory does a twisty shrug. 'Bookshops are all having a hard time these days. At least we've got regulars.'

Meaning Rory is under pressure. We'll check what 'all right' means to him. 'I'll definitely have to bring the nephews in to support you, so,' I say, smiling. 'What time did you finish up?'

'I close at six.'

'And what'd you do then?'

'I went back up to my flat and had a shower. I was, um, I had a . . .' Rory is turning a cute shade of pink. 'I was going over to a girl's house for dinner. A woman's house.'

'Ohhh *yeah*,' says Breslin, tilting his chair back and grinning. 'My man Rory's a playa. Tell your Uncle Don the whole story. Girlfriend? Friend with benefits? True love?'

'She's . . .' The pink gets deeper. Rory swipes his palms across his cheeks like he can wipe it away. 'Well. I don't know if I'd call her my girlfriend, exactly. We've only been on a few dates. But yes, I'm hoping it'll go somewhere.'

Present tense. Not that that means much; he's not a fool. I smile at all the adorable young love; Rory manages a smile back.

'So you made a bit of an effort,' Breslin says. 'Right? Tell me you made a bit of an effort, Rory. That shirt's fine for selling *The Gruffalo* to soccer moms, but if you want to impress your way into a babe's – well, into her good books, let's put it that way – it's not going to do the job. What'd you wear?'

'Just a shirt and a pullover and trousers. I mean, they were decent ones, they weren't—'

Sceptical look off Breslin. 'What colour? What kind?'

'A white linen shirt and a light blue pullover, and dark blue trousers? I'm normally a jeans guy, but Aislinn's . . . I knew she'd be wearing something a bit fancier, so I thought I should too.'

'Hmm. Sounds like it could've been a lot worse. You've got decent taste when you try, my son.' Breslin nods at the overcoat on the back of Rory's chair. 'That coat?'

Rory glances uncertainly back and forth between it and Breslin. 'Yes. I don't really have another proper winter coat. I got it at Arnott's, it's not just some . . . I mean, it's OK, right?'

'Not bad,' Breslin says, squinting critically at the coat. 'It'll do. You didn't wear those gloves with it, though. Did you? You didn't.'

Rory's head whips around to the gloves. 'Yeah, I did. Why? What's wrong with them?'

'Yeesh,' Breslin says, grimacing. He reaches across the table and pokes the gloves with his pen, flips them over. They look clean. 'Maybe I'm getting old; maybe nowadays all the cool kids go on dates looking like they borrowed their hands off a mountain biker. You really wore these?'

'It was cold.'

'So? You've got to suffer for style, Rory. You don't have a black pair? At least those wouldn't have stuck out like a couple of sore thumbs.'

'I looked. I thought I had black leather ones, somewhere, but I don't know where they've gone. These were the only ones I could find.'

We'll look too. 'Quit hassling the poor guy,' I tell Breslin. 'You take the gloves off as soon as you're in the door anyway, amn't I right, Rory? Who cares what they look like?'

Breslin rolls his eyes and sits back, shaking his head. Rory throws me a quick grateful glance. We're turning the interview room into familiar ground – even Breslin's slaggings are the type Rory has to have taken in school on a regular basis – and that's settling him. He's not a helpless little weenie, the way I thought from all that fidgeting and dithering at the start. It's more complicated than that. Inside his comfort zone, Rory does fine. Take him outside it and he stops coping.

I'm normally a jeans guy . . . Aislinn wasn't his comfort zone.

I say, 'So where does Aislinn live?'

'Stoneybatter.'

'Convenient,' I say, nodding. 'Just a quick hop across the river, and you're there. How'd you get there?'

'Bus. I walked down to Morehampton Road – it wasn't raining yet – and I caught the 39A up to Stoneybatter. It stops practically around the corner from her house.'

'Whoa whoa whoa. Rewind.' Breslin's eyebrows are up. 'Bus? You took the *bus* to her place? Way to impress a lady, Rory. Do you not own a car, no?'

Rory's going all pink and flustered again. I love blushers. 'No, I do, yeah. Just, I was thinking – I mean, if we had wine with dinner, and if I needed to get home—'

'You do? What kind of car?'

'It's a Toyota Yaris—'

Breslin snorted. 'Yeah? What year?'

'2007.'

'Jesus,' Breslin says, grinning into his notebook. 'Now I see why you took the bus. Carry on.'

Rory ducks his head and pokes his glasses up his nose. Apparently he's the type who takes wedgies meekly. When those guys finally snap, they do it right. I ask, 'What time did you leave home?'

Rory instantly sits up straighter. He's so glad to hear me doing the talking instead of Breslin, he'd tell me anything. 'Quarter to seven.'

Which is the most interesting thing he's said so far. His appointment with Aislinn was for eight. It doesn't take an hour and a quarter to get from Ranelagh to Stoneybatter, specially not on a Saturday evening. He could have walked in half the time.

'And when did you get the bus?' I ask.

'Just before seven. One got there as soon as I reached the stop.'

We can check that: CCTV on the bus. I write it down. 'What time were you due at Aislinn's place?'

'Eight, but I – I mean, I didn't want to be late. If I was early, I could always just walk around for a while.'

'Brrr,' I say, making a face. 'In that weather? Doing what?'

Rory shifts his feet like he can't get them comfortable. Talking about that extra time is turning him jumpy. I would only love to stamp Rory INNOCENT and chase off after Steve's gangster, but I can smell it, hot as blood: there's something here.

He says, 'I don't know. Just . . . making sure I could find the house, that kind of thing.'

I look puzzled. 'But you said her place was practically around the corner from the bus stop. That sounds like you already knew your way around.'

Rory's blinking hard. 'What? . . . No – no, not like that. But Aislinn had given me directions. And I'd looked up the map on my phone. It wasn't complicated. I just wanted to allow a little extra time, just in case.'

I leave a sceptical pause, but he doesn't jump into it. 'OK,' I say. 'So you got off the 39A in Stoneybatter – what time?'

'A little before half-seven. There wasn't much traffic.'

In plenty of time to reach Aislinn's house, kill her, and be back outside the door knocking and looking confused by eight o'clock. It even makes sense of turning off the cooker: Rory didn't want the fire alarm going off before he had time to act out his little play with the calls and the texts and presumably the worried pacing, for anyone who might be watching. That hot smell fills up my nose.

I glance over at the one-way glass, which stares blankly back. One look at Steve would have told me if his mind was matching mine. Instead I have Breslin, who's rocking his chair on its back legs and doodling in his notebook. I think about kicking the chair out from under him.

'You were well early,' I say. 'What'd you do?'

Rory says, 'I walked round to the top of Viking Gardens – that's Aislinn's road. To make sure I had the directions right. Like I said.'

'See anyone on Viking Gardens?'

'No. The street was empty. I didn't hang around there, though. I didn't want anyone thinking I was a burglar or a, a stalker.' Another jab at his glasses.

'Did you go into the road? Find Aislinn's house?'

'No. It's a straight road, a cul-de-sac – I could see the whole thing from the top; I didn't need to find the house in advance. And I wasn't keen on the idea of Aislinn looking out her window and seeing me there half an hour early. She would have had to invite me in, and she wouldn't have been ready, and overall it would have been really awkward.'

He's edgy as hell, but the answers are coming easily, no stumbling or backtracking. That doesn't mean much, though; not with this guy.

He's already told us he's the type who thinks ahead, goes through every hypothetical, makes sure he's got everything in place so his plans will run smoothly. If he planned a murder, he'd have his alibi story down pat; probably he'd do a walk-through a couple of days in advance. And if he didn't plan it, he would be well able to spend the night coming up with a good story and running through it a few hundred times. This guy's real comfort zone is inside his head.

'Plus she would have thought you were some obsessive freak who spent his spare time staring at her windows,' Breslin points out. Rory flinches. 'That's never a good look. What'd you do instead?'

'I was going to just wander around till eight o'clock. But then I realised I hadn't brought anything with me.'

'What, you mean condoms?' Breslin breaks into a big grin. 'Now there's self-confidence.'

Rory's head shoots down and he starts jabbing at his glasses again. 'No! I mean flowers. I didn't want to show up empty-handed. Aislinn had said not to bother bringing wine, but I'd been planning to buy her flowers in Ranelagh, except I forgot – I was concentrating so hard on what to wear and getting it ironed right and what time to leave . . . I only realised when I got to her road.'

'Awk-ward,' Breslin says, singsong. He's tilting his chair back again and playing with his pen.

'Well, yes. For a second there I was panicking. But there's a Tesco up on Prussia Street, so—'

'Hang on,' I say, confused. 'I thought you didn't know the area.'

'I don't. I— What?'

'How'd you know where the Tesco is?'

Rory blinks at me. 'I looked it up on my phone. So I headed up there—'

I know before Breslin opens his mouth that he's gonna come in. We're working well together: me keeping things chilled so we can get the basic info, him leaning in whenever he gets an opening to poke Rory with sticks, me standing under the piñata ready to catch whatever sweeties come tumbling out. I don't like working well with Breslin. It feels like he's suckering me all over again, in ways I can't pin down.

'Tesco flowers?' he asks. His face is halfway between a grin and a cringe. 'I thought you said this Aislinn's the fancy type.'

Rory shifts his arse on the chair. 'I did. She is. But at that hour—'

'She's the fancy type, she's been slaving over a hot cooker all day for you, and you're going to show up with a bunch of half-dead shocking-pink daisies? Come *on*.'

'Well, no, it wasn't what I'd planned. I wanted – Aislinn told me that when she was little her father used to take her to Powerscourt and they'd walk around the Japanese garden together, looking at the azaleas, and he'd tell her stories about a brave princess called Aislinn. So I wanted to see if I could find her an azalea plant. I thought . . .' A tiny rueful smile, down at his hands. 'I thought it would make her happy.'

'That's nice,' I say, nodding. 'Really nice. I'd say she'd have loved that.'

'Now that,' Breslin says approvingly, pointing his Biro at Rory, 'that's bringing your A game. That's the kind of thing that gets a guy places, if you know what I mean. That might even have made up for those.' The gloves. 'Shame you screwed it up. I'm betting Tesco doesn't stock azaleas.'

'I know it doesn't. But at that hour on a Saturday evening, nowhere else was going to be open. I thought even a bunch of ugly flowers was better than nothing.' Rory glances anxiously between the two of us, looking for approval.

Breslin grimaces and wavers one hand. 'Depends on the girl. If she's the downmarket type, sure, but with this one . . . Never mind; too late now. So you headed up to Tesco . . . ?'

'Yes. They didn't have a lot of flowers left, and most of them were what you said – big daisies dyed strange colours – but I found a bunch of irises that were OK.'

'Nothing wrong with irises,' I say. 'What time did you get to the Tesco?'

'About quarter to eight. Maybe just after.'

And we can check that, too. CCTV on the bus, CCTV in the Tesco: the whole timeline Rory's laying out is verifiable, and I wonder if that's deliberate. Those forgotten flowers were very convenient.

The Tesco is seven or eight minutes' walk from Viking Gardens: just enough to account nice and neatly for that extra half-hour.

If Rory rushed there or back – and we need to go looking for someone who saw him rushing – he could have shaved a couple of minutes off that walk. The actual murder took almost no time: two seconds for the punch, maybe ten or twenty to check Aislinn's breathing and her pulse, ten to turn off the cooker, gone inside a minute. It's the build-up to the murder that could have taken time; if there was a build-up.

If Rory is our boy, he's no routine rock-bottom-stupid wimp. He's nervous, but he's covering every crack before we can reach it, one step ahead all the way. If we're stuck with him, then at least we're gonna get a fight.

'Cutting it a bit fine,' I say. 'How long were you there?'

'Only a couple of minutes. I hurried. Like you said, I didn't have a lot of time left. Things like this are why I like being early.'

'Fair enough,' I say. 'So when you left Tesco . . . ?'

'I went back to Viking Gardens. I got there in time – I checked my watch: it was just before eight.'

'Was there anyone on the road?'

Rory thinks, rubbing at his nose. 'There was an old man walking his dog – a smallish white dog. He was heading out of Viking Gardens. He nodded to me. I don't think there was anyone else.'

Easy to check, again. 'So then what?'

'I went down the road looking at the house numbers till I found Aislinn's house – it's number twenty-six. I rang the bell . . .'

He trails off. I say, 'And?'

'She didn't answer the door.'

This time the blush comes up hot and fast. I can feel Steve behind the glass swaying towards that blush, positive that it means he was right and Rory Fallon is a holy innocent. I'm not so sure. That blush could be the memory of humiliation, or it could be the lie showing.

'Huh,' I say. 'Weird. What did you think was going on?'

Rory's head is going down. 'At that stage I just thought Aislinn hadn't heard me. I knew the bell was working – I could hear it going off inside the house – but I thought maybe she was in the toilet, or she'd gone out the back for some reason.'

'So what'd you do?'

'I waited a minute and then knocked. Then I rang the bell again. She still didn't answer, so after a few more minutes I texted her – I was wondering if I had the address wrong. I waited for ages, but she didn't text me back.'

'Ooo,' Breslin says, wincing. 'That's gotta sting.'

'I thought maybe she hadn't heard the text alert—' Rory catches the mix of pity and amusement on Breslin's face and ducks his head back down. 'It could happen. She could have been cooking or something, and left her phone in another room – those text alerts can be awfully quiet—'

'I'm always missing mine,' I agree. 'Pain in the hole. So did you try her again?'

'I rang her. The house is only a little cottage, one storey, so I thought she'd definitely hear the ring, no matter where she was. But she didn't answer.' Rory glances up, catches Breslin's dry grin and winces. 'I tried one more time – this time I put my ear to the door, to see if I could hear the phone ringing inside – I was wondering if she was even there, or if . . . But I couldn't hear anything.'

We'll check that. I say, 'What did you figure the story was?'

'I wasn't sure. I thought probably . . .' Rory's voice has almost vanished.

'Speak up,' Breslin says. 'The camera needs to hear this.'

Rory manages a little more volume, but he's still having trouble looking at us. 'Well. Aislinn cancelled a date at the last minute, a couple of weeks ago. She never said why; just that something had come up. And it was pretty complicated trying to schedule our other dates, as well – I'd suggest a day and it wouldn't work for her, or it would at first and then there was a problem – and sometimes she doesn't answer her phone . . . I don't know whether it's some mind-game – that really, really doesn't seem like something Aislinn would do, but obviously I don't know her that well yet – or whether there's something in her life that she's not ready to tell me about, like a parent with dementia or alcoholism who sometimes needs looking after at short notice?' No mention of two-timing, although the possibility has to have occurred to him. Maybe he's just dodging the slagging from

Breslin, but it's an interesting one to leave out. 'So I thought this was probably more of the same. Whatever that was.'

'And you standing there with your lovely Tesco irises,' Breslin says, almost keeping back a smirk. 'All ready for action.' Rory's head goes down farther.

I say, nice and sympathetic, 'Were you worried? That something had happened to Aislinn?'

Rory turns towards me gratefully. 'Yes. I was, a bit. That's why I asked, when you came in, whether this was about her. I was afraid she might have fainted, or slipped in the shower, or she might be too sick even to pick up her phone – I mean, that might have been the thing she wasn't ready to tell me about: some illness, epilepsy or . . . But I didn't know what to do about it. I couldn't ring 999 and tell them the emergency was that a woman wasn't answering her door to a guy she'd only known a few weeks – they'd have laughed in my face and told me it sounded like I needed a new girlfriend. Even I knew that was the most likely scenario. But I couldn't help imagining all the possibilities – I do that, even when it's not . . . Is Aislinn OK?'

He was out of his comfort zone, and he turned into a useless dithery little spa; or he wants us to think he did. I say, 'So what did you do?'

'There was a crack between the curtains, and I could see light inside, so I tried to look through the crack. I was a bit worried that the neighbours would see me and call the police, but I did have texts from Aislinn inviting me over, and I thought maybe the police coming wouldn't be such a bad idea, because then at least they could check and make sure nothing was up—'

This guy couldn't order a sandwich without tying himself in knots about the possible consequences of mayonnaise. 'What did you see?'

Rory shakes his head. 'Nothing. It was only a narrow crack, and the angle meant that all I could see was a bit of sofa and a lamp – the lamp was on. I didn't want to stay there too long; I just had a quick look.'

'Did you see any movement? Shadows? Any indication that there was someone home?'

'No. Nothing like that. The shadows were flickering a bit, but not really like someone was moving around; more like there was a fire in the fireplace.'

Which there was. I make a note to check whether you can see the flicker through the curtains. If Rory's our guy, he's got good self-control; a lot of people wouldn't have been able to resist the temptation to give us a mysterious intruder. 'So what did you do?'

'I texted her one more time, just in case we had got our wires crossed on the day or—' Breslin snorts. Rory flinches. 'I *said* just in case. I realise most likely I've been dumped. I already said I realise that. But *if* it was all some misunderstanding, and I went off in a huff and deleted her number off my phone, then we could both be missing out on something amazing. I didn't want to take that risk. I'd rather make an idiot of myself.'

'Looks like you got your wish,' Breslin says. 'You should've walked when she didn't answer the door. If she wants to fix the situation, let her do the work. Treat 'em mean, keep 'em keen.'

'I don't do that stuff.'

'No? How's that working out for you?'

I say, 'He's a decent human being, Breslin. That's actually a good thing. Rory: when she didn't answer that text, what'd you do?'

Rory says quietly, 'I gave up. It was gone half-eight, I was freezing, it was starting to rain – and whatever was going on, it wasn't going to make any difference if I stood there all night. So I left.'

'You must've been well pissed off,' Breslin says. 'Here's you hauling your arse halfway across the city on a shitty winter night, legging it up to Tesco and back, and she can't even be bothered letting you in? I'd be fuming.'

'I wasn't. I was more just . . . upset. I mean, I was a bit annoyed as well, but—'

'Course you were. Did you do any banging on the door? Any yelling? Swearing? Kicking lampposts?' And as Rory opens his mouth: 'Remember, we'll be checking with the neighbours.'

'No. I didn't do anything like that.' Rory has his face turned away, like not kicking Aislinn's door in makes him less of a man. 'I just went home.'

'Fair play,' I say. 'Some guys would've made tits of themselves in front of her whole road. Not the way to impress a girl. Did you catch the bus again?'

'I walked. I didn't feel like waiting for the bus, or having to see people. I just . . . I walked.'

Meaning no bus driver or passengers who could tell us if he was acting stunned or shaky, or if there was blood all over his gloves. I pull my eyebrows into a concerned shape. 'Jesus, I wouldn't fancy that walk. Right through town on a Saturday night, drunk eejits looking for trouble . . . No one gave you hassle?'

Rory's shoulders twitch in some kind of shrug. He's trying to vanish into his chest again. 'I probably wouldn't even have noticed if they'd tried. Some guy roared something right behind me, on Aungier Street, but I don't know what it was – I don't think it was in English – and I'm not sure he was talking to me. I was just . . .' The twitch again. 'I wasn't really paying attention.'

'Doesn't sound like you missed much,' I say. 'What'd you do with the flowers?'

'I threw them away.' All of a sudden the evening surges up in Rory's voice, turns it defeated and raw and horribly sad. Losing Aislinn has hit him hard, in one way or another. 'At first I forgot I even had them, and when I realised, I just wanted to get rid of them. I thought I should find someone to give them to, instead of wasting them, but I didn't have the energy. I shoved them in a bin. After all that.'

'A bin where?'

'On the quays. Yeah: I walked all that way basically wearing a sign that said "DUMPED", before I remembered the flowers existed. Hilarious, right?' That's to Breslin.

'I would've done the same,' I say. I flick an eyebrow at the one-way glass: Steve needs to send a couple of floaters to go through the bins on the quays, before they get emptied. There could be blood on that shitty bouquet. 'Only I would probably have stopped for a pint on my way home. You didn't, no?'

'No. I just wanted to get home.' Rory rubs his hands down his face. The strain is starting to get to him. 'Can you tell me what's going on?'

I ask, 'And you got home when?'

'I'm not sure. A bit before half-nine, maybe. I didn't look at my watch.'

Breslin says, 'Who'd you ring?'

'What do you mean?'

'When you got in. Who'd you ring to bitch about your big date going to shite? Your best mate? Your brother?'

'No one.'

Breslin stares. 'You're not serious. Ah, Rory, tell me you had someone you could ring. Because plenty of people get the old heave-ho somewhere along the way – it happens – but if you genuinely got home from a night like that and you couldn't think of a single bloke to ring for a good bitching session about women and the world ... well, that's just the saddest thing I've heard in weeks. Months.'

Rory says, 'I didn't ring anyone. I made myself a sandwich because for obvious reasons I hadn't had any dinner, and I sat in my flat looking out my window and feeling like the world's biggest fool, and imagining more and more ridiculous ways that everything might still be all right, and wishing I were the kind of person who could deal with this by going out and getting drunk off my face and getting into a fight or shagging some stranger.'

The savage humiliation in his voice bites at the air. It tastes good. If we get to him, it'll be through that: humiliation.

If Aislinn got to him, it was the same way. Finding out she was shagging someone else would probably have done the job.

'And at midnight, when Aislinn still hadn't rung me or texted me, I went to bed. The last thing I wanted in the world was to ring up one of my mates and tell him this story. OK?'

Breslin keeps up the incredulous stare for another minute. Rory looks away and pulls at his shirt cuff, but he keeps his mouth shut.

So far, Rory's been all about a nice checkable story, and he has to know we can check phone records. If he talked to anyone, it was in a way he figures we can't trace. I wonder if any of his mates live near his route home.

I leave it. 'Just so there's no confusion,' I say, 'can you confirm that this is the woman you were seeing? The woman whose house you went to last night?'

I pull a photo of Aislinn out of my file and slide it across the table to Rory. He glances up, wide-eyed, forgetting all about the flash of bitterness. 'Why do you have . . . ? You already— Did something – what—?'

'Like Detective Breslin said,' I tell him, nice but firm, 'we need to do this in order. Is this the woman whose house you went to last night?'

For a moment I think Rory's gonna grow a pair and demand some answers, but I don't break the smile or the stare, and in the end he blinks. 'Yeah. That's her.'

'Mr Fallon has identified a photo of Aislinn Murray,' I tell the tape.

'Let's have a look.' Breslin leans across to pick up the photo. His eyebrows shoot up and he gives a long, low whistle. 'Oh, my. Respect to you, my friend: she's a little corker.'

That takes Rory's mind off his questions. He hits Breslin with a hot glare, which Breslin doesn't notice – he's still holding up the photo at arm's length, nodding away appreciatively. 'She's beautiful. That isn't what I like about her.'

Breslin throws him a disbelieving glance, over the photo. 'Uh-huh. You're there for her sparkling personality.'

'Yeah. I am. She's interesting, she's intelligent, she's warm, she's got a wonderful imagination— It's not about her looks. Physically, she's not even my normal type.'

A snort explodes out of Breslin. 'Oh, please. She's *everyone's* type. Are you telling me you prefer them ugly? Given the choice, you would've gone for some fat hairy troll with a face like a smashed doughnut, but somehow you got stuck with this instead? My heart bleeds for you.'

Rory flushes. '*No.* I'm just saying I've never ended up with a girl who's so . . . well, so elegant. All my other girlfriends have been more the casual type.'

'Doesn't surprise me,' Breslin says, eyeing Rory's shirt. 'So how'd you pull this one? No offence, but let's face facts: you're punching well above your weight there. It doesn't bother you, does it? Me pointing that out?'

'No. I already said she's beautiful.' Rory is shifting in his chair, wanting Breslin to put the photo down. Breslin gives it another leer.

'She's a stunner. Whereas you . . . well, there's nothing wrong with you, but you're not exactly Brad Pitt, are you?'

'I know that.'

'So how'd you manage this?' Breslin waves the photo.

'We got talking. At a book launch in the shop, at the beginning of December. That's it.'

'Uh-huh.' Breslin gives him another sceptical once-over. 'What's your technique? Seriously. Any tips you've got, I'd love to hear them.'

Rory's getting ruffled: sitting up straighter, trying to stare Breslin out of it. 'I don't *have* a technique. I just talked to her. I never even considered that it might turn into anything. I know perfectly well that anyone would take one look at Aislinn and one look at me and bet any amount of money against us ending up together, because I thought the same thing. I only talked to her because she was off on her own in the children's section, and since it's my shop, I felt responsible for making sure everyone was having a good time.'

'And then,' I say, 'you clicked.'

I'm smiling at him, and it pulls an answering smile before he remembers. 'Yes. We really did. Or I thought we did.'

'What'd you talk about?'

'Books, mostly. Aislinn was leafing through a collection of George MacDonald fairy tales; I loved that book when I was little, so I told her that, and she said she loved it too – we'd even had the same edition. And from there we just . . . We both like magic realism, and we both like spinoffs, reworkings – Aislinn loved *Wide Sargasso Sea*; I was telling her she had to read *American Ghosts and Old World Wonders*. And she told me how, when she was fourteen, she got so annoyed at the ending of *Little Women* that she actually rewrote it and had Jo marry Laurie. She glued the pages into her copy, so that when she reread the book she could pretend that was the real story. She was funny, talking about that – how furious she was with Louisa May Alcott, till she found a solution . . . We laughed a lot.' Rory is smiling again, unconsciously.

He's yapping away like I'm his best mate. I know me and Breslin are doing the business, and I know Rory's what-if head is throwing out scenarios where one stroppy answer lands him in a cell full of *Oz* extras, but still: by this time, he should be digging in his heels and asking for answers, not sitting there handing over big wads of whatever we ask for. The accommodating type, the floaters said, but this goes beyond accommodating. The only ones who never push back are the ones who have something to hide.

I want to look at Steve. The one-way glass stares back at me.

'So you swapped phone numbers,' I say. 'And then . . . ?'

'We texted back and forth a bit, and then we went for a few drinks at the Market Bar. And we got on great again. It felt – I know this makes me sound like a teenager, but it felt like something incredible was happening. We couldn't stop talking. We couldn't stop laughing. We got there at eight, and we didn't leave till they threw us out.'

'Sounds like the date everyone dreams about,' I say.

Rory's palms turn upwards. 'That's what it felt like. Aislinn . . . She was telling me she used to be plain – that's the word she used, "plain" – and now every time a guy tries to chat her up, all she can think is that he wouldn't have gone near her a few years ago, and she can't get past that; she can't respect someone like that. She said with me it felt different; she felt like I actually would have talked to her exactly the same way, even back then – which I would have. She sounded . . . startled by it. More than startled: almost giddy. You see what I mean? We did click. It wasn't just me.'

That doesn't sound like the game-playing Rules addict I've been picturing. Aislinn's doing it again: getting blurrier with everything I find out about her. That, or she was feeding Rory bullshit, or Rory is feeding us bullshit.

Breslin says, 'And at the end of the evening?'

'I walked her to a taxi.'

'Come on, Rory. You know what I'm talking about. Did you get a little kiss on the way?'

Rory's chin goes up. 'How is that relevant?' He's going for dignified, but he hasn't got the oomph to pull it off.

Breslin snickers into his notebook. 'Not even a snog,' he says to me. 'You were calling this a dream date?'

Rory bites. 'We did kiss. All right?'

'Aah,' Breslin says. 'Sweet. Just a kiss?'

'Yes. Just a kiss.'

Breslin grins. I say, 'And after that night?'

'We kept texting. I invited her out for dinner. Like I said, it took a while to set it up, but we sorted it out in the end. We went to Pestle.'

'Very nice,' Breslin says, nodding. Even I've heard of Pestle, although I want those brain cells back. 'Did you sell a kidney?'

A sad flicker of smile from Rory. 'I thought Aislinn would like it. I wasn't thinking about it being super-trendy; I just chose it because it has an enclosed roof garden, so we could look out over the city and talk about, I don't know, all the people out there and what they might be . . . In hindsight, I misjudged completely. It must have seemed like I was doing the same thing as those other guys: judging her based on her looks. Do you think' – his face turns to me, suddenly wide-eyed – 'do you think that's why she . . . ?'

'Not enough info to tell,' I say. 'Did she seem like she was enjoying the evening?'

'Yes. I mean . . .' A shadow slips across Rory's face. 'She did. She really did. But she seemed like there was something on her mind, too; like she couldn't quite relax. Every time things were going well – when we started having a good conversation, or having a laugh – Aislinn would get this worried look, and she'd turn quiet, and I'd have to pick up the conversation from scratch and get it moving again. That was when I started wondering if there was something she wasn't ready to tell me, like a family situation or—'

'Or,' Breslin says, 'maybe she was starting to realise that she wasn't actually that into you. And every time she saw you thinking things were going great guns, she got worried because as far as she was concerned this was the date from hell and she didn't know how to break it to you.'

That gets to Rory. 'It wasn't the date from hell. I know I would say that' – Breslin's started to say something, but Rory raises his voice to force him down; he's getting ballsy – 'but I was there, and I'm not just fooling myself. Most of the time, we were getting on great.'

'If you say so,' Breslin says, almost holding back the twitch at the corner of his mouth. 'And at the end of that evening?'

'We kissed again. I assume that's what you're asking.'

The front legs of Breslin's chair come down with a bang. 'You *kissed*? She didn't invite you home with her? You mortgage your organs to take her to Pestle, and all you get is a snog up against a lamppost like a fucking teenager? If that's your idea of a date going well—'

Rory snaps, 'Two days later she invited me over to her house for dinner. You can check my phone: I've got the text messages right on there. Would she have done that if it had been the date from hell?'

Breslin's grinning, a wet open grin like hunger. He's loving this.

I feel it too. We're getting good at Rory, we know how to work him now; he's all ours. We can bounce him up and down, fling him into fancy shapes, like our very own little yoyo.

I don't want to bounce him too hard, not yet. I shoot Breslin a warning look and say, 'And the dinner invitation was for last night.'

'Yeah.' Rory's spine slumps; his little feisty moment is over. 'At first it was for last week, but Aislinn had something come up. So we switched it to last night.'

Breslin backs off a little, but not all the way. 'When we were talking about how you got to Aislinn's place, you said' – he flicks back through his notes – 'that you took the bus in case you had wine with dinner and you needed to get home afterwards. Meaning you weren't sure whether you were going to be spending the night at her place or not. Is that right?'

Rory's starting to go pink again. 'I had no idea. That was why I didn't bring the car – I didn't want Aislinn to think I was assuming she'd invite me to stay. Or that I was pressuring her to.'

I'm amazed this guy manages to get out of bed in the morning without working himself into a panic attack over the chance that he might trip on the bath mat and stab himself through the eye socket with his toothbrush and be left with a permanent twitch that'll ruin his chances of landing an airplane safely if the pilot has a heart attack and doom hundreds to a fiery death. Normally this shit makes me roll my eyes, but here it's gonna come in useful, as soon as we're ready to start pushing.

What-if-maybe crap is for weak people. It belongs to the ones who don't have the strength to make actual situations go their way, so they have to hide away in daydreams where they can play at controlling what comes next. And that makes them even weaker. Every what-if is a gift to anyone who's looking for a hold on you, and that means us. If a guy's whole head is in reality, then reality is the only route we can take to get to him. If he's letting his mind prance off down dozens of twisty hypothetical fairy tales, every one of those is a crack we can use to prise him open.

Breslin says, 'But you thought last night might be The Night.'

'I didn't have a clue. That's what I'm—'

'Come on, Rory. Don't bullshit me. It's your third date, right? You'd blown the budget on her, last time? She'd invited you over for a taste of her home cooking? Any normal guy's going to be expecting—'

'I wasn't expecting *anything*. The price of the restaurant has nothing to do with— Aislinn's not a—'

Rory is fun when he's pissed off: like a fluffy little attack gerbil. Breslin raises his eyes to the ceiling. 'OK, let's try this. Did you bring condoms?'

'I don't see how that's—'

'Rory. Don't get coy now. We're all grown-ups here. When you knocked on Aislinn's door last night, did you have a condom on you, yes or no?'

After a moment Rory says, 'Yes. I had a pack in my coat pocket. Just in case.'

'You've got your priorities straight,' Breslin says, sitting back and smirking. 'You forgot the flowers, but the johnnies: those you remembered.'

'You're showing your age, Breslin,' I say smoothly, smirking right back at him. 'Your generation was weird about safe sex. My and Rory's lot, we don't go anywhere without a three-pack, just on the off-chance.' Breslin throws me a narky look that's only partly put on. I say, 'Am I right, Rory? Still got them in your coat?'

If he's got them, that backs up the claim that this is the coat he was wearing last night. But Rory shakes his head. 'I took them out. When I got home and took off my coat, I felt them in the pocket, and I just . . .' He's breathing fast. 'I felt like I should have known all along that this was never going to happen. Just like you said.' That's thrown at Breslin, who tilts his head in acknowledgement. 'Like the only possible reason Aislinn could have been seeing me was to set me up for some awful candid-camera thing, and while I was knocking and texting and ringing like an idiot, she'd been behind that door with all her friends, all of them splitting their sides laughing at the loser who genuinely thought he had a chance with her.'

The emotion is real. It's gripping his whole body, ready to lift him off the chair by the scruff of his neck and slam him against the wall. That doesn't make the story true. That blast of humiliation could have hit him when he says it did, or it could have hit when he arrived early at Aislinn's and she didn't give him the welcome he was expecting; or it could have come weeks back, when she told him she was seeing someone else, or when they left Pestle and she didn't invite him home, and he decided to punish her.

Rory is still going. 'I threw the condom packet across the room. It made me feel ridiculous and disgusting and sleazy and . . . It's somewhere in my living room. I hope I never find it.'

I say, matter-of-fact but sympathetic – Cool Girl is big on matter-of-fact sympathy – 'If she genuinely didn't bother answering the door, that was a shitty thing to do.'

Rory shrugs. He's folding over his hands again. That rant emptied him out; he even looks smaller. 'Maybe. I don't know what happened.'

Breslin moves. Rory glances up in time to catch the smirk. He flinches away from it.

'No, seriously,' I say. 'You've got every right to be well pissed off.'

Rory says, 'I'm not even pissed off. I just wish I understood.' He looks exhausted, suddenly. He takes off his glasses and pulls down the cuff of one sleeve to polish them. Now that he can't see me properly, he has an easier time looking at me. Bare and half blind, his eyes look clean as an animal's. 'Just so I can stop making up scenarios. That's all I did last night. I couldn't make my mind stop it. I think I got about two hours' sleep.' Which would cover things nicely if anyone heard him moving around in the middle of the night, or saw a light on. 'I just want to know. That's all.'

I say, 'Why do you think we brought you in here?'

'I don't know.' Rory's spine tenses up. He can feel it: we're headed for the real stuff. 'Obviously, something's happened. Probably near Aislinn's house, since you were asking me what I . . . But I can't – there are too many – I mean, I'm hoping it's not—'

I say, and I don't make it gentle, 'Aislinn's dead.'

It hits Rory like a strobe light to the face. He jerks back in his chair, hands spasming in front of him – his glasses go skittering halfway across the table. For a second there I think he's having some kind of attack – he's the type who would carry around an inhaler – but he gets himself back. He grabs for his glasses and shoves them onto his nose; it takes him three clumsy tries, catching them when they fall off and fumbling to get them right way up and trying not to smear the lenses. Then he presses his palms together, jams his fingers up against his mouth and breathes hard into them, staring at nothing.

Me and Breslin wait.

Rory says, into his fingers, 'How? When?'

'Last night. Someone killed her.'

His body jerks. 'Oh God. Oh God. Is that why – was she – when I was knocking, was she – was the person still—'

I say, 'Now do you see why we needed to talk to you?'

'Yes. I— Oh *God*!' Rory's eyes snap into focus; focused on me, and huge. The penny's dropped, or he's decided to play it that way. 'You don't think – wait. No. Do you think I – am I a *suspect*?'

Breslin laughs, one cold note.

'What? What? Why is that funny?'

'Listen to that,' Breslin says, to me. 'He's all about how much he *cared* about Aislinn and her great personality, right up until we tell him the poor girl's dead. And just like that, it's all about him. Forget her.'

'I do care about her! I just – this wasn't—' Rory grabs for air. He looks like shit: white and ragged, staring wildly back and forth between us. I hope he brought his inhaler. 'I thought a *burglary*, maybe. Or a, an assault. I never—'

His hands go to his head, and he rubs the heels back and forth on his temples. He's breathing hard.

It all looks right. Shock and grief are clumsy, they're ugly, they're not pretty tears and a dabbing hanky. But Rory's had all night to build himself an armour suit of what-if and dress up in it. And, because he's used to focusing on what could have happened just as much as on what actually did, he could walk around in his made-up story like it's the true one.

The one place where his story cracked and peeled: around that half-hour between him getting off the bus and him knocking on Aislinn's door. There's something there. Everything else could play either way, innocent or guilty. That half-hour, the half-hour that matters, wasn't innocent.

The shock could be real and he could still be our guy. There's one obvious reason why he might have been expecting to hear about an assault instead of a murder.

I say, 'Why did you think there might have been a burglary or an assault?'

'Can I—' Rory's voice has gone thick. He swallows hard, but his chin is shaking. 'Can I please have a minute by myself?'

Breslin says, 'What for?'

'Because I just found out—' He jerks his head like there are small things flying in his face. 'I just need a minute.'

'You're doing grand,' I say. 'We'll only be a little longer. Hang in there.'

'No. I can't. I need—'

'We're asking you to help us out here,' Breslin says. 'Any reason why you have a problem with that?'

'I just need to clear my head. I just— Do I have to stay? Am I allowed to leave?' Rory's voice is spinning higher and louder.

Breslin's leaning back in his chair, watching, with a curl to his lip. 'Rory. Pull yourself together.' But Rory is beyond reach of the snap of disgust. 'This is just routine. It's not personal. We'll be having this same conversation with every single person who had anything to do with Aislinn. And I can guarantee you, the people who cared about her will want to do anything they can to help us. You don't?'

'I *do*. I just— I'm not under arrest, right? I can just go for a walk? And then come back?'

Not a total pushover, after all. Fluffy little Rory is well able to push back, when he really wants to.

He's one nudge away from trying to walk out. If he goes for the door, I'm gonna have to choose: let him go, or arrest him. Neither of those sounds good.

'Jesus, man, have you seen the weather?' I say easily. 'It's lashing. You'll get soaked. Plus, we'll lose this interview room, and then we'll all be hanging around for hours before we get another one.' Rory stares at me, too disoriented to work out what he thinks about that. 'Tell you what: we'll give you a few minutes to yourself, OK? Just to get your breath. It's a lot to take in.'

There's a small sharp movement from Breslin, but I don't look around. I give Rory a Cool Girl smile, enough sympathy to warm it but not enough to feel sticky. 'We'll have a cup of tea and come back to you,' I say, scraping back my chair and standing up, before he can come up with a decision. 'Can I get you a cuppa while I'm at it?'

'No. Thanks. All I want is—'

Rory's voice splits open. He presses the back of one hand against his mouth.

Breslin hasn't moved. Those pale eyes are on me. They say, clear as a death grip on my wrist, *Sit the fuck down*.

I say, without taking my eyes off Breslin's, 'We'll see you in a few, Rory. Hang in there.'

Then I turn around and go for the door. I leave it open behind me, but I don't look back. I'm halfway to the observation room before I hear the nasty, juddering scrape of Breslin pushing back his chair on the grimy linoleum.

Steve's at the one-way glass, with his shirtsleeves rolled up and red hair sticking out in all directions; he's been putting a lot into watching us. I head over to see what Rory's doing with his alone time. On the way my eyes hit Steve's, but only for a second that says *Later*.

Rory has his elbows on the table and his face in his hands. The jump of his shoulders claims he's crying. I can't see if there are actual tears.

'Well well well,' Breslin says behind me, swinging the door shut with a bang. 'I thought that went pretty well, for a first round. Nice work, Conway.'

Patronising fuck. 'You didn't do a bad job yourself,' I say.

'I'm not sure that was the right call, pulling out just when he's going to pieces. That's always a good moment to push for a confession.' Breslin loosens his collar with a finger and rolls back his shoulders. 'But hey: we got to him once, we can do it again. Am I right?'

'Not a problem,' I say. 'So: what's the betting?'

Breslin's head pops forward like he can't believe he heard me right. 'Say what?'

'The suspect, Detective. Guilty or .not. I'm asking for your opinion.'

Breslin's eyebrows are hitting his careful hairline. 'Are you serious?'

'About wanting your opinion? More or less.'

Steve has wandered over to the water cooler and is filling a plastic cup, watching us. Breslin lifts a hand. 'Whoa whoa whoa. Let's just stall the ball here. Are you saying you've got doubts?'

'I'm saying I'd like your opinion. If that's a problem, though, I can live without it.' I'm right back to wanting to throat-punch the bollix. The fine thread of alliance that built up between the two of us in the interview room lasted all of thirty seconds outside it.

'Talk to me, Conway. Are you trying to be super-careful, yeah? Make sure you've got all your bases covered? Is that what's going on?'

It's not a bad technique – make the other person explain herself, you've got her on the back foot right there – but this is what I mean about Breslin not being as smart as he thinks: I just saw him use it on Rory, plus it should have occurred to him that, what with me being a detective, I might just know the same tricks he does. I lean a shoulder against the one-way glass, where I can keep one eye on Rory, and stick my hands in my pockets. 'Do you think we should be?'

Breslin sighs. 'Well. I guess we've got to face it: one of the last things your rep needs is a ding for jumping the gun. But the *other* last thing you need is a rep for being so indecisive that you'll let your guy walk rather than put your balls on the line. Are you getting me?'

Steve says, doing mildly bewildered, 'Hang on a sec. You're saying you deffo think he did it, yeah?'

Breslin sighs exasperatedly and runs his hands over what's left of his hair, carefully so he won't bother it. 'Well, yeah, Moran. I kind of do. This guy was the victim's boyfriend, so that's Strike One. He was actually *at the crime scene* at the relevant time, he's not even trying to deny it, so that's Strike Two. He was wearing non-fibre gloves, same as our killer: Strike Three. He was wearing a black wool overcoat, and we've got black wool fibres on the body: Strike Four. And he basically admits that he was getting impatient for his ride, after all the time and money he'd put into this girl, and she wasn't showing any signs of giving up the goods. That's a great big Strike Five. I'm not a baseball aficionado, but I'm pretty sure it takes less than that to put a guy well and truly out.'

Steve is sipping his water and nodding through Breslin's list. 'I'd say it does, all right,' he says agreeably. His accent has got stronger. I put on the Thicko Skanger act too, now and then, but I do it for suspects, not for my own squad. Sometimes Steve makes me want to puke. 'I think I'll keep an open mind a little longer, but.'

Breslin lets the exasperation go up a notch. 'Open about *what*? There's nothing else *here*, Moran. There's our boy Fallon, there's a shitload of circumstantial evidence all pointing straight at him, and that's it. What are you being open-minded about? Aliens? The CIA?'

Steve pulls his arse up onto the rickety table, getting comfortable for the chats. I leave him to it. 'Here's the only thing,' he says. 'How'd the actual killing play out?'

'What are you talking about? He punched her. She hit her head. She died. That's how it *played out*.'

Steve thinks that over, brow furrowed – bit slow on the uptake, us skangers. 'Why, but?' he asks.

Breslin's head goes back and he bares his teeth at the ceiling, half-way between a smile and a grimace. 'Moran. Moran. Do I look like Poirot to you?'

'Huh? . . . Not a lot.'

'No. Because this isn't Saturday evening in front of the telly with a nice cup of tea and a digestive biscuit, and so I don't *care* about motive. I don't. And neither should you. You ought to know that by now.'

Steve scratches at his nose. 'You're probably right, man. I'd say you are. It's just I'm not seeing it. I like being able to see things in my head, know what I mean? Picture them, like.' He frames his hands in front of his eyes, to make sure Breslin gets the concept of picturing something.

Breslin takes a deep breath and blows it out slowly, so we can see how much he's putting into keeping his temper with us. 'OK,' he says. 'OK. Let's go ahead and spend some time *picturing* it.'

'Thanks,' Steve says, giving him a humble smile. 'I appreciate that.'

'Rory shows up with his shitty Tesco bouquet. Aislinn, who clearly wasn't the shitty Tesco type, isn't happy. She gets snotty. Rory's not having that – he's been blowing his budget and rearranging his schedule and racing around Stoneybatter in the rain to make her happy, but that's not good enough for Princess Special? He pulls out a Jane Austen quote about high-maintenance bitches, or prick-teases, or whatever literary types call girls like that. Aislinn slaps him down hard: she tells him exactly why he's not good enough for her, including why she hasn't let him into her knickers and why after this she never will. She goes one put-down too far, and bam.' Breslin mimes a little punch, not bothering to put much into it. 'And here we all are. Can you picture that OK? Yeah?'

'That'd work, all right.' Steve nods, picturing away. 'Only you'd think the bouquet would get a bit messed up, like, in all the action. He'd drop it, or something. We didn't find any petals on the floor.'

'So no petals happened to come off. Or Rory's got the brains to pick them up. We're not talking about a massive struggle; we're talking a bit of that' – Breslin makes a yappy-mouth sign – 'one punch and a few seconds of oh-shit. A couple of petals would have been great, but in this job you can't get too demanding. You need to work with what you've got, instead of fussing about what you haven't.' Breslin's giving Steve the beginnings of a smile, all ready to kiss and make up. 'Am I right or am I right?'

Steve says cheerfully, 'You're dead right, man. I'd just like to shake a few more trees and see if anything falls out, is all.' When Breslin rears away, rolling his jaw: 'I'm new, you know? I've got loads to learn. Might as well get in the practice while I can.'

'You're not that fucking new. You've both been on the job long enough that you should be able to handle your own cases without a babysitter. This kind of shit right here is why the gaffer decided you need one.'

'And we appreciate you taking on the job, man. Seriously. But I've gotta get there in my own time, know what I mean? Otherwise I'll never learn. Sure, what harm?'

'Moran. Come on. The *harm* is that you two are about to embarrass yourselves – and let's be honest here, it's not like you can afford to do that. If you actually let this guy walk out of here while you go shaking trees or whatever it was, you look weak as fuck. You look *unsure*. And not just to the rest of us. The longer you leave it, the more the defence is going to make of it: *Ladies and gentlemen of the jury, even the cops weren't positive my client was guilty, how can you not share their reasonable doubt?* Doesn't that bother you at all?'

In the interview room, Rory lifts his head and wipes his face with the heels of his hands. He's red and blotchy; the tears are there, for whatever that's worth.

Steve raises his cup to Breslin. 'Don't worry, man. We'll make sure the gaffer knows you did your best to light a fire under us.'

'*Whoa* there. Hang on a second. You think this is about me?' Breslin switches to a nice mix of stunned and wounded. 'You seriously think that's what I'm worried about? My rep?'

'Ah, God, no,' Steve says, giving him a big sweet smile. 'Your rep's amazing – stellar, is that the word I'm looking for? It'd take more than the likes of us to mess it up. I'm just saying, don't worry: we'll make sure credit goes where credit's due.'

'This isn't about *me*. I don't work like that. This isn't even about you – if it was just your reps on the line, then sure, I'd try to stop you making a hames of this for your own sakes, but in the end I'd have to let you make your own choices. This is about the *squad*. If you take a month to get up the balls to charge Mr Obvious in there, the media won't be yelling about how Conway and Moran need to get their act together; they'll be yelling about how *the Murder squad* needs to start taking its job seriously and actually protecting the public from scumbags. I'm hoping you two have at least enough loyalty to give a damn about that.'

Breslin's worked himself up into enough of a righteous lather that I can't tell whether he actually thinks he means that shite. I say, 'How's the squad gonna look if we charge the wrong guy?'

'Having to drop the charges,' Steve says, doing a cringe-face. 'Public apology, more than likely. Media yelling about how the Murder squad's a shower of incompetent wankers who don't care who they lock up as long as they get the solve. Witnesses afraid to come to us, in case they end up in cuffs because we're in such a hurry to charge anyone we can get our hands on . . .' He shakes his head. 'Not good, man. For the squad, like.'

Breslin sighs again. 'Conway. Moran,' he says, changing tack to go gentle. 'The guy is guilty as sin. Take it from someone who was putting scumbags away when you two were kids filling out your application forms for Templemore: he's our man. The question here isn't whether he did it. The question is whether you two are able to do what needs doing.'

I say, 'We'll all just have to keep our fingers crossed. Won't we?'

'OK. Listen.' Breslin leans back against the wall, gives us both the smile that melts witnesses. 'I know you guys haven't been getting an easy ride around here. Probably you thought I'd missed that, or didn't care, but you'd be surprised how many of us are pulling for you. I've always said you'll make a great pair of Murder Ds, once you find your feet.'

'Thanks, man,' Steve says. Steve gets basically no hassle, except what rubs off from me; Breslin just wants the pair of us paranoid. 'That means a lot.'

'Not a problem. You've just got to get past the routine bullshit. Newbies get hazed; it's part of the job. It's not personal.'

The slimy bastard is too thick to realise he used the same words to Rory Fallon, five minutes back, or else he thinks we are. And he thinks we're thick enough to believe our shitpile is just routine, or desperate enough to pretend we do.

'The lads just need to see whether you can take the heat. And this?' Breslin points at the one-way glass. 'This is your chance to show them. I know all the silly shite has to have knocked your confidence, but if schoolkid crap can take you to the point where you don't trust your own judgement enough to charge a slam-dunk like this one, maybe you'd be better off back in blue. Yeah, that sounds harsh' – lifting a hand like one of us tried to break in, which we didn't – 'but it's what you need to hear.'

I know better than to look at Steve. In the corner of my eye he's still peacefully swinging his legs and drinking his water, but I can feel him knowing better than to look at me.

Breslin wants us to charge Rory Fallon. He wants it badly. It could be because he's sick of babysitting the kindergarten case, wants to wind it up and go back to his pal McCann and their PhD-level fancy conspiracies and gang-boss shootings. Could be because he wants to shake himself in front of O'Kelly – *It took those two a month to crack their last domestic, with me on board it takes them a day, now give my ego a hand job and put me up for promotion.* Could be just that he's so in the habit of arm-twisting, he can't get through his day without that buzz. But.

I've been taking it for granted that whoever threw me to Crowley did it on the spur of the moment, for kicks, like whoever dropped my phone in my coffee back when I still left it on my desk. It didn't occur to me, till this moment, that a lot more thought could have gone into it.

Creepy Crowley is whipping this case up into a big one, and someone is egging him on. If I fuck up spectacularly, like for example if I charge Fallon when there's some great big chunk of exonerating evidence that somehow managed to vanish on its way to my desk, and if the papers somehow happen to get hold of the story, the whole country will explode with it. And there'll be the excuse the squad's gagging for: I'll be gone.

In an interview, this is where I'd be on my feet, stopping the tape – *Interview paused at 2.52 p.m., Detectives Conway and Moran leaving the interview room* – and getting me and Steve the hell out of there. We need a chat, right now. I watch Breslin blandly and wait to see what comes next.

'Here's what we'll do,' Breslin says. 'Moran, you go have a look through the CCTV, see if you can pick up Rory Fallon leaving the vic's place last night and track him through town – maybe we can figure out where he ditched the gloves. Meanwhile, Conway and I will have another go at Rory, try for a confession – shouldn't be a problem to us, am I right?' He gives me a big pally grin and, I swear to God, an actual clap on the shoulder. I nearly punch the presumptuous fucker. 'Even if we don't get it, no big deal: we've got plenty on him already. We arrest him, charge him, I get to tell the lads that when the chips are down you two can do the business, and I can pretty much guarantee you won't be getting any more hassle in the squad room. Everyone's a happy camper.'

He's a hair away from spelling it out for us: *You go along with me on this, and I'll sort out the lads for you.* This isn't just because he wants to get back to McCann, or because he wants to look pretty for the gaffer. He's itching to get Fallon charged.

And he's positive we're gonna jump on the deal. He's already tightening his tie and heading for the door.

I say, 'Here's what we'll do. Deasy and Stanton are making a list of Rory Fallon's KAs. If Rory's our boy, then the guy who called it in will be on that list. I'd like you to have chats with them all, see if you can identify the caller. Start with best mates and brothers if he's got them. If there's no joy there, you can work your way down.'

Breslin has turned round. He's staring at me, but he's managing to stay nice and neutral, ready to keep the matey stuff coming if we let him. When he's sure I'm done, he says, 'Why?'

I say, 'Because me and Detective Moran will take Fallon from here.'

Breslin looks back and forth between us – he's aiming for big dog who's been patient with the bold puppies long enough, but him having to look up at us takes some of the oomph out of it. He says, 'I'm going to need an explanation here.'

I'm opening my mouth on *Because this is our fucking case and the next time you try to give me an order you're getting a knee in the balls,* but Steve gets in there first. He says, 'You're dead right, man: we need to earn the lads' respect. And that's not going to happen if you get our confession for us. We appreciate the offer, but we're going to have to handle this one ourselves.'

Which I have to admit is better than my version. The second of taken-aback on Breslin's face gives me my control back. I tell Steve, 'Detective Breslin knows that, you thicko. Does he look like a rookie to you? He was testing us. He was trying to see if we'd wimp out and offload the tough stuff on someone else when we got the chance, or if we've got the nads to actually do our job.'

Steve's mouth opens. Then he bursts out laughing. 'Jesus! And me standing here like an eejit, giving you the big speech about earning the lads' respect. Fair play to you, man; you had me going, all right.'

Breslin's got a bit of a smile on his mouth, but those pale eyes still moving back and forth between us are cold and expressionless. He doesn't know whether he believes us or not.

I let myself crack a half-grin. 'He had me, too, at first. There's a reason he's got that stellar rep. Thanks, Breslin: we get the message, loud and clear. We'll do our job. And once we've done it, we'll see you in the incident room. Case meeting at four.'

I give him a pleasant nod and turn away, to the one-way glass. Overlaid on Rory, Breslin's reflection stays still, staring at me. My back prickles.

Then he shrugs. 'I'd love to think you know what you're doing,' he says. 'See you at four.'

The reflection turns and vanishes. The observation-room door clicks shut.

Me and Steve wait, listening, watching Rory fumble in his pocket and find a crumpled tissue and try to mop up the mess that's his face. Then I go to the door and open it fast. The corridor is empty.

Steve says, 'I don't like this.' His accent's gone back to normal.

I say, 'Me neither.'

'What's he playing at?'

'I don't know.' I leave the door open. I'm trying to pace, but the observation room is too small; every two steps I'm slamming off a wall. The stink has thickened till it's like another person in there, shoving us aside. 'Did you hear him? "I can guarantee you won't get any more hassle in the squad room . . ." He was trying to bribe us.'

'Why would he want Fallon charged? This badly?'

'I don't know. I didn't think he was one of the ones trying to fuck me up.' Steve has to see what goes down, what with not being in a coma, but I don't do heart-to-hearts; this is the first time I've talked about this shit straight out, and it doesn't feel good. 'But if we charge Fallon too soon, and then it all goes tits-up, and Crowley splatters it all over the country . . .' Even the thought – the burst of applause in the squad room, the smirk on Roche, the naked relief in O'Kelly's voice as he explains that this isn't working out – sends red zigzags across my brain. I say, 'That'd be one way to put me out of commission.'

Steve has split his plastic water cup and is folding it into shapes. He says, 'It could be just that: him trying to fuck us up.' The 'us' is cute – no one's on any campaign to fuck Steve up – but it gives me a quick ridiculous beat of warmth anyway. 'I've never got that vibe off him either, but. I always got the sense he doesn't give a monkey's about us, either way.'

'Me too. But if he was serious about getting rid of us, that's exactly the sense we would get. Breslin's no genius, but he's been at this a long time. He's well able to hide what he's at.'

'Or,' Steve says. 'If the gangster thing pans out . . .'

He leaves it there. The sharp crack of folding plastic jabs me in the ear.

Bent cops exist. Fewer in real life than on the telly, but they're out there. Everything from the guy squaring a speeding fine in exchange for match tickets, to the guy who's owned by a gang boss, body and soul.

If a gangster boyfriend killed Aislinn, the first thing he or his pals would do is ring their best bitch-boy and tell him to sort it out. The perfect way to sort it out, no loose ends, no worries, would be charging Rory Fallon and closing the case.

'Breslin,' I say. I've stopped pacing; stopped breathing, almost. 'Breslin. You think? Seriously?'

Steve lifts one shoulder.

'Nah. I don't see it. He's all about being the big hero. He wouldn't be able to handle seeing himself as the bad guys' pet cop. It'd blow his brain cells.'

Steve says, 'Breslin would find a way to see himself as the hero, no matter what he did. That's where he starts: with the idea that he's the good guy, so whatever he's doing must be right. Then he works backwards from there to figure out how.'

Which is true, but I never thought about it that way before – I've never spent this much time thinking anything about Breslin before. I don't like the feel it gives me, clamped onto the back of my neck. What Steve's talking about, it's not just Breslin who thinks that way; we all do. When you badger a statement out of some traumatised witness, or manipulate a mother into giving evidence that'll put her own kid in jail, you get to enjoy the buzz of winning without tying yourself in knots over the deeper moral subtleties, because you're the good guy in this story. Steve is shredding that into something different, something tangled and thorny; dangerous.

He says, 'And he's the type they go for. Wife, kids, mortgage . . .'

The gang boys don't bother with the likes of me and Steve, working-class singles on the way up; unless there's a gambling problem or a coke habit, we don't come with enough leverage. But Breslin has a high-maintenance blonde wife and three bucktoothed blond boys, like something out of an ad, and a house in a snazzy part of Templeogue. That's a lot of needs tugging at his sleeves, and a lot to lose if he were to change his mind down the line. Once he was in, even one toe, he wouldn't be getting out.

Breslin and McCann pull a lot of the big gang murders; they spend a lot of their time talking to seriously hard-core guys. It would be a miracle if, somewhere along the way, someone hadn't made Breslin an offer.

That same flex to the air that I felt in the squad room, straight lines buckling at the edges of my eyes. My heart is going hard.

I say, 'Yeah. He is.'

'Exactly the type. And a Murder D would be worth top dollar to a gang boss.'

Breslin wears good suits, but we all do. He drives a 2014 BMW and he bangs on about how his kids go to private school because he's not having them surrounded by skangers and immigrants who can barely speak English – and that's just the skangers, ha ha ha, no offence, Conway, Moran – but I always figured Daddy and Mummy were bankrolling him. He takes his family to the Maldives for holidays, but if I'd cared enough to think about it, I would've assumed he'd squared a few penalty points for his bank manager in exchange for a sky-high credit-card limit and no pressure to pay it off.

Me and Steve have been wanting an interesting case. This could be a lot more interesting than we bargained for.

Steve says, 'And if he's the one who fed Crowley his info, that would explain why.'

Enough mud in the water can take you a long way towards reasonable doubt. The air twitches, in the corners.

And I can't keep the grin off my face.

If Steve's right, then there's some high-level danger headed our way, from a bunch of directions at once. Gangs don't kill cops, it would draw too much hassle, but they don't have a problem firebombing your car to tell you to back off. And that's small-time, compared to what the lads will do if we dob Breslin in to Internal Affairs.

I can't wait for them all to bring it on. Danger doesn't bother me; I'll eat danger with a spoon. Breslin the puffed-up little tosspot, trying to twist me like a balloon animal, he made me feel like I was in a straitjacket and writhing to punch him. But Breslin the bent cop: he's a dare, a bad poison dare that no one with sense should take, and I've always had a thing for dares.

Steve's eyeing me like I've lost it. 'What? What's funny?'

'Nothing. I like a challenge.'

'So you think I'm right. You think he's . . .' Steve doesn't finish.

That sobers me up a notch. 'I don't know yet. We're way into the hypothetical here. I don't like hypotheticals.' I bite down on one thumb to get rid of the grin. 'All we know for definite is, Breslin wants this guy charged and the case closed, ASAP. We need to stall till we've got a handle on why. What you came up with back there, about doing our own dirty work: that was good. That should buy us some time.'

The twist to Steve's mouth doesn't look convinced. 'You think he went for it?'

'Not sure. I think so. I hope so.' The memory of Breslin's cold stare makes me bite down harder. 'Either way, that's the line we stick to: we're the thicko rookies who don't get how things work around here, and we want to do our case our way. Are you OK with that?'

Part of me expects Steve to squirm away. There's a decent chance that the bullshit here is all about me; as long as he plays it right, he can sidestep the blast and slot right into the squad once I'm a smoking crater, but he'll blow his chance if he convinces Breslin he's an idiot. But he grins. 'I can manage thicko rookie.'

'Right up your alley,' I say. The relief hits me harder than I want to think about. 'No acting required.'

'Hey, you use what you've got.' Steve tilts a thumb at the one-way glass. 'What do we do with him?'

Rory has finished his cry. He's getting antsy, popping his head up to peer worriedly around like a specky meerkat, wondering where we've disappeared to. He should be the biggest thing in our day. I practically forgot he existed.

I say, 'We have one more go. Like we told Breslin we would.'

'That means leaving Breslin to talk to his KAs. You think that's safe?'

If Breslin's looking to fuck up either Rory or me, there are a dozen ways that Rory's pals could be a pure gift to him. I say, 'Probably not, but what the hell, let's live dangerously. It was the only way I could think of to get rid of him. And I don't want him in with Fallon any longer. Fallon can't take being pushed around; if Breslin shoves him any more, he's gonna walk. And whether he's our guy or not, I don't want him thinking we're big scary bullies out to get him. Not yet, anyway.'

'"Whether or not,"' Steve says. 'You're not sure any more?'

I lift one shoulder. 'I was when I came out of there. Not a hundred per cent, but almost. There's something dodgy about him getting to Stoneybatter early – he didn't like talking about it, did you spot that?'

'Yeah. But the reaction when you told him Aislinn was dead: that looked real to me.'

'To me, too. But even if it was, that doesn't say he's innocent.' Rory's got his sodden tissue between finger and thumb and he's looking around for somewhere to put it. He gives up and tucks it in his pocket. I say, 'He might not have known he'd killed her. He throws the punch, she goes down, but when he checks her pulse or her breathing she's still alive; so he turns off the cooker to make sure the place won't burn down around her, and he legs it. He thinks she's just got a concussion or whatever; he spends the night praying it's knocked the memory right out of her head. And when he finds out she's dead, and all of a sudden he's staring down the barrel of a murder charge, he nearly shits himself.'

'That'd play,' Steve says.

'When I came out of there, I would've put money on it. But now . . .' Rory half-stands up, then sits down again, like standing might not be allowed. I say, 'You?'

Steve runs a thumbnail along the ribbing of the plastic cup and watches Rory try to stay sitting. 'The thing is, even if Rory is our guy, that doesn't mean there's no secret gangster boyfriend and Breslin's clean.' His voice goes down on that. We both glance automatically at the door: nothing. 'Assume the boyfriend exists, right? Even if he did nothing to Aislinn, he isn't going to want us sniffing around his business, checking his movements, telling his missus about his bit on the side . . . The second he finds out Aislinn's dead – if he calls round to her for a quickie late last night, say – he's going to put in a call to his guy on the inside and tell him to get it sorted, fast.'

'And the slower we get it sorted,' I say, 'the longer we've got to find out if there's something else going on.' Just saying the words lifts my heart rate.

'So we stall,' Steve says.

'Not stall. Breslin's right, we don't need a rep for getting nothing done. We'll just take it nice and easy. Whatever's going on here, I don't want Rory back in till we know every single thing we can get about this case. If we go at him again, I want us going in with enough ammo to blow him away.'

Steve nods. 'And right now?'

I check my watch: just under an hour till the case meeting. 'Right now we take him through his story again, see if he's got anything he wants to tell us, get his coat and gloves, try and convince him to let us go through his flat. Then we send him home and do this case meeting. After that—'

'After that, we get some fucking *sleep*. I'm wrecked.'

Saying it pulls a huge yawn out of him. I bite one back, but too late: it's hit me that I'm shattered too. My vision is jumping; I can't tell how far away the walls are. 'But Breslin's not,' I say. 'If we go home, we're leaving him in charge to do whatever he wants.'

'And if we don't, we're tipping him off.'

Steve's right. For a dead kid or a dead cop, you work twenty-four hours straight if you need to, then grab a shower and a quick kip and head in for another twenty-four. If you do that for every case, you'll burn out inside three months. Your basic murder gets an eight-hour shift, maybe twelve or fourteen if something interesting happens. If me and Steve go twenty-four hours for this, we might as well run to Breslin and tell him we think there's something dodgy going on.

I say, 'So what do we do about him?'

'Load him up with busywork at the case meeting. Keep him out of trouble.'

'Yeah, right. He'd love that. Big man like him—'

Steve's grinning. 'This isn't about his ego, remember? He told us so. It's all about *the squad*. He won't mind tracking down every passenger on the 39A, not when it's for *the squad*.'

I'm grinning too. 'Search every bin between Stoneybatter and Ranelagh: Breslin, for the sake of *the squad*. Go to the post-mortem: Breslin, for the sake of *the squad*. Type up statements—'

'Pizza run: Breslin, for the sake of *the squad*—'

We're both on the edge of a full-on fit of the giggles. If I relax that much, I'm gonna fall asleep right here on my feet.

'We'll keep him on checking out Fallon,' I say. 'If he gets through the KAs, he can talk to Fallon's old girlfriends, see if he's got any history of giving out the slaps—'

'He won't have.' Steve runs his hand under the water-cooler tap and over his face, trying to wake himself up.

'Probably not. But if Breslin wants Fallon charged this bad, he won't have a problem digging for dirt on him, right? That should keep him too busy to make trouble for us, at least for the evening. And we'll send a floater with him. Might make him think twice before he disappears any statement he doesn't like.'

There must be something in my voice. Steve glances up sharply. 'Has more stuff been going missing on you? Since that witness on the Petrescu case, like?'

'Nah,' I say – I'm not about to sob on his shoulder about the mean boys who stole my lovely statement sheet. 'That doesn't mean it won't. We need to be careful here.'

Steve is still watching me, palming drops of water off his jaw, and I feel like it's half a blink too long before he answers. But he says, easily enough, 'A floater won't stop Breslin from feeding Crowley info, if he's the one doing it.'

'I know that. What's your plan? You gonna follow him into the jacks, make sure he doesn't text Crowley with one hand while he's got his dick in the other?'

'Nah, the floater's a good idea. We can tell Breslin he needs mentoring.'

That gets a snort out of me. 'He'll eat that up. It might not work – Breslin'll probably wrap the guy round his finger – but it's better than nothing.'

Steve says, 'We need to keep Breslin away from Aislinn's electronics.'

Her phone, her e-mails, her social media accounts; the places where, if there is a gangster boyfriend, there might be something to point us his way. 'At the case meeting we'll make sure everyone knows we've got those,' I say. 'Breslin's probably already had a look through her phone, when he went to the scene, but there's nothing good on there as far as I could tell.'

'Tell you what else we need to do,' Steve says. 'We need to have chats with Breslin, whenever we get the chance. Or let him chat to us, more like.'

'Ah, Jaysus. Shoot me now.'

'We do. Get him talking. He's not an idiot, but . . .'

'But he loves the sound of his own voice,' I say. 'Yeah. Let him knock himself out enlightening us; you never know what might slip out. Chats with McCann, too, if the chance comes up.' McCann and Breslin have been partnering for ten years. They're tight. If Breslin wants Rory Fallon done, for whatever reason, or if he just wants this case to blow up in my face, McCann will know. 'Not that he's much of a talker, but you never know.'

'It's the best we can do. We definitely can't talk to Organised Crime now, not upfront.' Steve is biting a cuticle, staring at Rory without seeing him. 'You said you've got a mate in there. Can you get on to him? See if he's heard anything?'

'Yeah, it's not that simple.' I wet my palm at the water cooler and run it around my neck. 'I'll see what I can do.'

'And we don't type anything up.'

'God, no. Or leave anything on our desks.' I think about my statements, locked in my desk drawer; no one's gonna bother screwing with those again, they like mixing it up to keep me on my toes, but all of a sudden the diddy little lock feels like a joke. 'Or in the desk drawers. Notes stay on us.'

Steve bites down on the corner of his lip. He says, 'Jesus.'

This is all a load of nothing, shadows that could be thrown by something huge or by something barely worth tracking down, but the adrenaline is banging through me and I can't help loving it. I almost flick water at Steve. 'The face on you. Cheer up, man. This could be the best bit of action we've ever seen.'

'This isn't my kind of action. Hiding stuff from our own squad—'

'Chillax on the jacks,' I say. 'It's probably all a load of shite. Like I said: just being careful.'

Movement in the corridor. I'm at the door in two long steps, but it's just Winters walking an unimpressed little prick in a tracksuit to one of the other interview rooms. All the same: 'We better move,' I say. 'Before Breslin comes back to check up on us.'

Steve nods and tosses his mangled cup into the bin. I take one more look at Rory, who by this point is jittering like his chair is electrified. Then we head in to take it nice and easy for a while.

The interview room stinks of sweat and crying. 'Detectives Conway and Moran entering the interview room,' I tell the video recorder.

'Hi,' Steve says, taking a seat and giving Rory a sympathetic grin. 'Detective Breslin had to head off. I'll be joining you instead. Detective Moran.'

Rory barely nods. I say, pulling up my chair, 'How're you doing?'

'I'm all right.' His nose is stuffed up. 'Sorry for . . .'

'Not a problem,' I say. 'Are you OK to talk now?'

Rory gives me a red-eyed, accusing stare. He says, 'You knew all along. That I've been seeing Aislinn. That I was going to her house last night. You knew.'

Bless his middle-class little heart. He's genuinely miffed that officers of the force would deceive him. I say, 'Yeah. We did. I know that was a shitty thing to do to you, but we're investigating a murder here, and sometimes the only way to get the info we need is by doing things that aren't ideal. If we'd told you what was up, you might have gone cagey on us, and we couldn't risk that. You might know something vital, even if you don't realise it.'

'I've told you everything I know.'

He's actually in a sulk with me. I sit back in my chair and glance at Steve, handing over.

'You think you have,' Steve says, 'but that was before you knew what's happened. What I've found is, a shock like that, it can shake people's memories loose. Could you do me a favour and have another think back over last night? Just in case?'

Rory looks him over suspiciously, but Nice Boy Next Door gives him an earnest hopeful gaze back and Rory decides my bad behaviour isn't Steve's fault. He's all primed to like Steve anyway, just for not being Breslin. 'I suppose. I'm pretty sure there wasn't—'

'Ah, brilliant,' Steve says. 'Even the smallest thing could help us out. Did you notice anyone you can describe, while you were in Stoneybatter? Hear anything odd? Anything at all stand out to you?'

'Not really. I'm not very observant to begin with, and last night I was concentrating on . . . on Aislinn. I wasn't really paying attention to anything else.'

'Oh, yeah. I've been there. When you're just starting a relationship, specially one that's taking off like yours was, nothing else even exists.'

Steve is smiling, and it pulls a twitch that's almost a smile out of Rory. 'That's it exactly. You know what the weather was like, yesterday: it was a rotten evening, I was freezing, a tree dumped rain down the back of my collar . . . But I felt like I was in a wonderful story. The smell of turf-smoke, and the rain falling through the light of the streetlamps . . .'

'See? That's what I'm talking about: you remember more than you thought. And you were in Stoneybatter for a full hour, right? Half-seven to half-eight. You must've seen someone.'

And there it is again: the sudden involuntary twist to Rory's neck, the jab at his glasses. Steve brings up that extra time, and all of a sudden Rory doesn't like this game. That blood-smell hits the back of my nose again. The lift of Steve's head tells me he smells it too.

Rory's memory comes back: anything to distract us. 'I did, actually. I passed three women on Prussia Street, when I was on my way to Tesco. They were dressed like they were going out, and two of them had hair like Aislinn's, long and blond and straight – that's why I noticed them. They were sharing an umbrella and laughing. And when I got off the bus there were a bunch of boys in hoodies kicking a football on Astrid Road, around the corner from Aislinn's house – they didn't stop when I got close, so I had to step onto the street and dodge around them. But I don't see how any of them could be . . .'

Steve nods away like this is crucial info. 'You never know. They might've seen something. It's all good stuff.' I scribble in my notebook, crucial-info-style. There's a decent chance all these people are imaginary. 'Anyone else? Anything else?'

Rory shakes his head. Steve waits, but nothing else pops out. 'OK,' he says. 'What about your conversations with Aislinn? Take a second and think back over those. Did she ever mention anyone who bothered her? Someone at work who was a bit creepy, maybe? An ex who wouldn't take no for an answer?'

Rory is shaking his head.

'OK. Was there anything that seemed to make her uncomfortable? She ever get a bit cagey when any particular subject came up?'

'Actually . . .' Rory has relaxed again, now that we've moved away from the hot spot. 'Yes. When it came to her parents, Aislinn was . . .

Something was odd. She told me they were both dead – she said her dad died in a car accident when she was little, and her mum had MS for a long time and finally died of it a few years back . . . ?'

He glances back and forth between us, hoping we'll give him a yes or a no. We don't.

'But she seemed very uncomfortable talking about it, and she changed the subject straightaway. It could have been just because we didn't know each other that well yet, but I wondered if maybe there was more to the story – like if one of them was still alive, but with some problem, like I said. I mean, obviously I wasn't about to ask, but . . . I wondered.'

This isn't what Steve's angling for. 'Right,' he says. 'Interesting; we'll definitely check it out. Anything else?'

Rory shakes his head. 'That's the only thing I can think of.'

'You're positive? I'm not joking: any little thing could make a difference. Anything.'

There's a moment's silence. Rory catches his breath to say something; then he lets it out again. He isn't looking at Steve any more.

Steve waits, watching him, easy and interested as a pal in a pub. Rory says, suddenly and unwillingly, 'I just wish I knew what else you're not telling me.'

'Course you do,' Steve says matter-of-factly. 'All I can say is, we don't keep things back just for the laugh. We're doing it to catch the person who killed Aislinn.'

Rory's eyes come up, with an effort, to meet Steve's. He asks, 'Am I a suspect?' And he braces himself for the answer.

Steve says, 'Right now, everyone who had any kind of connection with Aislinn is a potential suspect. I'm not going to insult your intelligence by trying to claim you're the exception.'

Rory must have known, but it still lights him up with fear. 'I never even *saw* her last night. And I cared about her, I thought we were going to – why would I—'

Whatever he was thinking about telling us, it's gone. 'Fair enough,' Steve says reasonably, 'but we have to figure everyone we talk to is going to say the same thing. And one person's going to be lying. We'd be only delighted to eliminate you – the faster we narrow it down, the better – but we can't do it just on your word. You can see that, right?'

'Then how do you do it?'

'Evidence. We always need fingerprints, and on this case we're also asking for coats and gloves – obviously I can't tell you why, but they should go a long way towards crossing you off our list. You're all right with that, yeah? We can hang on to those?' Steve nods at Rory's gear.

Rory's taken aback, but Steve hasn't left him much choice. 'I guess – I mean . . . yes, OK. I'll get them back, right?'

'Course,' Steve says, reaching across the table to hook the gloves across with his pen. 'It might take a few days, just. OK if we have a look in your apartment for any others that we might need to eliminate?'

'I'm not . . .' Rory blinks fast. The strain and the airless room are getting to him; he's starting to have a hard time keeping up. 'Can't you just take these? They're the ones I was wearing last night, if that's—'

'See, though,' Steve explains, 'we're not just trying to take this particular coat off our list. We're trying to take *you* off our list. That means we need anything you could've worn, not just what you did wear. See what I mean?'

Rory pushes up his glasses to press his fingers into the corners of his eyes. 'Yes. OK. Whatever you need. I'd rather be there, though – when you're in my apartment. I don't like the thought of people . . . Is that all right?'

'Not a problem,' Steve says easily. 'The lads who bring you home can just take a quick look around while they're at it. We'll get on that as fast as we can, yeah? Get your prints done and get you out of here, back to your day.'

Rory's eyes close, against his fingertips. 'Yes,' he says. 'I'd like that very much.'

I toss Rory's gloves and his coat into evidence bags and head off to send them to Sophie, before he can change his mind. Then I type up his statement, and ignore the squad-room turds ignoring me, while Steve prints off a map so Rory can draw us his route home – as near as he can remember, or wants to – and takes him through his story one more time. I give the two of them as much alone time as we can afford, in case Rory's still holding a grudge against me, but when I come back into the interview room Steve throws me a minuscule shake of his head: nothing interesting has happened.

'Here,' Rory says, pushing the map across the table. He's looking rough. His lips are parched and the mousy hair is plastered flat to his head, like he's been running in heat. 'Is that OK?'

There's a careful line winding from Stoneybatter to Ranelagh, and a tiny tidy X labelled 'FLOWERS' on the quays. 'That's great,' Steve says. 'Thanks a million.'

'Have a read of that,' I say, holding out the statement and a pen. 'If it's all correct, initial every page and then sign at the end.'

Rory doesn't move to take the statement. 'Do you think . . .' He catches a long breath. 'If I hadn't left when I did. If I'd kept banging on the door, or if I'd called the police, or if I'd broken in. Would I have been able to save her?'

I almost say yes. If he's not our guy, he's such a godawful damp weenie, the kind who needs regular slaps across the back of the head just to keep him from vanishing up his own hole, plus he just wasted half our day by being in the wrong place looking guilty as hell. All I have to do is say yes, and he'll spend the rest of his life whipping himself with a more and more elaborate fantasy where he storms into that cottage in the nick of time and saves Aislinn from a herd of rampaging bikers and they live happily ever after and have 2.4 damp weenie kids. It's practically irresistible.

But if he is our guy, he's no idiot, and he'll find a way to use any info I hand him. 'No way to know,' I say. 'Here,' and I dump the statement under his nose.

He reads it, or at least he spends a while staring at each page. At the end, he signs like he barely remembers how.

It's headed for four o'clock. We get hold of the floaters who've been pulling CCTV footage – Kellegher and Reilly – and tell them what we want done with Rory and his gaff. Steve finds an old hoodie in his locker so Rory won't freeze his delicate self on the way home. Then we tell him how great he is and hand him over.

'You owe me a tenner,' Steve says, as we watch Kellegher and Reilly walk him down the corridor. From the back, sandwiched between their farmer shoulders and their cop walks, Rory looks like a nerd being marched behind the school to get a few slaps.

I check that I've got all the statement pages. 'Like fuck I do. Did you not see him bawling his eyes out there? Pay up.'

'Doesn't count. It has to be because he's petrified of us, not because he just found out his girlfriend *died*.'

'Since when?' Steve is right, but I feel like yanking his chain. 'Nah nah nah. You can't make up the rules to suit—'

'Since always. When did I ever try to get away with—'

'When did I ever try to stiff you just because I didn't like the timing of—'

Rory and the floaters are gone, in a jumble of footsteps echoing down the marble stairwell. I slam the interview-room door and we head for the squad room to get our stuff together. The corridor still feels like it's twitching with covered pits and pointed sticks, but that doesn't feel like such a bad thing, not any more.

5

I used to love the first case meeting, love everything about it. The pulse of the incident room, everyone taut as greyhounds at the traps; in that room every answer comes in closer on top of the question, every glance snaps round faster. The whipcrack of the jobs being assigned, *Murphy collect the CCTV footage, Vincent check gold Toyota Camrys, O'Leary talk to the girlfriend*, bam bam bam. The moment when I'd shut my notebook and say *Go*, and we'd all be out of our seats and halfway to the door before my mouth closed on the word. I used to come out of that meeting feeling like the bastard we were after didn't have a chance in hell. By this time, even the thought of it – floaters eyeing me up and down, wondering which of the rumours are true; me eyeing them back, wondering which of them is going to glom onto any slip-up, blow it up huge and barter it for a laugh and a pat on the back – turns me hangover-queasy and hangover-mean.

Incident Room C, but. I haven't been in there since I was a floater chasing down pointless non-leads for the big boys; I'd forgotten. The white light exploding down from the high ceiling, skating and flashing on the whiteboard and the tall windows. The sleek computers lined up straining for action, the throb of them pumping at the air. The desks polished till they look like you could slice your thumb open on the edges. One step through the doorway, and that room blows the fatigue off me like dust and recharges me till I spark static. Walk in there and you could solve Jack the Ripper. And this time I'm no floater, there to jump when some big man snaps his fingers; this time I'm the big woman and every bit of this is all mine. Just for one second, that room blindsides me into loving the job, a hard green painful love like it's growing from scratch all over again.

Steve's lifted face, lips parted in a half-smile like a kid at the panto, says he feels the same way. That's what smacks sense back into me. Steve falls arse over tip for anything beautiful, without bothering to think about how it got that way or why, or what's underneath. I don't.

I slap my stack of paper onto the boss desk, the double-length one at the head of the room. 'Gentlemen,' I say, loud. 'Let's get started. Who owns this?' I whip a coffee mug off the desk and hold it up.

Breslin is leaning against the whiteboard, holding court for Deasy and Stanton, the floaters who brought Rory in, and the pair we put on the door-to-door – a slight, fidgety dark guy called Meehan, who I've worked with before and like, and a prissy-faced newbie called Gaffney, who I've seen around and who's holding himself so straight that his suit looks like a prefect's uniform. Breslin, or more likely someone he was bossing around, has made a start on the whiteboard – shots of Aislinn, the crime scene, Rory, a map of Stoneybatter – and set out a heavy hardback notebook for the book of jobs, where we keep a list of what needs doing and who's supposed to be doing it. We even have an electric kettle.

'That's mine,' Gaffney says, bobbing forward to grab the mug and retreating fast, scarlet. 'Sorry about that.'

'Meehan.' I toss him the notebook. 'Book of jobs, yeah?' He catches it and nods. Steve dumps his stuff beside mine and starts handing out photocopies: the initial call sheet, the uniforms' report, Rory's statement. I head for the whiteboard and sketch out a fast timeline of last night. The floaters pick desks and settle fast: chitchat's over.

'The vic,' I say, tapping the photo of Aislinn with my marker. 'Aislinn Murray, twenty-six, lived alone in Stoneybatter, worked as a receptionist at a firm selling bathroom supplies to businesses. No criminal record, no calls to us. Assaulted yesterday evening in her home: Cooper's preliminary exam says she took a punch to the face and hit her head on the fireplace surround. Texts on her phone narrow down the time to between 7.13 and 8.09.' I move to Rory's photo. 'This guy here, Rory Fallon, he's been seeing her for a couple of months. He was due at her house for dinner at eight o'clock.'

'Stupid bastard,' says Deasy, grinning. 'A looker like her, he should've at least waited to kill her till after he'd got his hole.'

Snickers. Breslin clears his throat, with an indulgent smirk and a tilt of his head towards me. The snickers fade.

I say, 'You can make it up to him, Deasy, seeing as it matters so much to you. Next time we bring him in, you go ahead and give him a blowjob in the jacks.'

Deasy pinches at his tache and makes a sour face. The snickers rise up again, prickly and equivocal.

I say, 'Me and Moran and Breslin, we've just had a chat with Fallon. His story is that he was at Aislinn's door at eight, but she didn't answer, so he figured he'd been dumped and flounced off home to cry on his pillow.'

'Amazingly enough,' Breslin drawls, twirling his pen, 'we don't believe him.'

'Our working theory,' I say, 'is that Fallon arrived at the vic's place around half-seven, things went bad somehow, and he punched her. We're guessing he thought she was just knocked out; he legged it home and hoped she wouldn't call the cops on him, or wouldn't remember what happened.'

That has Breslin nodding along approvingly, giving the newbies' little theory his blessing. 'More like manslaughter than murder,' he says, 'but that's not our problem.'

'By early this morning,' I say, 'either Fallon's conscience got to him, or else he'd talked to a mate who wanted to do the right thing. An anonymous male caller reported to Stoneybatter station that there was a woman with head injuries at 26 Viking Gardens, and requested an ambulance.'

'My money's on Fallon doing it himself,' Breslin says. 'He's exactly the type who'd bottle it after a few hours, start trying to put things right just when it's too late.'

'The phone number came up private,' Steve says. 'Who wants to get on it?'

All their hands shoot up. 'Easy there, boys,' Breslin says, grinning. 'There's plenty to go round.'

'Gaffney, you take the phone number,' I say – I need to give the kid a pat, settle him after the mug thing. Meehan writes that down. 'Stanton, Deasy: you were working on a list of Fallon's KAs. How's that going?'

'Nothing surprising,' Stanton says. 'Mother, father, two older brothers, no sisters; handful of mates from school and college, a few ex-flatmates, long list of work colleagues and friends – mostly history teachers, librarians, that kind of thing. I'll e-mail it on to you.'

'Do that. Detective Breslin, you've already started talking to the KAs, am I right?'

'Both Fallon's brothers sounded appropriately shocked,' Breslin says. 'According to them, they knew about Rory's big date, but that's as far as they'd got; they were waiting to hear all the dirty details. They claim they didn't ring Stoneybatter station this morning, or ever, but then they would, wouldn't they? I've got them both coming in for separate chats after this.'

Breslin's planning on working a long shift, for a bog-standard case. 'If they don't pan out, keep working your way down the list,' I say. 'Start with anyone who lives near Rory's route home, where he could've got a surprise visit last night. And while you're at it, get the brothers and the best mates on tape. We need to run their voices and Fallon's past the guy at Stoneybatter who took the call, see if he recognises any of them. Can you follow that up?'

For a second I think Breslin's gonna tell me to stick my scut work, but he says, 'Why not,' although there's a twist to his mouth. 'Great,' I say. 'We need someone to go through CCTV – we'll put Kellegher and Reilly down for that; they're pulling all the local footage they can get, they might as well watch it.'

Meehan nods, writing.

'And someone needs to pull footage from the northbound 39A bus route yesterday evening: find the buses that stopped on Morehampton Road around seven, see if you can pick out Rory Fallon getting on, confirm what time he boarded and what time he got off in Stoneybatter.' The gym rat has a finger up. That whipcrack rhythm, the one I used to love: even though I know better, it still hits me like a triple espresso. 'Stanton's on that. And we need someone to head out to Stoneybatter and time the route Rory says he took from the bus stop: down Astrid Road to the top of Viking Gardens, then up to Tesco on Prussia Street, buy a bunch of flowers and head back down to Viking Gardens. Meehan, you're around the same build and age as Fallon; can you do that? Time it twice: once at your normal pace, once as fast as you can go.'

Meehan nods. Steve says, glancing back and forth between him and Gaffney, 'Did Rory's flowers show up in the bins on the quays?'

'I looked,' Meehan says. 'Gaffney kept going with the door-to-door. The bins hadn't been emptied since last night, by the state of them, but no irises anywhere. Some lad probably robbed them to give to his bird.'

'Or,' Breslin says, 'they were never in the bins at all: Rory Boy tossed them in the river, because he didn't want us pulling Aislinn's blood or hair or carpet fibres off them. Where are we on her KAs?'

'She didn't have any immediate family, or much of a social life,' I say, 'but her friend Lucy gave us a few names and numbers to start us off. Someone needs to go round to Aislinn's workplace, get her boss to come in and ID the body, and have the chats with all her colleagues. I want to know if she talked about Rory, and what she said.'

Steve says, 'And we need to know if any of the colleagues had a thing for her. Just on the off-chance that Rory's telling the truth' – Breslin snorts – 'someone might not have been happy that Aislinn had got herself a fella. And her colleagues were the only people she spent any amount of time with.' Nice touch. If anyone spots us doing something that doesn't point to Rory, we've got a potential stalker colleague to take the heat. It might even turn out to be true.

'Why don't you two cover the office romance,' Breslin says. 'Feminine intuition, and all that jazz.'

'Mine's in the shop,' I say. 'Transmission went. We'll just have to go with actual detective work. Deasy, Stanton, you head over there first thing tomorrow.'

'The other place Aislinn spent time was at evening classes,' Steve says. 'She could have picked up a stalker there. We need someone to work out what classes she took, make lists of all the other students or whatever they call them.'

'Gaffney, you take that,' I say. 'Me and Moran will handle Aislinn's phone records, e-mails, social media, all that—'

'I can make a start on that tonight,' Breslin says. 'I don't mind staying a few hours late, if that'll help put this case to bed, but I can't exactly show up at Rory's KAs' houses at nine in the evening looking for chats. I might as well get cracking on the vic's social life.'

My look clicks against Steve's for a split second, before his head goes down over his notebook. Breslin could just be trying to buff up his stellar rep – everyone always wants the vic's electronics, because more often than not, there's something good in there – or he could be looking to make me into the loser who couldn't find her own evidence. Or he could need to get rid of anything in there that points to a gangster pal.

Meehan has stopped writing and is looking back and forth between us, uncertain. 'Me and Moran have already started on it,' I say. 'We've been in since last night and we need to catch a few hours' kip, but we'll get back onto Aislinn's electronics first thing tomorrow morning. You've started on Rory Fallon, Detective Breslin; you might as well stick with him. We need someone to make a list of his exes and see what they've got to say about him, specially about what winds him up and what he's like when he doesn't get his way. If you can stay late tonight, why don't you get the ball rolling on that.'

Breslin has on a face like he's found a hair in his soup and knows the waiter is too useless to fix it. 'Why don't I do that.'

'Great,' I say. After a moment, Meehan's pen starts moving again. 'Detective Gaffney: first murder case, am I right?'

'It is, yeah.' He's from somewhere involving sheep.

'OK,' I say, sending the gaffer a mental thank-you for not bothering to get us floaters with actual experience. 'You stick close to Detective Breslin for now; he'll show you the ropes, help you get the hang of this.' Breslin nods pleasantly at Gaffney, no objections, but that means nothing. 'Can you stay late tonight, yeah?'

Gaffney sits up even straighter. 'I can, of course.'

'Anyone who can't?' No one moves. 'Good. We need someone to pull Aislinn's financials – Gaffney, start on that; you'll need to go through them anyway, for her evening-class payments.'

Breslin sighs, just loud enough to make it clear that I'm wasting valuable time and resources. Steve says, to everyone, 'We don't have a motive yet. The romance gone bad is the obvious one, but we can't rule out a financial angle. Rory mentioned that his bookshop's been having a hard time; and Aislinn's mate Lucy Riordan said she had a bit of cash stashed away. Rory could have asked her to put a few grand into the bookshop and got nasty when she turned him down, something like that.'

Breslin shrugs. He's started doodling on the corner of his notebook.

'We'll need Rory's financials, too,' I say. 'Gaffney, pull those while you're at it. Someone needs to get onto the phone company and start them tracking where Fallon's phone went last night: Deasy, got a decent contact at Vodafone? Someone to confirm Lucy Riordan's alibi with the rest of the staff at the Torch Theatre: Stanton, you handle that. Someone to talk to the staff at the Market Bar and Pestle, see if they can tell us anything about Aislinn and Rory's dates: Meehan, yeah? Someone to assign one of the uniforms from the scene to go to the autopsy: Deasy, you do that. It'll be early tomorrow morning; make sure he's not late, or Cooper will throw a shit fit.' Snorts from everyone who's met Cooper. 'Me and Moran will follow up with the techs, make sure we're kept updated. There'll be more, but those should get us started. Any questions?'

Head-shakes. They're fidgeting at the starting line.

'OK,' I say. 'Let's go.' Meehan claps the book of jobs shut. They swing to their desks, their phones, to Rory's statement, diving to see who can hit the ground running fastest. Incident Room C leaps with the energy ricocheting off the shining rows of desks, splintering on the windows.

And underneath all that, hidden and working away, the small ferocious buzzing of the thing at the back of my mind and Steve's, nudging for us to let it loose. Breslin's slick fair head is bent over his notebook, but when he feels me looking he glances up and gives me a great big smile.

*   *   *

Steve types up our report for the gaffer while I go through the stuff the floaters brought back. They're all competent enough, although Deasy can't spell and Gaffney feels the need to share every detail of everything, relevant or not ('Witness advised that she was taking her daughter Ava aged eight to visit her grandfather in St James's Hospital after severe stroke and saw Murray getting out of car . . .'). Nothing particularly interesting in the door-to-door: Aislinn was friendly with her neighbours – no bad blood over noise or parking spaces, nothing like that – but not close to any of them; a few of them saw a woman matching Lucy's description going into or out of her house now and then; none of them ever saw any other visitors. Aislinn never mentioned a boyfriend. They saw her going out semi-regularly in the evenings, all dolled up, but they weren't on gossip-swapping terms and they have no idea where she was heading or what she did there. The old couple in Number 24 are half deaf and heard nothing last night; the young couple in Number 28 heard Aislinn blasting her Beyoncé, but they say she turned the music either down or off a little before eight – they could pinpoint it because eight is the baby's bedtime, so they appreciated the volume control. After that, not a sound.

The old fella in Number 3 backs Rory's story, or bits of it: he was heading out to walk his dog (a white male terrier named Harold, according to Gaffney) just before eight o'clock last night, and he saw a guy matching Rory's description turning in to Viking Gardens. When he got back fifteen minutes later, the guy was still there, down at the bottom of the road, messing about with his phone. None of the other neighbours were outside in those fifteen minutes – Viking Gardens is mostly old people and a few young families, no one head-ing out on the Saturday-night batter – which means Rory could have been let into the house, killed Aislinn, and been back outside texting up a cover story by ten past eight; but I don't buy it. The part that turned him twitchy was earlier, before the Tesco side-trip. None of the neighbours were out in the road then, to see him or not.

Steve is still typing. Breslin's headed off for his chats with Rory's brothers, taking Gaffney with him and dispensing wisdom all the way; Meehan has buttoned his overcoat to the neck and gone off to time himself wandering around Stoneybatter, Deasy's having a laugh with his contact at the phone company, Stanton's laying down the law to someone from the buses. Their voices wander around the high corners of the room, turning blurry at the edges from too much space. The windows are dark.

My phone rings. 'Conway,' I say.

O'Kelly says, 'You and Moran, my office. I want an update.'

'We'll be right in,' I say, and hear him hang up. I look at Steve, who's slumped in his chair, giving his report a last once-over. 'The gaffer wants to see us.'

Steve's head comes up and he blinks at me. Each of those takes a few seconds; he's two-thirds asleep. For once he looks his age. 'Why?'

'He wants an update.'

'Oh, Jaysus.' The gaffer wants in-person updates when you're working a big one, which this isn't, or when you're taking too long to get a solve, which even if you're in his bad books should be longer than one day. This can't be good.

The rumours say I got this gig because O'Kelly needed to tick the token boxes and I tick two for the price of one – and those are the nice rumours. All of them are bullshit. When the gaffer brought me on board, he was down a D – one of his top guys had just put in his papers early – and I was Missing Persons' shining star, waving a sheaf of fancy high-profile solves in each hand. I was fresh off a headline-buster where I'd whipped out every kind of detective work in the book, from tracing phone pings and wi-fi logons to coaxing info out of family members and bullying it out of friends, in order to track down a newly dumped dad who had gone on the run with his two little boys, and then I'd spent four hours talking him into coming out of his car with the kids instead of driving the lot of them off a pier. I was hot stuff, back then. Me and the gaffer both had every reason to think this was gonna be great.

O'Kelly knows what's been going down, I know he knows, but he's never said a word; just watched and waited. No gaffer wants this on his squad, wants the sniping in corners and the grey poison smog hanging over the squad room. Any gaffer in the world would be wondering, by now, how he could get rid of me.

Steve hits Print on the report; the printer gets to work with a smug purr, nothing like the half-dead wheeze off the squad-room yoke. We find our combs, sort our hair, brush down our jackets. Steve has something blue smudged on his shirt front, but I don't have the heart to tell him, in case the effort of trying to clean it off kills him. I assume I've got whiteboard marker on my face, or something, and he's doing the same for me.

One of the reasons I don't trust O'Kelly is because of his office. It's full of naff crap – a framed crayon drawing that says WORLD'S BEST GRANDDAD, pissant local golf trophies, a shiny executive toy in case he gets the urge to make clicky noises with swingy balls – and stacks of dusty files that never move. The whole room says he's some outdated time-server who spends the day practising his golf swing and polishing his nameplate and working out fussy ways to tell if someone's touched his stash bottle of single malt. If O'Kelly was that, he wouldn't have been running Murder for coming up on twenty years. The office has to be window dressing, to put people off their guard. And the only people who see it are the squad.

O'Kelly is leaning back in his fancy ergonomic chair, with his arms draped on its arms, like some banana-republic dictator granting an audience. 'Conway. Moran,' he says. 'Tell me about Aislinn Murray.'

Steve holds out the report the way you would wave raw meat at a mean dog. O'Kelly jerks his chin at his desk. 'Leave that there. I'll read it later. Now I want to hear it from you.'

He hasn't told us to sit – which has to be a good sign: this isn't going to take all night – so we stay standing. 'We're still waiting on the post-mortem,' I say, 'but Cooper's preliminary says someone punched her in the face and she hit the back of her head on the fireplace. She was expecting a guy called Rory Fallon over for dinner. He admits he was on the spot at the relevant time, but he says she didn't answer her door and he hadn't a clue she was dead till we told him this afternoon.'

'Huh,' O'Kelly says. The hard sideways light from his desk lamp throws heavy shadows across his face, turning him one-eyed and unreadable. 'Do you believe him?'

I shrug. 'Half and half. Our main theory is she did answer her door, they had some kind of argument and Fallon threw the punch. He could be telling the truth about not knowing she was dead, though.'

'Got any hard evidence?'

Less than twelve hours in, and I'm taking shit for not having a DNA match. I dig my hands into my jacket pockets so I won't slap O'Kelly's stupid spider plant off his desk.

Steve says, before I can answer, 'The Bureau have the coat and gloves Fallon says he was wearing last night, and we're searching his route home in case he ditched anything. He gave consent for us to search his flat and take any other clothes that look interesting, so a couple of the lads are on that. According to the techs, if he's our guy we've got a good chance at blood or epithelials, or a fibre match to what they found on the body.'

'I've asked a mate in the Bureau to put a rush on his stuff,' I say, keeping my voice level. 'We should have something preliminary tomorrow. We'll let you know.'

O'Kelly matches up his fingertips and watches us. He says, 'Breslin thinks ye need to quit wasting everyone's time and arrest the little scumbag.'

I say, 'It's not Breslin's case.'

'Meaning what? You've got doubts? Or you just want to show everyone that Breslin's not the boss of you?'

'If anyone's stupid enough to think Breslin's the boss of us, I'm not gonna waste my time proving they're wrong.'

'So it's doubts.'

In the dark outside the window, the wind is picking up. It sounds like wide country wind, barrelling down long straight miles with nothing to stand in its way, like the squad is standing high in the middle of empty nowhere. I say, 'We'll make the arrest when we're ready.'

O'Kelly says, 'Doubts about whether you've got enough to make it stick? Or about whether the boyfriend's guilty at all?'

He's looking at me, not at Steve. I say, 'Doubts about whether we're ready to arrest him.'

'That doesn't answer my question.'

There's a silence. O'Kelly's one eye, metallic in the lamplight, doesn't blink.

I say, 'I think he's probably our guy. There's no way I'm gonna arrest him based on nothing but my gut feeling. If that's a problem, take the case off us and give it to Breslin. He's welcome to it.'

O'Kelly eyeballs me for another minute; I stare back. Then he says, 'Keep me updated. I want a full report on my desk every evening. Anything big shows up, you don't save it for the report; you let me know straightaway. Is that clear?'

'Clear,' I say. Steve nods.

'Good,' O'Kelly says. He spins his chair away from the desk, to one of the stacks of files, and starts flipping paper. Dust swirls up into the light of his desk lamp. 'Go get some kip. Ye look even worse than this morning.'

Steve and I wait till we're back in the incident room, with the door shut, before we look at each other. He says, 'What was that all about?'

I flick my coat off the back of my chair and swing it on. The floaters upped their rhythm when we came in; the room is all clicking keys and rustling paper. 'That was the gaffer getting all up in our grille. What bit did you miss?'

'Yeah, but why? He's never given a damn about any of our cases before, unless we weren't doing the business and he wanted to give us a bollocking.'

I throw my scarf around my neck and tuck the ends in tight: the dark at the window has a condensed look that says it's cold out there. O'Kelly's taken the shine off our bright new idea; gangsters and bent cops feel like a gymnast-level stretch, compared to just more people trying to screw me over. 'Right. And even after the bollockings, I'm still here. Maybe the gaffer figures he needs to up his game.'

'Or,' Steve says, quieter. He hasn't started packing up yet; he's standing by his desk, one finger tapping an absent tattoo on the edge. 'If he's been wondering the same stuff we've been wondering, maybe for a while now, but he doesn't want to say anything till he's sure . . .'

I say, 'I'm going home.'

*   *   *

From the outside, my gaff looks a lot like Aislinn Murray's: a one-storey Victorian terraced cottage, thick-walled and low-ceilinged. It fits me just about right; when I let someone stay over – which isn't often – I'm twitchy by morning, starting to feel the two of us barging up against the walls. The 1901 census says back then a couple were raising eight kids in it.

Get inside and my place has fuck-all in common with Aislinn's. I have the original floorboards – sanded them and polished them myself, when I first bought the gaff – and the original fireplace, none of this gas fire and laminate shite; the walls are scraped back to bare brick – I did that myself, too – and whitewashed. The mortgage and my car payments eat enough of my paycheque that my furniture comes from Oxfam and the low end of Ikea, but at least nothing is gingham.

I throw my satchel on the sofa, turn off the alarm and switch on the coffee machine. I've got a text from my mate Lisa: *We're in pub get down here!* I text her back *Pulled a double shift, gonna crash.* This is true enough – I've been up for more than twenty-four hours, and my eyes aren't focusing right – but I could still have done with a pint and a laugh with a bunch of people who don't think I'm poison. Except that's the reason I'm staying in. You spend long enough being treated like you're wearing a SHIT ON ME sign, you start to worry that the sign's developing a reality of its own and now anyone you talk to can see it. In my mates' heads I'm Antoinette the top cop, smart kickass successful Antoinette, nobody fucks with Antoinette. I want to keep it that way. I've turned down a lot of pints, the last few months.

Plus, odds are the gang in the pub includes my mate with the security firm. I don't want him offering me the job again. I'm not gonna take it – not tonight, anyway, not with that dare still flashing at me – but I'm not ready for him to take it off the table.

I should throw some dinner into me and crash out, but I hate wasting time on sleep even worse than I hate wasting it on food. I stick some pasta ready-meal thing in the microwave; while it heats up, I ring my ma, which I do every night, I'm not sure why. My ma isn't the type to bitch about her back problems or update me on which of her friends' kids are up the pole and what she found while she was emptying some middle manager's bin, which doesn't leave her a lot to talk about. Me, when I'm in a good mood, I tell her the basic outline of my day. When I'm not, I give her the details: what the wounds looked like, what the parents said while they sobbed. Sometimes I catch myself at the scene filing away the bad stuff, thinking this is gonna be the one that finally gets to her, gets even just a sharp breath or a snap at me to leave it. So far nothing ever has.

'Howya,' my ma says. Click of a lighter. She has a smoke while we talk; when she puts it out, we hang up.

I hit the button for an espresso. 'Howya.'

'Any news?'

'Me and Moran pulled a street fight. Couple of drunk fellas jumped another one, danced on his head. His eyeball was out on the footpath.'

'Huh,' my ma says, and inhales. 'Anything else strange?'

I don't feel like talking about Aislinn. Too much shite swirling around it, too much stuff I don't have a handle on; I don't tell my ma about anything I haven't got well sussed. 'Nah. Lisa texted me to go for a pint with the lads, but I'm shattered. Gonna crash.'

My ma lets that lie for a beat, just long enough to let me know I'm not getting away with it, before she says, 'Marie Lane said you're in the newspaper.'

Of course she bleeding did. 'Did she, yeah?'

'Not about any street fight. About some young one that got killed in her own house. The paper made you out to be a right gobshite.'

I swap out the coffee pod and hit the espresso button again: I'm gonna need a double. 'It's just a bog-standard murder. It made the paper because your woman was a blonde who wore a shit-ton of makeup. The journalist doesn't like me. End of story.'

A lot of people's mas would get a taste of the weakness, burrow in and suck out every last drop. Not mine. My ma just wanted to make it clear who's the boss of this conversation, and who needs to up her game if she wants to bullshit a pro. Now that she's made her point, she drops it. 'Lenny asked me again can he move in.'

Lenny and my ma have been together nine years, off and on. He's all right. 'And?'

She lets out a hoarse laugh and a blow of smoke together. 'And I told him he must be joking. If I wanted his smelly jocks in my room, they'd be there by now. He's talking bollix anyway; he no more wants to eat my cooking, rather get his dinners down the chipper . . .'

She makes me laugh about Lenny till she's finished her smoke and we hang up. The microwave beeps. I take the pasta thing and my coffee to the sofa and open my laptop.

I hit the dating sites. Over my own dead body would I do this at work – one glance over my shoulder, or one trawl through my computer when I'm out of the squad room, and I can already hear the whoops: *Jaysus, lads, Conway's doing the internet dating! – Yeah, frigid-bitches.com – There's a market for everything these days – For her? You serious? – Hey, we all know she gives a good gobble or she wouldn't be here, she can put that on her profile* . . . But if Mr Loverman exists, Aislinn met him somehow. Checking out her work colleagues and her evening classes won't cover the crim angle, and going by her phone and by Lucy, she didn't have much of a social life. Unless she found herself a gangster who was learning to crochet, the internet is my best bet.

I set up accounts using a throwaway e-mail address, Aislinn's description and a smirking blonde from Google Images, just in case our man has a type and goes looking for a replacement girlfriend, and I poke around for a while. The sites mostly use handles, not names – j-wow79, footballguy12345 – and Aislinn's description matches half the girls on there. I filter for age and type and skim the sea of duckfaced blond selfies till my eyes bubble, but there's no sign of her. *I believe in been positive in life whats for us wont pass us by lol . . . I like romance, spontaneity, respect, honesty, genuineness, good conversation . . . Looking to chat n just go with the flow message me you never know what might happen!!!*

The pasta thing has gone cold and slimy. I shove down the last mouthful anyway. Outside the window my street is dark, the street-lamps fighting the night and losing. The wind is punching around a paper bag from the chipper, slamming it up against a wall, holding it there for a second before tossing it down the road again. The old one from Number 12 hurries past, pushing her tartan shopping trolley, headscarf bent low.

I switch to the guys' photos and scan for a face that's familiar from work or from news stories: nothing, not that a high-profile gangster is gonna upload his pic on some dating site. *First time on a site like this not really sure what to say, looking for someone easy going no drama good sense of humour ... I'm a bit mad will say anything just a wild n crazy guy so if u think u can handle me give me a text!!*

These people are pissing me off. The neediness of it, all of them jumping up and down and waving their arms and doing their cutest little booty-shakes for the internet: *Me, look at me, like me, please oh please want me!!!* The because-I'm-worth-it shower (*Looking for someone tall, slim, very fit, no smokers, no drugs, no kids, no pets, must have full-time job and own car, must like fusion cuisine, speak at least three languages, enjoy bikram yoga and acid jazz ...*) are just as bad: ordering their relationships from the online menu because of course you have to have one, same as you have to have a state-of-the-art sound system and a pimped-out new car, and it's important to make sure you get exactly what you want. The only ones I can respect are the ones there on business: Ukrainian superbabes looking for older men down the country, with a view to marriage. All the rest could do with a good kick up the hole and a double shot of self-respect.

No one *needs* a relationship. What you need is the basic cop-on to figure that out, in the face of all the media bullshit screaming that you're nothing on your own and you're a dangerous freak if you disagree. The truth is, if you don't exist without someone else, you don't exist at all. And that doesn't just go for romance. I love my ma, I love my friends, I love the bones of them. If any of them wanted me to donate a kidney or crack a few heads, I'd do it, no questions asked. And if they all waved goodbye and walked out of my life tomorrow, I'd still be the same person I am today.

I live inside my own skin. Anything that happens outside it doesn't change who I am. This isn't something I'm proud of; as far as I'm concerned, it's a bare minimum baseline requirement for calling yourself an adult human being, somewhere around the level of knowing how to do your own washing or change a toilet roll. All those idiots on the websites, begging for other people to pull their sagging puppet-strings, turn them real: they make me want to spit.

I've got two private messages already. *Hi what's the crack?? So check out my profile tell me if u wanna chat.* The kid is twenty-three and works in IT, which makes him an unlikely candidate for Aislinn's top-secret squeeze. *Hello beautiful woman, I'd love to know what's under that stunning exterior. Me: spiritually evolved, very creative, world traveller, people tell me I should really write a novel about my life. Intrigued? Let's share more.* I recognise the profile shot: back when I was in uniform, I arrested the guy for wanking on a bus. Small city. I make a note to check out what he's been at lately, when I get a spare moment, but it doesn't feel urgent: there's no reason why Lucy would have gone squirrelly about this little creep.

I've hit the stage where the screen is warping and sliding in front of my eyes. I throw back the last of the cold coffee. Then I log into a very old e-mail account and hit Compose.

Hiya hun, how's tricks? Too long no see — love to catch up whenever your free. Let me know. Seeya soon – Rach xx

The 'From' address says rachelvodkancoke. I read it again. Don't hit Send.

The light in the room shifts: the motion-sensor lamps out the back have clicked on. I get up, kill the inside lights and move to the side of the kitchen window.

Nothing: just my patio. The white light and the tossing shadows turn it sinister: bare paving stones, high walls, the spreading tracing where an ivy plant used to be and the dark looming up all around. For a second I think I see something move over the back wall, the top of a head bobbing out in the laneway. When I blink, it's gone.

My heart is going hard. I think of Aislinn: young single woman, cottage in Stoneybatter, rear access via a laneway. Of the intruder who did a legger over her patio wall when he got spotted. I think of that spunkbubble Crowley splashing my photo across his front page, just in case anyone felt like waiting outside Dublin Castle and following me home.

I switch off the patio lights and check my gun. Then I slam my back door open, lunge across the patio, get a toehold on the wall and throw myself up onto the top.

I'm all ready to come face to face with anything from a junkie to Freddy Kruger. Instead I get the narrow laneway, dim in the faint yellow light from the streetlamp out on the road, and empty. Shadows and crisp packets banked along the edges, some kid's fourth-rate tag scrawled in blue on the wall. I listen: what could be fast footsteps, somewhere out on the road, or could be just the wind bouncing rubbish.

The kick of anger is half letdown – I was starving for that fight – and half at myself for being a moron. Even if this case magically turns out to be some serial killer's warm-up, tonight he's at home having some hard-earned R&R, not out looking for high-grade action. The bobbing head in the laneway was either fatigue warping my vision or some drunk having a piss; my motion sensor got tripped by the wind messing with rubbish, or the local half-wild cat on the scrounge.

I go back to my laptop. I sit there with my finger on the button for a long time, listening to the wind move outside my house and keeping one eye on the kitchen for the patio lights, before I hit Send.

6

First thing Monday morning, I get to track down my witness from the scumbagfest, haul him out of bed and coax him into coming in to the squad to give his statement all over again, this time with narky jabs about how he pays my wages – via the dole, somehow – and how I should have more respect than to go wasting his time like this. We both know that if I tell him to shut his face, he'll develop a bad case of amnesia about Saturday night. Even this little fucker can smell weakness off me. A couple of slaps would sort out his attitude, but I make myself save them for someone who matters.

Only half my mind is on him anyway. The day started off strange. It was still dark when I was leaving my gaff, thick cold fog filling the road, rolling it back to its secretive Victorian self: cars faded to smudges, lit windows and streetlamps hanging in the middle of nothing. And a guy at the top of the road, just standing there, on a morning when no sane person would be just standing. He was too far away for me to catch much; just a tall guy, facing my way, with a dark overcoat and a dark trilby and a set to his shoulders that said he wasn't young. Last night's adrenaline shot hit me again. I thought of the report on the guy climbing over Aislinn's wall: *medium build, dark coat, the neighbour thought he might be middle-aged . . .* By the time I manoeuvred my car out of the parking space and gunned it up the road, he was gone.

What sent something extra through me, what leaves me edgy and watching cars in my rear-view mirror all the way to the car pool and to the scumbag's place and back to work with him whining in the back seat, was the overcoat. Steve was right, there are a lot of guys who wear dark overcoats. They include just about every D I know.

There are a few reasons why a D could be staking out my road. Some of them are a lot more fun than others.

Just to brighten my day, Creepy Crowley is still trying to pump Aislinn into the story of the year. He's dug up a couple more photos of her – all post-makeover; Crowley and his readers don't get into a panting lather over dumpy brunettes in polyester skirt-suits – and a flood of hot-button clichés to pour over them, and he's got the front page of the *Courier* all to himself. A fair bit of it is hints about the cops, specifically me, not taking this seriously because we're too busy protecting the politicians and the elite to care about decent working people. Crowley has somehow got hold of a blurry shot of me back in uniform, policing a protest; the protest was a couple of hundred people rightfully pissed off about an emergency room closing and there was zero aggro, but there I am with a stab vest and a baton, which is all Crowley needs to prove his point. Unless we make the collar soon, the brass are gonna start feeling the pressure, they're gonna kick the gaffer, and the gaffer is gonna kick me.

I walk the scumbag witness out – he's still bitching about his ruined lie-in – and watch him light a smoke and slope off. It's headed for ten o'clock; the day is as strong as it's going to get, all feeble grey light choked with cloud. I lean against the wall outside, ignoring the cold biting through my suit jacket, and ring Sophie while I've got some privacy. I figure a drug lord's fat fingerprint in Aislinn's bedroom, or even a nice bloodstain on one of Rory's gloves, would do a lot to put my day on the right track.

'Hey,' Sophie says. 'OK if I put you on speaker? This vase needs to make it back to Galway in one piece for the O'Flaherty case, and I swear the idiots on evidence transport use this stuff for football practice, so I'm packing it myself. In a year's supply of bubble wrap. I'm in my office, so no one's going to hear us.'

'Sure,' I say. 'You got the stuff from our suspect, yeah?'

'Yeah. The grey nylon gloves and black wool coat he was wearing, and navy-blue trousers, two white linen shirts, a pale blue pullover, red wool gloves, wool Fair Isle gloves – seriously – and black wool scarf from his flat. Plus fingerprints.' Sophie does something that sounds like ripping off a piece of gaffer tape. 'Just so you know: Breslin rang me yesterday evening. He was looking for all the scene reports, plus Aislinn's electronics.'

The rough stone prods at my back through my jacket. 'What'd you give him?'

'What do you think I am? I gave him fuck-all. He came on like a headhunter, telling me how *delighted* he was that I was working this case, how none of the other techs are up to my *standard* – what kind of idiot thinks bitching about my mates is going to get on my good side?' Tape ripping again. 'I told him none of our reports were ready, what with this case not being the only one in the whole world, and the computer guys hadn't even started on the electronics. Which was true, or near enough. Breslin wasn't pleased, but he kept right on schmoozing. I swear, by the end of it I thought he was going to send me flowers.'

'I'm gonna have a nice chat with Breslin,' I say. I could kiss Sophie. 'How far have you actually got?'

'Reports are ready whenever you want them. I got my guys to work late. I figured if you're trying to keep this stuff away from that arselick – and I don't need to know why, I'm just saying – it might be useful if you were a couple of steps ahead of where he'd expect.'

'It is,' I say, lifting a mental finger at Breslin. 'You're a gem. Find anything good?'

Sophie makes a noise like a shrug. 'The black fibres on the vic's body are consistent with your suspect's coat, but that's not as special as it sounds: they're common as muck, they'd probably be consistent with half the black wool coats in this town. No match to his scarf. No blood on any of his stuff – meaning if he is your boy, those aren't the gloves he was wearing when he did the job. Sorry.'

'Them's the breaks,' I say. No surprise there: even Rory's bright enough to spot a bin and dump bloody gloves in it. 'We'll keep looking. Anything new from the scene?'

'Most of it you can read in the reports – a load of miscellaneous unidentified fibres, that kind of shite. We'll cross-check them with fibres from your suspect's place, in case of secondary transfer – a fibre from his carpet gets on his coat and from there onto her sofa, or wherever – and we'll check your suspect's stuff for fibres from the vic's place, but we haven't got to that yet. Dammit—' Rustling and a thump: Sophie fighting with her roll of bubble wrap. 'There's just one thing that's a little on the weird side. The place is clean.'

'She was having her new fella over for dinner. She cleaned up.'

'Not that kind of clean. I mean, that too; it looks to me like she was the housekeeping type to begin with – the top of the wardrobe's got almost no dust on it, that kind of Stepford crap – and then she did a full blitz for her date with Romeo. But I'm talking about fingerprints. You know how Moran wanted me to check the places an ex might've touched? The headboard, under the toilet seat?'

'Yeah.'

'Nothing. No prints on the headboard, not even the vic's – and it's gloss paint, it should hold prints. The doorknobs, the bathroom sink, the toilet seat, the fridge door, the condom packet in her bedside table: nothing but smudges.'

I say, 'Somebody wiped the place down.' The ghostly gangster boyfriend is starting to cast a shadow. Gang boys know all about wiping a place down for prints. Rory, who'd never been in that house before, wouldn't need to.

Sophie makes a noncommittal sound. 'Maybe. Or maybe Ms Stepford was just hardcore about cleaning. Either one would fit. I figured you'd be interested anyway.'

'I am,' I say. 'Any fluids on the bed?'

'Yeah. The sheets were clean, but we found stains on the mattress. Could be just her own sweat – you were there; she kept the place tropical – but if we're lucky, some of it'll be semen, or at least someone else's sweat.' Energetic rustling: Sophie is wrapping another layer around her vase. 'Even if we get DNA, though, there's no way to tell when it was deposited. If you can find out when she bought the mattress, you can get an outside limit, but beyond that . . .'

'Keep me up to speed on the DNA,' I say. I'm not getting my hopes up; that condom packet says we'll be lucky if anyone's semen ever made it onto the mattress. 'Thanks, Soph. What about Aislinn's electronics? Anything there?'

'Most of it's your basic bullshit. Nothing good on her mobile – searches on clothes shops and nightclubs, cutesy game apps full of fluttery fairies. No one who looks interesting in any of her photos, but I'll send you copies so you can see for yourself. Her Facebook is all selfies and which-*Hunger-Games*-character-are-you quizzes and "Repost this if you hate cancer" – what the fuck is that supposed to *do*? If enough people like the post, cancer'll just take the hint and become extinct?'

'Get us the login details, yeah? We need to check out her Facebook friends.'

'No problem,' Sophie says. 'It doesn't look like she had any best buddies on there – no private messages or anything; it all looks like colleagues and old classmates, the type where you post on their time-line once a year telling them they look amazing in their birthday pic – but knock yourselves out.'

If the gangster boyfriend is out there, he's doing a nice job of being invisible; but then, he might. 'What about her e-mail? Any love notes, sex talk, setting up appointments, anything like that? From Rory Fallon or anyone else?'

'Nothing like that. The Gmail account linked to her phone is full of order confirmations and special offers from fashion sites, mainly. The lovey-doviest it gets is some cousin in Australia who sticks x's at the end of her e-mails. You still looking at exes?'

'Keeping an open mind,' I say. A clot of tourists wander past with their heads tipped back and their jaws hanging, staring up at the Castle buildings. One of them points a camera in my direction, but I throw him a stare that almost melts his lens, and he backs off.

'We're only seeing what she left on there,' Sophie reminds me. 'She could have deleted anything that reminded her of the ex. E-mails, texts, photos.'

'I know.' Or he could have, on Saturday night. 'We'll get onto the phone company and get her records – I'd say Steve's doing that now. Send me her e-mail account details – cc Steve – and can you talk to her e-mail providers? Get the logs, so we can compare them to what's actually left on her accounts?'

'My computer guy's got friends in high places. I'll get him onto it as soon as I've finished this fucking vase. You should see it: four feet tall, porcelain pug dogs sticking out everywhere, covered in blood spatter. Which actually improves it.'

'What about my vic's laptop? Tell me there's something good on her laptop.' I'm cold; tasteless instant coffee from the incident-room kettle is starting to sound good.

'You want interesting evidence, get me an interesting victim. This woman lived a boring life. She spent a lot of time online, but she wasn't playing in any dodgy corners of the internet, as far as we can tell – my computer guy had a good look through the last couple of months of her history. A lot of time – like, a *lot* – on travel sites: she was reading up on Australia, India, California, Portugal, Croatia . . . She ran some searches on evening classes in Dublin, looked at arts courses in universities, did a load of shopping for discount designer clothes, read all the coverage on a couple of gangland trials. Desperate for thrills; fuck knows she wasn't getting them anywhere else.'

Which is what I thought when I found Aislinn's little true-crime library. I've forgotten all about coffee. 'Right,' I say, keeping that out of my voice. 'Can you remember what cases?'

'Francie Hannon, and Whatsisname with his tongue cut out. I'd forgotten what a field day the papers had with that one. I think it gave some of the reporters an actual hard-on.'

Both those guys were from the same gang, a nasty bunch of north-side boys run by a raving psycho called Cueball Lanigan. Both of them were Breslin and McCann's cases.

'Sounds like it did the business for our vic, too,' I say. If Aislinn got mixed up with Cueball's boys, she got off lightly. 'Anything else on the laptop?'

More energetic bubble-wrap rustles from Sophie. 'She read a lot of fan fiction. The sappy kind, not the sexy kind; my guy was sort of disappointed about that. He said he stopped reading after one where Juliet wakes up early, and she and Romeo live happily ever after.'

'Cute,' I say. 'Any dating sites?'

'Nah.'

'Message boards?'

'Nope. And my guy says no one's been messing with the internet history.'

'Can you take the search back a bit further? We need her history for at least the last six months. A year would be even better.'

Sophie blows out air. 'You sure? If you piss off my computer guy, he's gonna send you a list of every single URL she ever visited. You'll spend the rest of your lives checking out every page of every designer-outlet website in the universe.'

'That's why God invented floaters,' I say. 'Was that it for the laptop, yeah?'

'Don't rush me,' Sophie says, through tape. 'I'm getting to the good part. My guy went through her documents – the only mildly interesting thing in there is that she updated her CV a couple of months ago: looks like she was considering switching jobs. And he had a look at her photos. Most of them are the same stuff that's on her phone, selfies in clubs; but there's one folder that's password-protected. It was created last September and it's called "MORTGAGE", but who the hell takes photos of her mortgage? And puts a password on them?'

I don't even need coffee any more; I'm well awake. September: long before Aislinn met Rory, and not long after, according to Lucy, she hooked up with her secret squeeze. 'Camouflage folder name,' I say. 'To turn off anyone who went looking through her stuff. How are you doing on getting in there?'

'No joy yet. My guy's thrown the dictionary at that folder, tried various combinations of Aislinn's name and DOB, and nada.'

'Did you try the password from her Facebook account?'

'We haven't got it. Facebook and her Gmail were both already open on her phone; we reset her passwords by answering her security question – her mother's maiden name, for Christ's sake – so we can get in on other machines if we want, but we don't have the original passwords. And the providers won't have them, either; they're encrypted.'

'Is your guy still working on it?'

'Yeah, and he's going to crack it. This chick wasn't Jason Bourne; no chance she was up to my guy's standards. I'm just telling you: she was at least a little bit serious about keeping this folder locked down.'

'I've got faith in you and your guy,' I say. The adrenaline is rising inside me again; no matter how hard I try to stamp it down, part of me is picturing Sophie's guy cracking the password and coming up with both hands full of pics of Aislinn riding Cueball Lanigan, with Breslin counting cash in the background. 'Let me know when you get in there, OK?'

'As soon as.' Sophie rips one more strip of tape and slaps it down. 'That'll have to do. I swear, this thing's ugly enough, I kind of hope they do smash it. The world would be a better place.'

I go looking for Breslin. Bernadette says he's in the building, but there's no sign of him in the squad room – the chat deflates to flat stares when I open the door, rises up again under a layer of sniggers when I close it behind me – and he's not in the canteen. I head upstairs to check the incident room.

I'm on the landing when I hear that smooth voiceover drawl coming down the stairwell. Breslin, somewhere up above me, talking low.

I stop dead. Then I move carefully – the stairs are wide white marble, part of the old castle, every sound echoes – till I can see through the banisters. Breslin and McCann, at the top of the stairs, close together.

I'm meant to be grabbing any chance for chats with these two, but McCann doesn't look like he's in a chatty mood. He's slumped into his suit, hands stuffed in his pockets. Breslin is lounging against the banister rail with his back to me. From the line of his shoulders I can tell the casual slouch is taking effort.

McCann is muttering something that includes the words 'that bitch'. He sounds like he means it.

'I'm on it,' Breslin says. 'You sit tight and leave it to me. OK?'

McCann moves like his suit is clammy. 'She doesn't like being pushed around. If you try to—'

'I'm not going to push her around. It's not about that. It's about making her see that she's really only got one option here.'

McCann swipes his fingers along his eyebags, head falling back.

Breslin says, 'I'll sort her out. Everything's going to be back to normal in no time.'

As McCann brings his head up to say something, he catches my black suit against the white of the stairs, and goes still. 'Bres,' he says.

Breslin turns around, and a blank look slams down across his gob. 'Detective Conway,' he says. 'Nice of you to call in.'

'I had some leftovers from Saturday night to take care of,' I say. 'This isn't the JFK assassination; I'm not gonna clear my whole schedule for it. I need a word with you.'

'Let's do that. Walk with me. Mac: later, yeah?' McCann nods without looking up. Breslin gives him a clap on the shoulder and heads past me, down the stairs.

I follow him. When I look back, McCann is still on the landing, staring at nothing.

'McCann and his missus have been going through a bit of a rough patch,' Breslin says confidentially, under the clatter of our footsteps. 'You've probably heard the phone calls, right?'

I make a noise that could mean anything. We've all heard the phone calls: McCann muttering through a clenched jaw about being home earlier tonight, while his head sinks lower and lower over his desk and the lads snicker just loud enough.

'She doesn't like the job. Doesn't like the hours, doesn't like him coming home with his head full of dead little kids, all the usual – hard to blame her, right? McCann thinks she's winding up to an ultimatum: he transfers out, or she kicks him out.'

I nod along. It's bollix. This squad gossips like a bingo hall, but no one ever bothers filling me in. The two of them were talking about me: either how to make me close this case, or how to get me off the squad. The only question is why. 'Huh,' I say. 'What's he gonna do?'

'Well, he's not crazy about either of those options, obviously. I said I'll have a chat with his missus, settle her down. We've all been friends a long time; she knows I've got their best interests at heart.' Breslin does the benevolent smile of a guy who's got everyone's best interests at heart. 'I'm going to need your word on something, Conway. This doesn't go any further. McCann doesn't want his private life splashed all over the squad. You shouldn't have heard any of that' – the reproachful finger-wag is a nice touch – 'but since you did, you need to treat it with respect.'

'I don't do gossip,' I say. 'I leave that to the lads.' I'm itching to punch Breslin in both his faces, but I wanted a chat with him, and here it is. 'You think you're gonna get it sorted out?'

'Oh, yeah. They're mad about each other, underneath it all; they just need a little reminder of that. It'll be fine in no time. McCann's just worried.'

'Yeah. The pair of yous looked a bit stressed, all right.'

Breslin stops and gives me a stare. 'Me? What's that supposed to mean?'

I lift my hands. 'I'm only saying.'

'This is what stressed looks like to you?' He's pointing at his gob, which is halfway between disbelieving and disgusted. 'Your radar might need some recalibrating, Conway. What would I be stressed about?'

I shrug. 'How would I know?'

Breslin's not moving. 'No. You can't throw out something like that and then backpedal when I call you on it. What would I be stressed about?'

Stressed and defensive as hell, too, which is interesting. I decide not to point out that part. 'Whatever. The usual. Work. Money. Life.'

'My life is great, thanks very much. I love my work, unlike some – and if you think a few days with you and Ginger Boy is enough to change that, you're flattering yourself. Financially, I'm fine – better than fine; not a care in the world. I'm a happy man. OK?'

'Man,' I say. 'I'm only making small talk.'

Breslin stares me out of it for a long moment. Then: 'All right.'

He heads off down the stairs again, making me follow. 'Just a tip, Conway: we've all got our fortes. Small talk may not be yours.'

'Maybe not,' I say. So much for my heart-to-heart with Breslin. 'Anything you want to tell me about yesterday evening?'

'Rory's big brothers came in for the chats. The reports are on my desk, if you want to take a look, but there's nothing good in there. They both say Rory is a New Man who respects women and would never God forbid hit one; he's been dumped a few times – surprise, surprise – and he just got depressed about it, never angry. They know the bookshop's not in great financial shape; they claim Rory would have come to them for a loan if he needed one, not to his new bird, but they're both skint as well, so I don't see why he'd bother. I got both of them on tape so we can play them to Whatsisname at Stoneybatter, but to be honest with you I'll be surprised if he IDs them. I think they genuinely are as clueless as they're making out.'

'Great,' I say. 'Did you ring Sophie Miller looking for Aislinn's electronics?'

Breslin's face turns to me, eyebrows lifting in a warning. 'Yeah. Is that a problem?'

'I said me and Steve were on those.'

He stops on the landing so he can give me a proper stare. 'Ah, Conway, come on. I get that you want to keep the good stuff for yourselves, but this isn't playschool; you don't get to call dibsies on your special toys. This is the real world. What matters is getting the job done.'

'Yeah. And we're well able to do that.'

'Not last night, you weren't. The two of you were home getting your beauty sleep – I know, I know, double shift, but the fact remains, you weren't here, were you? And I was. I finished up with Rory's brothers, I set up appointments with the rest of his KAs, I put in a call for his phone records, and then I had a little time on my hands. So I decided to use it. You should be thanking me, instead of getting your knickers in a twist.'

I say, 'Did you find out anything useful?'

Breslin eyes me. He says, 'Miller didn't have anything ready.'

'Right. That's why I'm not thanking you. Also because I like knowing who's doing what in my investigation, so I don't make a tit of myself trying to get something done and being told someone else already did it.'

Breslin's jaw moves. 'Conway. You need to chill out. Just bear in mind that I've got a lot more experience than you do. If I do something, I think you can take it on trust that it's in the best interests of the investigation.'

'No,' I say. I can hear Steve in my head going *We need to get on with Breslin*, but I want to see what happens. 'I'm bearing nothing in mind. Unless I missed your promotion, we're on the same squad, and this is my investigation. Which means you're the cheeky little bollix who's getting above himself, and you're the one who needs to bear in mind who's who here.'

For a second I think I've taken it too far, but Breslin forces his face into weary resignation, like a teacher who should never have expected better from that problem student. 'OK, Conway. Next time I consider contributing a little extra to *your* investigation, I'll be sure and run it by you first.' Eye-roll. 'Does that make you feel better?'

'Yeah. It does.'

'Good. So could you maybe pull that stick out of your arse?'

'I . . . Jaysus.' I dial it right back, turn all sheepish. 'I didn't mean to . . .' I glance down the corridor, making sure no one's heard me being a bad little D. 'It's not easy, you know? Having someone like you on board. It's pretty intimidating. I don't always manage to . . . yeah. Manage to deal with it right.'

'Well,' Breslin says. He takes his time thinking that over, to teach me a lesson, but he's puffing out with self-satisfaction. 'I suppose I can see that. That's no excuse for getting defensive, though. We're on the same team here.'

'I know, yeah. I apologise.' I won't lick arse for the sake of getting wankers to like me, but for the sake of getting wankers, I can slurp with the best. 'And I do appreciate the help, and the advice. Even if I'm not the best at showing it.'

Breslin nods. 'All right,' he says, all magnanimous. 'We'll say no more about it.'

'Thanks,' I say. 'Where are you headed?'

'I've got appointments with more of Rory's KAs. If that's still all right with you.'

He's smiling, although there's an edge underneath. 'That'd be great,' I say. 'Thanks a million. See you later.'

And I give him a humble duck of my head and start back up towards the incident room. McCann is gone off the upstairs landing. I'm on the top floor and turning down the corridor before I hear Breslin's footsteps start again, echoing around the stairwell in slow cold claps.

* * *

The incident room is getting on grand without me, which probably should feel like a good thing. The floaters are busy little bees and making sure it shows: Gaffney is scribbling, Meehan's finishing up a phone call; Kellegher and Reilly are hunched towards their monitors, fast-forwarding through jerky CCTV footage. Stanton and Deasy are somewhere else, presumably at Aislinn's work. Steve has our boss desk all to himself, he's turned it into a nest of printouts and Kit Kat bars, and he's whistling peacefully while he works his way through them. He looks happy.

'Morning, all,' I say, throwing my stuff onto my desk. The floaters whip out smiles like they love me. If anyone's got to any of them – and someone almost definitely has: whatever Breslin's agenda is, the first thing he would need is at least one floater in his pocket – they're good at hiding it.

'Howya,' Steve says. 'Sorted?'

'Yeah.' I didn't give him details, just said I wanted some extra from the scumbag witness, and he didn't ask. 'Anything I should know?'

'Sophie e-mailed us some stuff, just now.' He lifts a page.

'I was talking to her, yeah.' I sling my coat over the back of my chair. 'One of her guys is gonna wangle us Aislinn's e-mail records. Have you got her phone logs?'

'Yeah. My guy at Meteor sent them over.' Steve examines his heaps of paper, pats the right one. 'Breslin pulled Rory's; he says there's nothing that jumps out, no calls to anyone but Aislinn on Saturday night, no call to Stoneybatter station yesterday morning, and no link to Lucy Riordan. He's working on getting the actual texts, see if there's anything in there.'

'Gaffney,' I say. 'Any word on the number that called it in?'

Gaffney jumps. 'Yeah – yes; I've done that, yes. I got hold of the number. But it's unregistered.'

Steve says, 'I can't see any reason why Rory would have a spare unregistered mobile. One that didn't show up in the search of his flat.'

While most of the gang boys have more unregistered phones than they can keep track of. 'You never know,' I say. 'But yeah: it looks like Rory probably wasn't the one who called it in. We'll pull full records for the phone, see if those give us some clue who owns it. Moran, can you get onto that?'

Steve nods, writing. Gaffney looks wounded, but that's tough: if that phone log is full of calls to drug dealers, me and Steve need to know before anyone else does.

'Meehan,' I say, 'you were timing the route Fallon says he took around Stoneybatter. How'd that go?'

'According to Fallon's statement,' Meehan says, spinning his chair round to face us, 'he got off the bus just before half-seven, and he knocked on Aislinn's door just before eight – that part's confirmed by the witness who was walking his dog. So that's half an hour for the whole walk – from the bus stop to the top of Viking Gardens, up to Tesco and buy flowers, back down to her house. When I went at a normal pace, it came out at twenty-seven minutes. When I went as fast as I could without actually running, I knocked six minutes off that.'

I say, 'Meaning Rory could have had almost ten minutes to spare.'

'More,' Steve says. 'Here's the good part. Stanton pulled CCTV from the 39A route and had a look, first thing this morning. Rory got on the bus at ten to seven, not just before seven like he told us, and he got off it at quarter past, not just before half. He could've misremembered, or just been estimating the times, but . . .'

'But he was obsessing about being late to Aislinn's,' I say, 'in case she got her feelings hurt and dumped him and his life was ruined or whatever. Nah: he didn't estimate, and he didn't misremember. He's got anything up to twenty-five minutes unaccounted for, and he was fudging because he doesn't want us knowing that.' That blood-smell flares at the back of my nose again. He's so tempting, Rory, all fluffy and big-eyed and just begging for the killer bite; it would be so satisfying to hammer on his door, drag him back in and shove his face up against the CCTV screen. 'Good. When we bring him back in, he'd better have a great explanation for what he was doing. Have we got footage from the area yet?'

'Yeah,' Kellegher says, leaning back from his monitor. Kellegher is long, freckly, laid-back, and useful enough that he's going to end up on the squad sooner or later. 'The bad news is, there's no cameras between the 39A stop and Viking Gardens, or between Viking Gardens and the Tesco – so we can't verify Fallon's route, or the timing. But we've got him buying the flowers in Tesco. He paid at 7.51, which matches his story.'

'No surprise there,' I say. 'He had to know Tesco would have him on camera; he wouldn't lie about that. We need to widen the area of Stoneybatter where we're pulling CCTV. Whatever Rory was doing in that missing time, it could have taken him off the route he gave us. Reilly, you can get on that.' Meehan reaches for the book of jobs.

Reilly glances out the window – it's getting ready to rain – and back at his monitor. 'I'm not done watching what we've got.'

Reilly was a year behind me in training college. He's a lot less useful than Kellegher, but I'm guessing he'll make the squad sooner, just going by how beautifully he'd fit in with this shower. 'Kellegher can finish that up,' I say. 'With twenty minutes to spare, Fallon could have got, say, half a mile off the route he gave us. Do a half-mile radius, to start with. See you later.'

Reilly's chin moves and he gives me a piggy stare, but he heaves himself out of his chair and starts disentangling his coat. 'Kellegher,' I say. 'Tell me you've got some good news to go with that.'

'Some, yeah. We've picked up Fallon in four locations between Stoneybatter and Ranelagh, on his way home. I've mapped them up there.' Kellegher nods at a new map on the whiteboard, complete with X's and arrows and a halo of grainy time-stamped photos. 'They're consistent with his statement.'

I take a look. The slight guy in the black overcoat has his head down, against the rain and his bad evening, but it's Rory, all right. In the earliest shot, on the northside quays, there's a smashed-looking bunch of flowers sticking out of his armpit; by the time he gets across the river into Temple Bar, it's gone.

'Do we ever get a look at his hands?' I ask.

'Nah. In his pockets.'

'Meehan,' I say. 'I need you to time Fallon's route home. I want to see if he could have taken a detour anywhere along the way – gone off to ditch his gloves, or called in to a mate. Kellegher: what pace is he going on the CCTV?'

'Brisk, I'd call it,' Kellegher says, considering the Temple Bar shot, where Rory's been shouldered off the pavement by a howling stag do wearing fake tits and waving beer cans. 'Not jogging or anything, but he wanted to get home, all right. Yeah: brisk.'

'You heard the man,' I tell Meehan. 'Viking Gardens to the Wayward Bookshop, nice and brisk, and record the times when you hit the places where the CCTV caught Rory.'

'I'm going to get fit on this one,' Meehan says, pushing his chair back.

'Make it brisk enough and you might beat the rain,' I say. 'Thanks. Kellegher, how much of that footage have you got left to watch?'

'Not a lot.'

'When you're done, go have chats with the people who were at the book launch where Aislinn and Rory met. See how it looked: whether one of them was doing the chasing, whether either of them said anything interesting about the other, anything you can pick up. Yeah?'

Meehan scribbles that in the book on his way out. Kellegher gives me the thumbs-up and hits fast-forward on the CCTV – little dark figures spin and bobble down the street like wind-up toys. I go back to our desk and have a look over Steve's shoulder.

'These are Aislinn's phone logs,' he says, tapping a pile of paper, 'and this is the stuff Sophie e-mailed us, what was on the actual phone. I want to cross-check, see if anyone deleted anything along the way.'

'Great minds,' I say. 'I was going to say that to you.' Lower: 'We need a chat. Not here.' Having to take my chats out of my own incident room is fucked up, but there's no way to know which of the floaters belong to Breslin.

Steve nods. 'We need to search Aislinn's gaff anyway.'

'That'll work. Let's go.'

He bins his Kit Kat wrappers, because he was brought up right. 'While we're in Stoneybatter, fancy showing me round your locals?'

'Why?'

'Maybe they went for the odd pint.'

The floaters look like they're absorbed in their jobs, but I keep my voice down anyway. It's getting to be a habit. 'Who? Aislinn and her fella? A guy having a secret affair, you think he's going to be snogging the girlfriend down the pub?'

'They were seeing each other for around six months, according to Lucy. You can't spend six months just staying in and shagging.' Steve digs around the desk, finds a photo of Aislinn and sticks it in his coat pocket. 'The pubs'll be opening soon. Come on.'

I stay put. 'Even if he exists, they wouldn't have gone to one of my locals. Lucy said Aislinn was all about the fancy club scene; a pub in Stoneybatter wouldn't have been her thing. To put it mildly.'

'So less chance of being spotted. And if he's married, then they were doing their shagging at Aislinn's place; if they got stir-crazy and snuck out for a quick pint, it'd be somewhere around there.' Steve throws his coat on, glancing at the window. 'The fresh air'll do us good.'

'We don't have fresh air in Stoneybatter. We're too cool for that culchie crap. And you think a barman's going to remember some chick who looked exactly like half the twenty-something women in Dublin?'

'You remembered her. And barmen have good memories for faces.' Steve pulls my coat off the back of my chair and holds it up, valet-style. 'Humour me.'

'Give me that,' I say, whipping the coat off him, but I put it on. 'And sort those.' I jerk my chin at Steve's printouts and flick him a warning look. He starts organising the paper into a stack.

Gaffney is looking over. I say, 'Gaffney, spread the word: case meeting at half-five. And go find Breslin. You're supposed to be shadowing him, remember? What are you even doing here?'

'But he said—' Gaffney looks petrified; the poor bastard is seeing his career going splat all over the carpet. 'I did shadow Detective Breslin, like, all yesterday evening, and this morning – I was taking notes for him, and he was explaining to me how ye work, and all . . . It was only when he was heading out – he said I was grand to work on my own now, and you'd probably be needing me here more than he needed me out there, so, I mean . . .'

Breslin was right, obviously: Gaffney is well able to pull financials and make phone calls without someone holding his hand, or he wouldn't be in the floater pool to begin with. But he's also well able to take notes during interviews, and Breslin isn't the type to turn down the obedient PA that he deserves; not unless he wants the freedom to nudge witnesses his way, with no one else there to notice.

Gaffney has run down and is staring at me pathetically. There's no point sending him after Breslin; Breslin will find some excuse to slither out of it, or he just won't answer his phone. 'You're grand,' I say. 'Don't worry about it. You've got plenty of jobs to keep you going.'

Gaffney starts trying to come up with something grateful, but I'm already headed for the door. Behind me, I hear the click of Steve's desk drawer locking, for whatever that's worth.

7

Me and Steve head for the car pool and our shitty Kadett. The web of laneways behind Dublin Castle is hopping: students dragging their hangovers towards Trinity College, business types talking too loud into too-big phones so we can all be blown away by their Bulgarian property deals, yummy mummies out for shopping sprees and skangers out for pickings. It feels good getting out onto the street, where any danger coming our way won't be personal, and I hate that.

'So,' I say, once we're a safe distance into the flow of people. 'Breslin doesn't want company today. He wants to be all on his ownio for those interviews.'

'For the interviews,' Steve says, sidestepping a couple having complicated relationship problems in Russian, 'or for whatever else he's doing. Not long before you got in, right? Breslin's mobile rang. He had a look and got this face on him—' Steve does a clamped jaw and flared nostrils: Breslin, pissed off and trying to cover it. 'He took the call outside. But before he got all the way out the door, he said, "Don't ring this phone."'

He's right: maybe not the interviews. Maybe there's something else Breslin has to do, or someone else he has to meet, along the way; something, or someone, that doesn't need Gaffney. My adrenaline kicks.

'You want to know what he did yesterday evening?' I say. 'He went schmoozing Sophie for the scene reports and Aislinn's electronics.'

Steve's eyebrows go up. I say, 'It could mean nothing. I had a word with him: he says he was bored, went looking for something to do – and obviously he's going to go after the thing that could turn him into the big hero here. But . . .'

'But he wanted that stuff.'

'Yeah. Badly enough to go behind our backs, even though he had to figure we'd find out.'

'Did he get anything out of Sophie?'

'Nah. There's not a lot to get. Stains on Aislinn's mattress, but even if we get DNA and it's not hers, it could be years old; no way to know. It didn't get there on Saturday night, anyway, or it'd be on the sheets as well, and they're clean.' The adrenaline is moving me at a clip that sends even the big-phone types dodging out of our way. 'The only thing is, the places you asked Sophie to check, the bed frame and the jacks seat? They're too clean. No prints, just smudges. Sophie says our guy could've wiped the place down—'

'Ah, score!' Steve does a fist-pump. 'No reason why Rory would be wiping down the bed frame, when that was his first time in the house—'

'Yeah yeah yeah, you're a genius. Or Aislinn could've just been a clean freak. Sophie says it plays either way.'

Steve still looks pleased with himself. 'Anything else?'

'You mean that says Aislinn's other fella was real?'

'Yeah.'

'Not so far. No sign of him on Facebook, not on her mobile, not on her e-mail.' A junkie has cornered two lost-looking backpacker types and is hassling them for cash; I snap my fingers in his face and point off down the road, without bothering to break stride or find my ID, and he takes one look at us and bobbles off obediently. '*If* he exists, they must've made their appointments by ESP.'

'Or Aislinn deleted all their messages,' Steve points out. 'Or he did. I've only started cross-checking the phone records, and I'm still waiting on the e-mails.'

'Couple of interesting things on the laptop, though,' I say. 'Don't get too overexcited, but Aislinn read up on a couple of gang cases. Francie Hannon and the guy with the tongue.'

Steve's face has whipped round to me. 'They were Cueball Lanigan's boys. Both of them.' I feel him get caught up by the same roller-coaster surge that's speeding me along the footpath, feel the buzzing of the thing in our minds build higher. 'And they were both Breslin's cases. If he ended up in Lanigan's pocket, right, and if

Aislinn was seeing one of the gang and it went wrong, the first thing Lanigan would do—'

'I told you not to get overexcited. I've put out feelers. If Aislinn was seeing someone from Lanigan's crew, I'll know soon enough.' Steve looks a little wounded that I'm not opening up, but he'll have to live with that. 'The other good thing on her laptop: there's a password-protected folder of pictures that she created in September. It's labelled "Mortgage—"' Steve laughs out loud, and I can't help a grin. 'Yeah, that's obviously bullshit. Sophie and her lot are still trying to crack the password; she'll keep us updated.'

'Did she tell Breslin about it?'

'Nah. Neither did I. And I'm not planning to.'

Steve says, 'So since September, Aislinn's been worried about someone going through her laptop. That's not Rory. She only met him in December, and he'd never been over to her place before.'

'Maybe,' I say. 'Or else the folder's full of naked selfies, and Aislinn wasn't worried about anyone specific: she just didn't want some junkie robbing her laptop and uploading her full-frontals.'

'Naked selfies for who?'

'For kicks, for a little extra income, left over from one of the exes, for someday when she's old and wrinkly and wants to remember what a babe she was. How would I know?'

'Or,' Steve says, 'it's photos of her with her secret fella. And she really, really didn't want anyone – including him – knowing she had them. Yet, anyway.'

I've been thinking the same thing. 'Blackmail.'

'Or insurance. If she was with a gangster, maybe she had just enough sense to know this could turn dangerous.'

'"If,"' I say. 'From now on, every time you say "if" about this case, you owe me a quid. I'll be rich by the weekend.'

'I thought you liked a challenge,' Steve says, grinning. 'Admit it: you hope I'm right.'

'I do, yeah. That'd make a nice change.'

'You do.'

We've slowed down behind a pair of gabbing old ones. I say, 'I'd only love this to come through.'

I've been trying not to say it out loud because I don't want to jinx it. Like a dumb kid; like one of those moaners who believe the universe has it in for them and everything is just looking for an excuse to turn to shite. I've never been that. This is new, it's stupid, it comes from the squad training me to look for booby traps everywhere – last week I left my coffee in the squad room while I went for a piss, came back and nearly had it to my mouth before I saw the floating gob of spit – and no way in hell am I gonna blab it to Steve. I don't fucking like being what anyone trains me to be; I don't like it at all. I keep walking and count tall guys in dark overcoats.

Steve says, 'But?'

'But nothing. I don't want to get too attached to the idea till we've got some actual evidence, is all.'

He starts to say something, but I'm done with that. 'Here's the other thing,' I say, dodging around the old ones and picking up the pace again. 'Remember I said I had a word with Breslin about ringing Sophie?'

'Oh, Jaysus. Will he live?'

'Ah, yeah. His makeup'll cover the bruises.'

'You were nice to him, right? Tell me you were nice to him.'

'Relax the kacks,' I say. 'Everything's grand. That's the interesting part. I wasn't nice to him – I was busting his balls on purpose – but he just kept on being nice to me.'

'So maybe he wasn't bullshitting us, last night.' Steve is trying on the idea for size and stretching hard to make it fit. 'Maybe he genuinely does think we're all right.'

'You think? I called him a cheeky little bollix who was getting above himself, and I said while he's on my investigation he needs to do what I tell him.' Steve lets out a snort of horrified laughter. 'Yeah, well, I wanted to see what he would do. I expected him to take my head off. But you know what he did? He sighed and said OK, grand, from now on he'll run things past me.'

Steve has stopped laughing. I say, 'Does that sound like Breslin to you?'

After a moment he says, 'It sounds like Breslin really wants to stay on speaking terms with us. Like, badly.'

'Exactly. And that's so he can keep track of what we're at; it's not because he's got faith in us to turn into lovely little team players, or whatever it was. When I found him, right? He was having a chat with McCann, and they shut up sharp when they saw me. Breslin gave me some crap about McCann's marriage problems, but I'm pretty sure they were discussing the quickest way to get rid of me.'

Steve shoots me a look I can't read. 'You figure? What did they say?'

I lift one shoulder. 'I didn't give enough of a shit to memorise it. McCann wasn't happy, Breslin was reassuring him that he'd have some woman sorted in no time and everything would go back to normal, McCann wanted him to hurry it up. That was the gist of it.'

'And you're positive it couldn't actually have been about McCann's wife?'

'It could've been. But it wasn't.'

Some wanker with a logo jacket and a clipboard bounds up to us, opens his mouth, takes a second look and backs off. I'm getting my mojo back. Two days ago he would probably have followed me down the street, badgering me for money to end Third World psoriasis and telling me to smile.

'OK,' Steve says. 'We've been wondering if Breslin could be bent—' Even this far from the job, both of us automatically glance over our shoulders. 'What if it's McCann?'

I didn't even think of that. For a second I feel like a fool – letting paranoia distract me from the real stuff – but that blows away on the rising rush of excitement: that bad dare, growing bigger.

'That could work.' I'm skimming through what I know about McCann. From Drogheda. A wife and four teenage kids. Not from money, not like Breslin – I remember him saying something sour, once, about cutting the crime rate to zero by making all the spoilt brats with their smartphones go into apprenticeships at fourteen, the way his da did. No Bank of Mum and Dad to fall back on if the car dies, the house needs re-roofing, the kids need college fees and a D's salary isn't cutting it. A gang boss looking for a pet would like McCann a lot. 'Or both of them.'

'No wonder Breslin took everything you could dish out,' Steve says. 'He can't afford to have us telling the gaffer we want rid of him.'

'If,' I say. 'If any of this is real.'

'If,' Steve says. 'How did you leave things with Breslin?'

'I apologised. Told him I was too intimidated by his awesomeness to think straight. He liked that.'

'You think he believed you?'

I shrug. 'I don't really care. If he didn't, he just thinks I'm a narky bitch, and he thought that anyway. He was looking for an excuse to be buddies with me again; I gave him one. We're good.'

We're at the car pool. Just in that short walk, I've spotted eleven tall guys in dark overcoats. Every one made me feel more like a paranoid idiot, but the whole bunch of them can't scrub away the prickle of warning when I think of the guy at the top of my road.

Steve says, in the gateway, 'What do we do?'

What we need to do, just for starters, is pull Breslin's and McCann's financials, pull their phone records, and have someone turn their computers inside out to find out if they've been accessing anything they shouldn't be. None of which is gonna happen. 'Keep working our case. Keep talking to them. Keep our mouths shut.' I wave to the guy who runs the car pool; he waves back and turns to look for the Kadett's keys. 'And I'm gonna see if I can make Breslin eat a bug.'

Aislinn's gaff has been processed hard. When there's someone coming home to a place, we try not to wreck it too badly – print dust gets wiped away, books go back on shelves – unless we actually want to shake people up; but when no one's coming home, we don't bother breaking out the sensitivity. Sophie's lot covered half the house in black print dust and the other half in white, carved away a rough rectangle of carpet where Aislinn's body was lying, sawed a long chunk out of the fireplace surround, stripped the bed and sliced gaping holes out of the mattress. In a cosy messy family home that stuff looks nightmarish, against nature, but Aislinn's house barely looked like a real person's gaff to start with; now it looks like a Tech Bureau teaching unit.

Steve takes the sitting room and the bathroom, I have the kitchen and the bedroom. It's quiet. Steve whistles to himself, and the odd sound trickles in from the street outside – a bunch of old ones happily bitching their way past, a kid howling – but not a squeak or a bump out of the neighbours; these old walls are thick. Unless there was a blazing row or a scream, there's no way the neighbours would have heard anything. A stealth boyfriend, one who'd been to her place before, he would've known that.

The search gives me nothing relevant. Your standard hiding places – packet of peas in the freezer, emptied-out canister in the spice rack, under the mattress, inside shoes – are blank. No love notes in the curly-wurly dressing table, no spare pair of morning-after boxers in the chest of drawers. In the wardrobe, no envelope of cash or package of brown waiting to be picked up; the best I come up with is a bunch of family photo albums shoved to the back of the top shelf, behind the spare duvet. I take a look, see if they give me any hints on where I saw Aislinn before, but no. She wasn't a good-looking kid: chunky, with skinned-back plaits, a bumpy forehead and an uncomfortable smile. For someone who put this much gym time and celery and hair products into looking the way Aislinn looked, that would be plenty of reason to hide the albums. There's no family pics up around the gaff, either; pukey fabric-prints of flowers and gingham chickens go on her walls, but her family goes at the back of the wardrobe. A shrink would love that – Aislinn wanted to bury her parents as revenge for abandoning her, or she had to bury her real self so she could reinvent herself as Dream Date Barbie – but all I care about is that no one else in any of the photos looks familiar. Wherever I saw Aislinn, her gaff isn't gonna give me any hints.

The weird part is that I'm turning up nothing irrelevant, either. The search always has a surprise or two for you, because everyone's got a couple of things they hide even from their nearest and dearest; the only question is whether the surprises have anything to do with the case. But there's nothing here that Lucy didn't give us – in fact, since I've found zero evidence of any secret boyfriend, there's actually less here than Lucy gave us. No dodgy internet diet pills, no niche sex toys, I haven't even found that copy of *The*

Rules. The biggest revelation is that Aislinn sometimes wore padded bras.

'Her paperwork's in shite shape,' Steve says, in the bedroom doorway. 'Everything's thrown together in a big box under the side table: bank statements, bills, receipts, the lot.'

I shove the albums back on the wardrobe shelf. 'Gaffney's pulling the financials; we'll go through them that way. Bring back the box anyway. We need to check the receipts, in case the guy who delivered the sofa got a fixation. Anything interesting?'

'Her will. DIY job, on a form printed off the internet. She left half of everything to Lucy, the other half to provide respite for child carers. Who knows if it'll stand up to probate.'

'Lucky for Lucy she's got an alibi.'

'Yeah,' Steve says. 'It's dated two months ago.'

'So maybe Aislinn was starting to worry that she was over her head in something dodgy, or maybe she just figured it was time she got all grown-up and had a will. Anything else?'

'She had a first-time passport application form, filled in. Photo and all. Ready to go.'

'So she wanted a sun holiday. Don't we all.'

Steve says, 'Or she knew she might have to get out of the country sometime soon.'

'Maybe.' I slam the wardrobe door. 'That's it? No escort appointment book? No wad of cash inside the sofa? No guy deodorant in the bathroom cabinet?'

He shakes his head. 'You?'

'Fuck-all.'

We look at each other, across the pretty daisy-patterned carpet and the slashed bed. 'Well,' Steve says, after a moment. 'Maybe the pubs'll give us something.'

We come away with the box of paperwork, to dump in the back of the Kadett before we canvass the pubs, and not a lot else. Me and Steve give good search, but I feel like Aislinn snuck something right past us, and no matter how many times I think back, I can't figure out what or where it could be.

★　★　★

I underestimated barmen and Aislinn, and possibly overestimated her bit on the side. The first few pubs we try, Steve gets blank looks and head-shakes, while I hold up my notebook all ready to take nonexistent notes and give him the told-you-so eyebrow. But the barman in Ganly's – a back-alley dive, ratty enough that it's managed to avoid the hipsters looking for authenticity and hang on to its clientele of huddled old fellas in saggy jackets – takes one look at the photo and taps Aislinn's face. 'Yeah. She was in.'

'You positive it was her?' Steve asks, throwing me a triumphant look.

The barman is maybe seventy, baldy and bright-eyed, with shiny armbands on his starched shirt. 'Ah, yeah. She ordered a peach schnapps and cranberry – said she was trying out all the mad drinks she could think of, see what she liked best. I told her if she was looking for excitement, she was in the wrong place. She settled for a rum and ginger ale.' He tilts the photo to the light, what there is of it. 'Yeah; it was her, all right. I had a good old stare for meself. Have to take my chances when I can; we don't get the likes of her in here all that often.'

'Am I not good-looking enough for you, no?' demands an old fella on a barstool. 'You can look all you like; I won't charge you.'

'The state of you. That's why I was staring at that young one: I need something to clear the sight of you out of my head.'

'When was she in?' Steve asks.

The barman considers. 'A few months back. August, maybe.'

'On her own?'

'Ah, no. A one like her, I wouldn't say she does spend much time on her own.' The old lad on the barstool lets out an appreciative cackle. The barman says, 'She was with a fella.'

That gets me another *Ha!* look from Steve. 'Do you remember what he looked like?'

'I wasn't concentrating on him, if you know what I mean. He was older than her, I remember that; forties, maybe fifty. Nothing special: not fat or skinny, or nothing. Tallish, maybe. He had all his hair, anyway, fair play to him.'

Which fits well enough with the guy climbing Aislinn's wall. I think it before I can help it: fits the guy hanging around at the top of my road, too.

Steve says, 'Would you recognise him if you saw him again?'

The barman shrugs. 'I might or I might not. I won't promise yous anything.'

I ask, 'Would you say he was her fella? Any holding hands, any kissing? Or could he have been just a friend, an uncle, something like that?'

The barman makes a face and wavers his head. 'Could've gone either way. No canoodling, nothing like that, but I remember thinking they were sitting awful close if they weren't a couple. And that she could've done better for herself.'

'Like you, wha'?' the old lad wants to know.

'What's wrong with me? I've still got my figure.'

'Maybe he was a millionaire,' Steve says. 'Did he look flush?'

'Not that I noticed. Like I said: nothing special.'

'What would a millionaire be doing in a kip like this?' the old lad demands.

'Looking for a proper pint,' the barman says with dignity.

'If he'd've found one, he'd've come back.'

'Has he been?' Steve asks.

'No. Only saw either of them the once.'

I say, 'What about me? Have I been in before?'

The barman narrows his eyes up at me and grins. 'You have, yeah. Summer before last, was it? With a load of other ones and fellas, sitting over in that corner, having a laugh?'

'Fair play,' I say. I stand out a lot more than Aislinn, but it's been longer since I was in. The barman isn't talking shite to make us happy; he remembers her.

'What do I win?'

'Read that, and if it's all correct, sign at the bottom,' I say, holding out my notebook. 'If you're lucky, you win the chance to come into the station and tell us the same thing on tape.'

The old lad is craning his neck to get a look at Aislinn's photo. He says, 'Is she in hassle, yeah? She after doing something on someone?'

'Leave it, Freddy,' the barman says, without looking up from my notebook. 'I don't want to know.' He signs his name with a trim tap of the pen at the end, passes the notebook back to me and picks up his glass-cloth. 'Anything else, no?'

Outside, Steve slides the photo of Aislinn back into his jacket pocket. He's thinking *I told you so* loud enough that he doesn't need to bother coming out with it. 'So,' he says instead.

'So,' I say. The thought of the incident room left to its own devices, or Breslin's, is making me antsy. 'That's all the locals. Can we get back to the squad now, yeah?'

'Yeah. No problem.'

We head back down the potholed laneway, towards the road. That rain is kicking in, nasty spitty flecks edging towards sleet – I hope Meehan was brisk enough to get done in time. A bubble of low-grade trouble is building up on the corner – kids who can't go home because they're mitching off school – but apart from them the street's empty. A marker-graffiti creature, all bared teeth and bug-eyes, stares us out of it from the shutter on an abandoned shop, between a missing-cat poster and some leftover summer-fair thing, dancing kites and ice creams grinning manically from their faded paper.

Steve's self-control runs out. 'The secret boyfriend's looking good.'

He is. I say, 'Or else that was some guy from Aislinn's work—'

'She worked way out in Clondalkin. Why would they go for pints in Stoneybatter, unless they were buzzing off each other and didn't want to get spotted?'

'—or a pal from her wine-tasting class, or whatever she was at in August.' The car is parked half a dozen pubs back. I pick up the pace. 'Those fancy clubs she liked, those are full of good-looking, rich young guys; Aislinn could've had any of them. Why would she be buzzing off some middle-aged fella who was nothing special?'

Steve shrugs. 'There's women who prefer older guys.'

'Rory's her same age, give or take.'

'She could've had a daddy complex before him. Remember what Lucy said: Aislinn's da leaving, that messed up her life. Maybe she went looking for a father figure. When that didn't turn out the way she was hoping, she switched to guys her own—'

'*Jesus.*' I nearly walk into a lamppost, slam a hand against it at the last second. '*That's* where I knew her from. That's where I fucking saw her.'

'What? Where?'

'Jesus *Christ.*' My palm is throbbing; the glossy paint of the lamppost feels slimy against it. I can hear the street-corner kids laughing at me, somewhere behind us. '*Her.*'

Missing Persons, two and a half years back. I was on the front desk one lunchtime, a sunny day near the end of my time on the squad; the breeze floating in through the open window smelled like country air, like the summer had thrown off all the layers of city to come cartwheeling in clean and sweet. I was listening to bouncy nineties pop trailing out of a sunroof, eating a turkey sandwich, thinking about that morning's happy ending – ten-year-old disappeared after a fight with his parents, we found him playing Nintendo in his best mate's bedroom – and about Murder waiting for me just a couple of weeks away. It felt like we were on the same side that day, me and the world; it felt good.

When the girl in the crap suit hovered in the doorway, I put the sandwich away and gave her just the right smile and 'Can I help you?', not pushy, just warm and encouraging. It worked: she dumped her whole story on my desk.

Her dad, such a lovely sweet wonderful man, how he taught her to play chess and he took her to Powerscourt waterfall in his taxi and he could make her giggle till she got the hiccups. The day she came downstairs in her school uniform and her mother was frantically ringing her dad's mobile for the hundredth time, *He never got home last night I can't find him oh Jesus Mary and Joseph I know he's dead* . . . The detectives who took statements and made reassuring noises about how most missing people come home within a few days, just need a bit of time to themselves. The few days turning into weeks and still no sign of SuperDaddy, the detectives' visits getting further apart and their reassuring noises getting vaguer. The one who finally patted her on the head and said, *You have great memories of him; we don't want to change that, do we? Sometimes these things are better left as they are.*

'That has to mean he knew something, don't you think it . . . ? Or at least he had an idea, even just an idea – doesn't it sound like that to you, like he knew what . . . ?'

Her leaning in across my desk, fingers woven together so tight the knuckles were white. Me shrugging, blank-faced: 'I wouldn't be able to speculate on the detective's thought process. Sorry.'

So she kept going. The weeks turning into months into years; jumping a mile every time the phone rang, spending every birthday waiting for the postman to bring a card. The nights listening to her mother crying on and on. The times she was sure she spotted him walking down the street, nearly leaped out of her skin before the guy turned his head and was some randomer and she was left gasping and paralysed, watching the one moment she wanted from the world dissolve to dust and blow away. One look at my face should have told her this was getting her nowhere, but she kept on going.

You get that, in Missing Persons: people who think seeing their faces, hearing them cry, will make you do your job better. You get parents who come in every year, on the anniversary of the day their kid disappeared, to find out if you have even one new scrap of info. It sort of works: you keep track of the anniversary, put in a few extra hours when it's coming up, do your damnedest to find something to give them. This chick was a whole other story. I had zero intention of busting my arse trying to help her find Daddy.

Which is what I told her, in a slightly more tactful way, wondering how hard I would have to blank her before she would fuck off out of my face. Files can't be released, Freedom of Information Act doesn't apply to police investigations, sorry, can't help you.

And of course then she whipped out the tears. Please couldn't you just look up the file, you can't imagine what it's like growing up without yada yada yada, and some Hollywood-style puke about needing to know the truth so it couldn't control her life any more – I can't swear she actually used the words 'closure' and 'empowered', because I'd stopped listening, but they would have fit right in. By that stage my happy buzz was well and truly wrecked. All I wanted was to shut the bitch up and kick her out the door.

Aislinn wasn't looking for a daddy substitute. She was looking for Daddy.

I say, 'Aislinn's da didn't just walk out on them; he went missing. She came in to Missing Persons looking for info. I was on the desk.'

'Huh,' Steve says, thinking that over. '"Just gone," Lucy said, remember? I never copped that meant missing. What'd you give Aislinn?'

'I gave her fuck-all. She was whinging at me, could I not look up the file and tell her what was in there, pretty please . . .' I feel it all over again, the rush of anger rising up from my gut and flaring under my ribs. I shove myself away from the lamppost and start walking. 'I gave her the name of one of the older guys who would've been on the squad back then, told her to come back on his shift, pointed her at the door.'

Steve has to lengthen his stride to keep up with me. 'Did she? Come back?'

'I didn't ask. Didn't give a shite.'

'Did you have a look at her da's file?'

'No, I didn't. What part of "didn't give a shite" isn't getting through to you?'

Steve ignores the bite in my voice. He dodges a yapping clump of Uggs and buggies and says, 'I'd love to see that file.'

That gets my attention. 'You think there's a link? Her da going missing, her getting killed?'

'I think that's a lot of bad shite to happen to one family just by coincidence.'

'I've seen worse.' I'm not sure I want this case to turn out interesting, not any more.

'If we're thinking about the gangster-boyfriend thing—'

It feels like the whole of Stoneybatter is yammering at me: WE WON'T PAY spray-painted on a patched garage door, woman laughing hysterically about butter from a bus-shelter ad, an old one from my street waving at me across the road – I wave back and speed up, before she heads over for a chat. 'We've got no evidence the gangster boyfriend ever existed. Remember? You made him up.'

'Yeah, but *if*. Go with it for a second. I'll owe you the quid.'

I don't laugh. 'Whatever.'

'Say Aislinn thought some gang was involved in disappearing her da. And say she didn't get any satisfaction out of Missing Persons.' Steve's being tactful. He means, say some bitch gave her the brush-off.

'Why the hell would she think that? She didn't say anything about gangs to me. She was all about how perfect Daddy was; she'd have lost the plot if I'd suggested he ever had a *parking* ticket. And the gang boys don't waste their time disappearing normal decent citizens.'

'Maybe she didn't know that. We know she was naïve; maybe she thought gangs were like the villains in stories, going around looking to grab people just out of badness. Or maybe she found out the da wasn't as much of a saint as she thought. There are normal decent citizens who get mixed up with gangs.'

I say, reluctantly, 'I think he was a taxi driver.'

The gang lads love getting taxi drivers on side. All their own cars are on watch lists, under surveillance half the time, occasionally bugged. A taxi man can ferry drugs, guns, money, people, all under the radar.

'There you go,' Steve says triumphantly, on it like a puppy on a treat. 'He gets tangled up with the bad boys, puts a foot wrong, ends up in the mountains with two in the back of the head. Missing Persons can't prove it, but they know the story, and when Aislinn talks to your mate he lets something slip. She decides to do a bit of her own investigating; before she knows it, she's in way over her head . . .'

'Her bookshelf,' I say. I'd rather keep my mouth shut and hope this whole bloody thing will go away, but I suppose Steve's earned his extra treat. 'Book on missing persons, right next to the one on Irish gangland crime. Both of them full of underlining.'

He practically bounces. 'See? See what I mean? Doing her own investigating.'

'Fuck this might-have crap,' I say, pulling out my phone. This is one of the ways I know, no matter what the shitbirds in Murder try to gaslight me into thinking, I'm not just some ball-breaking humour-less bitch that no normal person could work with: I got on grand in Missing Persons. I didn't make any bosom buddies, but I had a few laughs, a few pints, I was in on a medium-disgusting running joke involving one of the lads and a squeaky rubber hamster; and I can still ring up anyone I need to. 'The guy I sent her to was Gary O'Rourke. I'm gonna ask him.'

Gary's phone rings out to voicemail. 'Gary, howya. It's Antoinette. I'm gonna owe you a pint; I need a favour. I'm looking for a guy who went missing somewhere around 1998 or '97, give or take, so it might not be in the computer – make it two pints. Guy called Desmond Murray, address in Greystones, taxi driver, aged anywhere between say thirty and fifty. Probably reported by his wife. You might remember the daughter, Aislinn; she came in looking for info, a couple of years back. I need whatever you've got sent over to me ASAP. And can you tell your guy to make sure he gives the stuff directly to me or my partner Moran, yeah? Thanks.'

I hang up. Ten minutes ago, I was enjoying this case. I liked that; it made a nice change. And now, just like that whiny voice warned me, it's finding a way to turn to shite.

'The brainless fucking bitch,' I say.

Steve's eyes widen. 'Say what?'

'You know something? If I ditch this gig, I'm gonna set up as a therapist. A new kind, specially for people like Aislinn. For a hundred quid an hour, I'll clatter you across the back of the head and tell you to cop yourself on.'

'Because she might've got herself mixed up with a gang?'

'I don't give a shite about that, if it even happened, which you still haven't convinced me.' I'm crossing the road fast enough that he has to jog a step or two to keep up; a car whips past inches from our arses. 'No: because she was twenty-six years old and chasing after Daddy, whining for him to fix everything for her. That's fucking pathetic.'

'Come on,' Steve says, catching up on the footpath. 'This isn't some spoilt Daddy's girl ringing him to change her flat tyre. Aislinn's dad leaving pretty much defined her life, and not in a good way. We don't know what she went through; we can't—'

'I bleeding do know. My da split before I was even *born*. Do I look to you like I'm mooning about, dreaming up ways to find him and throw myself into his arms?'

Which shuts Steve up. It shuts me up, too. I didn't know that was gonna come out of my mouth till I heard it.

After a moment he says, 'I didn't realise. You never said.'

'I never said because it doesn't matter. That's my *point*. He's gone; gone means irrelevant. End of story.'

Steve says – carefully: he knows he could get hurt here – 'Are you telling me you never thought about him? Seriously?'

I say, 'I did, yeah. I thought about him a lot.' There should be a special word for that level of understatement. When I was little, I thought about him all the time. I wrote him a letter every week, telling him how great I was, how I'd got all my maths homework right and beaten everyone in the class at sprinting, so that when I finally found an address to send them to, he would realise I was worth coming back for. I walked out of school every day looking for his white limo to scoop me up and speed me away from the bare concrete yard and the aggro-eyed kids with their places already booked in rehab and prison, away to somewhere blue and green and blazing where wonderful lives lay in glittering heaps waiting for me to choose. Every night I lay in bed imagining them: me with scrubs and a stethoscope, in a hospital so blinding with white and chrome it looked ready to lift off; me going down a sweep of staircase to an orchestra waltz, in a dress made of spin and foam; me riding horseback along a beach, eating fancy fruit in a morning courtyard, shooting orders from a leather office chair forty storeys above my dizzy view. 'I thought the exact same as Aislinn: when he came back, that's when my real life would start.'

Steve, God help us, is trying to find the right level of compassionate. I say, 'Jesus, the face on you. Don't be giving me the big sad eyes, you sap. I was like *eight*. And then I grew up and copped myself on, and I realised this is my real life, and I'd bleeding well better start running it myself, instead of waiting for someone else to do the job for me. That's what grown-ups *do*.'

'And now? You don't think about him any more?'

'Haven't thought about him in years. I mostly forget he existed. And that's what Aislinn would've done, if she had the brains of a fucking M&M. Her ma, too.'

Steve moves his head noncommittally. 'It's not the same thing. You never knew your father. Aislinn's da was someone she loved.'

Probably he has a point, sort of, but I don't care. 'He's someone who was *gone*. Aislinn and her ma, they could've got on with life, figured they'd deal with the answers when and if they got any. Instead they decided to make their whole lives all about someone who wasn't even there. I don't care who he was; that's pathetic.'

'Maybe.'

'Fucking pathetic,' I say. 'End of story.'

Steve doesn't answer. We keep walking. Up ahead I can see the car, right where we left it, which is nice.

I want Steve to talk. I'm feeling for any difference in him: the distance he keeps from me, the angle of his head, the tone of his voice. The reason I don't tell people about my father, apart from the fact that it's none of their business, is that they hear the story and move me in their minds, either to the box marked *Ahhh poor pet* or to the box marked *Skanger*. Steve grew up a lot like I did – probably he was a little posher, lived in a council house instead of a council flat and had a da with a job and a ma who put those lace things on the back of the sofa, but he would have been in school with plenty of kids who didn't know their daddies. I'm not worried about him getting snobby on me. But Steve is a romantic; he likes his stories artistic, with loads of high drama, a predictable pattern, and a pretty finish with all the loose ends tied up. I wouldn't put it past him to imagine me as the tragic abandoned child fighting her way through her demons to a better life, and if he does I'm gonna have to smack him across the head.

He's not throwing me gooey looks, at least, or walking closer to support me through my pain. All I can tell, out of the corner of my eye, is that he's thinking hard. After a while he says, 'What if she found him?'

'What're you on about?' The relief makes me sound snotty.

'The secret guy Aislinn kept ditching Lucy for. The guy in the pub.' Steve goes round to his side of the car and leans on the roof while I dig for my keys. 'What if it wasn't a boyfriend, after all? What if it was her dad? She tracks him down, they're trying to rebuild their relationship—'

'Ah, Jaysus. That does it.' I want to floor it all the way to Rory Fallon's gaff and arrest the hell out of him, before it can turn out that Aislinn was having heartwarming reunion rendezvous with Daddy and I have to listen to all the syrupy details. 'That's four quid you owe me. No' – when Steve grins – 'I'm gonna lose my bleeding mind if I have to put up with this *if* shite any longer. I don't even want to *think* about Aislinn's da until Gary rings back and gives us the actual story. Meanwhile, you're not getting into this car till you give me my four quid.'

I jingle the keys and stare him out of it till he reaches into his pocket and shoves a fiver across the roof of the car. 'Where's my change?' he demands, when I pocket the fiver and unlock the doors.

'By the time we get back to HQ, you'll owe it to me anyway. Get in.'

'OK,' Steve says, swinging himself into the car. 'Might as well use it up now. So if the da wants to make up for years of not being there to protect Aislinn, and he doesn't like the cut of Rory—'

'Sweet fuck,' I say, starting the Kadett and listening to it bitch about being woken up. 'What if I pay you *not* to do this shite? Would that work?'

'You should definitely give it a go. I take cheques.'

'Do you take Snickers bars? Because at least you shut your gob when you're eating.'

'Ah, lovely,' Steve says happily. 'I'll be good.' I find the Snickers bar in my satchel and toss it into his lap, and he settles down to demolish it.

He doesn't look like he's thinking about what an inspiration I am, or what a tragic story. I know Steve is nowhere near the simple freckle-faced kid he plays on TV, but still: he looks like he's thinking about chocolate.

'What?' he demands, through a mouthful.

'Nothing,' I say. 'The bit of silence suits you, is all,' and I catch myself grinning as I swing the car into the flow of traffic.

8

We get back to an incident room full of nothing. Breslin is still out, presumably talking to Rory's KAs; the floaters come in and out, fetching more nothing and dumping it on our big fancy desk. Stanton and Deasy turned up nothing at Aislinn's work, no rumours of an affair with the boss or anyone else, no unrequited crushes either way, no office feuds, no stalkery clients. Meehan comes back from checking Rory's route home to report that his times match the CCTV footage, meaning Rory didn't take any major detours between Aislinn's house and the last time he was caught on camera – although we've got no way of confirming what time he got home or what he did afterwards, so we can't rule out a last-minute detour or a late-night excursion. Gaffney is running Aislinn's KAs through the system, which spits out a load of traffic tickets, a couple of minor drug possession charges and one guy who smashed his brother's windscreen with a Hoover. Reilly slouches in with more CCTV footage and a flat stare at me, settles down to watch some telly and occasionally lets out a noise halfway between a cough and a roar to remind us that he's here and he's bored.

I'm itching to look up Cueball Lanigan's boys on the system, but I'm not gonna do it: I'd feel like a twat taking the gang thing that seriously, plus the search would be logged for anyone to find, just like we found the search someone ran on Aislinn last autumn. Instead I go through the statements from the door-to-door again, properly this time, looking for the little things that need following up. I'm not finding them – Gaffney went to town with the highlighter pen on one woman's statement that she heard the guy in Number 15 roaring about killing someone a week or two back, but seeing as Number 15 has three teenagers, I figure we don't need to break out the waterboarding equipment just yet. Steve cross-checks Aislinn's phone records against her phone, and comes up with no discrepancies: no one's been deleting texts or call logs, not Aislinn and not our guy. No calls or texts from unidentified numbers, either; every number is in her contacts list – and we'll track down the contacts to make sure they are who the phone says they are – or else comes back to some customer service department. That has its good side – it's a nice punch in the face for Steve's cute little fantasy about an Aislinn-and-Daddy reunion – but I'd give a lot for just one text from an unregistered mobile saying *Meet me for a shag by the heroin stash at 8.*

Every investigation nets you plenty of nothing. You need that – it's the only way you can narrow down your focus – and normally it feels good, slashing the dead ends off your whiteboard, leaving the live stuff to leap out at you big and bold. This time, though, there's no slashing going on, just little bits of useless nothing splatting onto my desk like spitballs from some joker I can't catch. That soaring buzz is turning to edginess, making me shift and knee-jiggle and rub away imaginary itches against the back of my chair. I need something, anything, that'll zap away Steve's great big fluffy cloud of if-based babble and leave me with the stuff solid enough to stand on. Incident Room C looks empty to the point of ridiculous, the half-dozen of us dotted around a room that would take thirty easily, the high ceiling and the shining rows of desks shrinking us to dollhouse size. I'm starting to wonder if Breslin was taking the piss out of us, getting the luxury suite for a two-cent case that would have fit in that ex-locker-room shithole with space left over.

At two o'clock we send Gaffney out for pizza, and Stanton pulls up one of the sob radio shows on his phone for lunchtime light relief. Sure enough, they've got a big segment about Aislinn, leading into a general outrage-fest about how the country is getting more dangerous for decent law-abiding citizens and the Guards don't give a damn, complete with phone-ins from old ones who were mugged and left to die in pools of their own blood while uniforms stepped over them looking for a politician's hole to lick. They even have Crowley on, being profound about how our cavalier attitude towards Aislinn's murder and our oppressive bullying of geniuses like himself are both symbolic of the sickness of our society 'on an almost mythic level', whatever he thinks that means. For a minute there, while we all crease ourselves laughing, we forget what we think of each other.

'My cousin went out with him for a while,' Meehan says.

'Your cousin's got shite taste,' Reilly tells him.

'She does, yeah. She dumped him because he wouldn't wear johnnies. He said they were a feminist conspiracy to suppress masculine energy.'

Everyone cracks up again. 'Fucking beautiful,' Stanton says, reaching to grab another slice. 'I'm going to see if I can get away with that.'

'Not a chance,' I say. 'If even someone thick enough to shag Crowley didn't fall for it – no offence to your cousin, Meehan—'

'Nah, you're grand. She is thick. She lent the little bollix three grand so he could self-publish his autobiography.' That sets everyone off again. 'Never got a penny of it back.'

'What'd he call it?' Kellegher asks. '*Johnny, I Hardly Knew Ye?*'

'*Free Willy,*' I say. That gets a laugh with a startled edge, like half the floaters didn't think I was able for it.

'Here we go,' Steve says, swiping at his phone. '*Truth's Martyr*, by Louis Crowley— No, listen; there's a review. Five stars. "A searing, towering dissection of one man's odyssey to reveal the hidden shadows of Irish justice. If you care at all about truth . . ." Jaysus, it's longer than the book.'

'Anyone want to put money on who wrote that?' Stanton says.

'How do you reveal a hidden shadow?' Kellegher wants to know.

'You lot are just part of the conspiracy,' Meehan tells us all. 'I bet you go around trying to put johnnies on poor unsuspecting fellas on the street.'

Reilly beckons to him. 'C'mere till I stick one on you.'

'It'd take three of yours.'

'Here,' Stanton says, throwing a greasy paper napkin at Meehan. 'Suppress your masculine energy with that.' Meehan slaps the napkin away and it goes into Kellegher's coffee, and all of them start telling me that I need to write up the rest for harassment and creating a hostile workplace environment and wearing crap ties and farting in the unmarked cars. For that minute, the incident room feels like a good place.

'I'm sure many Guards are fine people,' Crowley tells us, from Stanton's phone. 'But when one of them practically assaults me, simply because I want to keep you informed on what they're doing about this beautiful young woman's death, then I think we all have to ask ourselves why she – or he, of course – is so desperate to control what we're allowed to hear. After all—'

Underneath the solemn voice, he's obviously creaming his chinos with delight: his story is taking on a life of its own, parallel to reality and getting a lot more traction. Reilly is grinning. 'That'll do,' I say. The laugh has worn off; Crowley is giving me the sick. 'Yous aren't a shower of schoolkids. Get some work done.' Stanton switches off the radio and they all turn back to their computers, throwing each other sideways glances and eyebrow-lifts about what a bitch I am, and the incident room goes back to normal.

The only bit of actual something that comes in is the pathologist's report. Cooper hates most people, but he likes me – probably out of pure contrariness, but you take what you can get – so he rings me when he finishes writing up the post-mortem, instead of making me wait for his report.

'Detective Conway,' he says. 'I was sorry to miss you at the crime scene yesterday.'

Which is my cue to apologise for not making it in time. 'We were sorry to miss you,' I say, snapping my fingers at Steve to get his attention. 'We got caught up in roadworks. I appreciate you ringing me, Dr Cooper.'

'The pleasure is mine. I trust the investigation is progressing well?'

'Not too bad. We've got a good suspect. I could do with a bit more hard evidence and a bit less if-then-maybe.' Steve makes a face at me. 'Any chance you can help me out there?'

'I think I can promise you a minimum of *if-then-maybe*,' Cooper says, with delicate disdain, like I used bad language. 'It is hardly my stock in trade.'

'That'll be a nice change,' I say, making a face right back at Steve. Cooper makes a small crunchy noise that could be a laugh.

'As far as hard evidence goes, the vast majority of the post-mortem examination provided no unexpected information. The victim was in good health, showed no signs of injuries received prior to Saturday night, had not had recent sexual intercourse, was not pregnant and had never borne a child.' Cooper takes a pause and clears his throat: with that out of the way, we're getting to the good stuff. 'As I suggested at the scene, she suffered two sets of injuries: one to the face, and one to the back of the skull. The pattern of the facial injuries is consistent with a punch. The salient fact about this punch is the degree of damage it inflicted: the victim's jawbone was fractured, and two of her lower left incisors were broken almost out of their sockets. Considerable force was required. I think we can safely say that the blow was inflicted by a man of above average strength and fitness.'

I mouth *Strong guy* at Steve. He raises his eyebrows at me: *That sound like Rory to you?*

'Those injuries, however,' Cooper says, 'would not have been life-threatening. The fatal injury was to the right rear of the skull. This injury is linear, approximately two and a half inches long, and made by an object with a sharp right-angled edge, consistent with the fire-place surround on which the victim was found. The blow caused a severe skull fracture leading to an extradural haematoma. In the absence of immediate medical attention, the increasing pressure on the brain resulted in death.'

'The victim took the punch, went over backwards and hit her head on the fireplace surround,' I say. 'How long would it have taken her to die?'

'Impossible to say. An extradural haematoma can cause death within minutes, or within hours. Given the severity of the injury, I would have expected this one to progress fairly rapidly; precisely how rapidly, however, there is no way to know. One possible indi-cator, however, may lie in the second injury to the right rear of the skull.'

'Whoa,' I say. 'Second injury?' Steve's eyebrows go up. I kick my chair closer to him, switch on speakerphone and put a finger to my lips. Cooper hasn't made up his mind about Steve yet; one wrong word out of him could end the conversation right there. I feel a weird, idiotic twitch of triumph, like the bad kid seeing her golden little brother in the doghouse while she gets the pats on the head for once. I slap it down.

'Restrain your excitement, Detective,' Cooper says. 'This second injury is minor – a slight contusion. Apart from that, it is practically identical to the first: linear, two inches long, made by an object with a right-angled edge. The two injuries are parallel, lying approximately a quarter of an inch apart, which explains why the second was not immediately obvious at the scene.' He sounds miffed at the thing for hiding out on him.

I say, 'So after the victim went down, either she lifted her head and then dropped it again, or else the killer did.'

'Mmm,' Cooper says. Steve is scribbling something in his note-book. 'Either is possible. The killer could certainly have lifted her head to check for signs of life, or she could have attempted to get up but been unable to do more than raise her head. I would expect the initial injury to cause unconsciousness – there was some intraparenchymal bleeding, which generally has immediate neurological consequences – but it is plausible that she briefly regained consciousness before death.'

Steve passes me his notebook. Steve is about the only cop I know who has legible writing – nice writing, full of definite, old-fashioned loops and dashes; I think he practises in his spare time. The page says, *Or: first a push – then the punch when she's down?*

I ask, 'Could the injuries have come the other way round? The killer initially pushed our victim, rather than punching her; she went over backwards, hit her head on the fireplace, but not hard. Then when she was down and stunned, he went after her and punched her in the face?'

'Ah,' Cooper says, enjoying that. 'Ah-ha. Interesting. And possible; certainly possible. Impressive, Detective Conway.'

'That's why they pay me the big bucks,' I say. Steve mouths *Hey!* and points at his chest. I turn up my palm and grin at him: *Nothing I can do, man, hate that.*

'Hmm,' Cooper says, and I hear pages flicking. 'In light of this new theory, I must revise my estimate of the killer's strength. *If* the punch occurred when the victim's head was already lying on the stone surround – rather than when she was free-standing, so to speak – it would have required considerably less force to inflict these injuries. Some strength would still be needed, but any healthy adult of normal muscular development could have done it.'

I'm giving Steve the eyebrows right back: that does sound like Rory Fallon. 'Sorry to make you rewrite your report,' I say. Cooper handwrites; none of us have the nads to invite him into the twenty-first century, so we get floaters to type up his reports.

'I would forgive worse sins for the pleasure of hearing an alternative theory that fits the facts so neatly,' Cooper says. 'The rewritten report will be with you as soon as possible. I wish you the best of luck in finding hard evidence,' and he hangs up.

Me and Steve look at each other.

'That's not manslaughter,' he says.

'Nope. Not if that's how it went down.' People get knocked down all the time, get up and hit back; no one expects that to kill. But if you punch someone in the face while the back of her head is up against a sharp stone edge, it takes some cojones to claim you thought she'd get up and walk away.

'And Breslin likes it being manslaughter.'

His voice has dipped low. He's right: Breslin jumped straight on the manslaughter scenario. Maybe because that's a better fit with Rory Fallon, and Breslin wants this to be Rory, just to make everyone's life simpler; maybe because he knows well that it isn't, but he thinks we're more likely to bite on the manslaughter story. 'Yeah,' I say. 'Let's see what he thinks of the murder version.'

'Do you see Rory Fallon doing that?' Steve asks. 'One wild swing, yeah. But going after her like that?'

'Whoever did this was raging,' I say. 'He snapped. We already knew that. And we're not looking for King Kong. Rory could've done it, no problem.'

'Could've. But we still don't have a good reason why he would've snapped, and as far as we can find, he's got no experience with violence. Something as vicious as that punch, it's not easy; not for someone who hasn't touched another person since he was nine and gave his brother a dig. It'd come more naturally to someone who was in practice.'

'Nah nah nah.' I give my chair a shove back to my end of the desk – even the wheels on the Incident Room C chairs work better. 'You heard Rory. All the most intense shit in that guy's life goes on inside his head. People like that, you can't go by what you see. We don't know what he's been practising in there; for all we know, he's spent years rolling out a whole alternative life where he's a cage fighter. When the pressure was on, it came popping out, and bang.'

The thought of that punch, bone crunching against stone, flashes through both our heads. Steve is right, it's hard to see Rory on the end of that, but that could be because neither of us wants to. 'This is why I keep telling you to quit the "if" crap,' I say. 'Hazardous to your health.'

'Don't worry,' Steve says, going back to his paperwork. 'In my fantasy life I'm the super-detective who never misses a solve.'

'Deadly. Now all we have to do is get you under enough pressure that he pops out.'

Steve glances over, and the abrupt, wry snap of the look startles me. For a moment I think he's going to say something, but then he shakes his head and starts running his Biro down a line of phone numbers.

Just to be clear: I know, and what with Steve not being a certified moron I assume he knows too, that we should be on our knees praying Rory Fallon is all there is to this case. If we find any evidence that Breslin is bent, we're in deep shite.

If you catch another cop breaking the rules, or the law, or both, your first-line option is to keep your mouth shut. This is what practically everyone does about the pissant stuff like squaring traffic tickets and running private background checks: you look the other way, because it's not worth the hassle and because sooner or later you could be the one who needs someone to blink. But even if we want to go that route – which I'm nowhere near sure I do – it's not gonna be that easy this time, not if whatever we find is tangled up with our murder case.

Your second option, the one you're supposed to take, is a visit to Internal Affairs. I've never tried it. I hear sometimes it gets the job done. Maybe once in a while it even gets the job done without word getting around and turning you into radioactive waste, and without you spending the rest of your life feeling like a rat.

Your third option is to have a chat with the guy, tell him he needs to knock it off, for the sake of his conscience or his career or his family or whatever. Maybe this one sometimes works, too. I can just see the look on Breslin's face if I go finger-wagging at him about what a bold boy he's been. If I don't drown in the spill of self-righteous outrage, I'll spend what's left of my career trying to look over both shoulders at once.

Your fourth option is to go to your gaffer, who'll presumably give you wise fatherly pats on the shoulder, tell you you did the right thing, and do either Option 2 or Option 3 for you. Seeing what my relationship with O'Kelly is like, and what his relationship with Breslin is like, I'm gonna go ahead and figure that – even if I wanted to go running to Big Daddy for help – this one is off the table.

Your fifth option is to drop a couple of hints and get in on the action. Maybe you actually want to join in the fun; maybe you just want a little off the top of the other guy's kickback, in exchange for keeping your mouth shut. I don't like money enough to sell myself for it, and I don't like anything enough to tie my life to some scumbag who's already proven he can't be trusted.

Your sixth option is to find yourself a journalist, one who has balls the size of watermelons and doesn't mind being pulled over for drink-driving every other day for the rest of his life, and go full-on whistleblower.

None of those sound good to me. I'm loving this chase, every second of it. I don't give a damn whether that means I'm a bad person. But I know if we actually catch what we're hunting, it's probably gonna rip our faces off.

I'm having a hard time sitting still. Every few minutes I turn my head to look at Steve, sprawled over his desk like a student, fingers dug into that orange hair, frowning down at his whirlpool of paper. I can't tell what's going on in there. A couple of times I actually have my mouth open to ask him: *If. What do we do if?* Every time, I end up shutting my mouth again and going back to work.

The energy in an incident room usually dips in the middle of the afternoon, same as the energy in any office, but today it stays running high. Partly it's the room, making us all want to prove we're up to its standards, but partly it's me. The mood comes from the top, and that dare is whirling in my mind like a bad-boy lover, speeding up my heartbeat every time it bobs to the surface, beckoning and menacing. The wicked grin of it keeps me working flat out, and when I finish fine-tooth-combing reports it keeps me up and moving around the room, adding to the whiteboard, grabbing tip-line sheets – some anonymous guy is positive he's seen Aislinn on a very specialised website, stamping on bugs, which sounds unlikely but which the lucky people in Computer Crime will get to investigate anyway. I check out what the floaters are doing, toss out snippets of well-done and try-this – I can do the managerial shite just fine, when I feel like it. I have a laugh with Kellegher, tell Stanton and Deasy how their interviews with Aislinn's colleagues were bang on. Breslin would be proud of me. The thought of him – he should be back soon – sets me circling again.

Steve's caught it too: he's on the phone, trying to light a fire under his Meteor guy for the full records on that unregistered phone. We could go out, burn off that fizz interviewing witnesses, but I don't want to go anywhere. I don't want to miss Breslin.

Gaffney has finished his list of Aislinn's evening classes – which if I wasn't in a good mood would be depressing as hell: Aislinn genuinely paid actual money for a class called ReStyle You!, with the exclamation mark, also for one on wine appreciation and something called Busy Babes Boot Camp – and he's ringing round for lists of students. I take the financials off him and go through them for anomalies, while Breslin's not there to look over my shoulder.

No unexplained sums of money into or out of Aislinn's current account. The only thing that sticks out is that Lucy was right, Aislinn had a fair bit of cash: she opened a savings account the same month she started work, back in 2006, and most of her salary went straight in there. In the last couple of years she cut back on the saving and spent the extra on chichi clothes websites, but she still had over thirty grand stashed away. She wasn't carrying any debt – the Greystones home paid for the Stoneybatter cottage and for her crappy second-hand Polo, and she paid off her credit card by direct debit. If she wanted to go travelling or go to college, she would have been well able to do it. She would also have been well able to lend someone a few grand, if someone had asked.

Rory's financials are more complicated than Aislinn's, what with the bookshop, and nowhere near as healthy. Nothing remotely dodgy-looking – if there are gangsters in this case, they aren't laundering their cash through the Wayward Bookshop just to make our lives more interesting – but the business is barely keeping its head above water: in the five years Rory's owned it, sales have dropped by a third and he's had to let his part-timer go. The salary he's taking would look scabby to a burger-flipper. Breslin wasn't wrong about that Pestle dinner blowing the budget.

We've already seen how hard Rory takes humiliation. If he went begging to Aislinn and she slapped him down, his inner Hulk could well have burst his good going-out jumper.

I'm about to call Steve over for a look – he's up at the white-board – when a skinny kid with tufty fair hair and a crap suit sticks his head round the incident-room door. 'Um,' he says. 'Detective Conway?'

'Yeah.'

He edges between the desks to me like he expects someone to grab him in a headlock halfway. 'Detective O'Rourke sent me, from Missing Persons? Sorry it took so long; I've been downstairs for a while, actually, but some guy – um, I mean, another detective? – he told me you were out. He said I could give it to him, but Detective O'Rourke told me just you, so I was waiting? And then I thought maybe I should check, like just in case—'

'I'm here now,' I say. 'Let's have it.'

He vanishes again. I catch Steve's eye as he turns from the white-board, jerk my head to say *Over here*. None of the floaters seem to be paying any attention, but I'm not gonna bank on that.

'What's up?' Steve asks.

'The file on Aislinn's da. Don't make a big deal of it.'

The kid reappears lugging a cardboard box that probably weighs more than he does. Steve leans over his half of the desk and messes with paper, ignoring him.

'Oof,' the kid says, dumping the box by my chair and staggering backwards. 'And this.' He pulls an envelope out of his pocket and hands it over.

'Thanks,' I say. 'The guy who thought I was out: what'd he look like?'

The kid tries to disappear into his suit. I wait him out. 'Um,' he says, in the end. 'Like, late forties? Five ten, average build? Dark hair, kind of curly, some grey? Stubble?'

Which sounds a whole lot like McCann.

There's no good reason why McCann should give a damn what anyone's sending me.

'Great,' I say. 'I'll have to let him know I'm in here this week. Thanks.'

The kid hovers hopefully, waiting for his pat on the head. 'I'll tell Detective O'Rourke you did a good job,' I say. 'Bye.'

He edges off. Steve says, 'What guy who thought you were out?'

'Someone tried to intercept this stuff.' I know I sound paranoid. I don't care. 'McCann, by the sound of it.'

I watch Steve's mind go through the same steps mine did. 'Breslin doesn't know we're looking into Aislinn's da.'

'Right. McCann wasn't after this, specifically; he was just going for it because it was there.'

Steve says, 'Breslin'll be back soon. You want to take this lot somewhere else?'

'Fuck that.' It won't do any good – if Breslin gets in while we're gone, someone's gonna tell him we disappeared hauling a great big box of paper. And besides, this is my incident room. I'm fucked if I'm gonna scuttle off to some closet. 'We'll read fast.'

I'm already ripping open the envelope. Steve pulls his chair towards mine – casually, checking his phone for messages at the same time, nothing important going on here.

The note says, *Hiya Conway, file on your missing guy. Word of advice as a mate, no back seat driving OK? You don't like anything keep your big gob shut. I did a bit on the case so any questions give me a ring. GO'R*

'Huh?' Steve says. 'Keep your gob shut about what?'

'No clue.' I stick the letter in my pocket, for the shredder. 'Might make sense once we've had a look through that lot.'

We read the initial report together, me keeping one eye on the room to see if any of the floaters are looking interested. The lead D was a guy called Feeney; I saw his name on old paperwork when I was in Missing Persons, but he retired years before I came on board. He's probably dead by now. If we need the inside scoop, we'll just have to hope Gary's got it.

In 1998, Desmond Joseph Murray was thirty-three years old, a taxi driver, living in Greystones and working out of Dublin city centre. The photos attached to the file show a slight guy, medium height, with neat brown hair and a sweet, lopsided smile. I barely clocked him in Aislinn's photo albums. So busy staring at her and hoping her face would trigger my memory, I missed what was right in front of me.

There's one family shot in there. The wife was small, dark, groomed and good-looking; very good-looking, in the big-eyed, pouty, helpless way that makes me want to heave. And there's Aislinn, with her too-tight plaits and a big grin, snuggled into the circle of her father's arm.

'You know who he reminds me of?' Steve says. 'Our boy Rory.'

I tilt the photo my way. He's right; they don't look alike, exactly, but they're definitely the same type. 'For fuck's *sake*,' I say. 'What a bleeding cliché. How badly did that stupid bitch need to get a grip?'

'She was trying to. Give her credit for that, at least.'

Clouds are building up, making the light at the windows shift and heave; the incident room feels precarious and at risk, a ship on a bad sea or an island house with a storm coming in. Something – that light, maybe, or Steve's quiet voice dissipating out through all the empty space, fading to nothing before it can reach the walls – something makes the words sound, out of nowhere, massively sad. I don't feel like giving Aislinn credit for anything, or like giving a fuck about her except in terms of basic professional pride, but just for that moment everything about her seems dense enough with sadness to drop you like a sandbag.

I say, 'What I think of her doesn't matter. Read.'

Just after three in the afternoon of the fifth of February, Desmond left home in his taxi to follow his usual Thursday routine: pick up his nine-year-old daughter Aislinn from school, drop her home, then head into Dublin to work until the closing-time crowds died down around one in the morning. He picked up Aislinn and dropped her off according to plan. That was the last his family saw of him.

Around four in the morning his wife Evelyn woke up, realised he wasn't there and started to worry. Desmond had a mobile phone, but he wasn't answering it; at six she rang the taxi company he worked for, but he didn't answer their radio either. At ten in the morning she rang the local uniforms. The initial report said 'informant was distressed', which is code for 'freaking the fuck out'. The local guys checked hospitals and stations, found nothing, and told her Desmond was probably taking a bit of time to himself and would be back by evening. When he wasn't, and the informant had got distressed enough that her doctor had to come round and give her a sedative, they called in Missing Persons.

'Matches Lucy's story,' Steve says. He scoops a thick wad of dusty paper out of the box, hands half of it to me and slides over to his own side of the desk.

'So far,' I say. 'Remember: go fast.'

Steve starts skimming. I swing my feet up on the desk and have a quick discreet scan of the room, over paper, but none of the floaters are looking our way; all of them are working away, busy as good little schoolkids, in the uneasy light.

Evelyn's statement swore the marriage was wonderful, childhood sweethearts living their happy-ever-after; the paper is gooey with how he still brought her red roses and told her every day that she was the love of his life. It sounds like bollix to me, but the neighbours didn't contradict her – no one had ever heard them arguing, nothing like that. The financial records came up clean: Desmond and Evelyn weren't rich, but they weren't broke, either. Their parents had left enough, between them, to pay off most of the Murrays' mortgage and Desmond's taxi licence – and those went for anything up to a hundred grand, back then. There were no other debts; the current account had no suspiciously large deposits and no weird withdrawals to say someone had been buying coke or hitting the betting shops. Desmond had no history of mental illness. He had no criminal record – a few speeding tickets, few parking tickets, what you'd expect from a taxi man. His friends said he was a happy guy, outgoing, worked hard and liked his work, had no enemies and wasn't the type to make any. Their version of the marriage didn't match Evelyn's – according to them, Evelyn basically kept Des prisoner, never wanted to do anything but cried for days if he did anything without her, freaked out if he didn't answer his mobile fast enough – but none of them had ever heard Des say anything about leaving her, although most of them figured he was just sticking around for the kid and would be out of there the day she left home. This case isn't sounding like a full box's worth of mystery to me. I spot Gary's signature, neater and younger-looking than the one I'm used to, at the bottom of a sheet.

'Statement from Aislinn,' Steve says. 'Look.'

It's signed in careful, round kid-writing. The day Desmond went missing, he and Aislinn didn't talk much on the drive home from school; she had a homework assignment that she didn't understand and she was worried about getting in trouble if she couldn't do it, so she was mainly thinking about that. She didn't notice anything odd about her da, but it sounded like she wouldn't have anyway. The only thing that stood out to her was his goodbye, when he pulled up in front of their gate and she opened the car door to get out. He told her he loved her and to be a good girl, same as always; but then he pulled her over to him, gave her a hug – not part of their routine – and told her to look after her mammy. He watched her to the house and he was still there, waving, when she closed the door.

'There's your answer right there,' Steve says. 'The guy did a runner.'

'Yeah, he did. So what's the rest of this shite?' I nod at the cardboard box, which is still maybe a third full. This is where I would expect the file to end. Grown man, no reason to kill himself, no history of mental illness, no enemies, a pretty obvious goodbye to his kid: normally you would send one last press release to the media and assume he's gone because he wants to be and he'll come home in his own good time, or not.

Only Missing Persons didn't stop there. They pulled Desmond's mobile records – which took a few weeks: mobiles weren't big back then, Ds didn't have contacts in the phone companies, so they had to go through the official channels – and tracked down everyone he'd contacted in months. Most of the numbers turned out to be either his mates or his regular taxi customers, ringing Desmond direct instead of going through the dispatcher, and they were all able to account for their whereabouts at the time of his disappearance.

The question was why anyone had asked them to. Missing Persons is chronically short on manpower, same as every other squad; normally they put it into the custody-dispute toddler or the walk-about Alzheimer's granny, not the midlife crisis. I say, 'The way they worked it. Does that seem off to you?'

Steve says, 'They were very bloody thorough.'

'Yeah. Getting alibis off his customers? They worked this like they thought it was a murder.'

'If Des Murray was on the radar for gang-related activity, even minor stuff, they would've pushed the case all the way. In case he was getting to be a liability, and someone gave him two in the back of the head and dumped him up the mountains.'

'I haven't found anything that points to gangs. You?'

Steve shakes his head. 'Me neither. They might not have put it in the file, though.'

Which is true enough. If Feeney didn't feel like handing over his case to Organised Crime, he would have kept any gang-related ideas to himself, same as we have. I say, 'Keep reading.'

Des Murray's cab showed up on a side street in Dún Laoghaire, which moved suicide a couple of notches up the list – Dún Laoghaire has nice long convenient piers – except that there was no note in the taxi. No signs of a struggle, either, and no robbery: there was thirty-four quid, which matched the afternoon's fares on the meter, tucked down by the gearstick. If Des had done a runner, he had left his wife and kid every penny he could.

The tip line rings; Stanton dives for it, listens, and explains that we don't think Aislinn Murray was ordering a vodka and diet Coke in a club in Waterford last night, on account of her deadness, but thanks for calling. A couple of the other floaters snort, down at their desks. No one looks up.

'Whoa,' Steve says – quietly, but the note in his voice snaps my head up. 'Here we go.'

I shove my foot off the desk, spin my chair over to his side. 'Let's see.'

It's a report on another of the contacts off Desmond Murray's phone. The number was a mobile registered to a Vanessa O'Shaughnessy, but it took the Ds a while to track her down. This turned out to be because she had left the country. She had taken a boat to England, on the sixth of February.

'Oh yeah,' I say. 'Bet that got everyone's attention.' It definitely gets mine. The ferry to England leaves from Dún Laoghaire.

Steve flips pages: report on Vanessa O'Shaughnessy. We skim fast. She was twenty-eight, a dental nurse, sharing a house in Dublin with a couple of other women. The photo shows a freckly redhead with a wicked, vivid grin – nowhere near the looker Evelyn was, but I'm betting you'd get a lot more crack out of Vanessa. Almost two years before Desmond Murray went missing, she had started ringing or texting him every Sunday afternoon. According to her flatmates, he had brought her to visit her ma, who had Parkinson's disease and was in a nursing home somewhere in West Dublin with no bus service, and they had agreed to make it a regular gig. The actual texts, once they came in from the phone company, bore that out: *Hi des, vanessa here, just checking are you still ok to pick me up at 3? . . . Hi vanessa, yes i'll be there, see you then.*

After a few months, the phone calls and texts started getting more frequent – twice a week, three times, then almost every day. The flatmates said Vanessa's ma had been getting sicker, so Vanessa had been visiting her more often. There was still nothing incriminating in the texts. *Hi, are we still on for tomorrow evening?* and *Yes please, I'll be ready at 7.* The odd smiley face; nothing more intimate than that.

'All business,' Steve says.

'It would be, either way. The wife knew he had a mobile. And she sounds like the type who'd check it.'

On the second of January, five weeks before Des Murray went missing, Vanessa's ma died. After the funeral, she told her housemates and her boss that she was ditching her job and moving to England, for a fresh start. On the sixth of February, she was gone and so was Des.

Report from the nursing home, saying Vanessa's ma had died unexpectedly, hadn't been getting worse over the last while, and Vanessa had never visited more than twice a week. Missing Persons called in a favour from someone's pal in England, who found out that Desmond Murray had applied for a taxi licence in Liverpool. Then they called in another favour from someone's pal in Liverpool, who went to Murray's address and verified that he was alive and well and shacked up with Vanessa O'Shaughnessy. And that's the end of the file.

'Surprise, surprise,' I say. 'Some guy got bored of his wife and swapped her for a newer model. No gangs there. And nothing to do with our case, either, as far as I can see.'

Steve says, 'But why didn't Missing Persons tell the family? Aislinn hadn't a clue about any of this. Why didn't they just say it to Evelyn Murray at the time?'

If you track down a missing person and he wants you to say nothing – and plenty of them do – then you're supposed to keep your mouth shut. Normally, though, you make sure the general idea gets across, if only because you don't want it on your conscience when some rent boy's ma ODs on her Valium because she's convinced a serial killer got him. This is exactly the kind of case that should have got a carefully worded hint – *Obviously we can't release details of the investigation, Mrs Murray, but I can tell you that we don't expect to be asking you to identify a body* . . . For some reason, Feeney and his boys decided not to go there.

'Unless,' Steve says. 'Unless there was something dodgy going on, and the Ds were protecting the family.'

'Or maybe they did tell the wife, and she didn't pass it on to the kid.'

'For fifteen years? Even when the kid was a grown adult? When she was desperate to find out what had happened to her da?'

I shrug. 'People are weird. You heard Lucy: the ma was ashamed that her husband was gone. Maybe she was too ashamed to tell her daughter why.'

Steve is licking his finger and flipping back through his pile of paper, occasionally pulling out a page or two to add to a stack on his desk. 'Nah. That note from your mate, about the back-seat driving? This is what he meant: the Ds didn't tell the family, and if you think they should've, keep that to yourself.'

'I do think the Ds should've told the family. It would've saved us a shitload of time and hassle.'

Steve glances up at that. 'They should've told the family, full stop. Even if there was dodgy stuff in the background, they should have dropped a hint that he was *alive*.'

'Maybe.' I start tapping my half of the file back into a stack. 'I'll ring Gary, ask him what the story was.'

'You don't think they should've?'

'I don't know. Do I look like the Pope to you? Fancy moral decisions aren't my job.'

'What would you have done if it was your case? Would you have kept your mouth shut? Seriously?'

'I would've transferred to Murder. Where this kind of shite doesn't come up.'

'I'd've told them,' Steve says. I go to dump my paper back in the box; he takes it off me, adds it to his and keeps flipping. 'No question. Aislinn's own da? Your woman's husband? They had a right to know. If they'd known what they were dealing with, it might not have messed up their lives, or anyway not as much.'

I'm pulling out my phone, but that brings my head round. 'Yeah? Because *what*? Unless they know where Daddykins is, they've got no choice except to lock themselves in the gaff and sit around obsessing about him? There's no way they could get on with their lives, no?'

It comes out with more edge than I meant it to. Steve stops messing with paper. 'Come on. I didn't say that. Just . . . if they're spending half their time waiting for the da to walk back in the door, and the other half picturing him dumped someplace up the mountains, then yeah, their heads are gonna be wrecked.'

I dial Gary's number and keep an eye on the door for Breslin. 'Then they shouldn't have spent their time like that. The Ds didn't force them to. Get a hobby. Knit something.'

Steve starts to say, carefully, 'I don't think it's—' but I hold up a finger: the phone's ringing.

Voicemail again. I refuse to start worrying about why Gary doesn't want to talk to me. 'Hey, Gary, it's Antoinette. We got the stuff; thanks. We've had a look; your guy can pick it up any time.' I'm not about to hand that box over to any of our floaters. 'And give me a ring when you get a chance, yeah? I've just got a couple of follow-up questions, and I'd rather run them past you than go chasing anyone else. Talk then.'

I hang up. 'If he doesn't want me hassling the original Ds, that should get his attention. And if there was anything dodgy going on, he'll let me know, to make me quit poking around.'

'This is all the main stuff,' Steve says, holding up the stack of pages he's pulled out of the file. 'I want photocopies. Just in case.' He sweeps a handful of random paper off his desk, shoves the statements into the middle and heads off at a casual lope, no hurry, nothing worth noticing here.

I kick the file box under our desk, till Gary can send the crap-suit kid to pick it up. There's no reason Breslin shouldn't see it – there's nothing to see, as far as we can tell – but I don't want him to. I tell myself that's just good sense, no matter what: if there's nothing in the file, I don't need Breslin giving us flak for wasting our time. Then I spread out Rory's financials again and pretend to be fascinated by them, for the benefit of Breslin's pocket poodle, whoever that is.

My instincts are good – not bragging: every D's are, specially every D who makes it as far as Murder – and I know how to use them. They've come through for me when all the solid detective work in the world would have run me into a brick wall. But this time they're being bugger-all use. Not that they're out of commission – every sensor is firing wildly, red lights flashing, beeping noises everywhere – but they just keep sweeping, can't pin anything down. Rory's keeping something back, but I can't tell whether it's the murder or not; Breslin's fucking with us, but I can't figure out why. I feel like I'm missing the bleeding obvious here, but the harder I concentrate, the more all the signals turn to noise. Something is scrambling them.

Another D, one with more experience than me, would be well able to do that. The other thing Ds are good at, as well as using their own instincts: wrecking other people's. Suspects don't make mistakes because they're morons, or at least not all of them. They make mistakes because we know how to baffle them into it.

Someone wants me to make a mistake. And I'm a couple of hundred miles out to sea with all my systems going haywire.

That doesn't faze me too much, not in itself. Danger isn't the thing scrambling my signals; it's the only thing keeping me clear-headed enough that I have a chance of navigating my way out of this. I watch Steve, heading back between the desks with a brand-new blue folder sticking out from his handful of random paperwork, and I really hope he works the same way.

9

Breslin gets in not long after, banging open the incident-room door and telling the world, 'Jesus Christ, the suspect's mates. Bloody history teachers everywhere. Anyone want to know about the curve of murder rates since the foundation of the Free State?'

It's like being a teenager and seeing someone you fancy: that slam of electricity, straight through the breastbone and in. 'Howya,' I say.

The floaters give Breslin the laugh he's looking for, but he doesn't bother acknowledging it; his eyes are on me and Steve. 'Any updates?'

'Cooper rang,' I say.

'And?'

'And two possibilities. Either a great big bodybuilder gave her a hell of a punch, she went over backwards and smashed her head on the fireplace. Or else someone – wouldn't need to be a bodybuilder – gave her a push, she fell on the fireplace with no serious damage done, and he went after her and punched her while she was down.'

That stops Breslin moving, and for a second his face goes blank. Behind the blank, his mind is going ninety. Same as me and Steve, he has trouble picturing Rory getting that hardcore, and he's not happy about it.

He covers it fast, though. 'Bodybuilder,' he says, with a wry snort. 'No harm to Cooper, but what a typical lab-jockey thing to say. If he'd spent any time in the trenches, he'd know that even a wimp like Rory can come up with one good punch, if he's pissed off enough.'

Which is what I thought, but coming out of him it sounds like something I shouldn't fall for. 'Maybe,' I say.

Breslin threads his way between the desks to us, giving Stanton a clap on the shoulder along the way. 'We'll have to ask Rory, won't we? We'll have fun with that, next time we get him in.'

'He won't know what's hit him,' Steve says helpfully. The blue folder has vanished into the paper on his desk.

'Any more than she did,' Breslin says, inevitably, but his heart isn't in it. 'I hear you've been getting deliveries. Anything nice to share with the group?'

Me and Steve look at each other, all puzzled. Steve says, 'The vic's phone records, yeah?'

'Not unless she made an awful lot of calls. McCann said you had a big box of something so special, the delivery boy wouldn't let it out of his hot little hands.' He nudges the corner of the box, sticking out from under our desk, with the toe of his shiny shoe. 'Would this be it?'

His eyes are hooded and watching me, just on the edge of too casual. There's no point trying to dodge, not unless I'm prepared to rugby-tackle him off the box; and anyway, all of a sudden I've had enough of tiptoeing around Big Bad Breslin, hiding my own investigation behind my back like a kid with a smoke when a teacher walks past. 'That? Aislinn's da went missing when she was a kid,' I say, and watch his face. 'Moran thought there might be a link. Like maybe a gang thing, or a reunion gone wrong.'

Breslin's eyes pop. 'A *gang* thing? Moran. Conway. Are you serious? You think *gangs* kidnapped Aislinn's dad, and then came back for her twenty years later? I'm loving this. Tell me more.'

He's just about managing to keep the laugh in. Steve ducks his head and goes red. 'Ah, no, it wasn't that we really . . . I mean, I just wondered.' He's back in gormless-newbie mode, but the redner is real.

Part of me is actually with Breslin on this, but I've got other stuff on my mind. His face, when I told him what was in the box: just for a tenth of a second, I saw his mouth go slack with relief. Whatever he's trying to steer us away from, Aislinn's da isn't it.

'So don't keep me in suspense,' Breslin says. He's still grinning. 'Whodunit? Drug lords? Arms smugglers? The Mafia?'

'The da did,' I say. 'Turns out he did a runner to England to shack up with some young one. And no reunion gone wrong: there's no unaccounted-for contact in Aislinn's electronics.'

I think I see that tiny explosion of relief on Breslin's face again, but before I can be sure, it's gone under a blast of jaw-dropped fake amazement. 'No!' He recoils, one hand going up to his chest. 'You're kidding me. Who would've guessed?'

He's overdoing it. Breslin is too old a hand for that. He wants, too badly, to embarrass us away from the gang idea.

'I know,' Steve says, doing a rueful nod-and-shrug thing. 'I do, honest. I just didn't want to miss anything, you know?'

'Shaking trees,' Breslin says dryly. The grin is gone. 'Wasn't that the phrase? I'm not convinced that's how the taxpayers would want us using their money, but hey, I'm not the one running this show. You keep shaking. Let me know if anything ever falls out.'

'Will do,' Steve says. 'I was hoping . . .' He rumples up his hair and looks hangdog.

Breslin shrugs off his coat and throws it over the back of his chair – he picked a desk good and close to ours, which makes me feel all special. 'There's a fine line between hope and desperation. You have to know when to let it go, as the song says.'

'It's gone,' I say. 'Does McCann want a go of the file, yeah? Before we send it back to Missing Persons?'

That gets me a stare. 'McCann was trying to help you out, Conway. It's called being nice. You might want to learn to accept it without throwing a wobbler.'

Steve moves in his chair, trying to beam peaceful thought-waves into my head. 'I'll send him a thank-you card,' I say. 'How'd Gaffney do, yesterday evening?'

'Fine. He's not the brightest little pixie in the forest, but he'll get there in the end.'

I say, 'Then how come you ditched him today?'

Breslin is giving his coat a brush-down and a few twitches to make sure it won't get creased – and to make sure we notice the Armani label – but that brings his head up to stare at me. 'Say what?'

'He was supposed to be shadowing you. He says you told him you didn't need him for the KA interviews.'

'I didn't. I can write and listen at the same time. Multitasking, Conway: it's not just for the ladies any more.'

'Good to hear. Gaffney needed you, though. That's why I told him to stick with you in the first place: I don't want some rookie screwing up because no one's shown him the ropes. Why'd you leave him behind?'

I'm expecting the same clamp-jawed fake matiness I got this morning. That's half the reason I'm giving him hassle: I want Steve to have a look at this. Instead, Breslin leans in conspiratorially, with a grin lifting one corner of his mouth. 'Conway. Come on. Cut a guy some slack. Every now and then a man's got an appointment he needs to keep all by his lonesome. Know what I mean?' And he shoots me an actual wink.

Meaning he stopped off along the way to stick his dick somewhere it shouldn't be. Which would explain not just him ditching Gaffney, but the person who shouldn't have been ringing his mobile this morning.

I don't buy it. In a squad where cheating strategies count as coffee-break chat, Breslin and McCann get called The Monks. The grape-vine says neither of them has ever even given the eye to a pretty uniform, or tried to chat up the Bureau babe who everyone tries to chat up. Breslin probably thinks me and Steve are too far out of the loop to know that. He's forgotten that we haven't always been Murder's resident rejects, and forgotten how kids longing for Murder suck up every drop of gossip about the tall shining creatures they might someday become.

'Say no more,' Steve says quickly, lifting his hands. He has on a grin halfway between embarrassed and impressed, but I'm pretty sure he's thinking the same thing as me. 'A gentleman never tells.'

'No he does not, Moran. Thank you very much.'

'Fair enough,' I say, matching Steve's grin. 'I guess it's not like Gaffney could do a lot of damage playing with paper in here. How'd you get on with Rory's KAs?'

'Great chats all round.' Breslin swings himself into his chair, switches on his computer and has a stretch while it boots up. 'They're a shower of dry shites, the type who correct your grammar and think three drinks is a wild night out, but I'd say they're too terrified of us to do any major lying. They all say the same things about Rory: the guy's a sweetheart, wouldn't hurt a fly – one of his mates told me he won't even watch boxing because it's just too distressing. What a pussy.'

Sounds about right: Rory doesn't like reality getting all up in his face. 'Even pussies lose the head,' I say.

Breslin throws me a finger-snap and a point. 'Exactly, Conway. They do. I was about to point that out myself. And all the KAs agree that their pal Rory was head over heels about Aislinn: he hadn't shut up about her since they first met. They say it like it's a good thing: aww, look, he was so smitten he would never do anything bad to his sweetie! I don't think it's occurred to them that there's a fine line between smitten and obsessed.' He glances up from pulling his notebook out of his pocket. 'Nice to hear one of you two admitting that the obsessed boyfriend on the scene might actually be a suspect. Detective Conway, do I get the sense you're getting just a leetle bit tired of tree-shaking?'

'Nah,' I say. 'It's good exercise. But like you say, unless something big falls out, Rory's what we've got. A bit more solid evidence, and we'll be good to go. Did you run the voices past the guy at Stoneybatter who took the call?'

'Yeah, about that. Just a word in your ear, Conway . . .' Breslin glances at the floaters and lowers his voice. 'You need to learn how to allocate resources appropriately. I know that sounds like boring manager-type crap, but you're running investigations now; like it or not, you're a manager. And it doesn't take a Murder D with twenty years' experience to hit Play half a dozen times.'

Someone's ego wouldn't fit through the door of Stoneybatter station. Steve moves again. 'Got it,' I say sheepishly. 'Will we send Gaffney? Just so he knows he's not in your bad books?'

'Now you're thinking like a lead D. Let's do that. You tell him, so he knows who's boss around here; how's that?' Breslin gives me his wise-teacher smile, which is kind and crinkly and would make me feel warm all over if I was dumber than a bag of hair.

'Thanks,' I say, all grateful. 'That'd be great.' I swivel my chair around – without looking at Steve, in case one of us gets the giggles – and call, 'Gaffney. Over here. Job for you.'

Gaffney nearly falls over his own chair, he's in such a hurry to get over to us. 'Here you go,' Breslin says, tossing him a voice recorder. 'Those are voice samples: Rory Fallon, his brothers and all his male pals.' He lifts an eyebrow at me and tilts his chin towards Gaffney, to make sure it's obvious that he's cueing me.

I say, 'Take that down to Stoneybatter station and see if any of the voices ring a bell with your man. If he's got any doubts, organise a voice lineup. Can you do that?'

Gaffney's holding the recorder to his chest like it's precious. 'I can, yeah. No bother. I will. I'll do that.' He's so busy head-flipping back and forth between me and Breslin, trying to work out who's the boss here, he can barely make sentences.

'Thanks,' Breslin says, whipping out the smile. 'Do me a favour: pick me up a sandwich on your way back. Ham, cheese and salad on brown, no onion. I didn't get a chance to eat lunch, and I'm starving.' He throws me and Steve another wink, as he pulls out cash to give Gaffney. 'Sorry, no change.'

It's a fifty. I'm close enough to see where he took it out of: a solid wad of them, in his shirt pocket, tucked inside a crumpled white envelope.

I was right about my voice message giving Gary a kick up the arse: five minutes later my phone lights up with his name. No way am I gonna take this call with Breslin sitting five feet away, and no way am I gonna make a big deal of taking it outside. I mutter, 'Fuck's sake, Ma, I'm at *work*,' to myself, swipe Reject Call and shove the phone back into my pocket too hard. I glance across, doing embarrassed, to see if Breslin heard; his eyes are on the statement he's typing up, but he's got a twitch of a grin on his face.

I wait fifteen minutes – I'd love to leave it longer, but it's five o'clock, and we've got the case meeting at half past – before I head out of the incident room, leaving my coat and my bag behind. With a bit of luck Breslin will assume I'm ringing my mammy back. I don't look at Steve. I'm hoping I don't need to.

· Outside it's dark; the whitish floodlights and the thick cold, and the odd civil servant scurrying home with his collar turned up, give the huge courtyard a queasy, ominous feel, some looming futurescape I've stumbled into by mistake and can't find the way out of. I find a shadow, wrap my suit jacket tight and watch the clock on my phone.

Four minutes later the door opens and Steve nips out, trying to keep a massive armful of paper under control and close the door behind him without letting it bang. 'About time,' I say, catching a page that's escaping.

'Let's get out of here. I'm supposed to be photocopying this shite. If Breslin goes looking for me—'

'That's the best you could come up with? Come on, quick—' We dodge around the corner of the building, laughing at our bold selves like schoolkids mitching, which I suppose is better than thinking too hard about the fact that Incident Room C is supposedly all mine and yet here I am freezing my hole off.

You can see the gardens from our windows, and in the courtyard we might meet Gaffney coming back from Stoneybatter. We head up to the square outside the main Castle buildings, where only tourists go – not that there are any tourists in this weather – and find a corner out of the wind. The buildings feel a hundred feet tall around us; the floodlights strip out colour and texture till they could be made of anything, beaten metal or slick plastic or thin air.

Steve dumps his paper on the ground, with a foot on the pile to stop it blowing away. He's in his shirtsleeves; he's gonna freeze. I hold the phone between us, dial and hit speaker.

'Hey,' Gary says. 'You got the stuff, yeah?'

Gary is ten years older than me and perfect for his job. A big chunk of Missing Persons is getting people who stay far from cops to talk to you – street hookers to tell you about the new girl who matches that teenager on the news, homeless addicts to drop by and mention the guy who tried to sleep on their patch last night and looked a lot like that poster and do they get a reward? Everyone talks to Gary, and he'll talk to anyone, which is one reason I pointed Aislinn his way. Another big chunk of the job is wrangling the friends and families, and Gary can calm down a room just by walking into it; I once saw him trace an idiot teenage runaway in ten minutes flat, by getting her hysterical idiot best friend to chill out enough to remember the internet boyfriend's name. He's a big guy, he looks like he could build a shed if you needed one, and he has the kind of voice – quiet, deep, a touch of countryside – that makes you want to close your eyes and fall asleep to the sound of it. Just hearing that voice winds me down a notch.

'Hey,' I say. Gary's in the Missing Persons squad room: I can hear the weave of chat, someone giving out, someone else laughing, a mobile ringing. 'Yeah, I got it. You're a gem. Just a couple of quick questions, OK? And do me a favour: can you go somewhere private?'

'No problem. Hang on a mo—' The creak of his chair, some comment with a grin built in from one of the other lads, 'Yeah yeah yeah,' from Gary. 'Smart-arsed little bollix wants to know if my prostate's giving me hassle,' he tells me. 'Young people nowadays; no respect.'

'Awww, Gar. It's OK. I respect you.'

'At least you don't mock my prostate. Never mock a man's prostate. That's dirty.'

'Below the belt, yeah?'

'Holy Jaysus. Is that what passes for humour over there?' A door shuts, and the voices vanish: he's out in the corridor. 'Right. What did you want to know?'

Steve has his head up, keeping an eye on the entrances to the square, but he's listening. 'First thing,' I say. 'You guys went all out on the Desmond Murray case. Everything looked like he'd skipped voluntarily, it turned out he *had* skipped voluntarily, but yous worked it like a murder. How come?'

Gary snorts. 'There's an easy one. Because of the wife, basically. Did you see the photo?'

'Yeah. She was good-looking.'

'The photo doesn't do her justice. She was a stunner. Not the kind you want to get in kinky underwear and shag senseless; the kind you want to look after. Open doors for her. Hold her umbrella.' Gary's voice getting fainter, water running, clink of cups; he's rinsing a mug in the kitchen, phone tucked under his jaw. 'And she knew how to work it, too. Looking at us like we were superheroes, going on about how she knew we'd find her husband and she felt so lucky to have us, she didn't know *what* she'd have done if her whole world had been in the hands of people she couldn't trust the way she trusted us – loads of that. Crying at all the right moments, and making sure she looked good while she was doing it – her husband's just gone missing, but she's still bothered to do her hair and her makeup and put on a pretty dress? She knew what she was at, all right.'

Sounds like Aislinn took after Mammy. 'You think it was all an act? She didn't give a damn about the hubby, just wanted attention?'

Gary clicks his tongue. 'Nah, not that. The opposite of that. I think she was genuinely desperate to get her husband back – she wasn't the social type, didn't have friends, didn't have a job, didn't have anything apart from him and the kid; without him, her life was bollixed. And she knew the best way to make fellas go out of their way for her was by being pretty and making them want to take care of her.'

'Cute,' I say. I can hear the coffee machine whirring – instead of bitching nonstop about the crap coffee, the way we do in Murder, Missing Persons threw in a few quid each and bought a decent machine. 'And it worked.'

'Yeah. That type doesn't do a lot for me, but a couple of the lads would've brought out the army to comb the country for her husband, if they could've. Tracking down a few mobiles, interviewing a few extra witnesses . . . that was nothing.'

He remembers a lot about this woman, for someone who wasn't into her. I keep my mouth shut – Gary brings out my nice side. 'So it wasn't because anyone suspected Murray might've been involved with gangs?'

Gary laughs. 'Jesus, no. Nothing like that. Pure as the driven snow, Murray was. When it came to the law, at least.'

I throw Steve a look. He grimaces: still unconvinced. He's got his hands tucked into his armpits to keep them warm.

I roll my eyes and say, into the phone, 'You sure you would've heard?'

'Thanks a bunch, Antoinette.'

'Come on, Gar, you know I'm not being a bitch here. But you had to be, what, twenty-six, twenty-seven? Out of uniform for like three weeks? The lead Ds weren't necessarily telling you everything that went through their heads.'

The faint clinking of Gary stirring his coffee. He says, 'Is that what it was like when you were here? You figure I held stuff back from you, just to keep the rookie in her place?'

I say, 'No. You would've told me.'

Missing Persons isn't like Murder. In Missing Persons, you don't work your case aiming to take down a bad guy; you work it aiming to get a happy ending. If it even looks like there might be a bad guy to take down, mostly it's not your problem any more – say a body shows up looking dodgy, you hand it straight over to Murder. You can go your entire career without ever using your handcuffs. That attracts a whole different type from Murder or Sex Crime, the squads where your mind is focused on the kill shot and happy endings aren't on the menu, and it makes for a whole different atmosphere. Missing Persons was never my kind of place, but just for a second I'm swamped by how badly I want to be back there. I can smell the good coffee, hear Gar hamming up 'Bring Him Home' after a happy ending while everyone shouts at him to shut up and take it to *X Factor*; I'm coming up with new places to hide that rubber hamster. Like a little kid, wanting to run home to Mammy as soon as the going gets tough. I make myself sick.

'Yeah, I would've,' Gary says. 'It was the same back then: if the lead Ds were thinking gangs, they would've told me. Where'd this gang idea come from?'

I keep my head angled away from Steve, in case that burst of wimp shows on my face. 'Murray's daughter, the one I sent to you when she came asking about him? She's after turning up murdered.'

'Huh,' Gary says, surprised but not shocked. 'God rest. She seemed like a sweet kid, way back when; sweet girl, when she came in to me. You think she got involved with a gang?'

'Not really. It looks like the boyfriend threw a tantrum, but there's some loose ends we want to clear up, just in case. We were wondering if she went looking for Daddy and trod on someone's toes.'

'No reason she would've. There's nothing that would've pointed her anywhere dodgy.'

I really wanted Gary to tell me that something, anything, was dodgy here. I can feel it soaking through me along with the cold, just how badly I wanted it. I can't tell whether I knew all along that he wasn't going to.

Steve whispers, 'The Ds. Why'd they keep their mouths shut?'

'Second thing,' I say. 'Any reason why yous didn't just tell them at the time where Daddy had gone?'

Gary makes an exasperated noise, through a mouthful of coffee. 'Antoinette. I wasn't joking you about the back-seat driving. It wasn't your case; how they worked it isn't your problem. You start shooting your mouth off about how you would've done it differently, all you'll do is piss people off. You think you can afford that?'

Meaning word is getting around. Missing Persons have been informed that I'm poison. Even if I wanted to transfer back there, the gaffer probably wouldn't take me. He knows I'm good, but no one wants a D who brings hassle with her. Whether it's her own hassle or other people's is beside the point.

I say, 'So don't make me go shooting my mouth off. Quit the hush-hush crap and tell me what was going on, and I won't have to talk to the other Ds.'

'There isn't any hush-hush crap. By the time they tracked Murray down, I wasn't working the case any more – I was only on board for the initial push – so I don't know all the details. All I heard is, they found him in England, tucked up in his love nest with the bit on the side. One of our lads gave him a bell: he was happy as a pig in shite, no intention of coming home, and he didn't want anyone telling his wife and kid anything. So they didn't.'

Gary takes the silence for disapproval – which it isn't: I wouldn't have got involved in that mess, either. It's some thicko part of me still hoping this isn't the whole story. He says, 'We're not family therapists here. You know that. It's not our job to sort out some fella's love triangle; it's our job to find the fella, and they did. They marked the case closed and moved on.'

Steve makes a wry face, up at the flat dark windows staring back: that's still getting to him. I ask, 'Without even telling the wife that Desmond was alive? You said she had all the Ds wrapped around her finger, jumping through hoops to bring her answers; but when they actually find some, they don't let her anywhere near them?'

'I'm just telling you what I heard. And I'm telling you not to go giving anyone shite about it. What's it got to do with your case, either way?'

'Nothing, probably. Like I said: just tying up loose ends. Shaking trees.' I flick an eyebrow at Steve, who narrows his eyes at me: *Very funny*. 'One last thing. I know it's been a couple of years, but can you tell me what you said to Aislinn when she came in to you?'

Gary slurps coffee and thinks back. 'She had a fair idea we knew more than we'd told her and her mam. She said her mam had died and she was desperate to find her dad. According to her, him vanishing had messed up her entire life. She wanted to track him down, look him in the eye and make him tell her why he did it. She wasn't sure what was going to happen after that – she said something about once he saw her he'd remember how close they'd been, maybe they could have each other back . . . But even if it didn't work out that way, according to her, once she knew the story she could move on. Make a life of her own.'

Sweet jumping Jesus on a pogo stick. I'm on Des Murray's side here. He probably split because the alternative was braining his whole sappy family with a poker. 'What'd you give her?'

'I told her I couldn't disclose any information from the investigation. But . . . sure, you saw her. She was in bits. She was trying not to cry, but she was right on the edge of it. She was begging me; for a second there I was scared she was going to go down on her knees on the floor of the interview room. In the end I put in a call, had a mate run Desmond Murray through the UK system, just to see was he dead or alive. No point in her chasing him all over the world if he was six feet under.'

Aislinn was Mammy's daughter, all right; she might have looked helpless, but she knew how to make people do what she wanted. Even I ended up handing over Gary's name and shift schedule. I'm liking her less all the time.

Gary says, 'And I thought, if he was still alive, I might drop her a hint that she'd do better hiring a private detective in England. Sure, what harm?'

Missing Persons: happy-ending junkies, the lot of them. 'And?'

'And he was dead. A few years back. Nothing suspicious, he just died – heart attack, I think.'

And that's Daddy out of the picture. I almost laugh out loud with relief. Instead I elbow Steve and mouth *See?* He shrugs: *It was worth a shot.* I roll my eyes.

Gary says, 'Left a missus – well, give or take: he never married your one he ran off with, seeing as he wasn't divorced from Aislinn's mam, but they were still together – and three kids.'

'How much did you tell Aislinn?'

He blows out air. 'Yeah, that wasn't an easy one. I figured it'd be a bit of a shock to the missus and the half-sibs, Daddy's past life turning up on their doorstep – and since the dad wasn't around for Aislinn to talk to, it's not like knowing the whole story would've got her what she wanted anyway. But I wasn't going to just throw the poor girl back onto the street – "Off you go and keep looking for your dad, good luck with that!" She had a right to know her father was dead.'

Steve turns up his palms with a flourish: *Exactly.* I mime wanking. 'So you told her.'

'Yeah. Just that much: that the system showed him as deceased. And that I didn't have any other info.'

'How'd she take it?'

'Not great.' I can hear the grimace in Gary's voice. 'To be honest, she went bloody mental – which was fair enough, I suppose. She was hyperventilating, for a minute there I thought I was going to have to call an ambulance, but I had her hold her breath and she got it together again.'

'No better man for it,' I say.

'Yeah, well. Sort of. She was still frantic – shaking, whimpery noises, all that. She wanted to know why no one had told her – had the lads been lying to her ma or were they really that useless, how had they missed something that I'd found in ten minutes flat . . . I told her the lads were good Ds, but sometimes an investigation hits a wall no matter how good you are, and info from other sources can take a while to make it onto the system . . .'

It's instinct, as automatic as blinking when sand flies in your eye: a civilian accuses another cop of fucking up, you deny it. Whether she's right is beside the point. You open your mouth and a lovely reassuring cover story comes out, smooth as butter. It's never bothered me before – it's not like a grovelling apology would have done Aislinn any good, or done anything at all except waste everyone's time – but today everything feels dodgy, ready to blow up in my face at the wrong touch; nothing feels like it's on my side.

I say, 'Did she believe you?'

Gary makes a noncommittal noise. 'Not sure. I just kept talking, trying to talk her down. I gave it loads about how at least now she had closure so she could move on, how she had every right to make a wonderful life for herself; and I went on about how her dad sounded like a lovely man and he'd obviously loved her a lot, and whatever had happened I was sure it had broken his heart to leave her . . . That kind of stuff. She didn't look convinced – to be honest, I'm not sure she heard most of it – but I got her calmed down in the end.' That voice, doing its job; he could've read her the duty roster and it would have done the same. 'Once she was fit to drive, I sent her home. That's it. See? There was nothing in there that could've made her think gangs.'

'Doesn't sound like it,' I say, at Steve, who shrugs again. His eyes are on a guy hurrying towards the main gate, too far away to recognise in this light, but the guy is fighting the wind for his scarf and doesn't even glance our way. 'Thanks, Gar. I appreciate it.'

'So can you go ahead and leave the other Ds alone? If you won't do it for your own sake, do it because you owe me one. I don't need them jumping down my throat about passing you their case files.'

Meaning Gary doesn't need me getting my cooties all over him. Part of me understands completely: no one wants to catch the plague. The rest of me wants to go over there, deck the fucker and tell him to grow a pair.

'Fair enough,' I say. 'Can you send that young fella back to pick up your file?'

'No problem. He'll be over to you now.'

'Nice one. Thanks again. Catch you next week for those pints, yeah?'

'Next week's a bit mental. I'll give you a ring when things settle down, OK? Good luck with the case. Sorry I wasn't more use to you.'

And Gary's gone, back to the squad room with his mug of real coffee, to take slaggings about his prostate and sing musicals and go after happy endings.

He won't be ringing me, and it sticks in deeper and sharper than I was ready for. I pretend putting my phone back in my pocket needs my full concentration. Steve bends to mess around with his pile of alibi paper. I can't tell whether he's actually being tactful, in which case I might have to kill him.

'So,' I say briskly, 'the gang theory's out, at least as far as Des Murray's concerned. If the Ds had had suspicions they didn't want to put in the file, Gary would've known. Des Murray went off with his bit on the side. End of story.'

'Sure,' Steve says, straightening up. 'But Aislinn didn't know that.'

'So? Gary's right: there's no reason she would have been thinking gangs. None. Zero.'

'Not if she was thinking straight, no. But she wasn't thinking— No, Antoinette, *listen*.' He's leaning in close, talking fast. 'Aislinn was a fantasist. Remember what Lucy said, about when they were kids? When things were bad, Ash came up with mad stories to make them better. She had to, didn't she? In real life, all she did was get pushed around by other people's decisions. The one place where she had any power, the *one* place where she got to make the calls, was her imagination.'

He's forgotten all about being cold. 'So she built up this whole fantasy: she was going to go on a quest and find her daddy, and she'd throw herself into his arms and her life would be OK again. That fantasy was what kept her going. And then your mate Gary blew it right out of the water.'

I say, 'You make it sound like he torched a poor helpless kiddie's favourite dolly. Aislinn was a grown adult – and by that time, her ma was dead. She could do whatever she wanted with her life. She didn't need the Daddy fantasy any more; it was only holding her back. Gary did her a favour.'

Steve's shaking his head. 'Aislinn hadn't a clue how to do what she wanted with real life. She'd had no practice. You heard Lucy: she was only starting to play with that in the last year or two – and even then

it was fantasy stuff, doing herself up like something out of a magazine and going to fancy clubs . . . So when Gary killed off her reunion
fantasy, she would've needed a new one, ASAP. And a gang story
would've been perfect.'

His face is lit up with it; he can see the whole thing. You have to
love the guy. Where I'm seeing a dead end, he's seeing a brilliant new
twist to his amazing story. I wish I could take my holidays inside
Steve's head.

'Maybe she decided her dad had been a witness to a gang hit, so
he needed to get out of town fast, before the gang tracked him down
– something like that. Plenty of drama, plenty of thrills, a great reason
why her dad left and why he never came back to find her—'

'Doesn't explain why he couldn't Facebook her, somewhere along
the way,' I point out. '"Hiya, sweetums, Daddy's alive, love you, bye."'

'He was scared to, in case the gang was watching her Facebook
account and they went after her. Yeah, *I* know it's bollix' – when I
snort – 'but Aislinn might not have. There's a million ways she
could've explained that away to herself. And you know the next
chapter of the fantasy? The next chapter's going to star Aislinn as the
brave daughter who goes into the heart of gangland to learn her da's
secret. Guaranteed.'

'Learn it how? By walking into some radge pub and asking if
anyone here knows anything about Desmond Murray?'

Steve's nodding fast. Another civil servant trudges past, but he
doesn't even notice; too hypnotised by his sparkly story. 'Probably
not far off. Anyone who reads the news would be able to figure out a
few names of gang pubs. Aislinn goes into one for a drink—'

'You think she had balls that size? *I* wouldn't be happy doing that,
and I can handle myself a lot better than she could.' This idea is
annoying me: us, two grown-ass professional Ds, chasing some idiot's
Nancy Drew fantasy all around town. My job is dealing with stories
that actually happen, getting them by the scruff of the neck and hauling them clawing and biting to the right ending. Stories that only
happened inside someone's pretty little head, floating bits of white
fluff that I've got no way to grab hold of: those aren't supposed to be
my problem.

'It's not about having big balls. It's about how deep she was in the fantasy. If that's her place, where she's in control, then she's not going to believe it could go wrong. Like a little kid – that's what Lucy said, remember? In Aislinn's head, she's the heroine. The heroine might get into hassle, but she always gets herself out again.'

'And then what? She just sits in the pub hoping the right guy comes up to her?'

'The way she looks, *someone*'s going to come up to her. No question. She flirts away, comes back another night, gets to know his pals; once she finds a guy who looks promising, she targets him. Actually—' Steve's hand whips up, fingers snapping. 'You know something? Maybe that's why she looked like that. We've been thinking she lost the weight and got the new clothes just because she wanted a fresh start, but what if it was part of a bigger plan?'

'Huh,' I say, considering that. It actually gives me my first fleck of respect for Aislinn. Anyone who turns herself into Barbie because that's the only way she feels worthwhile needs a kick up the hole, but someone who does it for a revenge mission deserves a few points for determination.

'The timeline would fit,' Steve says. 'According to Lucy, Aislinn started the makeover stuff two years ago, give or take. That'd put it not long after she talked to Gary and had to change her plan—' That finger-snap again. He's practically bouncing up and down. 'Jesus: her gaff. You know how she had no family photos? This could be why. She didn't want her boyfriend recognising a photo of her dad.' Steve's eyes are shining. I'm actually starting to hope we never pull a really good case; the excitement would make him widdle on my leg. 'And that's why she ditched the scumbag for Rory: she finally figured out there was nothing he could tell her. It all fits, Antoinette. It does.'

'Or else,' I say, 'the whole gang thing is bollix straight through. Once she talked to Gary and found out that her hugs and hot cocoa with Daddy weren't gonna happen, Aislinn took down the family photos because they wrecked her buzz, and she decided she just wanted a nice happy-ever-after fantasy. The kind where the ugly duckling gets a makeover, turns into a beautiful swan and finds herself a handsome prince. Except the handsome prince turned out to be a big bad ogre. That fits, too.'

But nothing's gonna wet-blanket Steve now. Way before I finish, he's shaking his head. 'Then what about Lucy? You think she made up the whole secret-boyfriend thing out of nothing? All the twitchiness, she was just putting that on?'

'Maybe,' I say. That spark of respect for Aislinn is fading; this whole theory is pissing me off worse and worse. I press my heel down to stop one knee jittering. 'I've got feelers out; if Aislinn was hanging with gangsters, I'll hear about it. And when Lucy gets up the guts to come in, we'll squeeze her harder, see what comes out. She won't be as happy about withholding information when it's all official and on the record. Until then—'

Steve is woodpecker-tapping two fingers off the wall; he's frustrated too, with me for not getting it. 'Until when? What if she doesn't come in?'

'We give her a couple more days to get good and stressed, and then we go get her. Until then, we stick to what we've got. Not what you think might just maybe be out there somewhere.'

He doesn't look happy. I say, 'What else do you want to do? Take a pub crawl around the gang holes yourself, ask all the boys if they were banging our vic?'

'I want to pull mug shots of Cueball Lanigan's lot, run them past the barman in Ganly's. He might remember more than he thinks.'

I shrug. 'Knock yourself out. Me, I'm gonna concentrate on how Aislinn's bullshit could actually come in useful.' I already have my phone out, swiping for Sophie's number.

'What? Who?'

Sophie's phone goes to voicemail. 'Hey, it's Antoinette. If your computer guy hasn't cracked the password on that folder yet, I might have a couple of ideas for him. Try variations on "Desmond Murray" or "Des Murray", and stuff to do with "dad" or "daddy" – finding Dad, looking for Dad, missing Dad. Our vic's father did a runner when she was a kid, and our info says she might have been looking for him. It's worth a shot, anyway. Thanks.'

I hang up. 'Nice one,' Steve says. He's looking a lot happier with me. 'If that folder's full of pics of dodgy geezers, *then* will you—'

'OhmyGod,' I say, wide-eyed. 'What if Aislinn thought her da had actually *become* a gangster? What if she thought he'd, like, dumped some poor schlub's body with his ID on it, and he was alive and well under a whole new evil identity?' And when Steve opens his mouth and leaves it that way, trying to figure out if I'm serious: 'You spa, you. Come on and get this case meeting done.'

We need to go back into the incident room separately, and let the cold and the outdoors smell wear off us first. I head for the jacks and slather on the hand soap till I reek of fake herbal goodness; Steve goes to the canteen for a cup of coffee. When we wander back to our desks, nice and casual, Breslin is pouring smarm down the phone at one of Rory's exes and barely glances up at either of us.

Only: my stuff is wrong. I'm positive I had Rory's bank statement on top, but now my notebook is overlapping it; and the notebook is open to my notes on Cooper's phone call, when I think I remember closing it. I look over at Breslin, but he's schmoozing away, convincing Rory's ex to let him come for a chat this evening, and doesn't even look my way. The more I try to remember what was where, the less sure I am.

Gaffney comes rushing in just in time for the case meeting, mottled and watery-eyed from the cold, to tell us how he got on at Stoneybatter station: he played the recordings of Rory, both his brothers, and all his best guy friends, and the uniform is ninety-nine per cent sure the call didn't come from any of them. 'Ah well,' Breslin says. 'Thanks anyway. I appreciate that. And this.' He starts unwrapping his sandwich. 'Beautiful.'

'I'd say I did more harm than good, like,' Gaffney says worriedly. He hands over Breslin's change, a great big handful of notes and coins. 'By the end, after he'd listened to all those different voices, he was actually having a harder time remembering what the original one had sounded like. D'ye know what I mean? Now, if we get more voices for him to listen to, he won't be able to—'

'Lineups'll do that,' Breslin says, honouring Gaffney with a smile. 'Not your fault, my son; it goes with the territory. You did fine.'

'Yeah,' I say. 'Thanks.' It comes out an ungracious grunt – not that it matters: Gaffney is too busy giving Breslin the hero-worship goo-goo eyes to notice I exist. All I can think is that of *course* the lineup wrecked our chances of getting an ID. Even when we have something, touching it crumbles it into nothing. More nothing, sifting down like fine dust, piling up in sticky drifts on the glossy desks, gumming up the swanky computers.

Before we head home, me and Steve give the gaffer his update. O'Kelly stands at the tall sash window, with his back to us and his hands in the pockets of his tweed suit, rocking back and forth on his heels. He looks like he's gazing out at the dark gardens, only half listening, but I can see his eyes in the glass, zipping fast between my reflection and Steve's.

When we finish talking, he leaves a silence that says he wants more. Steve's reflection glances at mine. I don't look back.

O'Kelly says, without turning round, 'I looked in on your incident room, around noon. Ye weren't there. Where were ye?'

It's been a long time since any gaffer made me account for my whereabouts like a fucking kid. Before I can open my mouth, Steve says easily, 'We did the search on Aislinn's gaff. Then we brought a photo of her round Stoneybatter, asked pubs and local places if they recognised her. See if anyone had spotted her doing anything interesting.'

'And?'

Steve lifts one shoulder. 'Not really.'

O'Kelly lets that lie for a few seconds. Then he says, 'This afternoon you got a delivery from some lad who wouldn't let it out of his hands. What was it?'

Bernadette's had a thing for the gaffer as long as anyone can remember; everyone knows she'll grab any chance to drop a word in his ear. She could've grassed us up; or not. 'Aislinn's father went missing when she was a kid,' Steve says. 'It seemed like a bit of a coincidence, so we took a look at the file.'

'Any joy?'

'Nothing. He ran off with a young one. Died a few years back.'

O'Kelly turns around. He leans back against the window and examines us. His shave went wrong this morning; his face is raw and flaky, like he's slowly eroding away. 'D'you know what ye're acting like?' he asks.

We wait.

'Ye're acting like you don't have a suspect. Flailing about, haring off in every direction after anything you see. That's how Ds act who've got nothing.' His eyes move from Steve to me. 'But you've got a perfectly good suspect right in front of you. So what am I missing? What's wrong with Rory Fallon?'

I say, 'Everything we've got on Fallon is circumstantial. We've got nothing solid tying him to the actual killing: no blood on his gear, none of his blood or hair on the victim, no injuries to his knuckles. We can't even put him inside her house. We've got no motive. We're still working on all of that, and if the Bureau comes back to me saying they found fibres from Aislinn's carpet all over Rory's trousers, then yeah, I'll be paying a lot less attention to other possibilities. But as long as it's all circumstantial, I'm gonna keep chasing down other scenarios and ruling them out. I don't want to get Fallon into court and have the defence whip out a witness who saw Aislinn having a massive fight with some guy who looks nothing like him.'

O'Kelly's pulled a handful of stuff out of his pocket – paper clip, twisted tissue, a pebble – and he's turning through it slowly, not looking at me. He asks, 'Why didn't you have him back in today?'

And it's been a long time since any gaffer made me explain my decisions, in a case that wasn't going off the rails or anywhere near it. If I was positive this was just O'Kelly giving me shite to try and nudge me out the door, I'd be raging; but I'm nothing like positive. I think of Breslin's roll of fifties, and of O'Kelly at the roster saying *Breslin's due in. Have him.* The air of the building feels like it's changing into something different, something gathering speed and ready to switchback any second; something I know I should have more cop-on than to love.

I say, just bolshie enough, 'Because I didn't want to. When we get everything back from the Bureau, then we'll haul him in and hit him hard. He's the nervy type; letting him stew for a couple of days won't do any harm.'

O'Kelly's eyes hit my face for a second, needle-sharp, and then flick away again. He pulls a battered throat lozenge out of the pile in his hand and examines it with faint disgust. 'I don't know what you're so happy about, Conway.'

Like I said: O'Kelly is a lot sharper than he likes pretending. I smash the expression off my face. 'Gaffer?'

'Never mind.' He stretches out his hand over the bin and opens it. The rubbish falls in with a dry rattle. 'Go on. I'll see ye tomorrow. Try and get somewhere.'

Driving chills me out better than almost anything, but this evening it's not working. The wind is pulling nasty tricks, dying down just long enough to let me relax, then slamming into the car like a shoulder-tackle, throwing gritty rain at the windows. It turns the traffic jumpy, everyone hitting their horns too fast and taking off from red lights too early, and throws off the pedestrians' timing so they're skittering between cars at all the wrong moments.

I get pulled over before I even get across the river. I've just gunned it through a yellow and at first I figure the uniform is having a twitchy day too, but the spit-take he does when I pull out my ID tells me there's more going on. He spills straightaway: some-one called in my car for dangerous driving, probably DUI. Some driver could have misread a reg number, in the rain and the traffic, except they described the car as well: black '08 Audi TT. No one misread that.

The uniform wants to run for his life, but I make him breathalyse me and put the whole thing down in writing, before someone rings Creepy Crowley and tells him I used my badge to duck a DUI. I could try tracking down the number that rang the station, but I already know it'll be unregistered – plenty of cops have burner phones, for one thing and another. I spend the rest of my nice relax-ing drive looking over my shoulder for the next blue light. It doesn't come, which means I get to look forward to meeting it in the morn-ing instead.

At least there's no one hanging around the top of my road this time, which is something. I unlock my door, switch on the light, drop my satchel, slam the door behind me, and as I turn back into the sitting room the three things hit me one after the other and all faster than a blink. Smell of coffee. Silence where my alarm system should be beeping. Movement, just a brush, in the dark kitchen.

I get my gun out – it feels zero-gravity slow, even though I know I'm going at top speed – and aim it at the kitchen door. I say, 'Armed Garda. Drop any weapons, keep your hands where I can see them and come out slowly.'

For the first second all I see is a scrawny little bollix in the kitchen doorway, shiny blue tracksuit, hands up above his head, I think some dumbfuck junkie has picked the wrong house to rob and the trigger is a cool perfect fit to my finger and I can't think of a single reason why I shouldn't pull it. Then he says, 'You need a better alarm system.'

'*Fleas*,' I say. I laugh out loud; if I was the hugging type, I'd hug him. 'You little *fuck*. You almost gave me a heart attack. You couldn't have just e-mailed me back, no?'

'This is safer. And anyway, too long no see.' Fleas has a grin the size of a dinner plate on his face. I can feel the matching one on me.

'How is this safer? I nearly shot you, you know that?' I holster up. I'm light-headed with the adrenaline spike. 'Jesus *Christ*.'

'I wasn't worried. I've got faith in you.' Fleas heads back into the kitchen. 'Will I make you a cup of coffee?'

'Yeah. Go on.' I follow him and give him a smack across the back of the head, not too hard. 'Don't you ever do that to me again. If I'm gonna kill someone, I don't want it to be you.'

'Ahh!' Fleas rubs his head, looking injured. 'I wasn't trying to freak you out. I would've waited in the sitting room, only I thought you might bring some fella home with you.'

'Yeah, right. Chance would be a fine thing.' I still have that grin on; I can't get rid of it. 'You hungry?'

'You're out of everything. I looked.'

'Cheeky bastard. There's fish fingers in the freezer; you want a fish-finger sandwich?'

'Deadly,' Fleas says happily, and starts pushing buttons on the coffee machine. 'Loving this yoke. I might get one of my own.'

'If mine goes missing, I'm coming after you.' I turn on the cooker and pull open the freezer. Fleas leans his elbows on the counter and watches the machine spew coffee like he's fascinated by it.

Fleas is a little runt who looks like his ma didn't drink enough milk when she was having him, which given the block of flats he's from is probably true. He got the nickname in training college – he was in my year – because he can't stand still; even waiting for the coffee machine, he's bouncing from foot to foot like he's itchy. The two of us got on, back in training. I wasn't there to make bosom buddies, and I didn't need morons saying I was shagging a guy into looking after me; but if it hadn't been for all that, we would have been friends.

Halfway through our second year, Fleas disappeared. The story we got was that he had been kicked out for being caught with hash on him – cue jokes about how you can put the skanger in a uniform, but you can't put the uniform into the skanger – but I didn't fall for it: Fleas was way too sharp for that. A few years later, when I got pulled off a desk to spend a few weeks being Fleas's cousin Rachel who would be only delighted to take a suitcase full of drug money to his boss's friend in Marbella, it turned out I'd been right all along. The sting went like clockwork, a few bad guys went down, and me and Fleas had a blast. Before I went back to my desk, we made Rachel an e-mail address so we could get in touch, if we ever needed to. We've never needed to before.

We take the coffee and sandwiches into the sitting room and stretch out at opposite ends of my sofa, with our feet up and our plates balanced on our laps. I've lit the fire; the wind is still going, but the thick walls turn it faint and almost cosy. 'Ahhh,' Fleas says, wriggling his shoulders comfortable against the cushions. 'This is lovely, so it is. I'm gonna get myself a nice place like this, one of these days. You can teach me how to do it up.'

Which reminds me. 'How'd you know where to find me?'

'Ah, now. Where would you be if I hadn't?' He gives me his crinkly grin. 'Murder now, yeah? The big time. How's that going?'

Meaning he's been asking after me, when he gets a chance. 'Grand. Beats giving out penalty points.'

'How're the lads? Any crack?'

I can't tell what that means. His face, full of food, gives away nothing. 'All right, yeah,' I say. 'What're you at these days?'

'You know yourself. Bit of this, bit of that. Remember your man Goggles? The little fat fella with no neck?'

'Jaysus, him.' That makes me laugh. 'You know he kept trying to chat me up, right? Every time you left me on my own, there he was, edging over and telling me he loved tall birds and the littlest jockeys have the biggest whips. He was always so bickied he kept forgetting he'd already tried and got nowhere.'

Fleas is grinning. 'That's the boyo. We finally landed him – we didn't even want to, he was still useful, but the thick eejit . . . Himself and his pal Fonzie were in a B&B in Cork, right? Parcelling up a load of Es that had just come off a boat?' He's got the giggles; it's catching, even before I know what we're laughing at. 'And Goggles was sampling the merchandise, only he went too far. Three in the morning, he's out in the front garden in his jocks, *singing* – I heard it was "I Kissed a Girl".'

By now I'm lying back on the sofa, laughing properly. It feels good.

'When the landlord goes out to see what's the story, Goggles gives him a hug, tells him he's only gorgeous, then legs it back inside, hops in bed with the landlady and starts playing peekaboo under the covers. The uniforms arrive, take him back to his room to sleep it off, and there's Fonzie crashed out in a chair and a hundred grand of Es spread out on the bed.'

'Ah, Jaysus,' I say, wiping my eyes. 'That's beautiful, that is. You couldn't just seize the haul and let the lads go, no?'

'We tried. The gaffer had half the squad looking for some way the uniforms had fucked up, illegal search or something, yeah? But they were watertight. Poor old Goggles is going down. Here' – Fleas points his sandwich at me – 'you should visit him, inside. Cheer him up a bit.'

He's messing, but it sounds like there's a corner of serious in there. 'I'll get him to do his Katy Perry for me,' I say. 'Cheer us both up.'

'Not from what I heard, it wouldn't.'

'Come here,' I say. 'Speaking of the lads. The *Courier*'s after running my photo. Is that gonna fuck you up?'

Fleas is the reason I don't let my photo out there. They did me up for the gig – curls, big hoop earrings, shitload of makeup, pink crop tops with CHEEKY and YOUR BOYFRIEND WANTS ME across the front – but still: better safe. He shrugs. 'No hassle so far. See what happens.' It takes a lot more than this to panic an undercover. 'I wouldn't say anyone recognised you. You're all fancy these days' – a nod at my suit, half impressed, half amused – 'and in fairness, it's been a few years.'

'Rub it in, why don't you.'

Fleas examines me critically, chewing. 'You're looking all right. Not great, now; you look like you could do with a holiday. Or a tonic.'

'I'm grand. I could use a bit of sunshine, just. What are the chances?'

'Or a change of scene.'

I look up fast from my food, but he's leaning to get his mug off the coffee table; I can't see his eyes. Undercovers are like that – they can't go at anything straight – but I'm pretty sure I get the message. Fleas knows Murder isn't working out. He thinks I e-mailed him because I need him to put in a good word for me on Undercover.

For a flash I think about straightening my leg and putting my foot in his guts. Instead I say, 'I'm happy enough with the scenery I've got. I'd love your opinion on one bit of it, though.'

'Yeah?' Fleas's tone hasn't changed, but something streaks across his face, something that almost looks like regret. 'What's that?'

'Look at this.' I sit up and stretch for my satchel, find a photo of Aislinn Version 2.0 and pass it to him. 'Her name's Aislinn Murray. Twenty-six, five foot seven, probably a middle-class Greystones accent. Seen her around?'

Fleas chews, bounces one knee and takes his time looking. 'Hard to say for sure; a lot of ones look like her. I don't think so, but. Who is she?'

'Murder victim.'

That stops his knee bouncing. 'Her? The one off the front pages?'

'Yeah. Her best mate says she had a secret boyfriend, the last six months or so. We're thinking it could've been a gangster. One of Cueball Lanigan's lot, maybe.'

He looks longer. Shakes his head. 'Nah. She wasn't with any of Lanigan's lads, anyway.'

'You're sure,' I say. I already know from his voice: he's sure. The warm cosy feeling is sinking fast. I could kick myself for dragging him out here for this.

'Hundred per cent. I'd've met her. Probably if she was with anyone from Crumlin or Drimnagh, too.'

'Maybe not. If she was keeping the relationship on the downlow, he might've been too.'

Fleas laughs. 'Nah nah nah. A bird who looks like that, anyone who's shagging her is gonna want the world to know. He'd be show-ing her off in the pub, at parties, every time he got a chance.'

'Even if he's married?'

'No problemo. No one expects these lads to be monks, know what I mean? Not even their wives. If someone's married to another of the lads' sister, then OK, he's not gonna shove his bit on the side in the brother-in-law's face, but he'll still be bragging about her to the rest of us. And the lads gossip like aul' ones. Everyone knows who's got a little side action going on.' He's still scanning the photo, but his knee is jiggling again: he's losing inter-est. 'She have any bling that's not accounted for? Rolex, jewellery, designer gear?'

'Not that I spotted,' I say. 'Her stuff was mid-range, things she could've afforded herself; nothing that said someone else was buying for her. But maybe she just wasn't into the sugar-daddy thing.'

Fleas snorts. 'Any extra cash?'

'Not that we've found. Her financials look clean.'

'Any trips away? A lily-white like that, the boyfriend wouldn't be able to resist using her to carry something. And if she's the type who'd go for a gangster, she's not the type who'd say no.'

I shake my head. 'Her best friend said she'd never been out of Ireland. We found a passport application form – first-time, not renewal. No passport.'

'There you go,' Fleas says. He passes the photo back to me. 'I'm not swearing on my life or anything, but if I was a betting man, I'd bet plenty that she had nothing to do with the scene.'

And there it is. The cosy feeling burns out to dirty ash.

I say, 'You can't swear to it, but. She still could have had connections.'

He shrugs. 'She could've, yeah. So could my ma.'

Fleas isn't like Steve; he doesn't make up ifs and maybes for kicks. If Fleas says something, it's solid.

There goes our beautiful gang theory, spiralling down the jacks with a long sucking sound. I thought I was ready for that.

Me spending the last day and a half thinking I was a big badass sniper deep in enemy jungle, swinging my scope from Breslin to McCann, my blood clarifying to pure adrenaline while I waited to see which one I should pick off. Idiot, five-star fucking cretin. No different from Goggles getting off his tits on his own shipment and turning himself into a lifetime punchline. The only thing I've done right, since the moment I got this case, was hold on to just enough sense to keep my gob shut. Every other thought I've had was a joke.

I stuff the photo back into my satchel – I don't want to see the thing any more. 'Can you keep an eye out anyway? See if anyone's a little off his stride this week, maybe, or anyone's spending more time in the pub, getting drunker than usual?' The begging under my voice is pathetic. 'She only got killed on Saturday evening, so whoever did it should be feeling it.'

Fleas has gone back to his sandwich. 'Might be, might not. Plenty of them are total psychopaths; could blow their own grannies' brains out and never break a sweat.'

'Someone knows about this who isn't a total psycho, but. A guy called it in to the local station, looking for an ambulance. If that wasn't our boy, it was a mate who he talked to.'

'Fair enough. I'll keep an eye out for anyone who's off form.'

He's humouring me, but he'll do it. 'If you spot anything,' I say, 'you e-mail me before you show up here. I swear to God, if I find you under my bed tomorrow night, I'm gonna shoot your bony arse.'

'Come here, but,' Fleas says, wiping mayo off his cheek with the back of his hand. 'I wasn't joking about you needing better security. I had that alarm disabled in twenty seconds, tops; took me maybe another minute to get past the locks. And probably you already know this, but there's some fella casing your road.'

The air in the room hardens, scraping at me like sandpaper. 'Yeah,' I say. 'I was wondering about that. Where'd you spot him?'

'I took a stroll past the top of the road earlier on, just getting the feel of the place before I headed in. He was hanging about. Like he was waiting for someone, only I got the vibe – you know the vibe.'

'Yeah.' We all know the vibe. 'Did you get a decent look?'

'Tried. I went to bum a smoke off him' – Fleas slumps forward, lets his face go junkie-vacant and whines through his nose, '"Here, bud, gis a fag?"' Back to normal: 'Only he saw me coming and legged it. Could've been he just didn't fancy the likes of me getting a hold of him, in fairness; but . . .' Fleas shrugs. 'Middle-aged fella, tall, medium build, pricey overcoat, big schnozz. That's all I could see; he was well wrapped up, trilby and a scarf over half his face. Again, that's fair enough, in this weather. But.'

'Right. But.' That rules out Creepy Crowley and his short arse and his slimy mac, anyway, which is a shame; I would've only loved a good excuse to mistake him for a stalker. 'I think it's this gaff he's watching.'

Fleas nods, unsurprised. 'I'd say so, all right. Got any clue who he'd be?'

I shake my head. 'I was wondering about some gangster looking to warn me off. With that *Courier* photo, anyone could've waited outside work and followed me home. But if you figure the gang thing's a dead end . . .' Every time I say the word 'gang', it sounds stupider. I stretch out my legs farther along the sofa and try to get back some of that relaxed feel. It's well gone. I can feel the sitting-room window behind my shoulder, the dark wind shoving up against it.

'They're a shower of bollixes, the *Courier*,' Fleas says. 'And just 'cause it's not a gangster, that doesn't mean it's not the fella who killed your girl.'

'I already thought of that. Do I look thick to you?'

'I'm only saying. You'd want to get that alarm sorted rapid. Get PhoneWatch or something.'

'No, thanks.' If PhoneWatch doesn't get an answer off you when there's a breach, they ring the Guards. I'd rather have a serial killer use me for parts than have the squad find out I went squealing for uniform help like some civilian. 'I'm grand. I got you good and proper, didn't I?'

'I wasn't here to kill you,' Fleas points out. 'Not the same thing. I know you're well able for anyone, and I pity the poor little bollix that takes you on, but you have to sleep sometime, yeah?'

'I'll get the locks looked at in the morning.'

'And the alarm.'

'And the alarm. Mammy.'

Fleas watches me, over the rim of his mug. For once he isn't moving. He says, 'Will I stay the night?'

There are a few different ways he could mean that. Tonight, all of them sound good. If it wasn't for the guy at the top of the road, wasn't for the shite I'm taking at work, I would say yes, one way or another.

I can't handle either of us thinking I need him there. 'You're all right,' I say. 'Thanks, but.'

'No one'll miss me.'

'Ahhh. Poor baby.'

'You sure, yeah?'

'Positive. Just: if you see this fella again on your way out, give us a text, yeah?'

'No probs,' Fleas says. He slides off the sofa, hitches up his track-suit bottoms and picks up his plate and mug. 'I'll get out of your hair, so.'

'Leave that. I'll do it.' I was going to make another round of coffee, but it's too late to say it now.

'Ah, no. My mammy taught me to tidy up after meself.' He heads into the kitchen. 'Thanks for feeding me. You make a gorgeous fish-finger sambo, so you do.'

I follow him. He's bent over the dishwasher, slotting his plate into place. 'Here,' he says, holding out his hand. 'Give us that.'

I hand over my plate. 'I'm glad you came,' I say. 'It's good to see you.'

'Same here. Yeah.' Fleas slams the dishwasher and straightens up. 'If I spot any of the lads acting a bit stressed, I'll let you know – swear to God I'll e-mail first, this time. Otherwise . . .'

I say, 'Otherwise I'll see you when I see you.'

Fleas gives me a grin and a quick, one-armed hug. His tough skinny arm and the smell of him – cheapo body spray, straight out of when I was fifteen – hit me with a blast of weakness that makes me glad he's leaving. Then he switches off the motion-sensor light, unlocks the back door and is gone, over the wall, neat and silent as a fox. I lock the door behind him and wait, but he doesn't text me.

IO

The next morning I lie in bed and think about staying there. I didn't get a lot of sleep; after I rang my ma and told her about Aislinn's mouthful of blood clots and smashed teeth ('Huh'), I spent half the night leaping up to investigate random noises – in this weather, there were plenty of those – and the other half trying to lie still and trying to decide who deserves a punch in the gob more, Steve for coming up with the gang theory or me for actually going along with it. By six in the morning my body is one hard knot. I haven't mitched off since school, but today I can't remember why not. Two things stop me: if I don't go to work, I'll run till my legs give out and then sit at home driving myself mental; and if I don't go to work, that's one more day I'll have to spend on this shitpile of a case.

I get into my running gear without turning on a light. Then I switch off the motion-sensor lights, slip out to my patio and go over the back wall. It's dark, the flat drained dark that comes before dawn, when even the night things – foxes, bats, drunks and dangers – have finished their business and gone to sleep; even the wind has died down to an uneasy, feeble twitch. I move up the laneway without making a sound and flatten myself in shadows to peer around the corner and down the street. There's no one hanging around at the top of my road; no one anywhere, in either direction, as far as I can see in the sick yellowish light. I go take a look down my road: no one there either.

Normally my run leaves me feeling like nothing but long muscles streaming with strength, able and beckoning for more, for anything, bring it on. That feeling is what gets me through my shift. Today the strength is nowhere. I'm lurching like a flabby first-timer; my legs drag like they're wrapped in wet sandbags, my arms flop and my breathing can't find a rhythm. I push harder, till my chest feels like it's ripping and a thick red seethes up over my eyes. I hang onto a lamppost, doubled over, waiting for it to clear.

I make it home at a jog – some part of my head tells me that if I drop to a walk, I'm screwed in ways I can't put my finger on. By the time I get back to my road, my legs have stopped shaking. The first layers of dark are starting to peel away, and windows are lighting up. There's still no one there.

I told Fleas I'd get my locks and my alarm system looked at. I meant it at the time, but somewhere since then I've changed my mind. The guy casing my gaff is the only thing left in my week that has potential. If he sees locksmiths and alarm techs swarming over my house, he'll know he's been burned; he'll find someone else to stalk, or get himself another hobby, or back off and wait a few weeks or months before he comes looking for me again. I need him now.

I take my shower, throw some cereal into me and head out for work. There's still no one outside.

I make it to work without getting pulled over – even wankers take a while to gear up in the morning. Outside our building, in the strange unfocused mix of early light and thick halogens, McCann is leaning against the wall and having a smoke.

'Howya,' I say, without stopping. McCann lifts his chin, but he doesn't bother talking, not that I expected him to.

He looks like shite. McCann isn't slick to start with, not like Breslin; he's one of those guys who always look like they're fighting back their natural state of scruffiness – five o'clock shadow by noon, greying dark curls that won't lie flat. Normally he wins the battle, because he obviously used to be good-looking not too long ago, before the jowls and the belly started loosening, and because everything he wears is always immaculate and ironed so smooth you could skate on it. This morning, though, he's losing. The five o'clock shadow has turned into full-on stubble; his shirt is creased, there's something brown and sticky on his jacket sleeve, and his eyebags are moving towards black eyes.

While me and Steve were sculpting our fancy twirly conspiracy theories, like a pair of mouth-breathers in an internet sinkhole, Breslin was telling the truth all along: McCann is in the missus's bad books. He's sleeping on the sofa and doing his own ironing. I could laugh, if the great big joke wasn't on me.

I have my hand on the door when he says, 'Conway.'

I stop in spite of myself. I want to hear, just for confirmation, what I already know he's going to say. McCann is gonna drop me a nice juicy hint that him and Breslin are on the take.

'Yeah,' I say.

McCann has his head back against the wall, looking out at the winter-scrawny gardens, not at me. He says, 'How're you getting on with Breslin?'

'Fine.'

'He says good things about you.'

He does in his arse. 'Nice to hear,' I say.

'He's a good D, Breslin is. The best. Good to work with, too: he'll look after you, whatever it takes. As long as you don't fuck him about.'

'McCann,' I say. 'I'm just doing my job. I'm not planning on fucking your pal about. OK?'

That gets one humourless twitch of his mouth. 'You'd better not. He's got enough on his mind already.'

And there it is. Took him all of twenty seconds. 'Yeah? Like what?'

McCann shakes his head, one brief jerk. 'Forget it. You don't want to know.'

Yesterday I'd have been drooling down my suit. Now all I can feel is a small, bitter flare of anger, too exhausted to last. Whatever Breslin's playing at, he's decided his approach isn't doing the job; so, just like he would with some slack-jawed suspect, he's sent McCann in to try a different angle. The scatter of cigarette butts at McCann's feet says he's been waiting out here for God knows how long, just to feed me a few lines out of a B-movie. 'Whatever,' I say. 'I'll have him back to you in one piece, fast as I can. Believe me.'

I'm turning away when McCann says, through his cigarette, 'Hang on.'

I say, 'What.'

He watches ash scud away across the cobblestones. He says, 'Roche nicked your statement sheet.'

'What are you talking about?'

'Your street fight from Saturday night. The last page of a witness statement went missing on you.'

I say, 'I don't remember telling you about that.'

'You didn't. Roche was having a laugh about it in the squad room, yesterday.' McCann reaches a hand into his jacket pocket, pulls out a folded sheet of paper and passes it to me. I unfold it: my statement page. 'With Roche's apologies. More or less.'

I hold out the sheet. 'I got the witness to redo it.'

McCann doesn't take it. 'I know you did. This' – he flicks the paper – 'isn't the point. Shred it, stuff it up Roche's hole, I don't care.'

'Then what is the point?'

'The point is, not everyone on the squad is Roche. Me and Bres, we've got nothing against you. You're not a waste of space like some of that lot; you've got the makings of a good D. We'd be happy to see you do well for yourself.'

'Great,' I say. It sounds so much like truth, matter-of-fact with just the faintest fleck of warmth, the gruff old dog who isn't about to get sappy but wants the best for the young learner who's earned his respect. If I hadn't seen McCann do his shtick in a dozen interrogations, and if I didn't know a million times better, I might even fall for it. 'Thanks.'

'So if Breslin tells you to do something, it's for your own good. Even if you can't see how; even if you think he's wrong. If you've got sense, you'll listen to him. D'you get me?'

McCann's eyes are on me now, bloodshot from wind and fatigue. His voice has condensed, concentrated. This is the important part; this is what kept him waiting in the cold for me to walk out of the blurry, layered light, to the place where he wants me.

'I get you just fine,' I say. 'I'm missing nothing.' I crumple the statement sheet in my fist and shove it into my coat pocket. 'See you 'round.'

'Yeah,' McCann says. 'See you.' He turns away again, dark sagging profile against the growing light. The dirty reek of his cigarette follows me into the building.

*   *   *

Me and McCann are both early. The cleaner is still hoovering the corridor; when I pass the squad-room door, the only sounds inside are patchy two-man chat and the perky squawking of drivetime radio. Incident Room C is empty except for Steve, sprawled at our desk, looking rumpled and hugging a cup of coffee.

'You're in early,' I say.

'Couldn't sleep.'

'Me neither. Any sign of Breslin?'

'Nope.'

'Good.' I'm not in the humour for Breslin. There's a stack of little plastic photo albums on Steve's desk: mug books. I nod at them. 'What're those for?'

'Gang lads,' Steve says, through a yawn. 'Lanigan's lot, mostly. I want to run them past the barman in Ganly's. Then I'll show them to Aislinn's neighbours, see if anyone recognises—'

I say, 'The gang theory's dead.' It feels like punching a bruise.

Steve's face looks slapped blank. He says, 'Wait. What?'

'Gone. Out the window. I never want to hear about it again. Is that clear enough?'

'Hang on,' Steve says. He's lifted his hands and forgotten them in mid-air, trying to get his head together. 'Hang on. No. Then what was Breslin playing at yesterday, ditching Gaffney? Don't tell me you actually believe he stopped off for a shag.'

I toss my satchel on the floor and throw myself into my chair. It feels good, watching this hit Steve. 'Maybe he was getting his nails done. Maybe he didn't go anywhere special; he just wanted to show us he wasn't going to take orders from the likes of us. I don't care either way.'

'And you saw him give Gaffney the cash for his sandwich, yeah? The roll of fifties? What was he doing with those?'

'Did you not hear me? I *don't care*. I don't care if he wants to carry around his entire savings fund in his pocket so the Illuminati can't get their hands on it. His problem. Not ours.'

'OK,' Steve says carefully. He's looking at me like I might have rabies. 'OK. What the hell happened last night?'

'Last night,' I say, 'I had a chat with a guy I know. He knows the gang scene inside out, and he says we can rule out that angle. Aislinn had fuck-all to do with gangs. End of story. On the *tiny* off-chance he finds anything to contradict that, he'll let us know, but we shouldn't hold our breath. And we should be very bloody grateful that we found this out before we made twats of ourselves in front of the entire squad.'

Steve looks like a lorry splattered his hamster. He says, 'How well do you know this guy?'

'Well enough. We go back.'

'Are you sure you can trust him?'

The face on him; like this can't be happening, not to his very own special pet idea. 'If I didn't fucking trust him, would I have fucking asked him for his opinion?'

'No. I'm only—'

'No. And do I look fucking brain-damaged?'

'No—'

'No. So when I say we can trust him, it probably means we can trust him.'

'Fair enough,' Steve says. His face has turned neutral; he's drawn back inside himself, which is what he does when he's pissed off. 'Let's do that.'

I leave him to sulk it off and go back to work, or try to. It's not clicking; I have to read every sentence three times before it sinks in. Normally I can concentrate through anything – squad rooms teach you that, specially the kind of squad room I've been working in – but what Steve said is pinching at me.

Fleas knows an awful lot about me and my career, for someone who's been deep under for years. I thought that was nice, him bothering to keep up. Which it might well have been; or it might not.

All of a sudden I'm second-guessing every step of our lovely cosy conversation, looking for cracks where the hidden agenda might have shown through: Fleas getting me to back off in case I jeopardise a drugs op, or just because he doesn't need my cooties all over whatever he's doing; Fleas brushing me off because he's gone rogue and he's protecting his new boss. I'm second-guessing myself, too, wondering if I actually needed to talk to Fleas for investigative purposes or if deep down I was just looking for an excuse to have a sandwich and a chat with someone who doesn't know I'm untouch-able. I don't believe in second-guessing and I don't believe in intro-spective crap, and I'm not happy about catching myself doing both. I wish I'd given Steve more hassle while I was at it. I hope he's feeling like shite.

I have a skim through my messages, the ones that have made it as far as my desk or my inbox. If someone's swiped the good stuff, he's been thorough. Cooper's revised post-mortem report; a couple of tips that will need following up – someone saw a woman who might have been Aislinn in a nightclub, a few weeks back, having a drunken argument with a guy who looked like a rugby player; someone else saw three teenage guys hanging around the top of Viking Gardens on Saturday afternoon, looking suspicious, whatever that means. Bureau reports: the stains on Aislinn's mattress aren't semen, meaning they're prob-ably sweat. The techs are trying for DNA, but they're not promising anything: Aislinn kept her place hot, mattresses aren't sterile, warmth and bacterial action could have degraded the DNA till it's useless. I have a hard time believing it'll make a lot of difference, either way.

A massive stack of paper that turns out to be a year's worth of Aislinn's e-mail records, to cross-check against her account in case anything's been deleted. That should keep someone busy until his brain – or hers – blows up. This kind of crap is why God created floaters, but if there's one tiny worthwhile thing to find in this case, Aislinn's electronics is probably where to find it. I split the stack in two and slide one half over to Steve, who says 'Thanks,' without look-ing up and shoves it to one side. I consider kicking the sulky little bollix under the table. Instead I spread out Aislinn's e-mail records and the printouts of her mailboxes on my desk and start going back and forth between them, working backwards, making sure every e-mail is accounted for. 3.18 a.m. on Sunday, sale notice from some makeup website, still in the inbox. 3.02 a.m. on Sunday, spam from an imaginary Russian babe looking for company, still in the inbox. I want to put my head down on the paper and sleep.

The floaters show up one by one, snap out of their morning fog when they see me and Steve, and get stuck into the jobs they picked up at yesterday's case meeting. I give Cooper's report to Gaffney to type up – I'm still pissed off with him for not getting a voice ID off the Stoneybatter uniform. Breslin sweeps in singing to himself, throws the room a cheerful 'Hi-diddly-hi, camperinos!' and tells me and Steve, 'Two of Rory's lucky exes down, yesterday evening; two to go. Who's the man?'

'You're the man,' Steve says automatically, turning over a page. 'Did you get anything good?'

'No surprises. Rory's a predictable little bastard. We'll see if the other two have anything nice for me.' Breslin leans against our desk and tries to read what I'm doing, upside down. 'What's all this, then?'

'Aislinn's e-mail records,' I say.

'Huh,' Breslin says. 'And?'

'And if you want seventy per cent off a fabulous goddess gown, I can tell you where to go.'

'Sounds like you're having a blast.' Breslin gives me his best movie-star grin, picks up Aislinn's sent e-mails and has a flick through them. 'Jesus, I see what you mean. This could get old. You want me to take over? You can have Rory's exes.'

'Nah.' I'm not even gonna pretend to get all suspicious. He's working hard for it, but I'm done playing Breslin's game. 'I've started; I'll finish.'

'Conway.' Breslin switches the grin to mildly rueful. 'This is me trying to show you that I do know who's the boss of this investigation. If you need scut work done, I'm offering to do it.'

'Thanks,' I say. 'I'm grand.'

After a moment Breslin shrugs. 'Suit yourself.' He has another skim through the e-mails, taking his time, and drops them back on my desk. 'Moran? You need to get out of the office for a while?' He turns Steve's paperwork round to face him and has a good look. As far as I can tell, it's Aislinn's e-mail records, even though I would've sworn Steve was ignoring them up until Breslin came in.

'Ah, no,' Steve says. 'I'm nearly done, sure. If I haven't died of boredom by now . . .'

Breslin shrugs and shoves Steve's stuff back to him. 'Remember,' he says, aiming a finger at me. 'I made the offer.'

'I will,' I say. 'Enjoy the exes.'

'Yeah, I'm not getting my hopes up. You should see the first two.' Breslin swings into his chair, makes oily phone calls setting up appointments, and sweeps out again. 'And I don't need backup today, either,' he says, tossing me and Steve a wink on his way past. 'If you catch my drift.' We both pull out automated smiles.

'What did he even come in for?' Steve wants to know, when he's gone. 'He could've made those calls from anywhere.'

His voice still has some of that flat note to it, but he's talking, which presumably should make me feel all warm inside. I say, 'He couldn't stay away from your pretty face.'

'Seriously. He just wanted to check out what we're doing. And try to take over the electronics. Again. What's he scared we might find in there?'

I say, 'I don't care.' And, when he opens his mouth again: 'I *don't care*.'

Steve rolls his eyes to the ceiling, shoves the e-mail records out of his way and goes back to whatever he's really doing. I try to pick up where I left off, but my focus is shot; all the spam is blurring into one endless Viagra ad. My legs are twitching to get up and move.

The one thing that's still kicking feebly inside my head: Lucy's story about Aislinn's secret boyfriend. That's where all the gang bollix started, and now that we've cleared away the bollix, the story is still there and it still needs explaining. It occurs to me, which it should've done two days ago, that there are other reasons why Lucy could've been cagey. Maybe the boyfriend is a married guy she works with – Aislinn met Rory through Lucy, after all; if she met someone else too, there's a decent chance it was the same way – and Lucy doesn't want drama on the job if he finds out she dobbed him in. Or maybe, just like I thought at first, he never existed. I think about hauling Lucy out of her flat and going at her hard, so she can tell me the boyfriend story was revenge on one of Aislinn's exes or a way to make sure we didn't neglect any possibilities, and I can take this whole staggering wheezing sidetrack out back and put it out of its misery.

That's when Steve's head jerks up. '*Antoinette*,' he says. He's forgotten all about sulking.

'What?'

He pushes a statement sheet across the desk. His eyebrows are halfway up his forehead.

I look down, where he's pointing. The statement is one of his photocopies from the day before, an alibi from one of Desmond Murray's taxi customers. The reporting officer's signature is a scrawl, but the name typed underneath is Detective Garda Joseph McCann.

My eyes meet Steve's. He says, very softly, 'What the hell?'

Ireland is small, the pool of Ds is small, it would be weirder if there wasn't at least one guy from the Desmond Murray case working Murder now. This explains why Gary was so keen for me to keep my mouth shut, anyway: if I go stirring up trouble, it's gonna be close to home. Beyond that I can't tell, through the last few months and the struggling light at the windows, whether this is another handful of nothing or whether it should set all my alarms screaming.

I say, 'We need to check the rest of what you've got from that file. Give me half.'

We flip fast and with one eye on the door. That scrawl is everywhere. If we'd been in less of a rush, we would never have missed it yesterday: McCann, McCann, McCann. He didn't get drafted in to give a hand with the initial push, like Gary did. He was right at the heart of this case.

Aislinn leaning over my desk, all big eyes and twisting fingers, going on about the detective who had patted her on the head and told her *You have great memories of him; we don't want to change that, do we? Sometimes these things are better left as they are . . .* That could have been McCann.

Steve is holding out a thick sheaf of pages, easily a third of what he started with. He says quietly, 'All of these.'

'Yeah,' I say. I lift my own sheaf, the same size. 'And these.'

Steve takes them out of my hand, tucks them back into the file and locks it away in his desk drawer, nice and easy. I'm not sure whether to slag him for paranoia or tell him to hurry up.

'Here's the big question,' he says. 'Have McCann and Breslin copped that Aislinn's missing da was McCann's missing person?'

I clasp my hands at the back of my neck to keep them still. None of the floaters are looking our way. 'I don't know. I was watching Breslin, when I told him that box was the missing-persons file. I'd swear he was relieved. *If* there's something he doesn't want us finding, it's not that.'

'You told him we'd looked through the file and found nothing good. Maybe he was relieved that we'd missed McCann's name.'

'Why? How would they even make the connection?'

'Breslin's telling McCann about our case, mentions the vic's name . . .'

'Like we said before: there's got to be dozens of Aislinn Murrays out there. You honestly think McCann would remember a name as common as that? After seventeen years? She wasn't even the missing person, or the family contact; she was just some little kid in the background.'

'He worked the Desmond Murray disappearance hard,' Steve says. 'It could have stuck in his mind.'

'So what if it did? There's nothing dodgy about the disappearance; there's not even *room* for anything dodgy. Why would they care if we link it up with our case?'

Steve is shaking his head. 'Nothing dodgy, except the Ds not dropping the family a hint. Say Breslin and McCann know McCann screwed up there, yeah? Maybe they think it played into Aislinn getting killed, somehow. Or maybe it's not even that: they just don't want the screw-up coming out. So they're trying to shove Rory Fallon down our throats and hope we swallow fast.'

Maybe it's the fatigue, the heat and not enough coffee, wrapping layers of fuzz around my brain; I can't tell whether the story rings true, or whether it just sounds good because Steve is putting a nice shape on it. He says, 'It probably would've worked, too – if you hadn't been working the Missing Persons desk that day, or if you didn't have that memory on you. We might never even have found out about Desmond going missing, never mind Aislinn trying to track him down.'

I would love to believe it. If Breslin is messing with this case, not with us – meaning me – personally; if there are no gangs involved, no bent cops, just some dumb screw-up McCann made seventeen years ago and doesn't want coming out now; then we've got the pair of them in a headlock, with a great chance at working out a deal that will make everyone very happy. For a second I can feel it, right through my body: the weight of the room lifting off me, the rush of strength hitting every cell like oxygen, *Let's see you try and push me around now motherfuckers*. Me finally holding the high cards, ramming them so far up Roche's hole that he'll be spitting aces for months, and the Murder squad unfolding at long fucking last into the place I've dreamed of coming in to every morning.

Only I don't believe it, no matter how hard I try. The room clamps back down around me – thick hot air, Reilly typing like he's beating the keyboard into submission. It squeezes that strength right out of me, squashes it into a wad and tosses it away.

I say, 'Yeah, that'd be fun. Only why would McCann and Breslin care? Maybe it wasn't nice of the Ds to keep Evelyn Murray in the dark, but they were going by the book. What's the worst that's gonna happen to them if it comes out now? "Here's a copy of the policy on victim sensitivity, have a read sometime"? It's not like they're gonna get reverted back into uniform, specially not after all this time.'

'Depends on *why* they kept Evelyn in the dark. I don't care what your man Gary says: that's weird, Antoinette. It is. When you worked Missing Persons, did you ever do that to a family? Get an answer and walk away from them without one single hint? Ever?'

Steve's head close to mine, and the squeezed-tight urgency in his voice: they feel idiotic, make me feel like a kid playing cops, with a cardboard badge and a bunch of gibberish learned off the telly. I shift away from him. 'So? McCann wasn't even the lead D. Even if there was a dodgy reason behind them making that call, the buck wouldn't stop with him.'

Steve says, 'How long's McCann been married?'

'Bernadette sent round a card for some anniversary, last year. Silver one, must've been. So?'

'So he was married back when he was working this case. Gary said a lot of the Ds were smitten with Evelyn. What if that went further, for McCann? What if he was stretching out the case so he had an excuse to keep seeing her?'

The heat and the clacking keyboards are piling more fuzz onto my mind, thick as insulation. I picture grabbing Reilly's keyboard and snapping it over my knee. 'Only the case didn't stretch out. They closed it as soon as they found Desmond.'

'They did, yeah, officially at least – and we even said it was weird they didn't do it sooner, remember? But maybe McCann told Evelyn he'd keep investigating in his free time, stay in touch, give her updates. Maybe there was actually something between them, maybe not; but either way, McCann might not want that coming out. His marriage isn't in great shape, right? And he's got a bunch of kids, hasn't he? If the wife finds out he was using his job to chase Evelyn Murray, she could use that to—'

I say, before I know I'm going to, 'Stop. Just stop.'

It comes out loud. One or two of the floaters lift their heads. I give them a snarl that smacks them straight back down again.

Steve is staring at me. He says, 'What d'you mean?'

I say, and it takes everything I've got to hold my voice down, 'All this shite is *imaginary*. Do you seriously not get that? Just about every single thing you've said since we got this case has been pulled straight out of your hole. Gangs and affairs and sweet Jesus Christ I don't even know what—'

'I'm coming up with theories,' Steve says. He's still staring. 'That's our *job*.'

'Theories, yeah. Not fucking *fairy* tales.'

'They're not—'

'They are, Moran. That's all they are. Yeah, sure, all of it's possible, but there's not one iota of hard evidence for any of it. Here you are talking my ear off about Aislinn being a fantasist, coming up with stories to make herself feel better about her shite life: you're doing *the same fucking thing*.'

Steve is biting down on his lip, shaking his head. I lean in closer, feeling the edge of the desk jam into my ribs, mashing the words into his face. 'Rory Fallon killed Aislinn Murray because they had some stupid spat and he lost his temper. Breslin and McCann are fucking with me because they want me gone. Desmond Murray has nothing to do with any of it. There's no thrilling hidden story here, Moran. There's nothing that's going to turn you into Sherlock Holmes tracking down the master criminal. You're a scut-monkey working a shitty little lovers' tiff, with your shitty squad giving you shite because they're shiteholes. The end.'

Steve is white around the freckles and breathing hard through his nose. For a second I think he's going to walk out, but then I realise it's not humiliation; it's anger. Steve is furious.

He starts to say something, but I point a finger right in his face. 'Shut up. And I should've known that right from the start – I *did* know right from the start, only like a fucking fool I let myself get carried away by you and your pretty little story. If there'd been even a sniff of anything good off this case, we'd never have got within a mile of—'

Steve throws himself back in his chair. 'Ah *Jaysus*, not this. "Everyone's out to get me, the world is against me—"'

'Don't you fucking—'

'It's like working with an emo teenager. Does nobody understand you, no? Are you going to slam your bedroom door and sulk?'

I can't work out how he's managed to live this long, whether he injects bleach into his ear every evening to burn the day out of his head and keep himself innocent. I say, 'You fucking spoilt little brat.' That widens Steve's eyes. 'All the imagination you've got going on, and you just can't imagine that other people might not have it quite as easy as you.'

'I *know* you don't have it easy. I'm right here, remember? I see it every *day*. There are people who give you shite. That doesn't mean that everything that ever happens is just an excuse to throw you to the wolves. You're not that fucking important.'

We're forcing our voices into something like calm. From a few yards away, where the floaters are, this would sound like just a routine work discussion. That only makes it more vicious.

'I get that you want me to be talking bollix, Moran. I get that. It'd make your life a whole lot easier if—'

'All I *want* is to stop walking on fucking eggshells. I *want* to stop turning cartwheels trying to put you in a decent mood, so you won't bite the head off anyone who comes near us—'

Steve cracking crap jokes when I'm in a fouler, till I give in and throw him the laugh he's angling for. I thought it was just him liking things to be nice, maybe even him liking me and wanting me to be happy. It hits me like a mouthful of sewer water: he was chivvying me into happy-clappy moods so I wouldn't kill his chances of buddying up with the lads. And I fell for it, time after time, had a laugh with him and felt better about the world. Steve doing his little dance and his jazz hands; me clapping right along, slack-jawed and grinning.

I say, 'Now we're getting somewhere. You'd love to believe you're trying to save me from myself, but when we get down to it, it's all about you being in everyone's good books.'

His head goes back in exasperation. 'It's *about* not making everything ten times harder than it needs to be. For me or for you. Is that so terrible, yeah? Does that make me an awful person?'

'Don't do me any favours. You're aiming for a big group hug and happy ever after, and you might even get them, but we both know it's not going to happen for me.'

'No,' Steve says flatly, 'it's not.' The anger compresses his words into hard chips, slamming down on the desk between us. 'Because you're so set on going down in flames, you'd make it happen even if the entire force loved you to bits. You'll light your own bloody self on fire if you have to. And then you can pat yourself on the back and tell yourself you knew it all along. Congratulations.'

He tries to shove his chair back to his end of the desk, where he can sulk in peace about what a demon bitch I am, but I'm not letting him away with that. I get hold of his wrist, under the edge of the desk. 'You listen to me,' I say, barely above a whisper, and I grip hard enough to hurt and have to stop myself gripping harder. Reilly has stopped banging his keyboard and the silence is stuffing my ears, my nose, making it hard to breathe. 'You arse-licking little fuck. You listen.'

Steve doesn't flinch or pull away. He stares back at me, eye to eye. Only the line of his mouth says I'm hurting him.

I say, 'You have no idea how badly I wanted this to be a gang case.

You can't even imagine. Because if it was a gang thing, then that would explain everything that's been going on. Breslin shoving Rory at us, the gaffer giving us hassle, McCann trying to swipe the old case file, Gary not wanting to be caught anywhere near me: they were trying to protect a bigger investigation, or a bent cop, or the whole lot of them were in the gang's pocket, I don't even care. But my mate in Undercover says there's not a sniff of a gang connection. Nothing.'

Keeping my voice down is hurting my throat, like something swallowed wrong and swelling. 'Do you get what that means? Breslin and McCann pulled all their crap *specifically, deliberately* to fuck me up. There's no other reason. All that bullshit with the roll of fifties and the secret appointments, you really want to know what that was about? Breslin and McCann are no more bent than we are. They wanted me to go chasing after them till I was in too deep to pull back, and then they'd haul me up in front of the gaffer – *Look, gaffer, she's been pulling our financials, she's been bugging our phones, she's a lunatic, she's a danger to the squad* . . . Job done: I'd be gone.' Saying it twists my stomach. I swallowed that shite whole, gobbled it down. 'And if it's got that far, if it's people like Breslin and McCann who I've never done anything on, if they're this serious about getting rid of me, then I'm done, Moran. I'm done. There isn't a way back. There's only one way this ends.'

Steve says, quietly and very clearly, 'Let go of me.'

After a moment I let go of his wrist. I was holding it so hard my fingers are cramped into position. They leave white marks on his skin.

Steve pulls his sleeve down. Then he puts on his coat, picks up his mug books and walks out.

A couple of the floaters lift their heads to watch him go and glance across at me, half curious. I give them a blank stare back and listen to the blood banging at my eardrums. As far as I can tell, I don't have a partner any more. It feels like everything in the room is jumping and jabbering and mocking me, tiny tinny chants of *ha ha ha*, because I should have seen this coming all along.

I put my head down and flip paper without seeing it. Words pop out of the blur at random – *inconsistent, sample, between* – and vanish back into it before I can figure out what they're for. The room reeks of cleaning fluid, rancid cigarette smoke off someone's coat, half-eaten apple left to rot overnight.

It doesn't hit me all at once. It comes like the slow cold of an IV crawling up a vein.

Steve, pushing from the start for us to gallop off chasing a nonexistent gang angle that could have cost me the case and turned me into a laughing-stock. Steve, who loves to be liked and is longing to belong in Murder, and who could have both in a heartbeat if only I was out of the way. Steve, in the car on the way to the scene, asking if I was going to take up my mate on the offer of the security job.

Steve, wandering off on his own into Aislinn Murray's kitchen, where he could have texted Creepy Crowley anything he wanted to.

There are stories about Steve. Small stuff, from years back, but people remember. Way back when we were in training college, I heard things: Steve writing half the essays for some inspector's kid, brown-nosing for good postings down the line. I put most of it down to the farm boys pouting about being beaten by a Dub one step from a skanger, and I didn't know Steve well enough to care either way. But then, when we were working that first case together, I heard more. Steve screwing over the lead D on a case so he could put some shiny stuff on his own CV, earn himself a payback favour or two, haul himself out of the floater pool into a squad. The guy who told me had an agenda of his own; I took a chance, ignored him and trusted Steve. I was right, that time.

That time, Steve had plenty to gain by sticking with me. He was looking for a way into Murder, starting to panic he was never going to find one. One day of working together, and I found it for him.

We felt right together, I thought. I liked the way, when one of us knocked down the other's idea, it always led into a new one, not a dead end. I liked how we were starting to know, without thinking, how to balance each other: what angle the other one would take in an interview, when I needed to ease back and let Steve do the work, when to come in and change the note. I liked the way he called me on my crap, not because his ego was tangled in his undies but because the crap was getting in our way. I liked the laughs. Once or twice – more – I caught myself daydreaming like a sappy teenager about our future together: about someday when we would get the decent cases, the genius plans we'd dream up to trap the cunning psychos, the interrogations that would go down in squad history. Big tough Conway going all misty-eyed; how the lads would have laughed.

I was a pushover. By the time I met Steve, Murder had already given me a good going-over; all it took was one bite of comfort, one scrap of loyalty, and I turned sloppy with relief, falling over myself to get Steve onto the squad. Of course working with him felt good; he had every reason to make sure it did. I knew Steve was the king of bending himself into whatever shape you want to see, I watched him do it every day, but I somehow convinced myself that this was different. I make myself want to puke.

He's got nothing left to gain by sticking with me, not now, and plenty to lose. Keyboards yammering, wind banging the window back and forth in its frame. Every pore in my body is prickling. When I run my hands over my head, my hair doesn't feel like mine.

I can't think. I can't tell if this is batshit paranoia or the bleeding obvious slapping me in the face. Two years of watching my back, watching every step and every word, in fight mode all day every day: my instincts are fried to smoking wisps. For a second I actually try to think of someone I could phone, ask what they think; but even if I wanted to do it, which I don't, the option isn't there. Sophie, Gary, Fleas: everyone I think of feels slippery and double, a picture flickering faster than my eyes can focus.

Reilly says something, and him and Stanton burst out laughing, big raw shouts like the lead-up to an attack. I can't stay in this room any longer. I try Lucy's mobile: switched off. I rake through paper till I find the contact info for two of Aislinn's exes – no one's tracked down the Spanish-student summer fling yet – and shove it in my pocket. Then I put on my coat and leave.

II

Aislinn knew how to pick them. Her exes make Rory look like an entire theme park's worth of thrills and spills. The first guy is an accountant for a software company that had a rough ride through the recession, going by the worn-out carpet and the water stains on the ceiling, but the buzz in the office says things are picking up. He met Aislinn in a sandwich queue when they were nineteen and went out with her for six months, but they both made it clear from the start that they weren't looking for anything serious; when they got bored they drifted off in their separate directions, no hard feelings and no let's-stay-friends. He remembers Lucy, vaguely, but they never had any problems and he can't think of any reason why she would have a grudge against him. He's nice-looking, in a forgettable way, and he seems like a nice guy; he says Aislinn was a nice girl, they had a nice time together, now he has a nice fiancée who he took for a nice dinner on Saturday night and he's never even looked Aislinn up on Facebook.

The second ex is maybe half a notch less boring. He works in a call centre, in a massive corporate office building plonked down in a field in the middle of nowhere; someone's genius business-park idea that got smashed in the crash, or someone's carefully planned tax loss. Four of the five floors are empty; the fifth has a few dozen drones in one corner, talking too loud because there's no one to be disturbed. For our chat, the guy brings me to some executive corner office, bare, with a film of dust covering the bed-sized desk. He met Aislinn through Lucy, five years back, when he was still trying to make it as a lighting operator. They had been going out for eight months, and he was starting to think this could be something special, when she dumped him. She said, and he believed her, that it was because she felt the same way: this was getting real, and what with looking after her sick mother, Aislinn didn't have the spare time or energy for something real. No contact since, not till he saw her on the news two nights back. He drifted out of touch with Lucy, too, when he quit theatre; not on bad terms, they just weren't particularly close to start with and didn't bother hanging out any more. On Saturday evening he was at a gig – we'll check the alibis, but I'm not expecting any surprises. The shock and the sadness and the tinge of wistful might-have-been ring true, but so does the distance: Aislinn was in this guy's past. He wasn't chasing her, looking to relight the fire, getting pissed off when he saw her preparing for a date that didn't include him.

Which is exactly what I expected. The interviews were good ones; I Cool Girled the exes into opening up about stuff they never planned on spilling. None of it is any use to me.

I walk back to my car through wide cold hush, the sound of wind in long grass building up from farther away than I can see, rolling in across the empty fields, over me and on. Normally it would make me edgy – too much nature gives me the creeps – but at last my head has the wiped-clean clarity I was looking for in my run, this morning. For the first time in days, maybe months, I can think.

I can't shake the feeling that it's because I've run Steve out of it. Without him at my elbow – tugging and yammering and pointing in every direction, peppering me with bits of babble that might or might not mean something and I have to figure out which – I finally have room to see straight. Under all that, all the maybes and the mirages, there are only two things worth seeing.

Rory Fallon, the sad little wimp. He's it; all there is to this case. That's why it keeps spitting up great clots of nothing: because there's nothing else to find.

And the second thing: this is my last case in Murder. I can outmanoeuvre Breslin and McCann and Roche and the whole foaming mob, for one more day, one more week, one more month; but sooner or later I'm going to put a toe wrong, and they'll have me. I think of a boxer, ducking and weaving away from every punch, faster and faster, till one blink and bang, blackness.

I'm not going to wait for the knockout, give Breslin or Roche or whoever the chance to do his smirking lap of honour around me. I'm going on my own terms. I'll finish this case and finish it right, tie Rory Fallon down so tight the best defence barrister in the country couldn't wriggle him free, go out with my head up. Then I'll ring my mate with the security firm and ask him if that job is still on the table. And somewhere in there, I'm gonna tell O'Kelly to fuck himself and punch Roche's teeth in.

For a second I wonder whether, while I was getting everything else arseways, I could have got Steve wrong. I wonder – not that it matters now – if this is what he was trying to distract me from, all along; if he didn't want me to notice that I was done. If the poor optimistic eejit actually liked working with me, just like I thought. If he had the same sappy daydreams, us taking down some Hannibal Lecter together without breaking a sweat, shooting our cuffs and swapping a nod and striding off to the next uncrackable case that needed the best of the best. The twinge that gives me is sharp enough that I hope I'm wrong.

The car is cold. Even after I slam the door, I can still hear that unceasing roll of wind through too much grass. Part of me wants to floor it out of there, but I can't think of anything I'm in a hurry to reach.

When I get back to the incident room, Steve is still gone. The floaters are eating lunch and bitching about some news story bitching about cops. Breslin is at his desk, with his chair tilted back and his feet up, finishing a sausage roll and flicking through the *Courier*.

'Ah,' he says, bringing his chair legs down and tossing his paper on the desk, when he sees me. 'Just the woman I've been waiting for. Been doing anything interesting?'

'Aislinn's exes,' I say, peeling my coat off. 'Nothing worth hearing. We'll check the alibis and cross them off the list.' The *Courier*'s front-page headline says WHO WAS COMING TO DINNER? Someone's told Crowley about Aislinn's date.

Breslin swings his feet off his desk. 'I need to stretch my legs after that,' he says, patting his stomach. 'Let's go for a stroll.'

'I've got notes to type up.'

'They can wait.' Lower: 'I've got something that can't.'

Maybe he's gonna offer to cut me in on his imaginary sideline. I don't bother putting much thought into whether to play along, seeing as it doesn't matter either way, and his way gets me out of that incident room. 'Why not,' I say, and enjoy the flick of surprise on his face as I turn around and head back out the door.

'So I talked to Rory's exes,' Breslin says, on our way down the corridor. I wonder where we're going for his chat. It's hit me this week, for the first time, how little privacy we all have from each other. People come and go in the canteen, the squad room, the locker room; the interview rooms have observation windows and audio feeds. I never realised before how you would need the squad to be part of you, close and reliable as your own body, in order to survive it.

'And?' I say.

Breslin grins. 'How did he put it? His usual type is more "casual" than Aislinn? I'm sure they're all very nice girls, but my God, I wanted to march the whole lot of them into some makeover show and tell the stylists to bring out the heavy artillery.' He heads down the stairs at a jog. 'You know those godawful hairy ethnic hoodies that students used to wear back in the nineties, to show you they were planning to go backpacking in Goa someday? I swear the last ex was actually wearing one of those.'

'They give us anything?'

'Yes and no. All of them say Rory was a perfect little gentleman: never hit them, never yelled at them, no controlling behaviour, no jealous rages, no turning nasty when he didn't get his way, none of that.' He turns down the corridor and cracks the door of Incident Room E, the shitty ex-locker-room. Empty. 'In here.'

He holds the door for me. I get the message: in here, where I would be already if it wasn't for Breslin helping me out. The place is hot and still stinks of sweaty gym gear; the tiny whiteboard is stained where someone used the wrong kind of marker, and all the chairs look sticky. I don't sit down.

'But here's the interesting part,' Breslin says, closing the door behind us. 'Two of the exes, including the most recent one, say they dumped Rory because he was too intense. One girl's exact words were "too full-on"; the other one said he was "taking things way too quickly". I thought she was being coy, but it turned out she wasn't talking about sex: she had no problem shagging his brains out on the second date, God bless her. The young people nowadays don't know how good they've got it.'

'So what was she talking about?'

'Basically, by the time they'd been seeing each other for a few months, Rory was starting to think this was some great epic romance, while the girl was still deciding whether she even wanted a serious relationship. She says she really liked him, but she was only twenty-four; she was just looking for a few laughs and some intellectual conversation – she's doing a PhD in Russian literature – with plenty of sex thrown in. She wasn't ready for someone who kept talking about how amazing it would be to go around the world together.' Breslin examines the wall by the door, flicks away a speck of something and leans against it. 'So she dumped him. The other girl said the same thing, give or take. I keep hearing how women are dying for a guy who's not scared of commitment, but it looks like Rory might be a little too much of a good thing.'

According to Aislinn's second ex, when the relationship started getting real, she was out of there – although she blamed that on the sick ma. 'So when Rory told us him and Aislinn fell madly in love at first sight,' I say, 'that doesn't mean Aislinn felt the same way.'

'Exactly. Remember what he said about their date at Pestle? Every time he thought they were getting on like a house on fire, she'd go quiet on him and he'd have to kick-start the conversation again? That sounds to me like the other side of the story – if only we could hear it – would go, "He kept getting way too intense, but hey, he's a nice guy, so I tried to give him every chance . . ."'

'The only thing is,' I say, 'that doesn't fit with what the best mate told us. She was positive that Aislinn was head over heels. And those texts on Aislinn's phone, about how excited she was, getting ready for Rory to come over? There's no hint anywhere that she was backing away. If Rory was full-on, Aislinn was fine with that.'

Breslin pulls out his phone, which is the size of his head and in a flashy stainless-steel case, and spins it in his hand. He says, 'I've got to admit something here. I've been going back and forth all morning on whether to share this with you or not.'

Yesterday, I might have bitten. Instead I keep my mouth shut and wait.

When he realises I'm not gonna beg, he sighs, spinning the phone again. Light flashes off it in oily grey streaks. 'I'm a team player, basically. People have this idea of me as some high achiever, but I'm actually a big believer in teamwork. But that only flies if the other people on your team are working the same way. Do you get where I'm going here, Conway?'

I say, 'I'm thick. Go ahead and spell it out for me.'

Breslin pretends to think that over. The heat and the stench are inflating into a solid thing pressing in on us. 'You're sure you want to hear this?'

'You're the one who says you've got something to tell me. Yeah, I'm positive I want you to just spit it out, instead of wiggling around it dropping hints.'

Breslin sighs again. 'OK,' he says, as a big favour. 'Here you go: you go into every interaction treating the other person like your enemy. Now we both know in some cases you've got decent reasons for that, but even when you've got no reason at all, you're straight into attack mode. That creates an atmosphere where even the most dedicated team player is going to think twice before he shares anything with you.'

In other words, it's my fault he's been concealing evidence from the lead D. Even if there was still a reason to play along, I've got nothing left to do it with. 'Spit it or don't,' I say. 'If you're not going to, then tell me, so I can go type up my notes.'

He stares me out of it. I can't even be arsed giving him a stare back. He's gonna tell me; he's only dying to. He's just seeing what he can wring out of me in exchange.

'Conway,' he says, putting in all the ferocious patience he can fit. 'Do you take my point here? At least tell me you get my point.'

'Yeah. I'm a bitch. I knew that already.' I move to go.

'All right,' Breslin says, smooth but fast. 'I guess I've got to know you well enough, this week, that I can take the rest as read.'

'Whatever.'

'Our boy Reilly. Remember how he was pulling CCTV footage for Stoneybatter?'

After a moment I take a step back, away from the door.

'Well,' Breslin says, with a touch of a smile to show we're buddies again. 'Reilly's turned out to be a bit of a bright spark. While he was at it, he pulled the last four weeks – or as much as he could get; some places had taped over it. And he stayed in till five this morning with his finger on the fast-forward button.'

The slithery fuck. I say, 'He better have a very good reason why I'm hearing this from you, not from him.'

'Ah, well. I'm going to ask you to cut the kid some slack there. I get the feeling he wanted to impress me.' Breslin almost manages to hold back the fat, self-satisfied smirk. 'No harm in that. Get in a few more years on the squad and you'll have newbies flexing their guns for you, too.'

I get the message: *If you last another few years.* I say, 'What'd he get?'

'Here's a taster,' Breslin says. 'This is just a quick clip I shot off the monitor; there's more where it came from.'

He swipes, taps, and holds out the phone to me. I take it.

Fuzzy colour footage, but I'm in the shop often enough that I recognise it straightaway: Tesco on Prussia Street. And I recognise the skinny guy taking a bottle of Lucozade out of the fridge and bringing it over to the self-checkout. The delicate profile, the angle of the head, the slight hunch to the shoulders, the drifting way his hands move: I spent hours focusing on every detail of him, just two days ago.

I say, 'That's Rory Fallon.'

'Him or his clone. And have a look at this.'

Breslin leans in, pinches the screen bigger and homes in on the time stamp. 9.08 p.m., 14/01/2015. Two weeks back.

I say, 'Rory told us he had to look up the nearest Tesco on his phone, Saturday night.'

'He did. He also gave us the very definite impression that he'd never been to Stoneybatter before.' On the screen, Rory scoops his change out of the checkout machine and glances around. For a second he looks straight into the camera. His eyes, blurred and wide and intent, stare like he can see me staring back. 'But like I said, this is just the tip of the iceberg. We've got him within a few minutes' walk of Aislinn's house at least three other times this month. His car went past a camera on Manor Street last Thursday evening, he bought his Sunday paper in the corner shop on the eleventh of January, and he had a pint in Hanlon's on the fifth.'

Rory squirming when we talked about his side trip to Tesco. I thought it was the timeline that was making him twitchy, but it was a lot more than that. Rory hadn't needed to look up local shops on his phone. He already knew them by heart.

'And that's not counting the times Reilly didn't spot, and the times that didn't get caught on CCTV, and the times more than four weeks ago.' Breslin takes his phone back. 'Talk about "too full-on",' he says. 'Rory's been stalking Aislinn.'

I say, 'Looks like it.'

'He wasn't bringing nutritious meals to Stoneybatter's senior citizens. Anything innocent, he would've told us by now.' He slides the phone into his pocket. 'Now, wasn't that worth sticking around for?'

'I'm gonna have a chat with Reilly,' I say. 'Then I want to see the rest of that footage. Then I'll pull Rory back in and I'll see what he's got to say.'

'Why don't we make that *we*. You and I, we'll see what he's got to say.'

'I'm OK on my own. Thanks.'

Breslin's eyebrows go up on that. 'On your own? What about Moran?'

'He's out.'

'Uh-huh,' Breslin says. 'You're making him shake his trees by himself now, yeah? I thought your patience was wearing thin, all right.'

'Moran's well able to take care of business on his own. He doesn't need me to hold his hand.'

Breslin's scanning me, amused. He says, 'I could've told you that you and Moran weren't right for each other.'

I say, 'I didn't ask.'

'Give that kid a dozen witnesses and a DNA match and a video of the murder going down, and he'd spend the next year making totally positively sure that the scumbag didn't have a long-lost twin and the witnesses weren't confused and no one spit in the DNA, just in case. I'm not knocking it; there are cases that need that approach. But you, on the other hand: you want to get stuff done.'

'I do, yeah. That's why I'm gonna go sort out Reilly and have a look at that footage, instead of having the chats about life in here. See you later.'

'Jesus Christ, Conway, can you un-bunch your panties just for one minute? I'm *on your side* here. You keep acting like I'm the enemy. I don't know where you got that idea, but I'd like to put it to bed.'

'Breslin,' I say. 'I appreciate you showing me the footage, and all that shite. But I'm gonna assume anyone on this squad is the enemy, unless I've got stone-cold proof that he's not. I'm pretty sure you can understand why.'

'Oh, yeah,' Breslin says. He cracks the door and checks the corridor: no one there. 'I understand exactly why. In fact, I understand a lot better than you do. Do you want to know the story I heard about you?'

He thinks he sounds tempting. I say, 'Why don't you just assume it was all bollix, and we'll go from there.'

'I do assume it's all bollix. But you still need to hear it.'

'I've made it thirty-two years without giving a shite about other people's bitching. I think I can manage a while longer.'

'No. You can't. Every time you walk into the squad room, when you think you're just checking your e-mail and drinking coffee, this story is what the lads are hearing in their heads. As far as they're concerned, this is who you are. And how's that working out for you?'

He wants to tell me the story, badly. Him and McCann have worked hard to make me think he's just a big-hearted guy, but that kind of offer – here, let me take a chunk of your life and rewrite it my way – that never comes out of the goodness of anyone's heart. I say, 'When I need a hand, I'll let you know.'

'It'll sting. I'm not going to lie to you.' Breslin has his sympathetic face on, but I've seen it before, in interview rooms. 'I can see why you might not want to deal with that.'

'I don't. I don't want to deal with anything except my cases. And I want that word with Reilly.'

I go for the door, but Breslin stretches out an arm to block my way. 'You had a run-in with Roche, your first week,' he says. 'Remember that?'

'Barely. Old news.'

'Except it's not. You underestimated Roche. Not long after, he told us that back when you were in uniform, you fucked up big-time. You were supposed to be guarding some drug dealer while your partner did a sweep of his house; you took off the cuffs so the suspect could go behind a hedge and take a piss, and he did a legger. Then you told your partner – Roche didn't name names; he's too smart for that – that if he put anything in the report, you'd have him up for sexual assault, claim he'd been grabbing your tits in the patrol car.'

Breslin lowers his arm and takes one deliberate step to the side, out of my way. I don't move, just like he knew I wouldn't.

'When your partner wrote you up anyway,' he says, 'you followed through: went to your gaffer. The shit hit the fan, the report got rewritten your way, your partner's stuck in blue for the rest of his career, and you got three weeks' paid leave to recover from the trauma of it all. Is any of this sounding familiar?'

The three weeks I spent being Fleas's cousin. And before that, there was a suspect – some idiot off his face on speed; I don't even remember his name, that's how big an impression the whole thing made – who did a runner on me and my partner. My partner was a good guy, in the uninspired way that stamps BLUE FOR LIFE on your forehead from your first day. Roche did his research, made sure the story tasted of truth just enough that people would swallow it whole.

Breslin says, 'About half the squad believes it. And they want you gone, asap, before you pull the same shite on one of them. They're very, very serious about it.'

He's watching me under his eyelids for a tear, a tremor, a sign that I want to kick Roche's teeth out the back of his skull. 'I was right,' I say. 'I could've survived just fine without knowing that. Thanks, though. I'll keep it in mind.'

That snaps his eyes open. 'You're taking this very lightly, Conway.'

'Roche is a shitball. That's not exactly breaking news. What do you want me to do? Faint? Cry?'

'It wasn't an easy choice, telling you this. I'm a very loyal person. There are plenty of people who would see this as a betrayal of the squad – and this squad means a lot to me. I want you to at *least* show a little appreciation for what I've done here.'

Another minute and he'll have himself worked into a full froth of outrage, and I'll have that to clean up before I can go back to business. 'I appreciate it,' I say. 'I do. I just don't get why you're telling me.'

'Because someone needs to. Your partner should've done it months ago – come on, Conway, of course Moran knows; you think Roche let him get through his first week without cornering him to tell him what he'd hooked up with?' He's still scanning for a reaction, cold hungry cop-eyes above the touch of smirk. Breslin's aiming to end this chat with me sobbing my little heart out or punching walls or both. All the energy he's putting into it; what a waste. 'Your partner's supposed to have your back. We wouldn't need to have this conversation if he'd done his bloody job.'

I say, 'Maybe he didn't see any reason why I needed to know.'

'What the hell? Of *course* you fucking need to know. You need to know *now* – no, fuck that: you needed to know months ago. You're on your last legs here. Are you *getting* this, Conway?' Breslin's leaning in, too close, the hulking loom he uses on suspects wobbling on the edge of a confession. 'You've still got a shot, but it's your last. If you pull your head out of your arse and quit treating me like the enemy, then we'll have this case put to bed by the end of the week. I'll be able to vouch for you in the squad room, and my word actually carries a fair bit of weight there. And then, if you can manage to act civil to the lads, then you'll be sorted, and you'll be an asset to the squad – and like I said, that means something to me. But if you keep blocking me because you've got some martyr complex going on, then this case is going to go to shit, and I'm not going to be on your side any more, because I don't *like* being associated with cases that have gone to shit. And then, not to put too fine a point on it, you're fucked.'

He leans back against the wall again, sticking his hands in his pockets. 'It's your call.' The knight in shining armour, all ready to rescue me, if only I would let him.

I don't get rescued. I'll take help, no problem, just like I took it off Gary and off Fleas. Rescue – where you're sinking for the third time, you've tried everything you've got and none of it's enough – rescue is different.

If someone rescues you, they own you. Not because you owe them – you can sort that, with enough good favours or bottles of booze dressed up in ribbons. They own you because you're not the lead in your story any more. You're the poor struggling loser/helpless damsel/plucky sidekick who was saved from danger/dishonour/humiliation by the brilliant brave compassionate hero/heroine, and they get to decide which, because you're not the one running this story, not any more.

I had Breslin wrong all the way. He's not out to sink me, not necessarily. He's out to own me.

This is what McCann was softening me up for, with his salvaged statement sheet and his heart-of-gold routine. Maybe Breslin has some squad split in the works, him against Roche, and he's building up his team. Maybe he's got a hint that the gaffer is putting in his papers – the golden boy would know – and he figures bringing the bad girl into line would boost his chances for the job. Maybe he's got nothing specific lined up, just figures I'm an easy opportunity and I'll come in useful somehow, down the line.

I could laugh, if I had the energy. I'm not gonna come in useful to anyone, not on this squad.

Breslin taps his phone pocket. 'Conway,' he says, more gently. 'I didn't have to share this with you, remember? I could have just pulled Rory in myself and gone at him solo. I'm sharing because I think it's better for everyone if you and I work together. Better for the case, for the squad, for you – and yeah, better for me.' He smiles, putting in just the right balance of fatherly warmth and professional respect. 'Let's face it, Conway: you and I, we make a good team. We did nice work together on Rory, Sunday afternoon. With this' – the phone pocket again – 'we can do a lot better.'

I'm gearing up to tell him where to stick his rescue effort, when I realise it doesn't matter. I don't have to worry about Breslin rescuing me, owning me, sinking me, any of that fancy crap; whatever he has in mind for me, I won't be here for it. He's right, we're good together, and all of a sudden I'm free to use that, without going into a tailspin about consequences like Rory bloody Fallon himself. This quitting thing is fun; I wish I'd thought of it months ago.

'OK,' I say. 'Let's do it. But we don't bring up that footage till I give the word. I want to save that.'

'No problem. You call it.' Breslin grins at me. 'This is going to be a lot of fun, Conway. When we show Rory this, he's going to wet his frilly knickers.'

'It's better than that,' I say. Breslin raises a questioning eyebrow. 'We've been looking for a motive, or at least something that could've triggered the attack. Right?'

Breslin blows air out of one corner of his mouth. 'Well. You have. I still don't actually care why he did it, as long as we can show that he did it.'

'Rory gets over to Aislinn's place,' I say, 'all amped up for the big night. He's a bit early, but that's no big deal; she lets him in, they're delighted to see each other. And then, somehow, the stalking comes out. Maybe he lets something slip that tells Aislinn he knows Stoneybatter. Or maybe she mentions having seen him around the area, and he doesn't cover it fast enough.'

It feels good, coming up with a story. I can see why everyone's so hooked on it. I've got the whole scene playing out in front of me like another video clip, but one I can tweak and nudge till everything about it suits me right down to the ground. 'Either way, Aislinn's not happy. She's already been having doubts about how full-on Rory is; she dismissed those, but this takes him over the line into whacko territory. She tells him to leave, and he loses the head.'

Breslin has his lips pursed and he's nodding away. 'I like this,' he says. 'I like it a lot. Conway, I think you're onto something here. I knew there was a reason I had faith in you.'

I say, 'Let's see what Rory thinks of it.'

Breslin smiles at me, a great big warm smile like I'm the best thing he's seen in months. 'Come on,' he says. 'Let's get out of here. This place stinks.'

I could drink the air in the corridor in one swallow, after that snot we've been breathing. Breslin shuts the incident-room door behind us with a neat contemptuous slam that says, *You won't be needing this place any more*.

Back in the incident room, I ring Rory and ask him, all friendly and casual, if he would mind giving us a hand by coming in for another quick chat. I'm all ready to knock down a bunch of excuses about how he can't leave the shop and he's got an appointment and he doesn't feel well, but he falls over himself agreeing to come in straight-away. He's just desperate to prove he's on our side, but I'm so unused to things being easy that it feels unnatural, almost creepy, like the world has slid a notch sideways and won't click back to reality. I want sleep, a lot of it.

Steve is still out. I catch some autopilot part of me actually hoping he'll show up before Rory does – I'll have to start off the interview with Breslin, what with him bringing me that footage, but I can swap Steve in before we get to the final push; we'll get a confession off Rory, show that ditzy fool Steve that I was right all along, he'll apologise and we'll go for a pint and everything will go back to normal— This is when my brain catches up and remembers that things aren't going back to normal, not ever again. The incident room lurches, light jumping and stuttering, the hum of the computers rising like sirens.

When I beckon Reilly over to my desk, he doesn't even bother faking an apology, just puts on a blank pig-face and stares over my shoulder, waiting for me to be done. I was all geared up to take his head off, but looking at that face barely hiding a sneer, all I can think of is Steve: Steve, on that old case years back, getting that key piece of info and pinning it to his lapel instead of bringing it home to the lead D. Reilly makes me sick. I don't want him ripped to pieces any more; all I want is him out of my sight. When I tell him to go back to the floater pool, his face – sneer slapped right off, raw burn of anger and humiliation rising – doesn't even give me a drop of satisfaction. The other floaters pretend they're concentrating on work while he gathers up his stuff and leaves, slamming the door on his way out. Breslin lounges at his desk and watches me, eyes hooded, pen between his teeth, all ready to tell me whether I've done the right thing or not. I don't ask.

The footage shows exactly what Breslin said it did: Rory, wandering around Stoneybatter when he shouldn't have been. I send Meehan to head over there, pull all the December CCTV footage he can get – there won't be much left – and start watching. Then I pick out the best shots of Rory, with time stamps, and print them off.

The phone on my desk rings: Bernadette, to say Rory Fallon is downstairs. 'He's here,' I say to Breslin.

'Let's do it,' he says, shoving his chair back. 'See you later, boys. We'll bring you back a nice scalp.'

The floaters glance up and nod, too quickly, scared I'll rip the throat out of anyone who makes eye contact. On my monitor, a blurry black-and-white Stoneybatter street moves in jumps – runner frozen in one corner of the screen, teleported to the opposite side in a blink; Alsatian caught in mid-piss, then vanished – till I hit Stop. The computers and the whiteboard and the floaters billow and shrink around the edges like thin fabric underwater, drifting farther away all the time.

12

Rory is in even worse shape than he was on Sunday. His hair still has that plastered-down look, his eyes are bloodshot and his skin is a dry, clothy white. He smells of clothes left too long in the washing machine. A smile jerks up on his face when he sees us, but it's a reflex, jittery and mechanical. We're gonna have fun getting him chilled out enough to be useful.

We start by taking him to the nice interview room, the one for shaken-up witnesses and victims' relatives. It's cute: pastel-yellow paint, chairs that don't hate you, a kettle and a hotel-style basket of tea bags and itty-bitty sachets of instant coffee. My First Interview Room, we call it. Even through his jitters, Rory feels the difference; he relaxes enough to take off his second-best coat and hang it tidily over the back of his chair. Underneath he has on jeans and a baggy beige jumper that's twenty quid's worth of knitted depression.

'Let's get through the paperwork first,' Breslin says, sliding a rights sheet and a pen across the table. Since Chief Jock is the intimidating one, he's armed with a big file bursting with everything that could come in useful, plus random paper for padding. Cool Girl is on Rory's side, deep down, so I've got nothing but my notebook and my pen. 'Sorry about this; I know you've already done it, but we need a new one of these every time. You are not obliged to say anything unless you wish to do so, but anything you do say will be taken down in writing and may be given in evidence. Just like last time. Is that all OK?'

Rory signs without reading. 'Thanks,' Breslin says, through a yawn and a pec-display stretch. 'I need real coffee, not that instant rubbish. Rory? Antoinette? What'll I get you?'

Normally I'd smack down the 'Antoinette' crap, but I know what he's at. 'Oh God, yeah, real coffee,' I say. 'Black, no sugar. And see if you can find a couple of biscuits, would you? I'm starving.'

'I'll raid O'Gorman's stash,' Breslin says, grinning. 'He buys the good stuff; no Rich Tea nonsense there. Rory, what'll you have?'

'Um, I—' A baffled blink while Rory tries to chase down the potential implications of hot drinks. 'Tea would be— No, coffee. With a bit of milk. Please.'

'Your wish is my command,' Breslin says, and hauls himself out of his chair with a groan. 'I could sleep for a week. It's this bloody weather. One decent bit of sunshine and I'd be a new man.'

'Have a look through O'Gorman's desk, while you're at it,' I say. 'See if he's got a couple of tickets to Barbados in there.'

'If he does, we're out of here. Rory, got your passport?' Rory manages to catch up and find a laugh, a few seconds too late. Breslin throws us both a grin on his way out the door.

I lean back in my chair, stretching out my legs in front of me, and pull out my hair elastic to redo my bun while we wait. 'Oof,' I say. 'Long few days. How've you been getting on?'

'OK. It's a lot to take in.' Rory's on guard. He hasn't forgotten that I'm the mean cop who didn't tell him Aislinn was dead. Steve would have had him cosy and chatting in no time.

Steve isn't the only one who can play nice. 'It is, all right,' I say. 'Do you want me to set you up with Victim Support, find you someone you can talk to? That's their job, helping people through this kind of thing. They're good.'

'No. Thanks.'

'You sure?'

'Yes. I'll be fine. I just . . . what I really need is to know what happened. I need to know that.'

'Well, yeah,' I say, with a rueful grin. 'Don't we all.'

Rory risks a fast glance at me. 'Don't you . . . ? Do you know yet?'

I sigh and give my head a massage, while I have the hair down. 'To be honest with you, no, we don't. We've followed a load of lines of investigation, and I can't go into details, but basically none of them are taking us anywhere. That's why we're calling back the people who were closest to Aislinn: we're hoping someone will be able to give us a fresh idea, kick-start things.'

Rory says, still wary, 'I'd only known her a couple of months.'

'I know, yeah. But a connection like you and Aislinn had, that counts more than years of sitting next to her in work and chatting about internet kitty pics.' I get the tone right: no syrup, just direct and clean and matter-of-fact. 'You understood her. That was obvious, last time we talked. You weren't just seeing some blonde with a faceful of fancy makeup; you saw straight through all that. You saw who she really was.'

Rory says quietly, 'That's what it felt like.'

'That's valuable, man. Me, I'm never going to meet Aislinn. I'm relying on people like you to show me who she was. That's how we'll figure out what could've happened to her.' I've forgotten all about putting my hair back up; too earnest about this conversation, too far into off-duty chat mode. 'And I'd say you've thought about nothing else, the last couple of days. Am I right?'

Rory bites at his lips. After a moment: 'More or less. Yes.'

'And the last couple of nights.'

A nod.

'Hang in there,' I say gently. 'I know what it's like. At first it feels like it's taken over your whole life, yeah? And you're never going to get your head above water again?'

The breath and the wariness go out of Rory together. His shoulders fall forward; he pushes his fingers up under his glasses to rub at his eyes. 'I haven't *slept*. I don't do well with no sleep, but I can't . . . I've just been walking up and down my living room, hours and hours – my legs are killing me. Late last night something happened in the street outside, a man shouting, and I thought I was having a heart attack; I genuinely thought I was going to die, right there leaning against my wall. I haven't been able to open the shop, I haven't even been able to go out of my *flat*, in case I make a fool of myself by fainting if someone slams a car door.' He gives me a glance that's meant to be defiant. 'I suppose you think that's pathetic.'

I do, but even more, I think it's gonna be useful. 'Me?' I say, startled. 'Jesus, no. I've seen a lot of people go through this. The way you're feeling, that's par for the course.'

'When you rang . . . I was actually relieved, do you know that? Which is obviously ridiculous, but all I could think was that now I don't have to spend the day . . .' His voice wavers. He presses his fingertips to his mouth.

'You're doing me a favour, too,' I say, with just the right amount of sympathy in the smile. 'In this weather, I'm a lot happier in here than out doing door-to-door.'

'All I can do is think about it. How it might have happened. I've come up with *dozens* of scenarios. That's why I can't sleep. When I close my eyes, those are all I can see.'

'Thank Jaysus,' I say, heartfelt. And when Rory looks up, eyes widening: 'That's what we do, yeah? We come up with theories on how this could have happened, and then we try to match them to the facts. Only this time none of them are matching, and I have to admit, I've run out of theories. I've been going mental trying to come up with more. If you've got any new ones, then for Jaysus' sake, throw them my way.'

That would give Steve a laugh: me, begging for all the if-then-maybe fantasy crap this guy can dish out. The thought of Steve jabs me up under the ribs hard enough to mess with my breath.

Rory manages a small, tugged-down smile. 'How long have you got?'

'Tell you what: start with your best shot. The one that, deep down, you think is actually what happened. If it's any good . . . Jaysus, I'll owe you big-time. And if it doesn't fly, and that fella's still not back with the coffee, you can throw the next one at me.'

He looks at me like I might be setting him up for some point-and-laugh joke. 'Seriously?'

'Of course, seriously,' I say. 'I told you: we rang you because we need all the help we can get. Anything you've got is better than a load of nothing. Unless you figure it was, like, aliens.'

This time the smile is almost real. 'No aliens,' Rory says. 'I promise.' I sit up and pull out my notebook, ready to catch the pearls of wisdom. 'Well. This is the one I keep coming back to. The thing about Aislinn . . .'

Saying her name makes him flinch. He takes off his glasses and polishes them, turning me and the room blurry and soft, easy to talk to. 'The thing you have to understand about Aislinn,' he says, 'is that she was the kind of person who made you daydream. When you were with her, you found yourself coming up with stories.' His back is straightening already; I've got him on home ground. 'I wondered if it was because she was a daydreamer herself – I could tell she was; it takes one to know one – but it was more than that. It was because she didn't mind slipping into your daydream. Coming along for the ride. She liked it.'

Which sounds like a load of bollix to me: no one likes being turned into a bit part in someone else's fantasy. If that reaches my face, Rory can't see it, not with his glasses off; but he says, like he heard me thinking, 'She did. Just to give you an idea: when we went for dinner, I said to her that it felt like we'd known each other for years. Aislinn said yes, she felt the same way – she said something like "Maybe we did meet, somewhere along the way. It's a small country . . ." So I said, "Maybe we played together when we were little. Six, maybe. In a playground, in autumn. Maybe you'd brought your doll along . . ." Aislinn was smiling, and she said she always did bring her doll to the playground, a grubby old thing called Caramel. So I said, "Maybe you put Caramel down on a bench, so she could watch you on the swings, and I was on the swing next to yours. And then another little girl came along and thought Caramel had been abandoned, and picked her up . . ."'

Remembering the doll's name would have been adorable in the groom's speech; in this context, it's well over the line into creepy. Rory's smiling faintly, back at the Aislinn in his memory. 'I told her the whole story. The two of us saw the other little girl taking Caramel away, so we escaped from our families and followed her and her mother onto a bus and all the way into town, running after her down O'Connell Street, into Clery's – I said a Guard went after us, but we dodged and hid inside a huge umbrella, and we foiled a pickpocket by tripping him up with the point of the umbrella . . . It turned out that the pickpocket had just robbed the little girl's mother's wallet, and they were so grateful to us, the little girl didn't even mind giving Caramel back to Aislinn. And she and her mother brought us home in a horse-drawn carriage.'

Holy Jaysus. By this time I would have been out of the restaurant and halfway home, on the phone to my mate Lisa, breaking my shite laughing and swearing off relationships for life. 'I see what you mean about the date going great guns,' I say, smiling away. 'That must've been lovely.'

'It was. I'm sure it sounds silly, but at the time it felt—' His chin goes up defiantly. 'It felt magical. As if the whole thing had actually happened, but somehow we'd both forgotten, and telling the story was bringing it to life again. Aislinn was laughing, adding in bits of her own; she kept saying, "We must have been starving, maybe the man at the doughnut kiosk in O'Connell Street gave us doughnuts," and "Maybe a dog almost sniffed us out under the umbrella, and we threw a bit of doughnut to make it go away . . ." Like I said: she was happy with me making up stories around her. She encouraged it. She brought it out in people.'

He makes it sound like the whole thing was as unthinking and cute as a smile, just Aislinn skipping along among the daisies scattering happy daydreams wherever she went. I'm not so sure. I think of her in Missing Persons that day, pelting me with everything that should have started my mind wandering off down stories: the mystery, the tears, the snippets of info about what her dad had been like, the scraps of childhood reminiscence. If I had bitten – and maybe I would have, if the Daddy crap hadn't rubbed me up the wrong way – I would have been a lot more likely to give her what she was after: *And then the genius detective solved the poor orphan girl's problem, and they all lived happily ever after.* It worked on Gary. Aislinn knew how to use her knack.

She didn't get me. I raise a mental finger at her and say to Rory, 'And you're thinking that might have had something to do with what happened to her.'

Rory is nodding hard. 'Yes. Yes. The thing about daydreams is that they don't last. One brush up against reality, and that's the end of them. I know I must sound ridiculously spacy to someone like you, but I do understand that much.'

A sudden slice to his voice, and a sharp flash of his eyes; gone almost too fast to catch, but I was watching. Rory isn't fluffy clouds and adorable endings straight through; he's got something solid and keen-edged at the centre. Just like Aislinn. That combination made the two of them a perfect match, and then it turned on them.

'For someone like me,' Rory says, 'that's not a problem. I spend half my time in my head anyway, always have. I realise that, too.' That edge again. 'So when I bang up against reality and it bursts my bubble, that's not the end of the world. I'm used to it. Deep down, I was expecting it all the time.'

Which sounds a lot like a sideways explanation for why it couldn't have been me, honest, Detective. You get them a lot. Mostly you get them from killers. I nod along, concentrating hard on all these valuable insights.

Rory says, 'But a lot of people aren't like that. It took me a while to realise, when I was younger: some people spend all their time focused on what's actually happening.'

'I know what you mean,' I say. Confidentially: 'You get a lot of cops like that. No imagination.'

That gets an automatic half-smile, but Rory's too deep in his story to pay much attention to me. 'So if a man like that were to run into Aislinn, he wouldn't know how to prepare for the fact that his bubble was, almost definitely, going to burst. And when it did . . .'

'I get you,' I say, doing a little focused frown. 'At least, I think I do. Tell me what you're picturing. Specifics.'

Rory draws patterns on the table with one fingertip. He says, slowly, 'I think he was someone who wouldn't even have come onto your radar, because he knew Aislinn so briefly. They meet in a night-club, maybe, or through her work, and they get talking. Maybe he gets her phone number and they meet up for a drink, or maybe it never even gets that far. But his mind's already gone wild spinning stories, and he's intoxicated by the feeling – especially since, to him, it's brand-new.'

By now Breslin is waiting in the observation room, rolling his eyes and muttering at me to get a move on, while our coffee goes cold. He can do some deep breathing. If Rory needs all day to talk himself into this, then he's gonna get all day.

'And then, for whatever reason, Aislinn decides not to go any further with the relationship.' Rory looks up at me. His fingers are pressing down hard on the tabletop. 'If you're not used to that reality check, it's devastating. It's like I imagine cold turkey would feel to a heroin addict: actual physical upheaval, as well as psychological. Your body and your mind, floundering.'

'So he goes after her?' I say.

Rory shakes his head vehemently. 'No. Not like that. Someone who would do that, attack a woman just for breaking up with him after an evening or two – that's a monster. A psychopath. And Aislinn wouldn't have got involved with a monster to begin with. Just because she enjoyed daydreaming, that doesn't mean she was oblivious to reality. This man must have been a decent guy. Things just got out of control.'

Your average innocent guy whose girlfriend's been murdered, he's gonna picture the killer as a foaming animal who deserves seven kinds of electric chair. Rory can't afford to. 'That makes sense, yeah,' I say, taking notes and nodding. 'So what does he do?'

'If he can't be with Aislinn, at least he needs more material for the daydreams. Something to feed them. She's mentioned where she works, so he starts hanging around outside there, to see her come out. One evening he follows her home.' Some new charge is revving up underneath Rory's voice, powering it, swelling it. I don't need to nudge him, not any more. 'And once he knows where she lives, it becomes an addiction. He can't stay away. He tries, but every few days he finds himself straying towards Stoneybatter, before he realises he's going to do it. He finds himself wandering around the streets thinking about her feet touching those same pavements; buying chocolate bars he doesn't want, just to shop where she does. He finds himself outside her house, watching her while she makes cups of herbal tea and does her ironing.'

He's keeping close to the truth, staying parallel, almost touching. Smart choice: it makes the story ring almost true.

'He gets used to it, being out there in the dark, curling his toes to keep them from freezing. Watching the light in her windows. Imagining himself turning the key in the door and stepping into that warmth, and her coming to kiss him. Imagining the two of them cooking dinner together in that bright kitchen. He finds a routine, a kind of equilibrium; a kind of contentment. He could live like that indefinitely.'

Rory has changed. No more timid little gerbil. He's sitting forward, hands moving in fast, clean, confident gestures; that charge under his voice has built till every corner of the room hums with it. For the first time I can see why Aislinn went for him. This shite is the last thing I'd want in a guy, but it's got power. Rory has risen up out of his beige huddle and become someone who would make you turn to look when he came through a door, and keep looking.

'And then,' he says. 'Saturday night. This man went to watch Aislinn, as usual, but what he saw was different. He saw her all dressed up and made up, glowing like a treasure chest. He saw her making dinner, not just for herself, but for two people; taking two wineglasses out of the cupboard and bringing them into the sitting room. He saw her singing into her corkscrew, dancing, shaking her hair around and laughing at herself. He saw how happy she was. How she couldn't wait.'

Getting ready singing into corkscrew like teenager w hairbrush. That smell of blood soaks the air again, butcher's-shop thick. Rory's imagination is good, but he's not clairvoyant. He was watching Aislinn on Saturday night.

'It would have knocked him breathless. He must have felt like the world was tilting, he must have thought he had believed in that daydream so hard that it had burst its way into reality . . . He wouldn't have known that that's not the way life works.' A bitter wrench to one side of Rory's mouth. 'He would have been sure that, somehow, Aislinn was wearing that dress and cooking that meal for him. And when he could breathe again, he would have stepped out of the dark and wiped the worst of the rain off his coat, and he would have knocked on her door.'

Nice ending. Rory folds his hands, takes a long breath and looks at me expectantly. He wants to leave it there.

I'm loving this interview. Not just because it's going well; I'm loving this interview because it's clean. No ifs and maybes twitching in the corners, gumming up the air, itching inside my clothes. No layers on layers of outside chances and hypotheticals to take into account every time I open my mouth or listen to an answer. Just me and the guy across from me, and what we both know he did. It lies on the table between us, a solid thing with the taut dark shine of a meteorite, for the winner to claim.

I say, 'And then?'

Rory's neck twists. When I keep watching him, eyebrows up and inquiring, he says, 'Well. And obviously Aislinn wasn't getting ready for him; she was getting ready for me. She hadn't so much as thought about him in months. So she would have been astonished to see him. Presumably she told him to leave. And that's when he snapped.'

I keep up the inquiring look. 'And . . . ?'

Lower, to the table: 'And hurt her.' That charge is ebbing out of the room, out of Rory's voice and his face, leaving him wispy and beige again. His lovely story has burst, just like he described, against the gravel-sharp reality of dead Aislinn. When the silence keeps going, even lower: 'Killed her.'

'How would he do it?'

Rory shakes his head.

'Rory. Help me out here.'

'Don't you already know?'

'I'm asking you a favour,' I say gently, leaning in to catch his eye. 'Pretend it's just a made-up story, OK? Like the ones you told Aislinn? Just finish it for me. Please.'

'I don't . . . All I know is he wouldn't have had a weapon with him. A knife or anything. He would never have been planning to . . . Maybe a, a, a lamp or something, something that was already there . . .' He runs a trembling hand across his face. 'I can't—'

He's not going to let slip that he knows how she died. No big deal; it was a long shot. 'Wow,' I say. I lean back in my chair, blow out a long sigh and run my hands through my hair. 'Man. That's some powerful stuff.'

'Is it . . .' Rory catches a deep breath. He pushes his glasses back on and blinks at me, trying to refocus. 'Could it be useful? Do you think?'

'It could,' I say. 'It could well be. I'm obviously not going to go into the details of what I'm thinking, but there's a chance you could actually have given us something really valuable there. Thanks for doing that, man. Thanks a lot.'

'No problem. Do you think—'

'Hello-ello-ello,' Breslin booms cheerfully, bursting the door open with his backside and swinging in with his hands full of mugs. 'Sorry I took so long; that shower of uncivilised gits can never be arsed bringing their mugs back to the canteen, never mind washing them out. I had to chase these down. On the plus side—' He hands out the mugs and sweeps a packet of biscuits out of his jacket pocket with a flourish. 'O'Gorman's stash didn't let me down. Ladies and gentlemen, I give you chocolate-covered Oreos. Who's your daddy?'

'Ah, you star,' I say. 'I'm only starving.'

'At your service.' Breslin tosses an Oreo to me and one to Rory, who of course fumbles it, drops it on the carpet and has to go after it. He stares at it like he's not sure what it's for. 'Get that into you,' Breslin tells him. 'Before O'Gorman comes looking.'

'Come here,' I say, dipping my Oreo in my coffee. 'Rory's got a theory.'

'Thank Jesus,' Breslin says. 'At least someone has. Any good?'

'Could be,' I say, through most of my biscuit. 'Long story short, he figures Aislinn was the type who could get a guy fantasising about happy-ever-afters a lot faster than normal. So there was some guy who Aislinn was seeing, so briefly that he hasn't made it onto our radar; and once she dumped him, this guy got in over his head thinking about her. Started watching her. When he saw her getting ready for her dinner with Rory, he convinced himself she was waiting for him. Knocked on her door, got a nasty shock when she wasn't happy to see him, and snapped.'

'Interesting,' Breslin says. He throws his biscuit into his mouth and chews meditatively, considering. 'I like it. It could work with a lot of what we know.'

Rory doesn't look encouraged. He's huddled in his chair, picking carpet fluff off his Oreo. The second Breslin walked in, he faded and shrank and twisted like a boil-washed jumper.

'Exactly,' I say. 'It's got that feel, you know? In this job, you learn to recognise when something feels right. Practically and psychologically.'

'We love that feel,' Breslin tells Rory. 'We've been hunting it all week. I've got to admit, my son, your theory is the nearest we've got to that feel. We'll get people digging deeper into Aislinn's incidental contacts – nightclubs, work connections. If this guy turns up, Rory, we owe you that ticket to Barbados after all.'

He leans back in his chair and takes a long slurp of coffee, sorting through his file. 'Meanwhile,' he says, 'since we're here, you mind clearing up a couple of small things? Just so we can cross them off our list?'

'Ah, Jaysus, you and your lists,' I say, rolling my eyes. 'Ignore him, Rory. This guy makes lists of what he puts in his *pockets*, so he can double-check that he hasn't dropped anything. Don't get sucked in. Get out while you can.'

'Don't knock my lists, you,' Breslin says, pointing at me. 'How often have they saved our arses?'

'Yeah yeah yeah.'

'Rory? Is that cool with you? Just a few more minutes.'

We all know Rory's not leaving, not with nowhere to go but round and round his flat and his head. He says, 'I suppose—'

'See?' Breslin says to me. 'Rory doesn't mind humouring me. Am I right, Rory?'

'Yes. I mean—'

'*I* mind,' I say. 'If I have to put up with one more—'

'Beautiful,' Breslin says. 'Suck it up, Conway.' He flips paper. I sigh heavily, twisting my hair back into its bun: business time.

Breslin was right, we're good in interviews. It shoves the message home: working well together means bugger-all else. I catch the smooth cold span of the one-way glass in the corner of my eye and wonder if Steve is behind it.

'Ah,' Breslin says. 'Here we go: lovely list. Question One. Rory: Saturday evening, Aislinn and one of her friends were talking about you calling round for dinner. Sounds like she was looking forward to it.' He gives Rory a smile, holds it till Rory more or less smiles back. 'Sweet. And the friend warned Aislinn to' – he pretends to check his notes – '"be careful OK?" Why would she do that?'

Rory stares, bewildered. 'Who said that?'

'Who would you expect to say it?'

'I don't – I wouldn't. I hardly even know any of Aislinn's friends. Who—?'

'Hang on,' Breslin says, lifting a hand. 'You're telling us that, if Aislinn's friends *had* known you, they'd have had a reason to warn her to be careful? What reason?'

'*No.* That's not what I said. They wouldn't have a—'

'One of them thought she did.'

'She didn't. None of them had *any* reason. At all.'

'Must've been a misunderstanding,' I say. 'Was there something the mate could've taken up wrong? A new fella on the scene, mates can get protective, start seeing red flags everywhere—'

'Or jealous,' Breslin offers. 'Maybe the friend's a hound, can't get a fella of her own; she gets her knickers in a knot and decides to spin some little thing to try and put Aislinn off you. What could she have spun?'

Rory passes a hand over his eyes and tries to think. He's abandoned his Oreo untouched; he's figured out that we're not playing that game any more. Me and Breslin are still all smiles, but the air in the room's changed; the pulse is faster and harder and it's Breslin setting it now, not Rory.

'The only thing I can think of . . .' We wait encouragingly. 'I told you last time: it was complicated, setting up dates with Aislinn. But I kept trying, even when she cancelled. I suppose that could have come across as . . . I don't know. Pushy? I mean, I know *Aislinn* didn't think I was being too pushy, or she would have ended it, but maybe one of her friends might have—'

'Whoa,' Breslin says. 'Slow down. You just said you kept pushing Aislinn for dates, even when she cancelled; but then you're telling us, if she'd told you to get lost, you would've gone. Which is it?'

'But— No. That's not the same thing. She *never* said she didn't want to see me any more. If she had, then of *course* I would have gone. Saying "I'm busy on Thursday" isn't the same, it's completely—'

Rory's winding himself into a tangle of indignation and defensiveness. 'Hey, you don't need to convince us,' I say. 'The mate's the one who was worried. We're just trying to work out why.'

'That's the only thing I can think of. That's *it*.'

Breslin gets up from the table and goes for a stroll, giving Rory two places to look. He says, 'Sounds a bit thin to me.'

'And me,' I say. 'The friend's not the hysterical type, you know what I mean? If she thought Aislinn needed to be careful, she had a reason.'

'Maybe . . .' Rory clears his throat. 'Um, if I'm right, about the guy watching Aislinn . . . Maybe Aislinn had noticed him, and mentioned him to her friend? And the friend was worried that he'd get angry about her having me over?'

Breslin stops and gives Rory a long quizzical gaze – Rory holds it, in a blinky way. He says, 'Did Aislinn ever mention an ex who gave her the willies?'

Rory shakes his head.

'Out loud for the tape.'

'No. She didn't.'

'Most women aren't gonna bring up the ex to the new boyfriend,' I point out. 'Makes you sound like a bunny-boiler.'

Breslin shrugs. 'Fair enough, I guess. She ever mention having a stalker?'

The word makes Rory wince. 'No.'

'Not once?'

'No. But she might not have wanted to – I don't know, scare me off—'

'What, she thought you'd run a mile just because some rando was hanging around? Would you have?'

'No! I—'

'Of course you wouldn't. And Aislinn, not being an idiot, knew that. You think she would've bothered her arse with you, if she thought you were that much of a wimp? Conway: would you want a guy who scared that easy?'

'Nah,' I say. 'I like them to have at least one ball.'

'Exactly. I'm willing to bet Aislinn did too.'

Rory's shifting. 'OK. Maybe she didn't, she might not have known the guy was watching her—'

'Maybe not,' Breslin says. He leans in sharply towards the table and Rory flinches, but he's only going for another swig of his coffee.

'Maybe not. In which case, we're back where we started: when the friend told Aislinn to be careful, she couldn't have been talking about the stalker ex. Who's never entered anyone's head but yours.'

Except that he did. It twinges like a sore tooth that I thought was fixed, sorted, gone: an ex entered Lucy's head. According to her story, he was part of the reason she sent that text.

Breslin puts down his mug with a hard, precise clunk. 'So,' he asks, 'what was the friend talking about?'

Rory shakes his head. He's subsided back into his heap.

'Out loud for the tape.'

'I don't know what she meant.'

'Shame,' Breslin says. 'That could really do with an explanation. But if you're sure you can't help us there . . .' A small pause for Rory to come in, which he doesn't. 'I suppose we can leave it, for now. Let's move on down my list, shall we?'

He leans over his notes and scans. 'Ah,' he says. 'That's right. Question Two.'

He pulls a piece of paper out of his jacket pocket and unfolds it with a snap that makes Rory's shoulders leap. He has another stroll around the room while he reads down the page, taking his time, wandering behind Rory to make him twist in his chair.

'Tell me that's not another list,' I say, rolling my eyes at Rory. No response.

'This,' Breslin said, tapping the page, 'this is Rory's timeline for Saturday night.'

Rory's shoulders stiffen. 'Oh,' I say. 'Yeah. That's not as big a deal as you're making out.'

'You might be right. Let's find out.'

'What . . . ?' Rory's voice wobbles. He clears his throat and tries again. 'What's the problem?'

'Ah,' Breslin says. 'This is going to get complicated, Rory, so stop me if you're not following. According to you, you got on the 39A just before seven, and got off it in Stoneybatter just before half-seven. Walked around to Viking Gardens to make sure of the route – that brings us to, say, 7.32. Headed up to Tesco for flowers: we've timed it at around a seven-minute walk, so you'd have got there by 7.40.'

Rory has stopped tracking Breslin's stroll. He's rigid, feet braced on the floor, staring ahead.

'Your statement says you spent "a couple of minutes" in Tesco; let's say you left around 7.43. Another seven or eight minutes to get back to Viking Gardens, maybe less since you said you were hurrying: you'd have been at Aislinn's door by 7.50. Are you with me?'

'If you're not,' I say, 'get Bres to write it down for you. Make him earn his wages.'

Rory says, without looking at me, 'I'm following perfectly well.'

'You are, of course,' Breslin says heartily. 'Except you told us you got to Aislinn's just before eight. What'd you do with the extra eight or nine minutes?'

And his shoulders slacken again. Rory thinks he's off the hook; he's loosening, body and mind, with relief. 'I haven't got a clue. I mean, God, maybe I got off the bus a little later than I thought, or took a bit longer choosing the flowers; or maybe I reached Aislinn's a few minutes earlier than I thought. Or all of those. I don't really notice exact times; I haven't been trained to, the way you have. I couldn't tell you within eight minutes what time it is *now*, or how long we've been here.'

Breslin rubs at his nose, embarrassed. 'When you put it like that . . .'

'See?' I say, to both of them. 'No big deal.'

'Professional deformation,' Breslin says, with a rueful little laugh at himself. I laugh too, Rory lets out a slightly hysterical half-laugh, we all laugh together. 'I swear to God, sometimes I think I've forgotten what it's like being normal. I mean, a normal person couldn't lose track of, like, *hours*, right? Or even half an hour? You couldn't have got to Aislinn's house at half-eight and thought it was eight o'clock. Ten minutes would be about the limit?'

'I suppose,' Rory says. He remembers his coffee and takes a quick, covert sip. 'Probably.'

'Huh,' Breslin says, turning over his piece of paper. 'I've got another timeline right here – get more of that coffee down you, you're going to need it.'

'So am I,' I say, raising my mug to Rory and throwing him a wink. 'Hang in there, man. The list's gotta end sometime.'

'Yeah, yeah. The sooner you two quit bitching, the faster we get through this.' Breslin moves round to my side of the table, getting into firing position. 'So. This timeline is built around CCTV. Which says you got on the bus at ten to seven, Rory, and you got off it in Stoneybatter at quarter past. That doesn't exactly match what you told us, but hey, like we said: a few minutes here, a few minutes there, to normal people . . .' He smiles at Rory, who's still relaxed enough to smile back. 'Except after that, the next time we can confirm your location is when you were caught on Tesco's CCTV paying for the flowers, at 7.51.'

Rory's smile is gone. He's starting to cop on.

Breslin's voice is getting more weight to it, words coming down on the table with thick cold thuds. 'Like we said, from Aislinn's place to Tesco is about a seven-minute walk. So if you were paying for the flowers at 7.51, you had to leave Viking Gardens by around 7.40. That leaves your movements unaccounted for from 7.15, when you got off the bus, until 7.40. Twenty-five minutes, Rory. We've just established that even a normal person couldn't lose track of *twenty-five minutes*. Do you want to tell me what you were doing for those *twenty-five minutes*?'

Rory is staring at the space between me and Breslin. He's clenched into one tight knot; his mouth barely moves when he says, 'I've already told you.'

'I thought you had,' I say, miffed. The thought of losing his lovely ally makes his breathing speed up, but he doesn't look at me. 'But now it looks like you've been feeding us a great big heap of shite. You want to try again, before we decide you might have a reason for not wanting us to know what you were doing that night?'

'I've told you what I did. I can't help it if it doesn't match your timeline.'

It's not a bad strategy: pick a story, plant your feet on it and don't budge, no matter what. Once you start shifting, we can shove you off balance, push you step by step to where we want you. We need Rory shifting.

Breslin swings his chair to the table and sits down in one fast sweep. I sit back: let him work it for now, while Rory wonders if I'm still his pal. He says, 'How'd you know Aislinn didn't have curtains in her kitchen?'

That gets through: Rory jerks and stares. 'What?'

'And the laneway out the back. How'd you know about that?'

'The— I didn't. I mean, I don't. What lane—'

'You described your theoretical stalker watching Aislinn cook the dinner and get out wineglasses: stuff she would have done in the kitchen, which is at the back of the house. You didn't have him watching her set the table, which is in the living room at the front. In other words, you knew the stalker would have been able to watch from the back of the house.'

Rory blinks wildly, bewildered. Breslin says, grinning, 'Dude, see that glass there? I was right behind it, listening, for your whole chat. Antoinette's a top-notch detective, but she's . . . how'll I put this without getting a punch?'

'Careful, you,' I say.

'Easy, tiger,' Breslin says, leaning away and holding up a hand to block me. 'Let's just say she's a little more willing than I am to believe that you're on our side. She's an optimist: she's been hoping all along that this case would turn out to be some great big fascinating mystery.' A slant of side-eye towards me, a hair's breadth of grin that could mean anything. 'Me, I've been around longer. I'm a suspicious guy – more of that professional deformation we were talking about. So I keep an eye on things. I heard just about every word you said. And I'm asking you: how did you know the stalker would have been watching Aislinn in her kitchen, unless you were the stalker?'

'I was *guessing*. It's – I mean, that's just, it's basic – basic common sense, if he didn't want the neighbours seeing him, that he would—' Rory's breath isn't working right. 'And the kitchen, that's where she's going to be preparing, isn't it, if I'm coming – which I *was*, I don't mean *if*—'

He's losing his foothold on that safe story. I say – a touch of worry, not happy with where things are going – 'Here's another thing. You talked about the stalker seeing Aislinn singing into her corkscrew. We know from her texts that that's exactly what she was doing that evening. How did you know about that, unless you were watching her do it?'

Breslin says, before Rory can get enough air to answer, 'Do me a favour: don't try and tell us you were guessing. Unless you're psychic, there's no way in hell you could guess that. Are you psychic, Rory?'

'What? No! How could – I don't—'

'Well, that's a relief. So tell us how you knew about the corkscrew.'

Rory shakes his head, panting and wordless. I say, 'Then I'll tell you. You watched Aislinn from the back laneway that evening. Am I right?'

After a long moment his head rocks, helplessly, on his neck: yes.

'That's how you spent the missing twenty-five minutes.'

Another nod. That one-way glass, splattering light into the corner of my eye again. I hope Steve is behind it. I hope he's scarlet right up to his hair.

'Out loud for the tape,' Breslin says.

Rory finds a pinch of voice. 'I just wanted to . . . I was just taking a moment. To let it sink in that this was really happening. That's all.'

'And the only way you could do that,' Breslin says, 'was by peeping through Aislinn's back window.'

He makes it sound filthy. Rory flinches. 'I wasn't— I was just standing there. Being happy. I don't know how to explain—'

'I guess I get it,' I say doubtfully. 'Sort of. It's not like you were watching her shower – or were you?'

'No! Even if I'd wanted to – which I *didn't*; I would have left if . . .' Breslin lets out an amused snort. Rory manages to ignore him by focusing on me. Telling the truth, or telling the story, has given him his breath back. 'Anyway, I couldn't have: the bathroom window is frosted. Aislinn was in the kitchen. She had music on – it was too windy for me to hear what, but I could tell it was something upbeat by the way she was dancing around, singing into . . . yeah. The corkscrew.' A glance at me, too sad for defiance. 'She was wearing a pink jumper and jeans, and she was taking things out of the fridge and opening them, putting them into pans, and dancing while she did it. After a bit she went out of the kitchen – I waited, and when she came back in she was wearing this blue dress . . . She looked – all blue and gold like that, it was like she'd just *appeared* in the kitchen, like one of those visions of saints that people used to have centuries ago. And she was smiling. And I couldn't believe that, in just a few minutes, I would be in there with her. She would be smiling at me.'

The grief goes deep, right to the heart of his voice. That means nothing. 'And then I thought of the flowers, and I headed for Tesco. And if I hadn't . . .' Rory grabs a fast breath through his nose, like he's been hurt. 'If I had just remembered that azalea plant, if I had just stayed there watching her— I would have been there. When he came. And I could have, I would have . . .'

His mouth starts to curl up. He presses his knuckles to it. I can feel Breslin clamping down a snide grin at the image of Rory throwing on his cape and tights and beating the shit out of the villain. Rory has presumably run through a couple of hundred variations on that scenario.

He says, through his fingers, 'But I didn't do any of that. I skipped off to Tesco like an idiot, and while I was gone someone came along and killed Aislinn. I may have *seen* him, but I didn't even take it in, because I was utterly oblivious to everything except my own happy bubble. And when she didn't answer her door, I waited and waited because I couldn't find a way to believe that she had changed her mind, when just a few minutes earlier she had been acting like she couldn't wait to see me. I was standing in the cold, trying to understand how that was possible, while she was lying inside, dead or dying. And in the end, instead of having the brains to realise that something had to be wrong and breaking the door in, I went home to feel sorry for myself. That's *it*. That's what happened.'

'Jesus, Rory,' I say reproachfully. 'Why didn't you tell us straight out?'

'Because I know how it sounds! I know it makes me come across like some . . . I can't expect you to understand what it was actually like.'

'I'm doing my best. It'd be a lot easier if you'd told us the truth right away.'

'I'm telling you now.'

Under the table, I touch my foot to Breslin's ankle. He says, without missing a beat, 'Well. Part of the truth, anyway. That wasn't the only time you watched Aislinn. Was it?'

Rory's eyes flash to him and to me and away to a corner. He picks fast. 'Yes. That was the first time.'

'No it wasn't.'

I say, 'That's why you needed your moment out the back, to take in that this was real. Because you'd watched her in that kitchen, and daydreamed about going in there, so many times before. Right?'

'Just like the guy in your scenario,' Breslin says. 'Your *hypothetical* scenario.'

'It *was* hypothetical. You *asked* me to imagine—'

'That moment must've felt amazing, did it?' I ask. 'After all those times when you'd had to turn around and go home again, in the cold . . .'

'It— Yes, it felt wonderful. But not because I'd been— I wasn't *stalking* Aislinn, I wasn't—'

Rory's starting to gibber again. 'Shh,' Breslin says.

'What?'

'Shh.' Breslin picks up his file. 'I want to show you something.'

He leans back and leafs through the file at his leisure, pausing occasionally to lick his thumb. Rory watches with his hands clenching the edge of the table, like he's ready to leap out of his chair, but he keeps his mouth shut. His control isn't completely gone.

'Here.' Breslin throws a handful of photos, big eight-by-tens, across the table. Rory grabs at them and sends them scattering. He catches one, takes one look and makes a high, startled whimper.

Breslin says, 'Pick up the rest of them.'

Rory doesn't move. His head is down over the photo, but his eyes aren't focusing.

'Pick them up.'

Rory moves automatically, stacking the photos one by one. His fingers are trembling.

'Look at them.'

He braces himself before he goes through them, but every image still gets a hard blink out of him. Breslin tells the video camera, 'I've just shown Mr Fallon images from CCTV footage taken in Stoneybatter over the past month.'

There's a silence.

'Rory. That's you in those pictures. We can all agree on that, can't we?'

More silence. Then Rory's head moves, just a twitch: yes.

'For the tape.'

'Yes.'

Breslin leans forward – Rory flinches – and brings down a finger on the top photo, the face staring straight into the Tesco camera. 'This is you. On the fourteenth of this month.'

'Yes. I was just buying, I was in there looking for—'

His mind is flailing for a new story. I say, 'You told us you'd never been to Stoneybatter before Saturday night. When you had to look up the nearest Tesco on your phone.'

His mouth moves as he tries to swallow.

Breslin's finger is still mashed down on Rory's photo face. 'So,' he says, pleasantly. 'Your pretty little story about the guy who got hooked on spying on Aislinn. That was based on real events, as they say on the telly. Right?'

'Not the – no. No. Not the part where—' His breathing is starting to get away from him again. 'I never, I—'

If he hyperventilates and faints on us, the paperwork is gonna take all night. I say, calm but firm, 'Rory. The part about the guy wandering around Stoneybatter to feel closer to Aislinn. You've been doing a bit of that. Yeah?'

'Yes. But—'

'Hang on. One thing at a time. The part about him watching Aislinn from the laneway: you did a bit of that, too. Yeah?'

'I just—' Rory's rubbing the back of one hand across his mouth, hard enough to leave red streaks. 'No. I—'

'Rory,' I say. 'Come on. You really want to tell us you were mooning around Stoneybatter for weeks, but you never went near Aislinn's actual gaff till the exact night she got killed? Because I don't like the sound of that.'

'No. Wait.' His hands fly up. He's so easy to shove, step by step, back towards the corner he's never going to get out of. 'I watched her just, maybe, just a few times. Only to—'

Breslin – he's pulled the photo over to himself and is examining it – says, 'But on Saturday night, Aislinn caught you out.'

That voice. Easy, almost a drawl, almost friendly. But it fills up the air, leaves no room for anything else. 'How did it happen? Did she come out onto the patio for some reason, see you hanging over her wall? Or maybe you said something about the trip to Tesco that made it obvious you knew your way around Stoneybatter. Maybe you said the kitchen looked nice with the new picture, or told her you love beef Wellington. And just like that' – Breslin lifts his hand, lets it fall onto the photo with a flat thwack – 'your dirty little secret's out.'

Rory's face is coated in a thin, sick shine of sweat. 'I was never. No. I wasn't in her house.'

Breslin ignores that. 'You walk into that house thinking you're walking into Paradise, and inside five minutes it's all turned to shite. Jesus, man. Ouch. I'm scarlet for you just thinking about it.' The sadistic curl at the corner of his mouth makes that into a joke. 'How did Aislinn take it?'

'She, *no* – she *didn't*. It never, it didn't happen, none of that – it—'

'I bet you remember the exact look on her face. I bet you can't get it out of your head. Was she disgusted with you? Scared of you? Did she think you were a freak? Or a psycho? Or a pathetic loser? What did she say, Rory?'

Rory tries to keep denying, but Breslin doesn't give him the chance. He's leaning across the table, close enough to make Rory smell his breath, his aftershave, the heat of his skin. 'What? Did she laugh at you? Tell you to get out? Threaten to call us? What did it? What pushed you over the edge?'

'I didn't *do* anything!'

It comes out as a wild yelp. Breslin stares. 'What the living fuck are you talking about? You stalked her, peeped at her, you call that nothing?'

'No—'

'Did she think it was nothing?'

'She didn't *know*! I—'

'That's a load of bollix. You keep babbling on about "needing a moment", but twenty-five minutes isn't a *moment*. Twenty-five minutes is more than enough time to take your *moment* out back, show up at Aislinn's door, shove your foot in your mouth, lose the head, kill Aislinn, clean up after yourself, realise you need to account for all this time, and head for Tesco. Which is exactly what you did.'

Rory's face is a strange mix of horror and something almost like relief. He's run this scene in his head a hundred times already. Now that it's taken shape and come to find him, it feels like something he already knows, all the sharp corners already rubbed smooth from so much handling. It's actually easier, this time; we're doing all the work for him. All he has to do is come out with his lines.

He says, 'I never hurt her.'

After Breslin's voice, his sounds weightless, a spindly thing floating on the hot air.

'But you did go into her house,' I say.

'No. I swear.'

'The Technical Bureau is processing the clothes you wore that night. What are you going to say when we find her carpet fibres on your trousers?'

'You can't. You won't. I wasn't in there.'

Breslin says, 'No one else was.'

'But the guy, the stalker guy—'

'Oh, please. Did you seriously believe you were the first person to think of looking at Aislinn's social life? Every guy who ever smiled at her, Rory, we've been all over him like a rash. Every one of them's been eliminated. Have you got one reason, just one tiny reason, why I should believe your stalker exists?'

A sudden jerk out of Rory, his hands coming up. 'Wait. Yes. There was a guy, on Saturday in the street I saw a guy—'

Our very own Pez machine: push open his mouth and out pops a brand-new story. I roll my eyes. Breslin laughs, a great full-blooded roar that slams Rory back in his chair. 'Right. Only then aliens abducted you and wiped your memory, and it's only just conveniently coming back.'

'No—'

'A piano fell on your head and you got amnesia.'

'I didn't—'

'On Sunday you told us flat out that you didn't remember seeing anyone in Stoneybatter except a bunch of teenagers playing football and some girls on a night out. There was no guy, Rory.'

Rory tries to talk, but that voice crashes through his like it's a spiderweb, leaves it in tatters. 'There's nothing but you. Every piece we turn over, it's got your face on it. The stalker was you, Rory. We all know it. Every single thing you told us about him, it turns out to have been you all along. The only thing left is the part where he knocks at Aislinn's door and it all goes wrong – and guess what? That'll turn out to be you, too.'

'*No it won't*. I was never in her house. Never.'

By this time he looks about a tenth of Breslin's size, but he's turned into all glare and chin. Not so easy to shove any more. We've found Rory's sticking point.

I move in my chair. 'There's one more thing I think is important,' I say, to Breslin.

'We don't need anything else, Conway. We've got plenty.' Breslin reaches across to sweep the photos away from Rory and slaps them into a stack. 'Let's just put him under arrest, go get some dinner and come back to this afterwards.'

The word *arrest* opens Rory's mouth, but only breath comes out. His eyes, white-ringed with terror, go to me. Shit just got real.

'Hang on,' I say to Breslin. 'Hear me out.'

'You're the boss,' he says, with a sigh. He leaves the photos and tilts his chair back, listening.

'OK,' I say. 'Aislinn had the cooker on, right? Making Rory that lovely fancy dinner.'

'Yeah. And?'

'And before Rory left, he turned it off.'

Rory starts to say, 'I wasn't—' but Breslin lifts a hand to shut him up. 'Right. That's important how?'

'The only reason to turn it off,' I say, 'would be that he didn't want the house going on fire. Now, if Rory knew Aislinn was dead, or if he didn't care whether she died or not – hang on a sec' – Rory's trying to talk again – 'then his best bet would be to let the place burn. The house goes up in smoke, so does any evidence that he was there: the fibres, the prints, the DNA, the lot. Anyone who's ever seen a cop show on the telly would know that. Amn't I right?'

'I'm listening,' says Breslin. To Rory, who's practically coming out of his seat: 'You might want to sit down and pay attention to this, pal. It sounds like it might actually do you some good, and just being straight with you, you can't afford to miss anything that'll do that.'

After a second Rory sits back. His chest is going up and down like he's been running.

Breslin asks, 'Are you going to let Detective Conway finish what she's saying?'

'Yes. I will.' When Breslin's raised eyebrow prompts him: 'Sorry. For interrupting.'

'My point is,' I say, 'the only reason Rory *wouldn't* want the place going on fire would be if he didn't think Aislinn was dead, and he didn't want her to die. Meaning he never intended to kill her.'

'Ah-ha,' Breslin says, nodding slowly. 'Now I see what you're getting at, Detective. You're right: it is important. Everything else we've got looks like murder, and a pretty nasty one too; but if you're right about why that cooker got turned off, then it's not murder at all. It's manslaughter.'

'Exactly,' I say. '*If* I'm right.'

'*If.* There's any number of reasons that cooker could've been turned off. Maybe Aislinn turned it off herself. Or maybe Rory's got a touch of OCD going on, can't leave a house without turning all the appliances off. But *if* you're right . . .'

We both look at Rory. He's glazing over. Too many stories logjamming in his head: he's starting to lose hold of them all. Up to a point, this works for us: if the guy can't keep track of what he's said about what when, he gets sloppy. Too far past that point, though, he just stops making sense. If we're gonna get anything out of Rory, it needs to be soon.

'I'm done, Rory,' I say. 'You can talk now.'

Breslin lets him open his mouth before he says, 'Actually, don't. You're about to tell us you were never in that house, and you need to think very, very hard before you do that. Murder is an automatic life sentence, Rory. Manslaughter is maybe six years, out in four. And if you don't tell us why you turned off that cooker, then we've got nothing, not one thing, that says this was manslaughter, and a whole lot that says it was murder. So I'm telling you, Rory, for your own sake: before you say one more word, take just five minutes to think.' And, when Rory tries talking again: 'Ah-ah. Five minutes. I'll tell you when it's up.' He shoots his cuff and looks at his watch. 'Starting now.'

Rory gives up. He stares into space, rocking a little with fatigue.

'One.'

Slowly the lines of Rory's face solidify. He stops swaying. Inside his mind, things are moving.

Breslin's made the wrong call. I know what he's at – he's hoping the forced silence and the fear will bear down on Rory hard enough to crack him – but it's the barrage of words and demands that was doing the job. Locking this guy into his own head is only giving him a chance to get his focus back and straighten out his stories. We're losing him.

'Two.'

'Forget it,' I say, bringing my hands down on the table with a bang. 'That's as much time as he's getting. Rory: look at me.' I snap my fingers in his face. He blinks. 'Why'd you turn that cooker off?'

Too late. Rory says, 'I didn't. I've never been inside Aislinn's house. I never hurt Aislinn in any way. And I want to go home.'

He stands up, wobbly-legged, and starts trying to pull his coat off the back of his chair. His hands are shaking; he keeps losing hold.

'Whoa there,' Breslin says. 'We're not done. Sit down.'

'I'm done. Am I under arrest?'

I can see Breslin opening his mouth on the words. 'No,' I say, and ignore his head coming round towards me. 'Not at the moment. But if you want us to believe your story, walking out on us isn't the way to go about it. You need to stay here and work with us.'

'No. If I'm not under arrest, I'm going home.' Rory manages to get his coat off the chair and drops it.

'Here's what we'll do,' I say, closing my notebook. 'You go home. Get some sleep. We'll talk to Aislinn's neighbours and see if any of them happened to look out their back windows and see you in the laneway between, say, 8.30 and 8.40. If they did, you're off the hook:

you wouldn't have had time for the other thing.' Obviously we've already talked to the neighbours, and I'm betting they would have mentioned some weirdo hanging around the laneway, but this doesn't seem to occur to Rory. 'Come back in to us tomorrow to sign your statement, and we'll do updates then. Fair enough?'

Rory pulls his coat around his shoulders, not even trying the sleeves. 'Yes. OK.'

'We'll come pick you up,' Breslin says, keeping it just the right side of a threat. He stands up and stretches. 'You're not planning to be anywhere other than your flat or the bookshop, are you?'

'No. I'm going nowhere.'

'Good plan,' Breslin tells him. He pulls the door open and sweeps his hand at it with a little mock bow. 'After you.'

Steve is in the doorway of the observation room, suit jacket over his arm, sleeves rolled up against the heat. His eyes meet mine for a long level second. Then we're past him and down the corridor, Rory speeding up towards the draught of cold fresh air coming up the stairwell, Breslin humming happily to himself under his breath.

Me and Breslin watch from the doorway as Rory heads off across the cobblestones. He looks small and messy, slams of wind flapping his coat and tangling in his hair, swerving him off course. It's practically dark. Just a couple of months of bodyguard work, and I'll have enough saved up for a holiday somewhere blazing hot in eye-shattering colours and very far away.

'Enlighten me,' Breslin says pleasantly. 'Why is this guy going home?'

I say, 'We're nearly there with him. He was right on the edge, till that pause gave him a chance to pull his head together – and if we could get him there once, we can get him there again. But if we put him under arrest, he's gonna get a solicitor in there, and we can say goodbye to any chance of a confession.'

'We don't *need* a confession, Conway. We've got enough circumstantial stuff to bury him alive.'

Which is probably true. I don't care. My last murder case: this one isn't gonna be tacked down with circumstantial this and reasonable inference that. I'm gonna hammer a stake right through its heart and leave it dead as dirt.

'I want one,' I say. 'We can afford to leave Rory till tomorrow.'

'Unless he jumps in the Liffey.'

'He won't. He still thinks I might wind up believing him. He wants that.'

Breslin watches me. 'Is he right?'

'No,' I say. The adrenaline buzz is ebbing fast; I can feel the post-interrogation crash getting ready to hit. It leaves a sucking empty spot that, if you're not careful, can feel like loss. I need caffeine, sugar, a dirty great burger. 'He's our man, all right.'

'He is. And I hope you know that cooker doesn't actually turn it into manslaughter, either. There's no chance that little pussy-boy was thinking straight enough, after *killing* someone, to worry about burning the house down. His brain was *juice*. He probably turned the cooker off because the food was starting to burn and the smell bothered him. Cooper's report still stands: could be manslaughter, *if* Rory managed to get up the strength for a serious punch, or he could've deliberately smashed her skull in when she was down. And the more I look at those pathetic excuses for muscles . . .'

'Not my problem,' I say. 'The lawyers and the jury can figure that one out. All I want is a watertight case that he killed her.'

'Well,' Breslin says, heartily enough that for a second there I think he's going to clap me on the back, 'that shouldn't be a problem to us. We'll get every warm body out there looking for backup evidence, we'll throw the lot at Rory, and he'll fold like a cheap lawn chair. And if he doesn't, hey, we'll have enough circumstantial stuff to make our case watertight anyway. Right?'

'Right,' I say. Rory is gone, around the corner towards the gate. The splatter of yellow light on the empty cobblestones makes them look slick from hard rain, dangerous.

Wheels turning in Breslin's mind, so heavy I can practically hear them. I keep my eyes on the place where Rory was until, finally, I feel Breslin move away and hear the door close behind him.

* * *

I ring Lucy from the women's jacks. This time she answers, but her voice is barely above a whisper and she sounds hassled; someone in the background is calling orders and there's a sudden blast of country music, cut off by an annoyed shout. The theatre has a new show opening that evening, they're having technical problems and Lucy really has to go (in the background: 'Luce! Any word on those parcans?'). She swears she'll be home all tomorrow, but I can't tell whether it's true or whether she's just saying whatever will get rid of me.

I'm gonna be banging on her door tomorrow morning before she's anywhere near hauling her hangover out of bed. I hope she tells me she made up Aislinn's secret boyfriend to make sure the investigation was good and thorough. I hope that, as I step out of Lucy's flat, Sophie rings me to tell me that Aislinn's password-protected computer folder turned out to be full of pictures of Daddy, scanned to make them handier for sobbing over.

Me, praying my most interesting leads will crash and burn. It feels against nature, like some parasite has slid into my head and is eating bits of my brain. But Lucy, and that folder: they're the last two stubborn unruly strands stopping me from tying everything into a neat bow, leaving it outside the door of O'Kelly's office with my badge on top, and walking away.

Steve is at our desk, checking e-mails. I sit down next to him and start flicking through the piles of paper that materialised while I was away. The floaters try not to let me catch them glancing over, wondering when the mad bitch is gonna lose it again.

The thick sheet of silence between me and Steve is growing edges like ripped tin. I say, 'So you saw Rory in there.'

'A fair bit of it,' Steve says, without looking up. 'Good interview.'

It doesn't sound like a compliment. 'Thanks,' I say. I catch Breslin's knowing eye on us: *You were never right for each other.* 'Where were you?'

'I ran the mug books past the barman and Aislinn's neighbours. No hits.' He waits for me to say *I told you so.* When I don't: 'Then I went and had chats with a few of the lads who worked the Des Murray disappearance – don't worry, I was subtle about it.'

'I'm not worried.'

Steve throws me a quick sideways glance, trying to work out how I mean that. 'Anyway,' he says, after a second. The tone to his voice, neutral, precise, arm's-length; I've heard it before, but to defence solicitors and slippery journalists, never to me. 'According to them, McCann had a bit of a thing for Evelyn Murray, all right. He was the one who pushed to keep the investigation going; he got very eloquent about this poor fragile woman with her life in ruins – and McCann isn't the eloquent type, so the lads remembered it. He even found her someone to buy Des's taxi plate, and made sure she got top dollar for it, so she and Aislinn weren't stuck for cash. But the lads are all positive it never went as far as an affair. Even back then, McCann was getting called Holy Joe; not a chance he was riding a subject's missus. They laughed at me for even thinking it.'

Another gap for my *I told you so*. I can't take any longer sitting there next to him, being polite to each other under Breslin's amused eye. I say, 'Did you find a reason to think any of this has anything to do with our case?'

'No.'

'Good. Then let's get this meeting done.'

I stand up. Even before I reach the front of the desk, the floaters have dropped their work and are sitting up straight, managing to be all attention without God forbid making eye contact with the rabid animal.

'OK,' I say, 'good news. It's looking pretty definite that Rory Fallon is our boy. He and the CCTV both say he's been stalking Aislinn for at least a month. That's how he spent the missing time before their date on Saturday night – or part of it, anyway: peeping in her windows.'

'Little perv,' Stanton says, grinning. 'Better swab her walls for DNA.'

A quick edgy smatter of laughs. 'Do it,' I say. Rory's leftovers might not prove murder, but they'll up our chances at trial; juries hate a wanker. 'He says he was hanging out in the laneway behind her patio, so get the techs to give that wall a good going-over – and try the wall under her kitchen window, too, just in case he got up the guts for a little close-range action.'

Stanton nods; Meehan puts it in the book of jobs. I say, 'Our new working theory is that, when Rory arrived in Aislinn's house, she somehow found out about the stalking. She told him to get out, and he lost the head.'

'Rory hasn't spilled the beans yet,' Breslin says, 'but he's come close. We're hoping tomorrow's the day.'

'Before we pull him back in,' I say, 'let's find out just how much stalking he did, and what kind. I need two guys walking Rory's picture around Stoneybatter to see if anyone recognises him from the last couple of months. He's got the bookshop to run, so we're mainly looking at evenings and Sundays. Try everywhere: houses, shops, pubs, offices where the workers might've crossed paths with him on their way out. Any community groups or bingo nights or sports clubs, track down the members.' Kellegher lifts a finger. 'Kellegher, you and Gaffney take that. And I want to know what Rory's phone's been doing over the last two months: when it pinged towers around Stoneybatter, whether it logged onto any wireless networks in the area. Stanton, while you're making calls, make those.'

The case has changed. Before, we were dragnetting, sifting through what came up and hoping there was something good in there. Now we're hunting. We've got the prey in our sights and we're closing in, and everything we do is building towards the moment when we'll have him pinned down for the kill shot.

That feeling, it's not some bullshit figure of speech. It lives inside you somewhere deeper and older and more real than anything else except sex, and when it comes rising it takes your whole body for its own. It's a smell of blood raging at the back of your nose, it's your arm muscle throbbing to let go the bowstring, it's drums speeding in your ears and a victory roar building at the bottom of your gut. I let myself love that feeling, one last time. I let myself drink it down, cram every second of it deep into me, lay away my store of it to last me the rest of my life.

'I want to know where Rory drinks,' I say, 'and what the barman and the regulars think of him – if he's got a rep for fixating on some girl, not taking no for an answer, if he's got a temper, anything that could be relevant.' Meehan's hand is up. 'Meehan, have that; it'll give

you a change of scenery from Stoneybatter. And I want to know what
the other Ranelagh businesses think of Rory. Whether anyone's got
any stories about him coming on a little strong to a customer in the
bookshop, or hanging about outside the bakery waiting for the pretty
one to finish her shift.'

'I'll do that,' Breslin says. 'Moran, fancy joining me?'

Steve looks up, startled, but Breslin gives him a bland smile and
after a second he says, 'Yeah. Sure.'

'Great,' Breslin says, throwing him a wink. 'Let's take this bad boy
down.'

I don't feel like going into my plans for tomorrow. 'I'll check in
with the Bureau first thing in the morning,' I say, 'see if they've got
anywhere with fibre matches and DNA.' And with Aislinn's computer
folder, which I also don't feel like mentioning. 'Meanwhile, someone
needs to stay on Rory's gaff – just for tonight and part of tomorrow,
till we're ready to bring him back in.' Breslin gives me an amused
glance. I don't actually think Rory's gonna throw himself in the
Liffey, or skip town, or ditch evidence we haven't spotted, but I'm
not gonna risk it for the sake of a few hours' surveillance. 'Deasy: do
that, or stick a couple of uniforms on it if you want, but tell them they
need plainclothes and an unmarked car.'

Deasy nods. 'OK,' I say. 'If we don't get a confession, this is the
stuff that's going to make the case. So give it your best. Thanks, and
see you tomorrow.'

In the second before I turn away, to get Steve so we can pretend
we're still partners while we report to the gaffer, the incident room
grabs me by the gut. For that second it glows warm and steady from
every corner with twenty years' worth of might-have-beens. Every
time I could have walked in there laughing with Steve, every shout of
triumph when I could have held up the phone record or the DNA
result we'd been waiting for, every thank-you speech I could have
made at the end of a big case: all of those rise up to find me, now that
they're unreachable.

I don't do that shite. I've got half a dozen excuses handy – no
sleep, no food, pressure, big decision, blah blah blah – but still,
that against-nature feeling prickles my skin like nettlerash.

'Let's go,' I say to Steve. 'The gaffer.' I head out the door without waiting for him, so we won't have to walk down the corridor together.

O'Kelly is polishing the dust off his spider plant, with one of those fiddly little cloths that people use to clean their glasses. 'Conway. Moran,' he says, barely glancing up. 'Tell me you're getting somewhere.'

'Yeah,' I say. 'Looks like we are.'

'About fucking time. Let's hear it.'

I give him the rundown. He listens, turning the plant to the light to make sure he gets every angle. 'Huh,' he says, when I'm done. 'And you're happy enough with that.'

One sideways eye has come up to me. I say, 'We'll have another shot at the confession tomorrow. Don't worry: we won't send the file to the prosecutors till we've got it locked down tight.'

'I didn't mean are you happy enough to send the file. I mean are you happy enough that Fallon did it.'

'Yeah,' I say. That eye, edged wet and red where the eyelid's starting to droop like an old man's. I can't read him; I can't make myself care whether or not he's in on Breslin's game. 'He did it.' I feel Steve's weight shift beside me, but he says nothing.

The gaffer eyes me for another long moment before he turns back to his plant. He tilts a leaf to examine it, gives one spot an extra dab. 'I thought you were waiting for something that wasn't circumstantial.'

Last night, I told him that, back when this case was a wild thing shooting out curls of possibility in every direction. It feels like years ago. 'That or till we eliminated everything else. We've done that.'

'You have.'

I say, 'There's zero reason to think that anyone other than Rory Fallon was involved.'

O'Kelly tests the point of a leaf on the pad of his thumb. 'All right,' he says. 'All right.'

He looks like he's forgotten us; I can't tell whether we've been dismissed. 'We could use another floater,' I say. 'I sent Reilly back to the floater pool.'

That gets the gaffer's attention. 'Why?'

'He found evidence. Instead of bringing it to me, or to Moran, he took it to Breslin.'

'Can't have that,' O'Kelly says. He doesn't try to hide the long glance at Steve. 'OK: I'll get you another one. Keep me updated.'

He turns his shoulder to us and works his fingers delicately into the plant, pushing the leaves apart to slide the cloth right down to the base.

Steve says, in the corridor, 'Zero reason to think anyone but Rory was involved.'

His voice still has that remote sound. 'Yeah,' I say. 'Exactly zero reason.'

'What about Lucy's mystery guy? The folder on Aislinn's computer?'

'I'm seeing Lucy tomorrow. I'll ring Sophie about the folder first thing. If either of them gives us anything solid, then we'll review.' I can hear the danger signs rising in my voice. 'But right now: zero reason. Zero.'

'The DNA on Aislinn's mattress.'

'That didn't get there on Saturday night, or it would've been on the sheets as well. It's got nothing to do with our case.'

Steve has stopped moving. He's looking off down the corridor at the window – dark sky, layered in a thick yellowish vapour of light pollution – not at me.

I say, 'You saw Rory in there. You heard him. Don't you fucking tell me you still have doubts.'

It takes him too long to answer. I leave him there.

I'm pulling my coat on when it hits me: Breslin made it through the entire afternoon without once trying to hint that he's on the take.

That should be a relief, but instead it jabs like a needle under a fingernail. As far as I can see, there's no reason why Breslin should have suddenly, in the couple of hours I was away talking to Aislinn's exes, decided to ditch his whole ornate cunning plan. He was doing a lovely job of setting me up – a few more nudges and, if it hadn't been for Fleas, I would have been right in position for the kill shot – and out of nowhere he dropped the whole project and wandered away. I flick back mentally through the day, my chat with McCann, the floaters' reports, checking for anything that could have made him change course: anything that might have tipped him off that I'd sussed him, or anything that could have made him decide I wasn't worth owning after all. There's nothing.

The only possibility left is the one jabbing deeper: Breslin knows, somehow, that there's no point to that shite any more. The words I'm going to say to the gaffer stink like burning hair all around me, brand my face with their growing shadow. Breslin took one look at me and knew, with those dense-packed twenty years' worth of detective instincts, that the kill shot had already been fired. He knew I'm worthless now.

13

All the way home I'm waiting for something, or someone: another uniform pulling me over, the lamppost guy leaping out in front of my car as I turn onto my road, Fleas sticking his head out of the darkness in my kitchen. Nothing happens. My street is a blank; as soon as I step into the house, I know it's empty. I clear it anyway.

I'm craving sleep, a lot of it, ideally with someone armed and trustworthy outside my bedroom door, but I'm not going to bed till I know I'm wrecked enough to crash out the second I hit the sheets. There's a whole list of stuff I'm not gonna think about tonight, but it covers so much territory and I'm so tired that my mind keeps getting mixed up and letting bits slip through. For half a second, before I pull myself up sharp, I wonder what Steve is doing.

There's fuck-all in my fridge, and me and Fleas killed off my emergency fish fingers. I ring my ma and tell her about Sophie's vase, which has blood spatter on it because two scumbags broke into an old woman's gaff and punched her in the stomach till she puked blood, to which my ma says 'Huh.' She doesn't bring up Aislinn and neither do I. While she smokes, I make coffee and a pile of toast, cut the green bit off an old chunk of cheese, and take the lot into the sitting room.

No wind shoving at the window tonight; it's died down, leaving a thick, still cold. I look out into the dark and think, *Come on, motherfucker. Come and get me.* I leave the curtains wide open.

I've got an e-mail from Fleas. *Hiya Rach! Great to hear from you. No news here, all the gang are OK, no one doin anythin special. Kinda busy at the mo but love to meet up sometime when we both have the free time. Take care sunshine xx.* Meaning no one in his corner of the underworld is suddenly drowning his sorrows or looking twitchy or sobbing on Fleas's shoulder about his dead girlfriend. And meaning bye, see you someday maybe.

Sophie's team didn't find any dating sites on Aislinn's laptop, but they haven't reported back on her work computer yet. I take a look at Random Google Blonde's accounts. She's doing well for herself: dozens of messages. About a quarter of them are dick pics, which are presumably meant to send her running for her smelling salts rather than to start off meaningful relationships, although you never know. Most of the rest are one-line nothing, guys shotgunning all the pretty girls who join up, hoping one will bite. Two of them are worth a closer look. No photos, careful wording about no strings and discretion: married guys looking for fun on the side, and looking for a girl who matches Aislinn's specs to join them.

I'm working on my reply when something moves, in the corner of my eye. I whip around, not fast enough. A big dark shape skims away from my window before I can get a decent look.

I grab my keys and dive for the door. By the time I get it open, the road is empty.

I head for my car, forcing myself to keep the pace casual: just getting something I forgot, no biggie. My breath puffs clouds into the air, but the cold doesn't touch me. I smell turf smoke and hear cars zipping past the top of the road and feel my leg muscles throbbing to go.

I'm pulling open the car door when the light twitches. There's someone under the streetlamp at the top of the road: a tall guy, hovering. I slam the car door and take one step in that direction and he vanishes, into the dark around the corner, going at a fair old clip.

I'm pretty sure I'm faster than him, but Stoneybatter is good for twists and laneways, and if he knows his way around, he's gone. Even if he doesn't, he can just nip into a pub, turn and stare with the rest if I come bursting in; what am I gonna do about it? I need to nab him on my own turf.

I go back inside, pull the sitting-room curtains almost closed and watch the road through the crack at one side.

If I get another shot, it'll be my last. One more close call and the guy's gonna know for sure he's been burned.

There isn't a way for me to do this on my own. I run through every backup option I can think of – Fleas, Sophie, Gary, my mate Lisa, all my other mates, the neighbours. I even consider my ma. I swear to God, for a quarter of a second I consider Breslin.

I can't do it. There's no one, on all that list, who I can make myself ring up to say *Hi, I can't do this, come help me*. To every single one of them, I'd be a different person after that call. The emptiness of my gaff feels dense enough to tilt it on its foundations.

The guy's got some self-control, at least: it's twenty-five minutes before a thicker darkness moves in the shadows outside the street-lamp's circle. In the same second I feel my heartbeat rise to it, I real-ise that I've known all along what I'm gonna do.

The thicker darkness settles and stays. I get out my phone, I take a breath and I ring Steve.

It takes him a few rings to pick up. 'Hi,' he says.

'Hi. Are you doing anything important?'

'Not a lot.'

He leaves it there. That carefully neutral voice, while he tries to work out, or decide, whether we're still partners.

I don't have time for fancy dancing. 'Steve,' I say. 'Listen. I need a hand.' It feels rough in my throat, but when I glance out the window, the guy is still there, motionless at the edge of the lamplight.

There's a long second of silence. I shut my eyes.

Then Steve says, 'OK. What's up?'

His voice has thawed two notches, maybe three. It's fucking ridicu-lous how relieved I am, but I don't have time to deal with that either. 'Some fucker's been casing my gaff for the last few days,' I say, 'and I've had enough. I can't go out there and get him myself; he's got a clear line of sight on every route I can take, and if he sees me coming he'll do a legger.'

Steve says, and he's put everything else aside to focus on this, 'But he's not watching for me.'

'That's what I'm hoping.'

'Where is he now?'

'At the top of my road.' Steve knows my gaff; he's never been inside, but we've swung by to pick something up once or twice. 'He was looking in my front window earlier on, and I've seen him down the laneway out the back, but he mostly hangs out at the corner. Tall guy, solid build, middle-aged, dark overcoat, trilby-type hat.'

I feel Steve clock the match to the guy who went over Aislinn's wall. 'OK,' he says. 'What do you want me to do with him?'

'Bring him in here. I want a word with him.'

'I'll be there in fifteen minutes, tops.' I can hear him moving already: pulling on shoes, or getting into a coat.

'Ring me when you're almost at my road. Let it ring once, then hang up.'

'Right.' Keys jingling; Steve's ready. 'Mind yourself.'

'Thanks,' I say. 'See you soon.'

I put my phone in my pocket, sit back down on the sofa and click shite at random on my laptop. The window feels like fingernails drumming at the side of my head. I don't look around. When my phone rings once, what feels like an hour later, I manage not to jump.

I stretch, stand up and wander over to the front door, out of sight of the window. I get out my gun and press my eye up against the peephole.

Darkness and the yellow door across the road, bulging insanely in the fisheye lens. The yappy little dog next door throwing a fit. Girls shrieking, somewhere far away. Then a fast jumble of footsteps coming closer, over the cobblestones.

I hold the doorknob and make myself wait till a wild flap of black rears up in the peephole. Then I whip the door open, two guys pressed close together stumble inside, and I slam the door behind them.

They trip on the rug, get their balance back and stagger to a standstill in the middle of my sitting room. Steve is gripping the other guy's coat collar with one hand and twisting his arm up behind his back with the other. Big guy, black hair going grey – his hat's gone missing somewhere along the way – long black overcoat. 'Get *off* me—'

'I've got him,' I say, and point my gun at the guy's head. Steve lets go and jumps back.

'For God's *sake*,' the man says, and then he turns to face me and all three of us go still.

He wasn't expecting the gun. I wasn't expecting him. I was all ready for anything from a serial killer to one of our own, but not for this guy.

I've never seen him before, but I've seen everything about him, every day: the strong curve of his nose, the hooded dark eyes, the long black slashes of his eyebrows. For a second it feels like some fucked-up practical joke; my mind, skidding, grabbing for handholds, wonders if the squad wankers somehow organised this to wreck my head. He's the spit of me.

Steve is staring back and forth between us. His hands are open by his sides, like he's not sure what to do with them.

I say, 'Steve. You can go.' My lips are numb.

The man says, 'Antoinette—'

'Shut the fuck up or I'll shoot you.' I tighten my hands on the gun. He shuts up. 'Steve: go home.'

Steve starts to ask, 'Are you—'

'Go. Now.'

After a moment he leaves, practically tiptoeing. The door closes softly behind him. Me and the guy are left looking at each other.

He adjusts his coat collar where Steve had a hold of it. 'Thank you,' he says. 'I'm not sure who that was—'

'I asked him to bring you in,' I say. 'I've had enough of you hanging around my road.'

He's not fazed. 'In that case, perhaps you both did me a favour. I'm not sure when I would have got up the momentum to knock on your door.'

His accent is educated English, with something else overlaid on top – Nordie, maybe Belfast. He hasn't spent the last thirty-two years in a palace in Egypt or a nightclub in Brazil. He's spent them a train ride away.

'Have a good look around,' I say. 'You want the full tour?'

He's examining my face, intensely enough that I twitch, wanting to smash in his nose with the gun butt to make him stop. He says, 'You're very like me. Do you understand that?'

'I'm not blind,' I say. 'And I'm not stupid.'

That gets a tiny satisfied smile, like me not being an idiot is to his credit. 'I never thought you would be.'

All that maths homework I saved up to drop at his feet. There's a silence, while he waits for me to say something, or maybe throw myself into his arms. I don't.

'This is a very strange moment for me,' he says. 'I've been looking for you for almost a year.'

'Wow. A whole year, yeah?'

'I did consider making contact at the beginning. I give you my word, I did. But I didn't know your name, and your mother had gone off the radar really very effectively. And at the time, given the various complications in my life, in many ways I felt you would be better off without—'

'And now, what, you need a kidney?'

A thin smile. 'The year before last, my mother and father died, within months of each other.' A smaller pause, for me to say sorry for his loss or feel bereaved or fuck knows what. 'Losing one's parents causes an immense shift in perspective. It brought home to me the value of their presence within my life, on a much broader scale than I had ever understood it before: the value of being rooted within a greater story than one's own. I became acutely aware, for the first time, just what I had deprived you of. As soon as I reached that realisation, I began looking for you.'

Those dark eyes, all intense and urgent and meaningful. No wonder my ma fell for it; she was only twenty. I'm not. The truth is he was feeling vulnerable all of a sudden, what with being next in line, and he needed someone who could make him feel like he wasn't gonna vanish into nothing. 'At one point I actually hired a private detective,' he says, 'but all I could give him was your mother's name, and—'

'You've found me now.'

'As soon as I knew how to find you, I came. I booked a hotel in Dublin and drove down that very day.'

The face on him says he expects me to be all moved. 'Shame you didn't find out a few weeks earlier,' I say. 'You could've got your Christmas shopping in.'

'Is that really necessary?' He nods at my gun. 'You must know I have no intention of hurting you. And it does put a damper on the conversation.'

There's a smile at one corner of his mouth, a smile that he expects to work. A charmer, this guy. Shame that gene skipped a generation.

'There's no conversation,' I say. If Steve had the sense to do what I told him, he's in his car and well gone by now, too far for this guy to chase him down and try to pump him for info. 'You're leaving.'

That takes the smile away. He says, carefully, 'I realise you must be angry with me—'

'I'm not angry. I'm done with you. Go on.' I motion at the door with the gun.

'No,' he says. His hands come up towards me. 'Let me stay. Please. Just for a little while; an hour. Half an hour. If you still want me to leave after that, I will.'

I say, 'Out. Now.'

'Wait.' He hasn't moved, but his voice sounds like a leap to bar the door. 'Please. I'm not going to pry. You can tell me as much as you like, or nothing – it's up to you. And I'll tell you anything you want to know – you must have questions. Anything. Just ask me.'

Here it is: my deepest and darkest, the one that no best mate or partner or lover will ever know. In that second I see what Aislinn saw. I see the moment she chased over barriers and through muck and out the other side of death; it bursts into my house like ball lightning and it sings in front of me, an arm's reach away. *What's your name, how did you and my ma meet, why did you go, where have you been, what do you do, tell me all of it, all* . . . I see me tilting like a hawk high in warm air, while below me he unrolls all my might-have-beens, for me to circle above at my leisure till every fork and tributary is stamped into my mind, reclaimed and mine. I see him opening his cloak to show me all the lost pages of my story written in silver on the night-sky lining.

'OK,' I say. I lower the gun. 'Yeah: I've got questions.' I can hardly breathe.

'And I can stay. Half an hour.'

'Sure. Why not.'

He nods. He waits, gazing at me too intently to blink, hanging for the questions like they're the best gift I could ever give him.

They would be. This is what my ma was telling me, through all her bullshit fairy tales. If I let him give me the answers, he'll own me. Everything in my life, past and future, will be his: what he decides to make it into.

I say, 'How'd you track me down?'

He blinks then.

'You said anything I want to know.'

He glances at the sofa. 'May I sit down?'

'No. First you start answering. Then I'll see.'

A wry quirk of one eyebrow, like he's decided to humour an over-wrought kid. I use that look on witnesses sometimes. 'All right. I went to my local shop on Sunday afternoon, to buy my newspaper. While I was in the queue, I glanced at the other papers on the stand. Your photograph was on a front page. I knew as soon as I saw you.'

It sends red straight through me: he's got no right recognising me. 'So?' I say. 'What'd you do?'

'I looked you up in the phone book, but you're unlisted. I was certain your work wouldn't give me any information. So I rang the paper and asked to speak to the journalist who had written the article. I told him who I was – I could hardly expect him to give me any information otherwise – and that I was hoping to get in touch but uncertain of my welcome.' A dry glance at the gun. 'With good reason, apparently.'

'And he just handed over my address?' Even for Crowley, that doesn't ring true; Crowley does nothing for nothing. 'What'd you give him?'

'I haven't given him anything.'

I know that crisp snap of denial, too; too well to fall for it. 'Yet,' I say. 'What'd you promise him?'

He thinks about lying, but he's too smart to risk it. 'The journalist said he could provide me with an address for you. In exchange for an interview after our meeting.'

I can just picture it. *Top Cop's Childhood Anguish*; side-by-side photos of my shitty block of flats and his detached house in a leafy suburb; *'All the time she was searching for the truth on the job, she was really searching for me,'* sobs long-lost dad. Not the front page, or anything; part of some glurge spread about fatherless women. Just thinking about it makes me want to puke. Crowley wouldn't even need to publish it; he could just wave it under my nose and demand every scoop I ever have, and know I would hand them over.

I say, 'And you said yeah, sure, no problem.'

'I wasn't overjoyed about the prospect. Baring my soul for some tabloid isn't something I ever envisioned myself doing. But I would have done much more than that to find you.'

He doesn't come across like an idiot, although you never can tell. I say, 'Or you could have just rung up my work and asked for me. Or sent me a letter.'

'I could have, yes.' He runs a palm down one cheek and sighs. 'I'll be honest. I wanted the chance to observe you for a while, before making that commitment.'

Meaning he wanted the chance to decide whether I was good enough to contact. If I'd had a fella in a shiny tracksuit, half a dozen screaming brats and a smoke hanging off my lip, he could have turned around and gone home: no harm, no foul, story ended before it began.

Maybe he even believes that's why he did it this way, but I don't. I know exactly what he was at. Playing this the approved way – break the news nice and gently from a distance, have a few careful getting-to-know-you phone calls, meet on neutral territory when everyone's comfortable with it, all that shite – that would've let me decide when and whether. This guy was never going to do that. He wanted this situation – wanted me – on his terms, start to finish. Unlucky for him, that gene didn't skip a generation.

I say, 'So you spent the next three days hanging around outside my gaff like a peeper.'

That flares his nostrils. 'I don't enjoy admitting it. But I said I would tell you anything you asked. I hope now you realise I meant it.'

'Your journalist buddy gets nothing. First thing tomorrow, you ring him and tell him you had the wrong woman. And make it convincing.'

His head lifts. Pride looks good on him and he knows it. 'I gave him my word.'

He wants me to beg, or stamp my foot and remind him he owes me more than he owes some hack. I laugh, one crack – I'm not going to give him more. 'What's he gonna do, sue?'

'Obviously not. But I prefer to fulfil my obligations.' When the corner of my mouth lifts: 'And I don't think either of us particularly wants him as an enemy.'

'Trust me: you'd rather have him for an enemy than me. You think I don't have friends on the force around your way? You want to spend the rest of your life being pulled over and breathalysed every time you get in your car? Brought in for questioning every time a kid says the bad man had brown skin?'

His mouth – wide hard-cut curves, like mine – has tightened. He says, 'This obviously means a lot to you.'

He leaves space for me to take the bait. I don't.

'All right. I'll tell the journalist I was mistaken.' He nods at the sofa. 'Now may I sit down?'

The cheeky fuck is already moving towards my sofa. 'Great,' I say. I lift the gun and point it at him again. 'You can go now.'

That startles him. 'But your questions. Don't you want to know—'

'Nope. Off you go.'

He doesn't move. 'We said half an hour.'

'I'm finished early.'

'Half an hour. That was the agreement.'

I laugh out loud. 'You should've got it in writing. Fuck off. Don't come back.'

His jaw sets. 'If you're trying to hurt me—'

'I'm trying to get you out of my gaff. If I want to hurt you, I'll use this.' I move my chin at the gun. 'Go on.'

For a second I think I'm going to have to do it. He's not used to backing down. Funny, that: neither am I.

I see the moment when he realises I'll do it. It widens his eyes and he eases back a step, towards the door, but he's not done. 'I understand that this has been a shock. Believe me, this wasn't the way I would have chosen to— Let me leave you my card. When you feel differently—'

His hand's going to his breast pocket. 'No,' I say, and train my gun on that hand till it stops moving. 'We're done. If I ever see you again, I'm gonna shoot you dead. Then I'll explain how terrified I was of my stalker, my friend Steve will back me up, and I'll sell the story of our tragic misunderstanding to your journalist pal for big bucks.'

Slowly his hand moves away from his pocket. He says, 'You're not what I visualised.'

'No shit,' I say. 'Bye.'

For a moment he stands there in the middle of my sitting room, staring at my sofa without seeing it, like he can't get a hold of what comes next or how to do it. He doesn't look like the spit of me, not any more. He looks like some middle-aged guy who's spent too long, the last few days, standing in the cold and imagining.

In the end he moves. With the door open he turns and I think he's going to say something, but he just nods and steps out into the night.

I go to the doorway and watch him to the top of the road. His hat is under the street lamp, rolling a little in the rising wind; he bends to pick it up like his back hurts, dusts it off and keeps walking, out of the light and around the corner. He doesn't look back again.

I wait five minutes, then another five, to make sure he's well gone. My hands are shaking – the cold is hitting me – and I make sure my gun's pointing behind me, into the house. When I'm positive he's not going to try coming back, I holster up and ring Steve.

He picks up fast. 'You OK?'

'I'm grand. Where are you?'

'I'm only in the pub round the corner – what's it called, the Something Inn. I thought just in case – I mean, I know you're well able, but . . . Is he, like, still there? Or . . . ?'

He wants to know if I've got a corpse on my sitting-room floor. 'He left. Can you come back here?'

'Yeah,' Steve says, too promptly – now the little spa thinks I want to cry on his shoulder. 'Be there in five.'

He's hurrying down the road in three, wind grabbing at his scarf. 'Jesus, relax the kacks,' I say, opening the door for him. 'The gaff isn't on fire.'

'You OK?'

'Like I already said. I'm grand. Did you leave your pint?'

'I did, yeah. I thought—'

His hair is sticking out sideways, all orange and urgent. 'You bleeding drama queen, you,' I say. 'Want a drink to make up for it?'

'Sure. Thanks.'

I head into the kitchen and go for the booze cupboard. 'Whiskey OK?'

'Yeah, fine.' Steve hangs in the doorway and has a good look around the room, to avoid looking at me. He says, to the kitchen window, 'I saw him. His face, like.'

'Yeah,' I say. 'Me too.'

Steve waits for me to say something else. I say, 'Ice?'

'Yeah. Please.' He watches me set out glasses and pour – my hands are rock-steady again. 'Did you . . . ? I mean, are you going to see him again?'

I pass him a glass. 'I'm guessing no. I told him if I do, I'll shoot him.'

The loud, startled snort that escapes Steve makes me realise how it sounds, and all of a sudden I'm laughing too. 'Jesus Christ,' Steve says, through a wave of laughter. 'I don't think that went the way he was planning.'

That makes me worse. 'The poor fucker. I'd almost feel sorry for him, you know that?'

'Seriously?'

'No. I hope he shat himself.' That leaves the pair of us helpless, leaning against walls. I wipe my eyes, knock back my whiskey and pour myself another. 'Here,' I say, holding out my hand for Steve's glass. 'You've earned it. I'd say you thought I wanted your help to dispose of a body, did you?'

Steve chokes halfway through his shot and doubles over, which sets me off again. He spills half of it, and my whiskey is too good to waste, but I don't care. I feel better than I have in a long time. 'The state of you,' I say, whipping the glass off him. 'You need to learn to hold your drink. Here.' I hand him his refill and head for the sofa.

'You genuinely are grand,' Steve says, turning serious and giving me a proper once-over. 'Aren't you?'

'Told you.' I lean back into the cushions and take a sip of my booze, tasting it properly this time. I can feel things shifting, in the back corners of my head: a change in the angles of light, weights rebalancing. Maybe tomorrow when I ring my ma, I'll tell her how I spent my evening. Now that ought to get a reaction.

Steve says, 'Then . . . ?' Meaning, *Then what am I doing here?*

I sit up. I say, and I've gone sober too, 'Something's after hitting me. About the case.'

That moment, when my vision slid and stuttered and I saw what Aislinn was chasing, in all its miraculous excruciating glow. In that moment I saw what me and Steve should have spotted a good twenty-four hours ago: what Aislinn saw when her chat with Gary sent her Daddy daydream splattering across the floor. When that soothing lifeline voice of Gary's reached her, in the middle of the wreckage. She saw the obvious next place to look.

Steve takes the other end of the sofa. He balances his glass between his fingers, not drinking, and watches me.

I say, 'Remember what Gary said, on the phone? He told Aislinn her da was dead, and she went to bits. So he kept talking, to calm her down: went on about how much her da had loved her, how he was obviously a great guy. Does that sound like it'd put her off missing her da? Make her go, *Ah, what the hell, I'll just leave it?*'

'Nah. Someone like her, that'd make her feel like she couldn't let go; there had to be something there worth finding. That's what I've been saying.'

'Remember what else Gary said to her? He went on about the guys working the case. How they were good Ds, how thorough they'd been. How if there was anything to find, they'd have found it.'

Steve shakes his head, eyebrows pulling together: *And?*

'If I was Aislinn,' I say. My heart is banging. 'If I was someone like her. I wouldn't go off chasing some half-baked gang fantasy for no good reason. I'd go after someone who I knew could give me actual info. I'd go looking for one of those Ds.'

There's a silence. Faint wind struggles in the chimney.

Steve says, 'How would you find them?'

'I'll bet you anything Gary named names. "I know Feeney and McCann, they're great detectives, I'm sure they did everything they could . . ."'

Steve says, like he's not breathing right, 'McCann.'

Another silence, and the wind.

I say, 'Aislinn rings up Missing Persons and asks for Feeney or McCann. The admin tells her Feeney's retired and McCann's moved to Murder. She's got no way to chase Feeney down, but it's easy as pie to find out where Murder's based and wait outside at the shift changes. She wouldn't even have needed to ask around to pinpoint her guy; the amount of time she'd spent thinking about this, she'd have recognised him. Even after fifteen years.'

'And then what? Say she tracked him down; then what?'

I shake my head. 'I don't know.'

Steve runs a hand over his head, trying automatically to smooth down his hair. 'Are you figuring he was the secret boyfriend?'

'I thought of that, but I can't see any reason she'd want him. We're back to the same old question: a girl like that, why would she go for some middle-aged cop starting a beer gut? Flirt with him to get the story on her dad: sure. But be his bit on the side for six months? Why?'

'She's trying to get closer to her dad, McCann's the only link she's got—'

'Jaysus.' I make a face. 'Now that's fucked up. I don't see it, but. Gary was a link to her dad, too, and she didn't pull anything like that on him. He would've said.'

'Maybe she was a badge bunny.' Steve is still running his hand over his hair, again and again. 'She comes in to talk to you and Gary, gets a look around, decides she likes the vibe . . .'

They're out there. Women, mostly, but I've run into a few guys along the way. You could have a face like a warthog and they wouldn't give a damn; they barely see you. What they're chasing is the buzz of second-hand adrenaline, second-hand power, the story that doesn't end with *And then he worked in the call centre ever after*: tell me who you arrested today, keep the uniform on in the bedroom and get your handcuffs out. They're easy enough to spot, but there are cops out there who love it; makes them feel like rock stars. And it lets them punch above their weight.

McCann would have been punching farther above than most, though. 'If that was all she was after,' I say, 'she could've gone down to Copper Face Jack's and had her pick of good-looking young fellas. Why him?'

'Because she didn't want some uniform who spent his day giving people hassle for not having their car tax up to date. Like we said before: after the life she'd had, she wanted thrills. She wanted a Murder D.'

I can see it. Murder are the big-game hunters; we spend our days going after the top predators. For these people, that makes us the top prey.

If that's what Aislinn was after, Steve has a point: she didn't have a lot of options. Murder is small: two dozen of us, give or take. Half are McCann's age, or older. No one's a supermodel.

All the same, I don't believe she'd have picked out McCann. Going by Rory and the exes, rough and silent wasn't her style. She would have skimmed straight over McCann and kept looking, gone for someone smoother around the edges, someone with a bit of chat to draw her in; someone like—

Someone like Breslin.

Breslin, with his lovely little wifey and three lovely little kiddies. Breslin, with plenty to lose if the badge bunny turned bunny-boiler. Breslin, pushing us to charge Rory Fallon and close the case.

I say, 'Oh, Jesus.'

'The only thing is the timing,' Steve says. 'If you're right and Aislinn got McCann's name off Gary, that was two and a half years ago. According to Lucy, she only picked up the secret boyfriend six months back. Why the gap?'

'Try this,' I say. 'Aislinn goes to McCann looking for info, he gives her the brush-off. She doesn't give up; every few months she's back, hassling him for more. Then one day she turns up at the squad, he doesn't feel like dealing with her, he sends his partner out to get rid of her for him. And Aislinn likes what she sees.'

Steve's face has gone immobile. It changes him, strips away the studenty perkiness so that for once I can get a good look at what's underneath. He's turned adult, sharp, not someone to mess with.

I say, 'Remember the neighbour who called in a guy going over Aislinn's patio wall? Male, medium build, dark coat, probably middle-aged; and probably fair hair.'

Steve says, 'Breslin the Monk. Having a full-on affair. You think?'

'Everyone says Aislinn was something special, when it came to sucking people into her fantasies. The woman had talent, and she had practice. And Breslin, he overestimates himself and underestimates other people. Those are the ones who get tripped up. If she decided she wanted him . . .'

'Yeah, but getting into something that risky? Breslin's very careful of himself.'

'He was careful. No calls, no texts, no e-mails, nothing. And remember how someone ran Aislinn through the system? Last September, right after she picked up her secret boyfriend? He was making sure she'd never been reported for stalking, harassment, blackmail, anything that said she might be a psycho.'

Something hard flashes in Steve's face. He says, 'Remember how you told Breslin to take the recordings of Rory's male KAs down to Stoneybatter? To see if the uniform could ID the guy who called it in?'

'Yeah. The pompous bastard palmed it off on Gaffney—' And I stop there.

Steve says, 'I thought he was too important for scut work.'

'Yeah,' I say. 'Me too.'

'That's what he wanted us thinking. It was nothing to do with that. He couldn't risk the uniform hearing his voice.'

That movie-trailer voice. *In a world* . . . Even the thickest uniform would remember that voice. Unless, maybe, someone made sure he was bombarded with possibles till his memory smeared beyond recovering.

Breslin called this in. My mind jams on that like a needle stuck on a record, hitting it over and over. This isn't just us playing imagination games. This happened. Breslin called it in.

I say, 'No wonder the call didn't come in to 999. He couldn't have a recording floating around.'

'And no wonder the secret boyfriend's invisible. Breslin wouldn't go leaving love notes, or sending Facebook messages. Unless there's something solid in that computer folder, we've got nothing.'

'We've got Lucy. She could confirm the relationship. Whether she'll do it is a whole other question.'

'Lucy.' Steve's head goes back as it hits him. 'Jesus Christ. And we were wondering why she was so cagey. She was trying to figure out whether we were pals of Breslin's.'

The whiskey tastes ferocious in my mouth, dangerous. I say, 'Because she thinks he killed Aislinn.'

Silence, a small one this time. My heart beats strong and slow in my ears.

Steve says, 'That doesn't mean she's right.'

'She was afraid of us,' I say. '"I don't know anything about Ash's secret fella, she told me nothing, we're not that close . . ." She was terrified that we were the cleanup crew, and if we thought she knew anything . . .'

'But she dropped the hint about the boyfriend all the same. If we were actually on the up-and-up, she wanted us looking around, not fixating on Rory.'

'Yeah,' I say. 'Fair play to Lucy. She's got guts.'

Steve takes a swallow of his drink like he needs it. 'Yeah, but enough guts to come out and say what she knows? It's been two days now, she hasn't been in touch about giving her statement . . . She wants nothing to do with us.'

'We need her. Without her, we've got fuck-all linking Aislinn to either Breslin or McCann. We can't exactly go showing her photo around the job, ask if anyone remembers seeing her with either of them.'

'The barman in Ganly's? He saw Aislinn with her fella.'

'He didn't see *them*. He saw Aislinn, with some middle-aged guy vaguely in the background. He'll never make the ID.'

'There's Rory,' Steve says. 'He's hiding something: that half-hour when he got to Aislinn's early, something happened there. Maybe he saw something, or she said something . . .'

'*Shit*,' I say, straightening up fast. 'Were you in the observation room when Breslin asked him for evidence that Aislinn had a stalker?'

'Jesus.' Steve catches his breath with a hiss. 'Yeah, I saw that. Rory started to say something about having seen some bloke on Saturday night, and Breslin shut him right down.'

'Breslin and me,' I say. 'I was right in there, backing him up, like a bloody idiot. But listen: the guy Rory saw, that can't have been Breslin. If it was, Rory would've recognised him on Sunday – or at least today, when he brought it up. And you and me would've seen that, if he recognised Breslin; we couldn't have missed that. Breslin's not the one who was in Stoneybatter Saturday night.'

'Huh,' Steve says. He's gone immobile again, only his mind moving, twisting and rearranging the case like a Rubik's cube. 'Try this. Breslin was Aislinn's fella. Over the last few weeks, he starts to suspect she's two-timing him. Maybe he checks her phone – it only had a swipe lock, remember? – and he finds the texts between her and Rory. And then, sometime last week, he finds Rory's text about the dinner date.'

'Breslin wouldn't like being two-timed,' I say. 'The ego on him; he wouldn't like it one little bit.'

'But he'd have better sense than to do his own dirty work.' Steve's eyes come up to meet mine. 'You know who he would've brought in.'

I say, 'McCann.' The thought of putting yourself in your partner's hands like that does something weird inside my head. I look at Steve and he looks different from ever before: his freckles are more vivid, the lines of his mouth are more definite, I can almost see warmth coming off his skin. He looks more real.

'Yeah,' he says. 'McCann.'

I say, 'Breslin sets up a beautiful alibi, just in case – what do you bet him and the missus had friends over, Saturday night, or went to a nice crowded restaurant? And McCann heads down to Stoneybatter to sort out that cheating bitch.'

'The way it went down,' Steve says. 'That can't have been the plan.'

There's a question in his voice. He means did they want Aislinn dead.

'Nah,' I say. 'Just for two-timing Breslin? He might've been raging, but I don't care how close him and McCann are: there's no chance McCann would get himself into something like this just because Breslin can't keep his mot in line.'

'So McCann was just planning to talk to her. Drop a few hints about why it's a bad idea to cheat on a cop. Maybe talk to Rory, too, warn him off. Just talk.'

He badly wants to believe that. A surprisingly big part of me does, too. 'Maybe,' I say. 'Probably. Only something goes wrong. Maybe Aislinn goes to scream and McCann panics, something like that.'

'And he hits her. Or pushes her down and then hits her.' Steve's hand is tight around his glass. This shit is hard to say, physically hard. It goes against the grain. Our throats want to close over it.

'When he realises what's after happening,' I say, 'he wipes the place down, legs it out of there and gets hold of Breslin. Once Breslin's finished throwing a wobbler and had a chance to think, he calls it in to Stoneybatter. He times it so Aislinn will be found when he's on shift, and he'll be there to keep an eye on the investigation. And that's where we came in.'

For a long time it feels like there's nothing else to say. It feels like there might never be anything to say; like the one and only thing we can do is sit here on my sofa, drinking whiskey, while a man shouts far away outside and that small nagging wind flutters in the chimney.

The house is getting cold enough that in the end I have to move, to turn on the heat. 'You take Rory,' I say, when I come back. 'You were getting on great guns with him there, on Sunday. I'll take Lucy.'

Steve scrapes at his glass with a thumbnail, thinking. 'Rory first. First thing in the morning.'

'Yeah. Then anything he gives us, we might be able to use it to crack Lucy.'

'Breslin,' Steve says. He looks up at me. 'What do we do with him?'

I can't even think of what I actually want to do with Breslin. I say, 'You've got a date with him to check out Rory's rep with the locals, remember? Once that's done, someone needs to chase up the rest of the people who were in evening classes with Aislinn. No harm letting Breslin do that now.'

'If Lucy or Rory IDs him or McCann . . .'

'Yeah,' I say. 'That's when it gets interesting.'

'Shit,' Steve says. It's sinking in: this is real, and we're stuck with it. 'Ah, *shit.*'

I start to laugh. The face on him is beautiful: like a good citizen coming home and finding a dead hooker and a K of coke in his bed.

'Jesus, Antoinette. What's funny? This is *fucked up.* We're talking about one of our *own squad.* Killing someone; *murdering* her, maybe.'

I'm laughing harder. 'No. Have you even— If this is true, what the *hell* are we going to—'

'You should see yourself. The state of you. Don't you dare have a heart attack in my gaff. The rumours—'

'*Antoinette.* What are we going to *do?*'

Obviously, I don't have a clue either. I would tell him we'll figure it out as we go along, except that seems unlikely. 'Cheer up,' I say. 'Maybe it'll all turn out to be nothing. Maybe you'll give Rory a nudge tomorrow and he'll confess on your shoulder. Bring tissues.'

Steve takes a deep breath and runs a hand down his face. 'It could be nothing. Right? It could. Breslin was shagging Aislinn, he went down there late Saturday night looking for his hole and found her dead, and he freaked out. Like anyone would. The rest is coincidence and rubbish. It could be.'

'It could, yeah.' It isn't.

'It could. This is all fairy-tale. There's no solid evidence; it's all maybe-what-ifs.'

He's grinning at me, but the grin is a complicated one. Steve knows some, at least, of what's gone on in my head over the last few hours. He's here anyway.

'Yeah yeah yeah,' I say. It comes out easy, but he's right, and it catches at me in places I can't see. 'Your money's still on the big bad drugs gang, is it?'

'Jesus,' Steve says. The grin is fading. 'I actually wish that had panned out. Just to keep our lives simple.'

'Ah, no. If our lives were simple, I'd still be bitching about it, and you'd be bitching about me bitching about it. This is way better.'

He makes a helpless sound somewhere between a laugh and a groan. 'God. All that shite with the fifty-quid notes . . .'

'Yeah,' I say. 'All that shite.' All Breslin's fancy hints that he was on the take: all to give me and Steve a nice dead end to chase. The first day, when I asked the whole squad room who had run Aislinn through the system, McCann must've shat a brick. First chance he got, he grabbed Breslin and the two of them came up with something that would account for the check on Aislinn, account for anything else we found that linked her to them, keep us occupied till Breslin could break Rory, and lead us exactly nowhere. Breslin must've had fun, muttering darkly into his phone, layering on the obvious fake stories about stopping off for a shag to let us dig out the non-obvious fake story underneath, watching us lick it all up.

And now I know exactly why Breslin threw away his red herring, this morning. It wasn't because he could tell I was ready to jump. It was because when he got back in from interviewing Rory's exes, his pocket floater – and if that wasn't Reilly, I'm gonna find out who it is – told him that me and Steve had had a row and Steve had walked out. Breslin knew I was the one who'd been closer to sold on Rory from the start, he made an educated guess that that had been a big part of the row, and he knew I'd be itching to have the last word on Steve. And to help me do exactly that, he had the CCTV evidence of Rory stalking Aislinn. He dropped the bent-cop bullshit and played hard to that, aiming to get Rory arrested fast and to keep me and Steve apart till the file had gone to the prosecutors.

And me, I was so busy bracing myself to fight anyone who was out to sink me or own me or generally use me as his very own dollhouse dolly, it never occurred to me that this might not be about me to begin with. I skipped right off with the nice man waving candy – Steve did too, in his own way – and if that cocky fuck hadn't been hanging around outside my gaff, or if I hadn't made myself ring Steve, or if Steve was a very slightly different guy, we wouldn't be sitting here.

'Thanks,' I say. 'For coming down.'

'You're all right. There was nothing decent on the telly.'

I kind of want to say sorry, but explaining what I'm apologising for and not apologising for would take too much hassle and embarrassment and overall shite. Steve might be thinking the same thing, I don't know. Instead I get the whiskey bottle and give us both a refill. We sit there, drinking, while the stuff we should probably be saying out loud gets itself done in the silence.

'Fuck me,' I say, suddenly realising. 'I'm half English.'

'And you're middle-class,' Steve says. 'Next time you go home, you're going to get the shite kicked out of you.'

'Shh. Nobody has to know.'

'They'll smell it off you.'

'Seriously,' I say. I'm looking at him. 'Nobody has to know.'

Steve gives me a straight look back. 'They won't.'

'Good.'

'Unless someone else talks. Do you know how your man tracked you down?'

'He got my address off Crowley,' I say. The taste of that makes me finish my whiskey. 'I need to sort the little wankstain before he blabs.'

'He's not a problem. We'll do it tomorrow.'

The *we* sounds good. 'It's gonna be a long day.'

'Yeah.' Steve takes a deep breath, throws back the last of his drink and head-shakes away the burn. 'I'll head. Get some rest for this one.'

'You're over the limit. Get a taxi, come get the car tomorrow.'

'I'll start walking, pick one up along the way. Clear my head.' He stands up and pulls on his coat. 'Are you coming to Rory's with me?'

'Yeah, I'll come. He still thinks I'm OK. Early, like seven? You need to get back in time for your date with Breslin.'

He nods. Breslin's name doesn't even bring back an echo of that horrified look; we're somewhere out on the other side of that. 'Seven works.'

He doesn't ask – even after me calling him for help because there's a nasty man outside my house, he doesn't ask – whether I'm gonna be OK on my own, or whether I want him to stay. If I was a totally different person, I might hug him or some shit for that.

'Text me when you're home,' I say, instead. 'Let me know you got in OK.'

Steve rolls his eyes. 'No one's lying in wait to *jump* me.'

'I know that, you spa. But I'm the one who dragged you out. I feel responsible. You want to get yourself jumped on your own time, go for it.'

'Thanks a lot.' He grins at me, wrapping his scarf around his neck. 'I'll text you.'

When he's gone I take my laptop to bed and shoot some Nazis. I don't even have to stop myself thinking about all the shit on my lengthening list of shit I don't want to think about. My mind is done for the night, shorted out; there's nothing left but a dial tone.

It's half an hour before my phone beeps. *Home safe. See you tomorrow.*

I text back *Yeah, see you then. Night.* I crash out practically before I can put down the phone.

14

Waking up the next morning feels like waking up the morning after moving house, switching squad, dumping someone: you know the world's changed, even before you remember how. The air has a different flavour to it, sharp and strange and resiny, a chilly bite at the edges. Even before you remember, you know to watch your footing with today.

I run like a machine, through the dark and the fine hanging haze of rain. This morning my body works like something separate from me, running itself perfectly with no need for any input. I push it, faster and farther than normal, and I'm not even winded. My mind can only see one step ahead: getting to Rory's place. Beyond that there's nothing.

Steve is early, quarter to seven, but I'm ready: caffeinated, fed, showered and dressed. I doubt anyone's watching my gaff, but when Steve knocks I practically reef him inside all the same, just in case.

'How're you doing?' I ask.

He nods. He's even paler than usual, but there's a going-over-the-top set to his jaw. 'You?'

'Yeah. You need anything? Coffee, food?'

'Nah, I'm sorted. Thanks. How do you want to do this?'

I say, 'Deasy's meant to have organised surveillance on Rory's gaff. I'd say he'll be doing it himself; he'd be lucky to get authorisation for uniforms, plus he'll want the pat on the head if anything good happens. And I don't want Deasy knowing you and me are working Rory together. He could be Breslin's bitch.'

Steve nods. 'We'll go in separately.'

'Yeah. And we're not in a good mood with each other.'

'I made up a photo array,' Steve says. He pulls a handful of thin card out of his bag. Eight clean-shaven middle-aged guys with greying dark hair, all caught full-face or almost, in stills pulled from video, against neutral backgrounds. Steve must have been up half the night finding the right shot of McCann and then combing the internet for good matches, making sure no one can say the array was skewed. McCann is third down on the left, wearing what looks like his court suit, staring darkly over my shoulder against thick cloudy sky. 'Printed off a bunch of copies, just in case.'

'Good,' I say. It fries wires in my brain, seeing one of our own squad where a scumbag belongs; it looks like a joke birthday card. 'You do one with Breslin? I might need it for Lucy.'

'Yeah.' He flips to another sheet, this one full of good-looking fair-haired middle-aged guys. Breslin's smirk is in the top right corner.

If I start thinking about how fucked-up this is, I'm gone. We can't look down.

I can see Steve thinking the same thing. 'Nice one,' I say. 'Let's do this.' And I open the door to let him out.

There's a black Mitsubishi Pajero with heavy tint parked opposite the Wayward Bookshop, in the dim stretch between streetlamps. Dawn is only starting and all I can see through the windscreen is a wide shape in the driver's seat, but when I knock on the window – keeping my head low, and the car between me and the bookshop – sure enough, Deasy sits up and cracks it.

'Howya,' I say. 'Any news?'

'Not a lot.' Deasy looks wrecked enough that I believe he's been awake at least most of the time. The air in the car smells of fish and chips, too much breathing, and there's probably a piss-bottle under the seat. 'That there, the grey door next to the bookshop, that goes up to his flat; the windows over the bookshop, those are his sitting room. He went to the Spar on the corner around nine last night, came back with a pint of milk and a sandwich. The little bollix looked petrified; kept looking around like someone might jump him. I nearly gave him a blast of the horn when he passed me, just to watch him keel over.'

That gives us both a good laugh. 'Lovely,' I say. 'That's where we want him. Any other movement?'

'He closed his curtains when he went in, but the light stayed on all night. Twenty past five, he came down and went into the shop. Hasn't shown his face since. Are you bringing him in?'

'Nah. Later. I just want to poke him a little bit, keep him on his toes. No reason why he should get a lie-in when I don't.'

The thought pulls a yawn out of Deasy. 'Speaking of which,' I say. 'Call someone to take over, and go get some kip.'

He looks startled. It strikes me that I may have been kind of a bitch to the floaters on this one, at least part of the time. When Breslin went looking for a stooge, I'd made it easy for him.

'Thanks,' I say. 'For covering this.'

Before Deasy can find an answer, Steve rolls up, with his hands in his overcoat pockets and a look on his face that no one could call friendly. 'Morning,' he says. 'What's the story?'

'No story,' I say. 'What're you doing here?'

'Just checking in. Wanted to see if Rory's done anything interesting.'

'He hasn't.'

Steve raises his eyebrows at Deasy, who's soaking all this up. 'What's he been at?'

Deasy opens his mouth, catches my eye and shuts it again. 'Ah. Not much.'

'Like I just told you,' I say. 'See you back at HQ.'

Steve doesn't move. 'Are you planning on talking to him?'

'I might.'

'I might join you.'

I jut my jaw up at the dark sky, but I manage to keep it together, what with Deasy being there and all. 'Do you not have a tree to shake, no?'

'Good one,' Steve says. 'Will we go in?'

After a moment I do a tight sigh. 'Whatever.' To Deasy: 'See you tomorrow.' And I head across the road without waiting for Steve.

He catches up with me outside the bookshop. The window is dim, just a faint glow coming from somewhere in the back. The display's laid out with a perfection that stinks of desperation: bestsellers temptingly overlapping bright-coloured kids' books, all those wacky cartoons and enigmatic heroines staring dementedly into the darkness. I shift away from Steve and lean on the bell.

Rory hasn't slit his wrists, anyway. He opens the door fast, and we watch his heart rate skyrocket when he sees us. He's wearing the same clothes he had on yesterday, jeans and the depressed beige jumper, and he's getting wimpy stubble. Being a suspect has hit the pause button on his life; the poor bastard is paralysed.

He says, breathless, 'I'm not ready. I wasn't expecting—' He gestures helplessly at his ratty grey slippers. 'I haven't eaten breakfast, or even . . .'

'You're all right,' Steve says gently. 'We don't need you to come with us. We just have a couple of leftover questions to ask. Can we come in, yeah? It'll only take a few minutes.'

Rory's panic solidifies into fear. 'I don't think I should talk to you without a solicitor. Not now that I'm a . . .'

'We're not going to ask about Aislinn,' Steve says, lifting his hands. 'Nothing like that. OK? Just, I didn't get a chance to talk to you yesterday, and you said something in the interview that got me interested.'

Rory blinks hard, trying to focus. Fatigue and fear are using up most of his bandwidth; his mind's slowed down to a crawl.

Steve says – lower, leaning in like someone might be listening – 'And I think we need to talk about it without Detective Breslin around.'

That gets Rory's attention; anything that Breslin wouldn't like has to be good. And there's Steve, all rumpled and earnest, looking like your most harmless pal. 'I suppose . . .' he says, in the end, moving back and opening the door properly. 'All right. Come in.'

The bookshop is two connecting rooms, not big ones. The front one is crammed with shelves – Rory's not gonna be getting any fat customers. Hand-lettered signs say THRILLER and ROMANCE into the darkness; posters of old covers and illustrations hang from the ceiling, swaying restlessly in the sweep of cold air we've brought with us. The light is coming from the back room; through the doorway it looks jammed even tighter than the front, books piled on shelves instead of lined up, wavering stacks on the floor, covers curling.

'That's the second-hand section,' Rory says, waving a hand towards the back. 'I was organising it. I couldn't sleep, and I couldn't stand staring at my sitting room any longer, so I thought I might as well do something useful.'

'Lovely shop,' Steve says, looking around. 'This is where you and Aislinn met, yeah?'

'Yeah. Right over there, in the children's section. She told me she loved bookshops. Magic, she said, specially small ones like this; you always felt like you might find the one book you'd been looking for all your life, at the back of some shelf . . .' Rory rubs at the inside corners of his eyes. 'If Saturday night had gone well, I was going to invite her here next time.'

And she could have helped him alphabetise the feng shui section. Jaysus, the romance. 'I was going to do a picnic,' Rory says. 'On the floor – I was going to move shelves to make room. Explore the second-hand stuff, see if we could find that book she'd been looking for . . .' Another rub at his eyes, harder. 'Sorry. I'm babbling. I didn't get any sleep.'

'You're grand,' Steve says. I take out my notebook and fade back a few steps, between a shelf full of sepia guys running in helmets and a shelf full of laughing women with good hair giving babies adoring looks. The dimness makes them stir and twitch in the corners of my eyes. 'Could we have the lights on in here?'

'Oh. Yeah.' Rory finds a switch by the door, and the lights flicker on. He looks even worse in the light, hunched and red-eyed, like he's been barricaded in here for years hiding from the zombie apocalypse.

'Thanks,' Steve says. 'Are you doing OK?'

Rory does some kind of movement that could mean anything.

'We won't take a lot of your time. I just wanted to ask you about your theory? The dumped guy watching Aislinn, getting upset when he found out she was preparing for dinner with you?' Rory flinches, remembering the slagging that theory took off me and Breslin. 'Yesterday, you started to say something about how you had a bit of evidence to back that up. Yeah?'

Rory glances over involuntarily to see if I'm gonna point and laugh again, but I'm all ears. 'A guy, you said,' Steve says, moving to catch his attention back. 'A guy you saw in the street on Saturday night. Yeah?'

'Yeah. There was a guy. I wasn't making it *up*. I saw him.'

Steve nods, leaning against a bookshelf. 'OK. When was this?'

'When I was leaving Viking Gardens. When I'd given up on Aislinn. I turned down Astrid Road, towards the main road, and I passed the entrance to the laneway that runs behind Viking Gardens. The laneway where . . .'

That involuntary glance at me again. 'Where you'd been hanging out to watch Aislinn,' Steve says matter-of-factly. 'And?'

'And there was a man coming out of the laneway. We startled each other – both of us jumped.'

Steve nods. 'What'd he look like?'

'Middle-aged. A bit taller than me, but probably shorter than you? He had curly dark hair, going grey. Average build, I suppose.'

McCann, coming from Aislinn's house.

He went out, and presumably in, the back way. The back door was locked when we got there; Breslin must have had a key to give him.

'Do you remember what he was wearing?' Steve asks. Easily, like this is no big deal, nothing at all.

Rory shakes his head. 'Not really. A dark coat. A light-coloured scarf, I think. The main thing I noticed was that he seemed . . . I thought he was on something. Coke, maybe, or . . . I mean, I don't know enough about drugs to know what does what, but he jumped a lot harder than I did, and his eyes were . . .' He flares his eyes into a wild, unfocused stare. 'If he wasn't on something, I thought he had to be . . . unbalanced. Either way, he was the last thing I wanted to deal with, right at that moment. I sped up and got away from him as fast as I could.'

'How close were you?'

'About from here to that door.' Rory points to the back-room door. Five feet, maybe six. Close enough for an ID; far enough, with no light but the streetlamp, for a defence barrister to hammer it down.

'Did he say anything? Do anything?'

'There wasn't really time. I was only looking at him for a second or two, before I got out of there. When I got to the corner of Astrid Road I looked back, in case he was following me, but he was going in the opposite direction. He was walking fast, with his head down, but I'm almost positive it was the same guy.'

'And all this would've been around half-eight?' Steve asks.

'Just after. I texted Aislinn one last time at half-eight, and then I gave her five minutes to answer. When she didn't, I left. So when I saw the man, that would've been between twenty-five to nine and twenty to.'

That gave McCann anywhere from thirty-five to fifty-five minutes inside the house. Rory had left the laneway and headed for Tesco around 7.40. Maybe McCann had seen him having his moment, watched and waited for him to leave; maybe he hadn't shown up till Rory was already gone. But by eight o'clock, when Rory knocked on the door and Aislinn didn't answer, McCann was in there.

He wouldn't have wasted time on losing the head when he realised what he'd done, not McCann. Ds are experts at slamming the emotions away for later, when we can afford them. As soon as he knew Aislinn was dead or on her way there, he would have taken off his shoes so as not to leave prints, grabbed a handful of kitchen roll and started wiping down every place where Breslin could have left a fingerprint. Turned the cooker off, because God forbid it should set off the smoke alarm before he was done and far away. Listened to the doorbell and the knocking, to Aislinn's phone chirping and ringing as Rory tried to find her, and stayed out of eyeshot of the windows. When he was done, he would have scuffed out any shoeprints he'd left on the way in, stuffed the kitchen roll in his pocket to dump in a bin on the way home, and slipped out the back door. Thirty-five to fifty-five minutes: plenty of time.

'How come you didn't tell us about this on Sunday?' Steve asks.

'Because . . .' Rory rubs at his mouth. 'OK. You see, I'd seen him before. Twice. In Stoneybatter. The first time was an evening maybe three weeks ago – I was looking for my chance to go down the laneway, and he was right at the top of it lighting a cigarette, so I had to walk around the block and try again. I was across the road from him, that time, so he might not have noticed me; I only noticed him because he was in my way. But the second time – I think about ten days ago – I passed right by him on Astrid Road when I was heading home, and we made eye contact. There was a good chance he'd remember me, if he had any memory at all for faces. I knew if I told you about seeing him on Saturday, you'd try to track him down – and if you did, he'd tell you about seeing me before, and then you'd know I'd been . . . I was hardly going to *tell* you about him. I was *praying* you wouldn't find the guy.'

What the hell? hovers in the air between me and Steve. What was McCann doing, hanging around Aislinn's gaff for weeks on end?

Rory takes the second of silence as disbelief. 'I was *scared*! "Oh, by the way, Detective, I was spending half my evenings wandering around Stoneybatter peering in a woman's window, and while I was at it I happened to notice another guy who might have been doing the same kind of thing, so you should really look at him . . ." I would have had to be *insane* to come out with that. Look what happened when you did find out.'

'I get it,' Steve says. 'I do. And by the time that had come out, and you tried to mention this guy . . .'

'No one was listening,' I finish for him. 'Yeah. I owe you an apology for that.' Rory blinks, startled, and then comes up with a clumsy nod. 'Lucky for us all Detective Moran picked up on it.'

'Do you think you'd recognise the guy?' Steve asks.

'Yes. Almost definitely, yes. I've been thinking about him constantly, ever since I found out about Aislinn.' Rory's swaying forward eagerly; he's our friend again. 'The more I think about it, the more I think he . . . I mean, his face, Saturday night: something wasn't right.'

Steve is pulling the photo array out of his bag. 'OK,' he says. 'I want you to have a look at this and tell me if the man you saw is on here. If he's not, say so. If you're not sure, say so. Yeah?'

Rory nods, gearing up to concentrate. Steve hands him the card.

It takes Rory all of two seconds. 'This guy. That's him.'

His finger is on McCann.

'Take your time,' Steve says. 'Make sure you've looked at all the faces.'

Rory does another scan because he's a good boy, but his finger doesn't move. 'It's him.'

'Are you sure?'

'Yes. I'm positive. He looks a bit younger here, but it's him.'

And there it is: a solid link. No if-then-maybe; this is the real thing, at last. It shakes the air as it thuds down between me and Steve, dense and tarnish-black and too heavy to move. We're stuck with it now.

Rory can feel us believing him. 'Do you think he . . . ? Who is he?'

'He's a guy,' Steve says. 'We can't go into details right now. Can you write down where you've seen the man, at the bottom there? Sign it and date it, and put your initials next to the photo you recognise.'

Rory leans the card on a shelf and writes carefully. 'Here,' he says, passing it back to Steve. 'Is this OK?'

Steve reads. 'That's great. We'll need you to come in and give an official statement, but not right now. You can relax.'

'You mean . . . ? Do I still have to go in to you later on?'

'I don't know yet. We'll see how the day goes. For now, just try and chill out a bit; get some kip, get some breakfast. I know that's easier said.'

'Am I still . . .' Rory's throat moves; he can't get the word out. 'Did you talk to Aislinn's neighbours? Did any of them see me, in the . . . outside her place?'

'Not yet. We'll get back to you. Like I said: try and relax for now.'

'Do you . . . you know. Do you still think I did this?'

Steve says, 'I need to ask you, man. Is there anything else you've held back? Anything at all?'

Rory shakes his head vehemently. 'No. That was it. I swear: there's nothing.'

'OK,' Steve says. 'If you think of anything else we should know, ring me straightaway. Meanwhile, all I can say is that we believe you saw this guy' – I nod – 'and we're going to follow up on it very thoroughly. Yeah?'

'Thanks,' Rory says, confusedly, on a long breath out. 'Thank you.'

I put my notebook away; Steve straightens the books that shifted when he leaned against them. 'Um,' Rory says, twisting his hands in the hem of that godawful jumper. 'Can I say one thing?'

'Sure,' Steve says.

'Me watching Aislinn. I know it sounds like ... But remember when I said Aislinn didn't mind being drawn into other people's daydreams? And you didn't believe me?'

He's talking to me. 'I remember you mentioning that, all right,' I say.

'When I watched her ... I was trying to do the opposite of that. I was trying to feel what it was like to live there, be her. Trying to slip into that. Instead of doing it the other way round, like everyone else had.'

He's wound himself into a tangle of jumper. 'Does that ... ? Does that make sense?'

It sounds like gold-plated self-justification bollix to me, but we need him on side, so I nod. 'It does,' Steve says gently. 'We'll keep it in mind.'

We leave Rory standing among his shelves, peering dazedly at us over the ranks of silhouetted badasses and spooky trees and women prancing in sundresses, like if we come back in a few hours they'll have closed over his head and he'll be gone.

Outside the door, I say, 'What the hell was McCann at? Messing about in Stoneybatter weeks ago?'

'Doing a recce, maybe,' Steve says. 'Getting the lie of the land, so that when it came time to do the job, he could get in and out without getting lost or getting spotted.'

'Except he did get spotted. A bunch of times. That's what Google Earth is for: so you can do your recce without getting your hands dirty.'

'Yeah, but we can check what he's been at on Google Earth. You can argue an ID; harder to argue with internet records.'

Deasy's black Pajero is gone; two streetlamps down, there's a white Nissan Qashqai that wasn't there before. That was quick. I wonder if it's Breslin in there, but I'm not about to check, not with Rory blinking behind the bookshop window. 'Listen,' I say, whipping around on Steve and pointing a finger in his face, 'meet you in twenty minutes, in that park where we had breakfast Sunday. Make sure you're not followed.' I jab him in the shoulder. 'Clear?'

'Whatever,' Steve says, rolling his eyes. 'Jesus,' and as I turn to stride off to my car, I see him throw his hands in the air in exasperation. Who knows whether it'll fool Breslin, or his eyes and ears in the Qashqai. I get in my car and gun it like I'm well pissed off.

I'm first at the park, and I'm pretty sure there's no one on my tail. The place is damp and near-deserted again, just a Lycra-wrapped cyclist stuffing down something depressing out of Tupperware and two nannies having what sounds like a bitching session in Portuguese while a clump of toddlers dig up a flowerbed. I pick the bench farthest from all of them and have a look through my notes on the Rory interview, while I wait for Steve.

The description that matches McCann. The times that give him anything up to an hour in Aislinn's place. All in my handwriting, in my regulation notepad just like the ones packed with notes about the scumbags who danced on the other scumbag's head and the rapist who strangled his victim with her own belt and all the rest of them. *Witness identified Det Joseph McCann.*

I flip to a clean page and ring Sophie. It's just gone half-eight, but she picks up on the second ring. 'Hey. I was going to ring you as soon as I got to work.'

'Hey,' I say. 'Does that mean you've got something?'

'It means you're on my shit list.' She's chewing and moving at the same time: breakfast standing up, while she throws her stuff together. Sophie's running late. 'Four o'clock this morning, my phone starts going apeshit: texts, e-mails, more texts, all from my computer guy. When I ignored them, because I'm *normal*, he started *ringing* me. The guy's great at his job, but when it comes to being a human, he's a total fucking incompetent. I finally had to turn off the phone. And so obviously the bloody alarm didn't go off, and I woke up like ten seconds ago.' Bang of a cupboard door.

'Ah, shite,' I say. 'Sorry. Want to give me the computer guy's number and I'll ring him every half-hour for a week or two?'

That gets a snort of laughter out of Sophie. 'If I thought he'd even notice, I'd say yeah. Listen, though: he got into your vic's double-super-secret pics folder. That's what he was doing till stupid o'clock.

You were right: the password was "missingmymissingdaddy", with a few substitutions thrown in for kicks.'

The shot of disgust catches me by surprise. It's the first thing I've felt all day. 'Brilliant,' I say. 'I love it when they're predictable. What's in there?'

Sophie slurps something. 'I'll forward you the stuff as soon as I get in the car. Basically, it's a couple of dozen photos of Post-it notes with numbers and letters on them, plus one photo of a piece of paper with what looks like a kiddie fairy tale. I don't know what you were hoping for, but this better be worth screwing up my day.'

'I can't tell till I see it,' I say, 'but it's gotta be worth something if she bothered hiding it, right? Thanks a million, Sophie. Forward me the stuff – throw in the dates and times when the pics were taken, if you've got time. I promise to tell you it's cracked the case wide open.'

'You better. I have to go because I can't find my other boot and I'm about to start smashing shit. See you 'round.' And she hangs up.

I check the *Courier* online, in case I need to block out some time to go break Crowley's face, but there's nothing there about my personal life. Apparently even an arrogant fuck like last night's knows when to back away. There's another vomit-blast of Aislinn stuff – Crowley's tracked down some old classmate to make generic sobbing noises about what a lovely girl Aislinn was; Lucy, good woman, must have told him to get stuffed. And there's a sidebar of unsolved murders from the last couple of years – for a second I think *The gaffer's gonna love that,* before I remember that by the end of the day this article is gonna be the least of O'Kelly's problems. I can't even start imagining what he'll think of me by then. It bugs me that that even occurs to me. O'Kelly's opinion isn't gonna play a big role in my future, but some base-of-the-skull part of my brain hasn't caught up with that yet.

Just for kicks, I experiment with wondering what last night's smug fucker will think when – if – he sees my name at the heart of the story on every front page. I try it delicately at first, like biting down on a broken tooth you've been avoiding for a long time. It takes me a minute to figure out I'm feeling nothing. I bite harder, wonder whether he'll be proud of me for taking down the bad guy, impressed with all the work I put into it, disappointed at what this'll do to my career, disgusted with me for ratting out my own: turns out I don't care. I go meta, try to resent that he left it too late even to let me have a reaction: nothing. All I feel is stupid, for wasting brain space on this shite. When I ring my ma this evening, I'm gonna dig up some old rubber-hamster story from Missing Persons, make her laugh, and say not one word about last night.

Steve comes through the park gate talking into his phone and looking around for me – the nannies give him the once-over, then go back to their conversation when they see me lifting a hand to him. He drops onto the bench beside me, shoving his phone into his pocket.

'Story?' I say.

'I left a message for my guy at the mobile company, the one who's tracking down full records on the phone that called in the attack to Stoneybatter. I'm hoping there's something on there to help us prove it's Breslin's phone. We should be so lucky, but . . .' The corner of his mouth twists down. 'Any news?'

'Sophie's guy got into Aislinn's password-protected folder. She says it's mostly numbers on Post-its; she's gonna e-mail me the pics now.'

Steve's face crunches into a quick grimace. 'Ah, shite. Shite. We needed that to be something good.'

'It still could be. Who's the pessimist now?'

''Cause Rory's ID . . . it won't be worth a lot. Any defence barrister's going to say Rory had passed McCann in the corridor at HQ, on his way in or out, so he knew his face from there and got mixed up.'

'Yep,' I say. 'Or he didn't just get mixed up: he was frantically trying to invent a fall guy, so he pictured someone he'd seen recently, to make the description sound realistic.'

'Yeah.' Steve hasn't moved since he sat down, not even to resettle his arse on the damp bench. He's concentrating hard. 'We need to try for a voice ID, off the uniform who took the call.'

'While you're with Breslin this morning, see if you can get a voice sample. Just record a minute of the conversation on your phone.

Then send it to me, if you can't get away from him, and I'll take it down to Stoneybatter.'

He nods. My phone beeps. 'Here we go,' I say, pulling it out. 'Keep your fingers crossed.'

'They are. Believe me.'

The e-mail says *Here*, and a list of dates and times. It has twenty-nine pics attached. I swipe through them: yellow Post-it, *8W* inside a circle. Post-it, *1030* inside a circle. Post-it, *7* inside a circle, in the background a sliver of purple that looks like Aislinn's sitting-room curtains. Post-it, *7Th* inside a circle, chunk of a thumb in one corner.

I say, 'Times and days.'

'Looks like.'

'Remember we were wondering how the secret boyfriend could've made appointments with Aislinn?'

Steve flicks the edge of my phone with one fingernail. 'Low-tech. The safest way.'

'And we didn't find any of these in the search of her gaff.' I keep swiping: *11, 6M, 745.* 'When Breslin knows he's got some free time coming up, he sticks a note through Aislinn's letterbox, letting her know what time she needs to be ready and waiting in her good lingerie. Then, when he gets there, he takes the note back and destroys it. Just like we said: he's careful.'

Steve reaches over and enlarges the *745* on my screen. 'You figure that matches Breslin's writing?'

'Hard to tell. There's nothing that clashes, anyway. And I've seen him write times like that, without the full stop.'

'Plenty of cops do that.'

'Yeah, but not a lot of civilians. That might narrow it down.'

'Even then . . .' Steve shakes his head. 'A handwriting expert's not going to give us a match on this much.'

'No way,' I say. I go back to swiping: *9F, 630W, 7.* 'And Breslin would know that. Again: not taking any chances.'

'No way he was planning on killing Aislinn from the start.'

'No, but he wasn't planning on leaving his wife for her, either. Breslin likes his life. He likes his kids. He likes his house, and his car, and his fancy sun holidays. Probably he even likes his wife, more or less. He liked Aislinn, too, but not enough to risk losing all the rest of it. If she went bunny-boiler on him, he didn't want her having any evidence she could show his wife.'

'He did a good job.' Steve doesn't look happy about it.

7, *745Th*, 8, and then: a plain sheet of white paper. Careful, even handwriting – not Breslin's; this looks like a match to the signatures and scribbles on Aislinn's paperwork. Every loop neatly rounded, every line so straight that she must have put a lined sheet underneath to guide her, keep it perfect. I screen-pinch it bigger and we read, me glancing at Steve for a nod when I'm ready to scroll down.

> *Once upon a time two girls lived in a cottage in the deep dark forest. Their names were Carabossa and Meladina.*
>
> *Carabossa ran barefoot in the forest all day and all night. She climbed the tallest trees. She swam in the streams. She trained wolf cubs to eat from her hand. She shot bears with her bow and arrow.*
>
> *Meladina never left the cottage, because a wizard had put a spell on her. Carabossa couldn't break the spell. No prince could break it. No good witch or wizard could break it. Meladina thought she would be trapped there forever. She looked out the cottage window and cried.*
>
> *Then one day Meladina found a spell book buried under the floor of the cottage. She started to teach herself magic. Carabossa warned her that the wizard was dangerous, and she should have nothing to do with him, but Meladina had no choice. It was that or die in the cottage.*
>
> *When she had learned enough, Meladina worked her magic and moved the spell from herself onto the wizard. He was trapped in the cottage forever, and Meladina ran out to climb trees and swim in streams with Carabossa. And they lived happily ever after.*
>
> *If I got the ending wrong, I need you to tell them. Love and more love.*

'What the hell?' Steve says.

I say, 'That's meant for Lucy.'

'Yeah, I get that part. But what's it mean? Like, Aislinn fell in love with Breslin – OK, that's the spell – and it kept her trapped. And then what? She got him to fall in love with her too? Or what?'

'I don't care. Lucy can explain all the cutesy fairy-tale crap. Because that's what this end part means: if shit goes wrong, Lucy needs to tell us – or whoever – the whole story. And it means Aislinn was scared. As far back as' – I tap at the phone, going back to Sophie's e-mail – 'as far back as the twelfth of November, Aislinn was scared things could end exactly like this. She made her will right around then, remember?'

'Too scared to leave him,' Steve says, trying it out. 'And that's the spell?'

'Scared he was going through her laptop, too, or she wouldn't have bothered with the password – not on something she wanted found. Sounds like a lovely romance all round.' I'm checking the dates on the note pics, too, while I'm at it. Ninth of September, 5.51pm. Fifteenth of September, 6.08pm. Eighteenth of September, 6.14pm. Aislinn getting home from work, finding a note, taking a photo, uploading it onto her computer and deleting it off her phone. Planning something.

'And her reversing the spell on him is her trapping him, somehow. Getting him locked up, maybe?' Steve has his eyebrows pulled together and his hands clasped on top of his head, thinking it through. 'The whole Rory thing was Aislinn trying to provoke Breslin into beating the shite out of her, so he'd go to prison, because that was the only way she could think of to get rid of him? Except she didn't think things would go this far?'

I consider that. It fits with what we know about Aislinn: naïve enough to think an idiot plan like that could actually work, just because it played so nicely in her head; spent such a big chunk of her life trapped by someone else's demands, she could have panicked when it happened again. 'It'd explain why Aislinn kept pics of the notes. Evidence of the affair, in case Breslin tried to claim he'd never seen her in his life.'

'Except why just the notes? Why not, I don't know, set her phone to voice-record a conversation? Or take photos of him naked in her bed when he crashed out?'

I could've gone my whole life without that mental image. The things this job puts you through. 'Scared he'd catch her at it,' I say. 'Or go through her phone before she could upload the file and delete it.'

'Dammit,' Steve says. 'Even one nude pic would've been hard evidence. This stuff . . .' He blows out a breath. 'Unless Lucy's got something amazing up her sleeve, we'll be lucky if we ever have enough for a charge. Never mind a conviction.'

He's watching the kids put dirt in their hair, with his hands clasped between his knees. The tense hunch of his spine says he's not happy.

I say, 'You don't need to do this.'

It needs saying. Last night, with me and Steve caught up in our adrenaline hurricane from the hunt and the realisation, I took it for granted we were in this together, all the way to the finish line. I think he did too. Today, with Steve dumping doom and gloom into this morning made of flat chilly sky and Deasy's watchful eyes and left-over rain dripping inside the park hedges, it feels like he should have a chance to change his mind.

His face turns towards me. Not blank; he's not trying to pretend the thought's never crossed his mind. Complicated.

He says, 'Neither do you.'

'I don't have a lot to lose here. You do. And it's my case.' It gives me a quick flash of something like pain, the fact that part of me can't stop thinking like a detective: my case, my responsibility. It'll wear off, somewhere down the line. 'You can throw a sickie. Get food poisoning. Go home, come back in a couple of days when the dust's settled.'

'We could both still get out of it. Tell Breslin that Rory's ID'd McCann as being on the scene, and we know McCann's not involved but we don't want to fuck him up by letting him get dragged into court as an alternative theory of the crime, so we're going to back off Rory and mark this one unsolved. Then tell Rory the ID didn't go anywhere. The gaffer'll give us a bit of shite for not getting the solve, but Breslin'll put in a good word for us. Bang: we're done. Like the whole thing never happened.'

He's watching me, and his face has that same immobility it took on last night. The scraping light finds crow's-feet and smile-lines I never noticed before. I can't tell whether he wants me to say yes; yes, let's flush this toxic godawful mess and walk away.

He's right: we could do it. We could even square it with our consciences, near enough. Like he said, we'll get a conviction around the same time we get a Lotto win. Even if we do, justice does nothing for the dead; nothing we do will make any difference to Aislinn. There's no family needing answers, not this time. And it's not like McCann and Breslin are going to turn into a rampaging serial-killer team if we don't take them down; they'll go back to being who they always were, and Breslin will go back to keeping it in his pants. No harm done, all round.

Except that, when you get down to it, I'm right where I thought I was when we figured Breslin and McCann were bent. If I keep my mouth shut, then they've put their hands on me and knotted me into someone else, living a whole different life, even if from outside it looks just like the old one. Breslin and McCann will be running me and my every day after all, whether they even wanted to or not.

I owe this case. I've got beef with this case. I need to shoot it right between the eyes, skin it and stuff it and mount it on my wall, for when my grandkids ask me to tell them stories about way back a million years ago when I used to be a D.

I can't make myself tell Steve I'm gone, not yet. 'Nah,' I say. 'I've started now; might as well finish.'

The sudden loosening in his face could be anything, relief or disappointment, till it resolves itself into a small, very sweet smile. 'I might as well come along for the ride, so,' he says. 'I've never had food poisoning; I'd only make a bollix of faking it.'

For some reason that gets me, solid in the gut. Not like I'm welling up, or any of that shite, but something swells hard under my ribs. Weird how, when I realised I'm leaving, it never occurred to me that that's gonna mean leaving Steve. Somewhere along the way I must've started taking the little bollix for granted, thinking he'd always be there, like a brother. I don't do that shite. Because the fact is, Steve won't always be there. Once I'm gone, we'll stay in touch for a while. We'll go for the odd pint, laugh too hard at each other's stories and have conversations full of awkward stumbles where he tries to talk tactfully around work and his new partner, and I try to get him to knock that shit off. Then the pints will get further apart, and then one of us will get into a relationship and won't be around as much; the texts will start with 'Hey, too long no see,' and all of a sudden we'll realise it's been a year since we met up. And that'll be, in every way that counts, the end of that.

I can't afford to be getting maudlin. 'You little goody-goody,' I say. 'I bet you never once mitched off school, did you?'

'Ah, I did. To visit my dying granny.'

I concentrate on the kids eating flowerbed, and the cyclist doing improbable stretches to show off his glutes to the nannies, till I can wipe my mind blank again. 'OK,' I say. 'Good. In that case, I'm gonna go show Aislinn's fairy tale to Lucy. You go play with Breslin. Tell him you and me called in to Rory – he's gonna hear anyway. Say I was giving Rory hassle about his exes saying he was too full-on; I was asking if he stalked them too, he denied it, the poor guy got all upset. Play it like you're still not totally sold on Rory, I'm still pissed off with you for having doubts, and you're still pissed off with me for dissing them. That way Breslin'll want to keep you close, and he won't be too worried about me going MIA for an hour.'

Steve's nodding, thinking it through. 'All sounds good. If he asks where you've gone . . . ?'

'You don't know. I told you it was none of your business.'

After a moment Steve asks, 'When do we pull the pin?'

'Today,' I say. 'It has to be. Breslin's expecting to haul Rory in later on, arrest him and start preparing the file for the prosecutors. If I don't do that, he's gonna start wondering why not, and then they'll be on guard.'

He nods. 'Who do we go for? Breslin or McCann?'

'I vote McCann. Unless Lucy comes out with something top-notch that we can use on Breslin. Breslin's been watching us for days now; he's got a lot better handle on us than McCann does. Plus, if we even hint any of this to Breslin, he's gonna throw the mother of all self-righteous tantrums, and I've had enough of those for one week.

We'll find a way to get him out of our hair for a while, and we'll tackle McCann.'

'OK,' Steve says, at the end of a long breath. 'OK. McCann.'

'And you'd better get moving, before Breslin starts wondering where you are.'

'Right.' He pulls the photo arrays out of his case and hands me a couple of each. 'Good luck.'

'Yeah,' I say. 'You too.'

For some reason me and Steve slap hands as we're leaving. We don't normally do that shite, what with not being sixteen, but it feels like we need something, on our way into this.

15

This time Lucy answers the buzzer fast. When she opens the front door, she's dressed – black combats and a hoodie again, but clean ones, and she's got Docs on. She looks at me, expressionless, and waits.

'Morning,' I say. 'Are you OK to talk for a while, or is this too early?'

She says, 'I figured you'd be earlier.' Then she turns and heads back up the stairs.

Her sitting room is cold, the uncompromising damp cold after a night with the heat off. It smells of toast, smoke – the legal kind this time – and coffee. The stuffed fox and the old phones and the coil of cable are gone; instead there's a record player and a stack of beat-up albums, a big cardboard box of flowery crockery, and a roll of canvas that touches the ceiling, coming unrolled to show a painted country lane disappearing into the distance. The room feels charged up with too many stories, jostling in the corners, pushing for space.

Lucy sits down first this time, grabbing the sofa with its back to the window and leaving me the one that takes the light – she learns fast. She's got her armoury lined up ready on the coffee table: pack of smokes, lighter, ashtray, mug of coffee. She doesn't offer me any. She sits still and watches me, braced for my first move.

I take the shitty sofa. 'I'm going to tell you some stuff I've been thinking,' I say. 'I don't want you to tell me whether I'm right or wrong till I'm done talking. I don't want you to say anything at all. I just want you to listen. OK?'

'I've told you everything I've got to tell.'

'Just listen. OK?'

She shrugs. 'If you want.' She makes a thing of settling herself back into her sofa, cross-legged, mug nested in her lap, ready to humour me.

I can play that game too. I rearrange cushions, shift my arse on my bockety sofa, find the best angle to stretch out my legs. Lucy winds tighter, wanting me to get on with it.

'So,' I say, when I'm good and comfortable. 'Let's start with your friendship with Aislinn. You two were a lot closer than you tried to make out. Her phone records say you guys talked or texted basically every day. You were proper friends; best friends.'

Lucy pokes her coffee with her fingertip, scoops out a speck of something and examines it. The solid black of her against the blue-and-rust-striped Mexican blankets, and the white-blond forelock falling in her white face, make her hard to see, like a blank spot in the middle of my vision.

'So there has to be a reason you didn't want us knowing that, on Sunday. And the point when you started claiming you and Aislinn weren't close was when you told us about her secret fella. Which has to mean three things. A, you know more about him than you let on. B, you're scared of him; you don't want him finding out you know anything. And C, you think he might find out through us.'

One blink, on the word *scared*. She rubs her fingertip clean on the edge of the cup.

I say, 'Me and my partner, at first we wondered if Aislinn was going out with some gangster.' The way Lucy's face closes down would tell me, if I didn't already know, how far off target that was. 'It took us till last night to click. Aislinn's married fella wasn't a gangster. He was a cop.'

The silence stays. I'm better at leaving it than Lucy; more practice. In the end she moves. 'Is that it?'

'Yeah. Your turn.'

'For what? I've got nothing to say.'

'You do. I can see exactly why you're scared' – that blink again – 'but if you wanted to keep your mouth shut, you would've. You told us Aislinn was seeing someone on the side because you wanted us to track him down. You didn't want to get in too deep; you were hoping that, if you pointed us in the right direction, we'd get there on our own. And we have.'

Lucy's eyes are still on her coffee. She says, 'Then you don't need me.'

'If we didn't, I wouldn't be here. I'm pretty sure I know who Aislinn was seeing. I'm pretty sure I know who killed her. But I can't prove any of it.'

'Or you're saying that because you want to find out how much I know.'

I say, 'You want to hear something I haven't told anyone? We've got lockers, at work. A couple of months back, someone jimmied mine open and pissed in it. All over my running gear and half a dozen interviews' worth of notes.'

Lucy doesn't look up, but I catch the flick of her lashes: she's listening. I say, 'Here's the part that matters. Murder works separate from the other squads; there's no one else in our building. And the locker room has a combination lock on it. One of my own squad did that.'

She looks up then. 'Why?'

'Because they don't like me. They want me out. That's not important. The point is, this isn't the telly, where cops are all blood brothers and anyone who gets on the wrong side of a cop ends up dead in a ditch while the rest of us lose the evidence. I don't have any squad loyalty. I'm not here to clean up anyone's mess. I'm just working my case. Anyone gets in my way, cop or not, I've got no problem running him down.'

'That's supposed to reassure me?'

'If I was just here to shut your mouth, I would've done it by now. One way or another. I already know you know something; if I didn't want it coming out, I wouldn't need the details.'

For a second I think I've got through, but then Lucy's face shuts down again. She says flatly, 'You're better at this than I am. I know that. I've got no chance of figuring out whether you're telling me the truth.'

I take out my phone, find Aislinn's fairy tale and pass it across the table to Lucy. 'Here,' I say. 'I think this is for you.'

I'm hoping to God it won't break her down again, because I don't have time to stick her back together today, but Lucy's made of tough stuff. She has to bite down on her lips once, and when she looks up at me her eyes are too shiny, but she's doing her sobbing in private now.

I say, 'That's Aislinn's handwriting. Right?'

'Yeah.'

'And it's meant for you.'

'Yeah. It is.'

I say, 'I don't understand all of it, but I get this much: if the story doesn't have a happy ending, you're supposed to tell me the rest. I think this qualifies as a pretty shitty ending.'

That gets something like a laugh, helpless and raw. 'Carabossa and Meladina,' Lucy says. 'When we were kids, and Aislinn used to make up stories about us having crazy adventures, those were our names. I can't even remember where they came from. I should have asked her.'

I say, 'If I wanted this story kept under wraps, I wouldn't have brought you that. You're right, there are detectives who'd try to bury the whole thing. You didn't get them. You got me.'

Lucy's touching the phone screen, just lightly, two fingertips. 'Can I have this?' she asks. 'Could you send it to me, or print it out for me?'

'Right now it's evidence. I can't go passing it around. Once the case is over, yeah, I'll get you a copy. I promise.'

Lucy nods. 'OK. Thanks.'

I hold out my hand. She takes one more moment with that message; then she catches a small tight breath and straightens her back. 'Yeah,' she says, and passes me the phone. 'The guy Aislinn was seeing was a Guard. A detective.'

Flash of her eyes, checking my reaction. I ask, 'Did you ever meet him?'

'Yeah. The same night Aislinn did. I wasn't going to let her—'

'Hang on,' I say. 'One step at a time. Do you think you could identify him?'

'Yeah. Definitely.'

I open my satchel and find the Breslin photo array. 'OK,' I say. 'If you see the man who Aislinn was going out with, I want you to tell me. If he's not there, or you're not sure, say so. Ready?'

Lucy nods. She's bracing herself for his face.

I pass her the card. She scans; then her face goes blank with bafflement. 'No. He's not here.'

What the fuck? 'Take your time,' I say. 'Are you sure?'

'I'm positive. None of these guys look anything like him. At all.' Lucy almost shoves the card back at me. She's gone wary again, wondering what I'm playing at. I'd swear it's real.

In the moment as I bend to put the card back in my satchel – wondering wildly where the hell I go from here, wishing I'd brought Steve – it hits me.

I pull out the other photo array, the McCann one. 'Try these guys,' I say. 'Do you recognise any of them?'

It takes less than a second: the scan, the quick burst of breath through her nose, the clamp of tension grabbing her whole body. 'Him,' Lucy says quietly, and her finger comes down on McCann. 'That's him.'

'The man Aislinn was seeing.'

'Yeah.'

'How sure are you?'

'A hundred per cent. That's him.'

'Write it down,' I say, passing her a pen. 'At the bottom of the sheet. Which number you recognise, and where you recognise him from. Sign and date it. Then initial beside the photo you're identifying.'

She writes neatly, steadily; only the fast rise and fall of her chest and the slight huff of her breath give away that her adrenaline's running wild. Mine is too. The big mystery about why McCann was hanging around Viking Gardens for weeks: gone. Aislinn's neighbour thought the guy climbing the wall was fair-haired, but yellow half-light from a streetlamp would turn McCann's grey streaks fair. The phone calls from McCann's wife giving him grief about missing another dinner, the slump to his back while Breslin promised to get rid of me, the state of him the last few days, it all fits.

The only piece that still won't drop into place is why the hell Aislinn wanted McCann; what the hell me and Steve have been missing, all along.

Lucy passes me back the photo array. 'Is that OK?'

'Yeah,' I say, giving it a quick read. 'Thanks. Now you can tell me the story.'

She takes a breath. 'What do you want to know?'

'All of it. Start from the beginning.'

'OK.' Lucy wipes her hands down her thighs – rubbing away sweat or the feel of that photo, I can't tell. 'OK. OK. I guess the beginning was maybe seven or eight months after Ash's mum died – so about two and a half years ago? Ash and I were out for a pint, and she said, "Guess what I'm going to do." She was ducking her head down and looking up at me like this, out of the corner of her eye, this bashful little smile – for a second I thought she was going to get a nipple piercing or something . . .' Lucy laughs, a small dry sound. 'If only. But then she said, "I'm going to find out what happened to my dad." Which was the last thing I expected. She was always making up stories about where he was, or the ways he might come back; but she'd never talked about actually tracking him down.'

I say – I can sound as empathetic as anyone – 'Maybe she didn't feel able to do it while her mam was alive. Looking after her would've taken all of Aislinn's energy; I'm not surprised she had none left for her da.'

Lucy's nodding fast. 'That's what I figured. I thought it could be a good idea – not finding him, specifically; there were too many ways that could go pear-shaped. But this was the first time she'd ever come up with a plan to go after something she wanted. I thought that had to be good, for her to learn how to do that. Right? That makes sense, right?'

'Total sense,' I say – and I actually mean it – and watch the relief rush through Lucy. 'She wasn't going to get a lot out of life till she did.'

'Exactly. So I said great idea, fair play to you. Aislinn told work she had a dentist appointment, dressed up in her best gear, and went in to the Missing Persons squad. They gave her the runaround at first, but finally this detective looked up her dad on some computer system and said he was dead. Aislinn was . . .' Lucy bites down on her lips, remembering. 'God. She was devastated. She rang work and said the anaesthetic had made her feel faint and she couldn't come in, and then she went home and cried all day. I went over there after work, and she looked like roadkill. Everything had gone out of her; she was just . . . lost.'

This is the part where I should probably feel bad: my callousness turning poor Aislinn's story down the path towards tragedy, blah blah blah. Yesterday, I would have felt fuck-all. Like I said to Steve: if she wanted to hook her life onto some guy who wasn't even around, that was her problem. But today, I don't know what it is. All of a sudden it feels like there were so many people nudging Aislinn from every direction: me, Gary, her ma, her da, on and on, all those fingers poking, shoulders barging, everyone shoving her life whatever way happened to suit them. It makes my skin leap like flies are covering it. And finally someone didn't bother nudging: her life didn't suit him, and he punched it right out.

Lucy says, 'I was scared she'd go back to just drifting along, you know? That this had been her one chance at actually getting hold of her life, and now it had been smashed like that, she'd never give it another go. So I said, like a fucking *idiot*, I said, "Maybe someone who worked on the case could tell you what happened to him." I was only trying to make Ash feel better. I just wanted to give her something to go after.'

That appeal is back in her eyes. 'Sounds right to me,' I say. 'That's probably exactly what I would've said.'

'I should've kept my stupid mouth shut. But at the time, I actually thought I'd done the perfect thing. Aislinn stopped crying, just like that, and dived for her phone. I went, "What?" and she said I'd just reminded her of something the Missing Persons guy had said. He'd mentioned the names of the detectives who were in charge of the case, when her dad first went missing. Detective Feeney and Detective McCann.'

Hearing the name in her voice touches the back of my neck, one icy drop. I say, 'And?'

Lucy says, 'She Googled them. She found Detective Feeney's obituary – she only vaguely recognised the photo, but it said he'd spent twenty-three years in Missing Persons, so she knew it had to be him. So that was a dead end. But Detective McCann . . . it took Ash a while to find anything on him, but finally she came up with a news video of him leaving court after some murder case – so she knew he was on the Murder squad now. And him she recognised straightaway. She'd forgotten his name – she just knew it was McSomething – but she remembered him spending a fair bit of time at her house, trying to talk her mum down. And she remembered him patting her on the head and saying, "Sometimes things are better off left. You've got great memories of your daddy, don't you? We wouldn't want to change that." Aislinn kept saying, "That has to mean he knows something, doesn't it? He definitely knew something." I said maybe, maybe not, maybe he was just trying to make you feel better about them *not* knowing anything, right? But she wouldn't let go of it. For weeks, that was all she talked about. Finally I was like, "For fuck's sake, just track down the guy and ask him."'

'And did she?'

Lucy shakes her head. 'No. She said if he hadn't told her back then, why would he tell her now? And it wasn't like she could force him to – the Missing Persons detectives had told her you couldn't use the Freedom of Information Act to find out about investigations. So Aislinn decided she'd have to go at him a different way: meet him "by accident", not tell him who she was, and get him talking.'

I've got an eyebrow up. Lucy says, 'I know, yeah. But Aislinn wasn't just planning to bounce up to him the next morning and hope he spilled his guts. She was *thorough*. This was her last chance; she wasn't going to blow it. She wrote down everything she could remember about Detective McCann – she had this notebook. She hadn't paid a lot of attention to him, himself, because she didn't think he mattered; but she used to sit at the bottom of the stairs in the dark, listening in while he and her mother were talking in the sitting room, hoping she'd get some clue to where her dad had gone. So she remembered bits about him. She remembered he was from Drogheda, and he took his tea with just a drop of milk, no sugar.'

McCann still does. For some reason that's the thing that sends a cold spike down my spine. That's the moment when it goes right through me: that guy is the same McCann who was waiting for me outside the Murder building yesterday morning, all stubble and restlessness. That missing-persons case followed him from the dim house with the silent kid listening, down every twisting road, all the way to our bright shouting squad room. That's the moment when I understand that McCann is our man.

'She remembered he was married, with two little boys – her mum asked him over and over, "And you wouldn't leave them, would you? You'd never walk away from your own wife and your own children?" and he always said no, he never would. She remembered his coat, this grey tweed overcoat – he'd leave it hanging on the banister, and she'd pick bits of fluff off it while she listened and stick them in his pockets – she didn't like him being there. But the big thing Ash remembered, the thing she wrote down with circles and stars all round it, was that he was into her mum.'

'Into her like what?' I ask. 'Like they had a relationship? Like he came on to her?'

'Jesus, no!' The instant squeeze of disgust on Lucy's face says it's true. 'This wasn't some Greek tragedy; Ash wasn't shagging her mum's ex. Just, in hindsight, she was pretty much positive that he'd fancied her mum. She figured that was why he spent so much time on the case. Even though he was married with kids, even though he was supposed to be professional, even though Ash's mum was going nuts trying to find her husband: he fancied her, and he went with it.'

'And Aislinn thought that was important.'

'Yeah. She knew she could use it. She said, "If he's that kind of guy, the guy who does stupid stuff for pretty women, I can be that. I'd have to change my look anyway; I can't have him recognising me and getting suspicious – not that he ever looked twice at me, he barely noticed I existed, but I'll only get one chance at this and I'm going to do it right." And she did.'

Lucy laughs, a humourless small breath. 'God, she did. She basically stopped eating, and she started going to the gym every day. Once she got thin enough that she was satisfied – too thin, if you ask me, but whatever – she went to an *image* consultant and got shown what clothes to buy and how to put on makeup and what colour to dye her hair. She came out looking like she'd been cloned in some creepy factory off the M50. I was like, "Why don't you just wear whatever you like best?" but Ash said no. She said, "I don't know what type he goes for – except my mum's type, and I can't look anything like her or he'll suss me. So I have to look generic. I have to be someone who any guy in the world would think was pretty, so even if he's not actually attracted to me, being with me will be too much of an ego-boost to resist. I'll have plenty of time afterwards to figure out what *I* like." I mean . . .' Lucy's hands fly up in frustration. 'What was I supposed to say to that?'

Part of me is actually growing some respect for Aislinn Murray. The core idea is idiotic shite, but the way she went about it: fair play to her. She wasn't the limp blob I pictured on that first day in her house, or the pushed-around kid I felt sorry for a minute ago. She was training, taking her time and doing whatever it took, to do some pushing of her own.

'That's some pretty obsessive stuff right there,' I say. 'Didn't you worry about her? That she was getting way too wrapped up in this?'

'Of *course* I did. When I thought she needed to start going after what she wanted, this wasn't what I had in mind. She spent like a year and a *half* trying to turn herself into what she thought some total stranger would fancy. It was *insane.*'

'Did you say that to her?'

'Ahh . . .' Lucy grimaces, rubbing both hands down her face. 'I did and I didn't. The last thing I wanted to do was start pushing Ash around, you know? She'd had a tough enough time getting a hold of what she wanted to begin with, without me telling her she had it all wrong. But after the image-consultant thing, I had to say something. I didn't exactly go, "This is fucking mental," but I made it pretty clear that I thought she was taking this too far and it would be a lot healthier to either go talk to Detective McCann straight out or else forget the whole thing. Aislinn just laughed at me. She was like, "Don't worry, silly! I know what I'm doing; I've got a plan, remember? All I have to do is get this sorted, and then the whole thing's finally *over* and I can start my real life! Do you want to come to Peru with me?" I was like, "Can we not just go to Peru straightaway, and forget this guy?"'

'But she wouldn't,' I say.

'No. She said she needed to do this. She kept saying – in her new accent; she used to sound Greystones, like me, but she was worried that Detective McCann might connect up the accent, so she'd started talking like that newsreader who does the weird pout thing – she kept going, "You worry too much! Look at me; don't I look happy?"' Lucy has a small sore smile on her, remembering. 'And she did; she really did. The happiest I'd ever seen her. Giddy, like a kid high on sweets, but still: happy. And she was making plans for afterwards – she'd never made plans before. Peru wasn't just a joke – I mean, the bit about me going was, because I don't have the dosh and I couldn't leave my job for that long, but Ash was going travelling, all right. She was doing research on all the different countries she wanted to visit, and on the college courses she was thinking about doing when she came back . . . This plan had her *galvanised*. So . . .' Lucy's shoulder moves in something like a shrug. 'Hard to argue with that.'

'The plan,' I say. 'What was it?'

'She was just going to flirt with this Detective McCann for a few weeks, go on a few dates. She wasn't going to try and seduce him, or anything, and she wasn't worried that he'd be looking for a shag – she said she was positive he'd never made a move on her mum, so he wasn't the type of guy who has actual affairs. He was just the type who likes getting attention from attractive women, and who laps it up even when he shouldn't. She said he'd probably run a mile if she even tried to kiss him.' The shadow of a smile, flicking Lucy's mouth. 'She was just going to give him attention. Loads of attention.'

'Smart,' I say. 'Aislinn was good at reading people.'

'Yeah, she was. It was because she'd never had a life of her own; she'd spent all her time watching other people, thinking about how they work. That was the only reason why I thought she might actually pull off her plan. I mean, this guy was a *detective*, he wasn't going to be the type to fall for any old shite; but if anyone could get him, it was Ash.' The smile deepens, but it looks painful. 'She was going to pretend she was one of those people who're fascinated by the police, so she could ask Detective McCann questions about all his cases – she'd gone through old newspaper articles and court cases to figure out what types of cases he'd worked on, and she'd bought *books* on all the stuff, so she could ask the right questions. And then she was going to gradually steer the conversation round to her dad . . . And then, once she found out whatever Detective McCann knew, she was going to quit seeing him. And go to Peru.' Lucy's head goes up all of a sudden, and she blinks hard at the ceiling. 'That was all. A few weeks of *attention.*'

Those true-crime books on Aislinn's bookshelf, the gang murders in her internet searches. Not for the thrills, after all, or to cosy up with one of Cueball's boys. I say, 'What changed?'

Lucy says, 'I knew Aislinn hadn't thought it through properly. It was like the fairy tales: the story just goes up to the wedding, and then they all live happily ever after. That's what Ash was doing. All she could think about was the big moment when she'd get this guy to tell her about her dad; everything after that was just this haze where life was perfect. I tried to tell her that it might not work out exactly like that; I tried. But . . .' She spreads her hands.

'She wouldn't listen.'

Lucy runs her hands through her hair, leaving it sticking out at ragged-kid angles. She says, 'We were sitting right here. Ash was where you are, all curled up in a blanket with a mug of tea – we'd been out clubbing, so it was late enough and we were drunk enough that I could say it to her. I went, "Ash, what if you don't like what you find out? It could be bad. Like really bad."

'It was dark – we just had on that lamp over there. All I could see was her face, staring out of the blanket. She didn't look pretty; she looked hollowed-out, starving, all bones and teeth, and way older than she was. And she said, "Luce, you don't think I get that? Seriously? I've thought about every single possibility. I get that the most likely thing is my dad killed himself and the Guards didn't have enough evidence to be sure, so they decided to say nothing in case they were wrong; or else he had a breakdown and ended up on the streets, and the Guards couldn't track him down and didn't want to admit it. I get that a Guard could have hit him with his car and they covered it up. I get that there's a chance some psycho killed him and buried him up the mountains, and the police had some reason for not wanting to know – it was mixed up with a big investigation, maybe – and so they never followed up. I get all that. I just want to know. So it'll be over. And then I can go do the next thing."'

'So you left it,' I say.

'Yeah, I left it. Probably I should've pushed harder – well, Jesus, *obviously* I should've pushed harder. Right?' Lucy spits out a furious little laugh. 'But the way she looked; like this plan was all she had, and she could gnaw it down to the bones and still be ravenous . . . I couldn't do it. I told myself maybe it would be fine: maybe this McCann guy wouldn't give her the time of day. Or maybe he'd see through her – I mean, seeing through people was his job, right? – and he'd tell her her dad had died saving a little blond kid from an evil drug lord, and she'd have a cry and move on, just like she thought.'

If only McCann had had the cop-on to do exactly that. 'But it didn't work out that way,' I say.

Lucy says, 'She played him like a jukebox. The big tough cynical detective, yeah? It only took her a month to get it out of him.'

'How'd she go about it?'

'She went online and found out the places where Guards drink – I think she asked on some discussion board; she made it sound like she just wanted to bag herself a cop, tee-hee. She got a list of places, and we had to check them all out.'

'"We,"' I say. 'You went with her?'

That sends Lucy's chin up. 'Course I did. You think I'd let her go by herself?'

'Nah. I'd have gone with my best mate, too. Just checking.'

She settles down. 'Some of the places were obviously wrong, like Copper Face Jack's – Guards go there, but they're all young guys on the pull. But there was one pub, probably you know it – Horgan's?'

'Yeah,' I say. Horgan's is a cop pub, all right: an old-style pub, all threadbare red velvet seating and sconce lighting, hidden away in the tangle of laneways around Harcourt Street, where most of the squads and the General Unit work. I used to drink there, sometimes, back before I made Murder. I saw McCann and Breslin once or twice. Back then I watched them like they were rock stars.

'Plenty of older guys drink there. So we kept going back. It was messy, because a couple of guys tried to chat us up – well, chat Ash up, basically – and we had to get rid of them, but not too hard, or else we'd get a reputation for being bitches and McCann wouldn't bother with us if he did show up. We played it like . . .' Lucy blows out air. 'It was Aislinn's idea. We played it like I was upset about something, a breakup maybe, and just wanted girl talk; that way she could blow off any guy who tried it on with her, and make it look like it was for my sake.'

She catches my eye and says, with a defensive edge on her voice, 'I wasn't happy about it. That's not my kind of thing, at all. But . . . Aislinn was good at bringing you along with her. One little step at a time, and all of a sudden, without knowing how I got there, I was in the middle of some play she was putting on.'

That cold touch on the back of my neck again. McCann – same as every Murder D; same as me – he's the one who writes the scripts. He wouldn't have liked opening his eyes one day and finding himself in the middle of someone else's play.

'And then,' Lucy says. 'The fourth time we went to Horgan's. I was sitting there pretending to be depressed and wondering how soon we could leave, and all of a sudden I felt Aislinn freeze. The breath went out of her; her drink went down on the table, bang, like her muscles were gone. I turned around to see if she was OK, and she said – barely even a whisper, I almost didn't hear her – "*That's him.*"

'He'd just come in the door. I recognised him too: his hair was a bit greyer, but it was the guy off the video, all right. He must have felt us looking, because he turned around. And Aislinn, straightaway, she did this' – Lucy drops her eyelashes, glances up from under them with a tiny smile, ducks her head away to sip her coffee. 'As quick as that. She was right on it.'

I say, 'And it worked.'

That rough laugh again. 'Jesus, yeah. It worked all right. Detective McCann did an actual double take, he was so stunned that this gorgeous woman was looking at him like that. And Ash giggled across at him, this idiotic giggle she'd been practising on all the other guys who tried it on. And when he went to the bar, she knocked back what was left of her drink and dashed up there, right beside him, to order another. And next thing you know, Detective McCann had paid for our drinks and he was bringing them over to our table.'

The fucking fool. 'When was this?'

'The end of July. We left after that drink – I didn't have to fake wanting to get out of there; it was probably the weirdest conversation I'd ever had. Ash gazing up at this guy and laughing her head off at everything he said, and him swelling up, thinking he had her wrapped around his finger, and all the time . . . But before we left, Ash gave Detective McCann – *Joe* – her phone number. He rang her the next day.'

'She was good, all right,' I say.

'Yeah,' Lucy says. 'She was. That was what really freaked me out. Watching her pull him in, so easily, like she'd been doing it all her life; and I realised that she had. Deep down, it was the same as when we were kids and she'd come up with stories to make things better. Just that this time, it was real. And I didn't like it. It felt— This sounds melodramatic, I know that, but it felt dangerous.'

No shit. I ask, 'Dangerous to her? To Joe? To you?'

Lucy says, 'Aislinn wouldn't hurt anyone. She— Ash was gentle.'

I'm not convinced. Gentle to start with, maybe, but someone who's been as hard on herself as Aislinn had been for a solid year and a half, she's not gonna go easy on anyone else. I let that go. 'That doesn't answer the question.'

'Dangerous to her. Maybe to Detective McCann, too, but I wasn't thinking about him; just about Ash. She didn't realise this was real. She didn't get the difference.'

That one is probably true. 'So then Detective McCann contacted her,' I say. 'And they met up again?'

Lucy asks, 'Is it OK if I smoke?'

'Go for it.'

She doesn't look at me while she disentangles her legs from the striped blankets, puts her coffee cup down, opens the smoke packet and finds a cigarette and shakes the lighter. She's still got time to play it safe: *I don't know the rest of the story, Aislinn wouldn't tell me, once she actually got her hands on Joe she got cagey . . .*

There's nothing I can say that I haven't said already. I keep still and wait.

In the end Lucy blows a long stream of smoke away from me and says, 'They met regularly. At least once a week, usually twice or three times.'

'Were you ever there for the meetings?'

'Not after that first time. I wanted to go, but Ash said I'd only cramp her style. Everything had to be about *Joe*.'

'What'd they do?'

'They weren't sleeping together. Not then. Nothing like that. They just talked. He'd pick her up – never at her place, in case the neighbours saw him; always down on the quays – and they'd go for a drive, up the mountains or somewhere. I didn't like that. I mean, you guys are always finding bodies up the mountains, right? He's picked up this girl, he's made sure no one saw him, he's taking her to the middle of nowhere . . . How serial-killer can you get?'

I ask, 'Did you have any reason to think he might be dangerous?'

Lucy shakes her head, reluctantly. 'No. Ash said he was always nice to her – a total gentleman, was the way she put it. She didn't exactly *like* him; she said he was way too intense about everything, even when he tried to make her laugh he was intense about it – but his stories were interesting, and he was an OK guy. He really cared about his work, and that reassured her: it meant he'd probably done a good job on her dad's case, so there would be something to find out, right?' A humourless little breath of smoke that could be a laugh. 'Jesus. No shit.'

I say, 'And he was OK with just talking? He wasn't trying to move the relationship into something sexual?'

'No. Ash was right about him not being the affair type: he never tried it on with her, not even a kiss. He was a romantic, she said; he liked being into her from afar. But he was into her, all right. Aislinn felt bad about it, what with him being married—'

'On Sunday you told us she'd have no problem shagging a married man,' I say. 'Never mind going for drives with one.'

Lucy doesn't bother with embarrassment. 'Yeah, I lied. I needed you to know that she'd be on for going out with a married guy, and I couldn't exactly explain why it was only this one particular married guy.'

Even when grief had just punched Lucy straight in the face, her mind was going ninety. She was well scared. 'Fair enough,' I say. 'So Joe wasn't coming on to Aislinn, but he was into her.'

'Oh yeah. He kept telling her how great she was, how gorgeous, how intelligent – what he meant was she acted like everything that came out of his mouth was pure gold, which of *course* she did – and how he and his wife didn't get on. He said the two of them had drifted into getting married when they were way too young, and they should never have done it, because his wife was too thick to understand his job and too selfish to get that he was doing something that mattered; all she cared about was that he wasn't around to help with the kids' homework or eat the dinner she'd cooked.' A wry twist to Lucy's mouth, around her cigarette. 'Yeah. So Aislinn took her cue from that. She piled it on thick about what an amazing job Joe had, how amazing it was to know someone who was doing something so important, and please would he tell her another story about how he had been amazing and solved an amazing case? And of course he did.'

Of course he did. Like Aislinn said: McCann is a romantic, at heart. He wanted to see himself riding down the green hill with light flashing off his spear, doing battle to save the world from itself. No way the job was letting him tell himself that story, not after this many years. His wife wasn't doing it either. Aislinn let him tell it to her instead.

'And then,' Lucy says, 'at the end of August, Aislinn decided it was time to go for it. She and Joe went for a picnic somewhere, and she started asking him what Missing Persons had been like, because it sounded so incredibly *mysterious* – she had it all planned; she'd written out her questions and learned them off by heart, she made me run lines with her the way actors do. She let Joe tell her a couple of stories while she gasped in the right places. She waited for him to come up with a bad one – some teenager who OD'd – and then she said ohmyGod, the family must've been totally in bits! How did he deal with it when the families were really upset?

Because *she'd* never be able to deal with families who were going through something like that, she'd just totally go to *pieces*, but she was sure Joe was just *amazing* at getting people through the absolute worst time of their lives, right? And once he'd told her some story about that, Ash said she betted that sometimes, when they didn't find the missing person, Joe stuck around for the family even after the case was officially over, because she knew he wouldn't just leave them to pick up the pieces themselves, right? And next thing you know . . .'

Lucy grinds out her smoke. Her voice has changed; she's wrung it dry, making sure nothing seeps in there that might break out of control. She says, 'It was that easy. They hadn't even finished their sandwiches, and Joe was telling her all about this poor woman whose husband ran off on her, left her with a little girl. The woman was the delicate type, Joe said – Aislinn could see him getting all misty, remembering – she wasn't able for a nasty shock like that. He went all out, trying to get the poor woman some answers, and he finally tracked down the husband. In England, living with some younger woman.'

I say, 'That had to hurt.'

'Yeah. It wasn't exactly what Ash had been hoping to hear.' A twitch of Lucy's mouth, like a flinch. 'But she could have handled it. She was ready for something like that; not as ready as she thought she was, but she would've dealt with it . . . Only Joe kept talking. He said he rang the guy up, gave him a bit of hassle about shirking his responsibilities, asked what they were supposed to tell the wife. And the guy said something along the lines of, "Just tell her I'm OK. Tell her I'm so sorry. And I'll get in touch when things settle down a bit." Which Joe knew he wouldn't; apparently the ones who do a runner without even leaving a note, they're the ones who never find the exact right moment to get back in touch.'

'Huh,' I say. Gary said – I'm pretty sure Gary believed – that Des Murray told the cops to say nothing, not one word, to his wife. 'Only Joe didn't pass on the message to Mrs Murray.'

'No,' Lucy says. 'What Joe did was, Joe decided it wouldn't be *good for her* to hear that. The poor helpless little woman wasn't able for that kind of news, don't you know; she would have been destroyed. He decided she'd be better off knowing nothing at all.' That tic at the corner of her mouth again. 'So that's what he told her: nothing. He was very proud of himself, for taking the whole thing off her shoulders.'

I just bet he was. At least when I palmed Aislinn off on Gary, I had the basic honesty not to do it for her own good. I did it because I felt like it, and fuck her. 'What did Aislinn do when she heard that?'

'She told me she almost smashed her glass and put the sharp end in Joe's throat, only her hands felt too weak to do it. So instead she said to him – all wide-eyed, all thrilled to hear such an amazing story – she said he had been so right, that had been so brave of him, so wise, that woman had been so lucky he was on the case. And then she told him she was getting a headache, and would he mind terribly if she went home and had a sleep? And he drove her back home and told her to take a Nurofen, and they both waved goodbye.'

'And she rang you straightaway,' I say. 'Yeah?'

'No. She came here. She was . . .' Lucy catches a hiss of breath, remembering. 'I've never seen her like that. I've never seen *anyone* like that. She was so furious she was screaming into the sofa cushions – all dolled up in this pink flowery dress, screaming, "How *dare* he, how *dare* he, who the fuck does he think he is" – mascara all over her face from crying, and her hair coming down out of this fancy twist, and she was beating the cushions with her fists, she was *biting* at them . . . Do you get that at all? I mean, do you get why she was raging?'

She's staring at me. 'Yeah, I do,' I say. 'I get it, one hundred per cent. He had no right to make that call.'

She keeps up the stare, eyes flicking back and forth across my face. I say, 'It would've been one thing if Aislinn's da had been dead from the time he went missing. McCann wouldn't have been taking anything away from her by keeping his mouth shut. But her da was alive. She could've got in touch with him any time. Her ma might not have lost the plot, if she'd known what was going on.'

Lucy says, 'More than that.' And waits, to see if I get it.

I do. I say – and I hear my voice saying it, into the small cluttered room that's getting colder – 'Aislinn had been thinking McCann kept his mouth shut for his own sake. Because a cop car hit her da, or because finding him would fuck up some big investigation. She could handle that; people do selfish shit, other people get caught in the crossfire, that's life. But then she found out McCann had done it *because* of her and her ma. Because he'd decided their lives should play out this way. Her and her ma, they weren't just collateral damage. They were the target.'

The light through the window is hitting me in the face, relentless, stripping me bare. I manage not to blink or move away.

Lucy nods: I've passed. 'Right. Fuck whether they might actually have an opinion, right? What they might want? He was the cop, he had the right to decide that for them. They weren't even people; they were just extras in his hero film. That was what had Aislinn losing her mind. That.'

Her voice has filled out again, ripe and pulsing with Aislinn's anger and her own. She'll tell me anything.

All that rubbish from the gaffer about me not being good enough with witnesses. This witness, who's got every reason to shut down on me, she trusts me enough to give me everything she's got. I wish that could still make me, even the smallest part of me, feel anything other than sad.

I say, 'And so her plan changed.'

Lucy laughs, one sharp breath. 'You know the first thing I thought, when she showed up on my doorstep sobbing her heart out and kicking the walls? *At least it's over. Thank God.* I didn't say that to Ash till I had her calmed down – which took forever; I had to listen to the whole story three or four times over, every detail, she couldn't stop telling me. But finally I got a shot of whiskey and a cup of tea into her – I mean, she looked like she could've used a massive spliff or a Valium or something, but I didn't have any and I just knew sweet tea for shock, right? It worked, anyway: she was still raging, but she settled down enough that at least she could sit still and she was only crying off and on, and I could get a word in edgewise. So I said, "Look, the only good thing is that now you know. Now you can leave it. Like you said."

'Ash practically came up off the sofa. Her hands were—' Lucy's hands shoot up, rigid claws. 'I thought she was going to go for me, or dig her nails into her own face, I didn't know whether to grab her before she could . . . But she went, "You think I'm going to fucking leave this?" – Ash doesn't swear. "I'm not done. I'm nowhere near— I'm going to *get that fucker*. He thought he had the right to decide my life – no. No. No. I'm not going to just lie down and take it, yes sir whatever you want sir do it to me harder sir— *Fuck* him." She was so angry she was panting, but it was a different kind of angry from before. She looked *dangerous*. Ash, like; the least dangerous person in the world. Her voice was wrecked from crying, this hard hoarse voice that didn't even sound like her – she said, "Now I'm going to do it to him. I'm going to make the rest of his life into *whatever the fuck I want*."

'I went, "OK, hang on, what?" And Ash said, "He's already half in love with me. I'm going to get him the rest of the way there. Then I'm going to convince him to leave his wife and get a divorce so that he and I can be together. I'm going to make him tell her all about me, so there's no way she'll ever take him back. And then I'm going to dump him."'

And there it is, the one piece me and Steve couldn't find: why Aislinn wanted McCann. 'Jesus Christ,' I say. 'There's no way that was going to end well.'

'I *know* that. I *told* her that. In those exact words.'

'I thought Aislinn was good at people.'

Lucy says, 'She *is*. That's what freaked me out the most. In order to come up with a fucking looper idea like that one, she had to have completely lost hold of everything she knew about how people work. She was so obsessed with the story in her head, the fact that there were actual people involved wasn't even a factor any more.'

She reaches for her smoke packet, not to open it, just to have something in her hands. 'I tried to wake her up. I said, "I thought Joe wasn't the type to have affairs." And Ash said, "He isn't. I can get past that. It won't be that hard; he's always dropping little hints about how he and his wife are basically staying together out of habit and he loves her but he's not in love with her, blah blah clichés. Which is just him trying to convince us both that it's totally fine for us to be going for drives together, but I can use it. I'll make him think he's the brave romantic hero breaking out of his meaningless marriage and turning himself into something special by following True Love. Him telling my mum that *he'd* never leave his wife and kids, *never*, the sanctimonious *fuck*, and all the time he knew— I'll have him dumping her by Christmas. Just watch me."'

I say, 'Being blunt here: she was planning on shagging his brains out till he couldn't think straight.'

That makes Lucy blink, but she says evenly, 'Yeah. She was.'

'Not everyone would be on for that.' Which is putting it mildly. There are plenty of undercovers, trained professionals, who won't shag the targets. For a civilian, Aislinn was hardcore.

Lucy moves on the sofa, like a spring is sticking into her. 'Ash was weird about some things,' she says. 'Sex, love, all that. She was all into reading romantic books that ended happy-ever-after, but when it came to her own life: no way. She said – ever since we were kids, she said it, and she meant it – that she was never going to fall in love. She went out with a couple of guys, but that was just for the experience – she didn't want to be thirty and a virgin who didn't know what a date felt like. The second the guys seemed like they might be getting serious, Aislinn broke it off.'

'Because of her dad,' I say. 'And her ma.'

'Yeah. She said look what it does to you, falling in love. Just look. It means someone else has hold of your whole life. At any second, like *that*' – a snap of her fingers – 'they could decide to change it into something else. You might never even know why. And you might never get it back, your life. They could just walk out and take it with them, and it's gone for good.'

Lucy's eyes are on nothing and her voice has changed, lightened and tightened: Aislinn's voice, quick and urgent, running under her own. She's remembering. For that second I want to nod to her – to Aislinn, not Lucy; that nod across a crowded room to the person you peg as a cop, to the only other woman there, to the only person dressed in your same style. The nod that says, whether you like each other or not, *You and me, we get it.*

Lucy says, 'I mean, I thought she was doing exactly that anyway: letting her parents have her life. She was going to deliberately miss out on falling in love, because of what they did. But Ash said I didn't get it. She said this was *her*, her own decision. She was right, I didn't exactly get it, but I did get that the idea of shagging Joe . . . it didn't mean the same thing to Aislinn as it would to most people. Sex wasn't something she was hoping would be special, or mind-blowing; she specifically *didn't* want it to be. And this, getting Joe, this was the most important thing in her life. So if sex could help her do it, why not?'

'Well,' I say. 'You said she'd never hurt anyone. This plan was going to hurt Joe's wife, and his kids. A lot.'

Lucy turns the smoke packet between her fingers. 'I know. I said that to her, that day. I thought it would stop her for sure.'

'Why didn't it?'

She shakes her head. 'It should've. When I said Ash wouldn't hurt anyone, I wasn't just being sappy, trying to make her into a saint because she's . . . dead. She genuinely was like that.' She turns the smoke packet faster. This is jabbing at her. 'I don't know. Yeah, she was obsessed, but still, I couldn't believe . . . But she just stared at me. Like I was talking gibberish. I still don't get it.'

But I get it. Lucy's right: Aislinn had got good at tangling people in her stories, building the relentless current that drew them in deeper and deeper, tugged them step by step towards the ending she could see waiting misty and beckoning on the far shore. She had got too good: in the end she tangled herself. By the time Lucy pointed out McCann's wife and kids, it was too late for Aislinn to pull free. Her own current had grown too strong for her. It wound around her ankles, her knees, rising, and it dragged her downstream to a shore she never saw waiting.

Lucy says, 'She'd wiped her face on her dress. This flowy pink dress that she'd bought specially for the big day, to make her look sexy and adorable and harmless and everything that would make Joe more likely to spill his guts – she'd spent two hundred quid on it – and she'd been smearing the skirt across her face like it was a tissue. It was covered in mascara and foundation and tears and snot. And all of a sudden Ash looked down like she was only noticing, and she went, "Jesus, what a mess! I'll have to get this dry-cleaned. Joe likes it; I'll need it again." And she found a tissue and started dabbing at the worst bits. Like she'd spilled tea on it, or something. She wasn't angry any more, or crying; it was like none of that had ever happened.'

'What did you do?'

'I begged her to please, please just give it a few days before she did anything. I thought once she got over the shock, she'd realise this was a terrible idea in like a hundred ways. I *begged* her.' Lucy's hand's clamped around the cigarette packet, and her voice has started to rise. She drives it back down to normal. 'But Ash – I swear she didn't even hear me. She got the worst of the crap off her dress, and then she found her phone and Hailoed a taxi. Then she got up and gave me a hug – a long hug, tight – and she said, right in my ear, "When I dump him, I'm going to tell him it's for his own good." And then she left.'

I say, 'And she didn't give herself a few days to get over it.'

'Inside a week,' Lucy says, 'she'd slept with him. I don't know how she convinced him. She said it wasn't hard; she made him think it was his idea, and she was the one who needed convincing. And afterwards she got upset – not too upset, just prettily tearful – because she was scared he'd hate her for getting carried away and doing such a terrible thing to his marriage, and she'd never see him again. So he got to reassure her that it wasn't her fault and he'd never think less of her and never leave her and his marriage was a mess anyway and blah blah blah. It all went perfectly.' There's a savage twist on the last word.

'And?' I ask. 'How'd the relationship go after that?'

Lucy flips open her smoke packet and pulls out another, glancing at me for permission; this is getting harder. I nod.

She says through the cigarette, tilting her head to the lighter, 'Well. The first thing was they stopped going for drives up the mountains, which was kind of a relief, except that instead he'd call round to Ash's house and they'd . . . stay there. Which wasn't a relief.' She tosses the lighter on the table and pulls hard on the smoke.

'How often were they meeting?'

'Same as before: maybe once a week, maybe two or three times. They didn't have a routine. Joe said he had to play it by ear, to make sure his wife didn't suspect anything.'

'So he wasn't planning on ending his marriage,' I say.

'Not yet, he wasn't,' Lucy says dryly. 'But Aislinn was getting him there. The second thing was that he started buying her presents. Only tiny ones – a little china cat with a checked bow when he saw she had checked stuff in her kitchen, things like that – because his wife looked after the money and she noticed every euro, she'd have been on it like a bonnet if Joe had bought anything big. But he kept going on about how he'd love to buy her a diamond necklace, and take her to Paris because she'd said she wanted to travel . . . And Ash said it wasn't just talk; he meant it. So she fed it. Told him how she'd always dreamed about having a diamond necklace, and printed off pictures of cheesy places they could visit in Paris.'

I think about the high frustrated yammer coming out of McCann's phone, again and again and on and on, while the squad lads mime whipcracking and McCann tries to disappear into his chest. A girl who acted like every word out of his mouth was pure perfection would have made a nice change. I remember that fugly china cat, pride of place on Aislinn's kitchen windowsill.

'The third thing,' Lucy says, 'was that at the end of October – *October*; that's three months after they *met* – Joe told Aislinn he loved her.'

The fucking idiot. 'I'd say she was pleased with that,' I say.

'Over the moon. She brought me out for champagne to celebrate. I didn't exactly feel like celebrating, but I went anyway, because . . .' Lucy leans her head back on the sofa and watches the smoke trickle out of her cigarette. 'I missed her,' she says. 'We were seeing a lot less of each other. Aislinn felt like she could never make plans, in case *Joe* wanted to call round. We weren't even talking any more, not properly. I mean, we rang each other, we texted each other, but it was all stupid stuff: are you watching this on the telly, did you hear this song . . . Nothing that mattered.'

She's still watching the curls of smoke ooze through the cold air, not looking at me. 'We were losing hold of each other,' she says. 'Just little by little, but there was nothing I could do to stop it, and I knew if this didn't end soon … All Ash could talk about was Joe, and I didn't want to hear the gory details. What I did hear, I didn't like.'

I say, 'Like what?'

'Like,' Lucy says. Her head moves against the sofa. 'She still didn't have Joe's phone number, you know that? He's all in *love* with her, he wants to drink wine with her in a café in Montmartre, but give her his phone number: oh, Jesus, no. He'd only ever rung her once, the day after we met him, and that was from a blocked number. After that, when he wanted to see her, he'd leave a note at her house. And then – get this – when they met up, he'd make her hand the note back to him so he could destroy it.'

But once Aislinn got stuck into her brilliant new plan, she started taking photos of the notes for her secret stash, before she handed them over like a perfect obedient mistress. McCann thought he was on everything, the big bad Murder D running a watertight operation. He underestimated Aislinn by light-years.

'Thorough,' I say.

'That's not thorough. That's fucked up. What kind of person even thinks of something like that?'

Ds are all about preserving evidence, not destroying it. McCann was already thinking like something else. I wonder if he noticed.

'Did it bother Aislinn?' I ask.

'Not really. I told her I didn't like it, but she brushed it off. She thought Joe was just paranoid that she might go to his wife – which she figured was fair enough, specially considering he was right. But I thought it was more than that. Joe wanted to be the one calling the shots. His way meant Ash had no say in anything: if he dropped her a note saying "Seven on Wednesday", she couldn't text him going, "Hey, I'm busy Wednesday, how about Friday?" All she could do was ditch whatever she'd meant to do on Wednesday evening, put on a pretty frock and wait at home. And sometimes, right?' Lucy's head comes up so she can watch me. 'Sometimes he didn't even give her that much notice. He just showed up at her door and expected her to drop everything and spend the evening with him. Ash thought it was just because his schedule was unpredictable, but to me it sounded like he was checking up on her. He wanted to see what she was doing when he wasn't looking.'

Her eyes are dark and speeding across my face, trying to catch hold of what I'm thinking. We both know what she's saying. If McCann decided to check up on his girl, Saturday night, he would have found candlelight and wineglasses and her polished to a glow, and all for someone else.

I keep my face blank. 'What happened if she wasn't there when he told her to be?'

'She always was. Like I told you before, she was ditching me all the time, the last few months. That was why.'

She ditched Rory, too, the first day they were supposed to have dinner at Pestle. *Really sorry, something's come up tonight!* Rory thought she was looking after her sick ma; we thought she was playing hard to get. I say, 'Did she ever do anything he didn't want her to?'

Lucy makes a face. 'Not really. I mean, her whole plan was based on being his dream woman.'

'No arguments? No disagreements?'

'I told you, he worshipped Ash. Going by what she said, they would've sounded like the perfect couple, if you didn't know better. The only time they had any kind of disagreement was once, maybe at the end of September? Joe picked up Aislinn's phone and started messing with it, and it was locked, like with a code. He wasn't happy about that, at all. He wanted to know if she was texting people about him.'

'What kind of not-happy are we talking about?'

One corner of Lucy's mouth twists, around her cigarette. 'Do you mean did he hit her?'

'Did he?'

She thinks about lying, but after a second she shakes her head. 'No. From what Aislinn told me, he never touched her, not like that. She never sounded like she was even worried that he might. And she would've told me – what was I going to do about it, call the cops?' She leans forward to tap ash. 'From what she said, Joe wasn't even angry about the phone; more freaked out. He said it was because of his wife: it's a small city, people gossip, you never know who might say something to the wrong person ... But Aislinn said he acted more like he was terrified the phone was full of texts to her mates about how she'd pulled this middle-aged fool who was going to erase her penalty points. Aislinn thought he wasn't totally convinced, at least not yet, that this was real.'

'McCann's a detective,' I say. 'Like you said. His instincts must've been telling him something was up. He just didn't want to hear it.'

A small, humourless laugh out of Lucy. 'No kidding. If only he'd had the sense to listen.'

'What did Aislinn do?'

'She begged for forgiveness like she'd run over Joe's *dog* – obviously she didn't put it that way, but I'm translating. She let him look through every text on her phone – which, yeah, I was delighted about: there was stuff in there that ... I mean, nothing major, but just texts about nights out that I didn't necessarily want a Guard to see.' A quick glance at me. Seeing as I don't care, I stay blank. 'That didn't even occur to Ash; all she cared about was getting Joe in deeper. And of course she started keeping her phone on swipe-lock. So he could see everything on there, any time he wanted.'

He had some willpower, not touching that phone on Saturday night. It hits me all over again how much of a fight me and Steve are in for. 'She was OK with that?' I ask.

Lucy lifts a shoulder. 'She didn't care. It was only for a few months, right? And Joe being obsessed was what she wanted; she wasn't complaining. But I didn't like it. A control freak like that ...'

She lets it fall. I don't pick it up. She's right, obviously: this should have been yet another alarm bell waking Aislinn the hell up. This guy who couldn't let a text or a Post-it go out of his control, how did she think he was gonna take it when she kicked him to the kerb? Her own floodwaters had risen so deep around her, they drowned it out. She underestimated herself too.

'By the beginning of December,' Lucy says, 'Aislinn said she was nearly there with Joe. He told her he loved her all the time, he was constantly going on about the great stuff he'd do for her when they could be together; he was *this* close to offering to leave his wife. And Ash – Jesus. She was on a total high, all the time: talking a mile a minute and screaming laughing at nothing and never able to sit still, she was like someone on speed. Not from having a guy wrapped round her finger – Ash wasn't like that; because her plan was *working*. She could hardly believe it. To her, it was like finding out that magic was real and she had it, she could turn pumpkins into carriages, she could turn princes into frogs and back again. Do you . . . Does that make any sense? Do you get it?'

'Yeah,' I say. 'I totally get it.' Out of nowhere I think of my first morning on Murder. Me in my new suit cut for victory, satchel swinging and shining, my heels on the footpath laying down a fast rhythm on the city swirl of buses and voices as I sliced straight through them heading for the Murder squad room waiting for me, finally, finally all my own. I could have done the walk to the door in ten-foot leaps. That morning I could have pointed at the Castle and made its roofs unfurl in great gold petals and trumpet blasts.

Lucy says, jamming out her cigarette, 'And then Rory came along.'

I say, 'Rory wasn't in the plan, no?'

'The Plan . . .' She spreads her hands with a flourish. 'I'd started thinking of it like that, in capital letters: THE PLAN, da-da-da-dum. No: Rory definitely wasn't in the plan. Rory was my fault. I dragged Aislinn out to that book launch – and it took some dragging – because I was hoping if she had a night off from sitting at home obsessing over whether Joe would call round, if she went out and had a laugh and a chat about normal stuff with people our age, then she might get some perspective. Realise how mental this whole thing was.'

'Meet a nice normal guy,' I say.

'It never *occurred* to me that she'd get that far. I was just hoping she'd have a non-insane evening. But one hour with Rory, and Ash was head over heels. She was totally freaked out by it – this was the last thing she was looking for, specially just when she was getting Joe where she wanted him. She couldn't even believe she'd spent that long talking to Rory. She had this rule about not talking to a guy for too long, in case he thought he was in with a chance – Ash figured that wasn't fair, when she wasn't on for a relationship—'

'You told us the reason she had that rule was because she liked to make guys work for it.'

Lucy shrugs. 'That was the best I could come up with. I had to tell you she cut off her chat with Rory halfway through the evening, because other people might've noticed that; but I wasn't about to tell you she wasn't into relationships, or you wouldn't have gone looking for her secret guy. And I couldn't exactly go into the whole thing.'

'Fair enough,' I say. For someone who doesn't like coming up with scripts, Lucy's done a lot of it, the last while. Aislinn got good at sucking people in, all right. 'So Aislinn didn't know what to do about Rory?'

That smile on one side of Lucy's mouth again, tender and bruised. 'No, she knew exactly what to do about him: give him the brush-off. But she couldn't do it. She thought he was the best thing since sliced bread. We went back to hers that night, after the launch, and she could not stop talking about him. She was all pink and giggly, like a kid, and she kept going, "What do I do? OhmyGod, Luce, what do I *do*?"'

'What did you say?'

The smile breaks up. 'By this time I had *no* qualms about telling Ash what to do. I went, "You ring Joe tomorrow and cut him loose. Tell him you can't live with yourself if you break up a marriage, some bullshit like that—"' Lucy's hands go through her hair again. 'I could hear myself sounding like her, making up stories . . . I just wanted her *out* of the whole Joe thing, before she pulled the pin and blew herself to bits. I told her, "And then when Rory rings you, which he will, you say yes I'd love to meet up thank you very much." I told her, "*This* is how you get your revenge on Joe. By not letting him lose you a guy you actually really like. By not letting him run your life any more." Right?'

'Sounds dead right to me,' I say. 'Sounds like she should've had it tattooed on her arm. But no?'

Lucy shakes her head. 'No way. Not a chance. And being honest, I could see why not. The amount Ash had put into this . . . All the planning, all the energy. All the starving herself. *Shagging* this guy she loathed, for *months*. And right when it was all about to pay off, when the explosions were about to go off and the big soundtrack number was about to kick in, I was telling her to ditch the whole thing?'

And she was telling Aislinn to give up the magic, just when she was about to start shooting fireballs out of her palms. 'That wouldn't be easy,' I say. 'I get that.'

'And then of course two days later Rory texted Ash, wanting to meet up. If she said no, he'd take it as a brush-off, obviously – and she couldn't exactly say, "Could you just give me a month or two while I finish shagging this guy into leaving his wife, then I'll be all yours?" She stalled him a bit, as much as she could without him thinking she wasn't into him, but in the end she said yes; yes, let's meet. And they went for a pint, and they had an amazing time, and Aislinn was totally smitten.'

'But she still didn't break it off with Joe.'

'No. She just started trying to nudge him along, hurry the whole thing up. She dropped hints about how much she missed him when he had to go home, and how she wanted to have babies and she wasn't getting any younger . . . She had to be extra careful, because the last thing she wanted was him getting all noble and giving her up because she deserved better, or getting paranoid that she was sticking holes in the condoms. It was—' Lucy's hands go over her face and she laughs into her fingers, a laugh with a sob caught in it. 'Jesus, it would've been hysterical, if it wasn't so insane.'

'How'd Joe react?'

'I was *praying* he'd do the grand renunciation. I was trying to send him *thought*-waves. I'm not even joking.' Another half-sob of laughter. 'But nope: Joe just followed right along where Aislinn was taking him. Three weeks ago – just after New Year's – he told her he was going to leave his wife.'

McCann, who used to brag to Aislinn's mother about how he'd never leave his family. She'd fed all that into the shredder. I say, 'I bet she was delighted with that.'

'Oh yeah.' Lucy wipes her hands down her face. This is taking a lot out of her. 'Yeah, she was over the moon. Except Joe wanted to wait till summer. One of his kids is doing the Leaving Cert; Joe didn't want him upset till that was over.'

'Meaning Ash would have six more months of trying to juggle him and Rory.'

'Yeah. She wasn't happy about that, at all. She cried – not hard enough to be ugly, of course, just a cute little tear – and she told him she knew there would be something else after that, men never left their wives, it was so hard to watch him go home to another woman, blah blah blah. But Joe wouldn't budge.'

'So what did she do about it?'

'God . . .' Lucy grimaces, eyes closing. 'Aislinn was so, so badly out of her depth. This was real stuff, you know? Twenty-five-year marriages, kids . . . There was no way she could keep up. Not a chance. All she could think of to do was keep Joe nervous, basically. She was still being Perfect Girlfriend, but every now and then she'd show him some Facebook picture of someone's baby and sigh, or she'd let it slip that some client at work had flirted with her . . . She just kept poking him, nice and delicately, with the chance he could lose her if he didn't get off his arse.'

I ask, 'Did she ever tell him about Rory? Even a hint?'

'You mean, to make the point that she had options?' Lucy shakes her head. 'No. I thought of that, too. I specifically asked Aislinn – warned her, more like – and she said no way. But I wondered if . . . I told you Joe wanted to be able to look through her phone. I wondered if maybe Ash was leaving a couple of texts from Rory on there. Just so, if Joe went looking . . .'

Which she was. Jesus Christ. I think about banging my head off the coffee table a few times. Naïve didn't begin to describe this girl.

'That was what worried me,' Lucy says, 'when Ash told me she had invited Rory over for dinner. They could've met anywhere, you know? If they wanted a shag, they could've gone back to Rory's. Why go where Aislinn knew Joe might show up?'

I say, 'Unless she was actually hoping for that.'

'Yeah. Maybe not even consciously, but she had to know it could happen. And she was getting desperate for this whole thing to be over. Every time she saw Rory, or even talked to him, she got more smitten. Deep down, all she really wanted to do was forget the whole Joe mess had ever happened, and go off and spend twenty-four hours a day snuggling and giggling with Rory. She just couldn't quite make herself let go of the Joe plan. Maybe part of her was hoping that Joe would call round, see Rory, throw a wobbler and stamp off into the sunset. Make the decision for her.' Lucy catches the look on my face. We've been watching each other for so long, we're getting good at each other. 'I know. You think I don't know? Like I said, she was miles out of her depth. She could've genuinely thought it would go down that way. Just that simple.'

Jesus Christ. 'If only,' I say.

Lucy says, 'He did it. Didn't he? Joe killed Aislinn.'

I say, 'You need to keep quiet about this whole conversation. No dropping hints to your mates, nothing. Is that clear?'

'Yeah, it is. I've kept quiet about this for months; I'm not going to start yapping now. I just need to know.'

I'm not gonna be McCann, doling out info in prissy little drips only when my all-knowing enlightened self has determined that it's for someone's own good. 'Yeah,' I say. 'I'm pretty sure he did.'

Lucy puts a knuckle to her mouth and nods for a long time. This wasn't a surprise, but hearing it out of my mouth changes it. It takes her a while to get used to.

She asks, 'Was it on purpose? Was he actually trying to kill her, or was it something where he just snapped and didn't realise . . . ?'

'I don't know.'

'Has he ever done anything like this before? I mean, not exactly like this, obviously, but—'

I say, 'You mean, should you have seen this coming.'

'Yeah.'

'I wouldn't have,' I say, 'and I know McCann a lot better than you do. I've never heard even a hint of a rumour about him smacking his wife around, or giving a suspect the slaps – and we all know who does that, when they can get away with it, and who doesn't. He's not a violent guy.'

'The thing is, I *was* scared this would blow up. I said to Aislinn . . .' Lucy catches a tight breath. 'Back in September, when she told me she'd got Joe into bed. I asked her – we were in the Flowing Tide, but it was noisy enough that we could talk – I said, "Have you told him I'm your best friend?" She said no, they hadn't really talked about anything except Joe and his general amazingness. I said, "Then don't.

Please. Make sure you tell him I'm just someone you go for drinks with, every now and then." Ash was like, "Why? I'm not going to pretend you don't matter to me."' Lucy's eyes close for a second on that. 'But I told her, "When you pull the trigger, he's going to be *raging*. He's not going to just go away and sob into his pint. You'll be in Peru or wherever, seeing Machu Picchu and shagging gorgeous backpackers; he won't be able to get to you. But if he knows I'm your best friend, he'll know he can get to you by doing things to me."'

"'Things,"' I say. 'What were you worried he'd do?'

'I didn't even get as far as specifics. I just . . . Me on my own in this flat, you know? A Guard could do whatever he wanted: plant anything, do anything. I didn't want to find out. I figured I was safest staying far away from the whole drama.' Lucy's head goes back. That dry flick of a laugh, up at the ceiling. That hasn't gone to plan. 'But that wasn't even the real point. The point was, I needed to get it through to Ash: *This isn't a game. I'm genuinely frightened that you're doing something that's actually, real-life dangerous.* I knew she didn't give a fuck that she was taking risks, but I thought maybe if she realised she could be putting me at risk as well, she might pay attention.'

'But even that didn't get through.'

'Nope.' A small jerky shrug. Even through everything else, that still stings. 'Aislinn said sure, OK, she'd drop in a mention of me, make sure Joe thought I was just some sort-of-friend left over from school. But she was only doing it to shut me up. She didn't think it was important. Like I said: all she could hear was the story in her head. Anything outside that was just . . .' Lucy makes a yappy-mouth sign with one hand. 'Just noise. And I should've known that.'

'Aislinn had got herself in deep,' I say. 'You did your best.'

She shakes her head like I don't get it. 'No. Where I went wrong was, I never thought of this. I knew Aislinn was playing with fire, and I knew Joe was the wrong guy to pull this shite on – someone who thinks he's got the right to decide whether or not you know where your own *father*'s gone, how's he going to react when someone else does the same thing to him? But I never thought of this. I thought maybe when Ash dumped him he might hit her, yeah. But mainly I was worried that he'd decide to fuck up her life. Have her arrested for some bogus reason, land her in jail, make her spend years and thousands of quid fighting made-up charges, then start all over again. That was what I thought, when you guys showed up here on Sunday: that Joe had called round to Aislinn's, he'd seen Rory there, and he'd found some way to have her arrested for something.'

'Makes sense,' I say. 'That's what I would've worried about, too.'

'And instead it was this.' Lucy has her fingers wound in the fringe of the throw, so tight they've gone white and lumpy. 'And now I keep wondering . . . what if I'd said the opposite to Aislinn, that night? If I'd said, "You make sure Joe knows how close we are." If he'd known that Ash was probably telling me the whole story. Do you think he'd have . . . ? Would he have stopped himself from . . . ?'

It would have made no difference. The split second where McCann decided to throw that punch was too small to fit any calculations. But I need Lucy feeling guilty.

'No way to tell,' I say. 'And no point in beating yourself up over it now. You just do everything you can to help me get him.'

Lucy's eyes come up to meet mine. She says bluntly, 'You said the other detectives want you out. Are you going to be around to get him?'

I say, 'I never have given one solitary fuck what the other detectives want.'

'Seriously. Because I'm not going to go in there and sign a statement about all this, and maybe have Joe fucking up my life, if it's not even going to do any good.'

I say, 'I can't guarantee you that McCann will go to prison. Even with your evidence, we've got maybe a fifty-fifty shot. But what I can guarantee you is that, if you put what you've told me into an official statement, his life won't just go back to the way it was. I'm gonna make absolutely fucking sure of that, and I'm not going anywhere till it's done. Is that good enough?'

After a moment Lucy lets out her breath and pulls her fingers free of the throw fringe. 'I guess it'll have to be,' she says.

'You've got my card,' I say. 'I seriously doubt McCann's gonna come after you; it'd be too risky and it wouldn't do him a lot of good, now that you've talked to me, plus he's gonna have other stuff on his

mind. But if anything happens that worries you, if anyone gives you
hassle or even if something just strikes you as weird, you ring me.
Yeah?'

She nods, flexing her fingers to get the blood back into them, but
I'm not sure she's really heard me. 'I wanted Ash to have that happy-
ever-after ending,' she says. 'I really did. Even if it was a million miles
away, with that backpacker in Machu Picchu. She deserved it. But it's
like she wasn't able to want that for herself, not till she got Joe out of
her way. She could barely even *see* the happy ending. That's how
huge he was in her head.'

'Or else she saw it just fine,' I say, 'and she wanted it, but she
wanted to get Joe even more.' This shrink-style crap is making me
antsy, or maybe that's just from sitting still hearing about people's
stupid sides when there's shit I need to be doing. I get up. 'I'll be in
touch when I need you to come in and give your statement. Till then:
thanks. I mean it.'

Lucy makes a small worn noise that could be a laugh. 'Look at
that,' she says. 'Here we are, you and me, getting Ash what she wanted
all along. I guess this was one way to get it.'

She walks me to the door of the flat, but she shuts it behind me
fast, without coming downstairs. Lucy's got some crying to do. Me,
I've got nothing to do except head down the lopsided stairs that smell
of soup and dead flowers, with Lucy's story hammering inside my
head while I try to work out what the hell I'm gonna do with it.

16

I get in my car and check my messages – phones go on mute during interviews, or Sod's Law says your ma will ring. Text from Sophie: *Got DNA profile from fluids on mattress. Male, not in system. Get me sample from your suspect we'll run comparison.* Steve's sent me an audio file of Breslin explaining to him how much potential he has and how he should be sure not to throw it away. Random Google Blonde has another four million depressing messages from the various dating sites. I delete her accounts.

I text Steve: *Ring me.* Then I sit there, running the heat to try and thaw my feet after Lucy's flat, and watch the people going past. They make me edgy. Dozens and dozens of people, they just keep coming, and every single one of their heads is crammed with stories they believe and stories they want to believe and stories someone else has made them believe, and every story is battering against the thin walls of the person's skull, drilling and gnawing for its chance to escape and attack someone else, bore its way in and feed off that mind too. Even the cute little student mincing along in her flowery dress, the shuffling old fella with his shuffling spaniel, they look Ebola-lethal. I don't know what the fuck is wrong with me. Maybe I'm getting the flu.

It's eleven minutes of this before my phone lights up with Steve's name. 'Hey,' I say. 'Can you talk?'

'Yeah. Not for long; I'm supposed to be talking to the staff in the newsagent. Breslin's only across the road, in the bakery. You get the file?'

'Yeah,' I say. 'Listen. Once I showed Lucy that note from Aislinn, it took her about a quarter of a second to ID the mystery boyfriend. Only it wasn't Breslin.'

Before Steve can ask what the hell, it hits him. 'Jesus. *McCann?*'

'Bingo.'

'What the . . . ? Why?'

I give him the fast version. At the end he says, after a moment of silence, 'Oh Jesus.' His voice sounds raw.

'Yeah, we can do that part later. You got anything I should know?'

Steve says, 'My guy at the mobile company e-mailed me. Full records on the phone that called it in.'

'Anything to prove it's Breslin's?'

'No. All the other numbers trace back to journalists. Including—' I know what's coming. I say it with him: 'Crowley.'

Breslin, the little shit. He's been top of the rat list from the get-go, but it still gives me a quick hit of anger. 'Let me guess,' I say. 'Early Sunday morning.'

'Quarter to seven.'

That pulls a hard crack of laughter out of me. 'And then he came in and gave us a lecture about squad loyalty. What a load of bollix. Breslin figured if the pressure around this case got turned up high enough, I'd sign off on Rory Fallon just to get it off my desk. He knew that little cocksucker Crowley would jump on the chance to give me shite, and he shoved me straight under Crowley's wheels. Gave Crowley the scoop, told him to go all out: hints that I wasn't up to the job, photos that made me look like a raving lunatic. The bleeding shitehawk.'

'Sounds about right,' Steve says. The tight-wound note to his voice means something's at him, but my mind's not on that. My Crowley problem didn't begin on Sunday morning.

'When were the other calls from that phone to Crowley?' I ask.

'There's just the one call. Eight to other journos, over the last year or so, but just the Sunday-morning one to Crowley.'

Crowley's magic appearances started last summer, and there've been four or five of them since. If Breslin's been using that phone to run his journos, he's not the one who's been running Crowley into my scenes; not until this one. Me sulking at my desk, convinced everything about this case was part of a big dark conspiracy against me. I feel like a gobshite all over again.

'Here's the thing,' Steve says. His voice has tightened another notch. 'How'd Breslin know we had the case?'

'Because he'd called it in to Stoneybatter almost two hours earlier. Even allowing for delays, paramedics, uniforms, whatever, it had to be hitting the squad by then.'

'No. How'd he know it was you and me? Crowley's a cute hoor; he knows the score. He wouldn't give serious trouble to O'Neill, say, or Winters, if one of them had pulled the case; he wouldn't want to burn his bridges with them and all their mates. You and I are the only ones he'd be willing to hassle. Ringing Crowley wouldn't have done Breslin any good, unless he already knew the case was going to us. And the gaffer only gave it to us just before seven.'

The silence lands hard. Down the line between me and Steve I hear wind, and a faraway kid screaming, and the hiss of emptiness.

'Maybe Breslin knew we were on night shift,' I say. 'He knows the gaffer always throws us the domestics . . .'

I can hear in my own voice how weak it is. Steve says, 'How'd he know the case wouldn't come in ten minutes later and go to one of the day shift?'

The squad room, waiting in cold early light for the day to begin. O'Kelly tossing the call sheet on my desk: *I picked it up on my way in, said I'd bring it upstairs to save Bernadette the hassle . . .* I say, and my voice sounds calm and clean and very strange, 'Breslin had talked to the gaffer.'

Steve says, 'Can you think of any other way he could have known?'

'Is there a call to the gaffer in the phone log?'

'No. He must've used his regular phone for that. He knew we'd trace the Stoneybatter call; he wasn't going to have the gaffer's number showing up on that same phone. He couldn't do anything about the calls to journos, but anyone can ring journos, and we can't make them reveal their sources; he figured those wouldn't come back on him.'

O'Kelly scanning the roster, hands in his pockets, rocked back on his heels. *You'll need backup on this one. Breslin's due in. Have him.*

I say, 'The gaffer knew all along. He put Breslin on the case to keep an eye on us.'

'Yeah,' Steve says. 'Yeah. Fuck, Antoinette.'

We can't afford to get angry or wired or anything else, not now. 'Keep it together,' I say sharply.

I hear Steve blow out a long breath. 'I know.'

'What time are you and Breslin gonna be back at the squad?'

'We're pretty near done here. Say forty-five minutes, an hour max.'

'I'll throw him a ball to chase. When he heads off, meet me in the garden outside HQ.'

'OK. Gotta go.' And Steve hangs up.

The people going past the car seem like they're speeding up, driven along by that unstoppable savage thrumming inside their heads. I still have that off-kilter feeling like a fever starting. I can't afford the flu today, any more than I can afford to lose the head.

I need to head out to Stoneybatter, but first I set my phone number to Private, ring the General Unit and ask them, in a timid little girly voice with a nice middle-class accent, if I could please talk to Detective Breslin about Aislinn Murray who got murdered. They put me through to the Murder Squad; when Bernadette answers and tells me Detective Breslin is out and she'll get someone else for me, I get all nervy and say no, no thanks, but could I maybe leave him a message? And she pats me on the head, more or less, and puts me through to Breslin's voicemail.

'This is Detective Don Breslin.' Smooth as a coffee ad. He probably did a dozen takes. 'Leave a message and I'll get back to you.' Beep.

I keep my mouth a few inches from the phone, just in case. 'Um, hi. My name's . . . um, I don't really want to . . . But I'm a friend of Simon Fallon – I heard you were asking him about his brother Rory? And – I mean, I used to hang out with Rory as well, and he did some things that probably you should . . . I never reported it, but . . . Simon said you were really nice. I'm in the Top House bar, in Howth? In beside the fireplace? If maybe you could come here? I can probably stay till like four. Otherwise, I guess I can try you some other time, or . . . Well. Thanks. Bye.'

I put my phone away and floor it for Stoneybatter. That should do it. Breslin'll get in, check his messages, cream his Armani suit, turn right around and zoom off to find out what terrible things Rory did to this poor girl. He'll leave Steve behind, in case she can't bring herself to spill her story to two big bad Ds at once. Forty minutes to Howth, at this time of day and in this weather. Say half an hour of waiting for Mystery Chick, or till four o'clock if we're really in luck. Then forty minutes back. For at least two hours, me and Steve will have McCann all to ourselves.

Ganly's is empty apart from the baldy barman, who's stacking glasses and humming along to Perry Como singing 'Magic Moments' on the radio. 'Ah,' he says, giving me a nod. 'It's yourself. Did I win?'

'You got into the next round,' I say. 'The woman you identified for me the other day: remember the guy who was in with her?'

'More or less. I told yous before, he wasn't the main thing on my mind.'

'Would you have a look at a few photos for me, see if you can spot him?'

'Your pal was already in yesterday, asking me the same thing. I was no use to him.'

'He said that, yeah. These are different photos.'

The barman shrugs. 'I'll have a go, sure. Anything to help the forces of law and order.'

I pull out a fresh copy of the McCann photo array. 'If you see the man here, tell me. If he's not there, tell me. If you're not sure, tell me. OK?'

'I can manage that.' The barman takes the card and gives it a long thoughtful gaze. 'Would you look at that,' he says. 'I'd say you've got him this time. This lad here.' He taps McCann's face.

'Are you sure?'

'I wouldn't stake my life on it, but I'd put fifty quid on it down the bookies. Will that do you any good?'

'I'll take it,' I say, finding a pen. 'Initial the photo you recognise. At the bottom, write down where you've seen him before and how sure you are, and sign.'

The barman writes, head bent close to the page. 'Can you think of anyone else who was in that evening?' I ask. 'Anyone who might have noticed the pair of them?'

'Ah, now. You're asking a bit much. I don't call the register at the beginning of every night.'

'I might have to come in and have chats with your regulars, some night. I'll try and keep it low-key.'

'I had a feeling that was on the cards, all right.' The barman passes me the sheet and the Biro. His writing is tiny and beautiful; it deserves fountain pen and thick yellowing paper, not this. 'If you're talking to this fella, tell him he's not welcome back in here. I'm not asking you if he did anything to that young one. I'm just saying people come here for a bit of peace.' He gives me one more long glance, as he picks up the next two glasses. 'I wouldn't have your job for all the tea in China,' he says.

The uniform in Stoneybatter station says the voice sample might be the fella who rang Sunday morning, except he thinks that fella sounded a bit different from this one, he can't explain how but not the same, maybe the voice was a bit higher and maybe it had a Meath accent, or else Kildare, it won't come back to him properly. No surprise there; even if we hadn't already smeared that pointless voice array all over his memory, I'm not the only one who can put on funny voices. We've got everything we're going to get.

It's lunchtime. I stop at Rory's favourite Tesco, grab two bottles of Coke and two sandwiches with plenty of meat in them – this could be a long afternoon – and head back to HQ. Sleety rain spatters my windscreen with big dirty spots, but by the time I get to the Castle gardens, it's stopped. I pick a stretch of wall among the bushes, out of sight of the windows, and use paper napkins to get the worst of the rain off it before I sit down and open my sandwich. A couple of small birds are hopping forlornly on the wet grass. When I toss them a chunk of bread, they panic and scatter into the bushes in a wild rattle of wings.

I'm only getting stuck into the sandwich when Steve comes through the garden gate, walking fast with his head down, like that's gonna magically hide the red hair from anyone at a window. 'Hey,' he says.

'Hiya. Breslin gone?'

Steve brushes at the wall and sits down beside me. 'Just legged it. He got a message from some girl in Howth?'

'Yeah. She's not gonna be much use to him. You have lunch yet?'

'Nah.'

'Here.'

I pass him the other sandwich. Steve takes it and holds it in his two hands, not opening it. 'Did you get anything good?'

'Tentative ID off the barman. No joy out of the uniform. Sophie's guys got a male DNA profile off the mattress.'

He says, 'What do we do?'

I say, 'We need to talk to McCann.'

There isn't a way around it any longer. In two hours, maybe three, Breslin will be back and suspicious and wanting to arrest Rory. Those couple of hours are all we've got.

Steve nods. He asks, 'How?'

We have so many weapons. You pick them up from watching other Ds, you sift them out of squad-room stories, you come up with your own and pass them around; you stash them all away safe, for the days when you'll need them. By the time you make Murder, you have an arsenal that could pulverise cities.

You come into an interview carrying a ten-pound stack of papers, so the suspect thinks you've got that much against him. You stick a videotape on top, so he'll think you've got video evidence. You flip through the papers, put your finger down and start to say something, catch yourself – *Nah, we'll save that for later* – and move on, leaving him to fret about what you're saving. You pull out a voice recorder – *My handwriting's only terrible, mind if I use this instead?* – so that later, when you turn it off and lean in confidentially, he'll think you're off the record; he'll forget all about the interview-room recorders, whirring away. You read imaginary texts on your phone and swap cryptic comments (*Happy days, the searchers got lucky*) with your partner. You do the fake lie-detector test with an app these days: give the guy some bollix about electromagnetic fields and have him press his thumb on your phone screen after each question, and when you get to the one where he's lying, you shift a finger and it flashes red graphs and *LIE LIE LIE*. You tell him the live victim is dead and can't contradict him, or the dead one is alive and talking. You tell him you can't let him leave till the two of you work this out, but if he'll just tell you what happened, he can be home on his sofa with a nice cup of tea in time for *Downton Abbey*. You tell him it wasn't his fault, you tell him the vic was asking for it, you tell him anyone would've done the same thing. You tell him witnesses heard him talk about how he loved kiddie porn, you tell him the pathologist says he rode the dead body till it started falling apart, you pummel him with the sickest shite you can come up with until he can't stop himself from shouting at you that that's all bollix, that wasn't the way it went; and then you lift one eyebrow and say *Yeah, right, then how did it go?* and you listen while he tells you.

All our weapons are useless this time. McCann's known the feel of them by heart, he's had them shaped to his hands by wear, since long before we ever laid eyes on them. We're going in bare.

I say, 'We talk to him. That's all we can do.'

'He won't talk back.'

'He wants to tell us his story. They all do. Deep down, he wants us to know that him and Aislinn, that was true love, and whatever she was playing at with Rory was a load of shite that was begging for a punch. So let's see how much of that we can get him to tell us.'

Steve says, 'We focus on the relationship. Nothing else. We don't go near Breslin being involved, or McCann'll go loyal and shut his trap. Just talk about Aislinn.'

'We've got one grenade,' I say. 'When Breslin found out that file box was full of the Desmond Murray case, he was relieved. Meaning he didn't know McCann had worked that case. Meaning two days ago, at least, McCann hadn't made the connection: he didn't know Aislinn was Des Murray's daughter. He didn't know she was playing him all along.'

Steve says, 'We save that.'

'Yeah. That oughta go off with a bang.'

The birds have forgotten their fright and come back to peck about on the grass. Breslin is across the river by now, heading north.

Steve asks, 'Where do we do it?'

This is what I was thinking about, all the way back here in the car, all the time I was waiting for Steve. 'Interview room,' I say.

His face turns towards me. 'You think? We could clear out the incident room. Or come out here, even.'

'No. We throw everyone out of the incident room, we might as well put up a sign saying there's some big secret thing going down. Anyway, from now on we need to document everything, if we want a snowball's chance in hell of making a case.'

'He'll know. The second we head for an interview room, he'll know.'

'He will anyway. No matter where we take him, there's no way we can make this seem like a nice friendly chat, not past the first thirty seconds. The moment we bring up him having met Aislinn, he's gonna know.'

The thought of that moment flicks across us like a small black splatter of sleet. It stops us talking.

We get the sandwiches down us, the Coke for caffeine. Then we go into the Murder building, in through the glossy black door with the combination my fingers could press in my sleep, nodding to Bernadette on our way past. We take off our coats and hang them neatly in our lockers, I take off my satchel and stash it away. Steve finds a copy of the family photo from the Desmond Murray case and tucks it in his suit pocket; I take photos of the arrays, on my phone, and then I shove them to the bottom of my locker and hope no one picks today to piss in it again. The twin metal slams of our locker doors echo, sharp and startled, against the tiles of the small dim room.

We go side by side up the wide marble staircase, our footsteps circling blurrily around the stairwell, to the squad room. We go in there with no stack of papers, no videocassettes, no voice recorders. We go in with our hands empty.

The squad room's almost deserted, everyone out on cases or on lunch. For a second there, it reminds me of early Sunday morning, just before the gaffer came in to dump this case on me and Steve. The quiet, just touched at the edges by the far-off drone of traffic; the white light of the fluorescents sealing the room against the thick grey press of cloud at the windows, charging the scattered paperwork and forgotten coffee cups with latent meaning. Me thinking how I could love this room, if only.

McCann is hunched in his corner, peck-typing. He looks worse every time I see him. Me, bloody eejit, asking Fleas to look out for anyone who seems like he's had a bad week. You could fit your case notes in those eyebags.

'McCann,' I say. 'Got a few minutes? We could do with a hand.'

He looks up from his computer and he knows.

For a second I think he's gonna shut us down: got work of my own to do, bye. But he needs to know what we've got. And he's the veteran; we're rookies, can't even get through this first step without cracking – Steve is shifting his feet, I'm rubbing at my mouth. McCann can't resist. He figures he can do this, not a problem, and walk away.

'All right.' He hits Save and stands up. O'Neill and Winters, examining a statement sheet across the room, barely even glance over.

'Thanks for this,' Steve says, on our way up the stairs. 'We really appreciate it.'

'Yeah. What do you need a hand with?'

'Aislinn Murray case,' I say, over my shoulder. McCann's face doesn't change. 'We need all the witnesses we can get. Is in here OK, yeah?' I push open the door of the nice interview room, the pastel-yellow one with the coffee sachets that we used for Rory the second time round, and give McCann a hopeful look.

McCann grunts. He picks one of the chairs on the detectives' side, with its back to the one-way mirror, and gives it a quick rock to see if it's a dud. 'I'll have tea,' he says, landing in it heavily. 'Drop of milk, no sugar.'

'You sure you're all right for this?' Steve asks, obediently heading for the kettle. 'Not meaning to get personal, but you're looking a bit rough, man.'

'Thanks.'

'The missus not doing your ironing this week, no?' I want to know, with a grin that could go any way. 'You in the doghouse?'

'I'm grand. How's your personal life?'

'Shite,' I say. Me and Steve laugh; McCann comes up with

something that's meant to be a smile, except he's out of practice. 'You're married twenty-five years, amn't I right? How do you do it?'

'Twenty-six. Is this what you wanted me for, yeah? Relationship advice?'

'Nah. You mind if we have this on?' I'm already turning on the video camera.

McCann's eyebrows jerk down; he didn't think we had the nads. 'Why the fuck do you want that yoke?'

'Because I'm paranoid. A few months back, right? I got stuck helping Roche interview some scumbag's mammy. I got her to drop the fake alibi; Roche told the gaffer it was him.' I pull up the chair opposite McCann, the suspect's chair. 'Now I video everything. I'm thinking of getting myself a body cam.'

'In fairness,' Steve says apologetically, dropping teabags into cups, 'it's best practice to record witness statements, when we have the—'

'Jesus Christ,' McCann says. 'Video whatever you want.'

'Ah, man,' Steve says. He's practically curling into a ball with embarrassment, puppy-dog eyes begging McCann not to hold it against him. 'I'm really sorry about this. We'd've only loved to not bother you with this shite. If it was only one bit of evidence, then we'd have just dumped it down the back of the file and left it to go away; we wouldn't have taken up your time. But ... I mean, it's coming at us from all directions. We figured we'd be better off getting on top of it now.'

'At least ye have the sense to make him the good cop,' McCann says to me. 'I can't see you pulling that off.'

Steve does an awkward laugh. 'No flies on you,' I say, shaking my head ruefully. 'No point in us trying to pull the wool over your eyes. We wouldn't waste our time, or yours.'

'You are wasting my time. What do you want?'

'That's you put in your place,' I say to Steve. He manages an embarrassed half-grin as he makes his way to the table, eyes on his carefully balanced double handful of mugs. He passes them out and pulls the spare chair around the table, next to me. McCann slurps his tea and makes a face.

'So let's clear one thing up straightaway,' I say, 'save us all some time. You were having an affair with Aislinn Murray.'

McCann sucks his teeth and stares at me, not bothering to hide the disgust. 'You little quisling,' he says.

What surprises me is that I can't even come up with a spark of anger at that. 'We've got a witness who saw you chat Aislinn up and take her phone number,' I say. 'She's ID'd your photo. We've got a witness who saw you and Aislinn having a drink in Ganly's together. He's ID'd your photo. We've got a witness who saw you in the vicinity of Viking Gardens at least three times over the past six weeks. He's ID'd your photo. All of them will ID you in a lineup if you make us take it that far. Do I need to go to all that hassle, or can we just cut to the chase?'

McCann drinks his tea and thinks. I can see him rearranging pieces in his head like a chess player, tracking each strategy a dozen moves down the line.

What he needs to say is 'No comment.' That simple. Put up a wall of that, let us throw piece after piece of evidence at it till we run out, then walk away. This is the one and only non-idiotic thing to do, and every detective in the world knows that. We've all had jaw-dropped conversations where we can't believe the moron actually talked to us, when all he had to do was keep his face shut and he could have gone home; we've all seen the pros fold their arms and repeat 'No comment' on a loop, till we give up and cut them loose. We've all thought it: *If that was me, no way in hell would I open my big gob.* We all know for a fact that if we ever get pulled in, innocent or guilty, it'll be *No comment* all the way.

McCann can't make himself do it. Once he says, 'No comment,' he loses hold of himself as the detective, maybe forever. Once those two words come out of his mouth, he's no different from any junkie shoplifter, any pervert groping girls on buses: he's the suspect.

He says, 'I knew Aislinn Murray. We met up a few times.'

'And that's it,' I say.

'Yeah.'

'Were you ever in her home?'

Cogs turning again, as he weighs up whether there might be anything we've managed to keep away from Breslin, any fingerprints he missed during his wipe-down, anything that could catch him out. 'Yeah,' he says eventually. 'The odd chat, cup of tea.'

'Ever shag her?'

'You got a good reason for asking me that question?'

Me and Steve glance at each other. McCann doesn't react.

I say, 'We got male DNA off her mattress.'

'It's not mine.'

'You mean you wore condoms. It's not semen. It's sweat.'

McCann goes back inside his head to think. I say helpfully, 'We're pretty sure Aislinn didn't sleep with anyone else in the last couple of years.'

Not a budge out of him, as he weighs and measures. Then he nods. 'Yeah. We had the odd shag.'

And that's the preliminaries done with. Everything we can afford to give up, all three of us, is laid out on the table. Like the brisk initial stage of a board game, sacrifice this to take that, till almost by cooperation you've cleared the board of the small stuff, readied it for the real battle ahead.

'Ah, man,' Steve says ruefully, raking his fingers through his hair. 'Ah, *man*. Of all the girls in this town, you had to pick one who was going to get herself murdered?'

McCann shrugs, swigs his tea. 'What can I say. She didn't seem like the type.'

'You should've said,' Steve tells him reproachfully. 'As soon as the case came in.'

McCann's eyes move across us both like we're not worth stopping for. 'If it'd been any other Ds, I would've.'

'It's not like we were going to ring your missus and grass you up.'

'That's what you say. You're telling me you'd have stood by your squad? Look where we are.'

'You know this needs doing,' Steve says, worried. 'It does. What do you want us to do? Ignore all this, go ahead with Rory, and have his defence dig this up and throw it in our faces halfway through the trial?'

'I want you to have some respect. Something like this, you want to bring it up, you do it in *private*. Not in a fucking *interview room*. With a fucking *camera* going. Jesus.' He shoots a narrow, furious glance at the camera.

'If I was any other D,' I say, 'I would've. But I've taken enough shite from this squad that nowadays, anything that matters, I'm getting it on record. We'll try and keep it to ourselves, but I can't promise anything till I know what I'm dealing with.'

It's the oldest line in the book. McCann's mouth curls. 'I'll keep that in mind.'

'So let's hear it,' I say. 'Start with the first time you and Aislinn met. When, where, how.'

McCann leans back in his chair, stretches his legs out and folds his arms, settling in. 'Horgan's. Last summer; I don't remember the date.'

'Don't worry about it. We can find that out. Had you seen her in there before?'

'No.'

'You would have noticed her.'

'Yeah, I would. All the lads noticed her. Probably some of the girls, too.' Snide look at me.

'I'm not surprised,' I say. 'I've seen photos. How'd you get up the brass neck to chat her up?'

'I didn't. She came on to me.'

I laugh out loud. 'Course she did. Gorgeous twenty-something, could have any fella in the bar, throws herself at some middle-aged guy with a faceful of wrinkles and a beer gut. She just won't take no for an answer; what choice has the poor guy got?'

McCann has his arms folded tight, not budging. 'I'm telling you. She wasn't forward about it – I wouldn't've been into that. But she was the one that gave me the eye.'

I've still got one eyebrow high. 'Jaysus, come on,' Steve says to me, reasonably. 'People have different tastes. Just because someone wouldn't be your cup of tea—'

'I like them young enough to be some use to me,' I tell McCann, throwing him a wink. 'And good-looking.'

'What do you do, pay for it?' We're starting to get to him.

'—that doesn't mean he's not some other girl's,' Steve finishes. 'It happens.'

'It does happen,' I admit. 'On the soaps. Every time I turn on the telly, there's some young babe hanging out of an uggo old enough to be her da. Does this look like the set off *Fair City* to you?'

'Ah, Conway. It's not just on the soaps. Real life, too.'

'If you're Donald Trump, sure. You been holding out on us, Joey? Are you a secret millionaire?'

He doesn't like the 'Joey', but he almost hides it behind a wry grin. 'I wish.'

'Not everyone's all about the money,' Steve says. 'Aislinn could've just liked the look of him. Nothing wrong with that.'

'Maybe. Do you look like George Clooney, Joey? On your days off, like?'

'You tell me.'

I grimace, waver one hand. 'Gotta tell you, pal, I'm not seeing it. So I'm dying to know: why would she go for you? Don't tell me you never wondered.'

McCann shifts. Unfolds his arms, shoves his hands in his pockets. He says, 'She was a badge bunny.'

We thought the same thing. Aislinn led the whole lot of us down her garden path. What me and Steve need to know is whether McCann believes it still.

'A girl like that goes hunting for a badge,' I say, 'and you're what she brings home? Seriously?'

McCann's jaw moves. 'I was there.'

'And so were plenty of others. Horgan's is wall-to-wall cops. So why you?'

'Because she wanted a D. She liked to hear about the job: what cases have you worked, what was it like, what did you do next? Gave her a thrill. You know what I'm talking about?' The grin's a nasty one. I don't blink. 'She picked me out because I was old enough, and dressed nice enough, that she figured I was a D – she knew her stuff, that one. When she heard I worked Murder, that was it. Her eyes lit up. I'd've had to hold her off with a garden rake. And you saw her: why would I want to do that?'

'Because you're married?' I suggest. 'I hear to some people that means you don't go sticking your dick in any hole you can find.'

McCann lifts one shoulder. 'We had a few shags. It happens. It was no big deal.'

Good call. If Aislinn was nothing but a shag, then there's no reason he would've killed her for having another fella. I ask, 'You do that on a regular basis, yeah? Cheat on your missus?'

'No.'

'Ever done it before?'

'No.'

'Then what was so special about Aislinn?'

'Never had a bird that good-looking try it on with me before. And me and the missus, we hadn't been getting on great. I figured, why not?'

Me and Steve throw each other a quick sideways glance, letting McCann catch it. I say, 'That's a lovely story. Romantic. But it doesn't match Lucy Riordan's.'

McCann shakes his head. 'Who's Lucy Riordan?'

'Aislinn's best mate. Short? Dyed-blond hair, cut up to here? Ring any bells?'

At that he laughs, teeth bared like an angry dog's. 'That little dyke? I'd say her story's different, all right. She wasn't Aislinn's best mate, whatever she told you. She's a hanger-on who was arse over tip in love with Aislinn, and she was raging that Ash had found herself a fella. Of course she's going to tell some story that makes me the bad guy.'

Steve says, 'Where'd you meet Lucy?'

'You already know that. Your *witness* who saw me meet Aislinn, you think I don't—'

'We need your version.'

McCann flings himself back in his chair, folds his arms across his chest again and stares at us, lip curling up. 'The two of ye are pathetic. Do you know that? Sitting there, trying your little interrogation techniques on me, going off on tangents— I was doing that to scumbags, *actual* scumbags, when ye were picking your spots and snogging posters of pop stars. Do you honestly think I'm going to fall for it?'

'It's not about *falling* for it,' Steve says, wounded. 'We're hoping you'll help us out here.'

I say, 'Where'd you meet Lucy?'

'Was that not in her *story*, no?'

'Ah, come on, man,' Steve says, leaning forward across the table. 'You know as well as I do, we're looking to scupper her story. You think we want you to be our man? Are you serious? If we find out you did this, we're *fucked*. You think we want to sit out in that observation room trying to decide whether we're going to charge one of our own squad with murder?'

McCann turns those deep-set eyes on me. He's got years more practice being expressionless than I do; I can't read anything there. He says, 'You've got no reason to love this squad. You're fucked anyway; might as well take someone down with you.'

Even though I know what he's at, the matter-of-fact tone sends something cold into me. I say, 'I've got no problem with you. You've never done anything on me.'

He nods. 'If you've got any sense at all,' he says, 'you'll walk away. That's me giving you my best advice; the same as I'd tell one of my own young fellas, if he was sitting where you are. I didn't do this, so you're not going to prove I did. If you try, all you'll do is fuck yourselves up. Forget leaving the squad; you'll have to leave the force. Maybe the country.'

We've all told a suspect his life is over if he doesn't do what we want. The cold works its way in deeper anyway. I say, 'Where'd you meet Lucy?'

After a moment McCann shakes his head, slow and heavy. 'Your funeral,' he says. 'She was in Horgan's with Aislinn – keeping an eye on her. Aislinn sitting there in her little shiny dress, sucking on her glass and enjoying everyone staring while she picked out who she wanted; and the other one with a puss on her, giving the filthies to anyone who looked twice at Aislinn. Aislinn told me after, she said Lucy dragged her to the pub because she wanted to cry on Aislinn's shoulder about how she couldn't get a fella ...' The corner of McCann's mouth goes up; for a second his face looks almost soft. 'She was a real innocent, Aislinn, in a lot of ways. She was like a kid. She honest to God thought Lucy was looking for a fella. Have you checked Lucy's alibi?'

'Yeah,' I say, and realise what I've admitted when I see his grin widen. 'Rock-solid. Sorry.'

'But you wondered.'

'We did our job.'

'Like you're just doing your job right now.' The grin's turned savage. 'I'll bet a hundred quid that Lucy one's trying to put this on me. What's she saying? I hit Aislinn? I treated her like shite?'

Me and Steve do the sideways glance again. 'Not exactly,' Steve says.

'Actually,' I say, 'not at all.'

McCann's face has gone back to blank. He wasn't expecting this.

'According to Lucy,' I say, 'you treated Aislinn like she was made of diamond. What you two had going on wasn't a few shags. It was the real thing. The big L.'

He laughs, a ferocious bark, loud enough to startle all three of us. He's trying too hard. 'Jaysus fuck. You believed that?'

'Are you saying you never told Aislinn you loved her?' Before he can answer: 'Careful. We've got texts from Aislinn to Lucy.'

'Maybe I did. I've got news for you, Conway: when a fella who's trying to get into your knickers says it's love, there's a chance he might be bullshitting you. Or has no fella ever bothered?'

'According to the texts,' I say, 'you and Aislinn saw each other a bunch of times in August, but yous didn't start doing the do until the beginning of September. If you were only there for the riding, what was that all about?'

McCann shuts down again, takes his time weighing up his options. In the end he says, 'I liked Aislinn. She was a good girl. Sweet. She was looking for thrills, like I told you, but she wasn't some vampire type getting off on the guts and gore. She hadn't had an easy life; her da died when she was only little, her ma had multiple sclerosis, Aislinn was one of those carer kids till the ma died a few years back. There hadn't been a lot of excitement in her life, so she wanted to hear about mine.'

I'd swear he believes that. I can feel Steve clocking it too: we've still got our grenade.

She told Rory the same story: dead da, MS ma. No wonder she skidded away from it so fast. Using it to get McCann where she wanted him was one thing; using it on someone she wanted in her real life, that was something else. But the story was getting stronger, getting away from her. It came out anyway.

'Me and the wife, we've been having a rough patch. It was nice to be around a woman who liked my company; nice to have somewhere peaceful to go, no one giving it all that about what a waste of space I am. Made everything that bit easier. That was what it was about, at first. Just the bit of peace.'

The pull at the corner of his mouth says we don't need to point out the irony here. I say, 'Where'd you hang out?'

'I'd pick Aislinn up somewhere near her place, and we'd go for a drive. It was summer; she'd bring food, we'd take it for a picnic down the country. We'd find somewhere with a view where we could sit and talk.' McCann's trying to keep his voice flat, but the longing rises up and he can't force it back down. He stops talking.

'Aah,' I say. 'Sweet. You never brought the poor girl for an actual meal, no? Or a drink, even? Just had her make you sandwiches and sit on the grass getting ants in her knickers?'

'She never had a problem with it, why should you? We went to her local once. I didn't like it. Dublin's still a small town. The wrong person sees you, he tells his missus who tells her ladies' club pals and one of them's your wife's best friend, and bang, you're sleeping on someone's sofa.'

'Because you went for a pint?' Steve raises his eyebrows. 'Sounds to me like you knew, deep down, this wasn't just friendly chats.'

McCann's lip lifts; it's meant to be a smile, but it edges on a snarl. 'Sounds to me like you've never been married. "Well, yeah, sweetheart, I did spend the evening on the piss with a gorgeous young blonde, but we were only chatting, honest to God" – you think that's going to fly? Not with my wife, it's not.'

Steve gives him a grin for that. 'Fair enough,' he acknowledges. 'I'm starting to think I should stay single.'

'You and everyone else.' But the grin fades fast. 'Me and Aislinn, I'm telling you: it started out innocent.'

'How'd that change?'

McCann shrugs. He's turning wary; we're moving into the edges of dangerous territory.

'Jesus, Moran,' I say, in an undertone McCann can hear just fine. 'He stuck his dick in her, is how that changed. He waited for his chance, and when he got it, he banged her like a cheap drum. You want the guy to draw you a diagram?'

McCann stretches his neck sharply; he doesn't like that. 'Jesus yourself,' Steve tells me, in the same undertone. 'I'm not asking for their favourite *position*. I'm just asking what made things go that way. This is the Monk McCann we're talking about. He didn't go in there planning to cheat on his missus.' He gazes hopefully at McCann.

McCann stares back. 'What do you think made it go that way? Man and a woman spend a bit of time together, they get to fancying each other, one day it gets out of hand—' I've got one eyebrow high. 'Laugh all you want. You tell me: why would Aislinn be with me if she didn't want me? Just like you said at the beginning: I'm not rich and famous.'

'You're a D,' I point out. 'To some people, that could come in useful.'

'I thought of that. I'm not a fool. I wondered if she might be dodgy and looking to get a cop on side.'

'So you ran her through the system.'

'I did, yeah. Go ahead and dob me in to the gaffer, if that's what it takes to make you feel big. But don't tell me you've never done it.'

'Ah, background checks,' I say. 'The foundation of every beautiful romance.'

'Like I said: I know I'm nothing special. I had to check. But Aislinn came up clean as a whistle. She wasn't even looking for me to square penalty points. She wanted nothing from me.' McCann spreads his hands. 'This is all I've got. If she wanted me, it was for this.'

Me and Steve let that lie just long enough, and come just close enough to looking at each other, that McCann gets edgy. 'What?' he demands.

'The affair,' I say. 'That began in September?'

'The beginning of September. Yeah.'

'Date.'

'I don't remember.'

I've made him lie, rather than sound like the sap who's clinging on to every tiny detail, and he knows we know. I let a flicker of a smile slip through, and see his jaw muscle roll.

'We'll leave it at the beginning of September,' I say, being generous, which gets another twitch of his jaw. 'And it kept going till last weekend. Any breakups along the way, anything like that?'

McCann has his arms folded again; his cop face is back, a flat slab. 'No. No problems. No arguments. Everything was great.'

'Autumn,' Steve says thoughtfully, examining his Biro. 'Winter. And not being crude, but you two weren't just chatting any more. I'd say the picnics up the mountains weren't doing the job for yous, were they? Where'd you meet?'

None of your business grits McCann's teeth, but he says, 'Her place.'

Steve frowns. 'None of the neighbours ever saw you.'

'Because I didn't want them seeing me. I went down the laneway behind Aislinn's house, over the wall, in by the back door. She gave me a key.'

And there's the autumn intruder. 'Fair play to you, climbing walls at your age,' I say, almost holding back a grin – McCann doesn't like that either. 'Better than the gym any day. How often were you there?'

He'd love to lie about that, but he can't risk it. 'A couple of times a week. It depended. On work, my family, all that.'

'How'd you make the appointments?'

'Sometimes we'd make plans for next time before I headed off. Other times I'd leave her a note saying when I could call round. Or if I got a free hour or two I wasn't expecting, I'd just go round to her.'

'Where'd you leave the notes?'

'Post-it in a 7-Up bottle, throw it over her back wall. She knew to check.'

'We didn't find any Post-its in the house.'

'I'd take them back when I got there. Get rid of them.'

I do startled. 'Why?'

'Why do you think? Because I've been in this job too long to leave evidence floating around.'

The cold flat glance says *And way too long to get tied in knots by the likes of you.* 'Jaysus,' I say. 'Lot of hassle for the odd shag.'

'Depends how good of a shag.' That nasty grin again, but I've seen McCann use it on suspects and it doesn't work on me.

'Why not ring Aislinn, or text her? Your number wasn't even on her phone. Why not?'

'Because I didn't want it there.'

'And why not go in her front door like a normal person?'

He eyes me with dislike. 'Why the hell do you think?'

'I'm asking you. Did she get off on the top-secret hush-hush vibe, yeah? Or did you get off on knowing she had to be ready for you to show up at any minute?'

'She didn't *have* to do anything. I wasn't her boss.'

I say, picking my words carefully, 'Would you not have been . . . angry, let's say, if she hadn't?'

McCann's jaw clamps. 'What d'you mean?'

'What I said. You had Aislinn sitting at home, day in, day out, ready to jump whenever you decided to pull the strings. If you had pulled and she hadn't jumped, what would have happened?'

'Nothing. Most of the time I let her know I was coming; it was only now and then that I called round to her out of the blue. If I'd showed up and she hadn't been there, or she'd been busy, I would've left and come back another time. End of story.'

I'm all sceptical. 'You sure?'

'Yes, I'm sure.'

'You wouldn't have given her the odd slap, no? Not to hurt her; just to teach her she couldn't mess you about.'

McCann says, 'I've never hit a woman in my life.'

'Hmm,' I say. 'OK. You made Aislinn set her phone on swipe lock because you wanted to be able to read her texts. Right?'

His head flinches to the side, a fraction of an inch, before he catches it and faces us square again. He doesn't like thinking about this. 'I didn't make her do anything.'

'Asked her to. Let's say that.'

'I asked her, yeah. She could've told me to stick it. She didn't.'

'And did you read them?' I'm hoping he didn't, mainly out of professional pride. I like to hope that if a Murder D set up a plan to walk in on his bit on the side with her bit on the side, he would've made a better job of it than this mess.

McCann buries his face in his tea, but I catch the faint flush under the stubble. Out of all the options, this is what gets to him: the image of himself grubbing around in Aislinn's text messages. He's still holding on to how he loved her; in his mind, that snooping is the one thing he's done to taint that. 'A few times. Nothing worth seeing, and I felt like a twat. I stopped.'

I believe him. McCann knew nothing about Rory, not till Saturday night. Aislinn's frantic plan to move things along did nothing at all. Lucy was right: she was miles out of her depth.

I ask, 'Do you make your wife keep her phone on swipe lock?'

'Don't get smart with me. No, I fucking don't.' The shame puts a snap in his voice. 'I wasn't *controlling* Aislinn. I just didn't want my wife finding out about us. That's why I checked the texts: I needed to know Aislinn wasn't telling her mates. That's why I went in the back. That's why I didn't want her having my number. I liked her a lot, even trusted her more or less, but not enough to put my whole life in her hands. I wasn't about to put myself in a position where, say she got too attached or had a bout of PMS or got ideas about blackmail, she could just take her phone down to my gaff and blow the whole thing wide open. Is that simple enough for you?' Which is his biggest speech yet. Trying to shove that memory away made him talky.

'So,' Steve says dryly, 'you're saying you had no plans to leave your wife for Aislinn, no?'

McCann lets out a short harsh burst of laughter, just too loud. 'Fuck that. Me and my wife, we have some hassles, but I love her. Love my kids even more. I wasn't planning on going anywhere.'

'So what were you going to do? Just keep on climbing Aislinn's back wall' – I snort; McCann gives me a filthy look – 'for the rest of your lives?'

'I didn't have plans. I was having a laugh, seeing how things went.'

'Even if he was planning on leaving his wife,' I point out to Steve, 'he would have wanted to keep Aislinn on the downlow. No point in giving the missus ammo for the divorce settlement.'

'Did you not hear me? There wasn't going to be a divorce settlement. Myself and Aislinn were grand exactly the way we were.'

I lift an eyebrow. 'Yeah? Did Aislinn think you were grand the way you were?'

McCann shrugs. 'Far as I could tell. If she didn't, she would've ended it.'

'You're having your cake and eating it, and she gets the crumbs. What kind of person's OK with that?'

'I wasn't taking anything away from her. We agreed from the start that she could see other fellas. Only fair.'

Nice move. Not a chance it's true. 'And she took you up on it,' I say. 'When did you find out she was seeing someone else?'

A quick blink: McCann needs to be careful here. 'After she died, only.'

Steve and I glance at each other and leave a silence. McCann's too old a hand to fall for that. He flicks us a sardonic look and waits us out.

'We'll go with that for now,' I say. 'So how did that make you feel?'

McCann snorts. 'What are you, my therapist?'

'Do you go to a therapist?'

'No, I don't. Do you?'

'Then you don't need to save the good stuff for him. How'd you feel when you found out Aislinn had another guy on the go?'

McCann's all ready for this one. He shrugs. 'No one likes sharing. But sure, I always used johnnies, so what harm?'

'Were you surprised?' Steve asks.

'Didn't think about that either way.'

'Lucy was surprised. When she found out about Rory.'

That gets a sardonic grin. 'Yeah. Bet she was only delighted: two guys between her and Aislinn now, instead of just one.'

Steve says, 'She was surprised because Aislinn was in love with you, man. Mad about you. Did you know that?'

A twitch of McCann's head, like that flew at him. He doesn't know any more whether that was true or not, doesn't want to think about it either way. He says – careful again, remembering those texts – 'Doesn't exactly come out of the blue.'

'She'd never been in love before. You were the first. Did you know that, too?'

'She might've mentioned it. I don't remember.'

'So,' Steve says, 'if she was head over heels with you, why was she having a romantic dinner with some other guy?'

McCann's good. It's only because I'm looking for it that I catch the snap of pain, quick and savage as a muzzle-flash. 'Who knows. Women are mental.'

'OK,' I say, tapping the edge of my mug and frowning at it. 'Let's think it through. Aislinn was in love with you, but not vice versa. Right?'

McCann's got his control back. He snorts. 'Jesus. Nah. She was a good girl, good company. The sex was great. That's all there was to it.'

'Did she know you felt that way?'

'I'd more sense than to say it to her, if that's what you're asking.'

'But she might've suspected. She wasn't stupid.'

'Might've. I wouldn't know.'

'If she suspected,' Steve says, 'she would've been devastated. First love: it's powerful stuff. That didn't bother you?'

We're picking up the pace. McCann hasn't missed it: his back's straightened, there's a focused blue flash to his eyes. For a second there I see him twenty years ago, all cheekbone ridges and dark stubble and those long-distance blue eyes, and I see why he still thought he might have a shot with Aislinn.

He says, 'I wasn't out to hurt her. But I wasn't there to babysit, either. Aislinn was a grown woman.'

'So could that be what her little thing with Rory was all about, yeah?' I ask. 'Trying to make you jealous?'

Shrug. 'Doubt it. Seeing as I didn't know he existed.'

'She kept texts from him on her phone. She might've been betting you'd read them.'

That raw flush again, the minuscule flinch of his head. 'Even if I had. Wouldn't have worked, and Aislinn had enough cop-on to know that.'

'Maybe she was using Rory as a distraction?' Steve suggests. I know, sure as I know where my hands are, that he's picked up on where I'm heading, he's right beside me. 'Trying to take her mind off you?'

'Could've been.'

'Meaning she did suspect you weren't in as deep as she was.'

'Could've done. She never mentioned it.'

I ask, 'Did she ever talk about you leaving your wife?'

'It came up. Nothing serious, just a mention.' He's stepping carefully again: the texts.

'And what did you say?'

'Brushed it off. Changed the subject. She didn't push it.'

'Huh,' I say. I lean back in my chair, have a swallow of my tea – gone cold – and take out my phone. I go into my e-mail, taking my time, and find the Post-it photos from Aislinn's secret folder.

Civilians' eyes dive on anything you bring out; they can't stop themselves. McCann's don't move from my face. I put my phone on the table in front of him. The small click of it going down snips at the air.

McCann waits till I sit back before he looks down. His face doesn't change, but I feel the pulse of bafflement and wariness off him.

I say, 'There's more of them. Swipe.'

He swipes, keeps swiping. Something else stirs, under the bafflement: a wretched twist of pain and something almost like joy. McCann thinks he's seeing proof that he got it all wrong; that Rory meant nothing to Aislinn. She was mad about him, after all.

After a dozen or so pics he takes a fast breath and shoves the phone back across the table. 'I get the idea.'

I say, 'Are these the notes you wrote to Aislinn, to let her know when you'd be calling round?'

Shrug. McCann settles back in his chair, hands shoved easily in his pockets, but the taut stillness holding every muscle gives him away. We're building up to the big push, and he knows it.

'I don't have to be a handwriting expert to know these are consistent with your writing,' I say, 'but I can get one to confirm it for me if I have to. I can also pull your shift times for the last six months and cross-check them against the times and dates when Aislinn entered those photos into her computer. I'll bet my paycheque every one of those notes will line up with a time when you were just coming out of work, or just going in.'

'So maybe they're my notes. So? I already told you I wrote them.'

'And made sure to destroy them,' Steve says. He's picked up my phone and he's skimming through the pictures. 'You thought, anyway.'

'Only Aislinn had other ideas,' I say. McCann's eyes close against that for an instant. 'Every time you left her a note, she took a photo, put it on her computer – in a special password-protected folder – and deleted the phone pic. Why would she go to all that hassle?'

Shrug. 'How would I know?'

'If you had to guess.'

'Souvenirs?'

That gets a laugh out of me. 'You serious?' I take the phone off Steve and wave it at McCann. 'This is what you think a girl keeps for a souvenir?'

'I don't know what girls do and don't do.'

'Trust me. It's not. So what was Aislinn at?'

After a moment McCann says, 'She could've been thinking of showing them to my missus.'

'You said she was happy with the way things were. Why would she want to do that?'

'I thought she was. Doesn't mean I was right.'

'You told us you were being careful in case Aislinn "got too attached and blew the whole thing wide open".' I spin my phone on the table. 'Looks like you were right to be careful.'

'Not careful enough,' Steve points out.

'Looks to me,' I say, 'like Aislinn was making plans. She figured if your wife found out, she'd give you the boot, and you'd come running straight into Aislinn's arms—'

'Would your missus have given you the boot?' Steve asks.

'Nah.'

Steve's eyebrows go up. 'Nah?'

'No way.'

'Man, you said earlier she'd throw you out if she even knew you were going for *drives* with Aislinn. If she found out you'd been *riding* her, for *months*—'

'She'd've given me holy hell. Called me every name under the sun. I'd've been in Breslin's spare room for weeks, maybe months. God knows I'd've deserved it.' The vicious scrape to McCann's voice says he means that. 'But we'd have sorted it in the end. No question.'

I've got an eyebrow up. 'Uh-huh. Easy to say that now.'

'It's a fact. She'd've made me beg, grovel, but she'd've taken me back. The kids—'

'Yeah, let's not forget the kids. How traumatised would they have been?'

That tightens his jaw. 'They're grown adults, or near enough. A few weeks of Mammy and Daddy fighting isn't the end of the world.'

'How would they have felt about Daddy fucking some girl young enough to be their sister?'

'Jesus,' Steve says, wincing. 'Guaranteed long-term estrangement, right there.'

McCann snaps, 'They wouldn't have found out.'

'No? Your missus wouldn't have mentioned it? She a saint?'

'Sounds like one,' Steve says.

'She'd want to be,' I say.

'She cares about the kids. She wouldn't have hurt them.'

We're going faster, harder, leaning forward, slamming the questions across the table. McCann's meeting us beat for beat, firing back answers without a second's pause, that blue glint grown to a blaze. He thinks this is it. He can see exactly where we're going, and he thinks this theory is where we're putting our money. All he has to do is kill off this one, and we'll be left in tatters.

'Either way,' Steve says, 'it'd be a lot easier not to go through all that hassle. Wouldn't it?'

'Yeah, it would. Lucky for me, that never came up.'

'Lucky,' I say, eyebrows way up. 'Is that what we're calling this, yeah? We've got a dead girl in the morgue, but hey, look how lucky you got?'

McCann throws me a disgusted glare and doesn't bother answering. 'In fairness,' Steve says, 'McCann dodged a bullet there, all right. I'd call that lucky.'

'He did,' I said. 'He definitely did that. Did Aislinn threaten to go to your wife, McCann?'

McCann's shaking his head, slow and definite. He's on solid ground here: doesn't need to worry about Aislinn's texts, because he's telling the truth. 'Never.'

'She just hinted.'

'Nah. Not even a hint.'

'You sure about that?'

'Yeah, I am. Positive. Ask Lucy the Lezzer, ask anyone you want: let's see you find one bit of evidence that Aislinn ever mentioned going to my missus. One. Just one.'

'We've got two dozen.'

'Those notes?' McCann laughs in my face, a wide-mouthed bark. 'Jesus, Conway, tell me you know better than that. How are those evidence of anyone threatening anything? *Maybe* Aislinn was planning on using them to twist my arm – you can't even prove that much – but she hadn't got around to doing it. I hadn't a clue those notes existed. I didn't even have access to them – password-protected, didn't you say? Computer Crime can go through the times when that folder was opened, show that they don't match the times when I was round at Aislinn's. Those notes are *nothing*.'

I'm shaking my head. 'Doesn't matter whether you knew about them or not. Aislinn could've sent copies to your wife.'

'She didn't. Check her computer logs, printer, work printer, anything she had access to. Bet you anything they were never printed out.'

'She could have e-mailed them.'

'Go ahead and check her e-mail accounts. You think Aislinn had my wife's e-mail address? How stupid do I look?'

'Or she just called round to your gaff when you were at work.'

'She didn't. Trace her movements, look for anyone who saw her round my way. Good luck with it.'

'Is your wife gonna say the same?'

That brings McCann up and forward, halfway across the table with his teeth bared in my face, in one savage move. 'Don't you fucking *dare* bring this to my wife. She knows nothing about Aislinn, and it's staying that way. Have you got that?'

'Routine procedure,' I say, raising my hands. 'I've got to follow up every lead.'

'Follow up whatever you want. But if you tell my wife about Aislinn, I'll wreck you. You hear that?'

'Look at that,' I say, with a touch of a grin. 'Looks like your missus finding out about your affair might be a problem after all.'

McCann's jaw clamps hard. He wants to hit me. I stare back, still grinning, and hope he tries.

After a moment his eyes cut away from mine. He eases back into his seat, rolls his neck. 'If you need to talk to my wife,' he says, 'talk to her. But you work around the affair. Even the pair of ye should be able to do that. Ask her if she's had any anonymous letters, any strange callers. I can tell you exactly what she'll say, but if you need to feel like the big boys for a day . . .'

Steve says, 'If you don't want us talking to your missus, man, then don't make us. You talk to us instead.'

'What does it look like I'm doing?'

'OK,' I say. 'Where were you Saturday evening?'

The grin lifts his top lip like a snarl. He leans back, folds his arms and laughs, up at the ceiling. 'Now we're getting to it. About bloody time.'

'Where were you?'

'Are you not going to caution me?'

'If you want. You are not obliged to say anything unless you wish to do so, but anything you do say will be taken down in writing and may be given in evidence.' That gets another vicious huff of laughter. 'Where were you Saturday evening?'

'None of your business.'

Which is smart: no alibi means nothing we can break. '"No comment,"' I say. 'Is that what you're telling us?'

'No. I'm telling you it's none of your bloody business.'

'What'll your wife say when we ask her whether you were home?'

'Only one way to find out.'

Steve says, leaning forward, 'We're not trying to catch you out here, man. We're asking. If you can prove where you were, we can stop this whole thing. We'll find a way that none of this ever has to come out. But we can't do that unless we know the story.'

McCann throws him a stare like he can't believe Steve actually tried that one on him. 'I've got nothing to say about Saturday night. Except I never hurt Aislinn. That's it. We can stay here all year and that's all I'll have to say to you.'

'It's not gonna be that simple,' I say. 'Remember that witness who saw you hanging around Stoneybatter over the last few weeks?'

'So?'

'That same witness saw you leaving the laneway behind Viking Gardens just after half-eight on Saturday night.'

That gets a snort. 'Rory Fallon. Was it?'

'You recognised him, yeah? When we brought him in?'

Brief shake of his head, wry click of his tongue: he's not falling for that. 'Nah. Bres mentioned that Fallon's been doing a bit of hanging around Stoneybatter himself, the last while. Bit of stalking. Right?'

Me and Steve don't answer. McCann nods, satisfied. 'That means he was possessive about Aislinn. More than that: obsessive. Probably he saw me going in or out of her gaff, one night, did he?'

We look back at him.

'Yeah. That would've sent him wild with jealousy. Saturday evening, when he got in her door, the first thing he did was confront her, ask her if she was seeing someone else. Poor Aislinn didn't deny it, or didn't deny it well enough, and . . .'

One hand closes into a fist and lifts off the table, just an inch, twisting.

'No wonder he's saying he saw me Saturday night. He'd say anything to get you looking somewhere else. And you'd be a pair of fools to fall for it. God knows no jury would.'

Steve says, and all of us hear the defensive note weakening his voice, 'No one's said we're falling for anything. We're only talking here.'

McCann leans back in his chair and stuffs his hands in his pockets, one corner of his mouth tugging upwards. He doesn't bother trying to keep the triumph off his face. He thinks he's seen everything we've got, held steady against it and blown it all away.

He says, 'What do you think happens if the squad finds out you were *only talking* to me like this? Over nothing but a few shags?'

'Ah, come on,' Steve says. He's practically begging. 'You're a witness. We had to talk to you. You know we did.'

'I'm a witness to nothing.'

'You knew the vic. You were *sleeping* with the vic. We couldn't just—'

'You ask me very nicely,' McCann says, 'and you don't go trying to scupper my marriage, I'll forget this ever happened.'

'We won't tell your wife about Aislinn. I swear.'

'Good call,' McCann says. He stretches, rolls his shoulders back. 'We done here, yeah?'

Steve gives me a quick, uncertain glance. 'No,' I say stubbornly. 'Seeing as we're here, we might as well finish up.'

'Five more minutes?' Steve asks McCann. 'Honest to God, it won't take longer than that, we've just got a few more—'

McCann laughs and spreads his arms. 'You want one last shot? Take it.'

'Thanks,' Steve says humbly. 'I mean, no, we don't – we just—'

I say, 'I want to ask you about Aislinn. What was going on in her head.'

McCann snorts. 'This psychological shite, Conway. Honest to God, you need to grow out of that. Rory Fallon got obsessed and lost the head. All the rest, what Aislinn was thinking, that's not your problem. Nobody cares.'

'Probably you're right. Humour me anyway, yeah?' McCann settles back into his chair on a long-suffering sigh. 'You told us,' I say, 'just a few minutes ago: when someone who's trying to get you into bed says they love you – like Aislinn said she loved you – chances are it's bollix. They've got a hidden agenda. Right?'

'Right. Only Aislinn wasn't trying to get me into bed. That just happened.'

'You ran her through the system, at the start. Because you thought she might have a hidden agenda. Right?'

'Right. And she came up clean.'

'She did, yeah. That was really enough to make you relax? You never wondered again, no? Girl like that, guy like you, and you genuinely figured she was on the up-and-up?'

'Maybe he genuinely did,' Steve says, examining McCann critically. 'Hormones, man. Scramble the brain.'

'Ah, he wondered,' I say. 'He wondered all the time. He hated himself for doing it, tried to stop – didn't you, McCann? But he couldn't. You know what I think? I think, deep down, he knew.'

McCann's lip lifts. 'You think I don't know what you're at? You've got some nerve, trying this shite on me. Go play with Rory Fallon some more. Get Bres to show you how it's done. See if you can learn something.' He shoves his chair back from the table. 'I'm done here.'

Steve takes the Des Murray family pic out of his suit pocket and lays it on the table. 'Do you recognise any of these people?' he asks.

McCann leans over and whips it up, ready to toss it back at Steve after one glance, but the photo catches him. He holds it between his fingertips and we watch his face, held to stillness with all his will, as he recognises Evelyn, then Des, and fumbles for what the hell they have to do with this. As that chubby little girl and her tentative smile start to ring a bell. We watch the tremor run through his mind, coming from deep inside the foundations, as he finally begins to understand.

Steve puts a finger on Desmond Murray. He says, 'Can you identify this man?'

McCann doesn't hear him.

I lean in and tap the photo. 'McCann. Who's this?'

McCann blinks. He says thickly, like his mind's too taken up to work his mouth right, 'Name's Desmond Murray.'

'How do you know him?'

'You already know.'

'We want to hear it from you.'

'He went missing. A long time back. I worked the case.'

'And this?' I move my finger to Evelyn Murray. 'Who's this?'

'The wife. Evelyn.'

'And this?'

My finger's on Aislinn. Steve's leaning across the table beside me, the two of us close in McCann's face, watching every twitch. There's a long silence before McCann says, 'That's the daughter.'

'Her name.'

One breath. 'Aislinn.'

A second of silence, while that falls through the air.

'You seriously didn't remember her?' Steve asks, incredulous. 'I know she'd grown up and all, but her face didn't even ring a bell? Her name? Nothing?'

After a moment McCann's head moves, side to side.

I say, 'She remembered you.'

He can't stop shaking his head.

'That's why she picked you out in Horgan's,' I say. 'Not because she was a badge bunny and you were a D. Because she wanted to know what happened to her da.'

'I wondered if maybe it started out as curiosity,' Steve says, 'or some fucked-up way of getting closer to her da' – that gets one sharp flicker of a wince, at the corner of McCann's mouth – 'and then, as she got to know you, it turned real.'

I snort. 'Hey,' Steve says, 'stranger things have happened. Is that what you're wondering, too?'

McCann lifts his head to look at Steve for a second. The flash of hope is terrible.

I pick up my phone again and swipe, methodically, feeling McCann fighting not to look, till I get to Aislinn's little fairy tale that she left for Lucy. 'Have a read of this,' I say, and pass it to McCann.

His eyes close once, for a second, as he reads. When he finishes, he reaches out and puts the phone on the table in slow motion, like a drunk. He doesn't look at us.

'Recognise the handwriting?' I ask.

Nod.

'Whose is it?'

After a second: 'Aislinn.'

'Yeah. And the bad guy in the story? The one who fucked up her life, and now she's planning on fucking up his? You know who that is, right?'

McCann says nothing. I can hear his breath, heavy puffs through his nose, in the thick overheated air.

When we know he's not going to answer, I say, 'That's you, McCann. Do you get that?'

Nothing. His hands are over the photo, covering it, so he doesn't have to see.

I lean in closer, tap the table in front of him. 'Pay attention to this part. I want you to be very clear on exactly why all this happened.'

One flicker of his eyelids. He's got blurry inklings, but not enough. He's desperate to hear the rest.

'Remember talking to Aislinn about her da's case?'

McCann says, 'I never named names.'

I laugh out loud. Out of all the things he could be worrying about, he picks that; God forbid we should think he was unprofessional. 'You didn't need to. She knew exactly who you were talking about; she's the one who steered the conversation there to begin with. Do you remember what you told her?'

He shakes his head, trying to think. 'How we tracked him all the way to England. How we found him with the bit on the . . . Aislinn never, she never said a word. Never batted an eyelid. Just kept listening, nodding . . .'

'Aislinn was good,' I say. 'Aislinn was a whole lot better at this than you realised. Do you remember telling her how you talked to her da? How he asked you to tell Aislinn and her ma he was OK, and you decided to say nothing?'

McCann's eyes have come up to me. 'You didn't meet Evelyn Murray. Delicate little thing, the shyest, sweetest – like someone out of an old book, the one who'd die at the end of consumption or one of them things, just because the world was too much for her. Made of glass, Evelyn was.' To the spreading grin on my face: 'Fuck you. I wasn't shagging her. Never laid a finger on her, never would've.'

'Whatever,' I say. 'If you cared that much about her, why not pass on the message?'

'Because finding out her man had run off with a younger model, that would've killed her. Smashed her to bits. I wasn't going to do that to her.'

I say, 'But you had no problem taking over the rest of her life. Everything she ever did after you walked in her door, every thought that ever went through her head, it had your fingerprints all over it. And you knew it would.'

I'm leaning in, across the table that's specially chosen to be narrow enough that I can get close, see every coarse hair of this fucker's stubble, I can smell the tea on his breath and the stale smoke on his clothes and the acrid reek of rage and terror in his sweat, I'm close enough to draw blood a dozen ways. 'Be honest with yourself, McCann: that's why you kept your mouth shut. Isn't it? You couldn't have Evelyn, but you loved the thought that you owned the rest of her life. Every time she woke up wondering whether Des would walk in the door today, every time she leaped when the phone rang, every night she dreamed he was dead, she belonged to you. Did you think about that sometimes, when your wife was a bitch and you were lying beside her daydreaming about sweet little Evelyn? Did it turn you on, knowing that whatever she was doing at that second, whatever she was thinking, you'd made her do it?'

McCann's staring at me, those bloodshot blue eyes. I've never seen hate like this before, not coming my way. I've only ever seen hate this intimate between couples, families. I've put my finger right between his ribs, onto his deepest hidden places. I've got him.

He says, low and clenched and right into my face, 'Fuck you to hell. It was for her own sake. You know what her man said about her? For his excuse? Said she'd been suffocating the life out of him for ten years. Said he was going mental, another few months in that house would've sent him off his chomp. You think I should've told her that? Let *that* own the rest of her life, instead? She wasn't the kind who could throw that off, move on. It would've wrecked her. At least my way let her keep some self-respect, remember her marriage the way she thought it had been. Gave her a chance.'

'Except,' I say, 'you got Aislinn as part of the package. You never even bothered thinking of that, did you? You took over Aislinn's life, too. Every day was what you'd made it into, and it was shite. Then she grew up and went looking for some answers, and then she found out who had deliberately kept them away from her till it was too late.'

McCann's mouth opens. We watch the moment when something spired and shining explodes with a tremendous roar inside his mind, jagged shards rocketing everywhere, burrowing deep into every tender spot.

I say, 'Let me tell you what Aislinn decided, the night you told her that story. She decided it was her turn to make your life into whatever the fuck she wanted. That's why the two of you started shagging, McCann. Not because hey, dick happens; because Aislinn figured you'd be easier to push around if you were pussy-whipped. And she was right. She nearly had you, didn't she? When were you going to tell your missus it was over? Was it going to be this week? Today?'

He can't talk. I lean in even closer and I say, softly and very clearly, 'The whole thing was a lie. Every time Aislinn kissed you, every time she slept with you, every time she said she loved you, it took everything she had not to puke. She forced herself to go through all that so she'd have her chance to give you what you deserved.'

McCann's head is down and swaying. His shoulders are hunched like a bleeding animal's, trying to stay on its feet.

'Now do you understand why she kept those photos?'

His breathing, like something out of a hospital ward, in the pretty pastel room.

'You were right: she was going to take them to your wife, if she couldn't make you leave on your own. One way or another, Aislinn was going to break up your marriage. And then she was going to welcome you with open arms and tell you that your wife never deserved you to begin with and you were better off with someone who'd treat you right. And once the dust settled, once the divorce papers were filed and your kids hated your cheating guts and there was no way your missus would ever let you in the door again, then Aislinn was going to dump you right on your arse and leave you there in the mess that was your brand-new life.'

Nothing, just that thick breathing. This is it. There's nothing left of McCann; between us and Aislinn, we've taken the lot. If he's going to talk, it's from this seething nowhere place we've brought him to.

Steve says quietly, 'You were in love with her. Weren't you?'

McCann's head lifts. His eyes move across us like he's blind. His mouth opens and he takes one shallow breath and holds onto it for a long moment before he says, 'No comment.'

It stays in the air like a dark spot. The room looks skewed to the point of insane, all those cute colours and smarmy little comforts straining to cover the grinning white interview-room bones – table, chairs, camera, one-way glass – underneath.

Steve says, 'When you walked in on her getting ready for Rory. Did that hit you out of the blue? Or did you already have your suspicions?'

'No comment.'

'Talk to us, man. What did she say? Did she tell you to get out and not come back? Did she laugh at you, for thinking a woman like her could love you? What?'

'No comment.'

He's not even trying to look at us, not any more. He's staring at the wall between our heads, blank-eyed, tuning us out so everything we say is just faraway babble. I've seen that look before, on rapists, murderers. The ones we're never going to break, because they know what they are and they're not fighting it.

'Where were you last Saturday evening?' Steve asks.

'No comment.'

The click of the door handle turning makes me and Steve jump. McCann doesn't move. Breslin stands in the doorway, rain glittering on his black overcoat, smiling at us all.

17

'Mac,' Breslin says. 'You're wanted in the squad room.'

McCann looks up at him. Their eyes meet for a second that shuts me and Steve out completely.

'Go on,' Breslin says. 'I'll catch up with you in a few.'

McCann pulls himself out of his chair, joint by joint, and heads for the door. Breslin gives him a quick clap on the shoulder as he passes. McCann nods automatically.

'Interview terminated at 3.24 p.m.,' Breslin says, strolling over to the camera. He reaches up and switches it off. As he turns to the water cooler: 'Well well well. Look who's best buddies again. Sweet.'

I say, 'I'd like to know what made you think we weren't best buddies all along.'

'You'll have to forgive me if I don't give a damn about your relationship right this minute. You just had the brass neck to accuse my partner—'

'We'll talk about that when I say so. Right now I want to know which one of the floaters went squealing to you, yesterday morning, told you me and Moran had had a row.'

'Reilly,' Steve says. 'Wasn't it? We started arguing, he stopped typing.'

I remember that, the sudden heavy silence where that witless clacking had been battering my brain. 'I told you Reilly was a bright spark,' Breslin says. 'Unlike me, apparently. I spent twenty minutes sitting in the Top House before the penny dropped. Fair play to you, Conway: you make a very convincing South Dublin airhead. I didn't know you had it in you.' He raises his water cup to me. 'I was lucky with traffic, though. Got back in time to catch the good parts of the show.'

He must catch a flick of surprise off one of us, because he laughs. 'You thought I got back from my road trip and came charging straight in to save Mac from you two big scary avengers? I was in the observation room. Because I knew Mac didn't need saving, seeing as he's done nothing – well, apart from sticking his dick in the wrong place, which isn't a hanging offence in my book. But I think we can all agree he's had a tough few days, so when I saw you two going all out to wreck his head, I figured it might be time to call a halt.'

He wanders over to the table, flicks up the Murray family photo to have a long look. 'Huh. No wonder Mac didn't recognise her.' He flips the photo back at the table, ignores it when it misses and spins to the ground. 'So,' he says. 'All the time I thought we were working together. All the time I was getting a lovely warm feeling about what beautiful interviews we pulled off with Rory. This was what was going on in your heads. Tell me: when you looked in the mirror this morning, you didn't taste just a little bit of sick in the back of your throats?'

Breslin doing what he does best. It feels strange, somehow it feels like a loss, that I don't have the faintest urge to punch his face in. 'And all the time I thought we were working together,' I say, 'all the time I was enjoying those beautiful interviews, you were keeping this back. You wanna throw stones?'

His eyes snap wide and he points a finger at me. 'No no no, Conway. Don't you try to turn this around on me. You've just proved that I was dead fucking right not to let you in. This *interview* . . .' His mouth twists up in disgust; he takes a swig of water to wash it away. 'Go ahead; tell me. What do you think you accomplished with this interview?'

I say, 'We got enough for a warrant on McCann's gaff.'

Breslin thinks that over, nodding. 'A warrant. Nice. And what are you planning on finding in there?'

'Those brown leather gloves McCann wears all winter? The ones I haven't seen once this week? Either we'll find Aislinn's blood on them, or we won't find them at all.'

'Wow,' Breslin says, raising his eyebrows. 'Impressive. I'd say Mac would be shitting himself if he heard that. Shall I save you some hassle? Would you like to hear what actually happened?'

'Love to,' I say. 'From McCann, but.'

Breslin clicks his tongue. 'Not going to happen. Mac's got more sense than to put it on the record – to be honest, after that little stunt you pulled, I'll be amazed if he ever wants to talk to either of you again, on or off the record. But I figure it'll simplify all our lives if you know the facts.'

Steve says, 'And it'll be unrecorded, unverifiable, inadmissible hearsay.'

'Them's the breaks. Do you want to hear this or not?'

Deep down, I don't. When McCann left the room he took something with him, some dark savage charge sizzling the air. Without him at its heart, the room's gone flat and sickly and stupid. I just want to walk out and keep walking, anywhere I don't have to think about what comes next or look at Breslin's self-righteous gob. I lean back in my chair and rub my hands over my face, trying to find some of that charge again.

'OK,' Steve says. 'Let's hear it.'

'Don't do me any favours.'

'We'd like to know.'

'Conway?'

'Why not,' I say. I take my hands off my face, but I don't have the energy to straighten up.

Breslin doesn't join us at the table. He tosses his water cup in the bin, sticks his hands in his pockets and starts pacing, a leisurely stroll, the cool professor explaining something to his enthralled students. 'Saturday evening,' he says. 'Mac had dinner at home with his family, and then he decided to call in to Aislinn. He got there around quarter to eight, give or take – he didn't check his watch. He went in the back door to the kitchen, same as usual. The lights were on and he could see Aislinn had been in the middle of cooking dinner, but she didn't call out or come to meet him. Mac went into the sitting room and found her lying there with her head on the fireplace.'

'Must've been a shock,' Steve says. Breslin shoots him a sharp glance, but Steve's face is blank.

'It was, yeah. Obviously.'

'Most people would've gone to bits.'

'Most civilians would have. Mac was devastated, but he kept it together. That doesn't make him a killer. It makes him a cop.'

'He also found the table set for a romantic dinner,' I say. 'That must've been a shock, too. What'd he make of that?'

Breslin says, in a voice meant to tell me his patience isn't going to last forever, 'He didn't *make* anything of it, Conway. To the extent that he even thought about it, what with his girlfriend's body lying there on the floor in front of him, he took it for granted the dinner was meant for him, just in case he decided to turn up, which he sometimes did. He thought someone had gained entry to the house, maybe a perv, more likely a junkie – let's be honest, it's not the nicest area, is it? – and Aislinn had come off worst. Later, it occurred to him that Aislinn might have been seeing someone on the side and it could have gone wrong; but at the time, that didn't even come into his head. As Moran just pointed out, he was in *shock*.'

Steve asks, 'Was Aislinn alive?'

Breslin shakes his head. 'Mac checked her pulse and her breathing straightaway – so yeah, he probably did get blood on his gloves, and he may even have got rid of them because of that. She was gone.'

Minutes or hours, Cooper said; probably progressed rapidly. It all plays, so far. It's bollix, but a jury might go for it.

I say, 'So he rang it straight in and got a team of Ds on the scene.'

He stares at me, those pale pop-eyes frozen too hard to blink. 'Don't be cute, Conway. Just don't. This isn't the moment. Maybe you genuinely believe that's what you would have done in his place, but it's bullshit. If Mac had called it in, he would have been at the centre of a murder investigation, meaning he would have been working a desk till this was sorted, however long that took. If the case didn't get cleared, he would have been finished as a Murder D: there's no way you can be an effective investigator when you're under suspicion yourself. He would have lost his wife and kids. Quite possibly he would have ended up going on trial; there was a chance he could've ended up going to *prison*. For *life*. And for what? He hadn't done anything; he didn't have any info that could help the investigation. He would have been throwing himself on his sword, personally and professionally, for *nothing*. If you genuinely think you're that much of a saint, I'm delighted for you. But I'm not convinced.'

The thing I'm not about to tell Breslin: I don't have a clue what I would have done. I can picture it, clear as nightmare: standing there in the middle of someone else's bloody wreckage, feeling it silt up fast and faster around my ankles, my calves, my knees, and thinking *No.*

I stare right back at him. 'What I would do doesn't matter. What did McCann do?'

'He cleared the house, in case the assailant was still inside, which he wasn't. When McCann was sure the guy was gone, he wiped the place down to get rid of his old fingerprints – honest to God, Conway, I'm going to need you to take off that superior disapproving face. I can't concentrate while I have to look at that.'

There's no expression on me at all; Breslin just wants me in the wrong. 'If you don't like my face,' I say, 'you can look at Moran. Or shut your eyes, for all I care.'

Breslin sighs, shakes his head and makes a big deal of turning his shoulder to me and focusing all his attention on Steve. 'So McCann wiped for prints. He had a look around Aislinn's bedroom to see if she'd kept any of his notes, which she hadn't – at least, not in the obvious places. He considered sticking around in case the assailant came back, but he decided that was unlikely enough that it wasn't worth the risk.'

Steve says, all puzzled furrowed brow, 'Why'd he turn off the cooker? That's been bothering me from the start.'

'So that any evidence wouldn't be destroyed—' I snort. 'Fingerprints aren't everything, Conway. McCann knew the killer could have left behind DNA, hairs, fibres, valuable stuff; he wasn't about to ruin that. And he didn't want the place to catch on fire and burn Aislinn to death, if by some tiny chance he was wrong and she was still alive. And . . .' Breslin smiles a little sad smile. 'He didn't say this to me, because Mac doesn't like looking like a sap any more than you or I do, but I'm pretty sure he also couldn't stand the idea of Aislinn's body being burned. He was fond of her, you know.'

'Aah,' I say. I half expect Steve to move, signalling me to dial it back, but he doesn't. Steve's gone past wanting to be buddies with Breslin.

'*Conway.* Just *stop.* I know you hate this squad and everyone in it, but think like a fucking detective for a second, instead of a teenage reject who's finally got one up on the popular girls. If Mac had killed Aislinn, why would he turn off that cooker? He would have turned it up to full and hoped the place burned to the ground.'

I say, 'What'd he do next?'

Breslin sighs through gritted teeth. 'He went out the back door, locked it behind him and went home. Don't bother checking the CCTV; you won't find him. Not Saturday night, not any night. It's easy enough to find out where the cameras are and plan your route around them. If it came to a divorce, Mac wasn't about to give his wife anything a private dick could turn up to use against him.'

It plays; of course it plays. Just like McCann's story does, and Rory's, and Lucy's. All these stories. They hum like fist-sized hornets in the corners of the ceiling, circling idly, saving their strength. I want to pull out my gun and blow them away, neatly, one by one, vaporise them into swirls of black grit drifting downwards and gone.

I ask, 'When did he tell you all this?'

'He phoned me as soon as his wife went to sleep. In fairness, Conway, it's not exactly like he could have that conversation while he was walking through town on a Saturday night. Or on the sofa with his missus watching telly beside him. He took the first chance he got.'

I say, 'And you believed him.'

That whips Breslin around to face me full-on. '*Yes,* Conway. Yes. I do believe him. Partly it's because of a little thing called loyalty, which you apparently haven't got the first clue about. He's my partner; if I catch him with a dead body at his feet and a smoking gun in his hand, it's my job to believe he's been framed. But mostly it's because I know Mac. I've known him for a long, long time. You'll be lucky if you ever have a partner you know like I know Mac. And there's *no fucking way* he did this.'

My eyes meet Steve's for a second. I can't tell whether Breslin believes that load, or whether he's convinced himself he does because he needs to be that guy, the noble knight standing by his partner through thick and thin. Probably it's the second one, which means it's here to stay. You can knock down a genuine belief, if you load up with enough facts that contradict it; but a belief that's built on nothing except who the person wants to be, nothing can crumble that. We could show Breslin video of McCann bashing Aislinn's face in, and the noble knight would find a way around it.

'Do you two get that? Is that going into your heads?'

'Yeah,' I say. 'And you called it in to Stoneybatter.'

'I did, yeah. And just by the way, McCann knew I was doing it, and he agreed. As soon as the initial shock wore off, he started thinking like a cop again. Because that's who he is. Not a killer. A cop.'

'Uh-huh. So why'd you wait till five in the morning? If McCann called you as soon as his wife went asleep, we're talking what, midnight? Why wait five hours?'

Breslin sighs and holds up his hands. 'OK. You got me. Good for you. I wanted to be sure I'd be there when the case came in to the squad. Obviously McCann wasn't going to come within a mile of the investigation, or the whole thing could collapse—'

'Honourable,' I say. 'I'm impressed.'

Breslin throws me a filthy look, but he doesn't bother answering. '—but we figured I should keep an eye on things. See if there was a moment when Mac needed to come forward, that kind of— Conway, why are you even bothering to listen to me, if you're just going to sneer at everything I say? Would you be happier waiting outside while I have an actual conversation with Moran?'

'See if there was a moment when you could send the investigating detectives off on a wild-goose chase, more like. This week must have been hilarious for you, was it? Watching me and Moran chase our tails—'

Breslin's across the room so fast I almost flinch. 'What are you accusing me of? No' – with a finger in my face, when I start to answer – 'you be careful. You be very fucking careful.'

I'm done with being very fucking careful. I slap his finger away, hard enough that I see the flare in his eyes when he thinks about hitting me, but no such luck. Steve's half out of his chair, but he has the sense not to come in. 'You've been obstructing my investigation. That's not an accusation, that's a fucking fact. You've been playing bent cop, so that if me and Moran found anything linking McCann to Aislinn, we'd have a beautiful dead end to chase till you could get Rory Fallon oven-ready. Waving fifties around, giving Gaffney the brush-off, inventing sketchy phone calls— Did Reilly hand you that too? Go running to you, squealing about how we were looking at gang members—'

Breslin laughs at the top of his lungs, right in my face. 'You think I needed Reilly for that? The two of you told me yourselves. First you demand to know who ran Aislinn through the system and why. And then Sunday afternoon, Moran, when the gaffer called you in, you know what you left open on your computer? A search for Dublin-based males aged twenty to fifty with a history of gang activity. And Monday morning, Conway, along you came, pouring on the fake concern about whether I was stressed over money troubles. You seriously thought I was too thick to put two and two together?'

In the corner of my eye I can see Steve's blazing redner. Mine probably matches it. Me poking every shadow with sticks, all ready for a poison nest of spies plotting to get me, and all that was in there was me not being subtle enough and Steve forgetting to hit Exit.

Breslin steps back and spreads his arms. 'If you think I obstructed your investigation, go ahead and file a complaint. What are you going to put in it? Breslin paid for his sandwich the wrong way? Breslin didn't want Gaffney hanging off him?' He's got a grin on him, a nasty one. 'If you saw anything dodgy there, kids, it was in the eye of the beholder. If you went chasing after some wild hare, that was all on you. Not my problem.'

Neither of us answers that. I can still smell Breslin's aftershave.

'If you don't have enough to file a complaint,' Breslin says, 'then I think you owe me an apology.'

I say, 'Now we're gonna tell you our story. And it's a lot better than yours.'

His face pulls into a grimace of pure disbelief. 'What are you talking about? This isn't about who's got the best *story*, Conway. This is about what actually *happened* on Saturday night. And I've already told you that.'

'Humour me. Don't worry, ours is shorter than yours, too.'

Breslin sighs, long and noisy, and makes a big thing of pushing mugs out of the way so he can settle his arse against the counter. 'All right,' he says, folding his arms. 'Go for it. Blow me away.'

'Saturday evening,' I say. 'McCann had dinner at home and then decided to call round to Aislinn. He hadn't given her any notice, but that wasn't supposed to matter: she was supposed to be available whenever he wanted her. He got there sometime after seven-forty, when Rory left the laneway to go to Tesco. McCann went over the wall and in the back door, same as usual.'

Breslin's nodding away, giving me a wide-eyed stare of disbelief: isn't this the same story he told us? 'Hang on,' I say. 'This is where it gets good. He found Aislinn all dressed up and cooking dinner, and he didn't get the welcome he was expecting: she obviously didn't want him there. McCann went out into the sitting room to see what was going on, and he found the table all set for a romantic dinner that he knew bloody well didn't involve him.'

'By that point,' Steve says, 'his whole life was hanging on Aislinn Murray. He was getting ready to leave his wife, his kids—'

'I'm guessing Breslin knew that already,' I say. Breslin rolls his eyes to the ceiling.

'McCann had ripped up what he thought was going to be the rest of his life,' Steve says, 'thrown it away, and rewritten it from scratch around Aislinn.'

'Gobshite,' I say, aside to Steve, and see the flash of anger in Breslin's eye.

Steve says, 'And she set it on fire.'

'I wonder how much she told him,' I say.

'Not the whole story, anyway. Not the bit about her da. You saw his face when we brought that out. Genuine shock.'

'Ah, yeah. She never got that far. But I'd say she made it pretty clear that her and McCann were done, and he needed to get the hell out, rapid, so she could bang her new fella in peace.'

'Ouch,' Steve says, wincing. 'No wonder he lost the head.'

'Anyone would. Anyone. I would.'

'Most people would lose it a lot worse than that. One second out of control, one punch? That's nothing. No way he could guess it would end like this.'

Breslin's still leaning back with his arms folded, watching us under his eyelids, with a wry smile twisting one corner of his mouth. 'It's a cute story. So this was just a silly little manslaughter, no big deal, and Mac should own up and take his slap on the wrist like a good boy?'

I say, 'What do you think he should do? Keep his mouth shut, go back to the squad and his missus like nothing ever happened?'

'I do, actually. Because your cute story falls apart the second I start looking at it like an actual *detective*. Psychologically, it makes bugger-all sense, and while I don't normally give too many fucks about the psychological stuff, in this case you've got literally nothing else, so I figure it's worth a bit of attention. First off' – he raises a finger – 'why would Rory come as some big shock to Mac? Enough of a shock to make him punch a woman in the face, hard enough to kill her? Mac wasn't in love with Aislinn. If you don't believe that, there's the fact that he had told Aislinn she was welcome to see other people – witness the fact that she invited Rory to her place, where she *knew* Mac might show up any time, rather than going over to his. If you don't believe *that*, you've got Lucy's evidence that Mac had access to Aislinn's phone, *specifically* because he wanted to check her texts. That phone is packed with weeks' worth of texts to and from Rory, including ones setting up that dinner date. And you're telling me Rory would've shocked Mac right out of his mind?'

I say, 'By the time Rory came on the scene, McCann wasn't reading Aislinn's texts any more. Too embarrassed, plus he hadn't found anything worth reading.'

'Yeah, I saw you humiliate him over that. You got him good there, guys. Well done.' Breslin throws us a few slow claps. 'But if Mac had cared that much about whether Aislinn had another guy on the side, I'm thinking he would have managed to overcome a bit of embarrassment and check her texts. Whether he felt like admitting it to you two or not.'

Steve says, 'Unless Aislinn had him fooled well enough that it never occurred to him she might be seeing someone else.'

'Sure. Which would mean he's not the jealous type, which would mean he wouldn't lose the plot when he found out. We're back where we started: it doesn't add up, psychologically. And the second problem.' Breslin raises another finger. 'Rory could've turned off that cooker because he didn't like the smell, or because his mummy trained him never to leave appliances on. Mac couldn't have. He's not some civilian pussy-boy who'd go to pieces and do dumb shit for no good reason. Even under serious stress, he was thinking straight – straight enough to wipe the joint for prints, remember. He wasn't going to touch anything in that house without a solid reason. If he'd killed Aislinn, if he knew that all the forensics would point to him and burning the gaff down could only help him get away with it, why the hell would he turn off the cooker?'

I say, 'So the smoke alarm wouldn't go off. McCann was thinking straight, all right. He needed time to wipe the house down – and more than that, he realised Aislinn's fella could come in very useful. A boyfriend on the spot, all on his own with no one to vouch for his actions, right around the time of the attack: man, that's a killer's dream.'

Breslin's shaking his head, doing a small smile of pure disgust. I don't care. 'The only problem was,' I say, 'seeing as McCann hadn't actually been reading Aislinn's texts, he didn't know exactly when the boyfriend was due to arrive. Even if he checked her phone and found the appointment time – which he didn't want to do, because the techs would be able to see that he'd done it, and when – that didn't guarantee that the boyfriend wouldn't be running late. If McCann left the cooker on, it might set off the smoke alarm – and Aislinn might be found – while this fella was still somewhere else, with an alibi. Even if McCann disabled the alarm, he risked having a neighbour or the boyfriend notice smoke and call it in while the boyfriend could still be excluded. The cooker had to be turned off.'

Breslin shrugs. 'I suppose you might be able to argue that. Like I said, it's a cute story. But that's all it is. There's nothing solid underneath. You can prove that Mac had an affair with Aislinn. Good for you. But when it comes to Saturday night, you can prove exactly bugger-all. You've got an ID from the prime suspect, who has every motive to drag someone else into this mess. You've got some bizarre convoluted story you heard from some woman who may or may not have been the vic's best friend, may or may not have been in love with the vic herself, and may or may not be holding a jealous grudge against the lucky guy who got to shag the vic. And if you actually get a warrant to search Mac's gaff, which I can't believe you'd be stupid enough to do, you'll probably have proof that he's lost his brown gloves. And that's it. That's what you've got.'

Silence.

'What are you planning to do with it?'

More silence.

'Yeah. That's what I thought.' Breslin fills himself another cup of water, and we listen to the bubbles force their way up the cooler. He takes a long deliberate sip before he says, 'I hope you two realise what you've done to this case.'

Neither of us bites.

'You've fucked it right up the ass. Do you get that? You'll never get McCann for this, because A, you've got no evidence that he did it, and B, he didn't do it, Fallon did. If you actually try going after Mac, the prosecutor will laugh your file right out of his office. If you some- how manage to get him into court – which you won't – the defence will pull in Rory Fallon and your *mountain* of actual *evidence* against him, and the jury will acquit before the jury-room door closes. Wouldn't you? Be honest. If you were on the jury, and the sum total of the evidence was what you've just told me, would you vote to convict?'

Me and Steve don't answer.

'Of course you wouldn't. Neither would anyone else in the country, except maybe the odd cop-hater who'd vote to convict him of being Jack the Ripper. But now that you've opened up this whole can of worms with Mac, you're never going to get Fallon. The prosecutors get him into court, the defence pulls in McCann – wrecks his marriage and possibly his career in the process, but hey, that's not your prob- lem, am I right? – and bang, reasonable doubt. Bye-bye, Rory. Have a nice life. See you when your next girlfriend pisses you off.'

He raises his cup to an imaginary Rory.

'You're done, kids. All you've got left to do here is pack up your case file and send it down to the basement – and, of course, find a good explanation to give the gaffer and the media for why this case has crashed into a wall and poor Aislinn won't be getting the justice she deserves. Are you proud of yourselves? Does this feel like a good week's work to you?'

We stay silent. There's nothing we could say that has any point to it.

Breslin sighs and strolls over to the video camera. 'The only thing we can do with this mess,' he says, 'is keep it from ruining McCann's life. Frankly, after what you've put him through for absolutely no good reason, that's the *least* you can do.'

He reaches up to the video camera, hits the eject button and pulls out the tape. 'Am I right that you had more sense than to log this interview anywhere?'

Steve nods.

'When you got McCann to come with you. You managed not to make it obvious what you were doing?'

Nod.

'You haven't taken an official statement from Lucy Riordan?'

I shake my head.

'Let's all thank God for small mercies,' Breslin says. He brings the videotape down on his palm with a flat rattle. 'So. The last hour or so never happened. You'll get rid of those photo arrays and take a nice appropriate statement from Lucy – I'm sure you can figure out a way to do that. I'll explain to the gaffer that you've been doing a fine job, but we're not getting enough for a charge that'll hold up, so we've decided to back-burner Rory Fallon for now, keep working the forensics and electronics, and hope something pops up down the road.' Or, more like, reassure the gaffer that he's got me and Steve under control, like he promised to all along. I can hardly stand to look at his face. 'The gaffer'll hold off the media till they find something else to gnaw on. We'll keep an eye on Rory, make sure his near miss keeps him scared straight. And we'll all live happily ever after.' Breslin brings the tape down on his palm again. 'Does that sound like a plan?'

After a moment I say, 'Yeah.'

'Moran?'

Steve takes a breath. 'Yeah.'

'It's not going to run into any glitches along the way. Am I right?'

I say, 'No glitches.'

'Good.' Breslin tucks the tape inside his jacket and heads for the door. With his hand on the handle, he turns for an exit line.

'It might be a while before you get this,' he says, 'but you two owe me big-time. I'm sure it doesn't feel like it right now. But a few years down the road, when Rory Fallon gets locked and spills his guts to his new girlfriend, and you're still here to make the collar, you're going to realise I'm the best thing that ever happened to you. I'll take my thank-yous then. If they come with a nice bottle of bourbon thrown in, it won't go to waste.'

Before either of us can come up with a sensible response to that steaming heap, he gives us a nod and he's gone, bang of the door and fast firm strides down the corridor, off to tell McCann that everything's gonna be just fine.

After a few moments Steve bends to pick up the Murray family photo. He says, 'I thought we had him there. McCann. When we brought this out. I really thought . . .'

'Yeah, I did too. It was good, that. It should've worked.' I let myself have five seconds to think about just how good that interview was; how good we were together, me and Steve. How it felt like we could read each other's mind. I give myself those five seconds to understand what I'm losing.

'"No comment,"' Steve says. He tucks the photo back into his jacket pocket, carefully, like it might matter again sometime.

I say, 'We should have seen it.'

Way back at the very beginning, when Lucy turned squirrelly about Aislinn's secret boyfriend, we should have seen it. Us running around chasing imaginary gangsters, whipping up drama about bent cops and shushing each other about complicated suspicions, when the obvious was jumping up and down in front of us, waving its arms for attention.

'I'm a fucking eejit for leaving that search on my computer,' Steve says. 'No sleep, the gaffer called us in, I got rattled—'

'No worse than me, trying to pump Breslin and making a balls of it. Don't worry about it.'

'If I hadn't started us down the whole gang road—'

I say, 'Even if you hadn't. I don't think we would've seen it.'

Steve said it days ago: Breslin is used to being the good guy, any story that gets room in his head has to grow out of that beginning. It's not just Breslin. All of us Ds know, certain sure, we're the good guys. Without that to stand on, there isn't a way through the parts of this job that are dark dripping hell. Breslin the bent cop, McCann the bent cop, those we could picture. There are cops who'll go that way, always have been; hazard of the job. But a killer cop, one of our own transformed into the thing we spend our lives trying to bring down, that's different. That wrenches the world inside out. Even me, and I've got years' worth of reasons to know that the police aren't always good guys: when it was there in front of my face, my eyes weren't able to see it.

Breslin and McCann at the top of the stairs, muttering about how urgently they needed this case nailed shut: a kid could have seen why. It never came near my mind.

Maybe Breslin really did believe McCann, when he rang out of the night with a story that was just barely plausible, and not just because he needed to be the noble white knight. Maybe he believed it because when the other possibility came into his mind, the only thing his mind could do was spit it out and leap away.

'Maybe not.' Steve is staring blankly at the place where Breslin was. 'Even if we had, it would've probably made no difference. It's not like there's extra evidence we could've got our hands on. We'd be banjaxed anyway.'

It would have made a difference, but. All the ways it would have made all the difference hang in my head, weaving together into one thick dark curtain. I haven't got a way to put it into words: what might be gone for good behind its slow sway; what these few days might have changed, if only we'd seen.

I say, 'I'm not done.' I get my phone out and I start skimming through my contacts.

Steve's eyes move to me, dark and doubtful. 'We're not going to get him. What Breslin said, it sucks but he's right.'

'I know.'

He starts to say something else, but I lift a finger: the phone's ring-ing. 'Louis Crowley,' says Creepy Crowley suspiciously. The back-ground noise sounds like he's in a pub.

'Howya,' I say. 'Antoinette Conway, Murder squad. I need to talk to you. Like, now. Where are you?'

I throw in a good pinch of suppressed desperation, to get him drooling, and it works. 'Hmm,' Crowley says. 'I'm not sure I have the time.'

'Come on. You won't regret it.'

The little prick thinks he knows exactly what's going on here, and he's gonna wring every last drop out of it. 'Well,' he says, on a sigh, loving this. 'I suppose . . . I'm in Grogan's. I'll be here for another half-hour. If you get here before I leave, I can give you a few minutes.'

'Great,' I say, letting the rush of gratitude slip through. 'I— Great. I'll be there.' And I hang up.

'Was that Crowley?' Steve asks. His eyebrows are up.

'I need to shut him down, remember? And I've got an idea.' I shove the phone in my pocket, stand up and tug the creases out of my suit. 'Come with me? I could do with backup.'

All of a sudden there's a twitch tugging at the corner of Steve's mouth. He says, 'Would this idea count as a glitch in the Plan?'

'I fucking well hope so. You coming or not?'

Steve shoves back his chair and stands up, grinning. 'Wouldn't miss it.'

No one is in the corridors; when we get our coats, no one's in the locker room. The familiar run of sound comes through the squad-room door, keyboards, phone calls, bitching, the printer; in the middle of it all is that smooth power-voice of Breslin's, raised in some punchline that gets a big laugh. Up in Incident Room C, the floaters are working away, busy little bees piling up paper that'll go straight down to the basement. Even reception is empty; Bernadette's on break or in the jacks. We walk out of the Murder building and no one even knows we're gone.

Crowley's on his own at a corner table in Grogan's, sipping a pint of Smithwick's and reading a bet-up paperback with SARTRE on the cover in massive letters, so everyone will get that he's on a higher plane. He pretends he doesn't notice us till we're practically on top of his table. 'Crowley,' I say.

He does a bad fake startle and puts the book down. Steve is a surprise, but Crowley covers OK: 'Ah,' he says, holding out his hand and giving Steve a gracious smile, ignoring me, to put me in my place. 'Detective Moran.'

'Howya,' Steve says, without taking Crowley up on the handshake. He thumps down on a stool, long legs sprawled everywhere, pulls out his phone and gives it his full attention.

I can see Crowley trying to figure this out. I sit down opposite him, prop my elbows on the table and my chin on my fingers, and smile at him. 'Howya.'

'Yes,' he says, with a nice mix of distaste and wariness; he's not getting the feed of desperation I promised him. 'Hello.'

'Nice articles you've been running. I've never been on the front page before. I feel like Kim Kardashian.'

'Hardly,' Crowley says, eyeballing me. 'You liked the photo?'

'Crowley,' I say. 'You're after making a bad mistake.'

This isn't going the way Crowley expected, but he holds up well – after all, he's still got the upper hand, whether I behave myself or not. 'Oh, I don't think so. If you don't want to look like a bully in the eyes of the nation—' Steve has fired up some game that's a mixture of beeping noises and cherry bombs; Crowley twitches, but he manages to hang on to his train of moral outrage. '—then don't try to bully the agents of free speech. It really is that simple.'

'Nah nah nah. I'm not here about the photo. My problem is a guy who saw the photo. He rang you up looking for my address, and you gave it to him.'

'Haven't a clue what you're talking about,' Crowley says. He folds his pudgy little hands on the table and smirks at me. 'How is your father, by the way?'

While I'm still being puzzled, Steve's head snaps up and he lets out a great big snort of laughter. 'He did not. Did he?'

Crowley's eyes zip back and forth between us. The smirk's fading. This is why I wanted Steve along: if I was here to beg Crowley to keep my deepest family secret just between us, I wouldn't have brought company. 'Who didn't do what?' I demand. 'And you, where do you know my da from?'

'Your man who rang you,' Steve says, to Crowley. 'He didn't actually tell you he was Conway's *da*. Did he?'

'Ah, for fuck's sake,' I say. 'Seriously?'

Steve starts to laugh properly. Crowley shoots him a poison look. 'That's what he said. He said he'd lost touch a long time back and wanted to reconnect.'

'And you fell for it?' I demand. 'Just like that?'

'He seemed legit. I didn't see any reason to doubt him.'

'You're supposed to be a *journalist*,' Steve points out, still grinning. 'Doubt's supposed to be your *thing*.'

'Jesus,' I say. 'I don't even like you, and I'm scarlet for you.'

'You got played, man,' Steve says, shaking his head and going back to his game. 'Played like a pound-shop kazoo.'

'Crowley,' I say. 'You're a walking fucking lobotomy. The guy who rang you isn't my da' – Steve starts laughing again on that. 'He's a scumbag from up North who I helped put away for a few years, and when he saw that photo it occurred to him that this was his big chance to get his own back. And you gave him my fucking home address.'

A lot of the air goes out of Crowley.

'He's been casing my gaff ever since,' I say, 'and last night I found him in my sitting room. You figure he was just there for the chats?'

'"Conwaaay,"' Steve says, in his deepest voice. '"I am your faaather."'

'Luckily for everyone,' I say, 'I sorted the situation. He's not gonna be back. The only problem I've got left is you. Me and my partner, we've been trying to decide what to charge you with.'

'Conspiracy to commit burglary,' Steve suggests, jabbing away at his phone. 'And assault, depending on whether your man was only planning on leaving a chocolate log in Conway's fridge or whether he was hoping to do very bad things to her personally. Or accessory before the fact. Or we could go for the lot, just for laughs, and see what sticks.'

Crowley's gone even paler and sweatier than usual. He says, 'I want to talk to my solicitor.'

'You're in deep shite here,' I tell him. 'Lucky for you, though, I've got a use for you.'

'I'm serious. I want to talk to my solicitor *right now.*'

'Hey, genius,' Steve says, zapping something with a nuke noise and a flourish. 'Tell us: does this look like an interview room?'

'No. Because I'm not under arrest. I know my rights—'

'Course you do,' Steve says. 'Since you're not under arrest, you've got no right to a solicitor. You've got the right to leave any time you like, obviously.' I shift my stool back helpfully, making room for Crowley to go. 'I wouldn't recommend it, but. If you do, we'll take this to our boss, and then you will be under arrest. And then you can have any solicitor you like.'

Crowley starts to get up. When we watch him with interest and don't try to stop him, he changes his mind.

'Or,' I say, 'you can do me a quick favour, and we'll forget the whole thing. I'll even throw you a bit of a scoop, just to show there's no hard feelings.'

'I'd go with that one,' Steve advises him. 'If it was me, like.'

'The favour,' Crowley says. Most of the pompous puff has leaked out of his voice. 'What's the favour?'

'You've been showing up at way too many of my crime scenes, the last while,' I say. 'Who's been tipping you off?'

Crowley nearly crumples off his bench with relief. He tries to cover by pursing his lips and doing scruples. Me and Steve wait.

'I'm not the kind of person who stirs up trouble—' That makes Steve snort. 'Unless it's morally *necessary.*'

'It is, of course,' Steve says cheerfully. 'You spill, Conway sorts out whatever beef the lads have with her, everyone gets to concentrate on catching criminals, justice is served. Plus you don't have to waste your time fighting charges; you can keep on fighting the good fight instead. It's morally all tickety-boo.'

'I'm not going to rat you out to your buddies,' I say. 'You can keep your cosy little relationships going. I just want to know who's fucking me about.'

Crowley makes a face at hearing Language out of a girl, but he's smart enough to keep his gob shut. He taps his lips with one fingertip and leaves another few seconds for his scruples to impress us. Then he sighs. 'Detective Roche lets me know when he thinks I might take an interest in one of your cases.'

No surprise there. 'Roche and who else?'

After a moment he says, reluctantly – hates to jeopardise his beautiful new friendship – 'Detective Breslin rang me on Sunday morning. He mentioned the Aislinn Murray case.'

'Yeah, we already knew that. Is he the one who gave you my home address? Or was that Roche?'

'I got it from a contact.'

'What kind of contact?'

'You can't make me reveal my sources. I know you people would love to turn this country into a totalitarian—'

Steve pumps his fist and goes 'Yesss!' at the phone. 'Sorry,' he says. 'You were saying? Totalitarian something?'

I say, 'This wasn't a journalistic source, moron. This was someone helping you to help a criminal break into my *house*. You think that's protected?'

'It could be. You don't know what else he told me.'

'Crowley. You want me to ask them instead?'

He shrugs like a teenager in a sulk. 'All *right*. Breslin.'

The little fucker. I should've punched him when I had the chance. 'How'd you get it out of him?'

'Oh, please. I didn't put him on the *rack*. When he rang me about the Aislinn Murray case, he told me you had a terrible tendency to dither – I'm only quoting.' Crowley holds up his hands and smirks at me. 'He said you could take months to close the most blindingly obvious case. Normally that would be your problem, but this time Detective Breslin was stuck on the case with you, and he didn't want his name associated with that nonsense. He needed pressure put on you to actually do your job – quoting again, Detective, only quoting! So I came up with a little bit of pressure.'

'No better man,' Steve says, to his phone. 'We could hardly think straight, we were that pressurised. Amn't I right, Conway?'

Crowley shoots him a suspicious look. 'And then, when the man claiming to be your father rang me—'

I say, 'That's why you were falling over yourself to believe he was actually my da. Here I thought it was just because the idea of shoving your greasy fingers into my private life gave you such a hard-on, you couldn't think straight. But you were figuring, if this guy was legit, then siccing him on me would turn up the pressure another notch. And you'd get a pat on the head and a nice treat from your handler. Am I right?'

Crowley prisses up his mouth. 'The tone you're taking is inappropriate and it's deliberately inflammatory. I'm under no obligation to—'

'You can stick my tone up your hole. You rang Breslin and drooled down the phone to him about how you could fuck up my personal life till my head was so wrecked, I'd sign off on anything; all you needed was my home address. And he couldn't wait to hand it over. Am I missing anything out?'

He has his arms folded and he's refusing to look at me, to show me that my behaviour is unacceptable. 'If you already know everything, why ask me?'

'Oh, but I don't know everything, not yet. Roche's been siccing you on my cases, Breslin did it the once. Who else?'

He shakes his head. 'That's all.'

'Crowley,' I say, warning. 'You don't get to buy your way out of this by throwing me two names. Spill, or the deal's off.'

Crowley does what's meant to be wounded nobility, but comes out looking like indigestion. 'I actually know when transparency is important, Detective Conway – and there are plenty of Guards who can't say that. Other detectives do contact me – there actually are some who care about the public's right to know – but not about your cases.'

I can't tell what sends up the sudden wild spurt of anger: the chance that he's lying, or the chance that he's telling the truth. I go in close across the table and I say, right into his face, 'Don't you fuck with me. Whoever you're skipping, I will find out, d'you get me? And you'll spend the rest of your life looking over your shoulder and wishing you'd gone for a career cleaning the jacks in Supermac's.'

'I'm not! I'm not skipping anyone. Detective Roche, and this time Detective Breslin. That's it.' It's the fear on Crowley's face that convinces me. He adds, bitchily, 'I'm sure you think you're interesting enough to deserve a mass conspiracy, but apparently not everyone agrees.'

My head feels strange, weightless. All this time I've been thinking the whole squad's out for my blood, the squad room is a curtain swelling with the enemy army behind it, I'm the lone fighter lifting her sword and knowing she's going down. Except every time I pull back the curtain, all I find is the same one wanker.

The lads throwing slaggings my way: I took it for granted the edges were sharpened deliberately and smeared with poison, carefully constructed to slice till I dropped. It never occurred to me that it was just slagging, with a bit of extra edge because I don't get on with most of them and because – ever since that first arse-slap off Roche, half of them watching, none of them saying a word – I haven't tried. Fleas, hinting to see whether I fancied coming back to Undercover: I assumed it was because he knew I was crashing and burning in Murder, I never once thought it could be just that we were good together and he misses me. Steve, spinning his what-ifs and watching them whirl, considering all their glinting angles: I thought, for a few hours in there I actually believed, he was using them to lure me over a cliff-edge so he could watch me go splat and wave bye-bye from the top. I'm glad my skin means him and Crowley won't see the blush.

I was doing exactly the same thing as Aislinn: getting lost so deep inside the story in my head, I couldn't see past its walls to the outside world. I feel those walls shift and start to waver, with a rumble that shakes my bones from the inside out. I feel my face naked to the ice-flavoured air that pours through the cracks and keeps coming. A great shiver is building in my back.

Crowley and Steve are both watching me, waiting to see if I'm gonna let Crowley off the hook. Steve's game is yelping for attention.

'OK,' I say. I want to walk out, but I'm not done here. I shove everything else to the back of my mind. 'OK. We'll go with that.'

Crowley says – the fear's vanished; he's straight back into hyena mode – 'You mentioned having a bit of news for me.'

'Oh yeah,' I say. My focus is back; this is gonna be fun. 'Have I got a scoop for you. You're gonna love this.'

Crowley whips out his voice recorder, but I shake my head. 'Nah. This is non-attributable. It comes from sources close to the investigation. Got it?' 'Sources close to the investigation' means cops. I don't want McCann and Breslin thinking Lucy's been talking.

He gets pouty, but I sit back and have a watch of Steve jabbing manically at his phone screen. In the end Crowley sighs and puts the recorder away. 'I suppose so.'

'Good man,' I say, sitting up again. 'Get a load of this. Aislinn Murray, right?' Crowley nods, filling up with drool, hoping I'm about to tell him she was raped in creative ways. 'She was having an affair. With a married guy.'

Crowley's only delighted to settle for that. He does a man-of-the-world head-shake. 'I knew she was too good to be true. Knew it. Girls who look like that, my God, they think they can get away with anything. Sometimes – oops, so sorry, Your Highness! – it doesn't work out like that.'

He's already rewriting the story in his head, whizzing through his best euphemisms for 'homewrecking nympho who got what she deserved'. Steve says, 'It gets better. Guess what her fella does for a living.'

'Hmmm.' Crowley pinches his chin and thinks. 'Well. Obviously a girl like that would have liked money. But I'd hazard a guess that she was even more aroused by power. Would I be right?'

Me and Steve are well impressed. 'How come you're not doing our job?' Steve wants to know. 'We could do with that kind of smarts on the squad.'

'Ah, well, not everyone's the type who can work for The Man, Detective Moran. I think we must be talking about a politician. Let me see . . .' Crowley steeples his fingers against his lips. He's got the whole story rolling out in his head, ready for ink. 'Aislinn's job wouldn't have taken her into those circles, so they must have met socially, meaning he's young enough to be out and about—'

'Even better than that,' I say. I have a quick glance around the pub, lean across the table and head-beckon Crowley in. When him and his patchouli reek get close enough for a whisper: 'He's a cop.'

'Even better,' Steve says, ditching his phone and leaning in beside me. 'He's a detective.'

'Even better,' I say. 'He's a Murder detective.'

'Not me,' Steve adds. 'I'm single. Thank Jaysus.'

We both sit back and smile big wide smiles at Crowley.

He stares at us, sticky little mind racing while he tries to work out our angle and whether we're bullshitting him. 'I can't run that,' he says.

I say, 'You're going to run it.'

'I can't. I'll be sued. The *Courier* will be sued.'

'Not if you don't name names,' Steve reassures him. 'There's two dozen of us on the squad, all guys except Conway here, and most of them are married. That's, what, sixteen or seventeen people it could be? You're safe as houses.'

'I have contacts who would be furious. I'm not going to sabotage my career.'

'Everyone on Murder already hates you, man,' Steve points out, going back to his game. 'Except Roche and Breslin, and just to ease your mind, it's not them. So it's not like you're going to burn any bridges.'

'You'll be a hero,' I say. 'Ireland's bravest investigative journalist, daring to take on The Man and strike a blow for truth and transparency, never even thinking about the risk to himself. It's gonna be great.'

'Think how much hoop you'll get,' Steve says. Crowley throws him a look of disdain.

I say, 'The story runs tomorrow. A married detective, not involved in investigating Aislinn Murray's murder but in a position very close to that investigation, was having an affair with her. If we need you to throw anything else in there at some stage, we'll let you know.'

And the brass will have no choice: there'll be an internal investigation. It won't find enough for charges, any more than we did, but at least McCann won't be prancing back to his marriage and his lifetime Murder billet like none of this ever happened. Aislinn's getting the job done in the end. I wonder if some part of her realised, in dark glints during the long nights when she couldn't sleep for planning, that this was the only way it could go down.

I ask, 'Is that all clear?'

Crowley's shaking his head, but it's at us and our crudeness and our general inferiority as human beings; we all know he's gonna do it. 'Great,' I say. I shove my stool back and stand up; Steve kills his game. 'See you round.' And we leave Crowley and SARTRE to get to work on his brand-new scoop.

Outside, the air is mild enough to trick you into turning your face to it, looking for warmth. It's only five o'clock, but it's dark and the streets are starting to shift into their evening buzz, clumps of smokers laughing outside the pubs, girls hurrying home swinging shopping bags to get ready for the night out. 'I want to ask you something,' I say to Steve. 'Do you know who pissed in my locker, that time?'

I never told him about that, but he doesn't pretend it's news. He watches me steadily, hands in his overcoat pockets. 'Not for definite. No one's going to talk about that around me.'

'Breslin said—' Breslin said of *course* Steve would've heard the stories, of *course* Steve would've told me if he'd been on my side. Breslin said a load of stuff. I shut my trap.

Steve hears the rest anyway. He says matter-of-factly, 'Everyone knows I got here because you put in a word for me. They see us working together. No one's going to try messing with that. They're not thick.'

It catches me with a warmth that almost hurts. 'Yeah,' I say. 'No.'

Steve says, 'From what I've walked in on, but, the locker was Roche.'

'How about the poster with my head Photoshopped onto the gash pic?'

'Yeah. Roche.'

'Right,' I say. 'OK.' I turn in a circle, looking up at the city lights painting the clouds a tricky grey-gold. 'All the other shite? Not the small stuff. The real shite.'

'Like I said: I wouldn't know. But I've never heard anything to say anyone else was in on it.'

I say, 'You never told me.'

That gets a flick of one corner of his mouth. ''Cause you would've listened, yeah?'

Steve hanging on to his precious gangster story for dear life, building it bigger and fancier and twirlier, waving his arms for me to look. Here I thought he was trying to cheer me up so I wouldn't get him in the lads' bad books. All along he was hoping, if he could just come up with a good enough alternative, maybe he could snap me out of convincing myself the whole case – the whole squad – was one great big conspiracy to shaft me. I can't decide which of us is the bigger spa.

'Huh,' I say. The air smells tasty and restless, all those places you could spend your evening, all the things waiting to happen inside those beckoning open doors. 'Would you look at that.'

'What?'

'I just wish I'd copped earlier. Is all.'

Steve waits.

I say, 'We need to talk to the gaffer.'

18

Me and Steve, back in the gaffer's office. It's down the end of a corridor; with the click of the door, the silence closes around us and we're a thousand miles from the rest of the squad. The layers of tat and clutter close in, too: spider plant, golf trophies, framed crap, stacks of pointless old files, and there's a brand-new snow globe holding down a heap of paper on the desk, souvenir of some grand-kid's holiday. In the middle of it all, O'Kelly, taking off his reading glasses to look at us.

He says, 'Breslin was in. He says you've hit a wall with the Aislinn Murray case; time to take a step back, hope ye catch a break some-where down the road.'

He gets it bang on, gruff and not exactly delighted with us, but holding back from the bollocking because Breslin told him we've done a good job. For a second there I could almost believe it's real, and all the rest is our imagination. The rush of fury pulls a sharp breath into me.

The gaffer watches us.

I say, 'McCann killed Aislinn Murray.'

Not one muscle of O'Kelly changes. He says, 'Sit down.'

We turn the spare chairs towards his desk and sit. The crisp whirl and click of Steve placing his chair is full up tight with that same fury.

'Let's hear it.'

We tell him what happened, while the darkness thickens at the window. We keep it very clear and very cold, no commentary, just fact stacked neatly on top of fact, the way the gaffer likes his reports. He picks up the shitty snow globe and turns it from angle to angle between his fingers, watching the shavings of plastic snow tumble, and listens.

When we're done he says, still inspecting the snow globe, 'How much of that can you prove?'

'Not enough to put him away,' Steve says. He's barely holding down the savage edge of sarcasm: *Don't be worrying, it's all grand.* 'Not even enough for a charge.'

'That's not what I asked.'

'McCann's connection to the old case is on file,' I say. The anger's slicing through my voice, too, and I'm not even trying to hide it. 'Gary O'Rourke and I can both confirm that Aislinn was trying to track down the story on her father. The affair's solid: we've got forensics and the best mate's statement, plus McCann admitted it. And we've got the best mate's evidence that Aislinn was only stringing him along. When it comes to Saturday evening, we've got nothing but Rory Fallon's statement about seeing McCann, which is worth bugger-all. McCann's saying nothing. Breslin says McCann found her dead, but no one's going to confirm that on record.'

O'Kelly's eyes flick up to me. 'Breslin said that.'

'An hour ago.'

He swivels his chair, with a long low creak, to the window. He could be staring out over the courtyard, at the slope of cobblestones and the proud high-windowed rise of the building opposite, the old solid shapes he has to know by heart; only for the darkness.

Steve says, like it's punched its way out of him, 'He rang you Sunday morning. Before you gave us the case.'

One flicker of the gaffer's eyelids. Except for that, we could think he didn't hear.

'We were a gift,' I say. 'The perfect stooges. Moran's a newbie, Conway's fighting a bad rep. Easy to point them in the wrong direction; if they come up with something you don't like, easy to twist their arms, make them back off and shut their gobs. Worst comes to worst, easy to smear them bad enough that no one'll listen to a word they say.'

O'Kelly ought to reef me out of it, for talking to my gaffer like that. He doesn't even turn. The desk lamp slides gold light down the brass desk plaque saying DET. SUPT. G. O'KELLY.

After a long time he says, 'Breslin said it was a mate of his.'

Neither of us answers.

He takes a deep breath and lets it out delicately, the way you do when you're dying of a cough, afraid if you do it wrong you might explode. 'Five in the morning, he rang me. He said his friend, one of his best friends, he had called round to his girlfriend that night. Found her in her sitting room unconscious, bet up. Pretty sure another boyfriend did it. I said, "What are you dragging me out of my bed for? Call it in, get the uniforms and the paramedics over there, see you in the morning." Breslin said he was going to call it in as soon as we hung up. But then he said to me, "My friend's got a wife and kids. He can't be linked to this, gaffer. It'll wreck his life. We need to keep him out of it."'

O'Kelly lets out a small, humourless snort of laughter. 'I said don't be giving me that shite about *my friend*; we all know what that means. But Breslin said no. He swore up and down: it's not me, gaffer. You know me, I don't step out on my missus. I'll put you on to her, she can tell you I've been with her and the kids all week-end . . . A lie that size, from a fella I know the way I know Breslin, I wouldn't have missed it. I believed him.'

He moves; the chair creaks sharply. 'I said, "Your mate says he didn't put a finger on her, just walked in and found the damage done. Do you believe him?" And Breslin said he did, yeah. Hundred per cent. Two hundred. A thousand. He wasn't lying then, either. And Breslin's no eejit. He's had plenty of practice spotting bullshit stories.'

There's a second of silence, while we all let that lie there.

'I asked him, "Then what are you getting into hysterics about? If your friend did nothing and saw nothing, there's no reason his name should ever come into this. The bird'll wake up and tell the uniforms who gave her the slaps, they'll pull the fella in, she'll refuse to press charges, everyone'll go home; rinse and repeat a month or two down the line. Your mate's grand. I hope it scared him shitless enough that he'll keep it in his trousers from now on."'

The cough breaks through. We wait while O'Kelly pulls a tissue out of his pocket and presses it to his mouth, makes ferocious revving noises to clear his throat.

He says, 'But Breslin was worried. He said his mate hadn't checked to see was the girl breathing. Too shaken up, too afraid of being snared; he'd just legged it out of there and rung Breslin. They had no way of knowing how long she'd been lying there. If she was dead, then his mate was fucked. He'd be dragged in, dragged through the muck, lose everything. All because he'd stuck his mickey in the wrong hole.'

The prickle of alert lifts Steve's head at the same moment as mine. Breslin told us McCann checked and Aislinn was dead, meaning he would have done no good by calling it in, so he wasn't a bad guy for leaving her bleeding on the floor. Both versions are bullshit anyway, but I'd love to know why he served O'Kelly a different flavour from us.

O'Kelly either hasn't noticed or doesn't want to. 'I said, "You want something. What is it?" Breslin said, "If she's dead, I need to be on the case. I'm not asking to be in charge. I just want to be around, so I can see what's going on, make sure my mate doesn't get dragged in if there's no need. If it's all cut and dried, there's no reason to ruin his life. If he's needed, I'll make sure he comes forward. I swear." He said, "I've got thirteen years of credit, gaffer. I'm calling it in now."'

The corner of O'Kelly's mouth twists as he remembers. 'Breslin's not the genius he thinks he is, but he's a good man. He's never let me down. Never asked me for a favour bigger than a plum slot for his holidays. If he wanted to cash in his chips on this one . . .' His shoulders lift, fall again heavily. 'In the end I said all right. I told him to watch himself, and watch his mate: I was going to be all over this one, and if I got any hints that anything was off, then he was gone and his pal was coming in for the chats. He said no problem. No problem at all. He told me how much he appreciated it, and how much he owed me, and a bit more arse-licking that I didn't take much notice of. And then he went off to call it in.'

Another story. None of the rest were true straight through, not one. Victims, witnesses, killers, Ds, all frantically spinning stories to keep the world the way they want it, dragging them over our heads, stuffing them down our throats; and now our gaffer.

I say – I haven't talked in so long that my voice comes out rough and patchy, dried out by the heating – 'You knew who the mate was.'

O'Kelly's eyes move to my face. They stay there like I make him too tired to look away. 'You tell me, Conway. When you started smelling something rotten, did you straightaway think, "Ah, I know, must've been one of my own squad"?'

The weight of his voice – *my own squad* – falls on me like the swaying weight of deep water. Twenty-eight years, O'Kelly's been on Murder; since me and Steve were sticky-faced kids pointing finger-guns at our pals. When he says *my own squad*, it means things I used to dream I'd understand someday.

I say, 'No.'

'And when you should've known. Did you think it then?'

'No.'

'No.' His head turns back to the window. 'Nor did I. But I wondered. I didn't like that; I thought less of myself for it, still do. But there it was. That's why I gave you the case: I needed to know. And ye were the only ones who wouldn't drop it like a hot potato if Breslin wanted you to.'

And we waded right in and did his dirty work for him. Maybe he expects us to be grateful for the vote of confidence. I say, 'Now you know.'

'You're positive. You'd bet your lives on it.'

Steve says, 'He did it.'

O'Kelly nods a few times. 'Right,' he says quietly, to himself, not to us. 'Right.'

I wait for it. Just for kicks, I try to guess which he'll whip out first: the fatherly wisdom, the squad loyalty, the man-to-man chat, the guilt trip, the bribes, the threats. I hope Steve's got no plans for this evening, because it could take a while before it sinks into the gaffer's head that he's getting nowhere. While I'm at it, I try to decide whether we should tell him it's already too late, so we can enjoy the look on the bollix's face, or whether we should play it safe and let him find out in the morning, along with everyone else, when the *Courier* comes out.

He swivels his chair to his desk and picks up the phone. His finger on the buttons is clumsier than it should be; his knuckles are swollen stiff. When someone answers, he says, 'McCann. I need you in my office.' And hangs up.

His eyes fall on us for a moment, in passing. 'Ye can stay,' he says. 'As long as you act like adults. You get bitchy, you're out.' Then he goes back to looking out the window, at whatever it is he sees out there.

Me and Steve glance at each other just once. Steve's face is quick and wary, all the angles sharpened. He doesn't have a handle on where this is going either, and he doesn't like that any more than I do. We swap a tiny nod: *Stay steady.* Then we sit still, listening to the faint singing hiss of the radiators and the slow rasp of O'Kelly's breathing, and we wait for McCann to come.

The knock at the door snaps the silence. 'Come,' O'Kelly says, turning his chair, and there's McCann in the doorway, jacket sagging, eyes sunk deep.

Two beats – one look at the gaffer, one at us – and he understands. His shoulders shift and roll forward as he gets ready for the fight.

'Moran,' O'Kelly says. 'Give McCann a chair.'

I stand up with Steve and we move to the side, against the wall. For a second it looks like McCann's going to stay standing, but then he yanks Steve's chair farther from us and sits down. Legs wide, feet braced, chin forward.

O'Kelly says, 'You should have told me.'

A fast raw flush springs up on McCann's cheekbones. He opens his mouth to spew out a flood of reasons, excuses, justifications, whatever. Then he shuts it again.

'How long have I been your gaffer?'

After a moment McCann says, 'Eleven years.'

'Any complaints?'

McCann shakes his head.

'Have I had your back, along the way? Or have I hung you out to dry when things got tough?'

'Had my back. Always.'

O'Kelly nods. He says, 'A civilian who's fucked up, he tries to hide it from his boss. A D in trouble, he goes to his gaffer.'

McCann can't look at him. The flush deepens. 'I should've. Straightaway. I know that.'

O'Kelly waits.

'Sorry.'

'OK,' the gaffer says. He gives McCann the curt nod that means *You're off the hook, don't fuck up again.* 'We're talking now, anyway. And I want to know what in holy hell has been going on here. These two' – he jerks his chin at me and Steve – 'they're trying to tell me you went pussy-blind: Aislinn Murray was out to fuck you over, you were thinking with your mickey, the whole thing went to shite. Is that true? This whole five-star clusterfuck, it's all because you weren't getting enough blood flow to the brain?'

McCann's jaw moves. He doesn't like that.

'Because I know you – or anyway I thought I did – and I say it's bollix. These two have come up with some story they like, and they're making everything they get fit the story.'

It tracks cold right down into my stomach, like swallowed ice. The story we told him, the true one, it'll never leave this room. By the time we walk out, O'Kelly and McCann between them will have sliced it to pieces and sewn it up into something unrecognisable, to set loose into the outside world. I knew it was coming, but it still hits home.

'Fact is, everything they've got plays a couple of different ways.'

One fast glance from McCann.

O'Kelly holds up a thumb. 'The photos of your notes. It's a safe bet Aislinn was going to take those to your wife, but all that says is she wanted you for herself. Nothing to say why.'

Thumb and finger. 'That fairy-tale yoke she left for her mate. That just says she felt trapped – and I don't blame her; you're a fucking eejit, putting the girl in that situation, like she wanted to spend the rest of her life being your bit on the side – and she was angry with you, wanted to turn the tables so you couldn't get away from her.'

A quick double blink from McCann. This is reaching him. Any second now, he'll be jumping on board with whatever O'Kelly's got planned.

Another finger. 'Rory Fallon. Aislinn could've been trying to get you out of her head. She had enough sense to know the two of ye were a bad idea all round.'

McCann's looking at him now. The drowning-man hope struggling on his face is terrible.

'Maybe this is just me doing my own wishful thinking. I don't want to believe you'd make a mess like this one, drag the whole squad into it, just for the sake of a ride. For you to fuck up this badly, then you and Aislinn, that had to be the real thing.'

Shame, mixed in with the hope.

'We can't ask Aislinn what was going on in her head. You're the only other person who was there; if anyone knows, it's you. So you tell me, McCann. Was it the real thing? Or are we all sitting here because you fancied a fuck?'

The clench of anger in his voice pulls it out of McCann. 'It was real. I'm not that bloody stupid.'

'Real,' the gaffer says. And waits for more.

'Maybe Aislinn did go into it wanting to fuck me over. Probably. Maybe she ended the same way – that mate of hers persuaded her, or, I don't know. But there was a while in there . . .'

McCann rubs his eyes. In the merciless light they look red and sore, like he's got an infection starting. He says, 'I couldn't believe it was happening. To me. I thought I knew the rest of my life like it had already happened. All the decisions that make a difference, I'd made them before I was twenty-five – the job, the wife, the neighbourhood, having kids. All that was left was for me to sit there and watch them play out. No twists left; no surprises.'

He lifts his head to look over at me and Steve. 'You won't get it now, you two. You're still young enough that anything could happen. But you'll find out. It's like being in a film, one of those third-rate ones where by halfway through you know exactly where it's headed, every step; you can't remember why you're even bothering to watch the rest. Because it's there, just; because there's nothing else to do. And then . . .'

He blinks hard, like that might clear his eyes.

'And all of a sudden someone lifts you right out of it and drops you into a different film. Different music, different colours. She was brighter. Always bright colours. And anything could happen.'

Steve says, 'So what you told us about just liking her company, that was bollix. You knew from the start that this was something special.'

McCann shakes his head. 'Nah. I didn't think that way. Not at first. I just . . . I loved being with her. Nothing more than that; I never thought of doing more than that. Just seeing her listen to my stories like they mattered. It reminded me of how I used to feel about the job, way back when. The look on her face: when I pulled a good case, I used to feel like that. Like what I did changed things.'

I risk a glance at the gaffer. His face is steady; the shadows of wrinkles and eye sockets turn it unreadable.

'OK,' Steve says, keeping the scepticism level well below bitchy. 'So how did that change?'

'One night,' McCann says. He brushes a hand over his cheek, like something fine and cobwebby is catching at him. 'One night. August. Aislinn said some guy had chatted her up at her evening class. Just in passing, she mentioned it – she wasn't into him, she'd turned him down. But that was when it hit me: a girl like that, of course she's going to want a fella. Not just someone for picnics and talk; a man who loves her. A man in her bed. Hit me like a ton of bricks, because I knew once she got him, I'd be gone.'

She made him think it was his idea, Lucy said. She did a good job of it.

'And then I thought: why not me? Why not? We were loving each other's company, couldn't get enough. There was chemistry there – even I could tell that. The way she looked at me, the way her breathing went when we accidentally got close— There was something.'

A sharp glance at me and Steve. That faint stinging red has come up on his cheekbones again. 'Probably it sounds pathetic to you: just a middle-aged fool head over heels for some young one, oldest story in the world. You weren't there.'

Every murderer says that to us, sooner or later. *You weren't there. You don't understand.* There's a small dry chip of silence while no one points that out.

I say, 'It was that easy? You said, "Hey, let's give it a go," and Aislinn said, "Sure, why not?"'

McCann shakes his head heavily. 'I don't know how I made it happen. You two, you keep talking like she hunted me down, but it wasn't— She didn't want to be some homewrecker. It took me a while to convince her she was doing no harm that hadn't been done years ago. When I finally, when we finally . . . that was when I realised: she honest to God cared about me. She . . . It . . .' A quick involuntary catch of breath. 'That blew me away. Just blew me away.'

The wonder in his voice. He sounds like a teenager, lifting with joy and amazement, he sounds so tender you could bruise him with one wrong touch. Time after time it's left me gobsmacked, how people will tell you things they should keep locked inside for life; how ferociously they need the story to be out in the air, in the world, to exist somewhere outside their own heads.

He says, 'It was real. All that shite you've got, that means nothing. One time I fell getting over her wall, scraped up my knee. Aislinn knelt down in front of me and washed it, so gentle. You think she'd've done that if she only hated my guts? Maybe she did, some of the time, but she loved me as well. People are complicated. She was more complicated than I realised.'

He's giving me and Steve a stare that's a challenge. No takers. The whole thing is pure double-dipped fantasy, but the last thing we want to do is take it apart. Me and Steve, scrabbling so hard to pull the true story out of the tangle, we forgot the false ones come with their own ferocious, double-edged power.

The gaffer nods. 'I would've put money on that. Nice to know I'm not losing the bit I have.' He resettles himself in his chair, adjusts his waistband over his belly. 'Now we've got that cleared up,' he says. 'Let's talk about Saturday night.'

McCann opens his mouth, but O'Kelly lifts a hand. 'No. Hang on. That's not what I'm asking you.'

McCann shuts up.

'Breslin told these two you found Aislinn dead. But he told me that you – that his *mate*, I mean – didn't even check for a pulse. Why?'

A shake of McCann's head, baffled and wary. This isn't what he was expecting. Not what I was expecting, either. I'm not sure, any more, that I have the foggiest clue what the gaffer is at.

'He wanted me thinking the mate was a civilian, is why. So he said the mate panicked and did a runner, the way a civilian would. The way no D would, ever.' O'Kelly shoots a sharp glance at McCann, under his eyebrows. 'You happy with that?'

A humourless twist of McCann's mouth. 'Not happy with any of this.'

'You shouldn't be. You let Breslin paint you as a civilian, to keep you out of hassle with your gaffer. How does that sit with you?'

McCann's jaw moves. 'Not great.'

'Good. Because it's not sitting great with me, either.' O'Kelly leaves that for a moment, but McCann's got nothing to add. 'And then, a minute ago, you said Aislinn made you feel the way you used to feel on a good case: like what you did mattered.'

Nod.

'Used to feel, you said. Meaning not any more.'

McCann's eyes are on the floor.

'Since when?'

'Don't know. A couple of years back.'

'What happened?'

O'Kelly's leaning forward, elbows on the desk, as close as he can get. Me and Steve aren't moving. We're not even in the room. This is between McCann and O'Kelly.

McCann says, 'It wasn't the job. It was me. What I said before: somewhere in there, it started feeling like everything I'd ever do was already set in stone. Middle of a big interview, out of nowhere I'd get this feeling like my mouth was moving by itself, like I was reading off a script and there was no way I could change it. It'd hit me that it didn't matter who was sitting in my seat, asking the questions; the ending would be the same if it was me, Winters, O'Gorman, anyone. Felt like I was vanishing. It wasn't that I stopped seeing myself as a D. I stopped seeing myself at all.'

The gaffer says, heavily, 'I should've spotted that.'

McCann says urgently, 'It never made a difference on the job, gaffer. I never slacked. No matter what, I gave it a hundred per cent.'

'I know.' O'Kelly leans back in his chair, runs a hand over his mouth. 'What were you planning? Transfer off the squad? Hold out till you had your thirty and retire?'

McCann's face upturned to him, like a kid's, begging. 'No. Gaffer, no. I thought midlife crisis, I'll work through it, come out the other side, get my head back— I wasn't going anywhere. Here till they drag me out.'

O'Kelly says – not brutal, just quiet and simple – 'That's out now.'

McCann bites down on his lip.

'I can't have you on the squad.'

After a long time, the smallest slice of a nod.

'And I can't palm you off on some other squad. Not knowing what I do.'

That nod again.

'And the story's going to come out, one way or another. Aislinn's mate: we can keep her quiet for a while, but sooner or later she'll cop that the case is going nowhere, and she'll find herself a journo to talk to.' O'Kelly doesn't look at me and Steve, doesn't act like he even knows we're there, but I wonder. 'And we'll have the Garda Ombudsman jumping down our throats. There'll be two inquiries, minimum: ours, and theirs. Breslin'll be for the chop.' That pulls a quick in-breath through McCann's nose, jerks his head back. 'What do you expect? Withholding evidence, and there's that phone call to Stoneybatter to prove it. He'll be lucky if he's not up on charges.'

'Gaffer,' McCann says. The raw desperation gashing his voice open; I can't look at him. 'It's not Breslin's fault. He did nothing, only stood by me. Please—'

'I won't be able to do anything for Breslin, McCann. I'm for the chop, too.' No self-pity in O'Kelly's voice; these are facts, no different from fingerprint results or alibi times. 'Unless I put in my papers before the investigation finishes up. In which case I won't be around to give Breslin a dig-out.'

'Christ,' McCann says, barely above a whisper. 'Ah, Christ, gaffer. I'm sorry.'

'No. Don't be getting maudlin on me. It's done now.' O'Kelly's face across the desk, all unmovable grooves and crevices, like something carved a long time ago to send a message I can't read. 'You've got a choice. You can go out like a scumbag. Or you can be a D one more time.'

The silence goes on for so long. The office has changed, shifted, the same way the cosy interview room did. Crayon drawings, tiny flakes stirring in the snow globe. Thin skin stretched over clean bones and clacking teeth.

McCann says, quietly, 'Saturday evening, after dinner, I told my wife I was going for a pint and I headed over to Aislinn's house. I went in through the kitchen; saw the dinner cooking, but I didn't think anything of it. There was music playing, dancy stuff, Aislinn didn't hear me come in. I went out into the sitting room calling her – quiet, like always, so the neighbours wouldn't hear – and I saw the table, set for two. Wineglasses. Candle. I thought it was for us. Should've known. I'm never over to her on Saturdays – mostly my wife wants to go out to a restaurant, only that evening she had a headache; no way Aislinn would've guessed I was coming. But all I could think about was seeing her.'

I risk a flash of sideways glance at Steve and meet him risking one at me, wide-eyed. We're the only ones gobsmacked here. McCann's voice doesn't even hold a flicker of surprise at what he's doing. The moment he walked into this room, he knew what O'Kelly would want from him. Breslin knew, too; that's why they didn't come to the gaffer with a version that had McCann in it, beg him to thin-blue-line it all away. Me and Steve were the only fools who didn't get it.

'And then she came out of the bedroom,' McCann says. 'Bright blue dress, beautiful; winter evening like that, nothing but grey and damp, and then this blue that'd light up your whole head . . . Her hair down, she knew I loved it like that. Putting an earring in one ear. I went to go to her, I . . .' His hands come up, sketching the offer of an embrace.

'Aislinn . . . she jumped a mile. Then she saw it was me. I expected her to laugh and kiss me, but the face on her; horrified. Like I was an intruder. That was when I started to cop: it wasn't me she was wait-ing for. She put up her hands to stop me touching her, and she said, "You need to go."'

He's breathing hard, the rush of disbelief hitting him all over again. 'I couldn't wrap my head . . . I asked her, I said, "What? What are you doing? What are you on about?" But she just kept pointing at the back door, telling me to go. I was begging her, don't even know what I was saying. I said, "What's happened? Just Wednesday night we were, three days ago, we— Have you had enough of me going home to my wife? Am I not spending enough time with you? I'll end it with my wife tonight, I'll move in, do anything— Was there something someone said about me, did your mate Lucy, I'll explain, let me—"

'But she was just shaking her head: no, not that, no, no, just go. She was trying to move me towards the kitchen, *herding* me, only I wouldn't, or I couldn't . . . I said – stupid, standing there, couldn't keep up – I said, "Are we done? Does this mean we're done?" And Aislinn, she stopped like she'd never thought of that. Startled. And then she said, "Well. Yes. I suppose it does."'

There's no way I'd risk a glance at Steve now. Neither of us is breathing.

'It felt like a joke,' McCann says. 'I was waiting for the punchline. But her face: she meant it. I said, all I could say, "*Why?*"'

'She said, "Go home." I said, "Tell me why and I'll go. Whatever it is, just tell me. I can't live wondering."'

'She looked at me and she laughed. Aislinn's got a lovely laugh, sweet little giggle, but this wasn't— This was something different. Great wild laugh, huge. She sounded . . .'

McCann's throat moves as he hears that laugh again, growing and growing to fill his head, unstoppable. 'She sounded happy. The happiest I'd ever heard her. And then she said, "You keep on wonder-ing. Now fuck off."'

He stops talking.

O'Kelly says, 'And.'

McCann says, 'And I hit her.'

Me and Steve, we went at McCann by ripping away what he believed most about his life, blowing it up in front of his eyes, and hoping there'd be too little of him left to hold out against us. Just like Aislinn had been planning. But when we took as much of McCann as we could, shredded him into the last thing he ever wanted to be, we left him with *No comment*.

O'Kelly offered McCann a way back to who he was. McCann's taken it.

He says, 'It wasn't murder, gaffer. It was manslaughter. I never meant her to die.'

The gaffer says, 'I know.'

'It never came to me that she might. Not till after.'

'I know.'

I'm taking in a breath to say it. Cooper's report. McCann is no bodybuilder. He landed that punch when Aislinn was down, head on the stone fireplace.

O'Kelly hears the breath. His eyes flick to me and he waits for what I'm going to say. His face still hasn't changed. Only the eyes, moving in shadow, look alive.

I shut my mouth.

The gaffer's eyes go back to McCann. He says, 'We need this on record. You understand that?'

McCann nods. He keeps nodding for a long time.

O'Kelly leans his hands on the desk to stand up. 'Time to go,' he says.

McCann's face turns up to him, quickly.

'I'll do it,' the gaffer says. Steadying, like a surgeon promising to cut it out himself, not to let the med students touch the scalpel.

McCann says, 'Maura.'

'I'll go see her. Soon as we're done.'

McCann nods again. He stands up. Stays by the chair, arms hanging at his sides, waiting to be told where to go next.

The gaffer tugs down his jacket, carefully, like he's got somewhere important to be. He switches off the desk lamp and looks around his office, absently, touching his pockets. His eyes fall on me and Steve like he forgot we were there.

'Go home,' he says.

*   *   *

We don't talk. Down the long silent corridor, the padding of our feet on the carpet like muffled heartbeats. Down the stairs, through the cold draught that fidgets in the stairwell, to the locker room: coats on, satchels on shoulders, locker doors closing. Back upstairs, the smiles and the nods and the few words with Bernadette at reception stuffing tissue packets and throat lozenges into her bag, ready to go home. And outside, to the wide sharp blast of city-smell and cold.

The great courtyard, the floodlights, the civil servants scurrying home. It all looks strange: small stark paper things, far away. A big solve does that to you, leaves the world scoured dawn-white, sand-white, empty except for the solve smooth and heavy as a deep-dived rock in your hand.

Only it's more than that, this time. The cobblestones feel wrong under my feet, thin skins of stone over bottomless fog. The squad I've spent the last two years hating, the mob of sniggering fucktards backstabbing the solo warrior while she gallantly fought her doomed battle: that's gone, peeled away like a smeared film that was stuck down hard over the real thing. The squad I would've chopped off an arm to join, the shining line of ass-kicking superheroes, that went a long time ago. What's left underneath is smaller than either of those, quieter and more complicated, done in finer detail. Roche, begging for a punch in the gob, which is high on my to-do list. The lads, each of them deep in his own mix of dodgy alibis and messy fibre evidence and the baby's chickenpox, occasionally glancing up to roll their eyes at Roche's bullshit or mine. The gaffer – it occurs to me that just maybe the gaffer throws the odd domestic our way, not because they piss me off, but because they have a good clearance rate and he wants our stats solid; or maybe, even simpler, because he knows we'll work the hell out of them. All of them, and Steve. And me.

We stand in the courtyard, hands in our pockets, shoulders up against the cold. We're not sure where to go from here; there's no rule book, no ritual, to tell us what comes after a day like this one. Above us the Murder windows are lit and alert, ready for whatever tonight's got in store. Somewhere up there O'Kelly and McCann are in an interview room, heads bent close, talking low and steady. Breslin is alone in the observation room, watching through the slow swell and ebb of his breath on the glass, not moving.

Steve says, 'He was looking after us.'

He means the gaffer, sending us home. 'I know,' I say. It'll be O'Kelly's name on McCann's statement sheet, O'Kelly's name on the book of evidence that goes to the prosecutor. When we walk into the squad room tomorrow, we won't be hissed out of it. Breslin will hate our guts, as long as he lives. The rest of them will watch O'Kelly, walking out of the building shoulder to shoulder with McCann to take him to booking, and understand.

Steve catches a sudden deep breath, blows it out again. 'God,' he says, and there's a shake in his voice that he doesn't bother trying to hide. 'What a day.'

'Look on the bright side. We're never gonna have a worse week than this one.'

That pulls a helpless bark of laughter out of him. 'You never know. We could get lucky: the Commissioner could get coked up and strangle a hooker.'

'Fuck that. Someone else can work it. Just Quigley's speed.'

Steve laughs again, but it's gone fast. 'The reason we didn't see it from the start,' he says, 'is because we were thinking like cops. Both of us.'

He leaves it hanging there, like a question. He knows. Here I was so sure I was some secret-agent-level closed book, keeping my big plan all to myself. I watch our breath spread and fade on the air.

'So,' Steve says, squinting up at a shadow crossing one of the windows. 'You putting in your papers?'

I can practically see the might-bes, bobbing like marsh lights over the cobblestones, skimming past the high windows, tricky and beckoning. Me in a suit that makes this one look like a binliner, striding through Harrods after some Saudi princess, one eye on her and the other on everything else. Me stretching out my legs in business class, checking exit routes in the hushed corridors of 24-carat hotels, lounging beside blinding blue sea with a cocktail in one hand and the other on the gun in my beach bag. All the might-have-beens, whirling in and out among the bars of the gate, and gone.

'Nah,' I say. 'I hate paperwork.'

I swear Steve's head falls back with relief. 'Jaysus,' he says. 'I was worried.'

I never saw that one coming. 'Yeah?'

His face turns towards me. He's as startled as I am. 'Course. What'd you think?'

'Don't know. Never thought about it.' Not once. And I should've. For a second I see Breslin in the interview room, practically lifting off his feet with fury, *There's no fucking way he did this*; Breslin in his dark sitting room, before dawn, muffling his voice on the phone to Stoneybatter station. 'Sorry,' I say. 'I've made a bleeding tosser of myself, the last while. A lot of ways.'

Steve doesn't even try to deny that. 'You're all right. We've all done it.'

'I'm not planning on doing it again.'

'That'll be nice.'

'Fuck off, you.' The cobblestones have lost that misty feel, they're centuries' worth of solid again, and the cold air hits my lungs like caffeine. I need to ring Crowley, tell him he's off the hook for the article, make sure he knows he still owes me a big one and I'm gonna collect. I need to ring my ma and tell her about last night, whether I want to or not. Maybe it'll give the pair of us a laugh. Maybe Fleas will e-mail me tomorrow, when he sees the headlines: *Hiya Rach, saw your news, delighted everythings workin out for you, have to meet up to celebrate x*. Maybe at the weekend I'll text Lisa and the rest of my mates, see if they're about. 'You know what I need, I need a pint. Brogan's?'

Steve hitches his satchel up his shoulder. 'You're buying. You still owe me for Rory not crying.'

'What're you on about? He bawled his eyes—'

'I thought you were done being a tosser—'

'Nice try. Doesn't mean I'm gonna be a pushover—'

'Ah, good, 'cause I was dead worried about that—'

I take one more look up at the rest of my life, waiting for me inside those neat sturdy squares of gold light. Then we start off across the courtyard, arguing, to get a few pints and a few hours' kip before it's time to head back and find out what's in there.

ACKNOWLEDGEMENTS

Even more than usual, I owe huge thanks to Dave Walsh, whose insights into the world of detectives gave me everything in this book that's true to life, and none of the elements that aren't.

I also owe huge thanks to the consistently amazing Darley Anderson and everyone at the agency, especially Mary, Emma, Rosanna, Pippa and Mandy; Andrea Schulz, Ciara Considine, Nick Sayers and Sue Fletcher, for their immense editorial skill, insight and wisdom; Breda Purdue, Ruth Shern, Joanna Smyth and everyone at Hachette Books Ireland; Swati Gamble, Kerry Hood and everyone at Hodder & Stoughton; Carolyn Coleburn, Angie Messina, the wonderful Ben Petrone, and everyone at Viking; Susanne Halbleib and everyone at Fischer Verlage; Rachel Burd; Steve Fisher of APA, the most patient man in LA; Dr Fearghas Ó Cochláin, for straightening out my haematomas; Sophie Hannah, for pointing me towards the title; Alex French, Susan Collins, Ann-Marie Hardiman, Jessica Ryan, Karen Gillece, Kendra Harpster, Kristina Johansen and Catherine Farrell, for every kind of support from practical to emotional to hilarious; David Ryan, top with smoked ham, bacon strips, ground beef, mushrooms and black olives, bake for ten minutes on pizza stone, serve with German Pilsner; my mother, Elena Lombardi; my father, David French; and, for more reasons every time, the man who can sort out the worst plot tangle before the starters arrive, my husband, Anthony Breatnach.

Look out for the first book to feature the tough, abrasive detective Antoinette Conway of the Dublin Murder Squad:

'A classic in the making'
Sunday Times